Continued...

I n every family there exists someone who is definitely a little different, someone who says or believes things others dare not say or perhaps never pondered. It is quite another thing when something that person said actually comes true and miracles are performed. What must have been the word on the street or village, and what must those who were close to Jesus and his family thought? Bill Kassel takes you there. Take a step back in time, and imagine how you would have thought had you lived in Israel some 2,000 years ago, dealing with the harsh reality of daily life in the cruel world of the Roman-occupied Middle East. When you heard stories of Jesus of Nazareth, would you have been a believer?

Dave Hartline
Contributor, *American Catholic*

M y Brother's Keeper is a book of history, and, yes, entertainment. Even though we all know how it will end, I can't put it down! It's one of those stories you find yourself thinking of when you go about your daily routine .... Whether you are a Christian or not, this is an awesome read.

Nancy Ryan
Book Reviewer, *Simply Hers Magazine*

I found it very interesting that the author chose to incorporate early Christian traditions held by both Catholicism and Orthodoxy .... The character on which the novel focuses is James, the half-brother of Jesus, known as "James the Just," who throughout the novel evolves from a knowledge-hungry young man to a very respected rabbi and the Jewish advisor of Pontius Pilate .... The author did a fantastic job exploring the motivations that drove Pilate to condemn Jesus to death although knowing He was innocent. The plot leading up to the Passion story is presented with great depth and reverence, meant to incite further discussion of what led to the sacrifice of Jesus and what its implications, whether political, social or spiritual, were.

Alex Szollo
International Book Reviewer, Romania

One might expect that, since anyone who has read the Bible knows how that story ends, there would be little incentive to keep turning the pages. For this reader, at least, the book was hard to put down. It's a tribute to the skill of the author that the characters are so believable and robust that one becomes emotionally involved with them. Although the events are set two thousand years in the past, there is an almost modern feel to the narrative. The complex characters, both public and domestic, could have stepped out of our lives, and the horror and cruelty of political repression are all too familiar in our time.

Diane Osbourne
Contributor, *Stubborn Things*

If I had lived in the time of Jesus, who would I think He was? What would I have believed about Him? Would I have espoused His teachings? It wasn't like being raised Christian in the 20th century. My Brother's Keeper made me realize in a fresh new way how hard it was, in Jesus' time, for many people—especially Jews—to believe in Jesus, and how amazing His mission really was.

Cheryl Nael
Ave Maria Radio

Kassel has created a vivid landscape for his characters that can be clearly seen felt and almost touched. The interaction between the characters is understated and dutiful, with silent respect. The reader can almost hear their thoughts in humble reverential tones. The relationships come across as genuine, the narrative moves along smoothly, and the storyline in engaging. All in all, a very good read.

Al Ferber
Poet & Author

My Brother's Keeper was, for me, a most gratifying reading experience. The book is beautifully written. And even with my limited early Christian history knowledge, I could tell that it had been exhaustively researched. I consider it a significant literary achievement. It was a privilege to read it.

Gordon Boardman
Artist & Writer

Other Novels by Bill Kassel:

Holy Innocents

This Side of Jordan

My Brother's Keeper

שומר אחי

A NOVEL ABOUT THE FAMILY OF JESUS

BY BILL KASSEL

Company.

Company Publications

ISBN 978-0-938984-06-1

Printed in the United States of America

Design, Cover, and Cover Graphic Symbol Copyright © 2017 by Bill Kassel

Note: The Hebrew characters shown on the cover spell out the phrase, "my brother's keeper."

Titles set in Trajan Pro. Text set in Baskerville.

FOREWORD
BY AL KRESTA

What consternation falls upon a family, a village, a society in which the Son of God presents himself as a member? Historical fiction must combine an engaging plot with well-drawn characters while also paying careful attention to the politics, customs, religious devotion, styles of clothing, civil laws and household codes, dietary habits, forms of labor and entertainment, civic rituals, and the social relationships of an earlier historical period.

Bill Kassel is a veteran novelist. He can handle all that. But in *My Brother's Keeper*, he has the added task of insuring fidelity to the Mystery of the Incarnation. It takes unusual skill to imaginatively strive to get behind the eyes of those closest to Jesus. Or to sympathetically profile the reactions of the Pharisees who, we often forget, were the most devout of the Jewish sects.

Kassel performs all these literary tasks with grace and a light touch that draws the reader into the Palestinian social and spiritual world of two thousand years ago. What kind of sibling rivalry exists when one of the children is the Son of God? How do you educate him when he is the Wisdom of God? He created the universe, but how does he learn to work with his hands? Kassel elaborates, adapts and embroiders, but never contradicts the biblical material. In the process he spins a yarn of intrigue and adventure that sets the protagonist—James, "the brother of the Lord"—struggling mightily (if mistakenly) to save Jesus from the gruesome death which we now know was the will of God all along.

My Brother's Keeper is a creative and stimulating form of meditation that entertains like a novel but edifies like a prayer. It's part of a vibrant movement by a new wave of serious Christian novelists to sustain (or perhaps, rebuild?) a Catholic educational/literary culture that has long been a key underpinning of our Judeo-Christian civilization. I am proud to encourage this effort.

If the author's name is familiar to listeners of Ave Maria Radio, it's because Bill Kassel has a long involvement with our communications apostolate, having written and produced several programs for us, and even sat in for me on my daily talk show, "Kresta in the Afternoon."

I believe Bill has taken a truly fresh approach to what is often called "the greatest story ever told"—imaginative and absorbing.

Enjoy it.

Al Kresta

Host, "Kresta In the Afternoon"
CEO, Ave Maria Communications

MY BROTHER'S KEEPER

Out of Zion the law shall go forth,
and the word of the Lord from Jerusalem.

(Isaiah 2)

PROLOGUE

The house of Joseph was located at the northern edge of the town on a grassy hill. There Avram the shepherd, of blessed memory, had once kept a sheepfold in which he would pen his animals until they were shorn or selected out for sale to Nathan, the butcher.

When Avram had owned the hill, before Joseph came from Bethlehem of Judea, the knoll was thought of as outside the town, half a Sabbath journey beyond the last house on the street. But Nazareth had grown. Being close to the great city of Sepphoris, it had prospered from work provided to craftsmen in the surrounding country by the Greek merchants eager to enlarge their villas, as well as by the legion command for construction of new billets for Roman troops in transit and the storage and distribution houses that supplied posts and garrisons throughout Galilee.

By the time Joseph came to Nazareth with his wife, Escha, new dwellings had already shortened the road up from town, and Avram the shepherd had recently died. Having no children, Avram's widow sold the land to this young carpenter and builder, and then went to the home of a kinsman to spend her own last days.

Joseph and Escha moved into the small limestone hut in which Avram had kept his fodder and sheltered himself against the rain. A new roof and door made the place habitable enough, but Joseph's building skills soon yielded another room, in which their first son, Josis, was born. That was followed by an upper chamber on the new section, accessible by a stairway running up the outside to a door at the top sheltered by a wooden enclosure. The original hut was given over completely to the purpose of a shop where Joseph daily plied his woodworking trade. A wall, built of the same limestone plentiful in the region, came next, enclosing a court with its own well, a small flock of chickens, and a she-goat.

The family grew—to five children, before long—in tandem with Joseph's spreading reputation as a man of superior craft, industriousness and reliability. As the years passed, he found himself spending less time fashioning carefully wrought wood furniture and household implements for the people of Nazareth, and more adding to the growing array of fine houses and public structures in Sepphoris.

Indeed, Joseph and his crews of workers were highly praised among the city residents, whom the Jews called Greeks whether they be Roman or any of the other nationalities represented among the foreign intruders. And if his neighbors in Nazareth felt some unease about Joseph's many dealings with pagans, feelings were soothed by the pagan gold he brought back to town. As the old expression went, "A workman deserves his wage," and it was Joseph who came to provide so much of it.

While he might not be considered a man of wealth to the measure of his Greek patrons, Joseph was a man of accomplishment. And with his indisputable piety—faithful in attendance at synagogue and study of Torah, despite so many demands of business upon his time—he was respected, someone to be turned to in trust.

Joseph and Escha lived in as much hopefulness and serenity as could be expected in a land under the control of a usurper king backed by a foreign force. Indeed, while Nazareth was close to the great imperial enclave of Sepphoris, it was much less touched by the intrigues and strife of Jerusalem, to which Bethlehem was located so near. A certain kind of peace prevailed here in the hills of Galilee.

And so it was in this sedate household that Joseph and Escha raised three sons and two daughters. Josis, the eldest, trained at his father's side, mastering carpentry skills and joining Joseph in the family business. Judas and Simon, being more drawn to country pursuits, brought sheep back to old Avram's grassy hill, their sheepfold abutting the outer side of the court wall. They also secured some seedlings of olive trees with the intention of establishing a grove.

All three of the sons took wives, and the wall became pierced with doorways into new dwellings built in a cluster, so that the house of Joseph grew into a compound of some size. Marriages were arranged for Lydia and Assia, the daughters, who thus made their homes with their husbands in the town. Grandchildren abounded on old Avram's hill, the boys learning to assist their fathers in the trades of the household, and the girls learning womanly skills at their mothers' sides.

And then, in the fullness of her days, Escha conceived unexpectedly and gave birth to a fourth son, James. But the joy of this late blessing was dampened by a sudden turn in her health. Escha's healing was not proper, and she was never fully strong after that birth. She collapsed on the morning of the child's circumcision, and had to be carried to her bed.

No one could say if her illness had been caused by James' birth. She vomited, passed blood, and ate less and less as painful weeks wore on. Lydia and Assia came from their homes every day to help their brothers' wives in caring for the baby and attending their mother, but to no avail. Joseph was heartsick to see her wasting in such a manner.

Finally, one day Escha pulled her husband close and whispered a few labored words. "This little James is the child of your old age," she said with great difficulty. "He is the last of me. He is what I leave to you, my husband. And you must love him like Jacob loved his favorite son. Promise me that you will not charge this child with my loss, and that you will love him always."

With tears in his eyes, Joseph took his wife's chilled and weakened fingers between calloused hands that were strong but now shaking from his great sadness and fear. "I will love him," he told her. "I will cherish this boy, and make him a great scholar and a man who is held in high regard. This I promise you, my wife."

Escha smiled and turned her face away to sleep. And by the time night had come upon the house of Joseph, she was dead.

PART I

UNDER HEROD

CHAPTER ONE

Whoever pursues righteousness and kindness
will find life and honor.

(Proverbs 21)

The Rabbi Ezra surveyed the small cluster of students, only four today. They sat on rough wooden benches in the mottled shade of an overhead screen of olive branches woven into a loose wicker. The crude shelter, set in the court that separated the rabbi's house from Nazareth's small synagogue, served as a classroom in pleasant weather. It did double duty as a harvest hut for the rabbi and his wife during the annual feast of booths.

He chose a random psalm to check his students' memorization. *The earth is the Lord's and all its bounty…* he began, leaving the line incomplete. The boys dutifully picked up from him—*the world and all who dwell in it*—reciting through to the end with only occasional stumbles among some of them.

"Better," said the rabbi, "better." Then he pointed at a small boy, the newest member of the class, just five years old. "And who is the King of Glory, Abner son of Benjamin? I don't think I quite heard you say it."

The little boy was startled at first and searched his memory. Then he recalled that he knew perfectly well who the King of Glory was. "The Lord of Hosts is the King of Glory, master," he said assertively.

"Yes," said the rabbi, smiling broadly. "The Lord of Hosts is the King of Glory. Very good, Abner son of Benjamin."

All the boys laughed.

Ezra straightened in his seat and gestured in the direction of the oldest boy. "Yesterday we heard the story of Cain and Abel," he said, "which was read to us very nicely by James son of Joseph."

At this mention, James turned his eyes down into his lap self-con-

sciously. He often felt slightly embarrassed when the rabbi compliment-
ed him. Ezra made it a point to praise all his students, believing kind
words a better encouragement to learning than the harsh criticism,
even scorn, on which some teachers relied. Still, James often sensed
that the rabbi was the merest bit quicker to recognize his accomplishments than those of his fellows. There was a reason for that, and it
made him somewhat uncomfortable.

It was well known to those familiar with the family of Joseph the
builder that James held a special place in his father's heart. But no one
ever observed any resentment expressed toward him by his brothers or
sisters. Indeed, it had often been remarked that Joseph avoided the error of their forefather, Jacob, who as Scripture recounted, doted on his
favored child in ways that sowed seeds of bitterness.

There was a certain sweet honesty about James that endeared him
to the adults in the family and made him a hero to the household children. Because of his scholarly bent and the diligence he brought to his
studies, no one ever begrudged the time he spent in ceaseless questioning of the Rabbi Ezra or pious reflection on the holy books, even when
it took him from chores in the compound.

That James would one day be a doctor of the Law was an assumption shared by all, especially Ezra. The rabbi was always willing to
invest time in the boy, over and above the hours spent in class. This
was partly due to his recognition of James' abilities, and partly out of
gratitude for some extra support provided by James' father.

Nazareth being a small town based principally on its surrounding
farms and herds, Ezra's students were often called upon to work in
the fields and so could not be counted on for regular attendance in
class. This made the stipends on which Ezra depended somewhat erratic. Since Joseph was deeply concerned for the continuity of his son's
schooling, he had a quiet understanding with the rabbi to make up the
difference whenever students were away and Ezra's earnings fell short.
It kept things going, regardless of how many students were present.

The supplement was invaluable and much appreciated by a humble
scholar with few opportunities for added income. To Joseph it was a
practical arrangement by which he expected no privileges for his son
beyond the privilege of learning. Still, Ezra couldn't help but feel a
special stake in this particular student. James was aware of that, and so

...een set for Catholic Authors of Michigan, a mini book

...u due to heavy snows in early February. The rescheduled event,

...guished Catholic authors, will be held Saturday, March 17 (St. Patrick's

AM/FM station covering south-central Michigan, in its studios located at 704 N. East Avenue, Jackson, on the grounds of St. Joseph Oratory.

...til 11:00 a.m. to 2:00 p.m. It is being hosted by Good Shepherd Catholic Radio, an

Guest authors are EWTN personality Teresa Tomeo, Catholic apologist Gary Michuta, Islam expert Dr. Brian Bradford, Catholic gardening specialist Margaret Rose Realy, and novelist Bill Kassel. They will be on hand to personally sign their books — which will be available for purchase — and talk about what inspired their writing.

Teresa Tomeo, who hosts the daily morning talk show, "Catholic Connection," has written several inspirational books, including *Beyond Me, My Selfie & I: Finding Real Happiness in a Self-Absorbed World; Intimate Graces: How Practicing the Works of Mercy Brings Out the Best in Marriage*; and others. She appears regularly on EWTN (Eternal Word Television Network), and speaks throughout the country with a special focus on women's issues and the corrosive influence of media and pop culture.

Gary Michuta is a popular catechetical speaker and religious education specialist. An expert on Catholic Church history and doctrine, he is a frequent guest on Christian radio and television shows. His books include *Why Catholic Bibles are Bigger*; *Hostile Witnesses: How the Historic Enemies of the Church Prove Christianity*; and *Making Sense of Mary*.

Dr. Brian Bradford is a renowned scholar of comparative religions, concentrating on the timely topic of Islam and the Middle East. His many books include *Muhammad's Jesus*, an examination of how Muslims understand Christ; and *Islamic Jerusalem: The Invention of a Holy City*, which argues that Muslim concern about Jerusalem's religious importance is an expression of Islamic supremacy.

Master gardener Margaret Rose Realy is a writer, speaker and retreat leader. Formerly coordinator of the St. Francis Retreat Center Garden Society in DeWitt, she is the author of *A Garden of Visible Prayer* and other books, and she writes regularly on gardening and spirituality for Catholic Digest, CatholicMom.com, and Patheos.com.

Bill Kassel is the author of *My Brother's Keeper*, a carefully researched historical novel about the family of Jesus. He is a Catholic journalist and media producer who runs a popular blog, "The Guy In the Next Pew."

Book sales during the *Catholic Authors of Michigan* mini book fair will be handled by staff members from the Catholic Shoppe of Jackson. Volunteers will be on hand to give studio tours, answer questions about the Good Shepherd Catholic Radio apostolate, and provide refreshments. For additional information call: 517-513-3340.

NOTE TO MEDIA: Participating authors will available for interviews during this event.

often wondered if a certain amount of this rabbinical attention might be more than was deserved by his actual scholarly gifts, ample though they were.

"What did all of you think about this story?" Ezra asked the class.

The group was silent. James too said nothing. He knew the day's lesson was aimed at the younger boys and the rabbi did not expect him to respond.

Ezra waited. Then: "Well, let us recall what happened in the story. Ephraim son of Joel, what did the two brothers do?"

The chubby boy, son of the town blacksmith, wrinkled up his face in thought. "They made sacrifice to the Lord," he said after a moment.

"That's right," Ezra said. "And what did they bring before the Lord?"

Ephraim thought again. "Well..." he said, "Cain brought crops, and..." His words dissolved into the silence of uncertainty.

"Yes, Cain was a tiller of the fields," the rabbi said. "And what was Abel?"

The strain of remembering was apparent in the boy's soft features, but all his effort yielded no result.

Ezra turned to another student. "Caleb son of Mathias, do you remember what was the work of Abel?"

"He was a shepherd," the boy answered quickly with a grin at his triumph over a classmate.

"A shepherd, yes," the rabbi said. "And what would a shepherd offer as a sacrifice?"

"He offered a lamb," said Caleb.

The rabbi clapped his hands together. "A lamb," he said, glancing at James, who was amused at the rabbi's playful and teacherly prompting.

"Now," said Ezra, "what happened when Cain and Abel made sacrifice? Was the Holy One pleased?" He pointed to Abner. "Abner son of Benjamin, did the Lord like what Cain and Abel brought Him?"

The boy hesitated. "Y—yes...?" he proposed warily.

"Did He?" asked the rabbi. "Remember the story which James son of Joseph read to us."

Caleb waved a hand to attract his teacher's attention. "The Lord liked Abel's gift," he said.

"Ah! Caleb son of Mathias recalls that the lamb of Abel was pleasing to the Holy One," said Ezra. "But what of the crops brought by Cain?"

"He didn't like them," said Ephraim, at last connecting with yesterday's reading.

"You're right, He didn't like them. And how did this make Cain feel?"

Caleb was about to speak again, but the rabbi looked at the boy, winked, and held a finger to his lips. Caleb smiled in satisfaction, understanding that his teacher realized he knew the answer.

"Ephraim son of Joel, Abner son of Benjamin, how did Cain feel?" asked Ezra.

"He felt bad," said Ephraim.

"Yes." The rabbi nodded his head solemnly. "He felt very bad. In fact, the story tells us that Cain's face fell." The rabbi's features became an exaggerated mask of comic sadness at which everyone laughed.

In such a back-and-forth manner, Ezra led the group through a recounting of Abel's murder at the hands of his brother and the Lord's banishment of Cain. He emphasized the seriousness of Cain's act, but took care not to present the tale in a way that was too frightening to the children whose minds it was his duty to nurture.

When the lesson was concluded, James lingered in the wicker-shaded enclosure. It was not unusual for him to remain behind to ask some question of his teacher or discuss the day's topic in more detail than would have interested the other students, even those closer to his own age. But today he sat quietly, gazing off in the direction of the synagogue building.

Ezra noted the boy's distraction. "Something burdens your mind, James son of Joseph?"

James turned to his teacher. "Oh...no, master," he said. "Not really. It's just that... Well, I have heard the story of Cain and Abel so many times, and..."

"Yes?"

"Rabbi, I have never understood why the Holy One should have rejected Cain's offering. Didn't Cain bring what he had to give, just as his brother did?"

"Do you think the Lord was unfair to Cain?"

"It seems like He favored Abel. And I don't know why."

Ezra sat down on the bench next to the boy. "This is a question the sages have pondered," he said. "Some note that the scriptures mention particularly that Abel offered the finest of his flock—where it's merely recorded that Cain offered crops, with no description of what they were or how good they might have been. So perhaps Cain was holding back his best and he deserved the Lord's rebuke."

"But we don't know that."

"This is true. We don't know."

"What if he did pick the best of his crops to give?"

"Mmm... He might have. But even if he did, there could be a problem in that also."

"How?"

Ezra seized upon an opportunity to push the boy into deeper reflection. "Well," he said, "here you must try to think like the sages who understand that Scripture teaches as much by what it doesn't say as by what it does. Suppose Cain had worked very hard, day in and day out, in all kinds of weather to make things grow, and then he chose very carefully so that he would be sure to set only his very best produce before the Holy One of Israel. And maybe, through all those days when he was toiling in the field, he had watched his brother lounging with his flock or leading the animals aimlessly about. Maybe all of this had made Cain feel that his efforts were better than those of Abel. Could it be the Lord saw that Cain was puffed up with his own superiority? Perhaps the Holy One knew that Cain had come to despise his brother even before the two made their offerings."

James examined the situation posed by Ezra. "My brothers are shepherds," he said. "They are farmers too, if you think about the olive grove they're trying to make."

"At which tasks do they work harder?" the rabbi asked.

"I'm not sure," James said. "With the olive trees they must dig and fertilize and water. With the sheep they must haul feed, and of course they have to sheer them. All of that is work."

"Yes. All of that is work," Ezra agreed. "So I guess we cannot really know what was in Cain's heart, and we cannot be sure why Abel's gift was pleasing to the Lord and Cain's not."

"Then what can we learn from the story, Rabbi?" James asked.

Ezra saw the boy's puzzled expression, and he smiled in a kindly way that was intended to encourage. "Perhaps what we can learn," he said, "is that the Lord has His own designs."

*   *   *

This time of year, classes were dismissed before the day's heat accumulated fully, so it was still morning when James arrived back at the family compound. He performed the usual entrance ritual, kissing his fingers and touching the scroll of the Commandment (called in Hebrew a *mezuzah*), the small piece of parchment bearing Torah verses and rolled inside a niche in the doorpost. He noticed that there were no children in sight, which struck him as unusual, since the court was normally alive with the din of childish play.

There were, however, two men standing in the portico of the house he shared with his father, who was at this moment addressing them, head slightly bowed in humble greeting. Approaching the portico, James recognized one of the visitors: Joachim, an aged neighbor and the wealthiest man in Nazareth, holder of vast estates on which perhaps a fifth of the farmers in the region were tenants. James' brothers, Judas and Simon, pastured their flock on part of his land.

The other visitor was a stranger, and an especially distinguished-looking one. Though clearly older than James' father, this man stood imposingly to the full extent of his tall size. His robes and turban were bleached a bright white, and the sash around his middle was an interlacing of cords in different colors woven with flecks of gold. James recognized it as a badge of status.

Joseph spotted his son, and made a gesture which the boy caught and understood. James ran to the side of the house, found a basin and sponge, and went to the well in the court. He filled the basin with water, and brought it to the portico. Joseph motioned the visitors to be seated, and they placed themselves side-by-side on a wooden bench whose edges were carved in a motif of vines and leaves. Joachim exhibited some slight difficulty in doing so.

The boy knelt down, removed their sandals, and proceeded to wash their feet with the sponge. Their nodding heads acknowledged the gesture of hospitality.

"My son, James," said Joseph, taking a stool and seating himself across from the visitors.

Joachim eyed the boy approvingly. "He has grown," the old man said. "What age is he now?"

"Soon to be twelve years," Joseph replied.

"So he will celebrate his maturity in just over a year then?"

Joseph nodded. "He looks forward to when he can be counted as one of the ten men for a service."

"Wonderful," said the tall, distinguished-looking visitor. "A fine son."

James completed the foot washing, stood with the basin, and bowed. He would not presume to refasten the guests' sandals.

Joseph put a hand on the boy's shoulder. "James," he said, "you know our esteemed townsman, Master Joachim."

It wasn't the most common thing for a young boy to be included in introductions among adults, but the warmth between father and son was evident to the visitors. James bowed toward Joachim, holding his tongue as befit his youth.

"But I especially wish for you to remember the day," Joseph continued, "when you were in the presence of the honored Zacharias, great priest of the Lord's temple."

James emitted a quick gasp, and his eyes went immediately to the tall man. The boy was duly impressed, as his father had known he would be. For such a figure to grace Joseph's home was an occasion to be spoken of down the generations.

Joachim smiled, amused at the boy's stunned reaction. "James studies the holy books with great diligence," he said to his companion. "Is that not true, Joseph?"

"My son has been a student of the Rabbi Ezra, here in Nazareth, since the age of five years. Ezra tells me that James has great prospects. He often has him lead the other boys in their recitations. When he is older, Ezra will find him a more learned master."

Zacharias smiled kindly at the boy. "A joy to you, Joseph, I am sure," he said. "But he should learn in Jerusalem. When the time comes, send him to me. I will see to a placement in one of the houses of study."

Joseph glanced at James and met the boy's eyes. Then he looked back at the exalted visitor. "I...would be forever grateful," Joseph said, unsure at what should prompt such a statement. Was it a sincere offer, or merely a social nicety?

James' face was reddened from the kind words spoken about him. He withdrew from the porch, carrying the basin.

The unsparing Galilean sun had brought the court near to its usual, cooking, midday temperature. But a slight breeze left Joseph and his guests cool in the shade of the portico. The two visitors sat quietly for a while, leaving their host in great perplexity about the reason for their coming. James shared his father's curiosity, though he shared it at a distance, listening from behind a large bush at the end of the portico by the stairway leading to the upper room.

Joachim appeared to Joseph to be somewhat unsettled, which could have been the effect of his poor health. He was indeed quite aged, his hands had a noticeable tremor, his skin was pale with many flaked patches, and the shock of fine, pure-white hair sticking almost straight out from under his cap was buffeted easily by even the slightest movement of the air. Joseph noted that he seemed as uncomfortable sitting as he had when he was shuffling slowly across the court. The old man had suffered the loss of his wife, Anna, not more than two years before, and it was said in the town that her passing had accelerated his long decline.

Joachim looked around the court, and then turned this gaze up to the sheltering roof overhead. "When you added this structure," he said, "it was just before the wedding of your son, was it not? What is his name?"

"Simon," said Joseph.

"Simon, of course. The flock. Forgive me. My memory..."

"We completed it in time for his wedding feast," said Joseph.

"I attended. I recall that."

"My house was honored by your presence. Simon is a father three times since then."

"Three times?"

"Yes."

"You are blessed."

"The Lord is generous," Joseph said.

"The Lord is generous," Zacharias repeated.

Joseph suddenly felt a flash of guilt. It was common knowledge that the wife of the famous priest had borne him no children, and he hoped that the joy of his own family life was not a reminder of that sadness. Joachim had been in a similar circumstance until late life. Then, a daughter. Joseph was glad he had instructed his sons' wives to keep all the children out of the court while the visitors were present.

Joachim stirred slightly on the bench, his face showing a fleeting grimace. "We have come, Joseph," he said, "I and my friend and honored kinsman, Zacharias— You are aware that my late wife was sister to Zacharias' wife, Elizabeth?"

"I am," said Joseph.

"Yes. Well...we wish to make...a request."

"Anything I am able to grant," Joseph said.

Zacharias laughed—very slightly, but still a laugh. "You are a most gracious man, Joseph. You must wait until you hear our request."

The priest's remark added to Joseph's increasing puzzlement over this visit. To James' as well. What an extraordinary thing that these men should come here. The carpenter had never before met Zacharias, though the holy man's fame had reached to Nazareth, as throughout all of Galilee and Judea. And as for Joachim—he was a neighbor, Joseph had served him with his carpentry skills, and his sons tenanted their flock in the rich man's fields. But to have him seated here was something very unusual.

"Yes," said Joachim. "It is not a small thing that I wish to ask you."

Now Joseph's curiosity was highly aroused. He waited in silence, but with impatience.

"Joseph," said Joachim, "you know that my daughter, Mary, has lived in the temple precincts. I and my wife, Anna, of blessed memory, had passed many years without the joy of children. Then the Holy One saw fit to bestow a gift. And such was our gratitude—and our relief, really..." He looked at Joseph with a sudden sadness of bitter reflection. "I once tried to make sacrifice in the temple, and the priest told me I was unfit because heaven had withheld children from my wife and me. You cannot imagine the shame."

"The shame was upon that priest," said Zacharias firmly. "I can only say that he was not of Abijah, my priestly division."

"I know, my friend, I know," said Joachim. "But that is past. When Mary came to us...after so long and painful a wait...my wife and I felt

it must have suited the Lord's purpose in a special way. The child belonged to the King of the Universe. We cherished her for three years...
three wonderful years...until she was weaned. That was all we had any
right to hold her as our own. We dedicated her to the service of the
Holy One, blessed be He."

"That was a great sacrifice," Joseph said. "It must have been very
difficult to give her childhood over to the temple."

Joachim's head moved slowly up and down. "Yes. This is true. Difficult. Still, we were confirmed in our decision when we delivered her to
the virgins' quarters." He paused, a hand going to his face, thoughtfully
fingering his white and tangled beard. "You would have been amazed,
Joseph. We expected the child to cry at our parting. Such a thing would
have been natural, what a child *would* do. But she waved us away. I remember her little happy smile. It was a strange thing...so very strange.
Her legs carried her up the steps as if she were dancing."

His face lit at the memory, and he started to laugh. "To be truthful, I
expected that *we* would cry—Anna and me—and embarrass ourselves
in front of the party that had come with us to make our presentation.
But we did not. We both experienced a most wonderful feeling of consolation. I have never been able to explain it, or to understand how it
should have come upon us, or why. Such things are beyond explaining."

Joseph, of course, was aware of the temple virgins and their life of
prayer, study and service. And he had often heard the gibes about how
the priests, for all their tithes and temple tax, would not be able to keep
the place running without the little girls and old women who knew
where the mops and brooms were kept. Mary was the only child from
Nazareth whom Joseph was aware served in the temple. But he had
known nothing of the circumstances of her going, beyond town gossip.
To hear these details from the lips of her father was moving.

To James it was all quite baffling. He had heard that this neighbor
girl was serving in the temple, but he found it hard to imagine a childhood spent separated from home and family, so far away in Jerusalem.
He could not imagine a young boy in such circumstances, much less a
girl.

Zacharias leaned toward Joseph with hands on knees. The priestly
turban gave his face, framed by his silvery gray hair and beard, an as-

pect of authority. "There is a problem now, however," he said.

"Yes," Joachim agreed, "a problem."

"Let us come to the point," the priest said to Joseph's unspoken agreement.

Despite being made privy to Joachim's family story—an interesting tale and a privilege to hear it—Joseph was no closer to understanding why these visitors were here.

Zacharias sensed a subtle impatience in their host. "Mary has reached nearly fourteen years," he went on. "For some time we have expected her to attain her womanhood and for her first flow of blood to begin. It is surprising that this has not happened already, but surely it will soon. This means that her stay in the temple will be concluded because the days of impurity will come. It is customary for the families of temple virgins to arrange marriages for them upon completing the term of service. Being pious and hard-working young women, they make exemplary wives and mothers. But..."

This hesitation prompted Joachim to speak again. "The problem, Joseph," he said, "is that Mary does not wish to marry. She insists upon carrying on with the dedication her mother and I made for her—that is, on remaining a virgin devoted to the Lord—even though there is no place for a girl her age in the temple."

"We can make no provision for her," said Zacharias.

Joseph took on a quizzical look. "As her father," he said, "do you not have the power to insist that she be absolved of this dedication? If you never intended for it to be lifelong, then—"

"Yes, I could do that," said Joachim. "I could do that. But...how can I explain... Mary is an unusual girl, Joseph. Gentle, but...intense. She feels deeply, and she is...insistent." The old man shrugged, his face in a crooked smile. "I am old, Joseph. Perhaps too softhearted? I admit it. I admit it. But I suffer with many infirmities, and I know...that the Lord will call me soon."

"You have kin," Joseph said. "Surely someone could—"

"There are clanship connections through which my properties are entailed," said Joachim. "But Elizabeth, Zacharias' wife, is the only *close* relative."

"We are old, ourselves, you see" said the priest. "One way or the other, Mary would be left alone."

"Even if I had relatives to take her," Joachim said, "how could Mary ever be assured that she could retain her virginity as she wishes? Whoever became her guardian could insist that she marry. I cannot have this, you see. My daughter's welfare must be looked after, her dedication respected. She is so young."

Joseph's curiosity was beginning to give way to unease. What did these men want of him? His three older sons all had wives, and his youngest was but a boy. And in any case, if the girl wished to remain unmarried, what had her commitment to do with him?

Joachim brought his hands together in the lap of his robes, Joseph's eyes following them. They were indeed the hands of an aged one, misshapen, trembling. He saw great pain in the fingers with their swollen joints under almost translucent flesh through which one could clearly discern the outlines of the bones.

"Joseph," said Joachim, now looking away, "it has been quite some years since the passing of your wife, Escha, of blessed memory. Yet, you have not remarried."

Joseph was silent.

"People in the town—I myself, in fact—well...it is often wondered if you might have had opportunities," Joachim said. "Surely, a man of distinction like yourself... You must have been approached. Many families would consider you... That is, the name of Joseph the builder is known throughout the whole of Galilee. You manage workers. You have authority, you have means. Yet you have remained unmarried." He looked directly at Joseph now. "Please, my friend, I know that I have no right to question you in such a way. Forgive me, but..."

"I have a family," said Joseph. "I am in middle life. Actually, a bit *more* than middle life."

"You are younger than I am," said Joachim. "Considerably so."

Joseph nodded. "That is true. And...yes, I have thought about what you suggest. The matchmaker has come to inquire on several occasions. But Escha, my wife... When she died, I just— Well, could another woman find a place in my heart? I don't know. I have never believed so."

"Joseph—if I may..." Joachim was at pains to avoid giving offense, and torn over having to venture into such a private area. Still, he pressed on. "What of a man's...*longing*...my friend? Again, I beg forgiveness. I have no right to question these things, no right at all. And of course, I speak only of the wholesome and proper feelings which a husband has for his wife. But...are such desires...behind you?"

Behind the bush, James' ears perked up, the inquisitiveness of a boy piqued at hearing his father probed along such lines.

Joseph looked from Joachim to Zacharias and then back at Joachim again. He saw no prurience in their faces. Indeed, their eyes bore into him with what was obviously a great sincerity of purpose.

"Surely," he said, "you cannot be thinking of *me* as a match for your daughter. I am well beyond the age even of being her father. I know that such marriages are not uncommon, but I have never thought them wise or fair, especially for the young girls. And besides, if Mary does not want a husband—"

"Mary's wishes are precisely of the essence," Zacharias said. "But... to the question, Joseph—do you no longer feel the needs of a man for a wife?"

Joseph was astonished. He sat quietly for some seconds. These men had come to ask him to marry Joachim's daughter. He hardly knew how to respond.

"My honored guests," he said at last. "Let me say that I am content with the life which the Lord has given me. He blesses me beyond measure. I am surrounded by my family—children, grandchildren. What more could a man of my age ask? What would be even *right* for him to ask? I have no wish to marry."

"Then, the question of desires..." said Zacharias, not letting the point drop.

Joseph was becoming annoyed. His visitors could see it in his face and in the rigid posture of his body on the stool. He had tried to answer their unwelcome queries in as discreet and dignified a manner as he could.

"Your forbearance and your forgiveness—please," Zacharias insisted. "The question..."

Joseph now felt embarrassment mixed with a feeling that was close to anger. Only his long and high regard for Joachim and the priestly status of Zacharias kept him from being overtaken by temper, something rarely seen in the steady and self-possessed carpenter.

"Let my contentment to remain without a wife be an answer to that question," he said. "Draw from it what conclusions you will."

A meaningful glance passed between Joachim and Zacharias, though whatever meaning it contained was quite beyond Joseph. The three men sat silently again for more seconds, Joseph trying to calm himself. Then Joachim, with an exertion that told of his age and weakness, straightened himself on the bench and spoke.

"My friend Joseph, please realize that our presence here, and these intrusive questions, reflect nothing but the utmost respect—which you surely deserve, and which you may be certain we have for you."

"Truly so," Zacharias added.

Again Joseph was without words.

Joachim continued. "My daughter is settled on her virginity. I cannot say that I understand her insistence, and as her father, I do not favor her choice. I would see her wedded to a fine young husband and grandchildren on the way soon after. Such is the outcome I prefer. Still, I respect the strength of her conviction, and I must assume that the hand of the Holy One is in it. Anna and I accepted the sacrifice of our child once, and I am prepared to accept it again. But my time is short, and Mary must be looked after. If a man were prepared to take her into his home—with no expectations that would compromise the discipline she wishes to impose upon herself—such a man would be doing a great kindness, both to Mary and to me."

"It would be a deed of the highest merit," Zacharias added.

Joseph's body lost its stiffness, and he made a long exhalation of breath. As presumptuous and startling as this proposal was, he recognized in it an honor, coming as it did from two men of such high standing.

"She would, of course," Joachim continued, "come with a generous dowry—"

Zacharias interjected, "That is, we do not wish in any way to imply, Joseph—"

"I do not take the words amiss," Joseph said. "Joachim is known to all as someone who is open-handed in the extreme. It is said he gives a generous portion of his income to the temple and its equivalent to the poor. I know he would be most unstinting to any husband, as befits his station and his good name."

"Indeed."

Joseph rose from the stool and walked to the front edge of the portico, standing with his back to Joachim and Zacharias, deep in pondering. James drew farther back around the side of the house to avoid his father's catching him listening in. The visitors glanced at each other again, then at Joseph, waiting for him to turn once more in their direction, which after a time, he did.

"Why do you make this request of *me*, Joachim?" asked Joseph. "We are both of the Tribe of Judah, but surely, that is not reason enough."

Joachim took time before answering the question, choosing his words with deliberation. "I asked myself, Joseph...to what man could I confidently entrust the care of my daughter? I considered several whom I had encountered over the years. Whom did I know that lived his life in accord with the Law of Moses? Who was faithful in fulfilling promises and meeting obligations? Who most had my trust?"

He paused again, stroked his beard, then held out a hand in Joseph's direction. "I have observed you in the execution of your craft and in the affairs of your business. I have seen you deal fairly with those who pay you for work and those who work for you. I have watched you at prayer in the synagogue, heard you read and discuss the holy books. I have observed the fatherly love in which you hold your family. I have sensed prudence, wisdom, charity. I speak here of righteousness, Joseph, *righteousness*. This is what I seek in the man who would care for my precious girl. And so, I come to you."

Joachim's words filled James with pride for his father. But Joseph was shaken. He stood with his eyes closed, almost ashamed to be in the sight of these two men. To hear such a recitation of his merits disturbed him deeply, because it echoed a struggle that had gone on within him all his life. He knew, deep in his heart, that Joachim's description of these qualities was accurate. He had always understood his own virtue. Yet he sought to walk humbly in the way of the Lord. *Humbly*. How can a man be humble when he knows that he is righteous? This was a quandary which Joseph had never been able to resolve.

Without opening his eyes, Joseph said, "It would be a great privilege to have the daughter of Joachim in our family compound." And then he did open his eyes. "We can accommodate her readily," he continued. "My sons and their wives will do their best to make her feel welcome. But marriage...this I do not know. Mary could certainly be regarded as an esteemed guest. A ward, maybe? Some sort of...adoption? Perhaps that would—"

Joachim reacted with a look almost of horror. "No," he said. "That cannot be. For you to adopt Mary while I still live—or for you to take her into your home under such conditions as you mention—this would shame me. People would get wrong, even malicious ideas. It is not without reason that those in other towns repeat the old joke that nothing good comes out of Nazareth. The gossip here can be vicious.

"And an arrangement must be made before I die," he continued. "I fear that Mary would not accept it when I am no longer here to persuade her. My daughter is a young woman of strong will. I must be honest and tell you this, right from the beginning, Joseph. She has a heart large enough to embrace the whole world, but she holds firmly to her own way once an idea has lodged itself in her mind."

"But of course this is a strength," Zacharias added quickly. "Mary has great attentiveness and devotion. I have observed it. She learned to weave while living in the temple precincts. She created several panels of the temple veil by herself. Everyone was impressed at her mastery of the craft—the fine work she was able to do, even though she was only a small girl at the time—and at how she persisted in a great and difficult task."

For a moment, Joseph found himself amused at these attempts at persuasiveness on the part of the priest. He knew that Zacharias was a trader when not serving in the temple. His caravans plied the routes to Idumea, Nabatea, the Arabian desert, Damascus, and many other parts far and near. It was obvious that the inclination toward selling did not fail him.

The carpenter returned to his stool and sat, his head turned down. Again, there was silence until, after more uncomfortable seconds, Joachim spoke.

"If you have any thought at all of marrying again, Joseph..." he said, "any at all—I mean to a wife who—" He left the awkward part unmentioned. "Well...I would certainly understand."

"No," Joseph said calmly, "I have no intention of that. In this time of life, my thoughts are not directed toward worldly pleasure. Without Escha...well... You see, I live in the world, and in so many ways, the world has been good to me. But now, my children, my grandchildren, my work—these are all the joy I ask of the world. I have no need of a wife in the way you suggest."

More silence. Joseph leaned forward on his arms, put his hands to his head, and thought—deeply. He understood that Joachim was a man of pride who would not make such a request as this but for the most tender concern. Joachim loved his daughter, the living sign of the Lord's blessing upon him, the focus of his faith and gratitude. It was hard for Joseph to think of him here in this house near to begging.

Joachim and Zacharias heard a murmuring from Joseph, very quietly, words they could at first barely make out but then recognized as words of prayer: "Blessed are you, Lord our God, King of the Universe..." Joseph's voice trailed off, and all was stillness again. More seconds passed. Finally, the carpenter lifted his head, looked at Joachim, and said, "I will take Mary as my wife under the terms you propose—if she will agree."

Joachim held up his hands as if to clap them together in joy and relief, but then he restrained himself. "Thank you, my good friend," he said, "thank you, thank you. You have made the path to my grave straight and peaceful for me. May your name be remembered throughout the ages."

"You do an important thing this day," Zecharias said. "The Holy One is pleased, blessed be He."

*   *   *

James could see that his father was disturbed in his heart. After returning from the evening service at the synagogue, Joseph had asked Salome, the wife of Josis, to bring him some fruit and bread to eat alone, for there were things on his mind and his hunger was very slight. Salome complied, but included some olives and uncooked vegetables, along with a few pieces of meat, knowing that her husband's father frequently under-judged his appetite.

Josis, Judas and Simon were at their respective tables, eating with their wives and children. James should have been at Simon's table this night, but he stayed behind, sitting in the shadows at the far corner of the lower room in the lodgings he shared with Joseph. A faint shaft of light, the last of the day, penetrated the open-shuttered window on the west wall, the lamp not yet lit.

James' eyes were on the man who had been his only parent. The boy carried no memory of his mother, since she had died mere weeks after his birth. And while he had been looked after by his sisters and his brothers' wives, his father was the one living soul around whom his life had always turned. Would things be different when the girl, Mary, was in their home? What claims would she make on his father's love and attention? Being young, James only partly understood what he had caught of the discussion about a man's desire for a wife. He had heard Joseph say that he had no such desire, so he assumed his father's marriage would not be quite like that of other men. But what *would* it be like?

And what expectations would the girl have of James? Would she consider herself his new mother? Would Joseph demand that he defer to this stranger who was only two years older than the boy? There were so many questions. Perhaps there were yet no answers. Perhaps that was all part of his father's unsettled mood.

A slight movement of James' foot caused a sound that roused Joseph's attention.

"My son? Are you there?" he asked. "I did not see you. Come out of the dark."

James stood and walked across the room, slipped off his sandals, and deposited himself on a mat near where his father was seated beside a low table.

"Did you eat in Simon's house?" Joseph asked.

"No, Father," said James. "I was not hungry."

"When are you not hungry?"

"Just tonight, Father." And the boy laughed nervously.

"Eat with me," said Joseph. "Salome has brought me more than I need. She always wants to fatten me like a calf."

Father and son washed their hands. Joseph took a small cup, drew water from a basin that sat beside the table and poured it over each of his hands, reciting the prayer for washing. James repeated his father's actions. Then each broke off a piece of the loaf Salome had provided, and recited the blessing of bread. They began picking from a tray in the middle of the table.

James considered how to address the subject of this person who was to come into the household. It was a delicate problem. Joseph would not like that his son had listened in on the talk of these visitors, but James very much wanted to understand the changes that lay ahead for the family—and for himself. He had to ask.

"Father," the boy ventured, "when will Mary come to our house?"

Joseph's eyebrows went up slightly, and his hand paused in delivering a morsel of lamb to his mouth. Then he smiled. "You are always the curious one," he said. "You heard my talk with the men?"

"Yes, Father."

Joseph thought of scolding, though he didn't think of it seriously. "No matter," he said. "You would have learned of these things soon enough. Have you told your brothers?"

"No, Father."

"Then please don't. I will tell them what is to happen."

"What *is* to happen, Father?"

When this morning's discussion on the porch had turned to specific details of Mary's coming, the voices of all three men grew softer, and James could not hear as much. He knew only that a marriage was to take place between his father and Joachim's daughter.

Joseph ate the piece of lamb, then said, "Mary will leave the temple before the turn of the new year. Then, a betrothal will be announced. A date for the wedding will be set at that time. There is no urgency, and I have projects that will take me way from Nazareth for several weeks. My journey has been planned for some time. We will marry after I return."

"Does Mary know?" the boy asked.

"Her father will speak with her," Joseph said. He reached to take some olives from the tray, then hesitated, aware once more of his lack of hunger, and clasped his hands together with his arms resting on the table.

James noticed. "You should eat, Father," he said.

Joseph looked at the boy fondly. "And so should you, my son."

"Then, we will eat together," James said.

Joseph smiled, and the two of them took food from the tray and ate. After a time, James, renewed his questioning.

"Do you think that Mary will want to marry you?"

"Mary is an obedient daughter," said Joseph. "And from what

Joachim and Zacharias say, it seems that she is a bright girl. If this is so, then she will see that it is the best way for her to live in the manner she— Well, she will see the rightness of the arrangement her father has made for her. I am certain she will agree."

"Where will she sleep, Father?"

"The upper room. That will be her home. I will set it aside for her use only. Mary has known a life of prayer and study. And since she can no longer have that in the temple, then she will have it in her own home. Or at least something as near to it as possible."

"The upper room is where you and I sleep," said James.

Since his relationship with Mary would be of a different nature than that with his late wife, Escha, Joseph had naturally assumed the girl would require separate quarters. He would, in consequence, remove himself to the lower level of the house. But only now did it occur to him that dedicating the upper room to Mary's exclusive use would mean evicting his son from the space in which parent and child had shared their nights since James was small.

"Oh. Yes. I— I am sorry, my son. I must confess, I did not think about..."

The expression on James' face made Joseph realize what disruption this would bring to the well-established order and rhythms of his son's life. It was a point of pride to Joseph that he had always been a good father, able to provide a secure home and an orderly pattern of living for his sons and daughters. He observed how some families paid little heed to the conditions in which their children lived. He knew that far too many of the urchins glimpsed on the streets of Nazareth slept in the straw of animals—and looked it. Now, Joseph felt that, in helping Joachim, a man whom he respected, he had ignored the needs of his own flesh and blood.

"I truly am sorry, my son," he said.

James saw guilt in his father's eyes, and it stabbed him in his heart. "Where will *you* sleep, Father?" the boy asked.

"Here. In this room," said Joseph.

"Than I will sleep here with you," James said. "This will be *our* home."

If there was effort in the smile which James showed to his father, Joseph accepted it as a sign of love.

"Yes, my son," he said. "This will be our home. Of course, Mary will be welcome in it."

"Yes, Father. Mary will be welcome."

Escha had been right. James was the child of his old age. He loved the boy in a special way, and he resolved that whatever adjustments might have to be made, he would let nothing become an impediment to his relationship with this last and cherished son.

CHAPTER TWO

Many a man claims to have unfailing love,
but a faithful man who can find?

(Proverbs 20)

What an odd feeling it was for Mary to be in her father's house, even on a visit. During all the temple years, she had seen it only two times—once when she visited during an illness her mother had suffered, and again when Anna died. It was true that she had a vague recollection of running around the fountain in the center of the court as a tiny child, but that was little more than a sequence of half-formed and fleeting images. The thought of living in this place on a permanent basis gave her a feeling that was odd, indeed. But her life in the virgins' quarters would draw to a close in a matter of months, and the only possibility of returning would be in late age, after the monthly flow of blood would have ended and she no longer faced recurring impurity.

Was she sad at the turn her life would soon take? Mary could not say that, exactly. This was her ancestral home, and in any case, she had always known—it had been made amply clear to her, as to all the other girls—that temple life was of limited duration. Each virgin would eventually leave, to be succeeded by another in an ongoing cycle of prayer, study, and service to the Lord in his earthly dwelling. It was the will of Heaven that she should return to her father's house, and she had been told that this brief visit—two weeks, arranged by Zacharias—was preparation for that time soon to come.

If she was to live here, Mary could certainly console herself that the home of Joachim was a nice place to live. Hiram, the steward, had taken pains to see that her room would be comfortable. The chamber was considerably larger than the simple cell she occupied in the temple precincts. Two tall windows brought air and light. Big, down-filled pillows and coverlets were provided. A bronze, Roman-style brazier sat in the center of the floor for warding off the chill of night. Hiram stressed that the master's daughter had only to ask and her merest need would be met.

It was all more than Mary was used to. It made her feel small— even smaller than she was, which was quite petite. It also made her confused about what she should be doing. At this time of the evening she would normally have been preparing for bed after returning from prayer with the other virgins. But outside the rarefied world of the temple precincts, only men met to recite the evening service, women being exempt from such religious obligations because of their household duties. Mary didn't know what, if any, duties she would have in her father's household. She had no sense of what to expect or what was expected of her.

Perhaps it was too soon to concern herself with all of that. Her father would no doubt make his will clear to her—share with her how he saw her life with him—that is, when they had the chance to speak at length. Joachim had met Mary in the court upon her arrival from Jerusalem with Hiram and two other male servants who had brought her. Father and daughter shared an embrace and a few words of greeting, then he placed his hands on her head and offered a blessing of welcome.

But she had been tired after the journey and taken aback to see how shockingly frail he had become. The change from when she had seen him at the burial of her mother was pronounced. Joachim realized the effect his appearance had on his daughter. He insisted that she rest, and she was pleased to oblige. Her expectation was that they would dine together, so she was surprised when Hiram led a serving girl into her room later with food for Mary to take alone. Her father ate irregularly these days, the steward explained, but Joachim would speak with her that evening.

In correspondence with her father, Mary had obtained his assurance that she could retain her virginity when she left the temple precincts. Whatever the other circumstances of this new life to come, she would continue in her devotion to the Holy One of Israel. She would pray and she would study. If Heaven willed it, one day she would go back to Jerusalem.

Mary turned at the sound of soft footsteps in the doorway. It was Joachim.

"My daughter," he said, entering.

The girl rose. "Father."

"Are you rested, my dear child? I hope this room pleases you."

"I am rested, my father. And the room is fine. It is big."

Joachim smiled. There was a stool under one of the windows, and he sat, easing himself down with a difficulty which Mary could not help noting.

"Yes. No doubt it is different from the quarters to which you are accustomed," he said. "Forgive me for coming to you so late. I slept. These days, I sleep a great deal. As you can see—as it must be plain to you—my age is heavy upon me."

"What can I do to help you, my father?"

"Your being here helps me, child. It is a tonic to my tired old body. I rejoice in your youth and beauty. It refreshes."

Mary would have blushed at the compliment, but for the ache she felt watching the old man struggling as he was.

Joachim glanced up at the window behind him, then back at his daughter. "The cool of the night begins to come," he said. "My bones feel the chill so quickly now. That is a surprise of age. When you are young, coolness is pleasantly invigorating. In age, it attacks."

"Shall I light the brazier, Father?" Mary asked, eager to serve.

"No, no. I won't stay long. Your journey was hard. You must be to your bed, and I to mine." He laughed. "There, you see? I will sleep again. It seems that is all I do now."

Mary tried to smile in return. Joachim gestured toward the floor in front of him. She sat.

"My daughter," the old man said, "I realize that you have just arrived. And all that lies ahead of you—after your days in the temple come to an end—it will be new and unfamiliar. I would not be insulted if you feel a bit unsure, even frightened."

"This is your home, Father. And so it will be mine—as you and Mother always told me."

"Yes, it is your home." He was thoughtful for a moment. "What might your life have been like if you had grown up here? What joy might we have shared—you and your mother and me?" Another quiet moment. "Well...we shall never know. You belong to the King of the Universe, and it is right that you have served him."

"And soon I will serve *you*, Father."

Joachim smiled again. "That is a thought to warm my chilled bones," he said, and reached out to touch the side of Mary's small face with its delicate, sharply delineated features, the dark hair, those big eyes. "But, my child, surely you can see that I am a sick man. It was a joy to me when my late life was blessed by the Lord's gift of a daughter. Now it is a sadness that you come again when so little of my life is left to me." He peered deeply into those eyes. "But that too is the will of the Holy One, blessed be He."

Mary tried to speak, but could find no words to counter what was so plainly true.

Joachim had hoped for inspiration on how to begin what he expected to be a hard talk, but none was forthcoming. It would have been a blessing to have Mary with him, to enjoy her vitality for a few precious months. But she would soon return to Jerusalem, and each day's pain and travail added weight to the truth he knew all too well, that the end of his life was near. He could not be certain that he would last until the close of the year and the completion of her term in the temple. No delay was possible in broaching a difficult subject. Artfulness and tact were luxuries which time did not permit him. Mary would have to be presented with her destiny.

"What is essential now," Joachim continued, "is that you be taken care of when I am gone."

"Father, please do not speak of such—"

"My daughter...it is unfair that change should heap itself so quickly upon change in the life of one so young and innocent." His smile, as he looked upon the face of his beloved girl, was one of perfect fatherly love. "But these things must be said. I will die soon. That is a fact which cannot be avoided. And it is why the honored Zacharias made provision for you to come to me now, just months before you are scheduled to leave the temple."

"It *was* unexpected," said Mary.

"And highly irregular, I am sure. Zacharias understands that you will soon be orphaned."

"Father, surely I will see you at year's end."

"If the Lord allows."

"And after that—your home...*my* home..."

"There are relations, Daughter," Joachim said, "—distant relations that have legal claim on my properties. I cannot be sure whether my lands will continue to be held in one parcel or sold off. You will receive a bequest, of course, and it is substantial. I have structured things in a way that is a bit unconventional, but my plans will not be contested. The servants will also have their reward for years of dedication. All of this will be covered largely by the disposal of the house. It is of no small value. But that means it will belong to someone else."

Mary was suddenly distressed. "Then...where will I live?"

Joachim held up his hand, and his face showed an expression with which he sought to be reassuring. "I have made an arrangement, my child. I'm convinced it is the best way for you to be protected and cared for. But the terms require that you consent to it willingly."

Mary was confused. Having just arrived in her father's house, and anticipating the end of her years in the temple, she was facing yet another change ahead. She realized that Joachim had the power to compel his daughter's acceptance of any arrangement he might have made. Indeed, he was under no compulsion to consider her feelings at all. But Mary sensed from her father's tone that she was being asked to make a choice of great significance to her entire life.

She raised herself to her knees. "What is this...arrangement...Father?"

Joachim looked at the small figure of his daughter who knelt before him, and he saw in her great strength. A memory of Mary as a three-year-old, climbing the temple steps with a courage of which she was not even conscious flashed into his mind.

"I have spoken with Joseph, the carpenter and builder...just a little more than a week ago. He lives here in Nazareth, and he...has agreed to take you...as his wife."

Suddenly Mary felt her entire being flush with alarm. "But, Father," she said in near fright, "you promised that I could retain my virginity. You swore I could continue in my dedication—"

Both of Joachim's hands went up this time. "Yes, Daughter, yes," he said quickly. "This is my pledge to you, and I keep it. I promise."

"Then...I don't under—"

"Joseph is an older man. He is widowed with children, most of them grown. He is a man of great piety and virtue. He has my complete trust. And...he promises that he will renounce all husbandly demands upon your person. You will live in your own quarters within the family compound. He will treat you as a daughter."

Mary searched her mind for any awareness of who this builder, Joseph, might be. But her life had been spent away from Nazareth, and there was no image or piece of local information to which she could attach a thought. She felt a spinning in her head. Married? She was to be married? Even under such terms as her father described—a husband who would claim no conjugal rights—this was too much for her to contemplate. In a very real sense, it was too much to be believed.

"I am confident that you will find great comfort and happiness in the house of Joseph," Joachim continued. "His sons and their families all live there. That is, three of the sons are married. With their wives and children they all live on the grounds. They each have their own quarters. And there is a younger son, as well. A fine boy, somewhat younger than yourself. He is a budding scholar."

Mary could hear her father's voice as he recounted the details of Joseph's home and family and the terms of his arrangement with this man who would be her husband. But it was as if he was talking from a distance.

"And of course," Joachim expounded further, "because his sons are there, you will remain in the family, even when Joseph has departed. The sons will care for you. They will have an obligation to you as their stepmother. So you will always be protected and have a home."

After some more minutes of elaboration, the old man recognized the dazed look on his daughter's face. He understood that the prospect of such an extreme shift in the direction of her life was perhaps more than she could take in all at once.

"But then," he said, "we can speak of this in the morning. It is much for you to think about, and you must rest."

"Yes, Father," she said vaguely. "I must rest."

Joachim gathered up his strength and pulled himself to his feet. "Please know, Daughter, that my greatest concern—my *only* concern— is for your well-being. I cannot go to my grave knowing that I haven't protected you, that I left you a prey to the teeth of those who might do you harm, as the psalm says. You are yet so, so young." He started to make his way slowly across the room to the doorway. "Please think of these things. We will speak more tomorrow."

She was still kneeling before the stool where Joachim had sat. He was out of the room when she finally collapsed back on her heels and said, in a quiet, distracted voice, "Yes, Father, we will speak more tomorrow."

*   *   *

Mary did not expect to sleep when she turned to her bed. For some time, her mind whirled with thoughts and wild conjecture about this new life her father had planned for her. But then, tiredness overcame her. Once asleep, she slumbered deeply the entire night, with dreams that were surprisingly pleasant. Light breaking through the two windows woke her gently, and she felt refreshed and calm.

She prayed the morning service upon rising, interrupted by the serving girl who brought a basin of water. The servant realized that she had disturbed her mistress, and was embarrassed. But Mary's gentle smile set the girl, who was about her own age, at ease, and she withdrew.

After Mary had finished her prayers and washed, she put on a clean white tunic and shawl, then went out to the court, where she found her father reclining on a divan. It was situated in the center of a small pergola with an overhead lattice from which wide swaths of cloth were suspended at their corners to provide shade. A low, round table sat beside him.

Joachim's face lit at her approach. "My daughter," he called. "Be seated. Food is coming. You slept well, I hope."

Mary deposited herself on a cushion. "Yes, Father. Very well."

"I am glad."

Joachim raised himself on one arm, which shook slightly under the effort. Mary reached toward him to help, but he waved her off.

"My child, I have sent word to Joseph, asking that he come to us this evening. We will dine, and you will see for yourself what a fine and noble fellow he is. Though if you asked anyone in Nazareth, they would confirm his honorable character."

It was obvious Joachim intended to persist in the effort to convince his daughter of the rightness of what he was proposing. Mary did not feel so much put under pressure by her father's single-mindedness as she felt sad for him. If this was a matter of such urgency, he must surely feel the angel of death close at hand. She thought about Joachim's wistful question of the night before. What might their life have been like if she had not spent her childhood in the temple? But such musings profited nothing, and she did not let herself dwell on the thought.

"Yes, my father," she said. "I am happy to meet this Joseph. I realize that you have my best interest at heart. And we shall see."

Joachim was encouraged by Mary's openness to his intention. The girl had always shown great wisdom—wisdom well beyond her years. It had been remarked upon in the temple.

Mary spent most of the day exploring her father's house and grounds. Hiram the steward set his young son, Mordechai, the task of leading the master's daughter on a tour. Mary lost herself in exploring barns, animal pens and the meadow where a small herd of cattle grazed. Mordechai took her to the top of a hill from which the whole of Nazareth could be viewed. She asked the boy if he might point out the house of Joseph the builder, but he was uncertain which it might be.

She did not converse with her father again during that day. The old man took to his bed once more, though not before urging Mary to rest herself when the sun would be highest in the sky. His urging reflected sincere fatherly concern, but he also wanted her to be fresh and at her best for the meeting with Joseph.

It was late afternoon, at the conclusion of her explorations, when Mary heeded his entreaty. She found a tray with fruit waiting for her in her room, but she ignored it and lay down on the bed. Not long after, she awoke, surprised to realize that she actually had drifted off to sleep. She sat for a time on the floor, praying. Anxiety had begun to take hold again, and she asked the King of the Universe to give her strength and clarity of mind for the decision ahead.

After praying, Mary went out to find the serving girl. She asked for water, that she might wash in preparation for the evening, and the girl quickly brought a basin. When she had finished cleansing herself, Mary dressed in the last of the three white tunics that were the main elements of her wardrobe from the temple. She would have to attend to laundry tomorrow, and she wondered if she would be permitted to wash her own clothes.

So far, all her needs had been met by the serving girl—whose name, it now occurred to Mary, she did not know. That would have to be rectified. The girl seemed shy and sweet. Perhaps she might be a friend. After all, Mary thought, was she, herself, not a servant in the temple? There were many chores along with prayer and study. Mary was well acquainted with the work of human hands.

It was Hiram who came to tell the master's daughter that her father desired her presence. Rising, she straightened her tunic, fastened her hair in back with a linen ribbon died dark blue, then took up a pale-blue shawl, which was the mark of the temple virgins, and draped it over her head. She followed the steward down a corridor and into the common room. Joachim was seated on the divan, brought in from the pavilion where he had reclined at the morning meal. There was a man standing by, holding himself erect, a walking staff in his hand.

Nervous as she was, Mary willed herself to not let her feelings show, but she was unable to restrain her eyes from going to the visitor. He was tall and muscular, with the large hands one would expect of a man who worked in timber or stone. Mary might have described him as handsome, for someone his age, which she could see was sufficient for him to be her father—though not nearly as old as her actual father. There was still color in the man's hair and beard, a fine black among the strands of gray. She doubted he was as old as Joachim had been when she was born. Still, in no sense would he be called young. Perhaps her father was right and she *could* be confident of having her virginity respected.

Joachim noted the girl's entry into the room and extended a hand in her direction. "Ah, the treasure of my life, my daughter, Mary." Then, turning to his guest, the old man said, "And this, Daughter, is my esteemed friend, Joseph, son of Jacob, of the line of David."

Joseph bowed his head. "I am honored to meet the daughter of Joachim."

Mary lowered her eyes demurely and bowed her head in return.

Joachim bade Joseph to place his staff down and set himself at ease on a chair made with curved wooden supports that crossed each other front and back in the Roman style, and a cushioned seat. He gestured for his daughter to join him on the divan. There was very little ease in any of them, since all understood the importance of this first meeting. A conversation then ensued with difficulty. They spoke of Mary's time in the temple, about which Joseph seemed genuinely curious. Then Joachim prodded Joseph into a long discourse about his family: his sons and their wives, his grandchildren, the life of his household, his business.

Joseph spoke of learning the carpenter's trade as a boy, of how his father had first assigned him the task of pulling nails from recovered timbers and broken implements, and straightening them for reuse. It was a lesson in frugality that had stayed with him through life—and also a lesson in carefulness. He would roll each nail on a stone, striking it on all sides until it was straight enough to be hammered into new wood without bending under a blow. He taught his own son, Josis, to do the same, and many were the fine Greek villas in Sepphoris whose headers and lintels were fastened by the proud and ancient nails of Nazareth. Mary laughed at the story, and Joseph seemed pleased to have amused her.

Most of the talk was between Joachim and Joseph, which was fine with Mary. Any self-possession gained living in the temple was not quite strong enough to overcome the natural shyness of a young girl in the presence of two older men. And anyway, she understood that too much womanly chatter was not held as becoming.

She quietly watched the interplay going on before her, sensing a confident nature in Joseph. And a warmth. He spoke about his family with great tenderness, which Mary found appealing. In her father she observed enthusiasm, an engagement in all this talk that seemed to lift him out of his decrepitude. She now fully understood that Joachim had much hope invested in this prospective match. This was his will for her. That much was clear.

Was it the will of Heaven? How could she know?

Servants brought in dinner, and the men continued to dominate the conversation as they ate. Mary continued to observe. When the meal was finished and they had said the blessing, she begged her father's leave to absent herself, and went to her chamber. It was her intention to sit for a few minutes to reflect and pray.

On entering the room, she saw that a vase of flowers had been placed on the small table near her bed. Lilies. They had always been a favorite. They grew in the temple precincts, and she had often collected them to decorate the virgins' quarters. Mary smiled when she saw the trumpet-shaped blooms, wondering if her father had directed that they be put there as a gentle encouragement to her positive evaluation of Joseph. Then she wasn't sure if he even knew about her love for lilies. There was no recollection of ever mentioning it.

Mary sat in prayer for a time, until she heard voices in one of the windows. She stood and peered out into the twilight. Joachim was walking in the court, haltingly, supported by the muscular arm of Joseph. The two men were still deep in their conversation. Watching them, she began to wonder at Joseph's willingness to participate in this arrangement for her care.

The talk at dinner had made it clear to Mary that he was in no need of any money Joachim might offer for her sustenance. And while widowed—for some years, apparently—he had his family, even a young son. James, Joseph had called him. These were all the comforts he should need to carry him to the end of life. And yet, he was willing to take a girl, young enough to be his daughter, into his home, and bind himself to a promise of chastity toward her.

Joachim was most certainly convinced of Joseph's integrity. And even after only this brief meeting, Mary did not question her father's judgment. There was something about this builder, this carpenter, that gave her—if not certainty—at least a kind of comfort, though she could not explain why. Comfort was something she dearly wished for at this moment. For, in truth, her situation offered no real alternative to marriage. Joachim was dying. Who would take her in?

But no. It was not resignation which Mary felt. She was experiencing something very different from just acceptance, from a mere facing of the inevitable. Suddenly, unexpectedly, she realized that she felt confident. Restored. Almost serene. It was the first time she had dared to feel any such way since realizing she was nearing the age when she must leave the temple.

Mary turned from the window, and her eyes fell on the lilies again. She went to the vase and snatched up the flowers, perhaps only in a small, unthinking effort to associate a tangible thing of earthly beauty and fond memory to the warmth which now radiated inside her. She left her chamber and went back to the common room, intending to wait for Joachim and Joseph to return. But then she spotted Joseph's walking staff where it lay behind the Roman-style chair.

The table had been cleared of the dinner remains, and on impulse, she set the flowers down on its surface. Then she went to get the staff off the floor and brought it to the table. Her hands reached to the back of her head, under the light blue shawl, and she untied the linen ribbon, setting her hair loose over her shoulders. Mary gathered up the flowers around the end of Joseph's staff, fastening them with the narrow, dark blue cloth strip. She propped the staff, with its new decoration, up against the chair for the men to find. They would understand its meaning.

Mary, the virgin daughter of Joachim, looked at this symbol she had created, crude and girlish as it was, and she grinned in satisfaction. Then she left the common room and returned to her bed chamber.

CHAPTER THREE

I have chosen him, that he may charge his children and his household after him
to keep the way of the Lord by doing righteousness and justice.

(Genesis 18)

Joseph's sons were perplexed at the imminent coming of Mary, though not at all surprised. They knew their father to be a man of charity. Indeed, it was held in the family that if angels came to test the hearts of men, as the holy books recorded, then a goodly batch had passed through their gate, found the food pleasing, and sent back word to others in Heaven to come and sample the fare. What else could account for the long line of down-at-their-luck relatives and misbegotten wanderers who had taken refuge in the house of Joseph over the years?

To Josis, much the eldest, it was a matter of some humor that this mere slip of a girl would be their new stepmother. "That is the sort of match made in royal families," he said. "I guess the blood of David still marks us as special."

His brothers laughed. Joseph smiled, but then waved the levity to a close.

"My sons," he said. "It is important that you understand the delicate nature of this arrangement. Mary's situation is unusual, and not one which most people would understand or appreciate. Some might even find it shocking that a young girl would refuse to marry in the usual sense, forgo children, live in so solitary a manner. They might think her a shameless child, one who is rebellious toward her father, unconcerned for her family name, even peculiar in her desires. Ugly ideas quickly become wicked words, and Joachim is at great pains to shield his daughter from suspicion and gossip."

"But Father," said Simon, "surely people could respect the pious intentions of a girl raised in the temple."

"If only!" said Judas. "I know plenty who are not so filled with regard for the temple. And they have reasons. There are complaints enough about priests living well on the temple tax. No surprise if people harbor ill thoughts about a house full of women within the precincts."

Judas' observation was solidly based. Resentment toward the temple ran deep, not least because the high priest was chosen, installed and maintained by the king. Herod, that reviled, half-Jew vassal of the Romans, had inveigled his way onto the throne. He was chosen by Marcus Antonius, conqueror of Jerusalem, as the least worst of the options available to govern the troublesome Jewish homeland.

That the high priest should be under the thumb of such a vile pretender as Herod was a festering sore on the body of Jewish religious life. No matter that the king had expanded and beautified the temple to an extent that made it legendary throughout the world. Most people were suspicious of the priestly administration. The separatist sect known as the Essenes had abandoned temple sacrifice entirely.

Joseph knew that Judas, his quiet second son, was inclined toward reticence and the least likely to offer his thoughts. "If your brother perceives the possibility of suspicion and rumor," he said, "we should all expect it. Tongues may wag about the difference in age between Mary and myself." He shook his head in acceptance of the inevitable joking. "So be it. But in all other respects, this marriage must appear ordinary. The world need not—and it *must* not—know that there is anything unusual between the daughter of Joachim and myself."

"But...Father..." said Simon hesitantly. "If after awhile...there are no...children?"

"That can be ascribed to my age," Joseph answered firmly. "If the explanation does not suffice... Well, let people think what they will of *me*. My duty—the duty of all in this family—is to protect Mary's honor and privacy. I know I can count on your help in that."

His sons nodded in agreement.

Then Josis added, "Our wives must be made to understand. They will treat Mary with the utmost warmth and consideration, I'm sure. But there will have to be explanations prepared for the children. And it would be most helpful if all our stories were consistent. What can be said about this new—" He paused, smiling again. "—*grandmother?*"

The others laughed.

"Not quite *grandmother*, I think," Joseph said, sharing in his sons' amusement. "*Mary* will do. Just Mary. The older children can be counseled against taking too close an interest in their grandfather's home life. And over time, the younger ones will come to understand how the pieces of a family fit together, no matter how complicated it all may seem."

Joseph turned to his youngest son who was seated to the side of his elder brothers. "James will set the example," he said, tipping his head in the boy's direction. "He understands the nature of this arrangement. His acceptance of Mary and his ease in the household will show that all is as it should be. The children will observe that and follow his lead."

"Yes, our scholar will handle things," said Josis, and stretched his arm over to the boy, knocking off his cap and tousling his hair playfully.

James picked the cap off the floor and, with a smirk, swatted it in the direction of his eldest brother. Everyone shared in the lightness of the moment. What the others could not see behind the horseplay was a deep division in the boy's feelings. James understood the trust which Joseph was placing in him, and he took it as a sign of his father's great love. At the same time, it was fearful to think that his family's high regard among the people of Nazareth might, to a considerable measure, be dependent upon him. His job was to influence the children in their acceptance of this new family member. Children observe, but children talk.

"In any event," Joseph said, "there is time. Mary departs for Jerusalem after Sabbath, and then there are yet many weeks until she completes her term and returns to Nazareth. But speak with your wives. If they have questions, have them come to me. I will explain further."

The brothers knew that Joseph had their wives' trust. Not one of the three women would hesitate to approach him with any concern—a situation not at all common. How many Nazareth wives would be so at ease with the family head? Many the wife who did all she could to avoid the imperious gaze of her husband's father—or worse, his mother. And so it was with surprise that each brother later encountered a reaction that was something a bit less than joy over the news of the family's expected new member.

Sarah, Judas' wife, found it very strange that any woman should wish to avoid having children. "Is it not odd," she asked her husband, "that this girl should dedicate herself to the Creator and yet turn from His command to be fruitful? What sort of piety is that? She has studied the holy books like a boy—does this make her despise her woman-hood?"

Salome, the wife of Josis, thought it was highly unfair of Joachim to have bound Joseph to such an obligation. "Your father deserves the comfort of a true wife in his old age, not the cares of raising a daughter he will never be able to give to another man," she said.

The strongest objection came from Simon's wife, Zipporah, young-est of the women. With three small children in her house, two not yet trained from soiling themselves, she saw this girl as an extra weight to be borne by the wives. "What does this mean for us?" she complained. "We all have our own to tend. Are we to serve this little princess from the temple who plans on having no babies?"

Next morning, the three brothers commiserated over their wives' reactions. And during the following days, Joseph too became aware that his beneficence toward an old and dying friend was not being re-ceived well within his own walls. He smoothed what feathers he could by taking each daughter-in-law aside to assure her that Mary was quite capable of caring for herself and might even prove a great help.

Joseph also brought his two daughters, Lydia and Assia, into his con-fidence, and found them to be only marginally more receptive to the news than their brothers' wives had been. Lydia closely echoed Sa-lome's concern about Joseph taking on this added responsibility. And while her sister professed that she was proud of their father's generous spirit, she too was worried that his act of kindness might lead to heart-ache. In the end, Joseph decided that he must entrust the peace of his family to the King of the Universe and the passage of time.

*   *   *

The weeks after Mary's return to the temple passed in the daily ac-tivities of life. There was a steady stream of orders for the finely crafted wooden furniture, tools and implements made by Josis, who had taken over the Nazareth shop. The eldest son had learned much since his boyhood introduction to the craft as his father's nail straightener. Josis had become a true master of the woodworker's art, Joseph conceding that his son's manual skills now surpassed his own.

Judas and Simon alternated days tending their flock grazing in the pasture rented from Joachim and nurturing the olive grove they were trying to establish beyond the east wall of the family compound. The wives saw to their daily routines of household chores and children. And James pursued his studies.

For Joseph himself there were the crews to supervise in Sepphoris and much consultation with clients over endless construction details and plan modifications. This was frequently done in the company of his able assistant, Lucillus, a gentile God-fearer whom most people referred to as Lucillus the Greek. That appellation was inaccurate. Lucillus was a son of Carthage, born a slave. But the name stood as a brief summation of a varied and accomplished life.

Quick-witted as a boy, Lucillus had learned to read and cipher by listening in on the lessons of the Roman child he had been assigned to serve on the island of Cyprus. He caught the eye of the child's father, a trader and owner of ships who took him from his youthful charge and set him a variety of tasks. As he grew into a sturdy lad with the black hair and dusky skin of his ancient race, Lucillus acquired greater trust and responsibility for his master's affairs.

The master eventually relocated his household and business to Palestine, setting up in a substantial villa in Caesarea. So fond had he become of his trusted servant that he granted Lucillus his manumission. When the master died, the son of the family, whom Lucillus had served as a child, assumed leadership of the firm. He proved much less a businessman than his father had been. The company foundered, leaving Lucillus with his freedom but no work.

The wanderings that followed brought Lucillus to Sepphoris, where he met Joseph, who recognized the gifts that had been apparent to the old trader. Lucillus became Joseph's right hand, keeping the books, managing the store of supplies, helping to estimate the costs of projects, and paying the crews. Another of Lucillus' duties—though an unofficial one—was tutoring James in Greek and Latin. He also shared with the boy the considerable stock of tales, poems, songs and philosophical sayings picked up on the many errands he had run for his late master along the imperial trade routes.

It was Lucillus who, some weeks after Joseph's meeting with Mary, accepted a letter carried by a messenger from Ein Kerem, the Judean town where Zacharias resided. He took the missive to Joseph, who was seated with James at the midday meal.

"Forgive this intrusion," said Lucillus, holding out the small scroll. "A message from the honored priest, Zacharias."

Joseph broke open the seals and handed the scroll back to Lucillus, asking him to read it aloud. The message began with customary greetings, followed by a request to be forgiven for the delay in writing after their meeting with Joachim. Zacharias had been overcome by a strange event, he noted, one that shook him deeply and robbed him of his voice. This, Joseph took as a reference to some kind of illness. Then Lucillus read that Zacharias reported a great and unexpected blessing that had come upon his house. Elizabeth, his wife, had conceived.

"Remarkable," Joseph said. "The wife of Zacharias is of advanced age. And she will have a child? Blessed be the Holy One of Israel. Zacharias and Elizabeth have always been without children. This is most remarkable, indeed."

Almost in passing, the priest expressed his joy at hearing that a contract for the marriage had been drawn between Joseph and Joachim. And then the message turned to Joseph's youngest son. Zacharias cited his comment about James coming to Jerusalem to study, and he repeated the offer to arrange for a teacher. "When James has attained his maturity," Zacharias wrote, "send him to me, and as I promised, I will find him a place in the school of a learned scribe."

James, his mouth falling open, stared at his father. "Can this be true?" he asked.

Lucillus looked up from the scroll. "Zacharias is a holy man," he said, "a man of honor."

"And of much gratitude, it would appear," said Joseph thoughtfully. He glanced at his son. "We must plan a great celebration for the day when you read in the synagogue. If you are going to study in Jerusalem, then celebrating will be in order. Not very many Nazareth boys have sat with the doctors of the Law."

"This will be a special thrill for Ezra, your teacher," said Lucillus.

"And for his Greek tutor?" said Joseph.

Lucillus smiled. "Quite special," he said.

"Then *you* shall be in charge of planning the big event," said Joseph.

"It will be my honor," said Lucillus, bowing broadly and sweeping one arm in front of him.

"Will it be like one of those grand Roman feasts you observed in your world travels?" Joseph asked teasingly, an eye on James.

"Perhaps not so grand as that," his assistant said. "Our scholar mustn't be led astray by pagan delights. We shall celebrate in a way befitting the dignity of the occasion."

James, not really aware that he was the being made the object of their humorous banter, asked, "May I invite the other boys in the school—and the Rabbi Ezra?"

"Of course," Joseph said, "all the boys and the Rabbi Ezra. And the Sanhedrin and a deputation from the court of Herod. It will be an important day for the town of Nazareth and all of Galilee."

"Perhaps the king himself will attend," said Lucillus, "and the Augustus as well. I have contacts in Rome."

Now James caught onto the joke. "But my friends *can* come," he asked, "and the rabbi?"

"It wouldn't be a celebration without them," his father said reassuringly. "Lucillus will handle the preparations. But you must continue to work hard at your lessons. There are many more months ahead before this feast. And if the honored Zacharias is willing to recommend you for study in Jerusalem, you must be prepared to do him credit when the time comes."

"I will, Father, I promise," said James.

The rest of the letter was an expression of Zacharias' satisfaction that Mary had consented to the arrangement made on her behalf, followed by an ardent appeal for the blessings of Heaven upon Joseph and his entire family. To that end, Zacharias promised to make an offering of thanks in the temple.

"Mary is an exceptional young woman," the priest concluded. "All who have known her in Jerusalem speak with the highest regard for her piety and virtue. I am sure she will enrich your household, and that you will never have cause to regret this great deed you are doing."

As Lucillus read the letter's formulary closing with its elaborate expressions of hope for good health and well being, Joseph pondered the reservations expressed by his daughters and his sons' wives. He experienced a momentary and disturbing thought that *women can be surprisingly clear of sight*. But then he pushed the notion from his mind.

CHAPTER FOUR

The angel Gabriel was sent from God to a city of Galilee called Nazareth, to a virgin betrothed to a man whose name was Joseph.

(Luke 1)

A loud pounding on the gate set the dogs to barking, and soon people stirred all throughout the compound. A baby began to cry. Simon, whose house was closest to the front, emerged into the court with a woolen blanket wrapped around himself from the shoulders. He opened a small port in the wooden gate and looked through to the midnight visitor outside.

"It is I, Hiram, steward of the house of Joachim," the man on the other side said excitedly. "Please forgive this late disturbance. I must see Joseph the carpenter. My master is gravely ill—I believe he is dying—and he begs that Joseph come to him with all speed."

Simon opened the gate and led Hiram across the court and under the portico to the foot of the stairway that led to the upper room where Joseph and James slept. "Father," he called up.

After a time, the bleary-eyed visage of Joseph appeared in the wooden enclosure at the top of the stairs.

"A thousand pardons, honorable sir," Hiram said. "My master, Joachim, begs your presence—and quickly, please, if you would be so kind. The end is near, and he needs to speak with you."

"A moment," said Joseph, disappearing back into the darkened room.

It had been several months since the dinner with Joachim and Mary, so Joseph wasn't surprised that the end was at hand. Since their marriage arrangement had been solidified, Joseph had prayed that his old friend might survive long enough to see his daughter return from the temple. The King of the Universe had blessedly granted that gift. But now the entire town was abuzz with Joachim's steep decline and imminent death.

"What is it, Father?" James asked with sleep in his voice.

Joseph took a heavy cloak from a line of hooks by the door, pulled it over his hastily arranged tunic to shield himself from the night air, then placed a knitted cap on his head. "Joachim is dying," he said to the boy. "I must go to him. Go back to sleep, my son." He stepped into his sandals, tied them, and started for the door, then stopped, looking back at the boy. "Pray for my old friend."

"Yes, Father, I will."

Joseph descended the stairway and followed the steward through the court and out the gate. Simon secured it behind them, then went to calm the dogs and inform the others, who had arisen at the noise, of what was happening. Joseph and Hiram made their way through the town to the imposing home of Joachim, located at the end of the market street. Hiram's son, Mordechai, admitted them, and the two men went directly to the master's bedchamber.

Hiram's wife, the servants, all the members of the household were present in the room, which was dimly lit by oil lamps and the red glow of coals in a brazier. Mary sat on the floor beside the fragile and sunken form of her father. She bowed her head silently to acknowledge Joseph's arrival. Then she touched Joachim on the arm and spoke gently.

"My father—Joseph is here. He has come, as you asked."

The old man stirred, looked up searchingly, and through dim eyes recognized his visitor. He spoke weakly. "Joseph, my son."

"I have come, honored friend," Joseph said, feeling a reaction within his viscera at how little there was left of the man lying so slight before him.

Joachim lifted a hand, just a few inches, but enough to gesture Joseph to his bedside. Joseph knelt on the floor next to Mary.

"The Holy One is calling me now," he said in a voice thin and weak.

Joseph could barely hear, but he answered, "Blessed be He."

"It is time to act on the contract."

"I understand."

"Mary should go to your home now."

"I have prepared her a home of her own," said Joseph, "within our compound. I will take her when you have gone into the arms of the

Lord."

Joseph looked at the girl, and she returned his glance to reconfirm her assent to the agreement. Then Mary turned to the man who had brought Joseph.

"Hiram," she said, softly but with a firmness and authority one wouldn't have expected in a young girl.

The steward signaled all the others to leave.

"Good. Good." Joachim heaved a labored breath, long and with a rattling sound. "You will care for my...beautiful treasure."

"Yes."

"Announce the betrothal."

"I will, Joachim."

"No one will fail to understand...that my passing..." He paused, expended the effort of another difficult breath, and then continued. "There will be...no questions."

"Of course."

"The marriage can be held...at an appropriate time. Arrange everything as it should be. Then no one will ever ask... And Mary... She will be free to live according...to the terms of the contract. There...will be no questions."

"No questions, my dear friend."

Joachim struggled to extend his hand toward Joseph, who took it between his own.

"Thank you, Joseph. The King of the Universe...will bless you greatly."

Joseph tried to speak, but felt a catch in his throat.

Then with supreme effort, the old man turned his face toward Mary. Joseph released his hand as Joachim tried to reach for the daughter he had possessed for so little time.

"Kiss your father, my child," he said weakly.

She leaned over and her lips brushed his forehead.

Joachim's eyes closed. "I go now," he said, then labored for a final breath. "Hear, O Israel...the Lord our God...the Lord...is...one..." And the thin voice trailed off into a quiet wheeze. Then silence.

Joseph looked at Mary, and he saw tears running from her eyes for the father she had never really known.

*   *   *

The Rabbi Ezra was sent for and, with Joseph and Hiram, rites were arranged for Joachim, of blessed memory. Joseph's presence, both at the burial and during the days of receiving, was much noted by the townspeople. It had not been known that there was a close relationship between the carpenter and the great landowner. In fact, the only apparent connection was the rental of Joachim's pasture by Joseph's sons, Judas and Simon.

And yet it was Joseph who led the prayers of mourning and was at Mary's side most of the time throughout the seven days. This occasioned some curious whispering, which grew into a cycle of speculation, which soon became a whirl of conflicting rumors. The rumors gained velocity when, at the end of the sitting, Mary moved out of her family home and took residence in Joseph's house. But conjecture was put to rest the following Sabbath, when it was announced in the synagogue that Joseph and Mary were to be married. Surely a girl so recently returned from the temple, with no other family in town, would need to be cared for. It was a natural thing for her to be taken within the walls of her future husband.

As Joseph had predicted, local sympathy was leavened by much jovial banter about the groom-to-be of mature years and his promised bride of such tender and beguiling youth. But the joking was spiked by occasional, more pointed, speculation as to how much of Joachim's vast holdings the fortunate carpenter stood to have come his way in the bargain. Some of this reached the ears of Lucillus, who reported it to Joseph, who waved it away.

"Vain fancies," he said with a shake of the head. "Everyone is curious about other people's affairs. Imagination knows no bounds."

Daughter of a rich man though she was, Mary had little in the way of personal possessions. The extent of her worldly goods was the few clothes she had brought with her from the temple. Not wanting to see the daughter of Joachim come to her new husband empty-handed, Hiram ordered that furnishings be carried from the chamber which had been provided for her in her father's house. These were installed in Joseph's upper room, recently cleared of his and James' belongings now moved downstairs.

Hiram brought some other furniture, as well, mementos of Mary's family home, which he thought it appropriate for her to keep. These included the divan, the Roman-style chair, and several other pieces. As space was limited in the lower room of Joseph's house, some of the items were placed under the portico and some stored in a shed next to Josis' workshop.

Hiram's last importation was the young serving girl, whom Mary had learned was named Hagar. Joseph hadn't considered that his bride would come with a servant, but on reflection he thought it shouldn't have been unexpected.

Mary, who still had not accustomed herself to being waited upon, expressed her discomfort to Joseph. "Hiram insists that I should have a girl to attend me," she told her future husband. "But in Jerusalem I attended to myself, and it has felt strange having someone fussing about. Still, Hagar is a pleasant, dutiful girl, and Hiram explained she is an orphan with no place else to go, now that my father's household is being dispersed. What is your will in this, Joseph?"

Though unanticipated, the only problem this situation seemed to pose was the question of where the girl would sleep.

Mary shrugged. "Hagar can sleep in my room."

"Well...until we can provide someplace for her," Joseph said.

"What shall I have her do?" Mary asked.

"Right now she can help you get settled," Joseph said. "After that... I'm sure there are ways for her to be useful. No doubt the family can think of many tasks. They will be pleased to have another set of hands."

Joseph was surprised to find that, when word of Hagar had spread throughout the household, his daughters-in-law were *not* pleased, but rather quite annoyed. The fact of a servant only compounded their reservations about Mary.

Once more it was Zipporah, wife of Simon, who made the harshest comment. "The princess has her own serving girl," she complained to her husband. "We shall see how helpful this Hagar is to the family when Mary wishes her linen aired or her bath drawn."

The brothers again found themselves commiserating over their wives' resentments, and again Joseph sought out each daughter-in-law. After encountering womanly skepticism at each of his three conversations, all he could do was pray that serenity might reign over his home.

It didn't. Joseph's attempts to introduce Mary into the daily life of the family met with an atmosphere of icy discontent. It soon became apparent that Hagar was an impediment to Mary's acceptance, which was Joseph's primary concern. He shared this conclusion with Mary, who urged him to give it more time.

"I don't think that Hagar is the problem," she said. "Maybe they just don't trust me because I was in the temple. People don't understand temple girls. They think we place ourselves above everyone else. But I will try to help them like me. I will show them that I don't put on airs."

"That may not be easy with your own serving girl here," said Joseph, whose unhappiness over the attitude of his sons' wives was clear to Mary.

In the end, she agreed it probably would be best if Joseph could find a different situation for Hagar. Two days later, the house of the Rabbi Ezra included a servant, on a stipend provided by Joseph the builder. This helped to assuage feelings, at least partially. Other seeds of good will were sown when Mary took it upon herself to approach the wives, offering them choice of Joachim's furniture.

"These pieces are very nice, but I have no use for them," she said. "And since I lived so long away from home, they stir no memories of my parents. Please—if you would care to have anything that is here, take what you wish. Consider it a blessing from my dear father."

While there remained a noticeable chill, Mary's gesture was a small further step toward relieving it, and Joseph dared to hope for better times ahead. It occurred to him that he had glimpsed in this young girl the gift of wisdom.

That was all to the good, because after Mary's third week in the compound, Joseph announced that he and Lucillus had to make a trip. A shipment of wood beams for one of the Sepphoris projects was to be received at the port of Caesarea. These pieces had been cut and shaped in Lebanon according to rigorous specifications. They would have to be inspected, and overland transport arranged. The entire process would likely be concluded in less than a month, depending on the arrival time of the ship. This was always variable, and someone had to be on hand at the port throughout the entire span of time during which the ship might arrive, since unattended cargo was likely to disappear. A date for the wedding could be set and made public upon Joseph's return.

Mary had taken over the care of Joseph's living quarters, and also tried to make herself available to the wives whenever they needed help with various household tasks. But the daily schedule of her prayers, which she maintained scrupulously, continued to set her apart from the other women. It seemed to them a very odd thing indeed for a girl to pray the services. There even was some shared anxiety among them that Mary might take it into her mind to pray with their husbands, which would be shockingly inappropriate. But who knew what presumptions might fill the head of a temple girl?

Salome expressed this concern to her father-in-law, who insisted such an idea was unthinkable. But admitting to himself that he couldn't really be sure what a girl of Mary's experience thought about such things, he queried Mary about her devotional practices—in as casual a manner as possible. She smiled knowingly, and assured him that her prayer life was entirely private. Joseph felt foolish for raising the question and more than a little annoyed at Salome for having prompted him to do so.

The only actual shortcoming that anyone could detect in Mary was a marked deficiency in cooking skills. She'd had kitchen duties in the women's residence, but only the most menial chores. She had never prepared a complete meal in her life. Consequently, she ate the food brought to Joseph's table by his daughters-in-law, which became another source or irritation among the women.

What the wives didn't realize was that Mary very much admired their ability to transform the fruits of the earth and the flesh of animals into appealing dishes for their families. But she recognized that each took great pride in her craft and guarded her own methods closely. Since their suspicions of her were already so firmly set, Mary hesitated in asking them for instruction. That left her dependent on their diligence, even as it seemed to confirm their assumption that she took them for granted.

So it was with a certain amount of apprehension over the simmering unease in his household that Joseph prepared for his journey to Caesarea. While Lucillus waited in the court, making adjustments to the straps that held their packs fastened to the sides of a donkey, Joseph gestured to his son, James, and took the boy aside.

"Be attentive to Mary," he said. "Don't intrude, but keep aware, and see that she is well. I am worried for her happiness here. I realize now that it will take time for all to be comfortable with this."

"I will watch, Father."

"I pray that things will be improved when I return."

"And I, Father."

"If there is a problem, speak with Josis. He is the eldest."

"Yes, I will do that. May the King of the Universe watch over you, Father."

Joseph embraced the boy, then departed with Lucillus.

*   *   *

Mary and James took their meals in Judas' house on the first day that Joseph was gone, and in Simon's on the second. Mary expressed her appreciation to both Sarah and Zipporah, offering compliments, which were accepted with restrained grace. On the third day, Mary lingered after the midday meal in Josis' house. When Josis and James had departed, she screwed up her courage and asked Salome if she might be kind enough to teach her a few things about cooking.

"I trust that Joseph hasn't told you he is dissatisfied with the meals he's been getting," Salome said with a sideward look.

Mary wasn't quite sure if the remark had been intended as a joke, and she was quick to reply nervously, "No, no—to the contrary. You are all such excellent cooks. Joseph seems delighted with the food, and I am also. And James, I'm sure. It is just that... Well, I have never learned to cook, and I feel I should know how...so that I can...do my part."

Salome could see the earnestness in the girl's face, and was struck by the thought that this was, after all, a mere child. Perhaps the women may have been too quick to judge Mary.

"Come back later and help me prepare the evening meal," she said, turning away.

Mary smiled, relieved, and offered a silent prayer of thanks to the Holy One.

Josis was surprised when, that evening at table, Salome mentioned how helpful his father's intended bride had been in preparing the meal.

"Oh?" He looked at the girl, whose eyes were turned down shyly. Then he looked at his wife, whose glance was also diverted. Then he looked at James, who, equally taken aback, returned his brother's surprised expression.

"That is...very good," said Josis.

Mary seemed to James especially cheerful when, later, he heard her up in her room praying the evening service. Her voice was louder than usual, with a lilting quality he'd not realized it possessed. Normally, what reached to the lower level was no more than a murmur, barely audible and certainly not sufficient to distract him from his own prayers, as her voice did tonight.

Unsettling as her sudden injection into the family had been, in the past three weeks James had observed Mary enough to decide that he did, in fact, like her. He felt bad at her obvious uneasiness, and he had prayed that his brother's wives could accept her. Salome's remark was a sign that perhaps things were turning in the right direction. He knew that, if it continued, his father would be pleased.

After completing his prayers, James went outside under the portico and sat on one of the stools, gazing across the court into the clear and star-filled sky. He and Joseph often took the evening air together for a while before turning in to bed. It was a time to be alone with his father, a time he cherished. Joseph would ask about the day's lessons with the Rabbi Ezra and tell stories of the family and his own childhood in Bethlehem. James was especially fond of Joseph's recollections of Escha.

Hearing about his mother always made for crossed feelings in the boy. He was captivated when his father would reflect on how beautiful and vibrant Escha was and how she so loved her children. It would make him feel, oddly, both warm and sad at the same time. And the sadder he felt for this woman he could not recall, whose appearance he did not know, the more he wished to hear of her.

He thought about that now, looking at the stars, and it occurred to him that Mary's situation was not entirely dissimilar to his own. Her mother had not died when she was an infant, as his did, but Mary had grown up separated from her parents. Was that why she had chosen a life without children? It seemed to James that such an experience would push her in the opposite way, making her want a family all the more. But no. Apparently not. It was strange. Perhaps he would speak with her about it one day—when he knew her better.

James became aware that the court was exceptionally bright. He stood up and walked to the corner of the house at the end of the portico where he could look up into the southern sky. There was a brilliant full moon, a desert moon, a moon for which caravaners pray to illumine the night and protect them from the stealthy approach of thieves. It seemed much brighter than usual, and especially large, the kind of moon that riveted one's gaze and was said to carry the mind away into strange musings.

The boy watched it for some time, examining the markings on its surface, which some called the face of the man. Then he realized he was tired and the hour was late. He walked around the side of the house to a screened area under the stairs that sheltered the privy. Then he went back inside the house and made his way across the room to a small oil lamp hanging over the table, and blew it out. He found his mat at the rear, lay down, and drew a blanket over himself. Sleep came in minutes.

*　　*　　*

James didn't know how long he'd slumbered. The chamber was still pitch dark, penetrated only by the indirect glow of moonlight in the small window. But something had broken his rest, some sound he could not name. Was it a human voice? Was it an animal outside?

He sat up on his mat, listening. There it was again. A voice. A wailing voice, though not loud. Were there words? He couldn't tell. But the voice was filled with feeling. Now frightened. Now happy. Frightened again. It was coming from above, he realized. Upstairs, from Mary's room.

James tossed his blanket aside, stood up, and groped his way across the dark space to the door and then outside to the foot of the stairs. He stood silently, straining to hear. Yes, it was Mary's voice. More of the strange, indecipherable utterances, then strained and rapid breathing, as if she had been sobbing, or perhaps laughing uncontrolled. Yet,

James had not heard her cry or laugh. Was she in the grip of some frightening dream?

"Mary!" he called.

No response, just more of the inexplicable sounds.

James would never presume to invade Mary's privacy. His father had made it clear that she was to be left undisturbed when alone upstairs. But the boy had promised to look after her, and these strange sounds were cause for alarm.

He made his way softly up the steps to the doorway, open but shielded partly by a curtain. He could see her sitting on the floor, her face turned upward and transfixed by a shaft of light from one of the two windows in the upper room. Her slim body was trembling, as if in the kind of fit he had once seen a man fall into on the street outside the synagogue. Now her voice emitted a quiet series of oddly shifting sounds, almost like the words from some unknown language. Yet, for all of this, the features of her face were still, formed into a joyous smile, her lips barely moving, eyes wide.

"Mary," he said. "Mary, are you dreaming? Are you alright?"

She sat in this rapt state for some seconds, unaware of his presence in the doorway. Then she seemed to awaken, and turned her head to look at him, speaking at last. "Yes...I am...alright."

James waited, watching, his gaze drawn to her face, locked on her eyes, which were made bright, almost iridescent, by the moonlight. Mary said nothing else, but rather sat quietly, the trembling and the odd sounds gone now.

After a time, the boy forced himself to turn away and started back down. He paused on the stair, glancing back, not understanding what he had seen, and feeling a disquiet that was like nothing he had ever experienced.

"Sleep well...Mary," he said.

CHAPTER FIVE

During those days Mary set out and traveled
to the hill country in haste to a town of Judah.

(Luke 1)

Mary was unseen the next morning. She remained in the upper room when James went to Simon's house to break his fast, and did not emerge until after her midday prayers, when she went again to Salome to offer assistance with the cooking in hope of further instruction. Salome set her to work grinding barley with a small stone wheel, showing her how the corns were to be milled in order to produce a flour fine enough to be baked into bread.

It was tricky work, requiring coordination between feet and hands to keep the wheel turning steadily and an uninterrupted conveyance of corns under the grinding face and thence into powder. But Salome figured if the girl truly wished to learn how food was prepared, this most basic of tasks was a good starting point.

Throughout the afternoon Mary toiled at the barley, Salome stealing an occasional peek at her as she worked. The older woman was taken by the look on Mary's face: concentration punctuated by an inexplicable smile. Perhaps she was lost in thoughts of her days at Jerusalem. Or maybe she was passing the time in continuous prayer. Or maybe anything—who could know the mind of a temple girl? Still, Mary obviously did not shy from the ordinary chores of life.

Salome began to think that perhaps Joseph was right and Mary would prove an asset to the family. After the sack of barley corns had been emptied, she inspected the girl's work and approved the fineness of the grinding, noting only a few fragments incompletely milled. She cut Mary's apology short. "Some always get through," Salome said.

"These will be sifted out." And then she had the girl slice vegetables for a soup.

When James returned from the house of the Rabbi Ezra, he spotted Mary seated on a bench in the court outside Josis' front door. She was cutting onions on a board set in her lap, eyes focused intently on the work but slightly moist. He started to speak, but then held back, noting the smile on her face despite tears from the strong, irritating scent. It was the same unearthly smile he had seen in the night. He stood for a moment, observing the girl's total concentration, and then was swarmed by a group of small nieces and nephews who were always happy when he came home from lessons.

In such a way did calm return to the house of Joseph. Each day, after devotions, Mary went to Salome for cooking lessons, and also offered herself for chores to Sarah and Zipporah. Each day James went to the Rabbi Ezra. Life proceeded normally, with Joseph's absence most directly affecting Josis, whose carpentry orders were becoming backed up as he provided what oversight he could to the building projects. Several times he went to Sepphoris, where he had to make decisions on behalf of his father and attend to Lucillus' duty of paying the laborers.

James accompanied him on one of those trips, running errands for his brother while Josis visited the worksites. Going to the city was a treat for which the boy was always eager. He found the noise and bustle of city life a fascination, and listening to street chatter let him exercise the Greek and Latin acquired from Lucillus. That was challenging, since there were so many different kinds of people from so many places throughout the empire and they all spoke in such distinctive ways. Legionaries, especially—some passing through Sepphoris from as far away as Gaul—pronounced their Latin words and phrases in accents tinged by strange languages which James could hardly imagine. They frequently departed completely from the legion argot in favor of their unknown native tongues. James strained to catch it all.

But there was something else that—perhaps because he was getting older—drew his attention on this trip, a side of city life that was less fascinating than disturbing. It was how people behaved when they came into contact with other groups. Greeks, of whatever nationality, tended to behave toward Jews in a most superior way, their facial expressions and their ways of speaking laden with condescension, even outright mockery. The boy overheard derisive words and observed rude gestures, even catching an unpleasant glance directed at himself.

Jews, for their part, maintained blank faces in the presence of Roman soldiers or even the ordinary Greeks of the city. But out of sight and earshot, they expressed feelings of resentment and disgust. They would make rude gestures of their own or speak in vulgarities. James saw one man spit on the street after passing a pair of Greek women.

He shared these observations with Josis, who acknowledged that this was the way of life in places where the nationalities rubbed up against each other. It seemed to be especially so in the cities, like Sepphoris, where Greeks dominated.

"Father tells our men never to express themselves in such ways," Josis said, "even when no one is around. He insists the workers avoid our clients and all other Greeks as much as possible. He says we are here to work, not give vent to anger."

"Do the men obey?" James asked.

"They respect Father," Josis said. "And they like their pay."

Aside from that one excursion, most days followed the normal pattern of studies and household activity. Those weeks without Joseph passed undisturbed by any noteworthy incident. Except at night. Mary had taken to singing in her room, softly enough that it was unnoticed by anyone but James immediately below.

At first it caused him some concern. Mary's voice, though a bit muffled, was a sweet presence as he laid on his mat in the dark, and he worried that it might be wrong to listen, since the sound of a woman singing could be considered immodest. But some of the songs brought back memories of his sisters singing to him as a small child. He reasoned—perhaps with a bit of self-serving—that since he had not yet attained his maturity, and since Mary was soon to be his stepmother, and since all of her songs gave praise to the King of the Universe, then listening might not be sinful. So he allowed himself to enjoy the sound.

While she sang mostly in a lilting and sprightly way, sometimes Mary's voice took on an eerily somber quality. James wondered if there was some deep sadness hidden beneath the good nature she showed the family. Or perhaps it was fear revealing itself occasionally in these nightly recitals. But then, wouldn't such feelings rise within her, so recently uprooted from the temple, bereft of her only parent, and set down in the middle of a new home? On such nights, the desire for Joseph's return exceeded the boy's normal longing for him. James truly wished that Mary might receive some solace, but he didn't know what to do for her.

Anticipation of his father's wise counsel was unrewarded, however. Nearly a month after Joseph's departure, Lucillus appeared at the gate of the compound. He informed the family that Joseph was detained at Caesarea. The ship bearing the consignment of carved beams had been delayed in its departure from Lebanon. Joseph had taken temporary employment with a local carpenter to stave off boredom while he was waiting, and Lucillus would assume direction of the Sepphoris projects until the master's return.

Josis felt a sense of relief, as he could now catch up on the pieces languishing unfinished in his workshop. James was disappointed, but he noticed that Mary suddenly looked strangely worried. There was no singing that night.

*   *   *

Still more time passed, extending Joseph's absence by almost three weeks. Lucillus was as much in the dark about the master's return as the family, but he advised everyone that, ship arrivals being extremely unpredictable, there was no cause for concern. At least plans were in place for conveying the expected materials from Caesarea to Sepphoris; there should be no additional delay involved in that. So Joseph could appear at any time.

Reassured but unsatisfied, James kept an anxious eye on Mary. Especially in the latter days, her spirits had seemed to dampen. The nighttime singing had become less frequent, with the sadder tone of her voice dominating, until the songs stopped entirely. Also, she appeared fatigued, and was less and less attentive to Salome's cooking lessons and other chores—so much so that the wives began to suspect that her enthusiasm for learning the domestic arts was waning and perhaps their first suspicions of her unreliability would prove right after all.

One day, Mary was still in her room when James returned from the morning meal at Judas' house. As he was folding the blanket on his sleeping mat, there was a sound of retching. He dropped the blanket, went outside to the stairway, and called up, "Mary, are you ill?"

She was silent. Then James heard the sound of more vomiting.

"Do you need help?" he called again.

Mary appeared at the top of the stairs holding a chamber pot and looking unsteady on her feet. The boy ran quickly up the steps.

"Let me take that," he said. "You are sick. How can I help you?"

"My stomach," she said. "Uneasy for some days. It passes after I lie down."

"I must get Salome."

Mary grabbed the boy's shoulder as he was turning away with the covered container. "No," she said. "I'm alright. Really I am. This will pass. It always does. Say nothing about it to anyone. When your father returns, I will tell him. He will know what to do."

"But Salome might be able—"

"Please, James!" Her voice was emphatic now, pleading. "Say nothing."

The boy looked into her eyes and saw genuine fear. What was it that had so panicked her? He wanted to insist on seeking help, but this picture of desperation made him hesitate to speak.

She repeated quietly but firmly: "Please."

James nodded. He turned, took the pot downstairs and emptied it in the privy.

Mary stayed in her room the rest of that day. She came downstairs only once to seek out some crusts of bread. She had set them aside from the leftovers with the intention of feeding the small birds that came to the sill of her window overlooking a terebinth just beyond the compound wall. Feeling settled now—and hungry—she ate the stale fragments. When she went back onto the portico, she noticed the chamber pot which James had rinsed out and left at the foot of the stairs. She picked it up and carried it back to her room.

That afternoon, James was on his way back from lessons, walking with two other boys who studied with the Rabbi Ezra. When they reached the square surrounding the town's public well, the other boys broke off and headed for a cobbled alleyway on the far side. James waved to his departing schoolmates and continued on to where the road began its rise up the hill toward his family's compound and then out into the countryside and eventually to Sepphoris.

He was nearly to the gate of his home when he spied some familiar shapes approaching along the road from the opposite direction. The boy's heart leapt at the realization that it was his father walking with Lucillus and the donkey. He ran to Joseph and threw his arms around him.

"Father, oh Father, how I have missed you."

Joseph was knocked slightly off balance and, recovering, laughed as he returned the boy's embrace. "My son," he said. "Surely all of Nazareth will think I had abandoned you."

"I am happy to see you, Father."

"And I you, my son."

As they reached the compound, Josis emerged from the gate. He smiled to witness the boy still clinging to Joseph. "Our scholar has been lonely," he said.

"So it would appear," Joseph said.

Josis went to his father and kissed him on the cheek. "Peace be with you, Father," he continued. "We have all prayed for your safety."

"I am well, as you can see."

"The shipment is received?"

"Partly. The rest is on its way."

"Two other carts are due tomorrow," Lucillus explained.

"Such an elaborate undertaking for a few timbers," Josis muttered, shaking his head. "These Greeks are so demanding."

"They love their decorative flourishes," Lucillus added. "Every carved leaf or flower petal is savored like a verse of Homer."

"But at such cost," said Josis. "Extra expense in the making, then to ship."

"Plus tolls at the city gates—both Caesarea and Sepphoris," said Joseph.

"The masters of the world grant themselves any indulgence," said Lucillus, taking his leave of the group with a wave and leading his donkey. "Peace be upon the house of Joseph."

They responded to Lucillus' blessing. Then Joseph and his two sons went into the compound, each kissing his own fingers and touching the small scroll. Everyone within rushed to greet the returning patriarch. Except for Mary. When blessings and warm wishes had been exchanged and all were assured that the mission had been completed safely and successfully, Joseph started toward the portico with James at his side.

"I trust Mary is well," he said. "Is she at her prayers?"

"I have not seen Mary since this morning, Father, but..."

The boy's hesitation prompted a flicker of concern. "James?"

"She was sick today, Father. She vomited. I had to clean her chamber pot."

"Sick? Are the wives treating her? They said nothing of it."

"They do not know."

"Why not?"

"Mary forbade me to tell them. She said she has been sick several times but it goes away."

Joseph looked at the boy quizzically, then he turned and went to the portico. James held back to give Mary privacy to explain her illness.

Standing at the foot of the stairs, Joseph called, "Mary?"

There was a pause, and then the girl appeared at the top. "Peace be with you, Joseph," she said. "You have returned safely. I am glad."

"James told me you were ill this morning."

"Yes. But I am better now."

"And that you have been ill before."

"Yes."

"You should tell the wives when such things happen. They will care for you. Or one of my daughters can come from—"

Mary interrupted him. "Joseph..."

"Yes?"

"Could you please come up? I would speak with you."

"Of course."

Mary went back into the room as her intended husband began to ascend the stairs. When Joseph came in, he found her seated on a low stool by the rear window. The girl appeared to him as if she were slightly ill even now. Or was she just nervous?

"Yes, Mary?"

Her face was turned away, her eyes closed. "Joseph," she said in a voice barely audible, "something...wonderful...has happened. But it is...difficult...to explain."

Joseph knelt down beside the girl. The way she was seated, with her knees drawn up under her tunic and her arms around her legs, made her look especially small and young—childlike.

"What has happened?"

He watched her. Her eyes were open now, focused on the wall. It was as if she were searching there for words that might serve to make clear a thought that was obscure or subtle. Joseph waited patiently, even as a worry began to come upon him that the girl might be facing a serious threat to her health, about which she hesitated to speak. And yet, whatever it was that had happened she described as wonderful.

"Shortly after you departed for Caesarea," she began, "I was visited."

"Visited? By Hiram, your father's steward?"

"No. Not Hiram."

"Then who?"

"It was a messenger, Joseph."

"From Zacharias—or some other of your father's kinsmen?"

"No."

"From the temple then." He could think of no one else who might send a message to her.

"Not from the temple, or from...relatives..."

Joseph waited. Finally, Mary turned to face him.

"It was a messenger of God, Joseph."

For Mary to use a term so closely linked to the Holy Name itself was unexpected, though perhaps this was a practice among temple girls. How those living within the precincts spoke among themselves was unknown to Joseph. But a messenger of God? Since the days of the prophets, those experiences were considered mainly the stuff of dreams. True visions were rare.

"This came to you in sleep?" he asked her.

"I was awakened from sleep."

Joseph smiled. "As I would have been."

"No, Joseph," she said firmly, seeing his lack of seriousness. "I was awakened from sleep by the messenger. It was then that I saw him and received his message."

Joseph sat now, supporting himself with his hands behind him on the floor and crossing his legs in front. Mary *was* young, wasn't she? Would an imaginative girl whose childhood had been spent in the temple be inclined toward angelic fancies?

"Mary," he said with fatherly kindness in his voice, "in my dreams I see myself awake. I don't think I have ever dreamed I was sleeping, though surely, one might dream about having just arisen. This is what happened to you."

Her gaze became more sharply focused, penetrating. "I was not dreaming, Joseph. I was visited by a messenger of God, and he told me something wonderful."

In that moment there was complete resolve in her eyes. But then, suddenly, it disappeared, and she turned her face away from her intended husband.

This quick change in her visage set Joseph aback. Girlish dream or no, all he could think to ask her was, "What did this messenger say?"

There was a long pause as Mary contemplated the difficulty of what she was about to divulge. This difficulty was considerable—no, *enormous*. In fact, she knew that the truth was actually quite unbelievable. And at the same time, she understood that her future, perhaps her very life, depended on Joseph believing it.

After the wait, during which impatience had begun, ever so slightly, to intrude upon Joseph's warmer feeling of fatherly indulgence—the girl turned her eyes back to him. With regained composure and hesitant courage, she framed up her words. "The messenger told me that I am to be the mother of the Son of God."

Joseph's face went slack. Mary, raised in the temple, the very heart of religious life, understood that the words she had just uttered were blasphemy. Indeed, their stunning effect could be read in the blank expression on Joseph's face. Unconsciously his crossed legs stiffened, pressing the edges of his feet against the floor and pushing his body back, away from the girl.

What delusion was this? Was Mary mad? Possessed? Was this what Joachim had meant when he described the intensity of her nature? Had the old man known his daughter harbored such ideas? Was that why she could be placed with no one else? Joseph wished to stop time, to give himself a moment in eternity to make sense of the thoughts coursing through his mind. He didn't know how he should respond to a child who could say such a thing.

And then, somehow, in the midst of a great surge of feeling, the kindness of his heart made him say quietly, "It was a dream, Mary."

She sat without speaking. She looked at this man—this gentle and generous man who had made a heartfelt promise to her dying father—and she knew that her words were turning his act of kindness into an insoluble dilemma. Then tears came to her eyes, because she realized that the explanation of the message she had received was not complete. She would yet compound his pain and confusion.

"No, Joseph," she said, "it wasn't a dream. What the messenger said was true. I know this is so. I've had only two times of impurity since leaving the temple. The third has not come. And for the past week I have been sick at mornings. I carry a child, the *Son of the Living God*. The messenger told me I should refer to him as *Emmanuel*, God with us."

Now Mary was speaking not of dreams, but of observable bodily facts. Even a girl new to the burdens of women would recognize when the blood that should have come did not. And James had verified her sickness. He said he had cleaned the chamber pot of her vomit in the morning, and there could be no mistaking that.

Joseph rose to his feet, his face flushed with anger. That Mary would utter blasphemy was bad enough. That she would offer it to explain away an immoral act was overwhelming deceit.

But still, she *was* young. She could be prey to a man of low intent. If she did carry a child, who could have done this to her? She had been here in the compound for these weeks, and in her father's house before that, and in Jerusalem before that. And since she said she had passed two times of impurity since leaving the temple, it must have happened while she was here.

Suddenly, he was swept by a horrible wave of guilt. His promise to her father was that he would protect the girl—the *treasure of my life*, Joachim had called her. Had Joseph failed so miserably at that task? Had Mary really been seduced, led into sin? Had he really been unable to prevent it, so blind as to not even imagine such a possibility, taken no precautions? He could hardly imagine a greater shame.

But who? Who could be responsible for this wicked thing? Joseph would at least know that, and he would take whatever action was necessary.

He turned to the girl again, resuming his kneeling posture before her. "Enough of messengers, Mary," he said sternly. "I do not see God with you in this. Tell me the truth. If you carry a child, whose child is it?"

Mary knew that the truth would not be believed. Yet, there was no other story to tell. What was, was. And in her heart she knew that it was unspeakably glorious, no matter how absurd or shameful it might appear.

Her eyes turned up into the face of this man whom she now feared might never be her husband, and with all her courage and honesty she said, "The Spirit of God came to me, Joseph. The messenger told me it would happen, and it did. I agreed to it. And now I carry the *Son of the Living God* within me. That is the truth, Joseph, and there is nothing else to say."

Her face, her manner, her voice—the entire presence of this small, childlike creature still on the cusp of womanhood was so disarmingly candid and open that Joseph was not sure if she was actually convinced that this was true, or if nothing had happened at all and Mary's senses had departed from her, or even if he himself was in the grip of a dream.

He struggled to stand again, feeling as if his head was spinning, and set his feet wider to counter the sensation that he might actually fall. When his balance returned, he walked to the door and, without looking back at Mary, went downstairs, passing James in the portico, not even seeing the boy. He entered the lower room now beginning to lose its light with the sun on the down-slope of its daily arc.

Joseph paced about the shadowed space, his undirected steps taking him to the doorway where the sight of James finally registered. That spurred a thought which the family head never would have believed it possible for him to entertain. Could one of his sons have done this to Mary? He recoiled from such a repellent idea, but the thought forced itself into his mind again.

Surely not James. The boy had been in the house with her all these weeks, but James was a mere child. There was not yet the slightest sign that he would even have the capacity.

The others—Josis, Judas or Simon? Could it be? Was it possible? He had raised them to manhood in the way of right and the fear of the Holy One. He knew these three men as he knew himself. It was *not* possible. He pushed the sordid notion from his mind. "James!" he called.

The boy turned with a start and entered the room, Joseph closing the door after him.

"Tell me, my son, do you know if anyone has visited Mary while I was away?"

"I do not know of anyone, Father," he said.

"Does she walk in the town or the countryside?"

"I don't think so."

"Not in the market street? Not to the well in the square?"

"No," the boy said. "We have our own well."

"Of course. But you are at lessons during the day."

"Yes. But Mary is with the wives then. Salome teaches her to cook."

"She has not gone to the house of Joachim?"

"No one is left there. The servants are gone, the house is empty. I have seen it myself when I've walked by."

Joseph searched his mind, struggling to imagine any possible opportunity for Mary to have met a man. "She has been nowhere?"

"To the synagogue on Sabbath."

"Does she go alone?"

"No. Only with Salome, Zipporah and Sarah. Always with them."

"And she goes nowhere else?"

"No, Father," said the boy, now deeply perplexed by this insistent questioning. "Mary is shy. When she is not with the women, she stays in her room. In the morning she prays, and often at night she sings."

"She sings?"

"Yes. Her voice is nice. I hear her when I'm lying in my bed. I— I enjoy listening to the songs, Father. I hope it isn't wrong."

That shook Joseph out of his agitation for a moment. A fleeting smile crossed his face, and he tenderly rubbed the side of his son's head. "We will speak of this some other time," he said.

But then, new anxieties flashed upon him. If Mary was truly with child, it would become known in the town, and she would be subject to the Law. The girl could be stoned. And just as the thought had crept into his mind that one of his sons might be responsible, that idea could occur to others. The entire family might be in peril.

What he must do was plain to him. He would put Mary aside quietly, end the betrothal in a private way. But first he would get her out of Nazareth.

"James," he said commandingly, "go to Lucillus. Ask him to give you something to eat, and then bring him back here after it is dark."

"But I am supposed to eat at Simon's house tonight."

"Eat with Lucillus. Then have him pack the donkey with supplies for a journey. Bring him back here only when the sun is completely down. And do not come to the gate. Go to the far side of the wall under Mary's window, and call for me there—quietly. I will pack some things for you. You will go with Lucillus."

"I am to travel?"

"Yes."

"But where?"

"You and Lucillus must take Mary to the house of Zacharias."

*   *   *

When James had gone, Joseph resumed his slow pacing about the room. Then he went to find some spare clothes for the boy, and rolled them up into a tight bundle. He took up pacing again, stopping after some minutes when it occurred to him that some explanation would be due Zacharias for Mary's untimely arrival. This should have been obvious, but he had overlooked it in his distress.

He found a small sheet of parchment which had been scraped of previous writing, though not thoroughly, brought it to the low table along with ink and a stylus, and set to writing. The room had become dark, so he lit the oil lamp with a piece of flint struck against a rough stone held at the wick.

Neither time, space, nor circumstance permitted much in the way of form or eloquence, so Joseph made a simple and direct appeal that Zacharias question Mary about a recent apparition. Her answer would make clear why his note was lacking in detail, and also why she was in need of seclusion. He begged the priest's wise counsel as to what steps he, as the girl's intended husband, should take both to satisfy the Law and to fulfill his pledge to Joachim that Mary would never come to harm. And he concluded with an urgent plea for a quick response, which Zacharias could place into the trusted hands of Lucillus.

Holding the parchment near the light, Joseph realized that traces of the earlier message, having to do with a business transaction of some months prior, were still visible under the fresh writing. His message would be plain enough to Zacharias, however, and this would have to do. He rolled up the sheet and tied it with a short piece of leather thong.

Leaving the small scroll on the table, Joseph went outside to the stairway. "Mary," he called to no response.

As he was preparing to go up, there was a sound behind him.

"Father?" It was Zipporah.

Joseph turned with a start.

"James and Mary have not come for the evening meal."

Joseph's hand stroked the side of his face anxiously. "I am sorry, Zipporah," he said. "James has undertaken a task for me. Something unexpected. And Mary is not hungry."

"No one has seen Mary today," Zipporah said. "Is she alright?"

"Yes. Yes. She is fine," Joseph answered, hoping his face reflected his words and not at all certain they had.

"Then...shall I bring *you* something to eat, Father?" Zipporah asked, less than assured.

"No. Yes. Bring some bread. And some dried figs."

"Surely more than that," she insisted.

"No, just that. And some dried meat."

"Dried meat?"

"Do you have dried meat?"

"Well...yes, but—"

"Dried figs and dried meat, then. And bread."

Zipporah eyed him, bewildered, shook her head, and started across the court to her house.

Joseph climbed the steps and, at the top, peered into Mary's room. She was kneeling in what appeared to be an attitude of prayer. Through the floor Mary had heard most of what was spoken between Joseph and James. What hadn't reached her ear she inferred, so a stack of clothing sat by the door, wrapped in a blanket and tied up with a cord. Joseph spotted the neat bundle, and he realized that little more would be required in the way of instruction.

"You will leave shortly with James and Lucillus," he said tersely, then went back downstairs.

*　　*　　*

When Joseph explained to Lucillus that he was to take Mary to Ein Kerem, which was near Jerusalem, Lucillus insisted they should have at least a second man with them.

"This is a long journey," he said, "and brigands are not unknown on those roads. Perhaps one of your older sons might come. Another pair of strong hands and two of Josis' stout gouging axes would be reassuring."

"Axes I can provide," said Joseph, "but all the others in the family must remain here. There are things to be explained which I cannot speak of with them yet. When I have clarity on certain points and the issue about which I have written the honorable Zacharias is resolved, then I will."

This made no sense to Lucillus. Joseph could receive no information until after whoever had gone to Ein Kerem returned. But he could see the master was upset, so he didn't raise the point.

"One of the gang men, then?" Lucillus asked. "How about Nachum? He is strong as an ox. He carries a mortar hod in each hand, and is quick on his feet. And I'm sending him to the sites irregularly just now, so he's available and would appreciate a few extra coins."

Joseph agreed. The party would stop by Nachum's house on the way out of town.

"Another thought, considering safety," Lucillus said. "You know that I love James, and a visit to the famous town of Ein Kerem would no doubt be enriching, but——"

A wave of Joseph's hand cut him off.

"You will be making stops," he said. "You may encounter Roman checkpoints where you'll have to declare yourselves. They set them up unexpectedly, whenever they have word of possible attacks on legion outposts or supply wagons in transit or other troublemaking. And at any place you find lodging—which you will especially need for the Sabbath—a young girl traveling with two men who bear her no relation would raise eyebrows. As for pagan Romans, the crude assumptions that would leap to their minds need not be mentioned. James will represent me. His presence will testify that this journey is a family endeavor."

"But he is only a boy."

"Nevertheless, with him along it will be easier for you to explain that you act on my behalf, taking my intended bride to the home of her kin in preparation for a wedding. You can say I am delayed on business and will follow."

Lucillus' head dipped to one side to acknowledge plausibility in this argument.

"Besides," Joseph continued, "James can stay close to Mary and shield her from direct inquiries. I do not want her speaking with anyone."

Lucillus' own eyebrows raised.

Joseph gave him a scrip full of gold coins for the journey, and then passed him the scroll he had so hastily prepared. "Give this only into the hands of Zacharias," he said. "And remember, let Mary speak to no one. For that matter, discourage her from speaking even when on the road by yourselves. And if the girl should say anything...*strange*...please, disregard it."

He gripped Lucillus' arm firmly. "I implore you, my friend," he said pleadingly. "You must trust me. This trip is necessary to protect Mary and to answer a very difficult question. I do not overstate the matter to say it involves life and death."

Lucillus looked deeply into Joseph's eyes and nodded again.

CHAPTER SIX

*"Joseph, son of David, do not be afraid
to take Mary your wife into your home."*

(Matthew 1)

The small party made its way through Nazareth, passing in and out of jagged shadows that dissected the moonlight giving the town a pale glow. Beyond the kiln of Reuven the potter, they set out into the countryside on the south road. James led the donkey bearing Mary while Lucillus and Nachum, armed with their walking staves, knives, and Josis' gouging axes, flanked the animal on opposite sides.

Food enough for three or four days travel was stuffed inside leather bags that straddled the donkey's haunches behind where Mary sat wrapped in a heavy cloak against the night chill. Their provisions included the bread, dried meat and dried figs provided by Zipporah, which Joseph insisted they take, even though Lucillus had brought ample supplies.

"The girl must eat," was his cryptic explanation.

Lucillus understood that Joseph wanted Mary away from Nazareth before dawn, but he realized that, starting so late, the party couldn't get far before fatigue overcame them. There was a dense grove set in a hollow some ways out of town and just off the main path, after the road began the first of its step-like descents from the green hills of Galilee. Tall trees and a thicket of scrub bushes, fed by a narrow stream running from a spring nearby, screened them from view as they spread blankets and took a few hours rest to prepare for the next day's walking.

Shortly after dawn, Lucillus was awakened by the sound of Mary's morning distress. He lay quietly under his blanket as the girl finished and then composed herself, James and Nachum still asleep. He felt confirmed in his suspicions about Joseph's haste to remove her from the scene.

The sun was on its rising arc by the time the party was underway again, but Lucillus accepted the delayed start as a reasonable price for strength renewed. And they would need strength. They made good progress throughout the day, entering into the Jezreel Valley, which the Greeks called the Plain of Esdraelon, a broad and fertile expanse of fields and meadows that cut the nation in half from the coast of the Mediterranean to the valley of the Jordan. That night found them by the River Kishon where several other groups of travelers were camped. The spot was famous as the site of Barak's victory over the army of Jabin and the Canaanite chariots.

Mary had ridden in silence, speaking only once when, with her stomach affected by the pitch and roll of the donkey's gait, she asked to walk. She took her meals similarly without words, except to say the blessings.

For his part, James was completely baffled by the whole situation. He did not understand why Mary had to be taken to the home of her relations, why it was necessary to leave in the middle of the night, or even why he should have been sent along—though he was pleased at the opportunity to visit Ein Kerem, a place he had never been but had heard much about. It was said that the village, near Jerusalem, was so lush and verdant that pomegranates, figs, olives and pears grew wild everywhere. Vineyards bore their fruits without tending. Whether such tales were true he didn't know, but he wished to find out.

The girl's silence was another source of mystery to him. Mary had said so little throughout the day, even though it was apparent to James that the journey was taxing to her. Some words of complaint, or at least an admission of weariness, might be natural. When they were preparing to bed down that evening, he asked if she was feeling alright. She merely smiled at him in a queer and unfathomable way, then turned her face up to the sky and started into what appeared to be a prayer, her lips moving soundlessly. He watched her for some moments sitting in that attitude, then shook his head and laid down to sleep.

The next day brought them to the start of the high road that led up into the hills and through the country of the Samaritans. Nachum expressed distaste for having to traverse infidel lands, common as the route was for those traveling between Galilee and Jerusalem. Lucillus, who had seen much of the world and its various peoples, reminded Nachum of the hard work Samaritan laborers had provided on several of Joseph's building projects. Nachum granted their strength and industry, but stood by his dislike for these lost cousins of the Jews.

The Samaritan village of Sychar came into view some time later. There they stopped to fill a water skin from the well which Jacob had dug after purchasing the land from the sons of Hamor. Though they could surely have used a rest, Lucillus insisted they press on, knowing that three Jews and a dark-skinned Greek would not be encouraged to linger.

Sustaining themselves on Zipporah's dried figs and meat as they walked, they continued through the high country of Ephraim with the goal of getting as far south of Mount Gerizim as they could. Lucillus considered whether they should attempt to continue walking into the night, since the following day's sunset would mark the start of Sabbath when no travel was possible. The farther they got, the better their chances of finding someplace more welcoming. But Mary was showing signs of weariness and had resumed riding on the donkey's swaying back.

"Are you able to continue?" Lucillus asked her.

She looked at him, and her face took on a strangely peaceful expression, not quite a smile.

"The Lord is my strength and my shield," she said, quoting the psalm. "We will go as far as you think best."

Lucillus nodded. "Let us keep on then," he said.

It was a brave effort, but after several hours of trudging through the dark and cold, Lucillus decided they would have to stop. This was not secure territory, however. They would rest, but he and Nachum would sleep in shifts, taking turns at maintaining a guard. The first watch would be his, he said, at which Nachum objected. Being quite tired himself by now, Lucillus did not resist the big laborer's kindness all that strenuously.

Two hours later, Nachum touched him gently on the shoulder, and the pair traded places. Lucillus watched over the small band until the first pink blush of morning glow. He then woke the others, and the journey resumed.

By the middle of the day they came upon an inn. It was not one of the massive khans that were set along the roads of Judea at regular intervals to service trading caravans and groups of travelers. This was a small lodge that took in the odd wayfarer—really just an out-sized farmhouse—a place where Lucillus had stayed before, run by a farmer whom he knew by name. Arrangements were made to rest through Sabbath. Their arrival was most timely. Mary was exhausted. She fell asleep until James woke her to come to the table where the farmer's wife was preparing to light the Sabbath candles.

*   *   *

Joseph was determined to avoid the questioning eyes of his family. The morning after Mary's departure, he left the compound early and headed for Sepphoris, leaving a note for Josis that he intended to spend the night with one of his foremen. He managed to make that stretch into a second night, but with Sabbath approaching, he knew he would have to return to Nazareth.

He arrived home in mid-afternoon. Salome spotted him in the court and asked if she could bring him some food after his journey. Joseph hesitated at first, but it was now long since he had broken his fast, and hunger forced him to accept some soup and bread. His expression of thanks to her upon its delivery was sincere but terse, almost abrupt.

She asked at which table he intended to take the Sabbath meal, extending an invitation to her own that made him feel somewhat uncomfortable. Joseph knew his presence in one or another of his sons' homes was unavoidable. He accepted Salome's offer with as much good humor as he could muster, and she returned to Sabbath preparations. He was grateful that she had asked no questions about his sojourn in Sepphoris or the unaccounted absence of James and Mary.

Aside from some restrained banter with his granddaughters upon entering Josis' house that evening, Joseph was quiet until he heard the Sabbath trumpet sound its final blast in the distance and Salome lit the candles. Then, as family head, he invoked the three-fold blessing. The meal proceeded with all the awkwardness he had anticipated.

While the family compound had been abuzz with all sorts of speculation, Josis and Salome took particular care not to pry, and their restraint showed. Joseph offered little in the way of casual chatter beyond a recounting of some problems he had been addressing over the past days at the work sites. When the meal was over, he removed himself from the table as quickly as pious practice and common courtesy allowed, returning across the court to his own house.

At this time on the eve of Sabbath, he would normally have immersed himself in prayer in the company of James. But with the boy gone, and under such a cloud of anxiety over Mary's confession, Joseph found it hard to focus on his devotions. He even applied the phylacteries improperly, turning the band that ran down his left arm an insufficient number of times.

He became annoyed at himself over the simple error. But he corrected it and persevered in his recitation of the psalms, eventually gaining a measure of quietude until he was ready for his bed. For all the conflict in his soul, sleep came within minutes of placing his head down. It was a sleep of greater depth and restfulness than any he had known since the death of Escha.

*   *   *

The blackness of the room didn't register on Joseph as he sat bolt upright on his mat, eyes wide open, the grip of his dream suddenly broken but the feelings it had evoked still present. *Such a dream!* So bright, so vivid, in stark contrast to the deathlike slumber by which he had been consumed until—

Until the messenger appeared.

Was this what Mary had experienced? If so, it wasn't surprising that she could be convinced she carried a child, even the child of God Himself. This had been enough to shake the heart of a grown man, so naturally, an impressionable young girl would be all the more effected.

But how was it they'd each had dreams so similar—hers announcing the unthinkable and his confirming that it was true? Was this vision merely a trick of the mind? Was it his conscience rebuking him for the harshness he had shown a confused child?

Or was it something else entirely? Something evil? Was it a demon that had come to him—and to her earlier? Such diabolical things were said to happen, even to those of right intent who would never think of dabbling in the realm of spirits.

And yet... And yet...

Mary had insisted it was not a dream, and she'd described the experience as something wonderful. Indeed, this apparition of tonight had left Joseph with the very same feeling. It *was* wonderful. Clear and vivid and wonderful. Could a demon so thoroughly mislead as to falsely uplift one's soul in such an ecstatic way? It didn't seem possible.

But then, none of this seemed possible.

And yet... And yet...

Joseph was suddenly convinced that what he'd experienced was real, even if, for him, it occurred in sleep, as it surely had. Weren't the holy books replete with tales of prophetic dreams? Even allowing for the rarity of such events, and for Joseph's certainty that he was no prophet, he had to admit that divine communication could happen.

But then what did *this* imply? Could it be that what Mary had told him was true?

Such a possibility was more than his mind could entertain in the black of night, roused so suddenly from sleep. It was too great and shocking a thought. It was beyond the wildest imaginings. And so he wouldn't consider it now. He *couldn't* consider it now. No. To the best of his ability, he would set it aside until he was able to speak of it with Mary. And this he would do as quickly as possible.

Yes. He would go after her. Leave now, in the middle of the night. He would run as fast as he could and overtake the party. Or he would reach them at the home of Zacharias. Either way, he would start immediately.

He stood up and groped about the dark room until he found the flint and stone. He was about to light the oil lamp when he was struck by the realization that it was Sabbath and this would be an impermissible act. He also realized that he would not be able to begin his pursuit until after the next sundown.

Suddenly Joseph felt horribly torn. He had to speak with Mary. His entire being ached to speak with her. He had to know if the apparitions were genuine. But this was Sabbath, and there could be no travel. He could not leave now. It was the Law.

Still, wasn't it understood that certain urgent needs overrode the Sabbath? Surely, messages from God were of sufficient urgency to preempt the restrictions.

But it was Sabbath, and every fiber of his Jewish manhood argued that the Law must be obeyed.

Joseph felt as if he was being butted back and forth by two huge, angry goats as he pondered this conflict. And then the answer became clear. If the messages were true, then there had been a reason that Mary was given into his care, a reason greater than providing Joachim a peaceful death. The most important thing he was being called to do was to be obedient to the will of the Holy One. And for him to transgress the Law would not be obedience. He had lived by the Law of Moses all his life, and he could not depart from it now. *Especially* not now.

Hard as it might be—painful as it might be—Joseph would keep the Sabbath.

* * *

With the quiet Mary had maintained since leaving Nazareth, James wasn't surprised that she secluded herself throughout Sabbath. She emerged from the small chamber over which Lucillus had haggled amiably with the farmer for her exclusive use—at extra cost—only to take meals.

James wondered at her detachment. At night, lying in the common area on an extremely thin sleeping mat just outside her door, he had thought about her singing upstairs at home. He still wasn't sure if his enjoyment of her songs was entirely appropriate, but he admitted to himself that he missed hearing her voice. Now that Sabbath had passed and they were underway again, the girl remained wordless as she rocked back and forth on the donkey, immersed in her prayers.

But this trip, sudden and unexplained as it was, provided much to distract the boy from thoughts about Mary and her strange silence— the landscape for one. As they approached Jerusalem, James observed how much more sparse and dry the country was than the green hills he knew in Galilee. He had walked this route with his father on previous occasions, but this time he made special note of how the garden plots, vineyards and orchards were largely confined to terraces lining the hillsides, rather than spread out on rolling land as in the north.

He also took interest in the different types of people encountered along the route—Greeks, Samaritans, Idumaeans, Bedouin tribesmen—all on their way to unknown places or converging on the great city of the Jews. At one point, the small party had to step off the road to allow passage of a column of Roman cavalry trotting by in purposeful haste.

Lucillus noted their standards, the crests on the officers' helmets, and the dark, un-Roman faces. "Auxiliaries," he said. "From Libya, I think."

"Pagans!" said Nachum, shaking his head dismissively. "Romans, Greeks, whatever. All foreigners in *our* land."

Lucillus laughed. "Am I not a Greek?"

"That is what people call you," Nachum said. "But you are not a Greek. You keep the commandments. The pagans laugh at that. They laugh at us. They think we have no religion because we are faithful only to the true Holy One."

"A single god doesn't seem like enough to them," said Lucillus.

"The King of the Universe is enough for anyone—*more* than enough."

"Well, the foreigners are here, and we build their houses for them."

"I'll take a fool's gold."

Again Lucillus laughed. "They have plenty of it."

"That they do," Nachum said, "lots of gold and lots of gods. I see their home altars. I see how they burn incense to the deities that watch over their grand houses built by Jews. They love all the gods. But what do the gods really mean to them? I think it is all just a show. It is what you do if you are a citizen of the empire. You make sacrifice on Caesar's birthday, and then you go out and get drunk. Some religion."

"Do the pagans not believe in their gods?" James asked.

"Some believe," said Lucillus. "Now it is true that for many the gods and their worship are, as our friend says, *just a show*. There are hypocrites everywhere. I am told that there are even some Jews who are less pious than they pretend to be. Isn't that so, Nachum?"

"It is. But we Jews do not fill our land with temples and images to make the nations think we are holy."

Lucillus continued smiling at the burly workman. "You are a philosopher, Nachum," he said, "a student of the human heart." He glanced at James who was looking up at his tutor with questioning eyes.

"I know devotion to the gods can appear false," Lucillus continued, rubbing his face thoughtfully. "But I have known many pagans for whom the divine will is important. And at the heart of it, they admit that all their gods are subject to one supreme divinity. So they are more like the Jews than it might seem. Some sacrifice with great seriousness when their need is great. They follow the auguries diligently when they face a big decision."

Nachum snorted derisively. "What can be seen in the entrails of beasts? Their auguries are meaningless, and their sacrifices are a waste."

"Jews sacrifice."

"We Jews deny ourselves the use of valuable things in recognition that life is a gift from the Creator, the Father of us all. Our sacrifices express our faith."

"As do theirs, my friend," said Lucillus, "in their way. It is not all show, not for those who truly believe. For them it is the root of life. It is what Rome stands for."

The party came over a rise, and the city loomed up in the distance beyond farms, olive groves and clusters of houses scattered across the knolls and hollows that marked the rough terrain before them. Within the grey walls snaking their way around the hill of the Lord, row upon row of tile roofs, interlaced as the threads in woven cloth, rose to a summit. There, shining like some great jewel set at the peak of a diadem, stood the temple.

To James the sight reflected the *compact unity* spoken of by the psalmist, the place where the tribes came up to give their praise. *I rejoiced when they said we will go to the House of the Lord.* Mary had her own quiet reaction to the sight: a pang of something like homesickness. But the boy felt his heart swell with the excitement that had seized him each time he'd visited the city with his father.

Then, perhaps as a consequence of his age and growing awareness, his eyes were drawn to a set of structures that stood erect and strong adjacent to the temple. These were the four watch towers of the Antonia Fortress. Built by Herod, named for Marcus Antonius, who had been the prime advocate of the Herodian regime, and home to the 600-man Jerusalem garrison, the fortress was a constant reminder of Roman presence and oversight, even of the temple itself. James knew that the ceremonial robes worn by the High Priest were actually kept in the fortress. This was one of many means by which the Romans exerted their control over the nation's religious life, the enthusiasms of which tended to find expression in civil unrest.

"The Greeks and their gods are everywhere, aren't they?" James said.

"They are part of our life," Lucillus answered. "Certainly, they have been part of mine."

"There are some who count the days until we are free of Greeks," Nachum said. "I do."

"Please count them quietly," said Lucillus. "We have to pass the checkpoint at the city gate."

*   *   *

After the sun set on the Sabbath day, Joseph returned to his house from taking the evening meal at Judas' table. He had gotten through Sabbath by maintaining a very uncharacteristic air of reserve, managing to largely avoid speaking about Mary and James. His one vague mention was that the girl had gone to visit her kinsmen and James was accompanying her.

Back in the shadowed lower room, he availed himself of the last faint evening light to gather some things for a trip. He took clean under-linen and rolled it up inside a spare tunic along with his phylacteries and a loaf of bread he had requested from a puzzled Sarah. Then, out of a small recess in the back wall of the room, he retrieved a short Syrian dagger in its scabbard. Finally, he laid down on his mat for a few hours sleep. He would leave with the sun.

In his anticipation of the trip and his continued preoccupation with the vision of last night, Joseph had difficulty getting to sleep. He tossed on the mat for a time, the questions he intended to ask Mary playing over and over in his mind. Eventually he settled into rest, once more to a depth of sleep he would not have thought possible.

The first glow of sunlight woke him, and he rose refreshed to pray an abbreviated version of the morning service without using his phylacteries. Then he put on fresh clothes, inserted the Syrian dagger into his belt next to a small scrip of gold coins, and gathered up the bundle he had prepared for the journey. He went to the door where he put on his sandals and took his walking staff propped against the wall. Going outside, he made a stop at the privy, then went across the court to Josis' house and rapped quietly on the door.

After a moment the face of his eldest son appeared, half awake and confused. "Father?" Josis said. "What is wrong?"

"My son," said Joseph, "I must go to Ein Kerem."

"Ein Kerem?"

"To the home of Zacharias, Mary's kinsman."

"Is that where Mary has gone?"

"Yes. You will have to attend to the building projects in my absence. I am sorry, but...it is urgent that I leave now."

"Of course, Father, but what——"

"All will be explained, my son. Please have trust in me."

"You know I have."

*   *   *

James, Mary and Nachum waited in the shade of some olive trees that stood in lines upon a hill overlooking the junction of roads that paralleled the north and west walls of Jerusalem. One of the city's gates was beyond. The donkey nosed in sparse grass seeking what forage it could. Lucillus had decided it was best not to subject Mary to the prying eyes of the civil guards, or worse, the Roman inspectors who observed all who entered the city, supervised the tolls on freight haulers and caravans, and detained at their discretion anyone who appeared out of the ordinary. So he left the trio at some distance and headed into the city alone.

Some recent incidents of violence had prompted added restrictions on entry. Lucillus was directed to a small side passage which had been set in the blocked gateway, a structure much like the chute through which cattle are driven for culling from the herd, known as the Eye of the Needle. Anyone seeking entry was required to queue up for individual checking and admission. He found himself about twentieth in an impatient line, all of whose occupants were annoyed at the security procedures and the gruff manner of the guards applying them. An amusing exchange between two travelers caught his ear.

"This is how they keep the city safe," said the first, an edge of sarcasm in his voice. "I could bring a camel through this door, and who would know what it carried?"

His companion nodded in agreement. "An extra *Caesar's head* to the watch, and no one would even ask."

"Well, be grateful for the civil guard," the first friend said. "A temple guard would demand *two* extra."

Both men laughed. Lucillus smiled quietly.

When he had been admitted, Lucillus went straight to the temple precincts. It had occurred to him that he couldn't be sure Zacharias was to be found at his home in Ein Kerem, not knowing the priestly schedule or what might be required of Mary's kinsman by his business affairs. Zacharias might be at the temple or someplace else in the city. In any event, directions to the priest's home would be helpful, since Joseph had provided none and probably didn't know where the family lived.

In the Court of the Gentiles Lucillus came upon a priest who knew Zacharias, confirmed that he was not on temple duty at present, and provided the information necessary to locate his house. Lucillus returned to where he had left the others in the olive grove outside the city walls, and after a short rest and the sharing of food from the donkey's pack, the party continued on around Jerusalem to Ein Kerem.

The town was indeed as lush as James had heard, although the orderliness with which the trees and bushes were set and the attention to their care which was clearly evident argued against their springing spontaneously from the earth. Still, the character of the area was a decided contrast with the rest of the gray, rocky country surrounding Jerusalem. James wondered what felicitous combination of soil, rain, breeze and sunshine might account for such plenty.

Zacharias' house was easy to find. It was, in fact, the most imposing structure in the vicinity—a two-story, limestone villa, fronted by a colonnade of fluted posts vaguely suggestive of the temple itself, and surrounded on all sides by its own impressive gardens contained within a wall whose arched gate opened onto the central plaza of the town.

A servant responded to a tug on the bell pull. Lucillus explained that they had brought a kinswoman of the master's wife and that he, himself, bore an urgent message for Zacharias from Joseph of Nazareth, the girl's intended husband. While Nachum remained at the gate with the donkey, the servant led Lucillus, Mary and James to the house, bade the younger two to remain under the shelter of shades that draped from the colonnade, and took Lucillus inside.

Mary found the comfort of a low stone bench, where she sat, tired from the journey, in the silence that had by now become her accustomed mode. James gazed about at the grounds and took several aimless steps, wandering along a side path, and feeling awed by more grandeur than he had ever experienced within a private domain.

After some minutes he heard a sound and turned to see a woman come out of the doorway. Her appearance was a curious mix: a deeply lined face and a head of silver hair, indicating advanced age, along with a clearly defined protrusion at the front. Such a bulge was something one would expect to see only on a much younger woman carrying a child, not on the thin, slightly frail body of this old lady.

Mary rose at her arrival and spoke some words unheard by James, to which the woman reacted with a start, grabbing her belly. James assumed this was Elizabeth, Mary's aunt. And he heard her say something that confused the boy, something about the *mother of my Lord* coming to her. Then she reached out, took Mary's hands in her own and seemed to bow before the girl.

He went back to the colonnade so that he might be introduced as the son of Joseph, which would be proper in the circumstances. Surprisingly, Mary did not acknowledge his presence. Instead she seemed to be reciting something.

"My soul declares the Lord's greatness..." he heard her say, and she went on at some length, a few of the lines striking James as familiar. He was confused by this display. Perhaps such recitations were a practice of greeting among the members of Mary's family. He couldn't be sure, of course. But when the girl had finished, the older woman's eyes were filled with tears, and she embraced her vigorously.

Inside the house, Lucillus was led to a chamber, the walls of which were lined with shelves, to await the arrival of Zacharias. The servant explained that, while the master would receive him, he was in the grip of a strange malady that had robbed him of his voice. Communication on his part would be by signs and writing, so patience was required.

"He can hear?" Lucillus asked.

"Perfectly," the servant said, turning to leave.

Lucillus waited, his eyes drawn to the numerous scrolls that filled shelves and lay in stacks on other surfaces around the room. His curiosity was aroused, and he wondered what knowledge they might contain. But his musings were short-lived. Zacharias entered.

"Honored sir, peace be upon you and all your house," Lucillus said, bowing before the famous priest.

Zacharias nodded and then seated himself behind a writing table that bore a tablet of wax held within a frame. There was also a stylus and a small roller with which smoothness could be restored to the wax surface for re-use. He gestured toward a chair, indicating that the visitor should sit.

Lucillus complied, drawing Joseph's parchment from under his cloak. He handed the small wrapped bundle to Zacharias. "From my master, Joseph son of Jacob," he said.

The priest untied the thong and opened the sheet, his eyes making a quick scan of the words. The traces of older writing underscored the urgency with which Joseph had composed his message. Zacharias turned a quizzical eye on Lucillus. Then he set the parchment aside and took the stylus, scratching it into the wax. He held up the tablet for Lucillus to read. "What is it that happened to the girl?" it said in Greek.

"My master was not specific," Lucillus answered tactfully. "But he is much in need of your wisdom. He carries a great burden on his heart."

Zacharias rose to his feet, held up a hand, palm out, indicating that Lucillus should wait, then left the room.

CHAPTER SEVEN

O the depth of riches both of the wisdom and knowledge of God;
how unsearchable his judgments and inscrutable his ways.

(Romans 11)

An air of something like rejoicing reigned in the house of Zacharias, which Lucillus, with his suspicions about Mary, found very surprising. Had he misread the situation? Did Mary's morning bouts of illness have a cause other than the presence of a child? If so, why had Joseph been so desperate to remove the girl from Nazareth?

It was clear that neither Mary nor her relatives were inclined to provide any answers, though Elizabeth had conveyed her husband's gracious invitation for Lucillus, James and Nachum to spend the next day resting from their journey before returning to Galilee. Lucillus was profuse in his thanks, but noted Joseph's eagerness for a reply to his message. Elizabeth merely smiled cryptically and expressed confidence that Mary's husband-to-be would be pleased when it came.

One could hardly decline the hospitality of such an exalted family, so the party spent a well fed and comfortable night followed by a further day of relaxation. Nachum found a grassy spot in the garden to enjoy the mild weather of this time in the year. On occasion throughout the day his rest was broken, quite amiably, by the provision of food and wine by the servants. James accepted Zacharias' suggestion, forwarded to him in writing, that the budding scholar might enjoy examining the priest's library. This privilege he shared with Lucillus who, as the boy's tutor, stood by to answer questions and help with any needed translating, since the collection included numerous documents in Greek. Even the donkey basked in the household's luxury, chomping on a seemingly unlimited supply of fodder.

Enjoyable as this respite was in such a magnificent house, enhanced by the pleasant setting of Ein Kerem, Lucillus remained curious, and a bit uneasy, about Mary and about the reaction of Zacharias and Elizabeth to her. He knew of her temple upbringing. Jerusalem was nearby, and Zacharias was a priest. Had the couple been close to her during those years? He would have assumed that the girls of the temple were kept fairly secluded, but he didn't know that for sure.

Then too, there was a certain awkwardness in Lucillus about his social and religious standing, relative to this great keeper of the Law. Judaism prescribed kindness and hospitality to all, even to the alien. And while Lucillus was not quite an alien, he also was not quite a Jew. He was merely a God-fearing gentile whose attendance at synagogue was regular but who did not bear the mark of the Covenant in his flesh. Even if the kindness of this priest was abundant, Lucillus did not feel entirely at ease.

James, on the other hand, was enthralled by this experience. While the reason for their trip remained a mystery to him, he was grateful for the opportunity to glimpse the home and daily doings of a leading religious figure—one who had held out the promise of entry into the inner circle of scholarly life. His mind was alive with the observations he would share with the Rabbi Ezra, and it stoked his eagerness for the day of his reading in the synagogue and the attainment of his maturity.

Throughout the afternoon Mary was the sole focus of her relatives' attention. Elizabeth had a divan carried out to the garden, over which the servants assembled a small pavilion of wicker screens. She insisted that the girl recline, ordered refreshments brought to her continuously, and peppered her with solicitous questions about her comfort and contentment. At one point, feeling rather dazzled by such fuss, Mary burst out laughing. James, who happened to be standing in the colonnade, noted her amusement, which pleased him after the days of silence.

Meanwhile, Zacharias came to the garden repeatedly with questions written out on parchment or scribed into the wax tablet. At various times both James and Lucillus saw the girl speaking to him at length, apparently answering his inquiries, the old man's head nodding solemnly. All of this seemed more than mere indulgence of a favorite niece. These exchanges held a significance, which James and Lucillus detected but could not understand.

Finally, that evening as Lucillus was preparing for sleep, Lemuel, the steward of Zacharias' house came to him bearing a scroll tucked inside a linen pouch. Both the scroll and the draw strings of its container were closed with wax seals bearing the signet of Zacharias.

"A message for Joseph of Nazareth," the steward said. "My master wishes you a safe and swift journey as you depart in the morning. He prays for your protection and offers his blessing upon the much favored house of Joseph."

"Please convey to him deepest gratitude for the great hospitality he has shown my companions and myself. May peace be upon the house of Zacharias."

At first light, Lucillus, James and Nachum were assembled by the front gate, Nachum loading the donkey with provisions for the journey brought out by a servant girl. They were about to depart when Mary appeared in the colonnade. She came across the garden to them.

"Thank you," she said, "for bringing me safely to the home of my relations. May the Holy One of Israel watch over you and keep you in His care." Then she said specifically to James, "Please convey my respect and affection to your father. Tell him I await his arrival eagerly."

"Yes, Mary," the boy answered. "I will tell him. Be well. I hope we will see you again soon. Peace be upon you."

While James accepted Mary's words as a simple parting sentiment, Lucillus took note of her expression of eagerness for Joseph's *arrival*. Was she merely stating her hope to see him again at some undetermined time in the future? If she did carry a child, who knew when that might be—if ever? On the other hand, could her words refer to something in Zacharias' well sealed message? Had the priest made a special appeal for Joseph to come? Was Joseph's presence somehow demanded? Questions heaped upon questions.

They set out on the road back to Jerusalem, James at pains to take in every view of the fertile haven they were departing. At one point, standing on a rise, he looked back and noted the contrast between the district of Ein Kerem and the surrounding countryside, which changed markedly over a very short distance. By the time they were again outside Jerusalem, rocky soil and sparseness of vegetation were the predominant features.

But there was no ignoring the dramatic presence of the great city. As they passed its walls, the boy felt once more a thrill of anticipation at the prospect of studying with the doctors of the Law. What arrangement would Zacharias make for him? And what might such an opportunity portend for his future?

He was deep in his thoughts about great things to come when Nachum called out, "It is the master."

Lucillus looked up. "Hmm?"

"Joseph. It is Joseph," the big laborer said, pointing forward.

James spotted him now. "Yes. It is Father!" The boy ran to him, Joseph taking his son in his arms.

"Peace be upon you, Joseph," Lucillus said when they had caught up. "But what are you doing here? I thought you wanted us to—"

"You have done well, my trusted friends," Joseph said, "everything I asked. But I received some additional information after you left, and it became necessary for me to make the journey myself."

"I am happy to see you, Father."

Joseph rubbed the side of the boy's head in his fatherly way. "And I you, my son." Then to Lucillus: "How was Mary received?"

"Remarkably well."

"And my message to Zacharias?"

"Whatever it was that you told him, his fervor over this kinswoman only increases the longer she is there.

Joseph nodded his head and smiled. "Has he told you anything?"

"Zacharias tells no one anything," Lucillus said. "Some malady blocks him from speaking."

"The illness persists?"

"He writes messages, Father," said James.

"And Mary? She has said nothing?"

"Other than a few words of thanks at our departure," Lucillus replied, "she kept the silence of the sphinx during the entire journey. She does speak with Zacharias and his wife, but we don't know what about."

"Mary is happy to be there, Father."

"With good reason," said Lucillus. "They treat her like your great ancestor would have treated the Queen of Sheba."

Again Joseph smiled. "Well, my friends," he said. "You must return with me to Ein Kerem." He patted the donkey on a haunch and gestured for the three to follow.

"Fine with me," said Nachum. "The house of Zacharias is a comfortable place."

"Shouldn't we get back to Nazareth?" Lucillus asked. "The projects."

"Josis has everything in hand, I'm sure," said Joseph over his shoulder. "I have important words to share with Mary." And he set a brisk pace, the others falling in behind.

James quickened his steps to parallel Joseph's stride. "Father, a very interesting thing did happen when we arrived."

"Oh?"

"When Mary was greeting her kinswoman, Elizabeth, she recited something. It was quite long, and at first I thought it was the *Song of Hannah*. At least it sounded something like that. But Mary said it in a different way and changed things. I never heard anyone give a recitation when they were greeting someone."

"Did Elizabeth recite anything back to her?"

"No, but she looked very excited about what Mary was saying." The boy scratched his head. "What could it have meant, Father?"

"I do not know. But unexpected things can happen, my son, many unexpected things."

Then Lucillus said, "Zacharias has given me a reply to your message." He handed over the sealed pouch containing the scroll. "You may wish to read it before you see him."

Joseph took the package, then stopped and said, "Yes. Everyone rest for a while. I will have a look at Zacharias' words."

He found a large rock off to the side of the road, deposited himself on it, snapped the wax tab that held the drawstrings together, and opened the pouch. Then he broke the seal on the scroll and read the priest's message as the others watched from a distance. Lucillus studied Joseph's face and observed his visage turn from curiosity to what seemed a look of deep satisfaction. He saw Joseph close his eyes and begin to rock forward and backward, mouthing words silently as in prayer.

What has come upon this family? the Greek asked himself in his thoughts.

*   *   *

Mary's face lit up at the sight of Joseph walking across the garden to where Elizabeth had her ensconced on the divan once more, shaded by the wicker panels. The girl rose to her feet. She and her intended husband shared a knowing smile as the distance between them closed.

"Peace be with you, Joseph," she said.

"Peace be with you, Mary."

"Do you know now?"

"The messenger came to me."

"And you believe?"

"I cannot think it otherwise than real."

"It is real."

"The marriage must take place at once," he said. "We cannot let any more time go by. People will make their calculations, and there must be no basis on which questions can be raised. The child's place in the family and in the synagogue must be secure."

"Yes, Joseph. Zacharias can arrange it."

"Is he not ill?"

"No, merely lost his voice. The Holy One has touched him—and touched Elizabeth as well."

"So he said in his message." Joseph gazed off toward the sky, then back at Mary, and then down at the ground. His head turned slowly from side to side. "But I must confess, I do not understand."

"We have all been chosen, Joseph," she said. "We have been chosen by God."

*   *   *

Joseph sat beside Zacharias on a bench in the garden from late morning until well into the afternoon, their conversation hampered by the priest's need to write out his words on the wax tablet in his lap. But eventually they worked out a plan for the wedding, which would be conducted in private within the next few days.

Since Zacharias would be unable to speak the marriage blessings, he sent his steward to Jerusalem with instructions to seek out Simeon, a scribe of advanced age and great holiness. With the decline in his physical capacities, Simeon spent most of his time in the temple praying for the consolation of Israel.

"He is a friend of many years," Zacharias wrote on the tablet, "pious and discreet."

Arrangements would have to be made to convey Simeon to Ein Kerem. "It will not be easy for one so infirm," Zacharias wrote, Joseph following the scratching of the stylus. "But I believe he will be eager to do it when I make the situation clear." He drew the roller across the clay, smoothing the surface, and then inscribed, "It will accord with certain assurances which he says he has received in his prayers."

"How much can we take him into our confidence?" Joseph asked. "There is risk in speaking of the messages we have received."

Zacharias nodded and then wrote, "Simeon is one of very few people whom I would trust to understand." Then, after rolling the surface clean again: "I believe this may be what he has waited for."

A litter carrying Simeon arrived late the next day. The frail form, crowned with wisps of feathery white hair, hardly seemed to require the combined strength of the four husky lads whom Lemuel had hired to bear it. But the old man's eyes were bright, his mind sharp. Immediately upon being helped from the chair, he began questioning Zacharias as to what was this exciting *purpose of the Lord* to which the priest's message had alluded.

Zacharias took him by the hand and led him into the house where he and Joseph shared the story of Mary's and Elizabeth's conceptions, the confirmations which the two men had received, and the role which Simeon was being called upon to play.

The old scribe sat quietly for some time, lost in a kind of wonder. It all came back to him—the conviction, felt over and over again as a promise from the Lord Himself that Simeon should not die until he had seen the Anointed One with his own eyes. He was convinced of it. He lived for that day alone.

Finally, he asked that Mary be brought to him. When the girl came in, he looked her up and down, slowly and carefully, as if assessing her worthiness for such an unimaginably important task as Joseph and Zacharias claimed she had been given.

She was so young, only just beyond childhood. And lovely. In the earliest blush of womanly ripeness, like an offering of first fruits. He considered the facts of her life: of a priestly clan, raised in the temple—he thought he recognized her from the precincts—her entire being dedicated to the Holy One of Israel. Surely, this was one such as the Lord would choose.

Perfect.

"You must promise that I can see this child," he said. "Alert me when you bring him to the temple."

Mary nodded, her eyes turned demurely to the floor. "You have my promise, sir," she answered.

"Then yes, I will conduct the wedding," said Simeon.

*   *   *

Zacharias and Simeon gave extensive consideration to whether Mary should go to the synagogue in Ein Kerem for the ritual bath normally required of a woman before her wedding. With the unprecedented circumstances of this particular wedding, neither the priest nor the scribe felt certain how the prescriptions of the Law would apply. Concerns about impurity associated with the female cycle seemed of less urgency since Mary and Joseph were beginning their married life without the expectation of normal marital relations. Their standing toward one another would necessarily be different from that of most husbands and wives. What were the ritual implications of that? Then too, didn't the fact that Mary carried the Child of the Most High suggest purity in the eyes of Heaven? Who could be more immaculate than she who was chosen to be the Lord's vessel?

Still, the Law had its obligations. In the end they judged that a ritual bath was, if not required, then certainly appropriate. Joseph too was certain he should purify himself, called as he was to be the guardian of this special child.

While the wedding would be conducted as inconspicuously as possible, Elizabeth insisted that some effort be made to create a festive atmosphere. She had the servants bring flowers from the garden to decorate the villa's common room. She arranged a special feast for those who would be in attendance: Mary and Joseph, along with James, Lucillus and Nachum, and of course, Simeon, Zacharias and herself. And she rigged a wedding canopy, using a large, ornate prayer shawl suspended from the tops of four poles. There might be no procession through the streets. No one would sing from the *Song of Songs*. But this would still be a celebration.

Her efforts were worthwhile—and successful. The wedding was joyous, if small and somewhat subdued. Mary beamed with the radiance of all brides, her youth and innocent beauty touching everyone in attendance, especially James. Perhaps for the first time, a suggestion of future joy—the joy which only life with a woman can offer—insinuated itself into his youthful heart. In a way which he did not fully understand, he felt himself envying his father.

By now it was clear to Lucillus, Nachum and, to an extent, James as well, that something extraordinary was happening. The hasty conveyance of Mary, the unexpected appearance of Joseph, the hushed consultations, the secretive wedding arrangements—everything suggested important, though hidden, motives. Lucillus especially, the worldly-wise Greek who kept his own counsel and who knew his employer as the most upright of men, was convinced that Mary was with child and that Joseph had decided to take her as his wife anyway.

But why? What conditions would prompt such an act? Lucillus understood the Jews and their fierce moral scruples. Something more was at work than Joseph's kindness or his commitment to honor a promise to Mary's father. Lucillus watched the ceremony unfold, he listened to the pledges and blessings, and he wondered. He wondered.

*   *   *

Very little seemed to have changed in the days after the wedding. Mary maintained her repose out in the garden, lying on the divan, as insisted upon by Elizabeth. And the furtive consultations continued, now between Mary, Zacharias and Joseph. Nachum, in particular, found it all very perplexing. While he had deduced Mary's condition, it was nonetheless strange to him that the bride and groom were not even sharing a bed chamber. If their behavior toward one another during the day embodied respect, even modest affection, the pair sought no privacy. It was hardly what one would expect of newlyweds, even newlyweds of such different ages.

He spoke his thoughts on the matter to Lucillus who took it upon himself to explain the agreement between Joseph and Joachim, of blessed memory, as the master had confided it during their sojourn in

Caesarea. Lucillus felt it best to nip Nachum's speculations in the bud, and he obtained a pledge that this information would go no further.

"I am not a gossip," the big laborer said with a hint of indignation.

When the time came to depart for Nazareth, Joseph asked Zacharias if Mary might remain in Ein Kerem for a time. Reflecting on the discord that had attended Mary's initial introduction into his household, he felt it wise to bring the rest of his family to some understanding of the situation before her return. That the Holy One had called this family to the honor of His service was a challenging enough idea. The divine origin of Mary's condition would be even less readily accepted. A bit of time might be needed for the facts to settle upon everyone's hearts, and it was essential that they did so.

Zacharias agreed.

For her part, Mary thought that remaining at the villa might actually be an advantage, the closer Elizabeth got to the birth of her own child—that is if Elizabeth would stop fussing and let her help. She suggested that she stay at least until Elizabeth's delivery, around Passover. Zacharias expressed his appreciation to her, and indicated that he would convince his wife to accept Mary's assistance.

And so, the morning after the first Sabbath following the wedding, Joseph departed Ein Kerem with James, Lucillus and Nachum, leaving Mary behind.

CHAPTER EIGHT

I will be with you as you speak,
and I will instruct you in what to say.

(Exodus 4)

Some inconsistencies were discovered in the carved beams brought from Lebanon. Several had not been cut precisely to specifications. Adjustments made to install them resulted in slight irregularities of appearance, which did not please the Greek client whose house was being built. Consequently, Josis had spent much of the two weeks since Joseph's departure in Sepphoris figuring out ways to disguise the flaws and placating a disgruntled customer.

"Shoddy Jew work," was the phrase that rang in his ears during several difficult negotiating sessions. Josis explained to the client, a mid-level official of the Roman civil administration, that the errors had been made in Lebanon, not by his Jewish craftsmen. In the end, he had to commit, on behalf of his father, to an adjustment in the fee for the entire building project, which restored some measure of grudging contentment. But with such distractions in Sepphoris and carpentry jobs piling up again in Josis' workshop, it was with extra joy that Joseph was greeted by his eldest son upon returning to the family compound.

"Peace be with you, Father. You should know how eagerly I thank heaven for your return."

Joseph had to smile. "I suspect there is more in this than the love of a loyal son."

"There is, Father," said Josis. "You are much needed." And he explained the problem with the beams, expressing his hope that he had done right in making adjustments to the fee.

"Was the customer satisfied in the end?" Joseph asked.

"More than he wished me to know, I think." said Josis. "Later that day I overheard him saying how the irregularities in the woodwork seemed to give his house more character."

"And saved him money," said Joseph, laughing. "You did what was necessary, my son."

Then, in a more subdued tone, Joseph asked Josis' assistance in organizing a meeting of the adults in the family, his sons and daughters and their spouses. "Mary and I have married," he told his son.

"Married? Where? When?"

"In Ein Kerem. And she has remained in the house of Zacharias to be of aid until her kinswoman, Elizabeth, delivers," he said.

"But why did you marry there, Father, without the family present?"

"I will explain all when everyone is assembled. And much more as well. There are things which they must know before Mary returns."

"What things, Father?"

"In time, Josis. In time. But please appreciate that this bears on the safety and the future of the entire family."

"As you wish, Father," Josis said. "I will speak with them."

It took two days for Josis to assemble everyone, during which time Joseph removed himself to Sepphoris from early morning to late at night, hoping to avoid inquiries he was not yet prepared to address. With his father gone, James became the focus of curiosity, especially among his sisters-in-law. Joseph had said nothing to indicate that the marriage should not be spoken of, so the boy did his best to answer their questions about the wedding. Why had it taken place so suddenly, and why in Ein Kerem, and why in such a private manner?

"It was how Father wanted it," James said with a shrug. "He had many long conversations with Zacharias. I suppose this was what they thought best. And the ceremony was very nice. Lots of flowers."

But why had Mary stayed behind? All understood that she would not be a wife to Joseph in the usual sense. Nonetheless, it seemed odd that a newly married woman should separate herself in this way. Would she not attend to her husband? Was his care to remain the responsibility of the other wives? Was this yet another sign of the queer presumptions one might expect of a temple girl?

James felt the women had leapt to conclusions that were very unfair to Mary. But events had unfolded so quickly and unexpectedly, and the air of mystery that surrounded the wedding was undeniable. He really had nothing with which to allay their suspicions. If only his father would come forth with an explanation that could answer everyone's questions, including his own.

The day of the family meeting Joseph spent extra time in the synagogue after the morning service. He prayed silently that he be given the words to convey this difficult story to his household with conviction and persuasiveness. All depended upon his being believed, and he didn't doubt for a minute the unbelievable nature of what he had to say. Unless others had received revelations similar to his own—and he harbored no illusions that anyone had—the onus was on him to make them accept that the Holy One of Israel had chosen this family, alone among all the clans of the Jews, for His own special purpose. Only then could they accept the child Mary was carrying and the circumstances under which she had conceived.

Upright as he was, Joseph might equivocate with those outside the family—let them assume what they would—but he could not lie to his own. To claim that the child was his would make it appear that he had violated his pledge to Joachim and maybe even forced himself upon an innocent girl placed under his protection. Likewise, to assert that Mary had changed her mind, abandoned a commitment that supposedly had been so strong as to induce her father to make this highly unusual contract, would say nothing good about her steadiness of purpose. Finally, and most important of all, Joseph could not permit anyone to believe that his wife had sinned before marriage. That would be unthinkable.

Such was the dilemma that occupied Joseph as he left the synagogue, heading toward the family compound. He searched his memory for a passage of holy writing which he might pray in preparation for the difficult task ahead. But nothing that came to mind seemed quite relevant to his situation. Closest was the psalm that offered assurance that a man could dwell in the tent of the Lord if he was truthful and kept a promise even when it was painful to do so.

When he reached his house, the gate was ajar. He touched the scroll and went inside. He could see that all the adults were present, sitting or standing in the portico. Except for James, who stood with his brothers, the children were all gathered at the far end of the court by the entrance to Josis' house, the older ones looking after the younger as Josis had insisted. There were more children than usual, since his daughters had brought theirs.

Enoch, the husband of Joseph's daughter, Assia, raised a hand in greeting. "Peace be with you, Father Joseph," he called.

"And upon all of you," Joseph replied. "I am most grateful you have come." He strode into the portico, giving a nod to Jubal, husband of daughter Lydia. "There are important things to speak about."

His sons had carried an assortment of stools and benches to the portico. The Roman-style chair that had come from Joachim's house was placed in a position of prominence. Assuming it was meant for him, Joseph sat on it as the others arranged themselves, the men on one side, women on the opposite. He looked about at each of his sons and daughters and their spouses, his eyes proceeding from face to face. While nothing was said, he could read curiosity, even anxiety, in their attentive expressions.

"My children," he began, "I know you are confused about events of recent days. I am sorry to withhold my explanation, but I felt that informing you all together was the only fair way."

This drew nods of assent, which Joseph found encouraging. Strangely, though he was head of the family and they his children, at this moment he felt very much like a child called upon to deliver a message he did not fully comprehend to a group of adults unlikely to take him seriously. It made him feel distinctly unsettled.

Then a passage from Jeremiah came to his mind: *The Lord said to me, "Do not say, 'I am a child,' for to whomever I send you, you shall go, and whatever I command you, you shall speak. Do not be afraid of them, for I am with you to deliver you."* He pondered the line for a moment, drew a breath, and continued.

"What I have to tell you is not easily understood," he said. "And I think that your acceptance of it will require more than mere trust in me."

This raised concern in several hearts, because Joseph held a position of utmost respect among all present. His two sons-in-law considered themselves—and were thought of throughout the town—as the most fortunate of men to have married the carpenter's daughters. And their trust in him had been vindicated on more than one occasion.

"Rather," Joseph continued, "I ask you to listen to me and consider what I have to say...as Jews."

Was there to be some sort of religious pronouncement? Perhaps having to do with the strange circumstance of the wedding? What was he about to tell them?

"We are fortunate—we Jews—not to be burdened with so many legends and fantastic tales, such as those the pagans are told. We are not raised on wild stories of the gods and their antics, their struggles and tragedies, their immoral delights, their dalliances with mortal women, and all the other nonsense by which the Greeks are so rapt."

Joseph's family had been amused by his comments on pagan folly before. He could speak with authority, having so many dealings in Sepphoris. This reflection brought smiles of familiarity to several faces in the group.

"Jews, on the other hand, are asked to believe very little, compared with the vast array of Greek myths. We know that all comes from the Creator of the Universe and it is His hand that guides our lives. Our fate is not at the mercy of flawed beings whose character is no better than our own and whose whims we must placate. The *Lord* is our shepherd."

Joseph's forthright manner of speaking sparked a thought within James, which the boy had entertained before: If his father's life had been different, he would have made an excellent rabbi. Clearly, this was the fount of James' own inclinations. If he could take full advantage of the opportunities promised by Zacharias, perhaps he could be the scholar Joseph should have been.

"And yet," Joseph continued, "there are certain things we are given to believe as Jews, things which are not the stuff of everyday experience. For instance, that Moses parted the sea so that the Children of Israel could escape from bondage in Egypt. Or that the lamp burned brightly for eight days in the temple, even though the oil was insufficient. These things are recorded, and we accept them, because we know the hand of the Holy One is in them. Yet they *are* extraordinary. It is because they are extraordinary that they have meaning to us and we celebrate them."

He paused, offered a quick, silent prayer for courage, and then went on. "I would ask you all...as Jews...to believe that something—that something similarly extraordinary—has happened within our family."

There was a stirring throughout the group, but no one said anything. How to approach this? Joseph decided that he would start with his own experience and then work back to the more daunting situation of Mary. "I have had a vision," he said. "It came to me in a dream, but I know in my heart it was more than a dream. I was visited by...the Lord's messenger."

Another stirring. No one now doubted that what Joseph wished to tell them was worthy of the suspense he had fostered. But this was their father, a man of pious devotion, yes, but a practical man of business as well, and not one given to vain spiritual imaginings.

Joseph explained further: "This happened after my return from Caesarea. And it came in the way of...confirmation...of a still earlier event. You see...Mary had told me that she too...had been visited. And the message she received...and which she conveyed to me...was disturbing. Shocking, actually."

He paused again, briefly, but did not allow hesitancy to take hold.

"It was because of what she said that I sent her away. I needed time to reflect on what her words would require of me. But after she departed...the messenger came again. And he assured me that what Mary told me was true. As unbelievable as it might be...it was true."

Still another pause, longer this time. Everyone watching Joseph's face could see deep unease in his expression, though they did not know its cause. They did not know that it was prompted by raw fear at having to make this revelation to those who had not shared his experience.

After an awkward silence, James, with the impatience of his age, spoke up for the group. "What did Mary tell you, Father?"

Joseph glanced at his youngest son. Of course it would be James to ask. Endlessly curious James. Then Joseph's eyes swept the group again, from face to face, finally settling on his own hands clasped in his lap.

"She told me that she had conceived the child of the Holy Spirit— *Emmanuel*...God with us."

Backs stiffened all around the portico. Joseph was right to have been shocked and disturbed. Zipporah rose to her feet.

"Mary spoke...*blasphemy*...Father," she said. "Such an idea... To say this thing—to even think it—a temple girl... This— This is— And you *married* her?"

Joseph's eyes were closed now. He knew the thoughts tearing at everyone's minds. They were all of the thoughts he'd had himself.

"Yes. I married her."

"But how— How *could* you?"

Simon rose and walked across the portico to his wife. "Zipporah," he said, touching her on the arm. Then, self-conscious in front of the others, he drew his hand away. "We will hear Father's answer."

Joseph looked up at his daughter-in-law. "I married Mary because what she said was true."

Zipporah's face was blank with disbelief, her expression not unlike that of the others. Silence fell over the group again until, after some seconds, Josis spoke.

"Father," he asked, "*is* Mary with child?"

"Yes."

"And you are convinced that her explanation for this is true?"

"Yes, I am," said Joseph, his eyes now trained directly on his eldest son. "I was not...not at first. When she told me these things I reacted much as Zipporah has. I was confused, and I was angry. And I was... I was guilty."

"Guilty?" Josis asked, incredulous. "You, guilty?"

Joseph nodded. "I felt I had failed in fulfilling my promise to her father. I had gone away to Caesarea and left her in Nazareth. I had not kept her from harm."

Josis was without a thought of how to respond, and there was another awkward, wordless moment.

Then Joseph spoke again. "I determined to put her aside...to end our betrothal with no public declaration...and to let her relatives care for her. I thought that by removing her quickly to Ein Kerem I could at least shield her from public disgrace here and— Well...I would not expose her to the Law if the sin was found out."

"But the sin *is* found out."

"*Zipporah!*" Simon said sharply.

"There is no sin," said Joseph. "My vision has confirmed this. The messenger assured me that Mary told the truth. The Spirit of the Lord came to her, and she conceived. No earthly man was involved. Her child is...the *Son of the Living God.*"

At these words a collective gasp was heard across the portico. Could their father, the devout and revered Joseph, be telling them that the King of the Universe Himself had chosen to make this household his own? That this girl who had come into their midst so unexpectedly was to bear a divine child? Such ideas were not only blasphemous, they were absurd. They were things only pagans could believe. Had their father spent too much time among the Greeks? Had he lost his mind?

Josis looked at this man who had raised him, loved him, taught him his life's craft, and he struggled to give the benefit of the doubt to what he had just heard. "I do not see how this can be, Father," he said gently. "Are you...certain...Mary is not lying? And that this confirmation was... real?"

All the others waited for Joseph's response, hoping for—what? That he would recant? That he would offer some proof? No one knew quite what it was they did expect.

Joseph took his time before answering Josis' question. He grappled for just the right set of words with which to take hold of his children's hearts, to inspire them with his conviction. He searched and he prayed. But before he could speak, James stood up.

"I believe you, Father," he said.

Zipporah turned and glared at him. "James, you are just a child," she said.

At this the boy's face flushed deeply. "I saw with my own eyes that Zacharias and Elizabeth believe." The reply to his sister-in-law had an assertiveness that surpassed his years. "Zacharias and Elizabeth rejoiced when Mary arrived. Elizabeth called her 'the mother of my Lord.' Why would she call her that? They embraced Mary, waited on her hand and foot as if she were a queen. And Zacharias is a holy man, a priest of the temple."

Joseph cast a sideward glance at the boy, and a faint smile crossed his lips. Dear James.

Then a word of support came from an unexpected source, the usually quiet Judas. "If we believe that the Holy One spoke to the prophets," he said, "can we not consider that our father might receive His message?"

Another pause, and then a comment from Assia's husband, Enoch: "Brother Judas has a point," he said. "The righteousness of Joseph the Builder is known throughout all of Galilee. If the Holy One were to send a child into this world, why not put him into the care of our father? Besides, do not all Jews pray that Messiah might come?"

Jubal, Lydia's husband, gave a quick, wry laugh at the mention of the Deliverer. "We have seen messiahs before, brother," he said, "and much tragedy to follow them. Many vain hopes have been raised, and much blood spilt."

"True enough," Enoch said. "But who knows for what purpose someone might be sent from on high?"

There was silence again. Then Josis said, "Judas and Enoch speak wisely. And James has reported what he witnessed for himself. Messiah or not, if this is the Lord's work, we will see the evidence in due time. We must be patient and wait for Him to reveal it."

Josis paused, understanding clearly now the reason for the haste of the wedding and for Mary not returning with her husband. "In the meantime," he continued, his voice bearing the authority of the eldest son, "we know our father, and we stand by him. Moreover, Mary is his wife, so we will welcome her when she returns to us."

Then he added with a meaningful glance all around, "Of course... this remains inside the family."

*   *   *

It could hardly be said that all were satisfied with Joseph's story. But most decided to withhold judgment on the man they knew so well and respected so highly. They would follow Josis' lead as best they could, waiting with as open a mind as possible.

This did not mean they were without doubts and questions. Zipporah especially felt the tug of conflicted feelings. She confided her anxiety to Salome and Sarah that Joseph's vision might be less a confirmation of Mary's claim than a troubling sign of advancing age with greater confusion yet to come. If that was the case, then what new burdens might fall on the wives? With a *divine child* to command her attention, would Mary even concern herself with the well being of her much-older husband?

Mary. This was Joseph's main concern right now. He realized that, if Mary's entry into the family had been contentious, her return, in present circumstance, promised even greater discord. Perhaps to crisis proportions, if Zipporah's feelings were any indication. He hoped that Mary's sojourn in Ein Kerem would provide time for the shock of his disclosure to subside. Elizabeth still had many weeks before her child was due, though at that point Mary's physical appearance would likely reveal her own state. Well, nothing to be done about that. At least everyone would be prepared for what, when she next appeared, would probably be quite conspicuous.

In the emotion of the family meeting, Joseph had not thought to relate what Zacharias and Elizabeth told him they believed about their own child, who was coming to them under extraordinary circumstances as well. They had received their own visions announcing Elizabeth's conceiving in old age. It was because Zacharias had expressed doubt at the possibility of such a thing that his voice had been taken from him. At least, that was what they believed. Now they were convinced that their child had a role to play as a herald of Mary's. If they were correct, then surely this provided some validation of the visions Joseph and Mary had experienced.

But no. Perhaps it was just as well he hadn't mentioned any of that. Perhaps it would have been too much, made the whole situation seem even more fantastic. To convey these things might merely have raised questions about Zacharias and Elizabeth. Joseph's children might assume that Mary's entire family was deluded. Or possessed. Better this drama unfolded gradually, one step at a time.

The immediate question—the one to be addressed over the coming weeks—was how to bring everyone in the household into agreement with Josis' promise that they would welcome Mary. This would be a test of Joseph's claim on their loyalty and confidence in him.

*   *   *

James had returned from Ein Kerem bubbling over with all he had seen and eager to discuss it. The first day back in class he shared his observations about the surprising lushness of the district, spoke of his excitement at being in the home of the famous priest, and described the remarkable documents he had perused in Zacharias' library. While the other boys found the report of his adventure modestly engaging, the Rabbi Ezra was deeply intrigued.

After the classmates were gone, James and his teacher discussed Joseph's wedding. Ezra was surprised to hear of the suddenness with which this sacred function had been carried out. His curiosity was piqued, and there was the slightest trace of professional disappointment, since he had assumed that he would officiate in binding Joseph to the daughter of Joachim. Still, he was most interested in the boy's animated recounting of the affair.

The morning after the family meeting, however, James' attitude was entirely changed. With his father's revelation of what had been behind the wedding and his eldest brother's insistence on strict confidentiality, the boy felt inhibited in speaking about anything related to the trip. Ezra noted this sudden reticence, so much in contrast with the previous day. He didn't probe him on it, but he got the distinct impression that James' enthusiasm had been intentionally curtailed. All of which added to the strangeness of this abrupt turn which Joseph's betrothal to Mary had taken, raising questions in the rabbi's mind.

Why was it done this way? The wedding of a man with the prominence of Joseph would surely be an occasion for the whole community to celebrate. And Mary's status as daughter of the wealthy landowner—even with her father passed away—would give the event even greater significance, the coming together of two leading families of Nazareth. No doubt Joseph understood the importance of that to the town and to the synagogue. Ezra would not presume to question any decision made by his patron, of course, but it all did seem extremely odd.

Just as it was time for James to go home, a figure appeared at the entrance to the synagogue court. Ezra rose at the sight of the visitor, a stout man with a silver gray beard who wore a brass badge suspended over his chest, marking him as a publican. This was someone Ezra knew well—too well, in fact—Eleazar, tax collector for the district.

"Peace be with you, Rabbi," the visitor said.

Ezra responded with measured politeness, "Peace be with you."

The look on Eleazar's face suggested that this call was a matter of business, not anything that touched on spiritual concerns or learned questions. But then, when the tax collector showed up it was always a matter of business, and generally unpleasant business at that. He and his ilk were referred to derisively as *tax farmers*. They bid on contracts from the Roman administration to collect the imperial levies within certain specified municipal areas. For their service they were given the right to add on their own charges. A common saying was that the only thing these farmers reaped was other people's money.

Eleazar held out a rolled-up piece of parchment tied with a ribbon and closed by an official-looking wax seal. "Rabbi," he said, "it is my duty to inform you that there will be an imperial census for the various jurisdictions of Palestine, by order of the Augustus. This document explains the details and the schedule. It is an official decree, which is to be read in the synagogue and then posted in a prominent place. All are to respond at the appointed time."

Ezra took the scroll and looked down at its seal. "I take it that Caesar is intending to favor us with new tax levies," he said.

"Caesar needs to know the scope of his realm and the number of people who dwell within it and depend on the security it affords," Eleazar pronounced imperiously. "We all enjoy that security, and we all must do our part to ensure it. Peace be with you, Rabbi." He turned and took his leave.

"What is happening?" James asked when the publican had gone.

Ezra tapped the scroll against the palm of his left hand. "We are being asked to give Caesar his due," the rabbi said, "or at least what he wishes to think is his due. What others think, we shall see."

*   *   *

Hearing about the census from James that evening, Joseph was perturbed. "New taxes," he said while seated at table in Josis' house. "This sort of thing inevitably brings trouble."

"Not without cause," Josis said. "Between the damnable charges for Herod's monstrous building projects, the temple tax, the head tax, and all the levies on property and crops, plus endless tolls and excises on anything transported and sold, people are bled dry."

"Herod built the temple," James observed innocently.

"And we never stop paying for it," said Josis.

Joseph sensed a fatherly need to step in. "Yes, James," he said. "The temple is Herod's crowning achievement. I myself, as someone who builds, can certainly appreciate its magnificent design and construction. But that project was a long and expensive undertaking. And while it can't be denied that the Holy One is properly honored by its grandeur, there are some who would call it a bit extravagant."

Josis tapped a finger emphatically on the table. "I do not think the Holy One would wish to see His people impoverished for the sake of a building," he said. "*Any* building."

"Well," said James rather weakly, "the temple *is* beautiful."

"When is this census to be held?" Joseph asked.

"The Rabbi Ezra said it would be around the Festival of Booths," James replied. "Each man must travel to the place of his birth to register his household in the tally."

"I would expect that," said Joseph. "But at that time of year, roads are usually clogged with people on pilgrimage to Jerusalem—Jews and gentiles both. To schedule a census then? The holy days will be disrupted, crowding will be worse, the entire country will be upset."

"Our Roman lords take no concern for how people live," Salome interjected.

"At least there will be no traveling for us," Josis said. "We were all born here."

"You and your brothers," Joseph said. "But I will have to register in Bethlehem."

Josis looked across the table vacantly, then said, "You are right, Father. I did not think about that. And Bethlehem is so near Jerusalem."

"Another walk for me," Joseph said with a shrug.

But Josis looked serious. "You will need to take care, Father," he said. "If there is trouble over this census, it will likely be in the district of Jerusalem."

"Perhaps I can attach myself to a caravan," said Joseph. "Don't worry, I will be cautious."

"Where does Lucillus have to go, Father?" James asked. "He was not born here at all."

"Probably Caesarea," said Joseph. "That is where he received his manumission."

The meal proceeded with more talk of Romans and taxes and the inconvenience of a census. What was left unspoken was any reference to the previous day's family meeting or Mary's child. Yet the situation hung in the air, demanding careful choices in words. There were moments when conversation seemed a bit forced.

After the meal was finished, Joseph took his eldest son out into the court. "Josis, I have been considering something," he said.

"Yes, Father?"

"Would you object to moving your workshop, my son?"

"My workshop? To where?"

"To the front corner of the court. I can bring in some men, and we can build you a larger structure, right next to the gate."

"Fine, Father. But why?"

"Well..." said Joseph hesitantly, "it is of course...customary...for a bridegroom to build his bride a new house...or add to the house of his father if they are to live with the family. And since so much about my marriage to Mary is...*not* customary...I thought... Well, your shop adjoins my house, and I thought that...with Mary's child coming, I could convert that space..."

Josis sensed—what, embarrassment?—in the way his father was speaking. This was a clear indication of the prevailing discomfort. The eldest son gave a knowing smile and touched him affectionately on the shoulder.

"Anything you wish, Father," said Josis reassuringly. "A bigger shop would be very welcome."

CHAPTER NINE

All went to be enrolled, each to his own city,
and Joseph also went up from Galilee.

(Luke 2)

The Sepphoris project which had demanded so much attention from Joseph and Lucillus was completed by early spring. Many shared the opinion that this was one of the handsomest structures in the city—well proportioned and not overly ornamented—adding to the reputation of the Nazareth builder. The Greek owner had by now forgotten all about the irregularities of the beams and boasted of how shrewd he had been in negotiating an excellent price for the work.

"Now these Jews know whom they are dealing with," he told a friend.

For his part, Josis was relieved that he had not been called upon to act for his father again in this matter. He contented himself with getting his tools, equipment and supplies moved into the new, larger shop which Joseph's men had erected in the front corner of the court.

Joseph also had his crew fix up the space Josis had just vacated, in preparation for Mary's return. With his young wife's prospects now changed from a life of prayer and study to one of motherhood, Joseph and James would sleep in the upper room, leaving the added area on the lower level for Mary's use in caring for her baby. James was happy to have their old quarters restored.

Worry about the census and the new taxes it would surely bring were starting to be felt throughout all of Herod's territories. Even though the count was still several months away, there had already been stirrings of unrest. These mainly consisted of angry but poorly organized groups calling on the people to refuse participation. However, there were rumors that the Zealot faction, the network of secret bands known as dagger-men, intent on overthrowing the Roman occupation, had plans for disruptive strikes on the counting stations.

To both encourage public cooperation and dissuade any would-be attackers, the level of Roman force was increased. Auxiliaries were brought in from Syria to supplement the garrisons, and there was some transiting of units between posts, mainly for the sake of increased visibility on the roads. But these early adjustments were minor. Spring and summer would pass before the census became an immediate concern, plenty of time to implement any other security measures necessary. Meanwhile, the new planting season and the approach of Passover provided other matters to occupy the minds of the populace.

Within the walls of Joseph's compound, one particular event claimed everyone's interest. Zipporah announced that she was with child again, the fourth for her and Simon. The effect of this news was mixed. It served to deflect attention from Mary, especially among the women. That was a source of relief for Joseph. At the same time, it underscored the contrast between the normal joy of family expectation and his wife's peculiar circumstance. He decided that, on balance, it helped the situation. And in any event, who could deny the blessing of a new grandchild?

Another point of anticipation for the family was the olive grove which Judas and Simon were developing. The earliest trees they had planted were finally of an age where the brothers expected their first decent crop, and they looked forward to this year's picking. Josis had promised his brothers that he would build them an olive press, and sitting prominently in his new shop were the timbers he intended to cut and shape for the framing.

James, of course, had his own milestone to look forward to. The celebration of his maturity would take place in the fall. Not only would this mark his full participation in the synagogue, if Zacharias lived up to his pledge, James would soon be sent to Jerusalem to study with some great doctor of the Law. His feelings about that swung between excitement and unease, since it would mean the end of childhood and the start of a new and very different life. But ambivalence was understandable in one facing such a turning point, even if still a few months away.

Joseph sensed his son's mood. To boost the boy's enthusiasm and divert him from his fears, he suggested that James and Lucillus begin planning for the day of James' reading in the synagogue. Not that the celebration should be too elaborate, Joseph cautioned. James agreed, but it did require some effort for him to keep a rein on his imagination.

The week after Passover, Joseph received a message from Mary. Elizabeth had given birth to a son, whom the parents named John. The courier, a guard of the temple, was provided with a meal, and his horse fed and watered while Joseph read Mary's note and prepared a response.

Mary asked if her husband preferred that she remain longer in Ein Kerem or if he desired her presence in Nazareth. Zacharias and Elizabeth, enthralled at the birth of their child—which, interestingly enough, had occurred on the very day of Passover itself—expressed their happiness at Mary remaining, if that was what Joseph thought best. Otherwise, transport would be secured for her. In closing, Mary noted that Zacharias had recovered his voice.

Joseph composed a note for the courier to take back to his wife. He wrote that he had explained her situation to the family. The reaction was what one would expect, and he believed all were doing their best to accept the truth of his account. He felt it would be helpful if she could return and work through any difficulties in having her received back into the household before she gave birth. And he noted that Zipporah was also with child, which might dispose the women toward greater sympathy for Mary's condition—at least that was his hope. Consequently, she should return to Nazareth as soon as it was convenient for her to do so. He would be most grateful if Zacharias could arrange for her safe conveyance.

Nearly three weeks passed before those arrangements came to fruition. Mary was reluctant to leave before Elizabeth had recovered fully from the delivery, which was somewhat hampered by her years. There was also a question about whether age would preclude the ability to nurse a child. Blessedly this proved no problem. Elizabeth's milk came in surprising abundance, and a wet nurse was not required.

Raised in the temple, Mary had never witnessed childbirth. Neither had she any knowledge of what was required in the care of a newborn. Elizabeth's experience proved a valuable opportunity for instruction before Mary would face her own motherhood, and she considered it a timely gift.

Mary's return was both unexpected and startling. Caravans regularly passed south of Nazareth, following the road that ran along the Jezreel Valley. But they rarely diverted up into the hill towns. Few could recall the last time a camel was seen in Nazareth streets. And so it was a novelty when one day a trio of the hulking beasts paraded by the synagogue and through the square.

The Rabbi Ezra was taken aback to see them lumbering along in their rocking, ship-like gait. The boys of the class, reacting to their teacher's wide-eyed visage, turned to watch the heads of the animals and their riders passing above the wall of the court. James was especially surprised to observe that the second camel in the train bore Mary.

He turned back to the rabbi. "It is my father's bride," said the boy. He stood, unthinking, as if to start for home, then stopped and looked at Ezra.

When word of Joseph's marriage had spread throughout the town, there was ample speculation about why the carpenter would leave his new wife with her relatives. The sudden, out-of-town wedding was extraordinary enough and certainly conducive to gossip. That Joseph would permit his young bride to be separated from him was beyond any sensible explanation.

Aware of this chatter, the Rabbi Ezra returned James' glance and nodded in the direction of the gate. "Perhaps you should go, James son of Joseph," he said. "Your father may need help getting his wife settled."

"Yes, Rabbi," said the boy.

He ran after the small caravan, past curious onlookers along the way, overtaking it at the edge of town. "Mary," he called.

She heard him, smiled down, and waved. "Peace be with you, James," she called from atop her swaying perch.

The train continued up the hill to the compound, drawing to a halt in front. James ran to the gate, touched the scroll quickly, and went inside. Josis, having heard the distinctive clanking of the camels' harness bells, emerged from his new shop, just within the walls.

"What is happening?" he asked.

"Mary is here," said James, running across the court to the portico past household children seeking out the sound. He found his father seated with Lucillus at the table inside the house, inspecting a set of building plans. "Father," he said, "Mary has arrived. She's on a camel."

"A camel?"

The two men rose and followed the boy out into the court and across to the gate. The children were already outside the wall, clustered around the big animals; their mothers close behind in a state of some concern. Words of caution were heard from the women.

The lead camel had lowered itself to the ground, its driver now standing beside the beast that carried Mary, motioning for it to sit as well. When it had settled, Mary swung a leg over the front horn of her saddle, the wooden frame of which bore a cushioned seat above the camel's hump. She held her robes tight to her legs for modesty, and climbed down, stepping over the packs that hung from the harness rigging.

Joseph stood before his bride. "Peace be with you, Mary," he said.

"Peace be with you, my husband," she responded.

He looked at the animals. "This is an unexpected mode of transport," he said, amused.

"Zacharias had me join a caravan headed for Tyre," Mary explained. "It is stopped awaiting the return of these men and their animals where the road from Nazareth meets the main highway to the seacoast. Then it will continue on."

The lead driver had detached two large bundles from the harness and brought them around to Mary. "Your possessions, Mistress," he said.

"Thank you for your care and your kindness," Mary said. "Please convey my gratitude to Master Zacharias."

Lucillus reached into the scrip he carried on his belt and took out two coins, which he gave to the driver for himself and his companion.

The man received the gratuity with a bow. "May the blessings of the Holy One be upon the house of Joseph," he said. Then he remounted his camel, signaled the beasts to rise, and the train set off back through town.

Josis and Lucillus each picked up one of Mary's bundles and carried them inside the compound as the children watched the camels disappear down the road. The wives each shot a quick glance at Mary's front, curious if any sign of her condition might show on her small frame.

Aware of their interest, Mary nodded to each woman in turn. "Sarah, Zipporah, Salome," she said, "peace be upon you all. It is good to see you again."

Each nodded coolly in response.

Josis and Lucillus had deposited the bundles in the main room by the table and departed when Mary and Joseph came in. Alone now, Joseph inquired as to his wife's wellbeing.

"I am very fine, husband," she said.

"The trip was not too difficult?"

"I found that riding on the cushioned saddle of a camel is more comfortable than on a donkey's back," she said. "It is softer. But you must hold on tightly against the swaying."

"And the child?"

"All seems well. I look forward to feeling him move. Elizabeth says it should happen within a few weeks."

Joseph showed her the added room—she had, of course, noted Josis' new shop in the court. As Mary inspected the converted space, Joseph cautioned her about the tension that permeated the household.

"I know that everyone wishes to believe what I told them," he said. "At least, they want to believe that I am not mad or that you have not bewitched me. But their willingness to accept you and the child remains to be seen. It is difficult for them, as I'm sure you realize."

"We ask them to accept what seems a blasphemy," Mary said.

"Yes," Joseph said, hands turned up in a gesture of resignation. "I understand their feelings. It is how I first reacted. And I realize that they will need time. They have received no messages of confirmation as I did. Meanwhile, things may be awkward for you."

She offered her husband a gentle smile. "The Lord is my rock, my fortress, my deliverer, my God, my strength, in whom I take refuge."

Then they spoke of Mary's sojourn in Ein Kerem, of Elizabeth's delivery, and the naming of the child.

"Elizabeth had insisted he be called John," she said. "Everyone wondered why, since there is no one named John in the family. But Zacharias wrote on his tablet that he agreed the child was to be called

John. It was very strange, my husband. At that moment he regained his voice."

Joseph shook his head. Just one more odd occurrence to ponder in all of this.

Mary shared an experience of which she was quite proud. She had learned to make the Sabbath bread.

"While Elizabeth was recovering from her delivery, I spent time with the servants in the kitchen," she said. "I must admit I had to be a bit evasive about it. My aunt would have been horrified if she knew I did household work there. Even when she herself was laid low, she kept trying to fuss over me. But I wanted to learn, so I swore everyone to secrecy." She laughed at the memory, then looked at Joseph. "Was that wrong, my husband?"

Joseph shook his head. "I think the deception was done lovingly," he said.

"Maybe I can demonstrate my bread-making to Salome," Mary said. "She was teaching me to cook before I went away. She might be pleased."

"Perhaps," Joseph said with something less than certainty.

*   *   *

Over the next few days Mary made tentative gestures toward each of the wives. She offered congratulations to Zipporah for the child who was to come. Zipporah received her words with a terse "Thank you," saying nothing about Mary's own state. Likewise, the blandest of pleasantries were exchanged with Sarah when Mary joined Joseph and James at her table for the evening meal. Her husband, Judas, tried to be more forthcoming. But he too was affected by the awkwardness of the evening, and focused his conversation almost exclusively on this year's anticipated olive crop.

Salome's first response to Mary's report of making the Sabbath bread was little more than a grunt. Then, seeing sincerity in the girl's face, she reproached herself for dismissing this accomplishment—quite obviously something Mary had considered an important bit of progress.

She put forth the effort to make her own expression more pleasant. "That is good," she said.

Mary, standing with head slightly down, turned her eyes hesitantly toward Salome. "Perhaps I could...help you...at Sabbath...this week?" she asked.

Salome eyed her back—this mere slip of a girl who so absurdly was her mother-in-law. Mary was indeed a child, the same child she had been before, sheltered, wide-eyed, well-intentioned, naive. Could she really have sinned? It didn't seem possible. Yet there was Joseph's admission, her hasty departure. The explanation he had given couldn't be true.

Could it?

"Come early on the morning of preparation," she said, turning away. "We will bake."

Mary stood quietly for a moment, the shadow of a smile washing across her face. Then she returned to her house.

*   *   *

As weeks passed and spring became summer, feelings about the census continued to harden. Concern no longer centered only on the likelihood of new taxes, though that was always a prospect capable of stoking resentment. Certain rabbis raised religious questions, noting how David's decision to conduct a similar count, with the aim of raising an army, had brought suffering to the people.

One scholar voiced his objections right in the temple. Speaking to a crowd that had gathered in the Court of the Gentiles, he shouted, "Only the Holy One Himself has the right to number the people." His listeners took up the point, chanting it over and over with increasing volume and emotional fervor. Eventually, temple guards were summoned to disperse the gathering.

Word of the incident made its way to Nazareth, raising the level of anxiety which Joseph's family felt about his impending trip to Bethlehem. News that additional Roman troops were being sent to police the census added to the fear, since a heightened military presence was as likely to provoke violence as suppress it. And all too often, when Romans took action, they showed little regard for the safety of innocent bystanders.

Joseph promised to find other men who would be traveling to register at towns around Jerusalem. He would be conscious of safety and not attempt the trip alone. This was as much reassurance as he could offer. In truth, he didn't know how many would have to make the trek in that direction, Nazareth not being someplace to which very many people moved from other areas. He had settled here himself only because of the promise of opportunity in nearby Sepphoris and the willingness of old Avram's widow to sell her property at an especially attractive price. But he asked Lucillus to inquire around.

Meanwhile, James took to perusing passages of scripture for his day of reading in the synagogue. He wanted to find a Torah portion that was special, something to which he could bring a fresh thought. The Rabbi Ezra offered several suggestions, none of which seemed quite right to the boy.

Then James remembered the talk he and the rabbi shared about Cain and Abel. The story stuck in his mind, perhaps because of his own brothers. But there was something else. It was Ezra's observation that the Holy One had his own reasons for accepting Abel's offering and rejecting Cain's, reasons not made explicit in the Scriptural account.

Later in the story Cain is banished for killing Abel, but he is not slain as one would expect of a murderer. Cain actually is given a mark that is meant to protect him. Did this treatment also suggest a higher purpose, inexplicable as it might be? Cain did go on to beget a line of descendants. He even built a city—a fact that was of mild interest, since James' own father was a builder.

The lesson seemed to lie in the unexpected way in which the Lord's will was worked out. Even a man who had done something as wicked as murdering his brother could still serve the Holy One's purpose. It was an intriguing idea and, James decided, one worth exploring. Ezra agreed, and he suggested some writings on which the boy might draw for his commentary.

*   *   *

A rumor began to spread that the Zealots now considered cooperating in the census a betrayal of the nation. No one could say for sure if there would be violent reprisals against individuals, but worry about the possibility was growing. Walking parties were organized for those traversing long distances. The organizers secured documents of passage from the Roman authorities so they would not be mistaken for protestors. In some cases, arrangements were made for armed soldiers to provide security, since troublemakers might infiltrate the groups.

Through his inquiries, Lucillus learned of one party coming from the coast through the Jezreel Valley. It would stop at towns and villages along the way to take on additional travelers, the better to ensure safety for all. Joseph could join it where the road from Nazareth connected. Lucillus found a similar party bound for Caesarea, and planned to travel with it himself.

It was clear that the impact of the census would be significant well beyond any simple inconvenience it imposed on daily life. The harvest would be complicated tremendously, since crops would have to be brought in and all threshing completed before the loss of field hands who might have to be counted in other places. Trade would come virtually to a standstill, with the roads clogged and many draft and pack animals diverted to the moving of people rather than the transporting of goods.

Joseph and Lucillus determined that disruption of work on their current projects would be minimal, most of the crewmen being locally born. But getting supplies would be a problem during the count and the weeks before and after. Joseph was especially concerned about a consignment of stone scheduled for delivery during that period. When the material might actually arrive was now impossible to say, though he thought it predictable that there would be another unhappy client.

With all his inquiries, Lucillus became aware of certain whisperings among the people in town. That Mary carried a child had apparently become known beyond the family compound, even though she hadn't set foot outside its walls since her return from Ein Kerem. The blooming of a fertile young wife, even one with a much older husband, was hardly surprising, but some noted that no announcement had been made in the synagogue.

Joseph's prediction that people would calculate was thoroughly borne out as speculation spread. Imaginings about the size of Mary's belly—which some people maintained, *on the best of authority*, was gigantic—validated the concern Joachim had expressed about the viciousness of

Nazareth gossip.

Lucillus dutifully, if reluctantly, reported what he learned to Joseph, who worried what effect this talk might have on the household. It didn't take long to find out. Sarah came to him in an agitated state to complain of some particularly nasty comments overheard in the market street.

"This bodes ill for the whole family," she said with consternation. "You must *do* something, Father."

He received similar reports, and a similar plea, from both of his daughters, Lydia and Assia. Simon weighed in as well, even though Judas had cautioned against burdening their father with idle gossip. And those who didn't come forth with such stories were now conducting themselves with a disquieting reserve. All chose their words with the utmost care whenever Mary was present, and avoided mentioning her name to Joseph when she was not.

Finally a remark, uttered outside the synagogue after the morning service, came to Joseph's ears directly. The speaker stopped in mid-sentence when he realized that Joseph was still within hearing distance. But Joseph didn't need the concluding words to make clear what was implied. His family had never before been touched by any sort of scandal, and yet people were indulging such foul thoughts. But if they wanted to talk, who could stop them? Joseph's concern was for the peace of his household, which he sensed was slipping away.

Surely he couldn't have been wrong in agreeing to take Mary. The divine origin of her child, the revelation by the Lord's messenger, the son of Zacharias and Elizabeth, given to them so late in life, as Mary herself had been given to Joachim and Anna—all of these things and more pointed to some greater design. For reasons known only to the Holy One, Joseph's family had been chosen to carry out a mission whose purpose and scope remained yet unclear.

It would not be easy. With this mission came risk. Hadn't the prophets been brought to strife in the Lord's service? How could Joseph not be surprised that his sons and their wives and his daughters and their husbands were so distressed? He had asked them to accept a claim that any righteous Jew—or any intelligent person, for that matter—would find improbable at best and, at worst, a damnable lie. They were all good, faithful people, not without their faults but sound at the core. That was their great strength and the strength of the family. But Joseph realized this was also what would make it hard for them ever to accept Mary and her child. And here was where the risk lay.

If his kin could not accept, then surely the townspeople, so quick to revel in their base conjecturing, might assume anything vile. How could the family not be touched by that? And what if a serious charge were to be leveled against his wife? Could they be counted upon to stand together in firm defense of her name when their own conviction was so lacking?

Perhaps he should have had her remain in Ein Kerem. People would have wondered why she stayed away, true, but they might not have found out she carried a child. Which might have made it easier on the family, better allowing feelings to be calmed and reservations to ease.

These thoughts weighed heavily on Joseph's mind as the time of the census drew near—and the time for Mary to deliver. What could he do? He was required to be in Bethlehem for the count, and he could barely think of bringing her along, heavy with child. Still, painful as it was to admit, he did not feel confident leaving Mary with his family. Never before had he wanted for trust in his own children. But he had to face his feelings.

Not unexpectedly, it was Zipporah who forced a difficult but unavoidable decision.

Occupying the lower level of the house, Mary had taken to reciting her prayers outside in the portico, especially when Joseph and Lucillus were discussing building projects at the table, as was their habit. Mary prayed with intense concentration, totally absorbed, the upper part of her body rocking forward and back, forward and back without her even being aware of the motion.

While she positioned herself discreetly by the large bush that grew at the corner of the portico, Mary was still visible. All the adults in the family had observed her in this attitude, each pondering to some degree the question of whether it was appropriate for a woman to be seen praying in such a manner—that is, like a man—even within the confines of the household.

Zipporah's reaction was more visceral. The sight of Mary's now large and protrusive belly seemed to her a stark contrast with the piety represented by the shuckling movements. The holy temple girl with child, and such a wild story given as explanation—it could only be regarded as hypocrisy in the extreme, and it made Zipporah feel actually ill. She shared her opinion with Salome one afternoon as they came in the front gate after a trip to the market street.

The older woman was torn. "You should not let such feelings take hold of you so," she said. "It does good neither for you, nor for the family. I know it's hard to accept what Father Joseph told us. But Mary seems such an honest and innocent girl. And who can say what the Holy One might do?"

Zipporah's laugh in response was tinged with cynicism. "You have a good heart, Salome," she said, "and so you take Mary under your wing. You want to believe. But tell me honestly, do you really think this story can be true?"

Salome hesitated. "I don't... I don't...know," she said.

Joseph happened to be inside the new carpentry shop with Josis. The words of his daughters-in-law passed easily through the open doorway and the light wooden planking of the walls. He glanced at his eldest son, whom he realized had also overheard. Josis concentrated intently on his work.

*   *   *

Lucillus and Josis both tried to talk Joseph out of taking Mary on the journey. After the painful incident of the conversation between his and Simon's wives, Josis was particularly eager to reassure his father that Mary would be safest at home.

"She will need the women, especially if she delivers before your return," he insisted earnestly. "I understand that feelings are strained. But Father, you must realize no one would leave Mary uncared for. She is your wife."

"Travel would be an ordeal for one in her condition," Lucillus added in support. "Please reconsider."

But Joseph was adamant. He would take Mary to Bethlehem, register for the census, and then go on to Ein Kerem. Bringing her back to Nazareth had been a mistake. Given the miraculous nature of all that had happened, Zacharias and Elizabeth would be happy to have her. They were convinced there was a connection between the birth of their son and the coming of Mary's child. Joseph was inclined to that view himself. Perhaps he would leave her there indefinitely. He would still be her husband, providing her with any necessary legal rights and protections. But maybe the Holy One intended for the two children to be raised together.

And so it was that Joseph and Mary departed from the family compound with Lucillus on the morning after the last Sabbath before the Festival of Booths. Mary was perched uncomfortably on the back of Lucillus' donkey. The Greek accompanied them down to where the road from Nazareth connected with the highway in the Jezreel Valley. There Lucillus continued toward the west to meet the walking party headed down the coast to Caesarea. Joseph and Mary awaited their party bound for the district of Jerusalem.

Several steps along, Lucillus paused for a moment and turned back for a farewell wave. He experienced a shiver of anxiety. But then he willed himself to smile, and continued on his way.

CHAPTER TEN

He took the young Child and His mother by night
and departed for Egypt.

(Matthew 2)

Aftel the months of tension, there was a definite sense of relief among the adults in the family—accompanied by a degree of guilt for feeling it—when Joseph and Mary departed for Bethlehem. But this soon gave way to fascination with an unusual effect that appeared in the sky. Each night for several weeks an especially bright star would rise in the east and appear to pause at a point in the general direction of Jerusalem, until finally it would disappear in the light of dawn.

The phenomenon drew attention throughout the country, and was remarked upon widely as something quite unlike anything ever noted within common memory. But eventually, the prominence of the star faded, and the sky returned to its normal appearance. Thoughts among the family members drifted back to the unresolved conflict over Mary. There was also some concern about what Joseph's attitude would be when he returned without her. He did not return, however. Nothing was heard of him for many weeks.

Even with a side trip to Ein Kerem after registering for the census at Bethlehem, Joseph should have been back long ago. Lucillus, who returned from Caesarea within days of his own registration, used his extensive contacts to seek out people who had been in the walking party with Joseph and Mary. He found several. One reported that the pair had stood in line with him waiting to be counted in Bethlehem. Nobody knew anything of their whereabouts afterward.

All in the family were worried, some harboring secret fears of the worst kind. Though the strong presence of Roman troops did succeed in keeping the anticipated troubles to a minimum, a few serious clashes had occurred. Predictably, these had gotten blown up into rumors of copious blood spilt, though it was unclear exactly how many attacks, how many casualties, and whether ordinary citizens were involved. Not all the rumors told of political acts. There were also stories of brigands pouncing on travelers who ventured into secluded paths or those unwise enough to attempt the trip unaccompanied.

For James, Joseph's unexplained absence not only held anxiety, it brought a particular disappointment. Celebration of the boy's maturity had been set for five weeks after the Festival of Booths. That day came and went. Lucillus cancelled the great fest they had planned, and called upon all the invited guests, informing them that a new date would be announced when Joseph returned. Meanwhile, the Rabbi Ezra asked James if he wanted to go ahead and read without the celebration, but the boy insisted his father should be present.

James was crestfallen and deeply worried. Joseph would never miss such an important event unless something serious had happened. It was the first time James had come face to face with the threats contained in life's uncertainty, and he was shaken by the experience. Sensing his brother's distress, Josis invited James to sleep in his house. But James declined. Even if he hadn't yet done his first reading, he was a man now, and a man had to take care of himself.

Josis put his hand on James' shoulder and gave a nod of respect. "That is true, Brother," he said understandingly. "Still...if you should need anything..."

James looked up into his eldest brother's eyes, paused and, speaking unsteadily, said, "Yes... I will..." Then, after a moment: "Do you think Father and Mary are... Do you think they're alright?"

"I don't know," Josis said. "We must pray for their protection."

*   *   *

Another rumor had begun making the rounds, a story that was inexplicable, if not outright bizarre, and yet maintained as true by a variety of seemingly reliable sources. It was said that Herod's minions were scouring the town of Bethlehem for male children, from newly born to two years of age.

As with most rumors, several versions circulated, the most benign of which described palace officials checking circumcision records and interrogating parents in a sort of follow-up to the census. The most horrific variant told of soldiers actually killing children, often right in front of parents forcibly restrained and wailing in grief and madness.

It would have been easy to dismiss the wildest of the tales as utter nonsense, except for the king's reputation as a scheming and heartless brute. Hadn't he killed members of his own family? It was Caesar himself who commented, "Better to be Herod's pig than his son." Those words became a joke when someone noted that dietary laws would hardly restrain the only-nominally Jewish Herod. "Perhaps the pig really would not be so much better off, after all" went the saying. "At least Herod's sons aren't likely to be eaten."

The significance of Bethlehem as the focus of these rumors was not lost on James when a classmate related the story about the children to him. In a panic the boy ran home, bursting through the gate without touching the scroll, and startling Josis in his workshop.

"Calm yourself," Josis said in response to James' rushed and frantic report. "Yes, I heard something about the king's soldiers looking for children. I don't know why they are doing it, or even if it is true."

"But my friend told me it happened in *Bethlehem*," James said breathlessly. "Father and Mary are in Bethlehem, and Mary carries a child."

"We don't know that they are still in Bethlehem. Father planned on going from there to Ein Kerem. Perhaps they are at the house of Zacharias. Or they could be anywhere."

After a few agitated minutes, Josis succeeded in getting James settled down. He promised the boy he would try to find out whatever he could, and Lucillus would as well. In the meantime, they must all be patient and continue to pray until some word came from their father.

The truth was, however, that others in the family had also heard tales of missing or dead children in Bethlehem. James was not alone in his anxiety. The deeper Josis and Lucillus inquired into the matter, the more it seemed that something strange had indeed happened, though the bits of information they gleaned were second-hand and varied widely. Confirmation came in a frightening way on the day of preparation for Sabbath. Early in the morning there was a loud and violent pounding on the gate, setting the dogs to barking.

"Open for the king's officer!" called a harsh, insistent voice as morning light broke over the compound.

Simon emerged from his house, hastily arranging his tunic, and opened the gate. There was a squad of six armed soldiers bearing shields of the Royal Guard. Their captain stood in front.

"We seek Joseph son of Jacob," said the officer. "This is his home."

"Yes," said Simon.

"Who are you?"

"I am Simon. Joseph is my father."

Other family members had come out of their houses. Zipporah stood in her doorway, three bleary-eyed children around her.

"Where is your father?"

"We do not know."

"You don't know?"

"He went to register for the census, and he has not returned. We have heard nothing from him."

"He registered in Bethlehem."

"Well, he was going to—"

"He did. We know this." The captain's eyes swept the court. "Your father has a young wife."

"Yes. Mary, daughter of Joachim."

"She was with him at the count."

Simon shrugged.

"She was. They were seen. And she has delivered a child."

"We did not know that. She still carried the child when they left."

Josis and Judas had come to the gate and were standing behind Simon. Their wives stood by their doors. Sarah held one of her children in her arms. James was in the portico.

"Your father's wife has given birth," said the captain. "We know that this happened at a lodging in Bethlehem."

"When?"

"Just after the Festival of Booths. It was a boy. His name is Jesus."

"Jesus?"

The officer looked at Simon, then at Josis and Judas. "This family is curiously ignorant of its father's movements."

"As my brother told you," said Josis, "we have had no word."

The officer grunted. Then he gestured to the soldiers, and they passed through the gate by the three brothers.

"We will inspect the household," the officer said. "You will cooperate."

The squad dispersed throughout the compound. Solders went into each of the houses. Sarah and Salome each followed after as they entered. The crying of a frightened child was heard from Judas' house. Sarah emerged again with a second child in her arms.

One of the soldiers, who appeared to be the captain's subaltern, whispered something in his superior's ear. Then he pointed toward Zipporah, who reacted with a start. Simon looked anxiously at his wife.

"No," said the captain to his man. "The child we seek has been born."

Zipporah's hands went instinctively to her belly.

"There are no children in this household under the age of two years?" the captain asked of anyone who would reply.

"None," said Josis.

The officer eyed him up and down. "You are..."

"I am Josis, eldest brother of the family."

The captain opened his hand, and the subaltern placed a sheet of parchment into it. The captain scanned the writing, then looked back up at Josis, saying only, "Yes."

Silence followed. The brothers stood awkwardly, nervously, unsure of what would happen next and knowing that whatever did happen, they would be powerless to do anything about it. The solders completed their search of the buildings in the compound and returned to the gate. One of them said, "They are not here, sir."

The captain gestured; his men went out into the street. He looked at Josis again, but said nothing. Then he turned and left.

Zipporah sank down onto the threshold of the doorway. Her body was suddenly taken over by a violent trembling she could not control. Simon rushed to his wife, kneeling down and taking her in his arms.

She looked up into his eyes, began to speak, hesitated, then said, "Mary. It's true."

*   *   *

Several days later, Lucillus came to Josis in his workshop. "I was visited early this morning by Lemuel, the steward of Zacharias," he said in hushed tones.

Josis put down the mallet and chisel with which he was working and looked intently into Lucillus' eyes. "What of Father?"

"He is in Egypt," Lucillus said.

"Egypt?"

"Zacharias waited until Joseph could get Mary and the baby out of the country before sending a message. The child Herod seeks is hers, though he probably does not know it. Lemuel said that Joseph wishes us to keep all the projects going and to continue operating the business. On no account should anyone in the family do anything that suggests we know where he is. He will contact us when he feels it is safe. Also, he sends his apology to James and instructs him to go ahead with his reading in the synagogue."

The two men looked at each other, the deepest gravity in both their expressions. This message could only mean that the family would not see Joseph and Mary for a long time.

PART II

UNDER ARCHELAUS

CHAPTER ELEVEN

An angel of the Lord appeared in a dream to Joseph in Egypt saying,
"Arise and take the child and his mother,
and go into the land of Israel."

(Matthew 2)

J ames toiled at the saw, working his way slowly through the hard, roughly hewn timber. The blister on his right hand was an annoyance, but Salome's ointment was helping it to heal, and James had by now disciplined himself to persevere with work in spite of the bumps, bruises and splinters of a carpenter's life. Still, he regretted his foolishness in spending days on the gouging ax with unwrapped hands. Josis warned him regularly about bare skin and repetitive motion, but the cloth strips were a nuisance, always coming loose and tangling the task.

Since his father's disappearance, now just over two years past, James had become Josis' helper, keeping the carpentry shop going when his brother's attention was diverted to the building projects. Mostly that consisted of preparation work—such chores as rough-cutting planks in advance of fitting and finishing, hollowing out pieces of burl for the shaping of wooden bowls, and of course, straightening nails.

Entering into the craft so late, James was well behind what an apprentice his age would normally have attained in proficiency. But that wasn't important. What mattered was doing his part for the family and helping to demonstrate to the people in town that the house of Joseph was committed to keeping all aspects of the business going and service dependable, even with the master absent.

Much of James' effort involved placating customers over delays in completion of orders, a common occurrence with his eldest brother so distracted. The young man's open countenance and sweet nature had a conciliatory effect, which Josis noted and often chuckled over.

"You are an angel, Brother," he once observed. "I am gone so much these days, and projects pile up so high, I fear to think what the folk of Nazareth would do to this shop if you were not so good at nurturing their patience."

Josis appreciated James' involvement for another reason as well. As the father of all girls, Josis had no son to rely upon as a helper or to train as his apprentice.

While James showed a bright outlook to customers, he often felt his heart stabbed by a recurring sorrow. Scholarly ambition had been cut short when his father failed to return. With Joseph and Mary gone, the family's link with Zacharias was broken. Josis thought it would be too presumptuous to appeal to the famous priest for the fulfillment of his promise to place James as a disciple of some scribe in the temple.

James continued to meet with the Rabbi Ezra, though now their get-togethers were more in the way of companionable talks than formal instruction. He read the books his teacher provided, and Ezra made inquiries through colleagues in Jerusalem about opportunities for further study. Given the family's prevailing circumstances, however, the rabbi didn't know if James would be in a position to avail himself of such a chance, even if one should arise. Ezra's own heart ached when he pondered the dejection felt by his dear student.

Josis sympathized with his brother's feelings as well. He encouraged him to hope and to continue setting aside time for study. Likewise, Lucillus tried to keep up James' language skills by speaking in Greek or Latin as often as was practical, prodding him to respond in kind. Still, a certain sadness clung to the youngest son, much as he appreciated everyone's understanding.

James kept the pushing and pulling motions on the saw even and regular, a piece of sheepskin now wrapped around the handle for protection. A line from the psalm repeated in his head, pacing the steady rhythm—*the heavens declare the glory of the Lord; the skies show the work of his hands*—carrying him away in the unbroken monotony. Josis had told him this was how to contain impatience when the wood was hard and progress slow. One needed just enough presence of mind to keep the blade from wandering off the scribed line, but not so much as to allow frustration to accumulate, which led to haste and error.

This length of wood was intended as a lintel for a new doorway which Josis' crew was cutting through one wall of a house in town. It was a rare Nazareth construction project, one of the few since their father had become so well established in Sepphoris. For such an installation absolute precision wasn't required. Still, the piece would have to fit the gap into which it was set, and it had to look neat in place.

Thinking of the purpose behind this chore brought a recollection. "Lift up your lintels, O gates," James recited out loud, "that the King of Glory might come in."

But it was Josis who came in, stirring James from his meditation. "How goes the work, Brother?" he asked.

"I am nearly done," said James.

"Good. My men are dressing the masonry around the side posts. They are about ready to insert the lintel." He inspected his brother's work and held up a hand. "Stop there," he said. "Turn the timber and cut down along the margin that remains. If you go deeper, the weight of the waste end will make the wood split."

They worked together to turn the heavy piece, then Josis supported the end while James completed his cut. When the blade had passed all the way through, they carried the sawn timber outside the shop, placed it onto a cart, and hauled it to the jobsite.

A craftsman by temperament as well as training, Josis tended to involve himself directly in the building projects. He would agree with Lucillus' counsel, offered regularly, that he should leave the work to the men and concentrate on the larger matters of planning and direction. But whenever he was at a site, he found it difficult to keep hands off. The crewmen were of two minds about this tendency. While they admired his willingness to share their labors, most would have preferred that he stay out of the way and let them get on with their tasks.

Josis had found it impossible to resist helping with this local project, which was a small contract involving the addition of a room. "These are our neighbors," he said to Lucillus. "They expect me to be present to see that the work is done properly."

Lucillus granted the point, but recognized a rationale for Josis to follow his natural inclinations.

When James and Josis arrived at the site with the newly cut lintel, they found the men huddled in conversation, their faces lined and serious. Josis asked if someone had been injured. A stonecutter named

Abner, from the nearby town of Japha, turned and came to him.

"No, Master," he said. "The wife of the homeowner was in the market street and heard some news. The king is dead."

*   *   *

Herod's death, soon confirmed by official pronouncement, brought conflicted feelings upon the family. On the one hand, it might mean that Joseph and Mary now could safely bring the child Jesus home to Nazareth. At the same time, it was not likely that the next occupant of the throne would be determined without strife.

Turmoil was already abroad in the land. Hadn't there been blood when the Roman eagle standard was displayed in the temple? Herod had thought merely to show his fealty to Caesar by posting the symbol of the empire. But it was a symptom of decline in a leader whose capacities were already on the wane—indeed, he was ill and in much pain at the time—that the king should have so misjudged how people would react.

Raising the eagle in the holy place was seen as akin to worshiping Caesar. That this offense was committed at Passover made the disgrace all the more appalling. Those who tore down the standard were acclaimed as heroes by the people, and Herod's Jerusalem cohort was unable to contain the explosion of anger that followed their execution by the Royal Guard. Some soldiers were killed in the effort. This brought in the king's entire force, led by his son, Archelaus.

That did not end the trouble. Word spread that the Roman garrison was using this violence as an excuse to seize the royal treasury under the pretext of guarding it, which caused further rioting. Few cared about preserving Herod's stash of wealth for him, but neither was seeing it fall into the hands of the hated occupiers an acceptable outcome. In addition, when the king finally reached the end of his agony and it became known that he had died, demands were heard throughout Jerusalem for the sacking—and even the heads—of several key officials whose personal corruption and maltreatment of the people had made them hated.

The swift transfer of a legion from Syria finally quelled the upheaval within the city, but by now the resentment of the masses was deep. Some three thousand of the rioters were said to have been cut down in the fighting or executed afterward. Clashes occurring in and around the temple precincts had caused fires, bringing substantial damage to parts of the sacred enclave.

It was a bloody, disgusting end to the reign of a bloody, disgusting monarch. Now the question was: Who would succeed him? Herod's children, those who had survived his malevolent scheming and murderous rampages, all had claims. Other relatives had aspirations. The choice of a successor would ultimately fall to Caesar. But no matter what Rome might do, the possibility of more unrest and bloodshed was all too real. A mood of revolt was spreading across the country, well beyond the royal capital.

Whether Joseph was aware of this ferment, or was considering a return to Nazareth now that Herod was gone, no one in the family could know. Which was cause for concern, since these were hardly safe days for an older man, a young woman, and a small child to be traveling the roads of Judea—indeed, even less safe than the census journey had been. If only there were some way of making contact. But it was impossible. Zacharias had provided no further information after his original message saying that Joseph and Mary were in Egypt. The family did not even know where in Egypt.

All that could be done was to continue praying for their safety.

*   *   *

Since Lucillus had first come to work for Joseph, he never doubted the prospects of the business. There had been steady growth in the number of contracts as the reputation of the Nazareth builder spread. But much of that success was tied to the confidence Joseph instilled in his clients. Even though his son was recognized as a hard worker and his attention to meticulous craftsmanship was every bit as great as Joseph's, the master's absence was taking its toll.

At the moment, there were only two projects underway in Sepphoris, both nearly completed, along with the small room addition in Nazareth. Nothing else was on the horizon. Lucillus had met with only one person seeking an estimate of costs, and that in the most inspecific of terms. No actual design had been rendered.

Of course, Lucillus understood that the slowdown wasn't attributable solely to the fact that Josis, and not his father, directed the business now.

The general mood throughout Galilee was adverse to elaborate plans and high expectations. Insecurity prompted by the Jerusalem clashes and the spreading unrest, uncertainty about the royal succession, and the ever-whirling rumors of Zealot plots made everyone nervous, Jews and gentiles alike—especially gentiles. As deeply rooted as some pagan families were in Galilee and Judea, they were keenly aware that they remained despised intruders and that any peace and safety they enjoyed depended entirely on civic stability enforced by Roman might. In the current atmosphere, investments in new homes or grand additions to older ones had dwindled. Lucillus was worried.

He discussed his anxiety with Josis who wondered if the business might shift its focus somewhat away from Sepphoris. Admittedly, the family's reputation there was favorable, but maybe other Galilean towns offered potential that had gone untapped. Or maybe they should look to the imperial enclaves along the sea coast, places like Caesarea or Ptolemais, which were more securely garrisoned and less effected by temple controversies, factional politics, or the intrigues of the Herodian court.

"I don't know if too many of your brother Jews have loose coins for building houses," Lucillus observed, "at least not in Galilee. Roman taxes weigh heavily enough, and the impact of the census has yet to be felt. The empire is large and the counting process long. But all expect that when Caesar has finished with his tallying of heads, purses will be emptier than usual. As for the coastal towns, we have never operated over such distances. There would be many added costs, and the problems of finding dependable laborers and managing the work closely would be difficult."

Josis agreed that the situation was not promising. But like his father, he was a man of faith. "We will trust in the Holy One to send us what we need," he said.

What they needed most immediately was word from Joseph, and it came unanticipated. The overseer on one of the Sepphoris projects was approached by a slave boy who handed him a leather sack containing a narrow parchment scroll.

"From my master, Albus Drusus," the boy said. "Please give this to Josis, son of Joseph the Nazareth builder."

The overseer passed the package on to Lucillus who took it to the compound where he found Josis alone in his workshop. Josis eyed it hopefully with the thought that it might be an inquiry about another building job. It was something far more exciting.

"This is a message from Father," Josis said with great joy when he had laid open the scroll on his work bench. "He and Mary are returning from Egypt with her child. He expects they will be underway by the time we receive this message."

Joseph reported that he was aware of what he discreetly called "the changed conditions." Josis and Lucillus took that to mean the king's death. Without being too explicit in a written message—which could, of course, fall into the wrong hands—Joseph suggested that he and Mary planned to be home before winter, traveling by a route that would not bring them across Judea.

It wasn't difficult to fathom Joseph's concerns. In recent months, an explanation had emerged about the search for male children born in Bethlehem. Herod had apparently been frightened by prophecies of a mysterious child who would become a new king of the Jews. Whether his fears had died with him or were shared by any of his possible heirs was unknown. But Archelaus, the son who most coveted the throne, now had effective charge over the district of Jerusalem, at least until the succession was finalized, and thus was able to exercise influence throughout the rest of Judea. It would be wise of Joseph to stay as far on the periphery of the royal territories as possible.

A closing request in the message was cautionary: to plan no celebration of their return. The less attention drawn, the better.

Josis looked up from the scroll. "I wonder if we should even speak of this to the rest of the family," he said.

Lucillus raised one eyebrow slightly. "Perhaps not," he said.

*   *   *

At that time, Joseph, Mary and the child Jesus were actually somewhat behind the schedule implied in the message. A vision had come to Joseph, giving him a presentiment of Herod's death. It wasn't long before the official word made its way from Jericho where Herod had spent his last, agony-filled days, to Alexandria where the three were living. Most of the large, long-established Jewish community greeted the news enthusiastically. No more of that half-Jew pretender and all his mischief. Many a prayer of thanks was uttered.

Joseph discussed with Mary the possibility that it might now be safe to bring the child home to Nazareth, and she expressed her desire to try. It had been necessary for Joseph to take up his old trade of working in wood to make his livelihood in Egypt. Upon completion of a carpentry project, a beautifully carved chest promised to the father of a young woman about to marry, the three set out for Judea overland, hoping to attach themselves to a caravan. Joseph heard of Archelaus' assumption of authority while they were lodged at a caravansary on the road to Gaza.

In caution, they returned to Egypt, to the city of Buto in the delta of the Nile, where Joseph knew they could obtain passage by sea. There it happened that Joseph encountered Albus Drusus, a Greek merchant for whom he had built a house some years before in Sepphoris. Albus was returning to Galilee, and agreed to carry the message which was eventually delivered to the worksite and passed to Lucillus.

After a wait of about two weeks, Joseph, Mary and Jesus set off on a coastal packet that called in at port cities from Egypt to Lebanon. It would carry them directly to Galilee, to the port of Sycaminum which was located at the foot of the great promontory called Carmel. A long day's walk from there would take them to Nazareth.

*   *   *

James knew nothing of his father's progress, nor even that the return was planned, since Josis and Lucillus had not mentioned the message to anyone else. Late of an evening, after taking his meal at Judas' table and praying with his brothers, he sat alone in the portico, staring dazedly into the sky. It was brilliantly clear, with more and more stars revealing themselves as the last faint glow of day faded beyond the horizon.

James often reflected on the different ways the sky appeared. Sometimes the stars seemed merely like spots, as though painted on the inside surface of a dome. Other times, the inky blackness seemed to have profound depth with the stars suggesting themselves as fires burning at unimaginable distances. Charting the heavenly bodies was a learned specialty among some of the sages, closely linked with the study of mathematics. James could understand why pagans attempted to divine the future from movement of the stars, even imagining them as gods.

It would not be hard to drift into those kinds of musings on a night like this. But James knew it was false and could only lead to confusion and harm. Didn't the fifth book of Torah prohibit looking up at the celestial array and exalting the sun, moon and stars? Do not be enticed into bowing down and worshiping the things which the Lord your God has apportioned to all the peoples under heaven.

Just then, a streak of light cut through the sky. James watched the trail until it disappeared. What would the pagans make of such a sign—a portent of some disaster ahead, or a promise of something good? Perhaps it might be taken to mark the passing of Herod. Or maybe it heralded the king's successor. James was aware that such fiery missiles occasionally struck the ground. But he figured this one had fallen so far to the west that, if it did reach the surface, it would likely plunge into the sea.

Off the Palestine coast, somewhere between Dora and Sycaminum, Joseph spotted the streak and indicated it to Mary who was covering her child with a blanket. The three were preparing to bed down along the bulwark of the ship under an extension of the fore where it overhung the main deck. They had secluded themselves behind a square of casks that were lashed together and covered with what appeared to be an old sail, oft-mended with patches over patches. Mary turned her face up, caught a glimpse of the streak, and lifted the little boy, pointing to the sky.

"Look, look quickly," she said.

But his eyes were heavy, and he didn't really understand what his mother wished him to see.

She kissed him, laid him down, and covered him again. He slept.

*   *   *

The sound of marching feet caught Judas' attention as he stood washing his face over a clay basin. He and Sarah had just arisen. She was dressing. Judas went out into the court and then to the front gate. Simon emerged from his house.

"What is happening, Brother?" Simon asked.

Judas shrugged, then opened the port in the gate just a crack and looked out into the road. A long column of legionaries was passing in quick step. He closed the port, knowing the risks of taking too close an interest in what Roman troops were up to.

"Soldiers," he whispered to Simon. "They look to be in something of a rush."

Legionaries passing through Nazareth would be headed for Sepphoris, probably coming from the district of Jerusalem. But most troops transiting through Sepphoris came either from Syria or from the sea coast. A cadre marching north suggested trouble.

Josis was in the court now, and Judas related what he had seen.

The eldest brother rubbed his face in thought. "There have been rumors that some incident happened in Sepphoris," he said. "Lucillus told me of a conversation he had with one of our clients yesterday. And the crewmen have heard things."

"What things?" asked Simon

"Zealot activities."

"One always hears of Zealot activities."

Judas pointed toward the gate with his thumb. "Maybe our friends out there have also heard about such things," he said.

It was later in the morning when Lucillus came to Josis' shop.

"Do you know anything of Sepphoris?" Josis asked.

"I tried to visit the sites this morning. But I was stopped on the way. The Romans set up a blockade. It seems the stories are true—attacks in town."

"What of our crews?"

"I have no knowledge."

*   *   *

Joseph was detained for some time by a squad of guards at the dock when he, Mary and the child stepped off their ship. What was his business in Sycaminum? Passing through. Where had he come from? Buto. Where was he headed? Nazareth.

The commander of the squad eyed him carefully, then glanced at the young woman and child. Deciding that the trio looked harmless, he signaled his men to let them pass. "Go no farther than Nazareth," he said.

"What is happening?" Joseph asked.

"Uprising in Sepphoris," the officer replied. "Jew bandits—damned dagger-men. They attacked the armory three days ago. Six cohorts have been sent in that I know of. Maybe more." A slight flick of his head indicated Mary and the child. "Take care for them," he said. "The countryside is alive." His expression was kind.

Joseph thanked him for his concern.

Then the officer glanced at Mary again. "Your daughter?" he asked. Joseph hesitated. "My wife."

The Roman's expression changed. He looked at Joseph and expelled some breath through his nose. "Very good, old man," he said with a laugh, then smiled at his men.

*   *   *

One of the laborers, whose name was Tobin, had succeeded in fleeing Sepphoris, avoiding the blockade and the Roman patrols. On reaching the family compound, he reported to Josis and Lucillus that he believed those crewmen who, like himself, lived outside of Sepphoris were probably being held by the legionaries who were going through the city trying to identify any insurrectionists at large. He assumed his fellow workers were unharmed, though probably not in the most comfortable of circumstances. However, he was worried about the crewmen who lived in the city. There had been much damage to the Jewish quarter, where a group of Zealots took a stand in support of their comrades holed up inside the armory.

Lucillus realized there could be no way to ascertain the fate of the crews until after the crisis had passed. And knowing the rough methods of Roman troops, he was anxious for their safety. He asked about the condition of the two houses under construction.

"When I last saw the site I was working at, all was well," Tobin said. "But there was fighting in the Greek neighborhoods. By now, who can say?"

Josis thanked him for the information, then sent him home.

*   *   *

Joseph had obtained a hard wooden club, the end part of a grain harvester's flail, before departing from Egypt. He kept it tucked reassuringly under his cloak along with the Syrian dagger, both obscured by a bulky travel sack slung over his shoulder, his right hand free to grab either weapon if needed. He and Mary made their way around the foot of Mount Carmel into the Jezreel Valley, keeping up as brisk a pace as they could with the child. Sometimes Joseph carried the little boy on his back. Sometimes Mary led him by the hand as he toddled along at her side. Joseph hoped to find some group of travelers they might join, but the expected foot traffic and pack trains normally seen moving in and out of a seaport city were largely missing.

Still, the farther they walked, the less endangered he felt they were. The presence of Roman troops could be sensed everywhere; this was not a day when brigands were likely to be about, stalking unwary passersby. They were challenged at several checkpoints along the way. Each time, Joseph had to repeat who they were, where they had come from, and where they were going. They took the occasion of one such stop to rest on a rise just beyond the Roman barricade. There they shared the remaining provisions which Mary had brought from Egypt, then put the child down for a nap before starting on again.

It was well into night when they ascended the final rise to Nazareth. The town was dark and slumbering as they made their way in and out of shadows along the cobbled street. They passed the house of Joachim. Mary experienced a strange sensation, realizing that her father's home was occupied again, by whom she did not know. Then they went by the synagogue, through the town square with its well—so much that was familiar, but now oddly distant of memory.

Finally, they came to the gate of the compound, barred as it should be in the night. Joseph hesitated at the bell pull, knowing that the sound would set off the dogs. But there was no avoiding a disturbance. He tugged at the rope.

Once the barking began, any hope for a quiet return was lost. The members of the household flocked around Joseph and Mary, even many of the children who had been roused by the commotion. Much embracing, many blessings of peace—and of course, eagerness to see this child Jesus who, it was now assumed, had been the cause of so much royal consternation.

With her own small son tucked half asleep against her bosom, Zipporah stood before Mary, attempted to speak, but hesitated. Then she went down to her knees on the ground, struggling slightly with the action because of her robes and the child's weight.

"Please forgive me, Mother," Zipporah said, a quaver in her voice. "I misjudged you. I was cruel to you."

Mary reached out and touched the side of Zipporah's face. She looked down at this woman, years her senior, and smiled. "Wife of Joseph, yes, but Mother?" Mary said. "Better sister. Friend."

Zipporah stood and embraced Mary with her free arm, the now-sleeping boy pressed between them. Joseph, who was nearby holding the child Jesus, watched this scene and experienced a feeling of great relief.

*   *   *

James was filled with questions as he and Joseph lay down on their mats in the upper room.

"Did Herod's soldiers really take the children?" "How did you get out of Judea?" "Where did you live in Egypt?"

"My son, my son," said Joseph, "all will be answered. But please... please...I must sleep. Mary and I have walked a great distance today."

"I have missed you, Father."

"And I you, my son." Then after a pause, lying in the dark: "You have grown, James. You are a man."

James was not so much a man that he didn't feel a lump in his throat. "Almost, Father," he said with difficulty, "almost."

Another pause, and then Joseph said, "I am so sorry that I did not hear your first reading in the synagogue. When the time is right, we will have the celebration we intended."

"It will be a celebration of your return as well, Father."

Then Joseph felt a lump in his own throat.

The two lay quietly, and James could hear his father's breathing change to the familiar rhythmic, rasping sound that had been the accompaniment of his nights for so many years. Now he related it to the sound of the saw which he had come to know so well. It was comforting to hear his father sleep once again, and eventually, he fell off himself.

CHAPTER TWELVE

Even though I walk through the valley of the shadow of death,
I will fear no evil, for you are with me.

(Psalm 23)

Joseph awakened much later than he had expected to the next morning. When he came down from the upper room, he found that the wives had brought food to the portico. His sons had carried the table out from inside the house. Mary was with the other women, showing them the packs of spices she had obtained from the market in Egypt for all to use, some imported from as far away as Persia. Salome held Jesus in her lap as she sat on the bench with the vine carvings. The boy chattered happily to her, amused at meeting this new person who took so much interest in him.

"Ah, you are awake, my husband," said Mary. "Everyone has been asking me questions, and I have told them they must wait to hear your words."

"We *cannot* wait, Father," said Simon. "We must know everything about Bethlehem and how you have lived these past two years."

Joseph laughed. "I am afraid you will have to wait a few minutes more," he said, and excused himself to the privy.

When he returned, he sat at the head of the table on the Roman-style chair. A basin filled with water had been set out. Joseph said the prayer for washing of hands. Then, taken by a thought, he looked up at Josis.

"Uh— The morning service?"

Josis smiled. "It is too late, Father. You have slept through it."

Joseph closed his eyes and laughed. "I count on the Holy One's forgiveness."

"He will grant it, Father."

Everyone gathered around the table, said the prayer of washing, then the prayer for the breaking of bread. Food was passed. Mary took Jesus back and held him at the table, placing a small wooden bowl in front of him in which she put bits of food for him to pick at.

Joseph recounted the happenings in Bethlehem, beginning with the registration for the census and finding shelter in a stable behind a lodge filled to overcapacity. "You would not believe the crowds throughout the entire Jerusalem district." He described the phenomenon of the star and the unexpected visits by strangers after Mary had given birth—shepherds and a trio of foreign astrologers who brought gifts of great value.

"Astrologers?" James asked, perplexed and not a little shocked. "But Torah forbids—"

"I know, I know," Joseph said, holding up a hand. "It was very strange. They said they had followed the star to where we were. But don't worry. They did not share their arts with us."

James accepted his father's word, but wasn't entirely comforted. Visited by pagan wizards? He wondered if it didn't raise the question of ritual contamination. But he kept the thought to himself.

Joseph explained that it had been his plan to take Mary and Jesus to the home of Zacharias, but they stayed at the inn until the day of presentation when they went to Jerusalem for the baby to be circumcised. There they sought out Simeon to fulfill the pledge Mary had made to the old scribe that he might see her child. They also encountered a widow named Anna whom Mary had known during her years in the temple precincts.

"Simeon made...a remarkable prophecy," Mary said, just then looking somehow disturbed, "about change and heartbreak to come."

Not wishing for his wife to dwell on a disquieting memory, Joseph continued his account. "We spent some time in Jerusalem, then returned to Bethlehem so that Mary could recover further," he said. "It was then the astrologers visited us. I am glad they came, and I am glad we were there to receive them. It was they who gave us the first indication of Herod's interest."

The king had gotten word of foreign mystics looking for an angelic child within his realm, Joseph explained. Since these were men of dignity in their homelands, Herod received them, questioning them at length about the signs and portents prompting their expedition. He insisted they keep him informed of their progress, which aroused their suspicions later supported by uneasy dreams. A dream of his own then convinced Joseph that there was danger afoot.

"We hurried to Ein Kerem to consult with Zacharias," he said. "Hearing of these wise visitors and the message that had come to me, he agreed that we should leave the country with all speed. There was a caravan bound for Alexandria. We left on it the next day, and when we arrived, we searched out my brother."

"Uncle Cleophas?" Judas asked.

"Yes," said Joseph. "He has lived in Alexandria for several years. He is a bit younger than I, and he has become quite renowned there for his skills as a stone carver. We stayed with him and his wife, Mary, and their children until we found a dwelling to rent. Zacharias had given me a letter of referral to the rabbi of the largest synagogue in Alexandria. That and Cleophas' recommendations aided me in finding work."

"What sort of work did you do, Father?" Simon asked.

"I made crates."

Josis laughed, nearly spitting out a mouthful of food, his eyes showing amazement. "*Crates?* The master carpenter, Joseph of Nazareth, making crates?"

Joseph smiled. "They were very good crates," he replied, to general laughter throughout the portico. "Actually, the crates are rather carefully crafted to protect the large, red-glazed pottery that is made in that region. Egyptian clayware is highly prized and shipped all over the empire."

"Your father did not make crates for long," Mary said with pride in her voice.

"I was able to obtain assignments for other kinds of carpentry projects," Joseph said with a shrug of humility, "also due to Cleophas' referrals."

"And to the quality of your work, my husband."

Joseph shrugged again. "Mary is proving to be a loyal wife," he said, teasing.

There was laughter once more.

"Father," said James. "I am curious. Were you in touch with Zacharias while in Egypt?"

"Yes. He was much concerned for our wellbeing."

"And yet...he never informed us of your whereabouts. And he never..." James' voice trailed off, the thought left unfinished.

Joseph looked at his youngest son whose face at that moment conveyed the distinct impression of disappointment.

"I know, my son," said Joseph. "Zacharias and I corresponded only occasionally, and always very discreetly. Our messages were carried by the master of his caravan that plies the route between Jerusalem and Alexandria, the one on which we traveled. Zacharias would entrust that task only to a man in whom he had complete confidence. You see, he felt it necessary to avoid drawing attention to his family tie with Mary, who had given birth to a male child in Bethlehem and who might be searched for. He knew that the palace had access to the census roles and also that Herod's tentacles reached into Egypt. Then too, Zacharias' own small son was within the range of age that the king was interested in. There was no guarantee the Royal Guard would confine its search to the neighborhoods of Bethlehem, Ein Kerem being not that distant.

"In the same way," Joseph continued, "Zacharias feared that contact with *my* family could draw attention here. Any one of you—or all of you—could have been taken and held as a means to force our return. He perceived a grave danger."

"Zacharias was wise," Josis said. "The compound was searched by a detachment of the Royal Guard."

Both Joseph and Mary looked at him with eyes widened.

"They knew you had registered and that Mary had given birth," said Josis. "They even knew the name, Jesus. But it's clear they knew no more than that. They were searching randomly."

"Thanks be to the King of the Universe that you are all safe," Joseph said with gratitude and relief.

"Father, do you think Archelaus will continue the search?" Simon asked.

"It seemed a possibility," Joseph said, "which is why we came by sea."

Josis mused silently on that small bit of information. By sea. This was what Joseph had meant in his note when he mentioned traveling by a route that would not take them across Judea.

"But now that we are in Galilee," Joseph said, "I think it unlikely we will hear from him. We saw no indication of such a search, either when we came off the ship in Sycaminum, or along the road. All the solders we encountered were concerned about the uprising. Perhaps Archelaus will be on his best behavior, at least until the royal succession is confirmed. I imagine he would not wish to be tainted by the incident of the children, which certainly fulfilled his father's bloody reputation. Archelaus has enough blood on his own hands."

Joseph now looked squarely at James. "Which brings me to another matter," he said. "The honorable Zacharias has not forgotten his promise, my son."

James drew in a quick breath.

"He has arranged for you to take a place as the disciple of a sage in the temple."

James' mouth fell open in anticipation.

"Perhaps you have heard of this doctor of the Law." Joseph was being playful, in the way he had often been with his youngest son in years past, fanning youthful eagerness. "Oh my...what is the name of that old rabbi? If only I could remember."

Mary smiled in a knowing way. "You torture your son, my husband."

"Well...it will come to me."

James was leaning forward to the point of almost toppling over.

"Ah yes, now I recall," said Joseph. "Someone named...Hillel."

Everyone was stunned. Hillel was the most learned rabbi in Jerusalem and one of the most respected scholars ever to sit on the Sanhedrin. Though he was now aged, his school was still considered the authoritative source for determinations on nearly all questions of ritual procedure, scriptural interpretation, or legal prudence. Only the great Shammai vied in prominence.

"Father..." said James, breathless, "how can this be? Hillel?"

"He is a close friend of Zacharias," Joseph said, setting all teasing aside. "But I assure you, my son, this is not just a matter of friendship connections, or even the tie to Mary. Zacharias has corresponded with the Rabbi Ezra and ascertained that you have the knowledge and ability deserving of such a place."

"The rabbi said nothing of this to me."

"He wouldn't. Zacharias secured his promise of trust."

James was speechless. He struggled to hold his emotions in check. The others in the portico shared the silence, until Josis decided he would take a playful poke at his brother.

"And James was becoming so good at straightening nails," he said. "Now I'll lose my helper."

All laughed.

Finally James was able to speak again. "When do I go to Jerusalem, Father?"

"You will need to wait just awhile longer, I think," Joseph said. "But perhaps, my son, these two years have taught you something of patience? Zacharias is aware that Mary and I intended to return home. When he feels confident in our situation, he will obtain instructions from Hillel's grandson, Gamaliel, who serves as proctor of the students. In the meantime, we will let the people of Nazareth discover that I am back—and let peace return to Galilee after this distress in Sepphoris. How all of that will affect us we cannot tell, so let us proceed carefully."

Everyone agreed on the wisdom in Joseph's caution.

Then Josis informed his father of what Lucillus and he heard about conditions in Sepphoris from Tobin, the laborer. After that, conversation turned to developments in the family during the past two years, which included Sarah's announcement that she was now with child.

*   *   *

Lucillus was deeply relieved at the master's return—both for the safe deliverance of Joseph, Mary and the child Jesus after their two-year sojourn, and for the good of the business. But he had been keeping attuned to the news now leaking out of Sepphoris, and each revelation was more troubling than the last. Sitting at the table, now restored to its place inside the lower room, he updated Joseph and Josis on the latest facts.

"There is much blood," he said, "much blood. Fighting was fierce. The Jewish quarter is in ashes, and the Zealots did not go down without taking their vengeance on the homes of the Greeks. Many neighborhoods were put to the torch. Even the royal villa was damaged. I was told by one of the checkpoint guards, an auxiliary whose unit was brought in from the Decapolis territory, that most of the gentiles have fled to Ptolemais."

Joseph sat across the table, listening with closed eyes as this account of human tragedy was laid before him. Josis merely shook his head slowly, continuously, from side to side. He too had heard some of the tales.

"Executions have already begun," Lucillus said. "The wounded among the insurrectionists were hacked to death, and those who were captured in decent shape are being crucified by the hundreds. The fear is that among them are many who took no part at all. The legionaries are not inclined toward making fine distinctions. And now it is said that all Jews will be removed from the city. I don't know if we will ever be welcome to work there again."

Joseph dismissed the last point with a wave of his hand. "We cannot think of that now. You say that two projects were still underway—what of our crews?"

"Five of the men who live in Nazareth have been able to return home," Lucillus answered. "Two are missing. Of the local Sepphoris men we have heard nothing."

"And probably never will," said Josis.

"That...is likely," Lucillus said. "There is word—only a rumor, but I think it plausible—that Jewish males from the city are being rounded up and taken as slaves."

"Fresh oarsmen for the imperial galleys," said Josis, "the men of Sepphoris."

"I fear so," said Lucillus.

"This is truly terrible," said Joseph, his forehead now in his hands, elbows on the table. "King of the Universe, preserve your people."

Over the next days, further details of the slaughter came to light as refugees from Sepphoris began appearing in Nazareth, mostly women, children and old men. Very few young men. The Rabbi Ezra suspended classes at the synagogue, turning its court into a shelter where the Sepphoris Jews could rest and be fed. The wives of the town brought food. For most of the refugees, Nazareth was a brief stop on the way to seeking out relatives in other cities. A few with Nazareth connections were taken in locally.

The wife of a craftsman from one of the Sepphoris crews found her way to the family compound with her two daughters. Joseph lodged them with Mary and Jesus. The woman told of how her husband had been cut down in the street right outside her house, caught in the middle of a clash between legionaries and a group of insurrectionists.

Mary comforted them as best she could. She taught the little girls some special prayers she remembered from the temple. They stayed for two days, then departed for Hebron with a purse of coins Joseph pressed into the woman's hand.

The horror of what had happened in Sepphoris became especially vivid to the Nazareth community when a proclamation was read in the square that the town was being called upon to bear witness to the outcome of the Zealot uprising. All the men, Joseph, his sons, and Lucillus among them, were forcibly marched to the highest point between Nazareth and Sepphoris. There they could see the road leading into the now-smoldering city.

On either side of the highway stood a column of crosses, frameworks and stakes, from which were suspended men and a few women, bloodied, beaten, nailed, moaning, crying. The witnesses were led between the rows of victims hanging as naked as slabs of meat on hooks in a butcher's stall, some already dead. Most were alive and writhing in agony and despair, hands pinioned above them, struggling to breathe as the weight of their bodies crushed their lungs.

Blood, pain, hopelessness, death—everywhere for as far as could be seen.

Legionaries on either side, holding their javelins horizontally at the ready, prompted the Nazareth group along this nightmare trail while a centurion bellowed, "*See and remember, men of Nazareth. This is the fate that inevitably comes to those who disturb the peace of Rome and oppose the will of the Augustus. I charge you to tell everyone you meet. Warn them of what defiance and banditry bring.*" Some of the witnesses were sickened, vomiting on the road in their revulsion. Even soldiers kept themselves from looking at the dead and dying for fear of reacting in the same way.

James, walking on his father's right, stared numbly, unbelieving, at this scene of inhuman cruelty which, in his young life, he could never have imagined. He looked up at one figure in particular, a lad not much older than himself. The mouth hung open, the tongue protruded. James could not tell if he was alive or dead, though the red eyes peering from a face bruised and swollen seemed to long for death.

A psalm echoed inside James' head, making it ache: *From the depths I cry to you, O Lord. Lord, hear my voice. Be attentive to my pleas for mercy.*

Amid all of this suffering and desolation, Joseph's eye was caught by an intricate pattern carved into the timbers that comprised one of the frameworks. It was somehow familiar, though smoke-blackened from fire. For a moment he didn't know why it arrested his attention. But then he realized that these were some of the beams which he'd had specially carved in Lebanon for the beautiful Greek house.

*   *   *

James was unable to sleep that night. His father slept only fitfully. At one point, Joseph woke to discover the mat beside him empty, its cover tossed away. He looked about the room illuminated sparsely by moonlight, and saw that his son was not there. Then he rose, went to the door, and descended the stairs. James sat on a stool in the portico.

"Son?"

James stared off into the court. He did not turn toward his father. Joseph stood silently, waiting for a response.

Eventually James spoke. "It was so horrible. People...living people. *Nailed*...like pieces of wood. Hanging uncovered. Waiting to die. How could anyone do such awful things to living people?"

Joseph nodded his head. Nothing to say. No answer to such a question.

"And they were Jews, Father. They were Jews like you and me."

"Yes, they were Jews."

"The Romans did not even drape a cloth over their naked bodies, not even the women. They left them shamefully exposed."

"Yes."

"How must those people have felt—even with all their pain and suffering... Exposed... The shame..."

"I know."

"And then that centurion speaking about the peace of Rome—the *peace of Rome*. Was that the peace of Rome? How could Caesar allow his subject people to be treated in such a way?"

"I do not defend what the legionaries did, my son," Joseph said. "I *would* not. What you saw was truly horrible. Rome is known to be brutal, and you have been a witness to that brutality yourself. But do not forget that it was the Zealots who attacked the city, killing many."

"And now I know the reason," James said, finally looking at his father. "I never really understood why they persist in fighting against the Romans. They speak of freedom and the purity of our land, of removing the yoke of Caesar. But to me these were all just words. Now I know what is behind those words."

Joseph took another stool, placed it beside James' seat, and set himself down on it. "The Zealots have a case, yes. We are a conquered people and treated unjustly in our servitude. We are oppressed, that is true. And it has been so for nearly half a century, since Pompey came with his legions to end the civil war. But *there* is our *real* shame, that the price we pay for Jews slaughtering Jews is bondage to Rome. Maybe this is the Lord's chastisement for our disunity and unfaithfulness."

"Father," said James, "you cannot believe that the Romans do the will of the Holy One."

"Who can say that what they think is for Caesar's good doesn't work to fulfill God's design?" Joseph said. "Hasn't it always been so? Hasn't good always been worked from evil? Joseph's brothers sold him into slavery, and their descendants became slaves in Egypt. But then Moses led us out and showed us the land which the Holy One had marked for us. Our fathers strayed from loyalty to the one true God, bowed down before foreign idols, and Jews were taken captive into Babylon. But then we returned and the temple was rebuilt."

"But the Romans are pagans, Father—cruel pagans."

"My son, you have seen a side of life which you did not know of before. It is painful, I realize."

James turned away and gazed into the court once more. "Pagans," he said. "Pagans and invaders. Conquerors. And our family—we have...built their houses. You... Josis... Lucillus... Even I have worked on pieces made for the projects in Sepphoris."

"Do you think it was wrong?"

"I never considered it so," said James. "It was merely the trade of our family." He turned back to look at Joseph, confusion in his eyes. "But now...I don't know, Father. I don't know."

Father and son sat silently for some time, both shaken, neither inclined to attempt sleep again.

Joseph searched his heart for some word of comfort to give his son—the child of his old age, as Escha had said, the one he loved and had so wished to shelter from *the terrors of the night and the arrows that fly by day.* Perhaps he sheltered him too well. Joseph had cherished the peaceful life of a small town like Nazareth set off in the hills of Galilee away from the tumult wrought by kings and legions and Zealots. This was a place where a scholarly boy could fill his curious mind with the books and teachings of the Rabbi Ezra or the sayings of the worldly Greek, Lucillus, and not be frightened by the daily strife of an occupied, exploited nation.

That was the childhood Joseph had been able to provide for a beloved youngest son. But that childhood was gone now. Two years of anxiety while Joseph and Mary were away. And now Sepphoris. It was a fearful threshold for a boy to cross into manhood. But James had crossed it, and there was no going back. Joseph pondered the change in his son's life, and hoped that what had been so jarringly experienced would not leave damage that was beyond repair. James had such prospects, so much to offer a downtrodden and brutalized people.

"Perhaps it is of little consolation at this moment," Joseph said, "but I do believe there is a role for our family to play in setting right these injustices which the Jewish nation has endured. And if our dealings with the Greeks have been in error, maybe it is how we will make amends."

James looked at him again. "What do you mean, Father?"

"Your new brother," Joseph said. "The strange and unexpected circumstances of his conception and birth point to a great purpose."

"Do you truly believe Mary's child is the Messiah?" James asked. "The chosen one of God?"

"Messiah?" Joseph said. "That I cannot say. But he has come to us for a reason—some mission in which we have each been given a part. You, me, everyone in the family. The things I have seen convince me."

James continued looking at his father for a time. Then his glance turned down toward his robe draped across his lap, and his hands came together, fingertips touching. He gazed, unfocused, through the empty spaces between them.

"Well..." he said, "we shall see."

CHAPTER THIRTEEN

Train up a child in the way he should go,
and when he is old he will not depart from it.

(Proverbs 22)

Just as the men of Nazareth were forced to witness the ghastly consequences of revolt, so were those from the other Jewish towns surrounding Sepphoris. Likewise, each community was given the responsibility of removing the bodies along the road running in its direction.

The Romans were determined that the Jews of Palestine learn a lesson from this gruesome display, and so left the bodies hanging for a week. As a result, most of the corpses were in very bad shape, having both begun decaying and fallen prey to carrion birds. The Rabbi Ezra and the synagogue elders hired a crew of gentiles for the unclean task of handling the dead, and designated a parcel of land outside the town for burial. A smell lingered in the air for days.

But, the human spirit being resilient, the people of Nazareth soon turned their attention away from the tragedy. Everyday affairs reasserted themselves in all families, eventually even in those that had suffered personal losses directly. No one would ever forget what happened, and for some the hurt would be deep. But life, as it always does, went on.

Joseph and his sons put their minds to developing income that didn't depend on Sepphoris. It was clear that the carpentry shop would now play a larger part in supporting the household, as would the sheep flock and olive grove. The wives came forth with the idea of reorganizing their daily baking routine with an eye toward producing bread for sale in the market street. Mary noted the weaving skills she had acquired as a young girl in the temple, suggesting this craft as a possible source of earnings.

Because of his long and critical involvement in the family business, Lucillus had been invited to take part in the meeting at which all these ideas were put forth. He recounted the talk with Josis, before Joseph's return, when they had discussed attempting to get building assignments in the imperial towns on the coast.

"There would be complications," he said. "Distance is an obstacle, to be sure. But with my contacts among the Greeks... Well, we could try."

Joseph had reservations. "In time, perhaps," he said. "Right now, I think the Greeks will not be eager to do business with Jews anywhere in the country. We should let this blood sink into the soil for awhile."

James had kept silent throughout most of the conversation, even seating himself off at the end of the portico, on the fringe of the group. The discussion of finding new work on the coast made him reflect once more on whether it was right to have dealings with Greeks. But his mind focused primarily on one question: How might the family's changed prospects affect his taking a seat in the school of Hillel?

When Zacharias did send word that he should go to Jerusalem, would he be able to afford the expected stipend? It was held among the Jews that a teacher should not be paid. To teach the Law was a religious duty for those who had knowledge of the Law. This ideal was rarely lived, but it was given honor through the common practice of remunerating the teacher for time he would have devoted to other pursuits if he were not teaching—a small bit of social hypocrisy that met everyone's practical needs.

James did not know how much would be required. And he worried that, whatever the amount, it might now be beyond his family's means. Would his future be sacrificed to the peace of Rome?

Then he suddenly began to feel quite selfish for thinking in this way. Yes, he had his dreams. But the family had its needs. Perhaps he *was* being called upon to make a sacrifice—Rome aside. He had waited two years for his father to return. He could wait longer.

"I can make calls in the other hill towns, Father," he said. "There must be many carpentry jobs we are not getting. Furniture, implements, repairs. I can make the rounds telling people about the excellent work you and Josis do. It might bring more business."

Joseph turned his glance toward the end of the portico and smiled.

"That is a fine idea, my son," he said, "but I think you will not be so available to us for that task. Once we hear from Zacharias, you will be off to Jerusalem. And until then, your time is better spent in studying the holy books with the Rabbi Ezra. You will need to be well prepared for what lies ahead of you."

"But Father," said James, "There will be costs, and right now, the family is—"

"The family is set upon you becoming a man who can serve the King of the Universe and our people," Joseph said. "That is how you will bring honor to this household, not by getting us carpentry jobs." Then, looking around at the group, he asked, "Are we agreed on this?"

By nods and sounds all indicated their assent.

"Do not worry about costs, my son. The Lord provides."

James was moved by his family's unity in showing support, though he was still uncertain as to how his father proposed to cover expenses. But the conversation shifted to other matters.

Later that evening James broached the subject again. "Father," he said, as they were preparing to turn in, "I know from working in the shop with Josis that the business has been slowing down. And now with this terrible thing that happened in Sepphoris—"

Joseph held up a hand. "Your regard for the family is a good thing, James," he said. "I bless you for that. And it is true that we have to make adjustments. Our building trade may never again be what it was. But we are not without means. For one thing, Joachim, of blessed memory, made an extremely generous bequest to Mary. Aside from money, it included the pasture in which Judas and Simon graze their sheep. So we are relieved of that rental expense and the land is added to our holdings of the compound and the olive grove.

"In addition," he said, "one of the gifts which the astrologers brought to Bethlehem was a quantity of gold coins. I would not call it a fortune, but it is an amount sufficient to be very useful. This money Mary and I have set aside for raising her child and seeing to his schooling. But she agrees that if the family should be in need, we will draw on it. Jesus is part of our family. I am raising him as my son. He is your brother. And whatever he becomes will in large measure reflect his upbringing among us. If the family were to suffer want, he would also. So it is important that our household be secure."

Joseph laid his hand on James' shoulder. "I tell you these things, my son, because you are a man now, and because I want you to be confident in facing the future. It is what I meant when I said that the Lord provides. I cannot stress enough that we all have our parts to play in the mission we've been given. Only the Holy One knows what *your* part may be, but He will ensure that you are properly prepared to play it."

*   *   *

During the two years Joseph and Mary were away, questions naturally arose in the town as to their whereabouts and the reason for their absence. Family members had fended off inquiries as best they could. The story given out was that, in marrying the daughter of Joachim, Joseph had also taken on responsibilities for liquidating certain portions of her father's estate. This required negotiations with Joachim's various far-flung relatives, which called for extensive travel.

It was Lucillus who, being steeped in Greek logic and worldly knowledge, had crafted this formulation. And while it was not in any sense true, it did have the virtue of seeming plausible to hill-town folk with little understanding of how wealth was disposed of.

Joseph did not feel comfortable maintaining such a ruse, but the story having been established by his family, he was stuck with it. As he reacquainted himself with his neighbors, however, he began to shade the tale more toward something that was at least not a blatant lie. It had been necessary, he explained, that he and Mary reside in Alexandria for a time, and there he worked as a carpenter—which was true—while they awaited resolution of certain questions—which was vague enough to be acceptable to Joseph's conscience.

This tended to redirect interest quickly. Egypt was a place that aroused great curiosity. The size and prosperity of Alexandria's Jewish community were well known. But what all found intriguing was how Jews had fared so well in the land where their forefathers had been slaves.

"The days of Pharaoh are long gone," Joseph would say, then turn conversation to other subjects. Thus he was able to avoid any suggestion that their travels had been connected to Mary's child, whose situation had to remain a family secret.

That secret prompted concern in the household. If the child Jesus was indeed the Messiah, or a prophet, or had been sent on some sort of divine mission, how was the family to deal with him? Lines of parental authority had always been rather blurred within the house of Joseph. It was understood that any adult at hand should intervene whenever juvenile conflict arose or some misbehavior needed to be brought to a halt. A serious infraction would be referred to the offending child's father for discipline, but the day-to-day business of keeping order was shared. All the children knew that their own parents would stand behind whatever action was taken by an uncle or an aunt, and so all the adults felt comfortable doing what was necessary. Introducing Jesus into their midst made them question the accepted practice.

Certainly, Jesus looked like an ordinary little boy, but Mary had called him the *Son of the living God*. How does one treat the *Son of the living God* when he's toddling around pursuing the mischief to which a two-year-old is normally inclined? How should he be restrained, guided, corrected? More worrisome, what of when he grew and his will, confidence and physical capacities increased? Most boys eventually assert themselves in some way, and often that presents a challenge, even in the best of families. What of a boy sent by the Holy One?

But then, would Jesus even know he was sent? Would he realize he had a special destiny? If not, when he finally came to understand his uniqueness, how would the knowledge affect him? How would he feel and behave toward those around him? Such questions the brothers and the wives discussed at length among themselves, until finally the eldest brought them to the family head. Josis and his father were working together in the shop. Joseph put up the draw knife with which he was shaping a plank for the back of a bench.

"We are perplexed, Father. It is apparent that Mary's child is special. No one doubts this now, not after all that has happened. But just as we still cannot account for why this boy was put into the care of our family, we are not at all clear about what the Lord expects of us."

Joseph laughed. "Neither am I, my son."

"Then how can we know the way we are to treat him? Is there something in the holy books which might guide us?"

"I doubt it," Joseph said. "What we face is extraordinary. The only situation that seems at all similar to me was that of Moses. But he was raised in the Egyptian way—in the way of Pharaoh's court—and we know nothing of that."

"Then what are we to do, Father?"

Joseph ran his hand along the contour he had been shaping in the wood as he thought about the question. "It does present a challenge," he said. "These first two years, Jesus has been almost entirely in the care of Mary. She is a wonderful mother, attentive to her child at all times and tender in her manner toward him. I cannot say I have ever seen her correct him. Rather, she guides him gently away from anything that could be harmful.

"But of course," he continued, "that is how one treats a baby. As a child grows, he is not always under the watchful eye of his mother. He encounters life's dangers, and opportunities to take the wrong path present themselves. It may be that the Holy One has made this child different. Perhaps Jesus will show that he is better able to discern right from wrong than other children are or to exercise better self-control. This we cannot say right now. Time will tell. But until it does, I think we must be to him as we are to all the children in the family. We must love him, we must teach him, and we must be prepared to guide him onto the right path. I cannot think that the King of the Universe would expect anything different of us."

*   *   *

After some months, unrest in Jerusalem had begun to settle. Harsh feelings about the affair of the eagle standard and all the bloodshed that followed it had given way to a general sense of relief that the tyrant Herod was gone. And while still young and new to his governing role, Archelaus showed some ability to manipulate the feelings of the people. He gave assurances to each of the various religious factions that he would hue more closely to expectations of how a ruler of the Jews should behave. These, combined with promises made to the leaders of each group, raising hopes of special advantage under the new regime, served to ease lingering resentment over the fact that it had been Archelaus who was responsible for so much of the blood that had been spilt.

In addition, by making some key alliances within the royal family, he was able to weaken the claims of his brother, Antipas, who at one time had been Herod's designated successor. Archelaus' position now appeared so strong that it seemed certain Caesar would confirm him on the throne, and rumors out of Rome suggested it would happen soon.

Observing these developments, Zacharias judged that the king-presumptive was likely feeling as secure as he could expect to feel, and so would not be troubled by his late father's fears about mysterious children. Consequently, the house of Joseph was probably safe now and conditions right enough for James to begin his studies in Jerusalem. So it was that on a spring morning a temple guard rode up to the gate of the family compound bearing a message.

James' reaction was unrestrained joy that took the form of leaping about the court, swinging his various small nieces and nephews around by the wrists, to the amusement of all the adults observing. That was followed by sprinting off to the synagogue to inform the Rabbi Ezra of this good news. Class was just getting underway when he arrived. The rabbi spotted James standing in the gateway and gestured him in.

"I have received word," James said. "I will go to the temple."

Ezra embraced him, which took the students by surprise. They knew their teacher as a warm and joyous person, but such a show of affection was unusual.

"Class," Ezra said, "our dear friend, James son of Joseph, will study in Jerusalem with the great Hillel. Such honor he brings to our school and to our town. May the Holy One bless his endeavors and favor him with much success."

James accepted the applause of the boys, some of whom had been students with him. Then he turned to Ezra.

"I thank you, Rabbi," he said. "I thank you for the words of support given to Zacharias. But I thank you for so much more than that—for your knowledge and for your care and for your friendship." Then he began to feel a choking sensation in his throat and a swelling in his eyes.

Ezra embraced him once more. "Serve the King of the Universe," he said quietly in James' ear. Give your life to Him. And if necessary, give your life *for* Him."

*　　*　　*

The celebration which originally had been planned to mark James' maturity and first reading in the synagogue was finally held, now in significance of his embarking on a new life of study and learning—and also, belatedly, for the return of Joseph and Mary. The cooking skills of the wives and Joseph's daughters were displayed to great advantage, all the guests diving into the heaps of food set out on trestle tables in the court. Lucillus engaged a group of musicians to accompany dancing carried on in separate areas curtained off for the men and the women. The Rabbi Ezra offered prayers and blessings for the scholar and his family.

All of Nazareth rejoiced at this great day that had come upon the town. Joseph's pride in his son was evident to all as he shepherded James about, greeting neighbors and friends who had come to share in the joy of his house.

During a quiet moment after the eating and revelry, when guests had felt the weight of the night and most had departed, Joseph stood alone in the portico. His thoughts went to Escha, and he addressed her in the depth of his heart. *Wife of my younger years, your child is grown. Now he will be a great scholar and a man of respect, as I promised you. Your work is complete. Rest, my wife. Rest in the arms of the Holy One. Rest.*

CHAPTER FOURTEEN

And now our feet are standing
within your gates, Jerusalem.

(Psalm 122)

It was the big laborer, Nachum, who accompanied Joseph and James to Jerusalem. He carried a stout staff of hard, knotted wood, more for protection than walking, and kept up a running commentary on the features of the countryside which he recalled from his last trek along this route. Could it have been three years since he, Lucillus and James had taken Mary to Ein Kerem and then returned with Joseph?

"It doesn't seem possible that so much time has passed already," he said. "It feels like we just walked this road."

"That is true," Joseph said. "But much has happened in three years."

"Much indeed, Master Joseph. Much indeed. I wish we were going to Ein Kerem. The house of the honorable Zacharias is a very pleasant place to rest."

Joseph laughed. "Not this time, Nachum, I'm afraid."

To James also the interval between the two journeys was a cause for reflection. He had been a spindly boy sent on a strange errand by his father, unexpected and unexplained. It was a trip that would presage so many changes in the life of his family. Now he was a young man following the same path through the hills of Samaria and Judea, but with a different destination. What did this excursion hold?

It was essential to Joseph that he accompany James on this journey. To place one's son into the hands of a learned master was a serious thing. It was not a task he would have assigned to anyone else, not even to Lucillus. Nachum was along for safety of course. The Jerusalem road was no more secure now than it ever had been when Herod ruled.

But father would deliver son to the house of study, as the schools of Jerusalem were called, in much the same way Joachim and Anna had delivered Mary to the temple when she was little.

And the sacrifice involved was similar. James would become a disciple of Hillel. The situation would be as if he had a new father. His life would be completely focused on the words of the rabbi, his attitudes and behavior adapted to meeting the master's expectations. Even his time would be committed totally. Joseph did not know when he might see his son again, once he left James in the school.

Nachum scanned the dry Judean countryside. "There," he said, pointing to the horizon. "It is Jerusalem. I see the towers. Beyond the hill with the olive groves."

Craning his neck and shielding his eyes to look, James felt a thrill of recognition, like the rejoicing mentioned by the psalmist, who speaks about counting the towers and reviewing the ramparts. He recalled a passage from the Prophet Isaiah: *You shall find comfort in Jerusalem.*

Was it comfort that awaited him? He really did not know what to expect. Hard work, to be sure. A revered sage would undoubtedly have high expectations of his students. But beyond that? James did not even know where he would be living. Zacharias had suggested the home of a business colleague as a possible place where a student might lodge. It would be looked into.

James had spent the recent weeks in a state of heightened anticipation tinged with a certain fear, distracted during the day, sleeping unevenly at night. Now the city was in view. Only the rest of his life was obscure.

They reached the gate outside of which James, Mary and Nachum had rested on their last trip while Lucillus went in search of directions to the house of Zacharias in Ein Kerem. There was no queue leading up to the eye of the needle, and the security chute was not in place. Instead, the main doors were wide open, everyone passing through with ease. But a watchful contingent of the Civil Guard was highly visible on the scene, at least a dozen sentries posted outside the arch. As before, legionaries manned the toll station just inside. Above the gateway hung a large banner bearing the signet of Archelaus.

"It seems the prince is welcoming us to the city," said Joseph.

"Not like last time," Nachum said, looking up at the standard. "Last time there was a long line of people waiting to be checked and admitted."

"Let us hope this is a sign that peace reigns in Jerusalem," said Joseph. "It is a hard enough thing that my son is leaving me. I would like to know that all is well where he will be."

"You must not worry so about me, Father," said James.

"It is a father's lot to worry," said Joseph, patting his son on the shoulder. "Perhaps you will know that for yourself one day."

They made their way through the crowded streets, so different from outside the walls where newer houses sat in loose clusters here and there along lanes that had begun to creep toward the countryside. Within, everything was tight, confined, ancient living quarters hard up against an endless variety of other structures, some streets so narrow and winding that it was difficult to see the sky or even to know whether it was still day.

Jerusalem was the center of the world, the Lord's city, built around Mount Zion, the Lord's footstool, or as the psalm put it, the true pole of the earth. The boundary line between the territories of Benjamin and Judah ran through the temple. It was said there were 500 synagogues inside the city confines, though that was probably an exaggeration.

This was a crossroads where armies and wayfarers and caravans from Arabia, Africa and the western lands of the empire converged on their way to everywhere else. It was the place to which, as Isaiah had written, the wealth of nations came. No wonder Caesar held onto it so firmly. It was an asset he could ill afford to let slip from the Roman grasp. But it was life and breath to the Jews. It had been fought over, bled over, died over throughout the ages. All Jews knew and ruminated on the words of the psalm: *If I should forget you, Jerusalem, let my right hand wither, let my tongue cleave to the roof of my mouth.*

Following directions provided by Zacharias, the three arrived at a sturdy block building set near the bridge that spanned the Tyropoeon Valley, a broad depression running the length of Jerusalem. The bridge made the temple mount directly accessible from the upper city, the neighborhood that was home to the Herodian palaces, the amphitheater, the opulent houses of so many leading Judean families.

"Is this the synagogue of Hillel?" James asked.

"It seems as Zacharias described it," said Joseph.

Not being an hour for prayers, all was silent. Nachum beat his fist on the tall wooden door carved with the seven-branched candelabrum. There was no reply, and the place appeared to be deserted. He pulled at the iron handle, opened the door, and peeked inside. The interior was dark with only a small spot of light shining from a lamp suspended at the far end of the space.

"Nobody here, Master," he said.

Then a voice came from the shadows. "Whom do you seek?" A figure appeared in the doorway, a fatherly looking man with a long beard, once black but now streaked in silver.

Joseph stepped forward with a slight bow. "We have been sent by the honorable Zacharias to Rabbi Hillel. I am Joseph of Nazareth. I bring my son, James, to submit him as a disciple of the learned master."

The man nodded. "This is the house of Hillel. I am Moshe, attendant of the synagogue. The master is not here. This is one of the days he sits with his students in the portico at the temple."

"Can we call on him there," Joseph asked, "or should we come back here at another time?"

"You need to see Gamaliel, grandson of the rabbi," said Moshe. "He makes all arrangements with the students."

"Is he to be found at the temple?"

"Go there. Ask anyone where Rabbi Hillel holds forth. Find Gamaliel, and speak with him."

"Thank you, kind sir," said Joseph. "Peace be with you."

They set off for the temple, crossing the bridge, and entered the Court of the Gentiles, a broad plaza surrounded on three sides by a roofed colonnade of pillars designed in the Greek style. The portion of this structure that ran along the south wall of the temple had two levels, creating a double-story arcade containing 162 columns and referred to as the Royal Porch. Joseph knew that the scholars sat in instruction on its upper level. He located a stairway, and when they reached the top, inquired of an old woman sweeping where Hillel's group might be. She indicated the far corner which was called the Pinnacle of the Temple, overlooking the Kidron Valley beyond the city walls.

Along the central corridor, they passed various clusters of scholars seated in dialogue here and there in the open spaces between the posts. Finally they reached an assembly of perhaps twenty young men in the place where the woman had said. Seated on the floor in batches interspersed between columns, they were all turned toward a man in black robes who sat on a stool with his back to a pillar.

Quite elderly and with a girth appropriate to his age, the man was vividly alert, the face behind his full white beard bright and expressive. He spoke with energy, eyes trained attentively on whichever of the young men he addressed, his smile and his animated hand gestures conveying a sense of friendliness and warmth.

"Is that the great Hillel?" James whispered to his father.

"I believe so," Joseph said, bringing a finger to his lips to signal quiet.

They listened as the sage conversed with his disciples. He put questions to several individually, and also asked for responses from the group in general. He took their inquiries, replying with terse but insightful comments that set heads nodding among the group.

After several minutes, a man came from around one of the columns and approached Joseph from behind. "May I be of service, my friends?" he asked in a quiet voice.

Joseph gave the man a quick glance. He was younger than the master, approaching middle age, but he wore the same smiling countenance.

"Peace be with you, sir," said Joseph. "We seek Gamaliel, grandson of Hillel."

The man offered a small bow. "I am Gamaliel," he said, "peace be upon you."

"I am Joseph son of Jacob. Perhaps you have received a request from the honorable Zacharias about—"

"The young man from Nazareth of Galilee, I believe?"

"That is correct." Joseph lifted a hand to make the introduction. "My son, James."

"Peace be upon you, James son of Joseph. We have expected you."

"Thank you, sir," James replied. "It is an honor to be considered for acceptance into this great house of study."

"Zacharias' recommendation was very enthusiastic," said Gamaliel.

James' head fell in humility. "Thank you, sir. I am honored by the kind words of Zacharias. He speaks too generously."

Gamaliel laughed softly. He glanced at Joseph, then back at James, and then, unexpectedly, at Nachum. "You, sir, are..."

The big laborer was taken aback at being addressed by the grandson of Hillel. "I am Nachum son of Hezekiah," he said uncomfortably. "I serve my master, Joseph."

"Welcome, Nachum son of Hezekiah."

James was confused by the diversion of Gamaliel's attention to Nachum. Joseph recognized it as a gesture of kindness and hospitality, but one which he sensed held a deeper point.

Gamaliel turned back to James. "Your reserve is creditable, James son of Joseph," he said, "as is your sense of gratitude. But I will give you a saying of our master to begin your time with us. If I am not for myself, who will be? And if I am only for myself, what am I? And if not now, when? These three questions make a man examine much about his expectations of his own person. For you, right now, the first is most relevant. Do not regard yourself so unsurely that you are impeded from moving forward. If so, you will never be able to ask the two questions that come after—or any others, for that matter. If you are truly a scholar, have confidence that you will prove yourself so."

James' eyes went to his father, and the two shared the recognition that these words meant James had been accepted into the company of Hillel. Then he looked back at Gamaliel.

"I will heed this advice, sir."

"Good," said Gamaliel. "Now then—we begin each day with the morning service. You will hear the crier at sunrise. We start one hour after, without fail."

"Yes, sir."

"We meet here in the porch on the first, third and fourth days of the week, and we are in the synagogue on the other days. Do you know where our synagogue is located?"

"We went there first and were directed here."

Gamaliel nodded. "You will begin with us there on the next Sabbath. Come for the evening service. That gives you three days to get settled. Have you someplace to lodge?"

"Zacharias has suggested the home of a friend. That is where we are to go next."

Again Gamaliel nodded.

"Sir..." James asked, looking at that moment, in spite of himself, the slightest bit timid, "what will I...do?"

This brought another quiet laugh from Gamaliel. "Of course," he said. "Since you are newest among us, you will attend to the master's needs—whatever he may require. My grandfather is aged, and so help with certain basic concerns is often necessary. For instance, he thirsts quickly. You will keep a skin filled with cool water and fill his cup when he calls for it. Also, you will help him get to his feet and steady him when he walks, especially on the stairs."

James was surprised to feel a small flush of excitement about being given the responsibility of meeting the essential needs of a great man. He realized some might consider such tasks as those of a slave, but he saw this charge as something unique.

"Most rabbis emphasize simple rote memorization of laws and judgments," Gamaliel continued. "But Master Hillel likes to engage his disciples more actively. You will listen to his speaking—to the questions he asks the other students and to the comments he makes about their answers. You may ask an occasional question yourself. But I advise you to think them out carefully and keep them succinct. And not too frequent. If he should ask you a question, do not make a casual reply. Answer in the most considered way you can. He will wait for you to gather your thoughts. And if he comments on your answer in a manner that confuses you, do not feel like you are stupid or foolish. The master never wishes to humiliate, but you will find that his comments make demands on you.

"You will be examined twice a year, in winter and in summer. We have just completed our summer inquiries. If, after the first testing, you are judged worthy to go on with us, you will be considered to rank among the accomplished students. You may then join more fully in the discussions. If at any time you should have problems or concerns, come to me."

James was now beginning to feel a bit dazzled. He had for so long looked forward to entering into serious scholarly life. But the realization that this path actually lay open before him, and that he was about to embark on it, was nearly overwhelming. Here he stood in the temple, in the porch of the sages. He was with Gamaliel, grandson of Hillel, the greatest doctor of the Law who was himself speaking just a short distance away. It was suddenly all James could do to stifle the desire to run, go back to Nazareth, work in Josis' shop, play with his nieces and nephews in the court, read books with the Rabbi Ezra.

Joseph, who knew his son's emotions so well, stepped in at that moment to turn the conversation toward an awkward but necessary subject. "Sir, what is the procedure as regards...the stipend?"

Gamaliel appreciated that Joseph had taken the initiative in this matter. "You realize," he said, "that the master does not seek payment for his instruction."

Joseph understood the convention. It was difficult for scholars to address the topic of money, but they had to live.

"Zacharias has advised me of the appropriate amount," he said, holding out a small sack filled with coins.

Gamaliel took the money with a nod, but without comment.

"My son will be at the synagogue," said Joseph.

They exchanged blessings, and Joseph, James and Nachum started to turn away. But then, the father in Joseph came to the fore, cracking through the wall of resolve he had built up in preparing to bring James to this fateful moment in his young life.

Joseph stopped, turned back to look at Gamaliel, and said hesitantly, "Forgive me, sir... If I might ask... I realize my son will be a disciple... that he will spend his time according to the rabbi's will. But...is it permitted for him to receive...visits? Or to come home...on occasion?"

Gamaliel was not surprised at the question. Indeed, other fathers had asked it.

"There are some rabbis," he said, "who believe that a man must turn entirely from his former life in order to tread the path of knowledge and wisdom. Master Hillel knows that the King of the Universe places each man within a family, and that neither knowledge nor wisdom is attained by turning from those to whom one has lifelong obligations. Your son will face a rigorous schedule, but within it there is room for a student to meet his responsibilities to those he loves."

A father's relief showed on the face of Joseph. "Thank you, sir," he said.

*   *   *

The lower city presented a different aspect of Jerusalem life from the temple precincts or the lofty neighborhood where the synagogue of Hillel was located. This was the industrious heart of the community, the center of craft and commerce. It was a warren of workshops and mills and market stalls and stock pens and garden plots, sprawling out from below the Royal Porch and down into the Tyropoeon Valley all the way to the southernmost city wall. This was home to the skilled artisans and laborers and merchants and traders who provided food, clothing, furnishings, implements, the necessities and luxuries to meet the needs of a great and prosperous city.

It was, in many ways, the real Jerusalem, where the diversity of everyday Jewish life could be seen. Jews from all the far reaches of the Dispersion were here—Jews from Babylonia, from Egypt, from Asia, Africa and Greece, even Rome itself, all identifiable by the inflections of their speech or the adaptations of dress acquired in the regions of the empire from which they came or to which they would soon return. And not only Jews. People of all colors and languages and lineages dwelled here, some briefly, some for all their lives. In this hive of bustling humanity a new clash of sights, sounds and smells assaulted the trio from Nazareth at every turn.

James' eyes and ears feasted on this mad variety as he made his way through the streets with Joseph and Nachum in search of the house to which Zacharias' message directed them. There were more types of people, more ways of speaking than he had ever encountered in Sepphoris. And while it fascinated, it also stirred a certain disquiet about how the world injected itself into the life of the Lord's city, and especially about the rightness of Jews living in such close proximity to the alien and uncircumcised. Perhaps these were thoughts he might bring to the Rabbi Hillel, once he was settled into the school and the time was right to make such an inquiry.

They came to a place where two streets intersected in an almost perpendicular way, a rarity in the lower city's random swarm of alleys and jagged lanes. There on the corner stood a stone enclosure, one face of which presented an archway outlined with a wide band of copper hammered in a geometrical pattern and burnished to a high sheen. The entry was closed by an iron grate wrought in a motif of intertwining grapevines. This fit the description provided, and they looked through into a court that was a curious mix of palm trees and flowering shrubs along one side of a stone walkway and stacks of what appeared to be metal ingots on the other.

"This looks like the home of a trader in metals," Nachum said. "Isn't that what the honorable Zacharias said this man is?"

"He did," said Joseph, reaching for the bell pull.

They were admitted by a servant, a young girl with skin the color of dark honey, shining black hair, and deep brown eyes. She reminded James of Lucillus, and he wondered if she was also from the North African coast.

The girl led them down the walk to a two-story house that spanned the far end of the long, narrow yard. She took them into the front room and indicated that they should wait, then disappeared down a passage whose opening was partially blocked from view by a screen. Some seconds later a man emerged. He was short of stature, with a balding head, insufficiently covered by his small cap, suggesting someone older than his actual years.

"Peace be with you," the man said. "I am Joseph, tin merchant. How can I assist you?"

"I too am Joseph—peace be with you. I am Joseph son of Jacob, from Nazareth of Galilee. These companions of mine are my son, James, and my man, Nachum."

Bows of greeting were exchanged.

"We have come at the urging of Zacharias, priest of the temple and kinsman to my wife, Mary. He is your friend, I believe?"

"Yes. Yes, he is. A dear, valued colleague and advisor," said the tin merchant, looking at that moment somewhat perplexed. "Are...you in need of metals...Joseph of Nazareth?"

"No, sir," said Joseph, "though I must tell you that I am a builder by trade and I found the metalwork at your gateway very striking."

The tin merchant nodded his thanks for the compliment. "It indicates to all who pass by the nature of my business and the quality of my goods. I import ores and metals from all over the empire, as far away as Britain."

James was impressed to meet someone with dealings in the most distant of Caesar's lands.

"My son," Joseph said, "has come to Jerusalem to be a disciple of the sage, Hillel, and—"

"Has he?" the tin merchant interrupted. "A privilege for you, young man, an opportunity which you should cherish."

"As I do, sir," said James.

"He takes his place in the house of study beginning next Sabbath," said Joseph. "But he requires a place to live, and the honorable Zacharias suggested that he might lodge with you."

Their host turned his head aside slightly and took on a thoughtful expression. "Perhaps," he said. "Perhaps. Zacharias knows that there are bed chambers in this house which I use to accommodate the agents who represent me in my acquisitions and sales of metals. They come and go, often at unexpected times, as I myself travel frequently. I would not be able to commit one of the rooms to a permanent tenant."

James glanced at his father.

"We understand, of course," Joseph said. "Then maybe you are aware of someplace else that—"

"No, no," said the tin merchant, holding up a finger. "No, no. Please do not misunderstand. A disciple of the great Hillel is not to be left wandering the streets, especially not one with a family tie to my esteemed friend, Zacharias. Let me think. There is a small hut in the front corner of the court. It is humble but snug. We have used it for storage. If the young man wouldn't be too disturbed by my many visitors or the hauling of materials in and out, it might meet the need. Come, let us inspect its condition."

He took them out of the house and down the path back to the front gate. On the right, the side on which greenery predominated, there was a stone structure with a tile roof, built out from the corner of the wall.

"This is quite more than a hut," said Joseph.

The tin merchant smiled. "Well, yes, I suppose. Only one room, but a door with a lock that is functional and a window with a shutter to keep out the chill." He peered inside. "A bit littered at the moment, but we can clean that up." Then he gestured for James to look.

"It seems very nice," James said.

"We can find you something to sleep on—in fact, there is a couch that is unused. It is in the house, just now, but we can bring it out here. And perhaps a chair and table. And a lamp, I think, as well."

Joseph looked inside. "It seems quite livable. We will visit the market stalls in the neighborhood for blankets and other necessities."

"Then here you shall stay," said the tin merchant, smiling. "When next I see Zacharias, I will inform him that James son of Joseph is my lodger. He will no doubt be pleased."

A conversation ensued in which a rental fee was determined, the modestness of which Joseph attributed to the friendship between Zacharias and James' new landlord. An amount sufficient to cover six months was advanced. Expressions of thanks were given. The tin merchant promised that the hut would be cleaned and ready by the morning of preparation for Sabbath. Then Joseph, James and Nachum departed.

*   *   *

The three found temporary lodging at an inn near one of the city gates. The next days were spent visiting the temple, exploring the city, searching out items James would need for his new quarters. A thick woolen blanket and sheepskin coverlet caught Joseph's eye in one of the stalls.

"These will help on a winter night," he said when James noted the sheepskin's weight. "The Jerusalem chill can take you by surprise."

Nachum spotted a small, footed iron cauldron. "Perhaps the metal trader will let you build a fire outside your door," he said. "You can make soup in this. And if it turns out to be of no use, sell it to him, and he can melt it down into an ingot. He will no doubt have a customer for it."

They all laughed. Indeed, there was much laughter as they made their explorations, purchased some dried foods, lamp oil and other supplies and James familiarized himself with the lay of Jerusalem. But amid the joking and pleasant time, James felt a gradual return of the anxiety he had experienced when they were speaking with Gamaliel in the temple.

On the morning of preparation they came once more to the house of Joseph the tin merchant to deposit their acquisitions in the hut along with the items James had brought with him from Nazareth, a few spare clothes, a new pair of sandals, and his phylacteries. They found a low couch placed along one wall of the now-spotless room, and a table and stool in front of the window, a lamp suspended from above. There was also a basin for washing, with a pitcher already filled with water, and a covered chamber pot. James looked around and expressed his pleasure at the change which had been worked in this place that was to be his new home. But his unease was apparent to a watchful father.

"You should be quite comfortable here," Joseph said eyeing his son.

"Yes...Father...I will be," said James. "And there is ample room for you and Nachum to spend Sabbath. We can spread the sheepskin out on the floor as a sleeping mat, and—"

"No, my son," said Joseph. "I think that Nachum and I should leave you now. A new life begins for you with the setting of the sun this evening. You must tread that path alone."

"But, Father—the Sabbath."

"If we start now, Nachum and I can reach the inn on the Samaria road by sundown. We will lodge there over Sabbath."

James was quiet for a moment, his eyes turned down. Then he took a breath, glanced up again, and said, "Yes, Father. You are right."

They shared a long look and then an equally long embrace.

"I will miss you, Father."

"As I will you, my son. But you are in the hands of the Holy One now, blessed be He. May the King of the Universe protect and keep you always."

CHAPTER FIFTEEN

She opens up her mouth in wisdom,
and the teaching of kindness is on her tongue.

(Proverbs 31)

A man of lesser faith than Josis might have been given to despair over what appeared to be his destiny—that he would never have a son. But Josis accepted the Lord's will, and he doted on his five daughters. One could even say there was a certain compensation in his circumstance, since he was free of concern about schooling for his children. Most girls learned all it was felt they needed to learn from their mothers. Rare was the young woman like Mary who was able to read and had broad exposure to the holy books.

Both Judas and Simon did have sons, and those who were old enough had spent time in the school of the Rabbi Ezra. But like most Nazareth boys, their attendance was sporadic, reflecting the seasons and the demands of family. Learning suffered especially when Judas and Simon needed help with the sheep or extra hands in the olive grove, as was frequently the case.

Mary had observed this situation when she first came to the house of Joseph, and she reflected on it during the months in Egypt. When she and Joseph returned, Mary suggested to the brothers that perhaps she might take upon herself the task of instructing the boys and girls of the family. Given the losses which the business had suffered in Sepphoris and the advantage in flexibility of schooling the children at home, her offer was accepted readily.

The brothers did hesitate somewhat over the question of whether the girls should participate. It was a commonly held view that too much learning tended to sow confusion and dissatisfaction in females, and that it could also reduce a girl's appeal to potential husbands, who might be less educated than the young woman under consideration. Then too, wasn't it said that a learned girl might be given to promiscuity? She could be so confident in her knowledge of Torah as to feel herself unbound by any moral restraint and so take her pleasure freely.

The wives, on the other hand, dismissed such ideas and were quite open to the prospect of having their daughters taught, especially reading, in which they saw a certain practical benefit. So the question was put to Joseph, who consulted the Rabbi Ezra. Ezra was sympathetic to the idea of teaching girls, though he had never made any public statement on the matter. He understood the risk of squandering rabbinic credibility in the eyes of those who depended on him for guidance. There was nothing to be gained by taking stands on issues of little urgency and great contentiousness.

"Between the two of us," he said to Joseph, "I have taught my three daughters to read. But I always tell them not to mention it outside the family."

And so Joseph rendered his judgment that Mary should include the girls of the household in her lessons, but the less said about it, the better.

Joseph appreciated Ezra's advice and, even more, respected his integrity in giving it, because Mary's plan did represent a loss to the rabbi. The special subsidy for James' education had ended with Joseph's diversion to Egypt and James' withdrawal from school to help his brother in the carpentry shop. Now, if Joseph's granddaughters were to be taught at home *along with his grandsons*, it meant that Ezra would be deprived of the small income to be gained from the boys' attendance, infrequent as it had been.

Over the years, there had been talk of some arrangement for support of the country's schools, either by the temple or by the royal treasury. But while all Jews agreed on the importance of learning, few looked forward to what would inevitably be the consequence of such a program: more taxes. Ezra's attitude paralleled that of most rabbis and synagogue attendants. Though they did the teaching, and thus would benefit from any official funding, they were reluctant to see taxes increased, even for so noble a cause as education. They did not wish the sour feelings which people bore toward the temple priests to be redirected toward themselves.

Ezra did have one source of hope for restoration of a relationship with his former patron, the little boy, Jesus. Joseph assured the rabbi that there were resources to fund the child's education. While Jesus would no doubt take part in his mother's teaching sessions when he reached the appropriate age, Joseph was certain that supplementary instruction would be called for. Without being too specific about why, Joseph made it clear to Ezra that he had high expectations of this boy. Perhaps Jesus would be as fine a student as James had been. Perhaps even better. The rabbi attributed Joseph's assumption to fatherly pride. He nonetheless looked forward to the day when Jesus would join the class.

In the meantime, Mary prepared to undertake her teaching enterprise. She obtained a few scraps of parchment as well as some planks of wood from Josis' shop, on which she wrote out selected verses from the story of creation. These the children would copy onto tablets, the frames for which were constructed by Josis. Simon provided clay for the tablets from a deposit he knew of, being intimately familiar with the fields surrounding Nazareth. The material wasn't as pure and malleable as the wax in tablets one could purchase in Jerusalem, but it would do.

Copying was the method by which Mary had been taught to read and write in the temple, and she had confidence in its effectiveness. She nailed up the planks and parchment scraps in the portico, using any portions of wooden framework that were exposed, and collected stools and benches from around the compound. She then scoured the countryside for thickets of a certain kind of wild bramble whose thorny projections could be used as writing implements.

Given the demands on the older children of chores and family needs, Mary knew she would have to keep the teaching sessions short, probably no more than an hour a day. And even at that, it was unlikely everyone could be counted on to show up all the time. Still, something was better than nothing.

The first session was well attended. In a show of support for Mary's effort, the wives had made sure all the children at least five years of age were present. Mary was not surprised to see Salome, Sarah and Zipporah seated at the back. They would naturally be curious about the elusive process of reading and want to know how their children were being taught. For her part, Mary was glad of the encouragement their presence offered the children.

As the days passed, the expected irregularities began appearing in attendance of the boys, but the girls were present consistently. As were the wives—though Sarah, with the discomfort of her growing belly, sometimes stood or walked about the far end of the portico, and Zipporah was often called upon to chase after her restless little boy, Noah, keeping him from one childish disaster or another.

The thought occurred to Mary that Salome, Sarah and Zipporah were not so much interested in observing their children's reading progress as in learning to read themselves. So she asked Josis to construct three more tablets, which she then handed on to the women. They were somewhat embarrassed, and not a little worried about their husbands' reactions to having wives learn to read. But they accepted the tablets and joined in the copying. They would even stand to recite when Mary called upon her pupils to speak the letters and words taken down.

Under a certain amount of motherly watchfulness while the class was in session, the children too young to participate in the lessons did what children do. Jesus and Noah were natural playmates, both being three years old, and they spent much time together in the court. But there were differences between the two boys. Noah was an animated child prone to inquisitiveness of a particularly active type that tended to lead him into mischief and call his mother away from the studies. Jesus, in contrast, was quieter, his curiosity of an interior sort.

It was frequently the case that, while Noah would be off chasing cockroaches, exploring the privy, or climbing the stairway to the upper room—any of which activities always brought a quick response from Zipporah—Jesus' attention would be drawn to the sounds emanating from the portico. From the start, he repeated what he heard the pupils saying, and soon Mary noticed that he was identifying the letters for himself. She suspected that some whole written words might be recognizable to him, though she couldn't be sure about that. She discussed these things with Joseph, who was not surprised.

"*Son of the living God?*" he said with a shrug.

"But he is a little boy," she replied. "It isn't natural that he should learn things so quickly."

"Yes, he is a little boy. But he is something else as well."

Mary's brow furrowed, giving her an expression that showed how vexed she was over this. "What effect will it have on him," she asked, "if he discovers he has abilities that greatly exceed those of other people? And how will others behave toward him if it becomes known?"

Joseph nodded and searched for words to assure her. "Perhaps... Perhaps this is the real challenge the Holy One has set before us. It is one thing to receive the *Son of the living God* into the world. It is another thing to bring him up in it." He touched her hand. "Right now, that task falls primarily to you, my wife."

"I know," she said. "Sometimes, when I hold him in my lap, he seems like any other child, and I revel in being a mother, as any woman might. But there are times I feel so poorly prepared for this that I wonder why the King of the Universe would have asked such a thing of me."

"Then the next time you take him on your lap," said Joseph, "pray for wisdom. Wasn't the Lord pleased when Solomon asked for wisdom? Pray that you might be a *seat* of wisdom upon which this boy can rest."

*   *   *

Judas was leading his flock from the sheepfold beyond the compound walls out for a day's grazing in the pasture when he was approached by a lad dressed in the Greek manner and wearing a slave ring. The young man asked directions to the home of Joseph the builder, and Judas pointed toward the entrance.

"You have found it," he said.

The lad went to the compound gate and tugged at the bell pull. "A message for the Nazareth builder," he said, holding out a scroll to Josis, who had answered the ring.

Josis instructed the young man to wait outside, though it was not really necessary to tell him. Greeks knew that Jews were not likely to welcome the uncircumcised into their homes. Such a petty people, and yet so filled with themselves. Even a slave had to laugh.

"Father," Josis called at the open door in the portico. He entered to find Joseph and Lucillus seated at the table.

Joseph untied the ribbon encircling the scroll and read the message. "It is from Albus Drusus, the merchant. He wishes to consult us about repairs to his house in Sepphoris."

"Albus Drusus?" Lucillus said vaguely. "The name...seems familiar, but I am not sure I—"

"We built his home some years before you joined us," Joseph said. "And it was Albus who carried my message from Egypt. I came upon him in Buto."

Lucillus tapped his forehead with a finger as he recalled the package passed to him by the overseer at the Sepphoris worksite.

"Can we take on a such an assignment?" Josis asked. "Now? In Sepphoris?"

"We would need assurance that Jews can enter the city and move about freely," said Joseph. "But Albus Drusus is of a practical mind. He likely has a way to obtain any necessary permissions. I don't think he would have considered us for this project otherwise."

"Perhaps I should speak with this Albus Drusus," Lucillus said. "I am Greek enough. No one will stop me in Sepphoris. I can return there with the messenger."

"Yes," Joseph said. "Speak with him and clarify the situation in the city. If he can provide us with assurance of safety, we will take the assignment."

Lucillus went to the gate, exchanged a few words with the young man, and then the two of them headed off along the Sepphoris road. They walked a bit in silence, and then the slave, whose name was Nonus, put a question to him.

"Do you work for this Jew?"

"Yes."

"Are you his bondman?"

"I have my manumission."

This seemed an odd circumstance to Nonus. "Why would you wish to be in the employ of a Jew?"

"Joseph is a decent man. Righteous and fair."

"He lets you go about as you wish in his house?" Nonus asked.

"Of course."

"Has he made you become circumcised?"

"No. But I keep the commandments."

"The commandments. Jews are a very peculiar people."

Lucillus laughed. "Yes, as Greeks see them, they are very peculiar."

After the crucified bodies had been removed from the Sepphoris road, the stakes, crosses and frameworks were taken down, stacked and burned. Piles of charred wood remained on either side of the route, and it gave Lucillus an odd feeling to pass between them.

They approached the city after some walking, and entered through what had been the Jewish quarter. Passage of months did not mask the extent of the great catastrophe. Very little remained standing. Heaps of rubble were everywhere, the leavings of slave gangs that had salvaged stone blocks, tiles, metal fittings, furniture, and whatever else was judged useful or valuable enough for the Romans to have confiscated. An officer leading a small detachment of legionaries eyed Nonus and Lucillus, but no one approached them or questioned them as to their movements or intentions.

The Greek neighborhoods were in better shape—at least they could still be thought of as neighborhoods—but there was much damage, with many buildings in ruin. Lucillus noted that the beautiful home for which the specially carved beams had been obtained was a burned-out shell. He shook his head in sadness and wondered about the fate of the Sepphoris crewmen, of which nothing had ever been heard.

Albus Drusus was found at his storehouse in one of the city's two market districts, a section of town which, it surprised Lucillus to observe, was pretty much fully functioning. The building appeared to have been untouched by the violence, and Albus had taken up temporary residence in it. Nonus introduced Lucillus and then withdrew, presumably to other duties. Lucillus conveyed Joseph's greeting and expressed his master's interest in the proposed rebuilding project and also his concern about the safety of Jewish workers in Sepphoris.

"Assure my friend, Joseph, that there would be no problems," Albus replied. "I will arrange for documents of passage. The city is restricted. But tradesmen from the surrounding towns and other Jews who have a legitimate purpose in being here are documented. There is no danger."

Albus handed Lucillus a sketch made in charcoal on a piece of old sail cloth showing the arrangement of rooms in his house and indicating where repairs and changes were required.

"Joseph will no doubt have kept the original plan," Lucillus said. "He is very careful in retaining any information related to a project. We can compare these notes with his records and give you a preliminary estimate of costs. It would help if I could see the structure myself. Perhaps your servant could take me to the site?"

Albus called for Nonus and then walked Lucillus out to the street.

"I have the utmost confidence in the fairness and accuracy of Joseph's estimate," said the merchant. "Contact me when you are ready. I'll get the needed documents for your men."

Nonus appeared, and Albus instructed him to take Lucillus to the site where the work was needed. The visit was brief but sufficient for Lucillus to assess the scope of the project. Back in Nazareth later, Lucillus reported the information he had obtained, describing the house of Albus as having received relatively light damage, compared to some of the neighboring homes.

"Other than one end of the structure which was brought down by fire, it seems the work Albus wants done is more improvements than restoration," Lucillus told Joseph. "It wouldn't really be that big a project. Still, it could give us an entry back into Sepphoris."

Joseph looked at the sketch on the sail cloth spread across the table, then turned his gaze out through the doorway to the court and said nothing for some seconds.

"You are hesitant?" Lucillus asked. "Albus assured me that it would be safe. There were troops about, but I detected no particular tension or hostility. Sepphoris seems a city in the process of recovering itself."

Joseph was still silent. Then he said, "Who is recovering the Jews?"

Lucillus' eyebrows went up, one slightly higher than the other.

"We are restricted from free access to a place that is within our own country," Joseph said. "We need documents of passage to enter." He gave a small, humorless laugh. "The peace of Rome."

"Peace of Rome?"

"Something James said." He was quiet again, then made a quick waving gesture with his hand. His expression changed to one of attention and resolve. "I still have the original plans. We will make a bid on this project. Albus has been kind to me. There is nothing to be held against him. We are craftsmen, and craftsmen exercise their craft."

*   *   *

But Joseph found an unexpected echo of his own reservations in a disturbing talk he had with Joel, the town blacksmith, two days later outside the synagogue after prayers. Joel had long been his supplier of nails and fittings, and Joseph mentioned casually that there might be an order coming—possible work in Sepphoris.

"Sepphoris?" the blacksmith said. "Haven't you finished with Sepphoris after the anguish that befell that town? I hear Jews cannot go there. How can you work in Sepphoris?"

"My client is a good and honest man," said Joseph. "He will obtain permission."

"A good and honest Greek?" asked Joel.

"There are some," said Joseph.

The blacksmith's face posted a sour memory. "Let me tell you something that happened," he said. "A group of scavengers, Beduin boys, came to offer me nails they had collected along the Sepphoris road. Can you believe it? Nails discarded after the bodies were removed. Crucifixion nails—thick spikes—baskets full. They thought I would buy them for the metal, to melt down. Well, I waved an iron rod in their direction, its tip red from the forge. I sent them scurrying away with their impure load of garbage. Crucifixion nails!"

He stood watching the scene replay inside his head. "That is what Sepphoris has to offer." Then he looked at Joseph. "Maybe I should have bought their blood-stained nails. I can think of nothing better for rebuilding that foul den of Roman thieves."

Joseph did not speak.

"You are my townsman, Joseph," said the blacksmith. "And you have always been my best customer. I will fill this order for your good and honest Greek. But I must admit that your business does not please me as it once did. Not if my wares are bound for Sepphoris. Not after what was done there."

CHAPTER SIXTEEN

Put not your trust in princes,
in mortal men, in whom there is no help.

(Psalm 146)

Archelaus' expectation that he would assume control of his father's kingdom was not fulfilled. Certain members of the Herodian clan, whose support the prince had believed he could rely on, came forward instead to endorse the claim of his brother, Antipas. Also, a delegation of prominent Jews, from both Palestine and Rome, petitioned the Augustus, insisting they would prefer their homeland be attached to the province of Syria rather than have it governed by *any* of Herod's heirs.

Archelaus felt betrayed.

All of which presented Caesar with a dilemma. The calm that had eventually descended after the riots and uprisings occasioned by the decline and death of Herod argued in Archelaus' favor. So did his attempts at placating the various Jewish groups with his pledges of greater royal deference to religious concerns. Those two factors might have tipped the scales, because Caesar was disposed toward Archelaus, recognizing in him the same grasping self-interest that had made Herod a perfect tributary vassal of Rome.

But in the end, these were not enough. Caesar felt Archelaus lacked that unique balance of adroitness and brutality with which Herod had been able to keep the Jews under some measure of control for thirty years. Archelaus had the brutality, but it was apparent he would never be the natural politician his father was.

Direct Roman governance was not desirable. Better a half-Jew dynasty than what the people would perceive as complete foreign despotism. So Herod's kingdom was broken up. Archelaus would rule as *ethnarch*—not king—of Judea, Samaria and Idumea. Other portions of the realm were given to his brothers, who were appointed *tetrarchs*. Galilee and Peraea went to Antipas, and the Decapolis, the territory of the ten cities, east of the River Jordan, went to Philip. In addition, certain key areas were set aside, designated as Roman administrative districts, overseen by the governor of Syria.

Most people took it as a sign of Archelaus' disappointment that he divorced his wife, Mariamne, and married Glaphyra, widow of his brother, Alexander. It was that Alexander who had fallen victim to their father's morbid suspicions about family members intriguing against him. Archelaus was already carrying on a less-than-secret dalliance with Glaphyra, who had caught his eye and inflamed his passions, even though her second husband, Juba, king of Mauretania, was still alive. While awaiting confirmation by Caesar, Archelaus had maintained a decorum of distance when seen with Glaphyra in public. Now decorum was thrown to the winds, creating a scandal and raising eyebrows among the doctors of the Law. Deference to religious concerns be damned.

The turning of public opinion against the ethnarch was not slowed even by Archelaus' deposing of the high priest, Joezer, a move which had been greatly desired by many of the rabbis and large segments of the people. Joezer had played a part in the bloodshed during the affair of the eagle standard. He was also seen as responsible for much of the corruption that had crept into the temple leadership. His downfall was applauded, but Archelaus didn't get the hoped-for credit. Rather, the move was seen merely as a means by which he could install his own man.

Such was the focus of public interest in Jerusalem during James' first months in the school of Hillel, though he would not have known it from listening to the words of the master. The great Hillel had long been a presence in the political life of the capital, but if the royal fortunes continued to interest him, he wasn't sharing his thoughts with his students. Perhaps it was mellowness of age, or maybe discretion learned through the delicate practice of surviving under Herod's volatile temperament. Or maybe the rabbi had truly attained such spiritual perfection that he was unmoved by the shifting of worldly power.

There was no lack of other sources for news on the latest events.

James had only to stroll the central corridor of the Royal Porch to hear gossip being passed among the students of the various rabbis—likewise the market stalls of the city, which the students frequented. Everyone had their views on the new ethnarch's prospects, opinions correlating generally with the profiles of the different houses of study.

The Aramaic-speaking schools, whose masters and students prided themselves on their fierce resistance to any sort of foreign influence, looked on Archelaus with utter disdain. He was seen merely as a less-imposing image of his wretched father. He was in thrall to all things pagan, unlikely to hold the allegiance of the people or maintain the peace, and so unlikely to retain the support of Caesar, grovel though he might.

To the Greek-speakers, particularly those who had come to Jerusalem from the western lands of the Dispersion, the only question was how smoothly Archelaus' regime would keep the tax monies flowing to Rome. Neither his pagan tendencies nor the allegiance of the people nor peace in the land mattered very much at all. The ethnarch's future was seen as dependent on how well his remaining territories fed Caesar's coffers.

That test was already underway. The count from the great census had been completed throughout the empire, and new levies were being collected. While Archelaus could hardly be blamed for a process set in motion before the death of his father, the mood of the people at this particular moment was not congenial to any governments, pagan, half-Jew or otherwise. Expectedly, there were rumors of new Zealot plots.

Taxes were a subject of intense discussion among the students of Hillel, and the master saw in this an opportunity to explore some aspects of a citizen's duty under the Law. The essential premise on which the obligation to pay taxes rested was that a kingdom was the possession of the king. Had it not been so since Samuel anointed Saul? The people had demanded a king to lead them, and the prophet laid down the price of their subservience. The king would have a claim on their lands, goods and crops, even on their sons and daughters. If the king owned the country, then to pay one's taxes was as if one were paying rent to a landlord; to withhold one's taxes would be as if to steal. While most people grasped the concept, it was not an idea that had much appeal, among either the public in general or Hillel's disciples.

"But Master," one student asked during a discussion of the new levies, "does this not suppose that the authority of the king is duly constituted? The people wanted a king, and so Samuel yielded to their will in selecting someone from among them. But Herod and his sons have been able to sustain their rule only by the will of Caesar. This is the power of a foreign empire imposed upon us."

"Do you think, then," asked the rabbi, "that we have no obligation to pay taxes?"

The student, whose name was Jedediah, kept silent for a moment, trying to compose a response which he thought the master would judge well reasoned. "It does seem right to pay taxes for purposes that benefit the people," he said. "If the city's walls need repair, for example, that would be a beneficial purpose, because the city must be secure."

Hillel smiled. The young man felt the penetrating gaze of the sage's all-seeing eyes, but he maintained his confidence.

"So the tax must be intended to achieve legitimate ends," the master said. "But is the distinction between right and wrong purposes always obvious? Might not a king or an ethnarch or a Caesar perceive a purpose whose rightness is not apparent to his people?"

"It is...possible," Jedediah said, "but in that case, the king should be able to persuade his people that paying the tax is necessary."

"The king might persuade you by means which you would not find pleasant," said Hillel to the laughter of all in attendance.

Seated at the rabbi's side with the water skin he always kept at the ready to fill his master's cup, James observed how Hillel's wit aided him in cutting through his students' polemics. He had seen it often enough by now that he knew to expect the master to follow with a deeper point. He was curious about what it would be, and his eyes shifted in anticipation between Hillel and Jedediah.

For his part, Jedediah was not entirely amused at the small joke, which seemed to have been made at his expense. Intelligent but somewhat prickly, he had not been so long a disciple of the great Hillel that he couldn't still be wounded by a jibe from the master. And a certain air of pride about him was often commented upon by his fellows.

"Is fear of punishment then to be the only justification?" he asked with the merest edge of pique in his voice.

There were some rabbis to whom any hint of annoyance or sarcasm would be sufficient reason to have a student whipped or even expelled. But Hillel's attitude was different. While his tolerance of youthful boldness was not without limit, he encouraged his students to probe, as long as they stayed within the bounds of respectfulness.

"Punishment is not a thing to be ignored, Jedediah son of Eli," the rabbi said. "Are we not enjoined to maintain ourselves in a condition where we are free to perform our religious duties? I think one would not find it very conducive to the practice of Judaism or the study of Torah to be confined in a prison or chained with a gang splitting rock in a stone quarry. Likewise, one hardly fulfills one's family obligations in such circumstances. A man is responsible to more than his principles."

In the rabbi's words Jedediah glimpsed endless complexities behind the question of paying taxes, complexities he had not considered before. He felt his facile arguments stripped from him.

"Yes, Master," he said sheepishly and turned his eyes downward.

Once again the rabbi had made his students see a larger truth. This was a wise man—a sage in the purest sense—the kind of rabbi James hoped to become. Of course, there were many years ahead before James could attain to that, many years at the feet of a master.

But would it be *this* master? In these few months with Hillel, it had become clear to James how much of an effort it took for the great man to keep up his rigorous schedule of teaching, synagogue duties, and other related activities. Hillel involved himself deeply, not only in the lives of his students, but in those of the men and women who formed his synagogue congregation. He was available to them for counsel in their personal, family and even business problems. And he made a special point of closely overseeing the charitable programs carried on by the synagogue to serve the poor of Jerusalem.

The dignity of the poor was a thing especially close to his heart. A story was told of how, with his own money, Hillel purchased a horse for a man who had once been wealthy but had fallen on hard times, so that the fellow should not be deprived of the daily ride he took for his health. The rabbi even assumed payment of the man's servant. Indeed, sympathy for the plight of those struggling with want had been cultivated in his youth when Hillel had been poor himself, working as a woodcutter in Babylon to gain the money needed for study in Jerusalem.

The connection with carpentry was of mild interest to James, given his family background, but it was Hillel's tireless efforts that impressed. With all his other obligations, the great man somehow found time for learned pursuits. The crowning scholarly work of his life was nearly complete. This was a compendium of the written and oral Law, with rules for scriptural interpretation, all organized into six canons, or *orders*, designed to aid judges and lawmakers in their decisions, especially where the points at issue were ambiguous or the holy books silent.

Such a labor, in itself, would represent a lifetime of accomplishment. How did the master keep up these exertions? How long would his dedication be rewarded with continued life? And what would happen when he was no longer there? Assumedly, Gamaliel would take over the school. But would he prove to be the match of his grandfather? As a teacher, would he be as wise, and as a man, so inspiring? These things James wondered while he savored the experience of being in the presence of the great Hillel, for however long that experience might last.

*   *   *

It was late of an evening when James arrived home, after working with some of the other students distributing food to several needy families. Since early in his tenancy in the stone hut, he had taken his meals in the main house. Chava, wife of Joseph the tin merchant, had observed how James was attempting to subsist on vegetables, flat bread, and dried meat. Her motherly instincts were roused, and she insisted that the young man join them at table. And since she knew that James' studies and his work with the synagogue gave him an irregular schedule, she instructed the servants to provide for him no matter how late he might come in.

He touched the scroll of the commandment inside the copper-clad archway, opened the iron gate, and came into the court. Approaching the main house, James was taken with a small start to see a man standing in the shadows by a stack of copper slugs, part of a consignment recently delivered. At James' approach, the man emerged from the dark.

"James son of Joseph?" he said. "I was told you might be along."

The man's face, as well as James could make it out in the dim light, seemed familiar.

"Sir..."

"It is I, Lemuel, steward of Zacharias."

"Of course. Peace be with you, Lemuel. It is good to see you."

"You have changed, Master James."

"I suppose I have. So many years have passed since we met in Ein Kerem. How do you happen to be..."

"My master has dealings with your landlord."

"Ah, the caravans. Yes, I was aware. There are many deliveries. And Joseph has told me of their long association. I trust the honorable Zacharias is well?"

"You may judge for yourself. He is within."

"Zacharias is here?"

"And he would very much like to see you," said Lemuel, indicating the door to the house.

James nodded his thanks and went inside. There sat Zacharias, the famous priest and James' patron, with Joseph the tin merchant. The two men smiled at James' entrance.

"My lord, Zacharias," said James, bowing slightly.

The priest raised a hand in greeting. "May the peace of the Holy One, Master of the Universe, be upon you, kinsman," he said.

James was surprised, and rather pleased, that Zacharias had referred to him as his kinsman. "It is an honor to see you again, sir," James said, "and to see you looking so well. The last time we met, your voice was impaired."

"Yes. A most extraordinary situation," said Zacharias.

"James, my boy," said Joseph rising, "our honored friend is most interested to hear of your progress. And I have told him of the joy which Chava and I share at having you in our household. Please sit with us. I will have food brought out."

Feeling slightly abashed at being the focus of such warm feelings, James seated himself on a cushion beside the low table. He inquired as to the health and wellbeing of Elizabeth and the child John.

"They are fine," said Zacharias. "The boy grows daily. What a delight it is to have a little one about. It makes me feel young, though I know that is only an illusion in which the Holy One indulges me."

"You will always be young," said Joseph, calling over his shoulder while heading for the kitchen to arrange for James' meal.

"Let us say that maintaining my youth requires more of an effort every day," said Zacharias.

James smiled.

The priest looked earnestly into his eyes. "Your father and Mary are well? And the boy Jesus?"

"To the best of my knowledge, sir, yes. It has been some time since I've seen them, of course."

"Of course—your studies with my friend, Hillel."

James nodded.

"Good reports of you."

This James found quite unwarranted. "Of me, sir? I attend my master," he said. "I strive to meet his needs. But I have not contributed very much to the discussions. I am still quite new."

"Hillel is a profound judge of character."

James didn't know what to say.

Joseph returned from the kitchen and seated himself at the low table. "Food will be taken out to the hut later."

"Thank you."

"And there will be some of those dates dipped in honey and nuts, of which you are so fond."

A smile of pleasure from the hungry young man.

"Our student," Joseph said to Zacharias, "a good eater."

There proceeded talk about what subjects were currently being discussed in the school of Hillel, how coming from small, remote Nazareth, one adjusted to life in Jerusalem, and James' recollection of being fascinated by the volumes in Zacharias' library. Then conversation turned to the caravans. James was intrigued to hear that, with the press of age, Zacharias was seeking to reduce his day-to-day involvement in the business and so Joseph would be taking an active role in the scheduling and managing.

James knew that Joseph had been involved in trading since coming to Jerusalem from his boyhood home of Arimathea. Zacharias had schooled him in the complexities of buying, selling and transporting. He had also helped him to develop his metals-importation specialty. Now it appeared that Joseph would be an active partner. In fact, Zacharias had devised a plan by which Joseph would eventually acquire the entire business, with provision for the support of Elizabeth and John.

It became clear that Zacharias was essentially making arrangements for when he would be gone. Was illness upon him, such that he expected to die soon? The thought was distressing, since Zacharias had been responsible for the great opportunity James was now enjoying. Also, he knew that Mary and his father would be sad to think that this holy and generous man who had done so much to aid and protect them might be nearing the end of his life.

"With all of these new concerns you lay upon me," Joseph said rather wistfully, "the one thing I will miss is traveling. I love the Lord's city and, of course, my dear Chava and my children—the joy of my life. I have often wished for more time to spend with them. Still, it has been a great blessing to see new places."

"No doubt," said Zacharias. "But now the time has come to return the blessing with service to the Holy One and his people. Under our arrangement your wealth will be secure. You are now in a position to give of yourself in this way."

"Of course, of course..." Joseph stroked his beard in thought, and there was worry in his eyes. "My dear friend, are you really sure I am qualified?" he asked the priest.

"You have my complete confidence," said Zacharias. "You are a man of piety and considerable learning. You are respected throughout the community. And even the extensive travel—it has given you a view of the world, which is not without value. So many of our people have no sense that there is anything beyond Judea, or even beyond Jerusalem. I will make the strongest recommendation on your behalf."

James was confused now. Joseph and Zacharias seemed to be referring to something other than the caravans or the importing of metals. Perplexity showed on his face, and it caught Joseph's attention.

"Ah, my boy," said Joseph. "You do not know what we're talking about. Forgiveness, please. I will explain. The honorable Zacharias proposes to put my name forth for a seat on the Sanhedrin."

This took James aback. The Sanhedrin. The highest deliberative council in the land, of which Zacharias was a member.

"I will be stepping down," said Zacharias. "That will leave a vacancy which must be filled quickly, since the required membership of seventy-one must always be maintained."

"My congratulations, Joseph," said James. "What an honor that would be."

"Not congratulations just yet," said the merchant laughing. "To be proposed is one thing, to be elected another."

"I believe the moment is propitious," said Zacharias. "Those of us who have urged reform are much encouraged by Archelaus' removal of Joezer from the office of high priest. It has long been felt that he abetted corruption in the temple."

Joseph's face took on a wry smile. "Doesn't the prophet Jeremiah speak of the Holy One lavishing *choice portions upon the priests?*"

"The portions of Joezer and his circle have been a bit too choice," Zacharias said. "And their influence within the Sanhedrin has too long secured their advantages. But now we need to solidify, and over time to expand, our faction. We must bring in younger men—younger than myself, at any rate—who see the need for doing things differently. I will submit your name, and I believe I can garner enough support for your election."

James had the feeling at that moment that he was witness to an important event, or at least to the preparations for that event.

"My generation is passing from the scene," Zacharias continued. "Those who replace us must lay the groundwork for what I believe are great changes to come." He turned a penetrating look on James. "Do you not agree, my young kinsman?"

A half smile of secret understanding set itself on James' face. "There are...signs of change, my lord."

Joseph held out his hands before him in acceptance of Zacharias' will. "Well, I hope I live up to your expectations, old friend," he said, untouched by the shared knowledge to which James and Zacharias had just given quiet assent.

CHAPTER SEVENTEEN

You shall not take vengeance or bear any grudge against the sons of your own people, but you shall love your neighbor as yourself.

(Leviticus 19)

The first husband of Efrat had been a weaver who taught her the skills of the trade before dying young. Since they had no children, her husband's brother took her as his wife, on the principle that one brother should not leave another without descendents. The second husband was unable to provide the hoped-for offspring before falling to the same illness, which ran in the family. Efrat then married a third time, and this husband also died without fathering a child. These things took place in a village far down the Jezreel Valley, and Efrat then came to Nazareth to live with a kinswoman, who herself subsequently died.

To have endured such a series of misfortunes would have been bad enough. But town gossip twisted this tale of sadness in such a way that people came to see Efrat as an embodiment of the old story about a woman who buried seven husbands, all of them brothers. Some suspected Efrat might be cursed. While they did buy the woolen goods with which she supported herself, the townspeople kept a cautious distance in their dealings with the pathetic widow in order to avoid any sort of contamination or the possibility of the evil eye. Efrat was very lonely.

The actual facts of her life were known in the house of Joseph because she was a regular purchaser of wool from the flock of Judas and Simon. Sarah and Zipporah made it a point to greet her kindly in the market street and take time to speak with her. Such efforts were accepted in the town as courtesy toward a customer, but were not really approved.

When Mary heard about Efrat, she sought out the woman, brought her cakes, drew her into conversation, discussing her own days of weaving in the temple, and sat with her in prayer right in her market stall. This was noted, the initial reaction being that it was a very unwise thing to do. After it happened on several occasions, people began to wonder what sort of affinity the young wife of Joseph might feel toward this woman around whom calamity seemed to gather. Old conjecture about the timing of Jesus' birth was revived, particularly in light of the fact that there had been no subsequent children. Curiosity about whether Joseph was too old to give her more naturally raised the question of whether he had given her the one.

Then there was Jesus himself, an unusually quiet child who was rarely seen in the streets of Nazareth, and only in the company of his parents on the way to or from the synagogue. Was it Joseph who insisted on limiting the boy's play to the compound, the olive grove, and the sheep pasture? Or was it Mary, temple girl and daughter of the wealthy landowner, Joachim, who made sure her precious son never mixed with the ragged urchins of the town? In truth, the child was isolated, but for a reason quite different from anything the townsfolk might have assumed.

Zipporah's son, Noah, in one of his adventures of daring exploration, lost his balance and fell from the compound's wall. It was not such a fall as to endanger his life, but he was left sprawled on the ground outside the gate, screaming in pain. All in the household came running to find the boy with his leg bruised and misshapen, the broken end of a bone bulging under the skin.

Taken by compassion for his playmate and wishing to quiet his cries, Jesus knelt down and laid hands on the boy's leg. Noah continued wailing, if in childish fright as much as anything else. But when Jesus removed his hands, the leg no longer appeared distorted in shape, and eventually Noah ceased crying and stood without pain or difficulty. All the adults present glanced about at each other, then at what had been an obviously injured limb, then at Jesus. It had *looked* like Noah broke his leg. They *thought* this was what they had observed. But now they were unsure.

"Well...what a most...fortunate thing," said Joseph, who had been among those rushing out at the screams. Then he advised, "Let us keep this between ourselves." To which all agreed.

At that moment, a neighbor woman returning from the fields where she had taken her husband his midday meal, called out from the street, "Is the boy alright? I saw him fall, and the leg appeared badly bent."

"Oh...he is fine," Joseph answered. "No harm...after all. Peace be with you."

He took Jesus by the hand, and as Zipporah led Noah back inside the compound, he whispered to Mary, "If this is a gift which might be demonstrated again, we must guard against it being witnessed."

"Yes, my husband," she said, "you are right."

The neighbor had occasion to mention this curious happening to others in the town—how the boy's leg was bent at an unnatural angle until Mary's son touched it. The story might have been put down to simple misperception but for her insistence on how unmistakable the deformity had been. It made the rounds of the market street, coming eventually to the ears of Efrat, who questioned Mary about it the next time she saw her.

"We too believed the leg was broken," Mary said vaguely and with noticeable ill ease. "But now it looks like it wasn't."

The incident served to resolve an issue that had been troubling Joseph. Jesus was approaching the age when it would be appropriate for him to begin attending the synagogue school. In fact, given his aptitude for recognizing letters, words and even whole sentences—to which the family had by now long become accustomed—he could very well have been in the class already. But Joseph was worried about the effect such proficiency would have on the other pupils, as well as on their parents when they heard about how advanced he was.

Joseph determined not to start the boy in the school, but rather to ask the Rabbi Ezra to instruct Jesus privately. This, of course, would prompt the question: *Why?* So despite his reservations, he took the rabbi into his confidence about Jesus' origins.

Ezra was without words when Joseph finished laying out the story. The angelic messengers, the mystical pilgrims following the sign of the star, the escape to Egypt with the help of Zacharias, the healing of the boy, Noah—these and all the rest of it Joseph shared. Surely this answered some questions, such as those about the hasty marriage in Ein Kerem, for which no explanation had previously been given. But a divine child living within Joseph's walls, possibly Messiah himself? How could such a tale be accepted?

Yet how could the words of such a respected man be dismissed? This was Joseph the carpenter telling him these things, his friend and benefactor, head of a family with which Ezra had been intimately involved for years, father of James who was especially close to his heart.

"I know, Rabbi," said Joseph, "that this is hard to believe. Even my children had difficulty coming to peace with it. But I assure you it is all true. Zacharias is convinced that the hand of the Holy One is in this. And when you have gotten to know the boy, you will see he is unique."

"But...*Son of the living God?*" asked the rabbi, incredulously.

"That is the phrase Mary used," Joseph said. "And after all that has happened...and all we have seen...I think it is not inaccurate."

Ezra rubbed his forehead with the tips of his fingers, tracing circular patterns as he weighed the words he had heard. If he did not know Joseph as the praiseworthy man of faith he was, such assertions would ring of blasphemy. And that thought made him realize the risk Joseph had taken in sharing such a story. Whether or not the child Jesus had actually been sent by the King of the Universe, it was clear to the rabbi that Joseph believed it was so. If for no other reason, simply because it *was* Joseph's belief, the possibility had to be considered.

The rabbi sat silently, reflecting on the various incidents recounted. He decided to set aside—for now—the more exotic ones, such as angels appearing and foreign astrologers following visions.

"The boy...*reads*," he said, "at four years old, he reads?"

"He is able to speak all the words from the story of creation which Mary scribed out for the children to copy."

"He hasn't just committed them to memory and can recite? I have known many small children who can do that."

"Mary points to the words at random, and Jesus identifies them. It doesn't matter which she picks. And some passages he is able to read in their entirety."

Ezra shrugged indecisively and then sat considering once more.

"And you are sure the boy Noah's leg was broken?"

"The lower portion was at an angle almost like a knee joint. It looked as if the bone might break through the skin."

"And after Jesus touched it?"

"Straight."

"No pain?"

"Noah walked with complete ease. Later I saw him running about in the court. And what a blessing. The child might have been crippled for life, the injury was that pronounced."

The enormity of what Joseph was suggesting began to dawn on the rabbi, and anxiety seized him. It was no small thing to consider what the coming of a prophet might portend. The prophets of old had suffered greatly, even to the point of death. And while the holy books were not specific on the matter, one could imagine the implications for their families and others close to them.

Assuming the story was true, Joseph and Mary had already evaded the Royal Guard during Herod's search for the Bethlehem children. No wonder they wished to limit awareness of Jesus and his unusual abilities. But if the child had truly been sent from on high, could that fact really be contained? What if word should reach Archelaus or one of his brothers? Or the Roman authorities? Or the Zealots? With conditions in the country as tense as they were, even a suggestion that the Deliverer had come could cause any number of extreme reactions.

Now Ezra grasped the extent of the trust which Joseph was placing in him. His face was screwed up into something that was almost a grimace, indicating his grave concern. "I will teach the boy," he said. "I will see if I perceive the holiness in Mary's child which you so clearly do." He stroked his beard slowly, thoughtfully. "But Joseph," he continued, "I am sure you realize that...if the boy has some special destiny as you believe...if he is a prophet, or if he is actually Mess— Well... you must understand what it could mean, to him and to your entire household."

Joseph nodded his head with a solemnity that matched the rabbi's seriousness. "We are all aware, Rabbi. Mary and I have discussed this, both between ourselves and with my children. Everyone sees the risks. But if we have been favored by the Lord...called to advance His great purpose..."

"And if the boy does *not* have this destiny?" Ezra asked.

"Then we are all mad, Rabbi," said Joseph.

*   *   *

As Lucillus had suggested, restoration work on the home of Albus Drusus did lead to other projects in Sepphoris. There was an urgent need for skilled craftsmen to rebuild the city, particularly in light of the stated intention of the Tetrarch Antipas to spite the insurrectionists by making Sepphoris even more grand than it had been before. While a call went out around the empire for artists and artisans to come to Galilee, Joseph, with his established reputation and his Jewish crews, was already close at hand.

After the initial security restrictions were eased and free entry of Jews for day work was permitted, Joseph and Lucillus began hiring laborers in Nazareth and other nearby towns once again. Men were glad for the employment, but the wanton brutality with which the legions had answered the revolt left a very bad taste. The exclusion of Jews from permanent residence in the city was another irritant.

Lucillus was the first to become aware of this mood. He detected some resentment directed at him by several of the workers who were new to the crews and did not know he was a God-fearer. But while he had, many times before, encountered the reservations which Jewish laborers had about working with a Greek, he was surprised to hear unkind remarks about Joseph. This was different, and it indicated how deeply conflicted the men's feelings were. Indeed, a cloud of guilt hung over the projects and the Greek gold they earned. The expression, *blood money*, was uttered by one worker, who nonetheless accepted his pay.

Whether or not to apprise Joseph of this situation weighed on Lucillus. He had always been scrupulous in keeping his master informed of anything bothering the men, so that needs could be met and problems addressed before they became large. But he well understood how important it was to reestablish the Sepphoris trade, both for Joseph's family and for the families of all who depended on the Nazareth builder for their livelihoods.

He was reluctant to risk dampening Joseph's enthusiasm. But at the same time, he realized that the master's own attitude about the Sepphoris projects was not without conflict. Joseph had shared with Lucillus how his conscience had been pricked by James' question about serving the Greeks.

"What is the right in this, Lucillus?" Joseph had asked. "We are not free, true. Our country is oppressed and exploited. But is the blood of

Zealotry our only option? Is peace impossible? Is forgiveness an illusion?"

Lucillus' response was less than emphatic, but it may have been the only one possible. "I have been a slave, and I saw men die in their servitude," he had said to Joseph. "But I hoped for something better, and the day came when I was free. Perhaps hope is all we have to cling to. And is not hope a gift of the Holy One?"

Under the circumstances, Joseph had accepted that as an adequate, if not altogether satisfying, answer. Reflecting on the exchange, Lucillus decided he had to speak with Joseph about the feelings of the men. He took the opportunity one afternoon as they were walking the Sepphoris road on the way back to Nazareth.

Joseph was not surprised. "Make them understand that I am as torn as they are," he said, and looked away with a sigh. "But we all must provide for our families. Perhaps one day—if the Holy One wills it—we shall be able to do that in our own free land." He turned his face back to Lucillus with an expression of uncertainty. "I hope this does not sound too resigned, my friend."

"It is what I love about the Jews," Lucillus said. "You are a practical people, adaptable and persistent. Suffer anguish as you may, practicality reigns."

This brought a smile to Joseph's face. But in his heart he knew that a change had come upon the small world in which he lived his life. There was a distance now between the members of his household and those outside the family. And it was increasing. The two-year absence, the whisperings about Mary, the new work in Sepphoris, and now Jesus' private instruction with the Rabbi Ezra—it all stirred suspicion. Joseph no longer felt comfortable in his own town. Unease was upon him even when he went to the synagogue for prayers or Sabbath services. But what to do? There was too much which could not be spoken of outside the compound, too much the family had to guard.

He extended a hand to touch the shoulder of his assistant, this loyal and perceptive Greek from Carthage. "And tell the men this, Lucillus," he said. "Tell them that I honor their feelings and I pray for their trust."

Lucillus absorbed Joseph's words, which he knew were heartfelt. But then their quiet exchange was interrupted by the clopping of hooves.

They turned to see three mounted legionaries riding at a quick canter from the direction of Sepphoris, and they stepped to the side of the road to let them pass. Lucillus recognized from their uniform adornments that the trio consisted of a centurion, a principales, and what appeared to be an immunes, a practitioner of a specialized technical skill.

"I have noted over these months that there are fewer and fewer troops in Sepphoris," he said. "I assume the Romans think the city secure now."

"Yes," Joseph said, "apparently they don't consider us a threat with our augers and gimlets."

Lucillus chuckled. "I suppose not."

They arrived at Nazareth and continued on beyond the family compound, Lucillus heading for his home, and Joseph bound for the forge to consult with Joel the blacksmith about a new order of metal fittings. They crossed the square, passing some women drawing water from the well in preparation for the evening meal. Then they separated, each to his own destination, with a word of purpose to meet in the morning.

Joseph walked past the synagogue and then by the place that had been home to Joachim. Since the late-night return from Egypt, seeing that house always caused Joseph to reflect on the path his life had taken after agreeing to Joachim's impassioned plea for his daughter's care. Finally he was at the far end of the market street. As he approached the smithy, two young men emerged abruptly from an alleyway and positioned themselves, one in front of him, one behind.

"You are Joseph, the builder?" the one in front asked.

"Yes."

"You build houses in Sepphoris?"

"I build houses wherever people need houses built."

"You have...too many dealings with Greeks."

A feeling of threat made Joseph's muscles tighten and gave him a tingling sensation across his back. He turned to the right, so that now the young men were standing to his sides. "Who is to say how many dealings are too many?"

"There are some people who can say. They are aware of your business, and they are displeased."

"Are they displeased with the wages I pay to hard-working Nazareth

Jews?"

The confidence of Joseph's response made the young man hesitate. But then he said, "They would prefer you make the money elsewhere."

Joseph looked piercingly into his eyes. "Tell that to my men, whose families must be fed."

"No..." said the young man, now with a note of hesitation in his voice. "I will...tell it to *you*." He drew a wide-bladed knife from beneath his cloak. "Take this warning to heart, Joseph, or—"

"*Hey!*" The call came from in front of the forge. It was one of the legionaries who had passed Joseph and Lucillus on the road.

"What is this?" The soldier hurried forward, sword drawn. "Put up your weapon, Jew."

The two young men turned to look at the Roman. The one who had been behind Joseph felt a sudden surge of panic and drew out a sling. He inserted a stone into the pocket, swung it over his head, and then let one end go. The stone shot toward the soldier, glancing down off the bill of his helmet, and hit him in the eye.

The man yelped in pain, then called, "Centurion!"

This brought the two other soldiers out of the smithy. When they saw their comrade injured and a glint off the blade of the knife, they drew their swords and came running.

The first young man looked at his companion. "What have you done?" he said in horror. Then he seemed to collect his nerve briefly and turned back to Joseph. "Be warned, builder," he said, brandishing the knife, and struck Joseph in the stomach with the fist of his opposite hand.

Joseph was taken by surprise, though the blow was only hard enough to knock wind out of him and set him off balance. He began to stumble, but caught himself on one knee as the attackers ran away up the alley, the two Romans in pursuit.

Joseph stood again, then went to the man with the wounded eye now streaming blood down his face.

"Soldier, can you see? Are you badly hurt?"

The man held his hand to his face. "All I can see on this side is blood. Get me some water to wash it away."

Joseph led him inside the smithy where Joel was standing near his forge, busy with the harness on one of the Romans' horses.

"What has happened?" the blacksmith asked.

"Water, Joel. Quickly." Joseph got the man seated, and when Joel came with a basin, began to wash out his eye.

"Were those bastards trying to rob you?" the soldier asked, wincing in pain.

"No. They said they didn't like me having dealings with Greeks."

"Dealings with Greeks?"

"I build houses in Sepphoris."

The blacksmith, standing by, pointed a finger, shaking it up and down in realization. "Oh," he said, "that was it. Those two were in here earlier. They asked if Joseph the builder would be coming by today. So that is what they were up to."

Just then, the other two Romans came back. The soldier Joseph was treating tried to get to his feet.

"Sit, Principales," the centurion said.

"Yes, sir. Did you get a look at them, Centurion?"

"They eluded us in that tangle of alleys and wash hanging on lines." He turned to Joseph. "What happened here, Jew?"

Before Joseph could reply, the principales said, "Damned dagger-men, sir. They attacked this fellow because he builds houses for citizens of the empire."

"Zealots?" the centurion asked Joseph. "Have you been threatened before?"

"No, Centurion. I was quite surprised."

"Has there been trouble with Zealots in this village—what is this place called?"

"Nazareth," Joseph said. "We've never had such problems here. And...actually, Centurion, I don't think those boys were dagger-men. Not real ones, anyway. They seemed more scared than I was, especially when the principales came after them."

"They attacked a Roman officer," said the centurion. "They could be crucified for such an act." He turned to the wounded soldier. "Can you ride, Principales?

"Yes, sir."

"Good. We must be at Jerusalem, and there are at least two days' travel ahead." He turned back to Joel. "Is my saddle clasp fixed?"

"Yes, Centurion," the blacksmith said.

The centurion reached into his scrip and took out a coin which he tossed to Joel. "We have no time to deal with this now," the centurion said to Joseph. "If you should have any other difficulties here, report it."

"Yes, Centurion," said Joseph. Then he turned to his rescuer. "What is your name, Principales?"

"I am Cassius Longinus of Cappadocia," he replied, getting to his feet.

"Thank you, Cassius Longinus," Joseph said. "Your help to me was timely and much appreciated. Peace be upon you."

The three Romans mounted their horses and rode out of town on the road to the Jezreel Valley.

CHAPTER EIGHTEEN

If we do as our kin have done and refuse to fight the Gentiles for our lives and our ordinances, they will quickly destroy us from the earth.

(1 Maccabees 2)

ames felt an overwhelming sense of relief that his examination had been successful and he was deemed suitable to continue in the school of Hillel. He hadn't known what to expect in the questioning, so anxiety was a constant companion, increasing steadily during the weeks leading up to the big day.

The master's aim in a first evaluation was not so much to assess the substance of a student's knowledge as to measure a young man's progress in developing his capacity to reason during those early months in the house of study. By the appointed time of testing, James' confidence in his own ability to think was so shaken he barely felt able to find his way to the synagogue, much less to reason through an explication of the Law.

So it seemed like he had been blessed by Heaven when the master led their dialogue onto—of all things—the story of Cain and Abel. This was the very subject James had pondered so often and discussed at such length with the Rabbi Ezra. He felt his confidence return as he drew a connection between the offerings set before the Holy One by Adam's sons and the requirement to sacrifice first fruits at the altar of the temple.

So far, so good. But predictably, Hillel pressed further. Did James see anything in the story which might signify a deeper moral dimension of Cain's sin in killing Abel?

James stammered his way through a desperate search of his thoughts. Eventually he struck on the contrast between Cain's earthbound labors as a tiller of the soil and the traditional implications of leadership—

even kingship—associated with shepherding a flock. Perhaps the killing of Abel was made even more tragic in that it deprived Cain of his brother's more elevated influence? Maybe Cain would have been a better person, not just by refraining from an evil deed, but by embracing the possibility of self-improvement? The idea seemed vaguely plausible, and James offered it with as much conviction as he could muster in the moment.

Hillel and his grandson, Gamaliel, shared a glance, each smiling slightly at James' proposition, almost Greek in its philosophical intricacy. It was the kind of thought that might come out of Alexandria or one of the other centers of learning where western thinking had penetrated Jewish scholarship. Perhaps this was the influence of the Greek freedman whom James had mentioned to Gamaliel as having played such a key role in his earlier education.

Then the master raised a point over which James had puzzled for years. "This is a story, James son of Joseph, which suggests much about the moral standing of man," Hillel said. "So please tell me this: After the death of Abel, why is it, do you suppose, that the King of the Universe, who surely possesses all knowledge, would ask Cain where his brother had gone?"

James stood in silence for the merest instant, and then he had a thought which had never come to him before, or at least had never come with as much clarity.

"I think the Holy One wanted to give Cain a chance to confess what he had done," James said. "I think He wanted him to repent, because with the Lord, forgiveness is always possible."

There were many brotherly pats on the back when the master declared that James would now be counted among the accomplished students. But along with relief, James experienced a distinct flash of disappointment that he would no longer be responsible for helping Hillel stand and walk, for giving him water, and meeting his other basic needs. These tasks would now be passed on to another young man joining the class and filling the position of newest disciple.

In all, the day left James in a kind of haze. When the evaluations had ended, he made his way down into the lower city feeling spent from the weeks of heightened anticipation, the tension of a face-to-face dialogue with the master, and then the relief of knowing he had been favorably judged. By the time he reached the copper-trimmed archway of Joseph the tin merchant, he was exhausted. The prospect of dinner held less attraction than a quick departure into sleep. But he knew that sneaking into his hut would not be appropriate, since his landlord had expressed a great interest in hearing about the testing.

Joseph was in a lighthearted mood when he met his tenant in the front room of the big house. James suspected the merchant might have been taking his evening's wine in something other than its customary dilution or more than the usual quantity. Joseph embraced him warmly.

"Tell me, my boy," he said. "How did you fare with the great Hillel?"

James was unable to withhold his smile. "If it pleases you," he said, amused by Joseph's exuberance, "I will be renting your stone hut for awhile longer."

"Ah, such good fortune," Joseph said, clapping James on both of his shoulders. "What a day this is. As it happens, I myself have news. I have been elected to the Sanhedrin."

"That is wonderful," said James, genuinely excited.

"The voting was yesterday, and the announcement was to be held until the next Sabbath," Joseph said. "But word was passed to me this morning. It seems our friend, Zacharias, twisted enough arms and told enough tales. And what do you know—they voted for me."

"Oh, surely they chose well," said James. "You deserve this honor. You are a man of many accomplishments."

"Yes, well...the importance of my accomplishments remains to be seen. But Zacharias—bless his generous heart—has confidence in me. Now I must live up to his expectations."

"I have no doubt that you will."

James took a cup of wine at his landlord's urging, and Joseph called for food to "satisfy our hungry scholar." His wife, Chava, brought in a platter, and she offered her congratulations when Joseph told her of James' achieving a permanent place in the house of study.

"So now you, woman, have two great men under your roof," Joseph teased his wife, "Hillel's star pupil and me, a counselor of the people. You must treat us with greater respect."

"Bah!" said Chava, deflecting her husband's banter. "Nothing has changed. All I see are the same two hungry men, exactly alike—although the counselor of the people has a bigger belly."

Joseph slapped his hands together. "Ah, how the woman loves me," he said jovially.

James laughed at their playful give and take. Through the months he'd been part of this household he had observed the ease and warmth of the tin merchant's marriage, maintained despite years of extensive traveling. He also saw the love Joseph and Chava had for their children. It all put James in mind of his brothers and their wives, which brought pleasant memories of home. But it also stirred up old wonderings about what his childhood might have been like if his mother had lived.

When James had eaten enough to feel full, he begged indulgence to go to his bed.

"Of course, my boy," Joseph said. "An exciting day for both of us. You must be worn."

Then, at the doorway, as James was about to depart, Joseph put a hand on his young tenant's arm. "One thing, James," he said. "This new service on the council—I will be relying heavily on Zacharias for guidance, as you might suppose. But he thinks it best for me if his influence is not too overt. You see, he has spoken out on various matters that cry for reform, and in the process raised some resistance. It is his wish that I, as a new member, should not be tarred with any resentments that accrue to him.

"This being the case," Joseph continued, "I might call upon you for some help—if you are so disposed, my young friend."

"Of course," said James. "What sort of help?"

"Well, for one thing, it would be useful to have a trusted man who can transmit information discreetly between Zacharias and myself," said Joseph. "Particularly so, if that fellow is bright and can provide me with his own impressions of how the honorable Zacharias reacts to the questions on which I seek his judgment. You have Zacharias' trust, and you have mine. You would be a perfect conduit between us."

James was honored by the request but concerned about one point. "I...would be delighted to do what I can," he said, "but there would be limits on the time I can devote. My obligations to Master Hillel and my duties at the synagogue—"

"I don't think we need worry much about that," Joseph said. "Master Hillel may no longer involve himself directly in Sanhedrin affairs, but he follows developments closely, and he shares Zacharias' view about the need for improvements. In any event, he may see the value of your service, both in aiding us and in preparing you for the brilliant future that lies ahead of you."

Having only just received confirmation that he would even continue as a disciple of Hillel, James was rather less certain that the master assumed he had a *brilliant future*. But that was something he could hardly bring himself to think seriously about at the end of this exhausting day. He departed Joseph with an exchange of good wishes, and set off in search of sleep, the desire for which was rapidly overtaking him.

*   *   *

The next morning found James heading for the temple, refreshed after a good night's slumber and basking in the satisfaction that yesterday was behind him. He observed the hustle and bustle of the lower city coming to life, the air filled with the cries of vendors hawking their wares to women out for an early round of the shops and stalls. He entered the temple through one of the south-wall gates under the Royal porch, and was ascending the stairs to the upper level when he encountered his fellow student, Jedediah.

"Peace be with you, Jedediah son of Eli," he said in a sprightly tone that echoed his spirits. "I trust you have recovered from our ordeal of yesterday? Praise be to the Holy One that we both did well."

Jedediah, who apparently did not share his mood, made no reply. Instead, his mouth twisted into an expression of annoyance, and after a moment of tense silence, said, "I have endured three of these evaluations, James son of Joseph, and I have liked each one less than the one before."

"They are very trying," James said. "I was wracked with worry for days."

Jedediah stopped abruptly on the stairs. "And why should we be so wracked?" he said. "Cannot Master Hillel see that we are progressing in the studies? Why are we put through such a trial twice each year?"

James shrugged. "It is a requirement."

"It is a humiliation," Jedediah replied, "and we get enough of that in the class."

Such a display of acrimony was surprising, and seemed to James uncalled for. But he had often noted Jedediah's strong sense of pride and the quickness with which it became wounded.

"I do not think the master wishes to humiliate us," James said, attempting to sooth his colleague. "Rather...I think he is preparing us for when we are in the position of having people turn to us for our insights and advice. A rabbi must be confident in his own judgment and make his thoughts understood."

"Perhaps," Jedediah said, only partially placated. "But sometimes I wonder at the worth of this whole business. Every day we sit parsing the fine details of the Law and squeezing the most abstruse moral precepts out of the holy writings. Meanwhile, the land is trampled by foreign intruders, Jews are crushed into the dirt. What does wordplay with the master really matter in the face of such injustice?"

This unexpected turn in the conversation brought an image of the Sepphoris crucifixions to James' mind. "I have seen Roman cruelty, Jedediah," he said. "I have seen it at close hand, and I know what our people have suffered."

His classmate's curiosity was aroused.

"But," James continued, "the people need leaders, and that is what Master Hillel is helping us to become. So—"

"Yes, yes, of course you're right," said Jedediah with sudden interest. "Tell me, James, what is this cruelty you have seen?"

James wavered for a second, not eager to dwell on the chilling experience. Then he said, "My town, Nazareth of Galilee, is close to the city of Sepphoris where the revolt took place. When Quinctilius Varus sent in his legions from Syria, they rounded up most of the Jews and either sold them as slaves or crucified them—with scant regard to whether they actually took part in the attacks. All the men of Nazareth were forced to witness the executions so that we would spread word of how dangerous it is to disturb the...*peace of Rome.*"

"Well then..." said Jedediah, "you *have* seen Roman cruelty. You understand the injustice that weighs so heavily upon us."

James' eyes fell. "Yes, I am afraid I do."

"It must have been a terrible thing to see."

"It was."

"Interesting. Interesting." And with that, Jedediah turned away to climb the remaining stairs. "Interesting."

James looked up and watched him disappear into the central corridor. *Strange fellow,* he reflected—a thought he'd had several times before. Jedediah was bright and imaginative, a scholar of sufficient merit to have earned a place in the house of Hillel. But he was older than most of the others in the class, and sometimes his heart seemed to be elsewhere.

As James neared the far corner of the colonnade where Hillel's group met, he was approached by Gamaliel.

"James son of Joseph," the master of students called.

James turned at the sound of his name. "Peace be with you, Rabbi."

"My congratulations once again on your fine showing," Gamaliel said, gesturing James apart from the accumulating knot of students. When there was sufficient privacy, he said quietly, "You may feel free to deal with any messages which might need to be conveyed. Return to class when your errands are complete. Just try to let me know if you will be gone for any extended times." He turned and walked away.

How unexpected. Someone had consulted with Gamaliel about his being the carrier of messages. Evidently, this was what his landlord had meant when he said not to worry about the commitment of his time to Hillel or the synagogue.

*   *   *

It was an impossible hope on Joseph's part that word of the attack in the market street would not get back to his household. The incident had been observed by several people, even though it occurred late in the day when business was already completed in most of the stalls. All of Nazareth was buzzing over the incident by next morning. Variations of the rumor described everything from a mild altercation to the bloody death of the carpenter at the hands of a knife-wielding gang of bandits. In most versions at least a full squad of legionaries had come to Joseph's aid.

The family was shaken. Mary was emphatic in insisting that her husband should not leave the compound unaccompanied. The others agreed, despite Joseph's protest that he didn't believe the attack had been a serious effort, and anyway, others in the family could just as well be targets if someone really held a grudge.

"Simon or Judas could be assaulted in the pasture," he said.

"That may be, Father," Josis replied, "but you are head of the family business and the one whom people first think of as dealing with Greeks. And you've already had one confrontation."

Lucillus suggested that Nachum accompany the master making business calls in town as well as when traveling to and from Sepphoris. "Even Zealots would be loath to tangle with him. He is a sweet soul, but he is a bull."

It took awhile, but Joseph finally agreed, with the proviso that if he was to be guarded, similar precautions must be taken for all. So it was decided that Nachum would watch over the master and also accompany the wives on their visits to the market street. When Nachum had to be with Joseph, one of the brothers would go with the women. Children would be kept within the walls, except for the sons of Judas and Simon when they were needed to help with the sheep or the olive grove, and then they would be with at least one of their fathers. Jesus would always be accompanied to the synagogue for his lessons with the Rabbi Ezra.

"How long do you think this must go on?" Joseph asked Lucillus.

"As long as caution dictates," his assistant advised.

"And what about you, my friend? Aren't you in danger?"

"I think not," said Lucillus. "To those who know me, I am a God-fearer. And to those who don't know me, what is the value in killing a Greek who works for a Jew? If I wished to frighten Jews out of dealing with pagans, I would kill the Jew."

Joseph glanced at Lucillus through slitted eyes, one side of his mouth turned up in wry amusement. "Your adventures in the Roman world have given you a fascinating shrewdness," he said. "As the old expression goes: *gentle as a dove, but wise as a serpent.*"

"I strive to do my best, Master."

In spite of Joseph's unease with being guarded, he determined to accommodate himself to Nachum's constant presence for the sake of the family's peace of mind. Nachum, for his part, approached his new assignment with the utmost diligence, constantly scanning the streets for any suggestion of threat wherever he ventured with the master. So serious was he—and so conspicuous—that Joseph asked if he might be a bit more restrained in his watchfulness.

"Please try not to scowl," Joseph said. "I think you are beginning to frighten people."

"Sorry, Master," Nachum replied. "I will try to look friendlier."

The attack on Joseph did have one beneficial effect. It served to remind people of their respect for the Nazareth builder, and even more so, the importance of his dealings with the Greeks. There was no denying the dependence of so many families on that trade, discomfiting as it may have been. Indeed, the prospect of losing this source of local wealth was most unsettling.

And wasn't that the dilemma faced by an entire nation? Jews hated the legions, cursed the imperial taxes, and longed to cleanse daily life of pagan influences. But Caesar brought them the world's handiwork and opened markets for their own. A web of roads connected the disparate lands of a vast empire, and a great net of secure sea lanes had turned the Mediterranean into Rome's lake. Thus, it was possible for goods and gold to move in all directions.

Industrious Jews had learned to use these assets effectively. Clanship and business ties linked all communities of the Dispersion, making Jewish families prominent in commercial affairs to an extent that far exceeded their numbers in the empire. But this very success divided the people as well. Aramaic-speaking Jews of the homeland disdained the accommodations made to a pagan world by the Greek-speaking Jews of the Dispersion. And the worldly Greek speakers bemoaned their recalcitrant brothers who refused to accept life as it was in the day of Caesar. Such differences didn't stop either side from doing business with the other, but they made for ongoing frictions.

Those in the Dispersion who were perceptive understood why the Jews of Palestine felt themselves so besieged. Since the return from exile, the people had been seared by wars and foreign invasions, torn by internal rivalries, and oppressed by rulers of dubious legitimacy. Now they not only faced Caesar's rapacious taxes, they had to bear with a half-Jew vassal monarchy whose corruption reached into the temple itself.

No wonder they guarded their religious traditions, clung tightly to long-set devotional practices, and defended ancient teachings against even the minutest deviation. And no wonder that—despite being a warm and hospitable people, given both by habit and by scriptural warrant to welcoming strangers—the Jews of Palestine were deeply suspicious of ideas considered novel and resentful of anyone seen as willing to compromise.

This outlook was held to an extreme by the Zealots, as it appeared Joseph's experience had demonstrated. The dagger-men dedicated themselves to freeing the Jewish nation. Yet attacks on Jews showed that they were not above drawing the blood of those very people in whose name they claimed to act. Had Zealotry come to small, out-of-the-way Nazareth? If the dagger-men had attacked Joseph, who might be next?

Yet Joseph couldn't shake the impression that what happened to him was not Zealot work. Oh, it was possible that his assailants were simply new to the business of inspiring terror. Perhaps intimidating a carpenter had been some kind of training or initiation. Either could have been the case, Joseph had to admit.

Still, the whole thing was so poorly conceived. Zealots were known for decisive action, even if it proved futile in its long-term effects. But these two young men had seemed so tentative. Even if the assault hadn't been interrupted by the Roman soldier, what did they hope to achieve? And what of their weapons, a sling and a wide-bladed knife that looked better suited to cutting vegetables than carrying out an assassination? The entire incident somehow didn't ring true.

For the time being, however, Joseph would have to live with the security arrangements set in place, if only to satisfy his family.

*   *   *

Well into the night by now, James returned from the small house near the amphitheater where Zacharias resided during periods of temple service. This was his first visit to the priest's city quarters, and he had been struck by the simplicity of the dwelling, compared with the sprawling villa in Ein Kerem. He entered the gate of Joseph the tin merchant, walked up the center path, noticing a new consignment of metal ingots stacked along the one side, and admitted himself into the main room of the house.

His landlord peered up from a stack of scrolls and parchment sheets that littered a work table recently acquired for the correspondence that tasked a counselor of the people. "What says my honored friend about this new proposal?" he asked.

"Zacharias has reservations," said James.

"So have I. What are his?"

James found a stool, pulled it up near the table, and sat.

"He appreciates that because the temple sits on its own mount it is somewhat isolated from the commercial districts," James said. "So it is no doubt inconvenient for people coming from outside of the city to exchange their Caesars heads and other pagan money for coins that are ritually pure and suitable for giving. But this idea of permitting money changers to set up within the court troubles him. He pointed out that there was no allowance for such vendors in Herod's original plan for the rebuilding of the temple, and such a thing has never been done before."

Joseph looked unhappy. He stroked his beard in thought. "It is ironic that, in my first session on the Sanhedrin, I find myself standing against a proposed change. This measure is being put forth as a reform—*for the convenience of the people.*"

"Zacharias sees the same irony," James said. "But he is afraid that once the temple grounds are thrown open to commerce, there will be no limits to what can be transacted. He predicts that merchants will be selling sacrifice animals right inside the temple walls."

"Yes, yes," Joseph said resignedly. "As a man of business, it pains me to admit it, but he is right. The trade could be lucrative."

"He also questions the motives of some who are proposing this," said James. "Surely the bankers want it. They make no pretense about their self-interest. But he distrusts the priests on the Sanhedrin who are most enthusiastic about the idea."

"Their motives are no mystery to me," said the tin merchant. "This is an opportunity to skim a nice bit of cream for the temple priesthood."

James smiled. "I think Zacharias agrees with you on that, but he didn't wish to impugn his colleagues quite so directly."

Now Joseph smiled. "Zacharias is a kind man. But he knows as well as I do how his brothers on the priest council sit with their mouths watering for any new source of income."

"Well," said James, "perhaps you could propose that fees generated by the exchange of monies be applied to a special fund—assistance to the poor, maybe? It might help to discourage this move while it avoids putting you in the position of opposing the measure directly."

A snicker came from the tin merchant. "Your time with Hillel has been well spent, James," he said. "You are becoming very subtle."

This messenger function had proven useful. Zacharias' advice, transmitted through James, had helped the new counselor find his footing in the early weeks. But Joseph was mindful of James' primary obligation to Hillel. He tried to schedule these errands in the late evenings or the very early morning hours, depending on Zacharias' availability. In that way he didn't divert the young man too much from his duties at the synagogue or his time in the house of study.

From James' point of view, this was a rare opportunity to observe the inner workings of the Sanhedrin, as well as to get more closely acquainted with his benefactor, Zacharias. In a way, he was becoming a sort of adjunct to the household in Ein Kerem. On his several runs, he had been welcomed warmly and fed amply. Elizabeth would pepper him with questions about Mary and Jesus, on which he unfortunately had little to say, being largely out of touch with the family. And he always managed to find a few minutes to spend with the boy John, which called up memories of happy days in the Nazareth compound.

James also enjoyed being in the confidence of his landlord. He was beginning to discern, behind Joseph's good humor, a great wealth of worldly experience and a considerable depth of human understanding. Zacharias was right that the years of doing business in foreign lands had been excellent preparation for the wheeling and dealing of the council.

And though Joseph was new in his office, his characteristics were being noticed by some of the other members. A few whose eyebrows had arched disdainfully at the prospect of a *tin merchant* serving on the exalted body, when Zacharias first put forth his name, now were at least willing to give the benefit of the doubt. James felt a vicarious pride in that.

The one aspect of this service which James found disturbing was his realization of how deeply ran the people's animosity toward the temple leadership. Growing up, James, like any Jewish child, had revered the temple as the Lord's dwelling place on earth and viewed with a certain awe those who conducted its sacred rites. That these were men of piety and holiness was beyond his questioning. And if he had considered it possible for human frailty to be found among the priests and Levites, his assumption would have been that such flaws were rare, quickly recognized, and cleansed with the utmost meticulousness and contrition.

Now he was privy to a seemingly endless litany of complaints and resentments over temple corruption, many of which found their way to Joseph's new table. James was beginning to understand the extent to which the nation's religious life was manipulated by the Roman occupiers, by Archelaus, and by various other actors within the royal circle. It was becoming clear what a staggering amount of wealth flowed through the temple coffers, as well as how many of the leading priestly families took their cut.

The situation was as intractable as it was distorted. Hadn't Archelaus sacked the high priest, Joezer, only to replace him in that office with Joezer's own brother? What a dousing that had been to the hopes of the reform element. James had not yet fully come to grips with his own disillusionment.

Viewed in this perspective, the proposal to admit the money changers seemed entirely logical, indeed inevitable. James realized that, as a new member of the Sanhedrin, Joseph would have minimal influence on the council's deliberation. Established protocols would make it unlikely that he would get the chance to speak more than a few words on the matter—if that. The most he could do was vote with the opposition.

"The real question for me now," said Joseph, "is whether voting *No* will simply tag me as a troublesome newcomer, an upstart to be disregarded and distrusted."

"Or a man of conviction?" James said.

"Can junior members have conviction?"

"I think Hillel would say that, without conviction, there is no point to serving on the Sanhedrin."

"No doubt he would—as would Zacharias, for that matter." Joseph pushed his seat back from the table to stand. "So I will vote against this proposal, although it will pass anyway," he said smiling. "I may as well accustom myself to futility early in my tenure. There are bigger fights ahead, to be sure. Meanwhile, my young helper, you need some dinner. To the kitchen."

*   *   *

James was in the temple next morning, as clear-eyed as could be expected after his long night of consultations and message carrying. Gamaliel noted less involvement in the discussion than was typical of James and assumed he had been on another of his nocturnal errands. Sluggish as he was, the subject of the day did prompt James' interest, if not his active participation. The question at issue was under what circumstances divorce could be permitted. Hillel laid out his criteria, drawing distinctions with those maintained by the rival school of Shammai.

Divorce was anathema to the Shammaites, who recognized adultery as the only possible justification for severing such an essential bond. Hillel's view, on the other hand, was that as long as it wasn't simply being used as a pretext for abandoning a wife, and when appropriate measures were put in place to ensure the woman's sustenance, divorce could be permitted for what he called *serious* reasons.

He was as pained as anyone when marriages broke down, Hillel said in answer to questions about the rationale behind his view. But weren't the implications of a total ban on divorce obvious? Even the Shammaites admitted that their strict position removed an essential curb on wifely misbehavior. And didn't this place women in peril? Wouldn't husbands be more inclined to beat their wives, perhaps severely, if the ultimate legal corrective was unavailable?

Several points were raised in the dialogue on which James would have liked clarification. But this morning he found it difficult to muster the energy to ask. His detachment was hardly unique. Students often had to work long hours to support themselves in their discipleship. The master frequently found himself looking into blood-shot eyes and vacant morning expressions. It was a tribute to Hillel's skill as a teacher that he was able to engage sleep-deprived minds as well as he did.

At the end of the morning session, James was on his way down the stairway, still tired but by now somewhat clearer in his thoughts. His fellow student, Jedediah, was at the bottom, the strap of a leather bag slung over his left shoulder.

"James," he called. "Have you a plan for your midday meal?"

"Only to go home," James answered.

"Perhaps you might join me." Jedediah held the bag out in front of him. "I have extra. We can find a quiet place to enjoy the day."

Such an invitation was without precedent, Jedediah normally being firmly disinclined toward chumminess. And James had noted several recent occasions when Jedediah was absent from class altogether—which he had attributed to demands of work.

"This is the day the Lord has made," said James with a wave of the hand to indicate acceptance. "Let us exult and rejoice in it."

They found a shaded spot in a cluster of low fruit trees near the city wall, shared prayers, and sat to eat. From the bottom of the leather bag Jedediah drew out flat breads and a pot of spiced bean paste to spread on them. There was also a small skin of wine and two wooden cups.

Pouring wine into one of the cups, Jedediah said, "I was interested in the remark you made recently about crucifixions at Sepphoris." He handed the cup to James. "You said you were forced to witness them?"

James took a sip of wine. "Yes," he said. "All the men of my town were marched at spear point on the road that runs from Nazareth to the city. Crosses and frameworks were set up along either side. The legionaries made quite a show of their brutality. They were intent on impressing us. They wanted us to speak of this horror we had seen to anyone who would hear."

Jedediah poured himself a cup of wine, then handed a flat bread to James. "It must have been a very jarring experience," he said.

"It...was the stuff of nightmares," James replied with a noticeable catch in his voice. "I really don't like to think about it."

His companion nodded solicitously. "I am sorry to call up painful memories," he said. "But this is the cruelty our people live with."

"Yes, it is," James said tersely, spreading bean paste with a wooden paddle.

A silence hung between them, and then Jedediah said, "Someday our land will be free."

"Someday," said James.

"When Messiah comes," Jedediah said.

"That is our hope," said James.

He had stuck the paddle into the bean paste. Jedediah took it and began to scrape up some paste for his own bread.

"There are people who work to hasten the day," Jedediah said.

James glanced up from his food. "Messiah will come in the Lord's own time."

"Of course, of course—blessed be His holy name. Still...there are things which can be done in advance. Things to...prepare the nation. To...make straight the way."

Was there a point to such observations, which surely made for uneasy luncheon chatter? Then too, had there been a point to Jedediah's invitation beyond the simple offering of food?

"Much of what has been done in the past involves violence," James said. "And as my father observed at the time, it was violence that brought on even greater violence. The insurrectionists attacked the armory in Sepphoris. The Romans responded."

"But whose violence really came first?" Jedediah asked. "Was not the attack on Sepphoris a response to the exploitation of our land and the violence done to our people? Caesar has held us in bondage for a long time. Roman injustice has deep roots, and it is continual."

That point was certainly beyond dispute.

"True," James said. "And I will say that what I witnessed on the Sepphoris road made me think about resistance in ways I had never thought before. I understand why some take up arms against Rome. Men's hearts burn for freedom and justice. Direct action has its appeal, no doubt. But the question is: Can resistance succeed? If blood is to be spilled—and it surely will be—is it merely to be spilled in vain? I am not convinced that resistance can accomplish anything beyond more suffering and heartache."

Jedediah took another sip of wine. "That is a fair and honest view," he said. "But of course, it depends on what kind of action is taken. And even when results are limited, action can still serve useful purposes. It can inspire the oppressed to hope for better times ahead. And it can remind the oppressor that there are limits to his own freedom to act. Those things, in themselves, are worthwhile."

James tried to read the expression in Jedediah's face. It was a faraway look and quite inscrutable.

"Perhaps so," he said. "I admit that my mind is not settled on the question. I wonder what Master Hillel would say about the effectiveness of violence. He is a man of peace."

Jedediah responded in a voice with little inflection, the inscrutable look unchanged. "A man of peace, yes... And a great survivor."

An odd remark. James felt the slightest bit disturbed by it. He was somehow pricked by a need to defend their rabbi.

"Hillel has never hesitated to speak the truth or stand on principle in any forum," he said. "That is no small thing in the conditions under which we live. No one can question his courage."

Then Jedediah seemed to snap out of his detachment and spoke with greater attentiveness. "As I never would, let me assure you," he said earnestly.

After an awkward pause, conversation turned to the morning's discussion of divorce. James acknowledged the master's explanation about needing to discourage husbands from using physical force against their wives. But he observed that, should he ever marry, he could not imagine divorcing.

"Marriage should be lifelong," he said.

Jedediah's eyes opened wide in a mockingly shocked way. "James," he said teasingly, "James, James, James—I pray the master never finds out that you, of all people, might grant that Shammai has a point."

James laughed. "Perish the thought," he said.

Amiable as Jedediah was being, the pleasantness of this midday interlude had somehow been used up. For James a question remained as to why his fellow student had suddenly become so uncharacteristically sociable. And this peculiar interest in James' experience on the Sepphoris road, what accounted for that?

But then, as he'd observed before, Jedediah was a strange fellow.

CHAPTER NINETEEN

How beautiful you are, my darling!
Oh, how beautiful! Your eyes are doves.

(Song of Solomon 1)

One wall of the booth where Efrat the weaver sold her cloth in the market street consisted of a tightly interlaced wicker screen which had been made by the occupant of the next stall, the basket maker, Uri. Techniques for creating baskets not being dissimilar from Efrat's craft, she admired the quality of the workmanship and thought the partition an appropriate surface against which to display her own wares. She wished the opposite side of her stall was also made of wicker—it was wood—and she had inquired of Uri about making a matching screen to put there. They discussed an exchange of merchandise, but had never come to actual terms.

A secondary benefit of the wicker was that it permitted passage of the breeze, which on humid days in Galilee was a blessing. It also permitted passage of sound, and so the chatter and dickering that took place in Uri's stall made their way readily to the ear of Efrat. This she considered a small compensation for being largely avoided by Nazareth folk. If she could not share actively in the life of the town, she could at least satisfy some of her curiosity about people's comings and goings.

A surprising amount of local gossip and private knowledge regularly came to Efrat's attention through Uri's wicker screen. If she was a malicious sort—and if her situation was such that she interacted more fully with others—she could do serious damage to some people's reputations. Things being as they were, she kept her own counsel.

Except with Mary. The young woman's kindness and girlish charm prompted a loquaciousness otherwise unseen in Efrat, who had come to anticipate Mary's visits eagerly. And while Joseph's wife was not disposed to seek out gossip—and in fact she sometimes found it necessary to change the subject when Efrat's tales veered in calumnious directions—Mary appreciated the weaver's alertness to what people in the town were thinking and talking about. Given the family's circumstances, that information had value.

So it was that Efrat felt herself filled with excitement over a bit of news which she expected would bring great relief to her friend's heart. And she was delighted to spot Mary perusing the goods of a seller on the opposite side of the market street, accompanied by Nachum. When Mary finally stopped by, Efrat gestured for her to sit and bend an ear closely.

"I have heard something important," Efrat whispered.

"Oh? What is that?"

"The attack on your husband was a hoax."

"It was not real?"

"It was intended merely to frighten. The two boys who did it were hired for the task."

"But what could be the reason for such a thing?"

"Because of what Joseph builds—for the *Greeks*. I heard talking in the booth of Uri the basket maker."

"Who—" Mary stopped herself from asking the obvious question. "Efrat, please don't tell me who it was. I don't want to know. If it was a neighbor, I wouldn't wish to place blame or harbor resentment."

Efrat felt a distinct flash of disappointment at not being able to reveal the identity of the plotter. She had so hoped to regale her friend with that juicy fact.

"Just tell me *why* it was done," Mary said, "if you know the purpose behind the hoax."

Efrat struggled with her conflicted feelings, reluctantly contenting herself with being able to pass on what information Mary would accept. She cleared her throat and continued whispering. "It was Sepphoris, of course. The— The...*person*...was upset over what the legionaries had done there. The crucifixions. He wanted to take his anger out on someone, and good sense told him it had better not be on the Romans. He said to Uri that he paid a couple of boys—nephews from another town—to come and frighten Joseph. He figured that if Joseph stopped working for the Greeks it would be harder for Sepphoris to be rebuilt. But after the boys were nearly captured— Of course, he could not have known those soldiers would be inside the smithy. After that, he felt guilty about almost getting his nephews into terrible trouble. You know what would have happened to them if they'd fallen into the hands of the legionaries."

"They would have been crucified for attacking one of the officers."

"That is what Uri told him. And then...*the man*...said he felt guilty about the whole thing and that it was probably a stupid idea in the first place. He said he had nothing against Joseph, really. He was just angry at the Romans. He wished he'd never had his nephews do it."

"Well," said Mary, "I hope those boys keep out of Nazareth, because other people saw them and might be able to identify them. Then the Romans could decide to look further into this matter, and it would be tragic if two young men lost their lives over a foolish stunt."

"And the one who put them up to it as well," said Efrat, still struggling with her desire to reveal the name.

"Yes, and him too," Mary said. "It would be tragic indeed."

*　　*　　*

"Do you think she knows what she's talking about?" Joseph asked.

Mary gave that some thought. "Efrat is perhaps...a bit overly fixed on affairs of the street," she said. "But please realize, my husband, that she is a woman much rejected. These little scraps of second-hand experience are all she has, and that is a sad thing. But she possesses a sharp ear, and in some ways, listening in on other peoples' lives has made her quite wise. Efrat is a source I trust."

Joseph rubbed his hands together, cracking his knuckles. "I wish you had let her tell you who was responsible," he said. "After the anxiety this incident has caused in the household, I—"

"Do you really wish that information, Joseph?"

He looked into her youthful face with its innocent but knowing countenance which by now had become so familiar to him.

"Hmmmm..." A crooked expression came upon his own face, a pinched smirk with one eyelid slightly drooped. "I will live by your advice," he said, "wise daughter of Joachim. The town is small, and we have all been touched by Roman cruelty. Perhaps forgiveness is what's called for in these times."

Mary's eyes fell demurely, and a soft smile crossed her lips. "As you say, my husband."

*   *   *

Lucillus maintained an unexpected reserve about Efrat's revelation.

"Do you not see it as good news?" Joseph asked, surprised at the lack of enthusiasm. "I thought you would be pleased that I was right and this was not the work of insurrectionists."

"Oh, I am pleased about that." His face seemed to suggest otherwise.

"So...then?"

Lucillus' finger traced the seam between two planks in the surface of the table. "It is, of course, a relief that your life was not in actual danger," he said. "But—hoax or not—someone in town thought to make Joseph the carpenter a target of their anger. In other words, someone took it into his mind that you are complicit in the crimes of the Roman occupiers, merely because you build their houses. If such a thought could occur to one of your humble neighbors in little Nazareth, perhaps it could also occur to someone with the actual means to do you harm. After all, it happened once already."

He raised a hand to forestall Joseph's objection. "I understand that we now know the story to be false. But most people don't. They see this incident as a failed attempt. And the instigator, whoever he is, will hardly be inclined to come forth and correct that wrong impression. Not with the possibility of reprisals from the Romans over injuring that officer. So it isn't impossible to imagine someone else hearing of the attack and deciding to finish the job others left incomplete."

"We cannot live our lives in fear," Joseph said, "especially knowing that nothing actually happened."

"I understand. But I would hope that you are not so relieved by the news from this weaver woman that you disregard caution. Then too—"

He set his palms flat in front of him, fingers spread, forearms on the tabletop. "Perhaps there is a blessing here. The protective measures prompted by this hoax do provide a certain rationale for the aloofness people observe in your family. And don't forget, you have more than one reason for setting yourselves apart from the rest of this community. I am speaking, of course, about Jesus—his extraordinary situation and his remarkable gifts. Maybe it is not a bad thing if townspeople attribute the separation of Joseph's household to concerns about safety, rather than assuming you have something to conceal. It could be for the best if the boy grows up less observed by neighbors than would otherwise be possible in a small town."

Joseph straightened in his seat across the table from his assistant. "Oh. Well... That is a very interesting point, my friend. Years unseen are years unreported."

"Precisely."

Joseph turned his face aside and scratched the back of his head. "So I suppose I must accustom myself to Nachum's eager protection?"

"He does seem to have taken well to his new job as bodyguard."

"*Too* well," said Joseph with a grin. "He's beginning to terrify small children and animals."

*   *   *

Discussion in the Sanhedrin over allowing moneychangers to set up on the temple grounds provided an opportunity for the newest member to make his first address before the assembly. Another counselor, one of Zacharias' friends and allies, suggested during his own oration that the views of, as he put it, *someone who has recently come to us from the heart of the people* might provide fresh perspective. He then recognized his new colleague. Naturally, it had all been arranged by Zacharias.

The newest member's remarks were thoughtful, cautionary and short, befitting someone of junior status. They stressed the importance of balancing the people's needs with protecting the decorum of the Lord's House. "The Holy One is watching us, blessed be He. His expectation, my brothers—and that of the people we serve—is for us to be watchful that a small convenience does not become a desecration."

Formulary and predictable. As such, it succeeded perfectly in reassuring the members that a man of restraint and propriety had joined their august fellowship. That he had voted against the proposal didn't matter one way or the other, since passage of the measure had been assumed from the start. Thus, the newest member was able to free himself from the dismissive appellation, *tin merchant*. After this debut, he would be referred to by all his colleagues in a more dignified manner as Joseph of Arimathea.

"I was positively inspiring, my wife," Joseph called to Chava, as he seated himself in anticipation of the evening meal. "You would have been proud of me."

"I would have been *bored*," she called back from the kitchen.

Across the table, James chuckled at their banter. "It appears that you at least avoided making any enemies with your first vote," he said.

"Yes, my eloquence accomplished that much," said Joseph. "Did you hear that, my wife? I said *eloquence*. I was indisputably eloquent."

Chava had come into the room with a covered dish, followed by the serving girl who carried a tray laden with other vessels.

"Bah!" said Chava. "*Eloquent* is just another word for *long-winded*. And *that* you have always been."

"Ah, how the woman loves me," said Joseph.

Prayers were offered, dinner shared, and conversation pursued. Joseph laid out some of the issues he expected to be brought before the Sanhedrin over the next few weeks.

"There may be more trips to Ein Kerem," he said. "I will need the advice of my friend, Zacharias on several questions."

James accepted these upcoming missions with a nod, but Chava had reservations about the burdens being placed on their tenant.

"You take this young man from his studies too much, Husband," she said. "The good nature of his master, Hillel, is not without limits."

"Hillel supports our efforts," Joseph replied.

"Even so... Even so..."

"I have kept close counsel with Gamaliel," James said. "So far, he has had no objections."

"Mmmmm... Even so..."

"My dear Chava is a mother," said Joseph. "Mothers worry, James, and she cannot help mothering you."

Chava glanced at her husband tolerantly.

"Still," he continued, "a mother's instincts are not to be ignored. I will try to organize my correspondence with Zacharias so as to perhaps make things easier on my messenger."

In the way common to wives of long duration, Chava's face could be read as, *We'll see.*

James would not have said it, but he appreciated Chava's intercession on his behalf. Much as he enjoyed playing the role of liaison between Joseph and Zacharias—and for all the insights gained into the workings of the Sanhedrin—he had become a bit apprehensive about the demands on his time. He knew that his sleeplessness was showing in class. And while Hillel had given no indication that he was annoyed by the many absences and late appearances, James could not help but worry. To be part of that great house of study was the rarest and most prized opportunity he could imagine, and he would not have wanted to put it at risk.

Since there were no errands scheduled for the remainder of this week, James made it a point to show up early at class sessions, to take part more fully in the discussions, and to put in extra time at his synagogue duties. But on the morning after Sabbath, just as he was rising, the serving girl, whose name was Amara, came to the stone hut.

"I have a message from my master," she said. "He needs you to go to Ein Kerem this evening. The great priest, Zacharias, has information of importance on a vote in the council."

"Of course," said James, still somewhat clouded from sleep. "I will depart when the afternoon session is finished."

The girl excused herself, and James watched her scurry back to the house. She was from Leptis, on the African coast, a year or two older than himself. And while her dusky coloring and Greek name always put him in mind of Lucillus, her slight build recalled Mary. Like Lucillus, Amara had been born into bondage. James' landlord had acquired her in the course of his many business travels, and brought her home to assist Chava, then promptly gave her manumission. In gratitude, she followed the way of the God-fearers.

Amara was one of the few young women with whom James came into contact regularly, and he found his eyes drawn to her whenever she was present. Of course, girls he passed in the street also attracted his attention, much as he tried to remain focused on Hillel's words or whatever task he was about.

The thought had occurred that, at his present age, if he were living in Nazareth, the matchmaker would likely be inquiring about the carpenter's son. It was hard for James to think of himself as marriageable, though he admitted the idea was not displeasing to him. But such a consideration was something to be left for the future. There was much to accomplish before he could seriously ponder a wife and family.

That afternoon's session was cut short, which happened from time to time when fatigue overcame the seemingly tireless old sage. The energy Hillel was able to muster at this stage in his life was impressive. Nonetheless, there were boundaries beyond which his aged body simply did not permit him to go. This change in schedule freed James to depart for Ein Kerem earlier than he had planned, and he arrived at the villa before sunset.

His intention was to see Zacharias, obtain the information for Joseph, and convey it back to his landlord as quickly as possible—thence to an early sleep. However, Elizabeth greeted him warmly and invited him to linger for the evening meal to be taken in the company of some guests. Having been accepted so thoroughly into the household, he could hardly refuse.

Zacharias was pleased to introduce James, whom he referred to as *a kinsman from Galilee*, to the three visitors. For his part, James noted that these tablemates were another sign of the priest's far-reaching influence. Chief among them was Samuel of Rabbah, that city of the Decapolis, beyond the Jordan, which the Greeks called *Philadelphia*. Zacharias explained that Samuel, a large, powerfully built man with a raven-black beard, was his partner in the operation of caravans plying the routes to Arabia and the eastern seaports.

James expressed his honor at meeting one who shared in Zacharias' critical trade from which all in Jerusalem drew benefit.

"The young man is a disciple of my honored friend, Hillel," Zacharias explained.

"Ah, a young man of distinction," said Samuel, clearly impressed.

Samuel's wife, Niva, a plump and earthy type who looked to James as if she would be more at home carrying water from the well in the square at Nazareth than sitting here in this elegant house, expressed a giggling pleasure at meeting *a scholar from the north*.

James thanked her for the kind designation.

It was the third member of this trio who arrested James' interest, however.

"My daughter, Avigail," said Samuel.

A pair of deep blue eyes under full, dark lashes contrasted with the milky complexion of a truly stunning face. James had never encountered such a visage. The features were sharply delineated and prominent but somehow delicate at the same time. What could be seen of her hair beneath a pale green veil was black as the father's beard.

It was Elizabeth who perceived the astonishment which the girl had brought upon James, and with which he was clearly struggling. She saw his eyes lock onto this breathtaking display of youth and beauty and his mouth fall open.

Barely able to speak, James forced a small bow of the head and mumbled, "Mistress..."

Elizabeth stifled a laugh and tugged gently at the sleeve of his tunic. "James is tenant to my husband's associate, Joseph of Arimathea."

Her timely intervention pulled the young man out of his stupor. He closed his eyes—and his mouth—and tried to shake off the effect of this startling female presence, a force he had never before felt so powerfully.

"Ah yes," replied Samuel. "I will be seeing Joseph in Jerusalem."

"An important contact for you to make," Zacharias said. "You will be dealing with him, since I am gradually transferring many of my functions. And he will have to learn more about the Arab trade."

"I understand he has succeeded you on the Great Sanhedrin," Samuel said.

"And has made a promising start," the priest replied. "I think that Joseph will become a figure of respect, over time."

This precipitated a dinner conversation about competition between the Great Sanhedrin in Jerusalem and the Sanhedrins of the various cities.

"The local councils are important, and they have their fields of competence," Zacharias said, "but they must always yield to the Great Sanhedrin on certain key points that involve all the Jewish people."

"It seems there is often reluctance to do that," Samuel observed.

"Quite so," said Zacharias. "It is an ongoing source of contention."

Interesting as this exchange might have been, James found himself constantly distracted by the vision across the table, even though Avigail sat silently, eyes in her lap, in a manner befitting a modest, obedient daughter. In fact, that discreet posture only enhanced the power of her allure.

After dinner, when James had excused himself and was preparing to take his leave, Elizabeth pulled him aside and spoke to him in a soft voice. "She is lovely, is she not?"

James suddenly felt very self-conscious. "Well...yes. I— She is a very pretty girl."

"Avigail and her mother will be our guests for several weeks while Samuel is traveling throughout Palestine on business for my husband."

James said nothing.

"It is just a fact I thought you might find of interest."

Still he was silent.

"Perhaps, when you are again in Ein Kerem, you will have occasion to speak with her—properly chaperoned, of course."

Throughout the entire walk back to Jerusalem, James found himself in a state of some distress. Had it been sinful for him to be so taken with a beautiful girl? Was what he had experienced raw lust? He realized he had barely participated in the table conversation, and hoped Samuel and Niva attributed his reticence to shyness rather than suspecting he was preoccupied with their daughter.

Then too, what was the moral validity of physical attractiveness in itself? Beauty was a gift from the King of the Universe, instantly recognized and always admired. Even the holy books commented on it. Solomon's Song waxed eloquent in praise of human comeliness. Of course, that particular bit of writing was approached with caution, the rabbis placing careful limits on how and when it might be read. And what did *that* say about the power of beauty?

Without doubt, beauty could be a grave temptation to wrongdoing. One had only to consider the wickedness of David, so in thrall to the wife of Uriah the Hittite. Or for that matter, the current scandalous conduct of Archelaus carrying on with Glaphyra in complete disregard of propriety. Could virtue be sustained when confronted by overwhelming feminine loveliness, the kind of perfection James had witnessed in Avigail? Perhaps these were matters he should put to Master Hillel. But then, that would raise the question of why he was asking, and James wasn't at all sure he would want to go into that. Certainly, not in the class.

His mind so rattled by such thoughts, James had little to say to his landlord when delivering the packet of information given him by Zacharias.

"Did my honorable friend and advisor have any comments?" Joseph asked to distracted silence. "James?"

The words were distant and barely heard.

"James?"

Finally Joseph's inquiry cut through the fog.

"Oh. I am sorry, Joseph. Please forgive me. I have much on my mind, and it has been a long day. Zacharias had guests, and so there was no opportunity to speak privately. He just gave me these materials."

"Guests?"

"Samuel of Rabbah and his family."

"Ah," Joseph said. "The eastern caravans. Zacharias has spoken of this Samuel. He wishes me to meet with him."

"Yes. Samuel will be calling on you."

Joseph nodded. "Fine. Fine." Then he smiled. "Did you by any chance see his daughter? I have heard from some of the caravaners that she is a most dazzling young woman."

James was self-conscious again, as he had been when Elizabeth spoke with him after the meal. "She...is very...pretty."

This reserve was not lost on Joseph.

Fortunately, tiredness overcame James' preoccupation, and he slept deeply and well. The next morning he felt clearer-headed, able to push the image of Avigail to the periphery of his thoughts, though she was not entirely out of his mind. From time to time during the day, his question about the moral validity of beauty poked at him, with no answer discernible. He tried not to let those thoughts become too much of a distraction, because there were other matters to engage him.

Today's discussion in the class focused on an intriguing question: Can someone acquire moral obligations without doing anything that prompts them? The master referred to a case that concerned a farmer who planted a field belonging to another without obtaining the owner's permission.

Shammai had held that the planter was entitled not only to his harvest, but to claim *even the fixtures* on the land, based on the premise that he had significantly improved the property. Hillel's own opinion had been that such an improvement gave the planter no rights over the property itself, but that the owner should provide a just compensation.

A vigorous discussion ensued. One student maintained that the effort and expense involved in working the land might entitle the planter to his crop, but he saw no way in which the property owner could be thought to have assumed any liability for actions he didn't authorize. Another declared vociferously that, since the planter had arbitrarily usurped the owner's prerogatives over the property, he was behaving in a manner that was essentially criminal. Wasn't this illegitimate use of someone else's land a certain kind of theft?

Hillel explained that even though the landholder had not given his permission to plant in his field, the act of making the land productive was an unsolicited gift and so imposed an obligation on the owner. The point was provocative, as the master's explanations generally were, and he suspected that time and reflection would be required for some of his disciples to fully grasp and accept the underlying moral precept.

James sat reflecting on the scenario presented. The wisp of a smile on his face drew the master's attention.

"James son of Joseph," Hillel said, "have you a thought to share about our problem?"

The smile firmed itself up into something more resolute. "Master," said James, "I see a contrast between the claim of rights and the spirit of charity. Perhaps you are suggesting that the landholder is called upon by the Holy One to overlook this assault on his prerogatives in favor of gratitude for the planter's effort, which made the owner's property more valuable."

Now Hillel smiled, throwing a quick glance at Gamaliel. "A useful insight, James son of Joseph, and one which we might all take into consideration as we ponder the problem."

"The eminent James son of Joseph reveals his wisdom again." It was Jedediah, once more waiting at the base of the stairs after class.

James waved away the sarcasm. "Not so much wisdom, I assure you. It is just that I am starting to anticipate the master's line of thinking."

"A useful thing, that," said Jedediah. "I know of no one in the class who would not like to anticipate the master's thinking." He laid a hand on James' shoulder. "You are making your mark, my friend. You truly are becoming a leader. And I mean that in all seriousness."

The compliment took James by surprise. He paused for a moment, groping for a reply, but Jedediah did not wait for it to come.

"Walk with me to the market district," he said. "The afternoon is pleasant, and I must purchase something for my evening meal."

Given the unexpected note of sincerity, James felt obliged to accept his fellow student's invitation. They made their way down into the Tyropoeon Valley and through streets still busy with late shoppers but beginning to thin as people—mostly women—made their last purchases and headed home to the evening's cooking.

Observing the presence of so many females around him, James entertained the notion that perhaps Jedediah might have a thought on the question that had occupied him since being confronted by the loveliness of Avigail. Jedediah was obviously trying to be friendly, so maybe it would be appropriate to share a confidence. And as this classmate was somewhat older, his reflection could be helpful.

"Jedediah, I have had an experience which I found disturbing."

"Oh?"

"I met an extraordinarily beautiful girl."

"Ha! I should not wonder that you are disturbed. Beautiful girls are always disturbing."

James stopped in the street. "Yes. Why *is* that?"

His companion laughed. "Because they are beautiful."

"No, Jedediah, there is a serious point here. The entire time I was in the girl's presence, I could not take my eyes off her. Then afterward, I wondered if it was sinful to be so preoccupied with physical attractiveness."

"Did you behave improperly toward her?"

"No, I did not even speak to her."

"Did you leer at her in a way that would make her uncomfortable or disgrace your family?"

"No... At least, I don't think I did."

"Then where is the sin?"

"Well... It is just that an image of her face has kept creeping into my mind ever since. I cannot put it behind me."

"You are a young man, James. The Holy One has ordained that young men should be captivated by young women, especially beautiful young women. That is why we have matchmakers—to make matches, which make families."

"But I am not in a position to think about such things. I am a student. I have commitments, and I am without means."

"Everyone of Hillel's disciples has commitments, and I doubt that any of us has much money. But we are all men, and I assure you we all think about such things."

Jedediah's straightforward response provided little in the way of an answer to James' question, but somehow it did bring a feeling of relief.

"I suppose you are right," he said. "Perhaps I am overly troubled."

"Don't let it weigh on you." Jedediah pointed a finger to indicate that they should follow a particular street that veered at an angle to the right. "But I do understand your concern. Will there be other occasions to see this girl?"

"I have to admit I hope so."

"Then enjoy the sight, but guard your feelings. A wise man exercises discipline over his desires. And as you say, there are commitments."

James nodded.

They came to a place where the street widened out into a plaza, the sides of which were lined with market stalls and the wagons of vendors offering produce from the countryside. A number of small carts and stands were also scattered about the open space. At the far end of the plaza was a synagogue which James knew was where one of the other rabbis of the Royal Porch based his house of study.

"This is the best marketplace in Jerusalem," said Jedediah sweeping his hand about. "Whatever you need can be purchased here—*if* you have money, of course."

"And as *you* say, very few of us have much of that."

They shared a laugh.

"But I need nothing today," James said. "I will eat at the table of my landlord this evening, as I usually do."

"A very hospitable arrangement."

They stopped at several locations in the plaza, and Jedediah bought a few items, the combination of which didn't seem to James like much of a dinner. Finally, they came to a large covered stall located at a corner near the synagogue.

Jedediah browsed about, inspecting the fruits and vegetables for sale, apparently unsure of what he wanted. He poked into a bin filled with meal, and sniffed at some bundles of herbs hanging from the overhead beams. He haggled with the vendor over the price of pomegranates, was undecided, and looked around again. From time to time during all this searching, he glanced out in the direction of the synagogue, then turned his attention back to the items.

James was becoming impatient. "What do you wish to eat?"

"I am not sure," said Jedediah, glancing over James' shoulder at the plaza once more. "But these choices must not be rushed. Food is important. The King of the Universe expects us to take proper care of our bodies."

He continued his browsing, but now he no longer seemed quite as relaxed and amiable as he had been. In fact, watching him, James got the impression that Jedediah was slightly on edge—which hadn't been apparent before—perhaps impatient about something.

Just then, a clamor of noises, including one that sounded like a cry of pain, caught James' attention. He turned and looked out into the plaza. Two men were in front of the synagogue entrance hunched over, moving their arms in quick jerks. James could see the figure of a third man on his knees between them, collapsing to the ground. Other people in the open space and emerging from the synagogue had become aware of the activity. Someone called out, and the two men suddenly left their fallen companion and ran off, the glint off a knife blade catching James' eye. With his last sight of them before they disappeared down a side street, James realized their faces were concealed by wide bands of cloth.

A crowd formed around the figure on the ground. There were cries for help and a woman's scream. James thought he saw blood.

Jedediah was behind him now, whispering in his ear. "Quickly. We must go."

"What is happening?" James asked.

"That man was attacked. The Civil Guard will be here. We must leave—now."

"But we did nothing."

"It does not matter. They will detain everyone who was close by. You don't want to sit in prison while they figure out who did what, or maybe be tortured until they get the truth. Archelaus' henchmen are not very bright, but they are persistent. Follow me."

He grabbed James' arm and pulled him to the rear of the stall and out into an alleyway behind. They made their way quickly through the tangle of passages, farther down the Tyropoeon Valley, around and through several neighborhoods. Finally, by a series of other alleys and passages, they emerged onto the wide street near the house of the tin merchant.

"There," said Jedediah. "Where you live. Go in, and say nothing. I will see you tomorrow in the class." He scanned the street in each direction, then slipped around the corner and was out of sight.

James hurried to the gate, then paused. He looked around himself, as Jedediah had done. No unusual activity was visible. Just a few scattered people heading here and there, unknowing, unconcerned. A cart pulled by a donkey, driven by an old man. A child carrying a bundle of sticks for someone's evening fire. All was calm. All was as it would normally be where these two Jerusalem streets crossed.

Only James was different. He opened the gate without thinking to touch the scroll of the commandment, and went inside directly to the stone hut, throwing himself down on the couch.

What had just happened? Had he witnessed someone murdered? Right there in the plaza in broad daylight? Right in front of a synagogue?

And who was the man? Who were his attackers? Were they Zealots? All of these questions roiled his mind, convulsing him, frightening him.

Then in the midst of this turmoil, a small, almost insignificant thought poked itself into the back of his consciousness. It occurred to James that he hadn't realized Jedediah knew where he lived.

CHAPTER TWENTY

There is no fear of God before his eyes.
He so flatters himself that he knows not his guilt.

(Psalm 36)

In the morning, all Jerusalem was abuzz with talk about the killing. When James arrived at the synagogue of Hillel, near the temple bridge, he learned that the victim had been a tax collector about whom it was said that he inflated his assessments and also that he regularly defiled himself by cavorting with Greek women. The first claim appeared to be more firmly supported, but there were those who held that if the charge of corruption was true, why shouldn't the other allegation be believed? A Jew who made himself a tool of the Roman occupiers, exploiting his own countrymen, was capable of anything.

And yet, this tax collector had been attacked immediately after praying in that synagogue on the market plaza. James had been there and seen the assault for himself. Was this a pious man unjustly maligned and cruelly murdered? Was he a hypocrite who could cheat people one minute and offer prayers the next? James didn't know what to believe.

The morning session began with continued talk on the subject of obligations, a few of the students raising additional points about the story of the unauthorized planting. Hillel answered all their questions, elaborated on his comments of the day before, and expanded the discussion to cover obligations to family, to the larger community, and eventually to the King of the Universe, the ultimate object of every Jew's obligations.

Sometime in mid-morning, James noticed Jedediah leaning against a post in the rear of the synagogue's meeting hall. He hadn't spotted him earlier, and assumed he'd come in late. Jedediah stood facing in the general direction of the master, but his eyes wandered unfocused about the room, and he didn't seem very deeply engaged in the talk. He was gone before the end of the session, and was absent throughout the entire afternoon.

It was when James had completed his evening synagogue duties, which this week consisted of helping to distribute sacks of dried beans to families in need, that Jedediah finally appeared again. James spotted him in the twilight sitting on the parapet at the near-end of the bridge.

"Where have you been?" James asked his classmate.

"Attending to private business."

"You missed some interesting discussions in class."

"I caught their flavor this morning."

"Yes, I saw you."

James eyed his companion curiously, sensing a certain air about him that aroused unease. For his part, Jedediah glanced furtively along the bridge toward the temple and then in the opposite direction, seemingly trying to confirm that they were alone.

"How are you feeling, James, after our adventure?" he asked.

"I must say I found the experience disturbing."

"Yesterday you spoke of being disturbed by a pretty girl."

"This was a bit different."

A smile on Jedediah's face. "He was a traitor, you know—that tax farmer."

"So I have heard."

"He made a big show of being a pillar of the synagogue, but he robbed people. That was how he made his living. He robbed people for the Romans, and he robbed them for himself."

James was quiet for a moment. Then he asked, "How did you know where I live? I cannot recall ever discussing where my lodgings are located."

"I was aware that you room with the new Sanhedrin member. Isn't it common knowledge?"

"It is no secret. But in all that running yesterday, we somehow arrived right at my front gate. I could not have so readily found my way home through those obscure passages—certainly not in a panic."

"I am very familiar with the city."

This time it was James who looked around to be sure no one was within earshot. "You knew that attack was going to happen. You took me to the spot, and you made sure to linger there until it did."

Jedediah's smile again—without words.

"You wanted me to see it, Jedediah. Why?"

"I thought it would be...instructive."

"Instructive?"

"Yes, to both of us," Jedediah said. "It would give you some idea of what actions might be taken to advance the cause of freedom in our land. And to me— Well, I wanted to see how you would react to the experience."

His voice had a coldness now as he spoke, a chill of death which James had never detected before. He could see that Jedediah was here at this bridge to do business. Private business.

"Alright," James said, "I took note of the demonstration. What did *you* learn?"

"I am confirmed in my opinion," said Jedediah. "Remember how I told you yesterday that you are a leader?" He tipped his head forward as an affirmation. "You *are* a leader, James. Watching someone killed may have been startling to you, but it did not bring you to your knees. You would have stood right up to the Civil Guard and told them all you saw. Naively perhaps, but without fear. And you were in no panic when we made our way through that maze of alleys and passageways. You could see I knew where I was going, and you came along, doing whatever was necessary. Even now, you stand here calmly, demanding that I explain myself, when you realize quite clearly that I am involved with the insurrectionists. That fact should fill you with fear. But it does not."

Jedediah was right. James wasn't afraid, though reflecting on the situation, he granted that maybe he should be.

"What do want from me, Jedediah?"

"I would like you to consider joining in our cause. The qualities that make you a leader—the same things that make you a scholar—could be of use in accomplishing great things for our nation. Men would follow you, James. Your voice would be persuasive, just as it is in the class. Hillel and Gamaliel recognize your gifts. I can see they do."

"I wish to be a rabbi."

"And *what* a rabbi you could be. Imagine gathering a great throng of disciples and building them into a movement for the freedom of our nation—of the *Jewish People*, James. It would be far better than any synagogue."

"That is an elaborate vision, Jedediah—too elaborate for me. I'm only a disciple myself, a disciple of Hillel. Remember those commitments we spoke of?"

Jedediah hopped off the parapet and stood facing James. "Stay with Hillel," he said. "It is the best thing you could possibly do. Study and succeed and gain his certification. I can think of nothing more powerful than a rabbi ordained by the greatest sage in Jerusalem rallying the Jews to cast off Rome's oppressive yoke. What authority such a man would have. All over the country people would flock to our cause."

Enthusiasm had replaced the coldness. Jedediah was now fired with excitement at the possibilities he was presenting. But to James the whole idea seemed absurd.

"Have you such influence among the Zealots that you could possibly suggest *me* for such a role?" he asked.

Jedediah offered a tight, truncated laugh. "Influence? I have very little," he said, "at least right now. And in any event, there is much less to have influence over than you might imagine. People speak of *the Zealots* as if there is a vast organization. In reality, there are many different groups, most very small, and each with its own aims and procedures. They do cooperate—sometimes quite effectively. But all the while, they compete for members and support. And *that* is the real tragedy. We will never drive out the Romans until someone can unite these factions strongly and permanently behind a single leadership and a comprehensive philosophy of resistance, a message of hope and liberty which all can understand and embrace."

"And you think I can accomplish this?"

With an exhalation Jedediah relaxed, leaning back against the parapet, arms crossed, showing a calm confidence in his thoughts. "Maybe we can accomplish it together, my friend. You have a mind that is capable of wonderful insights and formulations. I have... Well, let us say that I have *practicality*. The two of us would make an effective combination."

James eyed his classmate up and down—this strange fellow of many moods who was asking him to be a leader of revolt and terror. But then, did he really want James to lead? Perhaps his plan was to find someone who could merely serve as the face of his own ambitions. James did not find either prospect appealing.

"I once told you, Jedediah, that I understand why men wish to take up arms against the foreign occupiers. I share your desire to free our land of oppression, and not only the oppression of Rome. We are every bit as oppressed by a depraved royalty and corrupt religious leaders. In fact, it might interest you to know that, in my small way, I am working to ease some of the pains our people feel under those burdens."

The corners of Jedediah's mouth curled up into a smile once again, though now one that was knowing, shrewd, almost sinister. "Ah, those mysterious comings and goings? I have wondered what you were up to, and why Hillel and Gamaliel tolerate your highly irregular schedule so indulgently. I will assume it has something to do with this tin merchant-landlord of yours."

"But I think," James continued firmly, "that whatever improvements are possible would be best made without the bloodshed that seems to be the main result of this movement you champion. I have witnessed the consequences of revolt. And while there may come a time when taking up arms is unavoidable, I do not choose to lead others in bringing it on."

At that, there was an uncomfortable silence between them. Jedediah's smile vanished. He looked squarely at James, nodding his head almost solemnly, as if he had come to a decision. For the first time in the conversation, James felt a wave of anxiety, and he found himself, quite involuntarily, looking to see if Jedediah had a weapon.

But then his companion's mood changed into something unexpected. Jedediah's face took on an entirely pleasant expression. His manner now seemed almost carefree, and he said casually, "Well then, perhaps you are not ready for what I propose. I guess it was premature to invite you into this now. But, it was worth a try. You go on working to ease the people's pains and lighten their burdens. I wish you well and hope you succeed. But if your outlook should ever change, James—if you should come to see the limitations of what you are doing and...the *potential*...in an insurrectionist approach—you might want to reconsider my offer."

James was perplexed at this quick, almost indifferent, step back from the bloody proposition which had been set before him. Could Jedediah let it go so easily, as if James had merely declined the offer of a pleasant ramble through the olive groves?

"Do you not fear that I might reveal your involvement with the Zealots or your knowledge of the murder?"

"Not at all," Jedediah said. "I will be gone after this. My time in the house of study is finished. Actually, I made up my mind to leave when we had our last examinations. I am tired of Hillel's endless mumblings and of being probed and questioned and corrected and made to feel incapable of thinking. I am tired of the meaningless chatter and of dissecting abstract points of the Law while our nation is dying. I've stayed only because I was interested in you, James. But now there is other work to be done—more...*business*...to be attended to. Besides, I know you will say nothing."

"How can you be certain?"

"Because you are a Jew and you hate Rome as much as I do. That hatred comes from the same place as your aversion to bloodshed: the Sepphoris road. You may not be ready to join us, but you will not lift a hand against us. I'm confident of that."

He went to the end of the parapet and started down a stone stairway that led into the Tyropoeon Valley beneath the bridge. Then he stopped, turned around, and said, "Goodbye, James son of Joseph. Perhaps we will meet again. In the meantime, peace be upon you. And may the Lord guide you in right paths for the sake of His name." With a parting grin, Jedediah disappeared into the shadows below.

*   *   *

Darkness was dense upon the lower city by the time James arrived home. He had lingered at the bridge, replaying the exchange with Jedediah over and over in his head, and then made his way through the streets, hoping to avoid the night watch. The medal hanging from a cord around his neck under his tunic, indicating that he served a member of the Sanhedrin, protected him from being held in violation of the curfew. He could roam the city at will, as he did frequently with his message errands. But this was not a night on which he would have wanted to explain his business to the Civil Guard. Not after the killing. And especially not with the knowledge he now carried.

Inside the gate, he considered whether he should go to the house for something to eat. He knew that a bundle of food would have been set out for his late-duty night, and the pangs in his stomach left no doubt he wanted it. But with Jedediah on his mind, he did not wish to run into Joseph. His problem was solved when he spotted the serving girl inside the doorway.

"Amara," he called quietly, "could you please bring me something to eat in the hut? It is late, and I need a bite before retiring."

"Yes, Master James." And she fetched the bundle of food along with a small jug of wine.

Sleep was fitful, and by the next morning, James determined that he must say something to his landlord. Jedediah had assessed his feelings accurately. James had no desire to hurt this strange young man. And he admitted to himself during a sleepless period in the night that they did share a common hatred of Rome. This realization James found disquieting. Certainly the Sepphoris crucifixions confirmed his resentment of the occupation, even giving him cause to question his family's long service to foreign clients, as he had discussed with his father. But *hatred*—he had never analyzed his feelings in such terms. He would give it further reflection.

For now, he needed advice, and he needed to share this confidence. The appalling thought had occurred to him that Joseph of Arimathea might possibly be tainted, should it ever come to light that someone who was part of his household was even remotely connected to a Zealot. At that moment, Joseph was standing in the court speaking to one of his agents in the metal trade. James waited until the conversation was completed and the man departed.

"James, my boy, peace be upon you this beautiful morning."

"And upon you, Joseph. If I might have a word?"

Joseph sensed, from the seriousness in James' eyes, that this word would best be conveyed in private. They walked together down the path toward the front gate.

James related how, over several weeks, he'd had conversations with a fellow student, culminating in the stroll to the market plaza of two days before. He told how he witnessed the attack on the tax collector and realized that his classmate had brought him there to see it.

"You mean this fellow possessed advance knowledge of the crime?"

"Yes. He wished to gauge my reaction to seeing someone murdered."

"Your friend is a dagger-man?"

"I don't know if he, himself, has taken part in any such acts. But he admitted to me that he is associated with one of the Zealot groups."

"Was he trying to recruit you?"

"Yes. And I declined."

Joseph shook his head in disbelief. "This is a disciple of Hillel?"

"He was. When I confronted him last night, he told me that he was leaving the house of study. I imagine he is leaving Jerusalem as well—probably already gone. He said he had no fear of my reporting him to the authorities."

"So you are not in danger."

"I do not believe so."

Joseph set himself carefully down on a stack of iron ingots and immersed himself in thought. After some seconds, James intruded into his reverie.

"I was uncertain of what I should do, Joseph. I have no wish to bring harm to this fellow, but I would not want to be a liability to you if my contacts with him were—"

Joseph dismissed that concern. "Everyone knows someone, or the relative of someone, who is said to be a Zealot. Most often it is not actually true, but it makes for exciting gossip. And there is no connection between you and this student, other than that you were both disciples of Hillel. That is so, yes?"

"Aside from our sharing a midday meal once, absolutely none."

"Then on that basis, it could be argued that Hillel is more closely associated with the insurrectionists. And besides—not that it justifies what was done—but there *is* substance to what your acquaintance said about the murdered man. It is widely known that he was corrupt. I know it to be true, myself."

James now felt some sense of relief mixed in among the whirl of his emotions.

"All the same," said Joseph, "do not reveal this fellow's name to me. We will assume that he is gone by now. And if so, there is nothing more of which you have knowledge that could help in the investigation of this attack, so there's no reason to speak. Anyway, the Civil Guard are themselves corrupt—corrupt, incompetent brutes, to be truthful. And

I surely would not want you to go to the Romans. They would likely treat you as if you were part of the murder plot, or force you to become an informer. I will not see you put at risk, and Zacharias wouldn't either."

Joseph stood once more and patted James' back in a gentle, fatherly way. "The best thing is to keep this between ourselves." He gave a resigned sigh. "Such is life in the Lord's city, my boy. Caution and circumspection are virtues in this place. So do not be too upset by it all."

"Yes, Joseph."

"But if you should be approached by the Zealots in the future, alert me right away. Let us hope that this former student has lost interest in you. If not, a second contact might require us to get you out of Jerusalem."

"I will tell you if I ever hear from him again."

*   *   *

James knew that this was a day when the Sanhedrin sat as a court of law to hear criminal charges and civil complaints. Those sessions could run long, so he was surprised when he went to the house for his evening meal to see that Joseph was there, accompanied by a guest.

"James, I believe you know our visitor."

"Peace be upon you, James son of Joseph." It was Samuel of Rabbah, the eastern caravan operator.

"And upon you, sir. I am honored to see you again." Then to Joseph James said, "I did not expect you to be back from the council."

"Fortunately, the complainant in what was expected to be a long case withdrew his charge," Joseph explained. "He very wisely settled before coming to the court. When I returned I found Samuel waiting. He and I have been discussing the Arab routes. Zacharias asked him to instruct me about the eastern reaches of the trade. I am amazed to learn that some of the goods our caravans haul from the Arabian ports come from as far away as the land of the Ch'in."

"Really?" said James. "The vast eastern empire? I have heard the legend of the long wall."

"It is no legend," said Samuel. "There is such a wall. Some of the seafarers have shared tales of its enormity. They say it is guarded by troops that ride their horses along the top. And it would take many days to travel the entire length, if one can imagine such a thing."

"Astounding," said Joseph. "Even Rome, with its huge cities and endless roads, can boast of no such building accomplishment."

"Yes, but from what I hear, there is great turmoil among the Ch'in right now," said Samuel. "There are revolts and the overthrow of governments. Much blood, much blood. We are seeing very little of their goods these days."

Dinner conversation included many digressions from the business of the caravans into Samuel's colorful tales of exotic lands beyond the Arab waterways: India, the Spice Islands, even a strange island nation far to the east which was said to be ruled by a witch queen. James expressed his fascination at hearing about such wondrous places, born and raised as he was in simple, little Nazareth. What he found most to his interest—though he didn't mention it—was Samuel's remark that his travels for Zacharias across Palestine and up into Syria necessitated his wife and daughter being hosted in Ein Kerem for several weeks. This echoed what Elizabeth had mentioned, and it stirred James' hope for more trips to the villa.

At the end of the evening, when James was about to depart, Samuel came forth with an unexpected offer. "James," he said, "I will be visiting the ports of Ptolemais and Tyre. This will take me through the Jezreel Valley, which I believe is very near to your home village. I cannot be certain when I will be in the vicinity of Nazareth, since I have to make other stops on the way, which may necessitate my remaining at those locations for a time. But I could, if you like, deliver a message to your family. I am spending the night and one more day here as a guest of our noble council member. If you wish to prepare a letter, I will be happy to carry it with me."

James was overjoyed at the prospect. "Oh, that would be a great kindness, sir," he said. "I have not been in touch with my father and brothers in many months. Whenever you can deliver it, I am sure they will welcome you thankfully."

And so the lamp that hung over James' table in the stone hut burned late into that night.

CHAPTER TWENTY-ONE

Many waters cannot quench love,
rivers cannot wash it away.

(Song of Solomon 8)

Dissatisfaction had been growing steadily as it became clear how truly onerous were the new taxes imposed after the census. With assessments much steeper and collection methods more heavy-handed, resentment had taken hold, creating a rare unanimity that crossed virtually all the lines of class within Jewish society. Even those who were better off shared in the discontent, because they were losing a key advantage they had enjoyed under the tax-farming system—the only advantage.

It had always been that arrangements might be made with a local collector for flexibility in the payment schedule. The tax farmers would advance money when particular payers were in arrears, making payments on behalf of favored clients and collecting later. Predictably, the price of this *kindness* would be a high premium, over and above the tax, but it kept the authorities away while scrounging around to raise the needed resources.

Now the collectors were under pressure themselves. With larger payments due, their private pools of funds were inadequate to meet the increased demand for credit. They called for full payment on the spot, with taxpayers often caught short. Seizures of property were occurring at an alarming rate, even among the wealthy. Among the lower classes, whole families were being sold into debt bondage. The situation was made worse when Archelaus imposed a surtax to cover new royal construction projects. The ethnarch, who had inherited his father's proclivity for building, hoped he could raise the needed funds under cover of the increased imperial levies. It was a stupid idea that fooled no one.

Tax collectors attempted to deflect the public's wrath by making their own dissatisfaction known. This ravaging of the nation's wealth, they claimed, was the ethnarch's fault, since he bore ultimate responsibility for meeting Caesar's tax demands in Judea, Samaria and Idumea. While there was no disagreement about Archelaus' servility to Rome or his own ravenous appetite for the people's money, it became a common saying that perhaps the killing of that corrupt publican in the market plaza was a method of protest worth repeating. This idea was hurled in the face of more than one tax farmer. The collectors quickly set aside their criticisms of the ethnarch in favor of demands for royal protection.

So it was that, late of a night somewhat less than two weeks after the murder, a flaming torch came arcing through a window in the home of a tax farmer who lived in Hebron. Damage was limited to burning of the window coverings and one small rug, but there was no mistaking the message intended. Word of the incident spread rapidly throughout all Judea.

When James heard about it, he wondered if this was some of the other work Jedediah had said needed to be done. Perhaps the murder he'd been tricked into witnessing was the first step in some new Zealot initiative. But in truth, feelings had become so raw that insurrectionist sentiments would hardly have been needed to prompt a second assault on a tax collector. Anyone might have thrown that torch.

Joseph of Arimathea and his reform-minded fellow counselors insisted that the Sanhedrin should take action before public anger reached the boiling point. They put forth a resolution demanding that the ethnarch rescind his surtax. The measure was defeated. They then called for a temporary reduction in the temple tax to at least partially offset the increased civic and imperial assessments. That idea never came to a vote. They were left with suggesting a rather weak plea to petition Caesar requesting an unspecified adjustment in the new levies to offer some relief. This too failed.

Zacharias was increasingly distressed as he watched the situation deteriorate, and his anxieties weighed on him in a way that was clearly visible. Each time James saw him, the priest seemed older. Zacharias' fervor was undampened, however, and he kept James in motion conveying messages back and forth between Ein Kerem and Jerusalem, the correspondence broadening beyond Joseph of Arimathea. It now included other members of the reform faction to whom Zacharias felt compelled to offer his insights and advice.

Spending less and less time in class, James worried about his position in the house of study. But Gamaliel assured him of the master's sympathy with the attempts to address the tax crisis, insisting that James should focus on the need at hand. His place was secure.

The trips to Ein Kerem did have one decidedly pleasurable feature: they provided opportunities for James to glimpse the lovely Avigail. But that pleasure was not unmixed. The more he caught sight of her—always fleetingly and at a discreet distance—the more deeply this stunning girl became impressed upon his mind. The image of her face intruded into his thoughts at unexpected times, even making appearances in his dreams. He had never experienced such a persistent preoccupation, and it troubled him seriously.

Arriving late at the villa one morning because Joseph had been delayed in preparing his note to Zacharias, James found the priest was still in bed. Elizabeth explained that her husband was resting from an episode of sickness in the night.

"I am worried about him," she said. "He has lost much in vigor of late, James, and he is experiencing many pains and discomforts. His appetite has decreased, and there are digestive difficulties. It is all this concern about the Sanhedrin. I urge him to put it beside him, but he won't listen to his wife. What man does?"

James handed her the note from his landlord, and asked her to give it to Zacharias. She did so, returning a few minutes later.

"He asks that you remain, James. He will prepare a reply, but it might be awhile before he is able to rouse himself from bed. So please, come rest in the garden."

James accompanied her out to the colonnade, where he knew to expect shade and the gentle breezes of this verdant, hillside town. As he stepped through the door, the young man felt his heart leap at the sight of Avigail seated on a wooden bench, her mother standing nearby.

"Niva, Avigail," Elizabeth said, gesturing in his direction, "you recall our dear student, James son of Joseph."

The women nodded their greetings as James struggled to compose himself, caught as he was in the gaze of those deep blue eyes.

"Peace...be with you...both," he managed in some difficulty.

He should have expected that the women would be lounging out-doors. He should have suggested he would wait for Zacharias in the library. He should have anticipated, and then avoided, this awkward situation. But then, why would Elizabeth lead him into the company of two women who were not his relatives and with whom he had no legitimate reason to mix? Samuel was not here. Zacharias was not here. This was not appropriate, at least it wouldn't have been considered so in Nazareth. On top of that, here was this hauntingly beautiful face which had been lodged in his mind for days.

James stood with his hands clasped in front, head down, eyes trained on his feet, trying to avoid looking at Avigail, and feeling desperately uncomfortable.

"Sit, James. Be at ease," Elizabeth said, then wandered off with Niva along the colonnade exchanging amiable chatter about some flowering shrubs growing in pots at the base of each post.

Avigail sat silently, her face turned aside. Finally, after several un-settled minutes, she spoke. "Would you care to sit?" she asked, pointing to a bench set at an angle to her own.

"Thank you," James said nervously, and seated himself.

Silence again, James' discomfort growing with the amount of time passing by. Once more it was Avigail who took the lead.

"I was most interested to hear that you are a disciple of the famous sage, Hillel," she said.

"Oh...yes. I am."

"Do you study in the temple?"

"Yes...and at the master's synagogue... We meet in both places...on different days."

She absorbed these simple facts with a soft smile.

Allowing himself a quick glance, he perceived that her eyes—and such lovely eyes they were—seemed to convey sincere interest. It did not appear that she was just making conversation, though it would have been fine with him if she were. Under the circumstances, it was essential that someone did.

After another agonizing pause, Avigail asked, "What is he like?"

"He?"

"Hillel."

This gave James something specific to talk about—a topic on which he was always pleased to speak. "Hillel is the greatest rabbi in the world." His voice was charged with both enthusiasm and relief. "He is a man of true holiness, and yet he is unsurpassed in his shrewd understanding of everyday life. To be included in his house of study is the greatest opportunity I can imagine."

"I am sure."

"Yes... It is...an honor."

Again Avigail smiled. She inquired about subjects discussed in class, the way in which sessions were conducted, how Hillel treated his disciples, what aspects of the studies James found most interesting. James went on relating his observations and experiences in reply to these inviting questions.

Avigail seemed genuinely intrigued by the whole experience of rabbinical training, and James was grateful for her curiosity. More to the point, he was grateful for her ability to keep him talking in spite of his fear that he might collapse into a quivering heap any moment.

At one point, a serving girl approached and stood by, waiting quietly so as not to interrupt. At a break in their conversation, she asked if the mistress and the master might desire anything to eat or drink. James accepted a cup of wine diluted with fruit juice. Avigail declined with an expression of thanks to the girl that struck James as especially gracious. He had always felt that kindness to those in positions of service was the sign of a charitable heart. The words of appreciation Hillel would give him when he had attended the master were always encouraging.

After the servant departed, James felt awkward again, not being sure of how to pick up the conversation. But Avigail came to his rescue once more.

"It must be wonderful to study with such a teacher," she said, "in so elevated a way. My reading is very limited."

"Do you read?" he asked.

The question was entirely innocent, since James was well acquainted with the studious nature of his father's wife, Mary. But Avigail reacted in a way that took him by surprise. She was embarrassed to have let slip an admission of this talent.

"Well, I— I read...the psalms," she said hesitantly. "We have a scroll of the psalms in our house at Rabbah." Her eyes shifted quickly, peering about the colonnade almost guiltily. "I learned to read by following the words as my father would recite the psalms...when I was a child. He would read to me often." She looked at James imploringly. "Please... don't let anyone know I told you. Mother says it is...not becoming...for a girl to read."

Avigail's face bore a bright blush of red, her eyes were closed, and her hands fidgeted nervously in her lap. The poignancy of her confession, with its sudden, childlike loss of confidence, gripped James' heart. At that moment he was able to see beyond the physical beauty. He felt a powerful surge of empathy for this young woman who was ashamed of possessing a skill which he considered one of the greatest blessings in life.

"Oh no," he said. "Do not think that. Reading is the most wonderful thing. It is a gift from the King of the Universe. You should read *all* of the holy books."

"Well," she said, "if I were a man...I would read more. If I were a man, I would love to study in the way that you do."

She was merely trying to reestablish a facade of womanly deference appropriate in speaking to a man outside her family. But common as such a remark might have been for a girl to make, it took James aback.

He gave a quick shake of the head. Then he said in a breathless, whispery voice, almost dreamily, as if to himself alone, but loud enough for her to hear, "I cannot begin to imagine you as a man."

Avigail's eyes came up, and her glance locked on James' for the briefest instant. Then they both quickly looked away. Blessedly, the serving girl returned.

"Sir, Master Zacharias will speak with you now."

James excused himself, shaken. He rose from his seat and hurried into the house. Avigail remained sitting on the bench, the beautiful face now blank as she pondered a new emotion she'd experienced in the presence of this open and warm-hearted young man.

*   *   *

Over the course of months, finding time when he could, Josis had nearly fulfilled the promise he'd made Mary to carve all 22 characters of the Aramaic alphabet in wood. The letters already completed were

hanging in the portico. He was working on the next-to-the-last letter—
shin—when someone came to the compound. Setting down his carving
knife, he went to the gate.

The man who stood just beyond was almost the size of Nachum
and, in a way, of even more formidable appearance. Josis eyed the
niche beside the gatepost, assuring himself that it contained the club
weighted with an iron spike driven into its tip, which was one of the
precautions prompted by the attack on his father.

"Peace be upon you," said the man. "Is this the house of Joseph the
carpenter?"

"It is," Josis answered, trying not to let wariness show.

While all the adults in the household knew that the incident outside
the smithy had been a sham, they shared Lucillus' view that a real try on
Joseph's life was possible. Caution had eased with the passage of time.
But now, taxes were stirring discontent in Galilee, though to much less
an extent than in Judea, since this was Antipas' territory and Archelaus' surtax did not apply. Still, it wasn't unreasonable for the family
to worry about a renewed focus on Joseph's dealings with the Greeks.

"I am Samuel of Rabbah, partner to Zacharias in the caravan trade.
I bear a message from Joseph's son, James, disciple of the great Hillel."

"My brother?" Josis' elation was plain to the visitor.

"If you are another of Joseph's sons."

"I am, sir. I am Josis, the eldest. Peace be with you. Please enter. You
are most welcome in our home."

Samuel turned and held up his hand to signal the two riders accompanying him, one holding the reins to the horse which had been his
own mount. "Please wait, my friends," he said, and touching the scroll
in the gateway, he entered the compound.

Josis led him across the court to the portico, and knocked on the
door of the house. Samuel took note of the carved letters on display.

"Father?"

"Come." Joseph was inside with Lucillus, examining the plan for a
house under construction in Sepphoris. The workmen had discovered
slight discrepancies in some of the measurements, and there were fitting problems between stone and timber which required adjusting.

"A visitor, Father. He comes from Zacharias, and he bears a message
from James."

"Samuel of Rabbah," the visitor said, following Josis into the room. "I operate the caravans of the Arabian routes in partnership with Zacharias, kinsman to your wife."

"An honor, sir," Joseph said, rising behind the table. "May all your house know the peace of the Holy One, blessed be He."

"And yours, also." Samuel reached into a pouch that hung at his side, drawing out three parchment sheets rolled together and bound by a thong. He handed the bundle to Joseph. "I recently had occasion to speak with James, a fine young man who does you credit. Knowing I would pass this way, I offered to carry a message on his behalf."

"Bless you," said Joseph, "I am most grateful, both for your service and for your generous words about my son."

Joseph offered refreshment before Samuel should continue on his journey, but Samuel declined with thanks.

"My men and I have far to go before the fall of night," he said. "But the graciousness of the house of Joseph is much appreciated."

"Please know that your kindness in bringing me these words from my son is also much appreciated. We have had no contact in some months, and— Well...the concerns of a father..."

"I understand entirely," said Samuel.

After a few pleasantries and some answers to Joseph's questions about the welfare of Zacharias, Elizabeth, and their son, John, the visitor took his leave. Josis led him back to the gate, and with his two mounted companions, Samuel departed.

Curiosity sent Josis immediately back to the house. By the time he arrived, Joseph was seated at the table flattening the parchment sheets spread before him. Mary was also in the room now, and Lucillus was hunched over Joseph's shoulder looking down on the letter.

"What is James' news, Father?" Josis asked.

Joseph scanned the sheets. "I will have to read his message with greater thoroughness. But at first glance, it appears he has been busy. Well, what is this? The student has become involved in politics. His landlord, Joseph the tin merchant, has been elected to the Sanhedrin, and James assists him."

"The Sanhedrin?" said Mary, impressed.

Lucillus laughed. "I knew our scholar was destined for great things. I hope his Greek comes in handy."

"The Sanhedrin doesn't do its business in Greek," said Josis.

"The *world* does its business in Greek," Lucillus said. "Make no mistake about that."

"Well, *we* have Greek business right now," said Joseph, setting James' letter to the side. "Have the men re-cut the roof trusses, Lucillus. The masons were not as accurate as they usually are, but any alteration of the stonework now would take too much time and add too much to the cost. Our customer would not be happy about that. Explain to him that, structurally, the house is entirely sound and these few alterations will not be visible when the finish work is complete. If he is not content with that, we can adjust the contract."

"I will see him in the morning."

Josis was impatient to hear his brother's words. "Now, Father, the letter. What else does James say?"

"Perhaps," Mary interjected, "we should gather the whole family to hear James' news?"

Joseph looked up at her quizzically. "What if there is something private for my eyes only?"

Mary's hands were on her hips. "My husband," she said, "what is private in this family?"

Now it was Josis who laughed. "Your wife has a point, Father."

And it was a point with which Joseph could not disagree. "Alright," he said. "Get everyone together."

Later, when all had assembled, Joseph read the letter out loud to the group. Everyone was excited to hear of James' adventures—his progress in the house of study, his work at the synagogue, his service as contact between Joseph of Arimathea and Zacharias. About this duty James was circumspect, but all gathered that he was performing an important function.

That evening, when the compound was quiet and Mary was getting Jesus ready for bed, Joseph sat at the table again, rereading James' letter by the light of the lamp. His heart was filled with pride at his son's activities and accomplishments. At the same time, in a small, silent, secret way, it ached for the little boy who had so long been the center of a father's life.

And without expecting to do so, Joseph found himself beginning to well with feeling. His eyes started to burn, and a tear ran down his cheek. He wiped it away, then rolled up the letter, and sat gazing off into the darkness of the room. He was startled by the light pressure of a small hand on his arm, and he turned to see Jesus standing beside him.

"Do you miss James, Father?" the boy asked.

Joseph gathered himself, cleared his throat, and said, "Yes. I do."

"I miss him, too," Jesus said.

This was surprising. Everyone in the family spoke of James, so Jesus had always heard much about him. But he had been so small when James left for Jerusalem.

"Do you remember your brother?" Joseph asked.

"Yes," Jesus said. "He used to play with me."

With a nod Joseph said, "That is right. He did."

Jesus looked at Joseph with a smile that was at once innocent and knowing. "Do not be sad for James, Father."

Joseph was gripped by the child's loving concern, and he felt a brief constriction of his breath. He choked back the emotion, took the boy in his arms, and said, "How can I be sad when you are with me?"

Mary was standing in the doorway to the sleeping room watching this exchange.

*   *   *

No matter where he went, it seemed to James there was no avoiding controversy over taxes. The marketplaces were filled with fevered discussions, as were the temple courts. Disturbances were reported daily, with royal troops beginning to have greater visibility in the streets of Jerusalem. James found no respite at home, since the situation weighed so heavily on Joseph of Arimathea. And of course, it was the focus of all the messages James was carrying between Joseph, Zacharias and the allied members of the Sanhedrin.

The subject intruded constantly on class discussions, much to the vexation of Hillel, who felt he had covered its legal and moral aspects thoroughly and wanted to move on to other points. He attempted one ploy to redirect discussion, drawing an analogy between the paying of taxes and the making of offerings in the temple.

The master made note of his disagreement with Shammai over what constituted an appropriate sacrifice of grain, wine or oil. Hillel's position was that a fortieth of one's harvest was a generous offering, while Shammai insisted one had to give at least a thirtieth. By Shammai's measure, a fortieth was as undistinguished a sacrifice as a fiftieth, and giving a sixtieth was so niggardly as to suggest avarice. This was being far too rigid, Hillel insisted, and too legalistic as well. Didn't the Scriptures declare over and over that the Holy One was not moved by sacrifices but by the motives of the heart?

Under normal circumstances, the dispute would have sparked a lively exchange among the students, who always enjoyed comparisons of the master's teachings with those of his greatest rival—the more arcane the points and more subtle the distinctions, the better. But minds were set firmly on taxes and the unrest they were causing. There was no refocusing their attention.

James wondered whether people were as upset outside of Judea. In particular, he hoped that conditions in Nazareth were not such as might create problems for his family. It was so difficult to obtain any accurate news over distances, other than rumors, which flowed constantly, though with little reliability. He found himself hoping for Samuel of Rabbah to return from his travels in other parts of the realm. Samuel would have passed through Galilee, and hopefully, would have delivered James' letter to the compound. He must surely have gotten impressions of how things were going in the north.

Desire for information was the one and only reason James had for wishing to hear from Samuel, however. To the contrary, Samuel's return would mean Avigail's departure, and that was something James desired not at all. Sitting with her, strolling together in the garden, sharing reflections—always with Niva and Elizabeth properly attendant in the colonnade—had become cherished highlights of James' trips to the villa.

It did not take long for him to realize that providing opportunities for such interludes had been Elizabeth's plan all along. She was obviously intent on playing matchmaker, and saw in these two young people the potential for quite a good match. It was equally apparent that Avigail's mother was similarly inclined, or at least willing to follow Elizabeth's lead in exploring the idea.

What was not clear to James was why the two women might favor such a pairing. A scholar had little to offer in the way of prospects.

Even his status as a disciple of the great sage offered no particular advantage in framing his future, beyond lending a certain vague prestige. And no one had reason to assume that James came from wealth, even if his family could claim Davidic descent, their business was well established, and his father enjoyed a good reputation.

But then, why had Zacharias been willing to take such pains on his behalf? The great priest had opened the door to study with Hillel, directed James to Joseph of Arimathea for a place to live, made him virtually a member of the Ein Kerem household. It had all been because of Elizabeth's kinship with Mary, and because of the mysterious connection between the boys, Jesus and John.

Had Elizabeth confided to Niva the expectation of some great change ahead and her conviction that James' family was to play a key role in bringing it about? There were no answers. But James had to admit to himself that he didn't really care, as long as he could enjoy these visits with Avigail. She was an utterly charming girl, and the more he got to know her, the greater the depth he perceived.

Avigail was intelligent, witty and pious, with a great curiosity about the precepts of the faith and the will of the Lord. Once she had gotten over her embarrassment about being able to read, James persuaded her to take advantage of this sojourn in Ein Kerem to broaden her exposure to the holy books. He obtained permission from Zacharias for Avigail to peruse the priest's library.

Zacharias' willingness to open his holdings to this inquisitive girl helped to ease her mother's reservations about reading, and Avigail plunged hungrily into the great trove of knowledge. Her subsequent talks with James were peppered with questions about the wondrous ideas she was discovering and the picture she was getting of the Chosen People and its divine destiny—far more detailed than any she had ever encountered before.

Unexpectedly, James found himself in the role of teacher, and he felt absolute delight in being Avigail's *Hillel*. In a way, he was also her *Lucillus*, teaching a few Greek phrases to help clarify philosophical concepts. Their conversations steadily grew in length, sometimes pushing James' returns to Jerusalem well into the night.

The experience raised a fundamental question about Jewish life: *Why was it customary to shield girls from learning?* The argument about education undermining female virtue didn't really make sense, and in fact, contradicted reality. Wasn't it the lot of women to be the first teachers of the young? Wouldn't at least a modicum of formal learning make them better able to instruct their children, as well as to better understand, encourage and assist their husbands, especially if their husbands were scholars?

That thought brought James to an abrupt halt. *He* was a scholar. Had the possibility of being Avigail's husband really gained a grip on his heart? Were Elizabeth's matchmaking efforts drawing him toward something for which he clearly knew he was not ready—which he was not in a position to consider?

This was troubling. If he were to pursue obtaining Hillel's certification and establishing himself as a rabbi, marriage was out of the question for years. And yet, James was finding it more and more difficult to pull himself away after his visits with Avigail—even to attend to his duties, and he had already been having enough trouble balancing his obligations to the class, to the synagogue, and to Joseph and Zacharias.

How could he permit himself to think about marriage? But then Jedediah's remark flashed into his mind: *We are all men, and we all think about such things.*

CHAPTER TWENTY-TWO

The Lord is near to the brokenhearted,
and saves the crushed in spirit.

(Psalm 34)

I t was clear that the Sanhedrin could do nothing to alleviate the tax crisis. The interests of far too many of its members—both priests and laymen—were tied tightly either to the royal family or to the temple. The reform faction was too small and too weak to cut through the web of advantage and indebtedness Archelaus had spun in securing his office. Both the royal surtax and the temple tax would continue undisturbed.

Appealing to Caesar might have been worthwhile. Rome had been sympathetic to Jewish claims in the past. Hadn't an arrangement been made years before exempting Jews from conscription into imperial military service? The Augustus might have at least listened to an alternative tax proposal offered by a unified Sanhedrin. But the Sanhedrin wasn't unified, and without support across the membership, such an effort would be pointless.

A spirit of dejection lay heavily upon Joseph of Arimathea, and he wondered if it had been a mistake agreeing to have his name put forth to succeed Zacharias on the council. True, it had brought him into a kind of leadership role—mainly through dispensing the advice provided by the great priest to his fellow reformers—most unexpectedly so, considering his newness. But what had he really been able to accomplish?

Personal frustration was the least of Joseph's concerns, however. Incidents of violence were occurring nearly every day. One tax collector was dragged from his home in the middle of the night and beaten almost to the point of death. Messages were appearing on walls throughout Jerusalem calling for open rebellion.

James had not made a trip to Ein Kerem in more than two weeks, since it was determined that nothing could be done in the Sanhedrin. This was for the best. The present danger made passage across the city a dicey proposition, especially at night. The Civil Guard and royal troops were out in force and very much on edge. Anyone could be suspected of being up to no good, and soldiers were not always scrupulous in withholding force until questions were answered.

Also, with gangs of insurgents prowling about in the dark, actually looking for trouble, the possibility of blundering into some confrontation and being assaulted was all too real. The Sanhedrin medallion James wore might protect him from arrest by Archelaus' men, but it could get him killed by those with a grudge against anybody associated with civil or religious authority.

The need for caution provided James with a rationale for doing two things he knew were necessary: concentrating on his studies and staying away from Avigail. Not being with her was painful. There was no convincing himself otherwise, because she was on his mind constantly. But his feelings for her were outpacing his situation in life, and he sensed that she reciprocated his growing affection.

What to do? He could not possibly go to Samuel and ask for her hand. There was no way of knowing when a wedding would ever take place. How could a marriage contract even be written? With no resources of his own and his father so far from Jerusalem—and under current conditions, with little hope of even contacting him—how could financial commitments be made to secure a bride?

James was sinking into a mire of emotion. The sense of being overwhelmed was creeping upon him again, like the first day he came to find Hillel in the temple—that old feeling of wanting to run home to Nazareth. Of course, he had not run home when faced with the enormity of a new life. But at that point, he had only himself to think about. The present circumstance involved another person: Avigail. More than that, it involved her family and his. He would just have to think the situation through and consider his choices—such choices as he had.

In light of unrest in the city, Gamaliel announced that class sessions would be shortened so his disciples need make their way to the temple or the synagogue only during those hours when the streets were full and conditions safest. Similarly, food distribution and other services usually provided for the poor in the evenings would take place during daylight hours until the crisis had abated. So James found himself with time on his hands. Consequently, most of his waking thoughts—and a good many of his sleeping thoughts as well—were focused on the question of whether he could ever have a future with the beautiful and intelligent girl who sat in Ein Kerem reading Zacharias' books.

*   *   *

The property owner, whose house was on the same Sepphoris street as that of the merchant, Albus Drusus, and to whom Albus had recommended Joseph, was delighted with the construction and eager to move in. His wife was already making plans for a banquet intended to show off their new home, though setting the date of the affair depended on completion of the floor in the dining hall. The Greek mosaic artist to whom Lucillus had contracted that job was excellent, but notoriously slow. No matter. This project was a success. Alterations carried out to make the timbers fit within the improperly measured stonework were not visible to any but the closest inspection. They affected the appearance and integrity of the structure not at all. The customer was happy—another triumph for the house of Joseph.

It was the afternoon before the start of Sabbath, and Joseph was returning home in the company of Lucillus, Nachum and two of the workers. Lucillus' scrip bulged with gold coins, the last payment on the project. They passed through what, before the great uprising, had been the Jewish quarter of the city. Most of the buildings wrecked in the fighting had been cleared, with new construction accomplished on many of the sites. Those that had survived the fires and house-to-house combat with only partial damage were by now refurbished and bore new occupants—no Jews, of course. How much had changed, with untold heartache in the process. And yet, the city went on.

A rhythmic thumping from behind caught Nachum's attention. He turned to find its cause. "Let us get off the street," he said. "Legionaries." He grabbed Joseph's arm, pulling him to one side. "Quickly, Master."

They hurried off the road as the column approached at medium step, several hundred spear men, four abreast. The foot troop was led by a cluster of mounted officers followed by the aquilifer, bearer of the standard that identified this as an imperial cohort. These were not auxiliaries, but long-service professional soldiers, citizen-volunteers, *exercitus Romanorum*. Many of these men would likely have begun their careers on the Italian peninsula or in the colonies close by and seen action throughout the empire. A train of supply wagons brought up the rear, suggesting that the unit had traveled some distance and likely had a fair pace to go.

"From Tyre, perhaps," Lucillus speculated. "Somewhere on the coast."

"Where do you suppose they're headed?" Joseph asked.

Lucillus' brow furrowed thoughtfully. "Jerusalem."

Joseph did not like the sound of that. This was a heavy column of tough, battle-scarred veterans. If such a cohort was headed for Jerusalem, it meant that the stories circulating about unrest in the city were true, perhaps even understated.

Arriving at the compound, Joseph found Lucillus' judgment confirmed. Sarah reported that the soldiers had stopped to water at the fountain in the town square. A neighbor, speaking with one of the legionaries, learned that there was rioting in Jerusalem and that Roman troops were converging on the capital to restore order. A picture of James came to Joseph's mind. There was cause for a father to worry.

*   *   *

Conditions in the capital had become much worse. It was like the affair of the eagle standard all over again. Archelaus misread the people's mood in much the same way his father, Herod, had done. A combination of events, including the eventual death of the beaten tax collector and increasing avoidance of tax payments among the populace convinced the ethnarch that tough action was needed. Several homes in Jerusalem and farms in the surrounding areas were seized, families sold into debt bondage, the fathers tossed into prison.

Bystanders at the scene of one confiscation, egged on by insurgent agents, began throwing rocks. When the guardsmen drew swords, weapons appeared among the crowd and an actual battle broke out. A guardsmen was killed. Royal forces came to the aid of their comrades, slaughtering six of the rioters. That night, the sky over Jerusalem was aglow from fires burning around the city. Guard posts were attacked, homes of civic officials and tax collectors put to the torch. Shops, granaries and market stalls were looted.

Archelaus appealed for help from the Roman garrison, but the 600-man force billeted in the Antonia fortress was insufficient to quell the violence, which by now had spread throughout the city. When word of the disorder reached nearby towns like Bethany and Hebron, similar, though less extensive, eruptions occurred there.

The chaos went on for more than a week, with Archelaus virtually a prisoner in his own palace as clashes between rioters and royal troops raged outside. James, now confined within Joseph of Arimathea's walls, was sick with worry about Avigail. He knew that Ein Kerem was home to many people of great wealth and influence, and so maintained a well-paid and effective civil watch. But that very concentration of such important personages could be a reason why some dissident group might wish to foment trouble there. He hoped appropriate precautions were being taken at the villa.

The arrival of legion cohorts from throughout Palestine finally restored order. It was Roman brutality applied in its usual effective way. The commander of the combined forces handed Archelaus a note from the governor in Syria saying that tax collections were suspended, the ethnarch was to take no further actions that might inflame the populace, and a request for instructions had been sent to Rome. The meaning of this was clear. If Archelaus was to take *no actions*, in particular the filling of Caesar's coffers, then Rome's instructions, when they came, would not likely strengthen his position.

Would he be deprived of his authority, reduced to a mere figurehead? His status as *half a Jew* had won him the ethnarchy, if not the kingship. Was he now to be half a man?

Archelaus pondered this situation and decided that the solution to his problem lay in rallying the people behind him, challenging as that might be under the circumstances. He issued a proclamation that since normal life in Jerusalem had been so completely disrupted, with business brought to a standstill, food would be provided for a month, purchased by the royal treasury and distributed around the city free of charge. Royal troops and the Civil Guard, preempted in their security functions by the legionaries, were sent out about the countryside to purchase foodstuffs, paying liberally and collecting an ample supply.

The impact of this generosity on farmers and housewives was positive—as it was on certain officers, into whose pockets much of the ethnarch's money was diverted, a simple matter under the pressure of the situation and very lax oversight. But no one could be certain just how much peace Archelaus' magnanimous gesture would buy in the long run, especially when the month of free food came to an end.

After several days passed quietly, the Roman forces permitted a loosening of some security restrictions. Early on the first morning that the city was reopened to unrestricted traffic, James heard an insistent pounding on the front gate and hurried out of the stone hut to see who was there. Much to his surprise, it was Lemuel, Zacharias' steward.

"Master James," he said, "I must speak with Joseph."

Upon admitting Lemuel, James could see that the man was red in the face from running, and very distressed.

"Has anything happened at the villa?"

"Quickly, Master James," Lemuel said, pointing toward the house.

Joseph was up and had heard the commotion. He stepped through the front door just as James approached with the steward. "Lemuel," he said, "have you come from Ein Kerem alone? Is that safe?"

"It was unavoidable, sir." Lemuel stopped, caught his breath, and bowed. Then he said, "My master is very ill. He asks for both of you to come right away."

*   *   *

James was startled to see how much his benefactor had declined in the weeks since he'd last been to the villa. Zacharias lay on a divan, weak and manifestly in pain. He had endured the discomfort of being carried outside to the colonnade, intent on receiving his two colleagues with as much dignity as possible. Now he struggled to hold up a hand in greeting.

"Peace be with you," he said in a shallow voice.

Joseph of Arimathea knelt by his mentor. "Honored friend," he said, "forgive me. If I had known you were so ill, I would have been at your side."

"How could you have come?" the priest said. "The turmoil of these days... You were needed in the council."

"I have tried to bring your wisdom to the council," said Joseph, "but I have not done well."

Zacharias managed a smile. "You have done very well," he said. "You have done as well as any man could. Perhaps these are not days for wisdom. Only for endurance."

With effort, he gestured the two men to lean close. James knelt next to Joseph.

"Listen," said Zacharias. "A change is coming. You must take heed of it and proceed with caution. I am told that Archelaus will be deposed. The source of this information is reliable."

"Who will succeed as ethnarch?" Joseph asked.

Zacharias attempted to speak, but his voice broke into deep, rheumy coughing. When he recovered, he said, "No one. Caesar is finished with Herods in Jerusalem. It is probable that Judea will be ruled directly from Syria, though—" coughing again "—that is not certain. Archelaus' territories may be broken up or—" He was deeply fatigued, but he persisted. "A new...administrative district...may be created."

"Direct rule in Jerusalem?" Joseph said. "The Romans have always tried to avoid that. Maybe Caesar will wish the Sanhedrin to assume greater authority. This could be a good thing."

"I fear not," Zacharias said. "The Sanhedrin...is too much like the Senate of Rome...at least from Caesar's point of view. And Caesar... has trouble enough with that fractious body." He winced in discomfort, took a deep breath, and continued. "The Augustus prefers...his puppets...and there are puppets ready at hand. The high priest...and his inner circle. You will see them taking greater power. They have long made...their accommodation with Rome."

"The Sanhedrin will not be pushed aside," Joseph said indignantly. "The priests already have too much influence. The council will not stand for it."

"You'll find, my friend...that the council...will have little to say in the matter. The shameful ineffectiveness over Archelaus' surtax shows... how divided and corrupted...the Sanhedrin itself has become."

Joseph could not dispute the point.

Zacharias laid his hand on Joseph's. "You and the others must con-

tinue to...speak for the people," he said. "You must do what you can.
But you must proceed...carefully. Very carefully. The priests will be
even more guarded...and suspicious...than the ethnarch. They will be
wary of any change...or of anything they perceive as a challenge...to
their authority...or their relationship...with Rome...no matter how innocent a thing it is. Rome will always be in the backs of their minds...
and they are not wrong in that. The eagle casts its shadow...over all the
House of Israel."

The gravity in Joseph's face showed he was taking the words of this
wise man with the utmost seriousness.

Zacharias turned to James. "Kinsman," he said, "I have further need
of you. You must take a message...to your family."

"My family?"

"They must know that I have made an arrangement for my son,
John."

"Arrangement...?"

"He cannot stay here in Ein Kerem."

"But Elizabeth——"

"Elizabeth is old. When she departs, the boy's destiny...would be
taken into other hands. Perhaps even before she departs."

James was puzzled. "I don't understand."

"John is the son of a priest. By all measures of tradition...and expectation...*he* should be a priest." Beads of sweat had formed on Zacharias' brow and were running down across his face, indicating the great
labor required for him to keep speaking. But still he pressed on. "I have
not always been a friend of...the inner circle...but I have been blessed to
enjoy a certain...prestige...in the temple and among the people."

"You are beloved, my friend," said Joseph, "a model to all in the living of a righteous life."

Zacharias touched his hand again and smiled.

"Some would see it as a victory, of sorts..." he continued, "to have
the son of Zacharias in their care...to raise him in the way they...would
have him go. It would be as if I endorsed all their actions. And I will
not have that."

Weak as he was, Zacharias mustered his energies to peer deeply, pen-
etratingly into James' eyes. "It would not suit the Lord's purpose, kinsman...*as you well know.*"

A glance told James that Joseph was now the one who was puzzled.

"But my family in Nazareth," he said, "perhaps they could raise John. Galilee is far from Jerusalem."

"It is not a question of distance," said Zacharias. "If I sent him to... Britain...the distance would not stop them from...claiming the boy. He would be found...and taken to the temple to fulfill...what is, in fact...his lawful destiny...to be a priest. No. He must be cared for by men whom no one in the temple...would challenge. I am sending John to Jericho to live with...the Essenes."

The Essenes, that sect representing the most extreme form of piety, men who attempted to live in such pure fidelity to the precepts of the Law that they organized themselves into communities set apart from the mass of the Jewish people—they were the most vocal and persistent critics of the temple priesthood, implacable foes.

Joseph found Zacharias' intention shocking. "But, my friend...to do such a thing— You would be repudiating the religious leadership of the nation. All you have stood for. Your son would be...an outcast."

Zacharias' eyes closed. The pain on his face was more than physical. "I know this," he said. "I understand it all too well. It is much to lay upon a little boy...my loving child...the pride of my life. A greater burden than he should bear. But he has...a different destiny...a higher mission to fulfill."

He opened his eyes again, looking squarely at James. "You must share your family's secret with Joseph. Explain all that...has happened. He will be your most reliable ally."

James looked at his landlord. "I will," he said.

What was this relationship that existed between Zacharias and James—and apparently James' family as well? Had there been more behind the priest's sending this young man to Joseph's home than merely a desire to help a student? And the way James had been welcomed into Zacharias' household. Joseph knew that Elizabeth and the wife of James' father were blood relatives. But what Zacharias was saying now suggested a stronger tie than that.

The priest was near exhaustion. "I must rest," he said. "But Lemuel...will provide the details of what I...have arranged...with the Essene community. Joseph...you and I will discuss...the caravan business...in awhile. But perhaps...I might nap for a time."

"Of course," Joseph said. "I will sit with you, dear friend."

"A comfort," said Zacharias, and then, "James...Elizabeth would speak with you."

"Of course." He rose from where he knelt and went inside the house.

Elizabeth was in the central hall, talking with two servants, giving instructions about resetting the braziers in her husband's bedchamber to ward off chill. These days, Zacharias found himself shivering with cold at all times other than the very height of the day, as right now when the sun was most intense. She sent the servants on their way and turned to acknowledge James.

"I am glad you've come," she said. "You can see that the end is near."

"Yes, I can."

"He has told you about John?"

James nodded in the affirmative. "But what of you? Will you stay here in the villa?"

"I will go to Jericho. We have land there. I will be under the eye of the Essene community. John will be in their direct care for the purposes of his instruction."

"And to keep him from the temple priests."

"That more than anything."

"I will inform my family of these arrangements."

"Yes, please do," Elizabeth said. "It is vital that Mary and your father are aware of John's situation and able to be in contact with him... when the time of the Lord's purpose is at hand."

"You have my assurance." James looked around the hall. "Where is Avigail? I did not see her or her mother in the garden."

Elizabeth turned away for an instant, James catching the abruptness of the move. "That is something else I have to speak with you about," she said.

James felt the hairs of his back signaling trouble.

"Samuel returned from the journey he took for my husband," Elizabeth said slowly, knowing that this news would be difficult for James to hear. "It was just at the time when we had word that violence was gathering. One of his caravans was set to depart for the east. He thought it best to get Niva and Avigail away from the Jerusalem district as quickly as possible."

"Oh..." James said blankly. "I— That is a disappointment. But I suppose Samuel...acted for the best. Avigail should not— I would not want her in danger. Her father was wise."

James' mind whirled with conflicting thoughts. While he wasn't in a position to propose marriage, he hadn't really considered how he would get along without Avigail, once she returned home. And of course, she would have had to go home eventually. Didn't he realize that his opportunity to decide on whether he wanted a future with her was of limited duration? Had he been so shortsighted? But what should he do now? Should he attempt to contact her father? Should he go to Rabbah? Even if he did, his situation would be unchanged. He still could not marry.

Elizabeth interrupted his musings. "There is...something else, James."

He looked at her warily.

"One of the stops on Samuel's journey was in the tetrarch Philip's new capital, which they call Caesarea-Philippi," she said. "We did not know—even Niva didn't know—that Samuel has been in correspondence with someone there. It is a landowner...a man of great wealth who has vast holdings, there and in several other areas in the Decapolis territories. The man deals in certain tradable commodities grown on his farms, and Samuel knew him through the caravans, which carry his produce. This man has a son...of marriageable age."

James felt a tightening around his heart. Distress was in his eyes.

"Oh, James... Samuel returned with a marriage contract for Avigail. She is to marry the man's son."

Elizabeth burst into tears. "James, forgive me," she said. "I was foolish to have encouraged you to seek out Avigail, to have made times for you to be together. I only thought that you were both— I could see that the two of you are so alike. And then I even convinced Niva. But I— I have done you a terrible wrong."

*   *   *

James spent the rest of that day alone, sitting in the garden. Elizabeth instructed that he should be undisturbed, but had food sent out to him. He did not eat much. That night, he was many hours getting to sleep.

Next morning he broke his fast in the company of Joseph, taking that occasion to explain all of the peculiar circumstances involving the two boys, Jesus and John. Joseph's reaction was expected: disbelief in the implausible facts set against high regard for the information's source—very much what the Rabbi Ezra had felt when he was admitted into the secret.

Sanhedrin affairs compelled Joseph's return to Jerusalem, but James remained at the villa. Joseph sent word to Gamaliel, informing him that the impending death of Zacharias and some important business related to it would keep James away from the class for a period of time that was, at this point, unknown. Gamaliel sent a return message asking Joseph to assure James that Master Hillel understood.

*   *   *

Within a week of James' arrival in Ein Kerem, the great priest, Zacharias, of blessed memory, was gathered to his fathers. The size of the crowd processing through the streets of Jerusalem for his funeral would be spoken about with wonder for years.

Immediately after the interment, Elizabeth, in the company of James and the steward, Lemuel, handed John over to a man named Pinchas, an Essene elder and distant relative of Zacharias, and two other representatives of the Essene community near Jericho. The boy was taken away from Jerusalem under cover of darkness. The next day, Elizabeth prepared for her own departure and the closing of the villa.

James left for Nazareth in the company of three burly and well armed guards, hired by Lemuel from the watch in Ein Kerem. While they were on the Samaria road, a cohort of Roman troops entered the palace of the ethnarch in Jerusalem. A tribune informed Archelaus that he would be retired from office. On Caesar's order, Archelaus was removed to Gaul.

PASSAGE OF MORE THAN TWO DECADES

PART III

UNDER PILATE

CHAPTER TWENTY-THREE

I and the children whom the Lord has given me are signs and portents in Israel from the Lord of hosts, who dwells on Mount Zion.

(Isaiah 8)

Officiating in Jerusalem was a generally unpleasant experience for the prefects who ruled Judea. Each of the four who'd held the post since Archaleus' removal more than twenty years prior, found it expedient to minimize contact with the quarrelsome, often hostile, Jews of the capital. They spent most of their time in Caesarea, the provincial administrative center. There they could enjoy the refreshing coastal breezes and the gleaming white, colonnaded buildings that, if not quite authentically Roman, had been elegantly designed by Herod's best architects and at least suggested home.

And the people. Caesarea was overrun with Jews—no denying that—but mostly of a more civilized variety. Many of Caesarea's Jews were returned from the overseas communities which the self-designated *Hebrews* of Jerusalem referred to derisively as the Dispersion. Even those who were native to Palestine and had never been abroad were of a type more willing to bathe in the streams of cultural refinement flowing from the west since Alexander. All spoke Greek, many Latin. The presence of such companionable Jews, along with the corps of clerical functionaries, many of Italian origin, and the staff officers in charge of the military cohorts under provincial command, allowed the prefects to find comfort in their coastal enclave, while avoiding Jerusalem as much as possible.

The one pleasure to which a prefect could look forward whenever it was necessary to—as the Jews put it—*go up to the City of the Lord* was staying at the prefecture, the sprawling and elegant complex that had once been the royal palace. This dazzling edifice, on which Herod had lavished every imaginable luxury, served as the Jerusalem billet for Caesar's vicar. Its gilded halls and lush garden courts provided compensation, of a sort, for having to deal with the impossible demands, endless complaints, and bitter resentments of a nation that simply would not be satisfied.

The Rabbi James of Nazareth had first visited the official residence during the term of its last occupant, Valerius Gratus, shortly after taking over as proctor of students when Gamaliel succeeded his grandfather, Hillel, of blessed memory. Gratus, to his credit, had always made it a point to acquaint himself with the leading Jewish civic, religious and scholarly figures.

At that time, James had been included as Gamaliel's adjunct, among a group of scribes and Levites received in the prefecture's outer court. On later occasions, as his personal stature increased, invitations of courtesy came directly. Gratus knew that James was associated with the most respected house of study in Jerusalem, and it was rumored that he had links with the reclusive and highly unaccountable Essene community. James was someone Gratus felt it worthwhile to cultivate.

Evidently, the departing prefect had urged his successor to do the same, because James now stood at the prefecture's main entrance. The officer of the watch examined an invitatory letter James had handed him, bearing the seal of the new *Praefectus Iudaea*, Pontius Pilate.

"Admit the honored rabbi," he called to the two soldiers attending the gate. He returned the parchment to James, and accompanied him into the court. There he bade the visitor make himself comfortable while he went to get the prefect.

A shaded pavilion created from staked poles and suspended canopies was set up in one corner of the court near the foot of a narrow stairway leading to a terrace at the near end of the main building in the complex, known as the praetorium. The pavilion was furnished with benches and chairs for Jewish guests. All understood that pious Jews would never willingly venture more deeply into this pagan realm than the outer court for fear of uncleanness. Likewise, they wouldn't accept the graciousness of food or drink. To the Romans it smacked of ingratitude for simple hospitality, but it was a fact of life in Jerusalem.

James stood under the canopies, gazing around the court. His eyes were drawn here and there, glimpsing the various servants, operatives and legionaries caught up in the flurry of activity that always prevailed when the prefect was in residence. A few glanced back at this visitor, so out of place in the white linen robe James had long adopted as his uniform, his head in the turban that wrapped his long hair. If they could see that hair, which no one ever did, they would recognize the same streaks of gray that highlighted his beard, equally untrimmed.

The loss of his chance to marry Avigail had seemed to James a sign that he was meant for a life, not just of study in the Law, but of chaste adherence to it. He was encouraged in this by a certain indirect exposure to the ascetic practices of the Essenes. In his effort to follow the progress of Zacharias' son, John, growing up in the brotherhood's community near Jericho, James had maintained a correspondence with Pinchas, the boy's principal teacher.

Their letters not only dealt with John's welfare, but touched matters of religious philosophy and discipline. While James never considered joining the brothers, his exchanges with Pinchas provided a measure of inspiration. James attempted to approach the Essene level of dedication by taking, and then continuously renewing, the Nazarite vow. As with Samson of old, no razor touched his hair.

After some minutes, James spotted a figure descending a wider stairway across the court leading down from a wing of the praetorium. The man was of medium height and stocky build with notably muscular arms visible under a toga edged in royal purple. His face was the classic Italian rectangle punctuated by a high forehead and that characteristic, slightly hooked nose which the Jews referred to as *Roman*. He was followed by the officer of the watch.

When the pair reached the canopied pavilion, the officer snapped to attention and pronounced in introduction, "Pontius Pilate, Prefect, Legate of the Augustus, Tiberius Caesar," and then, shifting his position slightly, "the Honorable Rabbi James of Nazareth, representative of the School of Gamaliel of the Chamber of Scribes and master of the Synagogue at the Crossed Streets."

"My humble residence is honored by the presence of such a distinguished scholar," Pilate offered with ceremonial grace.

"Your kind invitation is greatly appreciated," James responded, "especially considering the press of duties you must face in taking up your new post. I thank you most sincerely—peace be upon you."

Now that the formalities of greeting were past, the prefect dismissed his subordinate and gestured for the visitor to seat himself wherever he liked. When they were both comfortable, Pilate said, "Your Greek is flawless, Rabbi. I was told you are fluent in several languages. It eases my task considerably, since to my disadvantage, I am not yet familiar with your colorful tongue."

"I was fortunate to be tutored from an early age," said James. "My father employed a Greek freedman who was quite learned."

"A great benefit," Pilate said, nodding thoughtfully, "to master the language in which so much of the empire's business is conducted and its knowledge shared. I understand that many of your people refuse to learn other languages, and that even those who know some Greek often decline to use it."

"This is true," James said. "It is even the case that some houses of study forbid discourse in Greek. That is a loss, because it imposes a limitation on what young men can learn."

Pilate looked at him appraisingly, taking note of a surprising air of sophistication that did not reflect what he had heard about Jewish religious scholars. Gratus may have been wise to take an interest in the Rabbi James.

"At the same time," James continued, "I would hope the prefect can appreciate that foreign influences have not always touched the Jewish nation in positive ways. If we have tended to turn inward as a people, even resisting knowledge which might be adapted to our good, it has not been out of mere resistance to change. Rather, we seek to protect a way of living that has sustained us through the most challenging of times. It is like our practice of moral discipline in which we strive to avoid situations that might dispose us to wrong behavior, or even cause us to think about it. We call that *setting a hedge around the Law.*"

How delicately put. Pilate could see the Rabbi James was a man of considerable tact. In the most subtle way, and in their very first conversation, he had told Caesar's vicar that the Jewish people would live their own lives regardless of Roman power or the overwhelming dominance of its Greek culture. The prefect didn't allow himself to smile, but he determined he would make getting to know this Greek-speaking scribe a priority.

"I am curious, Rabbi, about this *Synagogue at the Crossed Streets*," Pilate said. "That seems an odd designation for a religious house."

By a slight tip of his head and the raising of one eyebrow James acknowledged the point. "No doubt, Prefect," he said. "When we first began, we intended that only as a means of identifying its location. It sits on one of the few corners of the city where two streets intersect in a perpendicular way, rather than veering off at angles as most do. But after a time, it began to feel appropriate. You see, the establishment is a house of seclusion, a place where men come when they are pondering large decisions or seeking to focus more deeply on their interior lives. In other words, when someone has reached a crossroads."

"Clever," said Pilate. "It is affiliated with the school of Gamaliel."

"And his synagogue."

"Yes... A synagogue affiliated with a synagogue. I'm not sure I—"

"Our house is not a synagogue in the usual sense," James said. "We have no congregation, though there is a room we use for services when at least ten men are present. At other times, that room serves for private prayers and contemplation. There are also chambers for lodging guests."

"I realize that you Jews do not equate your practices with those of foreign cults," Pilate said, "but followers of other gods also undergo that kind of withdrawal from the world. I myself once sojourned in a sacred reserve in search of auguries to aid an important decision."

James said nothing in reply to that bit of personal revelation, but merely sat with a vague, noncommittal expression. Pilate took this as another sign of tactfulness, realizing that a pious Jew would not address a gentile religious exercise. Whether the prefect was genuinely interested in the house of seclusion or merely wished to draw him into conversation, James couldn't tell. But Pilate kept asking questions.

"How did you conceive of this establishment?"

"Actually, the idea was suggested by my father's widow—"

"Mmmm?"

"—a remarkable woman who has spent much of her life in prayer and contemplation. Her name is Mary."

"You father's...*widow*—she is not your mother?"

"His second wife. My mother died when I was an infant."

"I see. And this...Mary...resides in Jerusalem?"

"In Nazareth, my hometown. She lives in the family compound, with my three brothers and their families." James paused, then: "Four brothers, really. Mary has a son, though at present he is traveling."

Pleasantry piled upon pleasantry as the prefect sought to ingratiate himself with James. "And where is Nazareth?" he asked. "I am working to familiarize myself with the local geography, but I have not encountered that town as yet."

"Nazareth is not in Judea," said James. "It is in Galilee. In the hills near Sepphoris."

"Ah—Antipas' territory. Then we are both boys of the countryside. My family originates in the Apennine mountain region." It was a nice note of commonality, even if it did not ring quite true. James knew that Pilate was descended from a noble family of the Samnites, an ancient, non-Latin people of the Italian interior. As such, he held Equestrian rank, a knight of the empire. His boyhood countryside experience would have been rather different from life in Nazareth.

But so the conversation went for the better part of an hour. James was surprised that the new prefect should devote so much time to a purely social exchange with an individual rabbi. There were no politics, no probing for information, no striking of authoritative poses to let the Jew know who held the power. It was all very pleasant—enjoyable, really. James found himself musing over the irony of spending a genial interlude with the chief agent of Caesar's oppression. He'd had that thought before when in the company of Valerius Gratus, another affable Roman.

It was no accident that James would receive Pilate's attention. He held a unique position among Jerusalem's religious and scholarly leadership. He was not a priest, and in fact, he conscientiously maintained his distance from the temple elite, though he made sacrifice in the temple regularly. Neither was he a member of the Sanhedrin, having declined nomination several times. Nor had he founded his own house of study. Yet he was known throughout Judea.

James the Just, he was called by people of every social class and every religious party—Pharisees, Sadducees, Essenes, even Zealots—and there was no hint of mockery in that appellation. Broadly admired for his learning, wisdom and personal sanctity, he was free of the suspicion which people tended to harbor toward religious figures, even those they followed. He was trusted, and so consulted often on a wide range of questions. All paid heed to his advice, holding his powers of judgment and his spotless conduct as examples to be emulated.

Though he had been a disciple of Hillel and proclaimed his ongoing association with that great school, now presided over by Gamaliel, he was spoken of with respect by scholars of all affiliations. And while the priests regarded his aloofness from their circle with wariness, they would never utter a skeptical word about him publicly. He was, in short, a man of significance whom it would behoove Caesar's vicar to know well.

After a time, the officer of the watch returned to inform Pilate that his attention was required elsewhere in the palace. James assumed this had been prearranged as a means of drawing the interview to a polite close. Prefect and rabbi both expressed their pleasure at the opportunity to meet. Then, in what James took as a particularly gracious gesture, Pilate asked if he could call upon James for his guidance, in the event he faced some question that might benefit from the rabbi's expertise in Jewish religious concerns.

"I would be honored," said James as they both rose from their seats, "to help Rome better understand the special virtues of my people."

Pilate smiled at that, turned in a crisp, military way, and departed across the court and up the broad stairway, the drape of his toga billowing behind him. James' smile was unnoticed by the officer of the watch, who saw him back to the gate.

*   *   *

It was mid-morning when James reached the Synagogue at the Crossed Streets. The copper band around the archway, which had once identified this as the home of the tin merchant, was still in place, kept bright with regular polishing.

Joseph of Arimathea had maintained the house as his Jerusalem residence for several years after purchasing the villa in Ein Kerem from Elizabeth and relocating his family there. The stacks of ingots were long gone, Joseph having moved the metals trade to a site more convenient to caravan arrivals and departures. Sometime later, James approached his landlord with a proposal about establishing a house of seclusion, noting that the idea had been Mary's, inspired by her days in the temple precincts. James asked to rent the property, but Joseph embraced the project enthusiastically, allowing him complete use of the house for that purpose and securing another residence for himself when he was in the city.

Just as when he had first come to Jerusalem as a student, James continued to reside in the stone hut. It was a strikingly humble abode for a man of distinction, and enhanced his renown, adding self-denial to his widely recognized piety.

Upon arriving home, he went directly inside to a stack of letters that awaited his attention. There were inquiries about points of the Law as well as requests for advice on personal or family matters from people all over the Jerusalem district and beyond. He read through the notes, writing out his replies, most of which would be delivered by a student assigned to him by Gamaliel. James found it ironic that this messenger, named Asher, hailed from the town of Sennabris in his own native Galilee. Perhaps Galilean lads had a gift for such errands.

Asher did not carry all of James' messages. Eager for a word from the great rabbi, petitioners often specified that they would come to pick up the responses themselves or send their own messengers. This was especially true of those who lived outside the district and wanted to spare James any need to make delivery arrangements. Others prevailed upon him to speak in person. Hence, James never knew when a man, or even a woman, might appear at his gate. But he had learned to live with unexpected interruptions, often from agitated people in urgent need of guidance. He had become adept at calming their anxieties. Among the men, some discovered for themselves the answers they were seeking after a few days' of quiet reflection in the Synagogue at the Crossed Streets.

By late afternoon, James had worked his way through nearly all of the day's missives. Only three remained to be read. He picked up a small scroll, the seal on which was well known to him. This letter was from the Essene elder, Pinchas.

The first message James had received from Pinchas in some time, it expressed concern about odd behavior observed in the only son of the priest, Zacharias, of blessed memory. During recent months, Pinchas reported, John had become increasingly separated from the others in the community. Such was his zeal for Essene austerity that he had taken it to a far extreme. He was living as a hermit, wandering up and down the Valley of the Jordan preaching to anyone who would listen. His only clothing was an animal skin and leather belt. And he subsisted entirely on wild foods he collected for himself, such as honey combs and the few types of locusts that were acceptable under the dietary laws.

At first dismissed by people in the region as an oddity—and as someone who was probably quite mad—John had lately begun to attract followers. Many admired his self-mortification, responded to his impassioned calls for repentance, and flocked to receive a novel form of ritual cleansing John conducted at a place called Bethany Beyond the Jordan. At times, the crowds at this river site were quite large.

Pinchas explained that the Essene brotherhood was worried about the attention John was gaining. Notoriety of this sort contradicted the community's normal practice, which was to screen its devotions from public view and keep outsiders away. Especially troubling was the word they'd received that John's activities had piqued interest among the temple leadership. This James knew to be true. Pinchas' letter confirmed a rumor he had heard about some Essene wild man causing a stir up and down the river. The high priest had sent agents to investigate.

James hadn't realized that the object of so much curiosity was the son of his one-time benefactor. But his reaction to this news from Jericho was not the distress that fairly leapt off the parchment he held in his hands. He suspected that John's behavior indicated neither madness nor excessive Essene fervor. Perhaps it signaled the setting in motion of that great plan which Mary and his father had discerned in the circumstances surrounding the births of John and Jesus. Perhaps the Holy One was at last preparing to act. If so, the action was a long time in coming. But then, the Lord had His own time, which always defied men's expectations.

If this supposition was correct, speaking with the family might be in order. A trip to Nazareth would be most untimely and rather difficult, filled as James' days were with the needs and pleadings of so many people. But if this turn in the life of Jesus' cousin did reflect the divine will, it could not be ignored. The Rabbi James sat pondering this possibility and the complications which leaving Jerusalem would entail. Finally, he resolved that he did need to consult the family. He especially needed to consult Mary.

*   *   *

For years there had been debate about whether direct Roman governance made the country safer than when Judea was under royal authority. Some argued, for instance, that the possibility of facing Caesar's retribution caused those intent on committing highway robbery to consider the idea more carefully. And it was true that the visibility of Roman troops had increased. The breakup of the royal forces after Archelaus' removal had left security gaps which the prefects filled by dispersing legion cohorts more widely around the country. Valerius Gratus had also reinstituted the practice of routine patrols, which had declined since the days when Palestine was first brought into Rome's *community of nations*.

On the other hand, except for crimes involving sedition against the empire, the actual administration of justice was still in Jewish hands. Anyone taken by legionaries would be turned over to the Sanhedrin in the nearest town or to the Great Sanhedrin in Jerusalem. If their offenses were serious enough, criminals indicted by the local councils could still end up in Jerusalem. So in practical terms, not much had really changed.

Regardless of whether greater military presence actually made for greater deterrence, wise travelers still journeyed in groups. James checked with Joseph of Arimathea about when a caravan might be scheduled to set out on the route to Tyre or one of the other northern seaport cities, thus providing him companionship—and, more to the point, *security*—on a walk to the hills near Nazareth. Joseph's response was to arrange mounted transport directly to the family compound.

"James," he said, "a man of your stature does not walk the Samaria road behind a camel, or even the road into his own village."

He held up a finger to forestall any objection from James, who was about to protest that his only interest was safety.

"You will be borne in a suitable manner," Joseph said firmly.

James acceded to his dear friend's insistence. And so it was that he found himself tucked into a cushioned seat on the swaying back of a dromedary bound for Galilee attached to a caravan that made a regular run between Jerusalem and Caesarea Philippi. Joseph had altered its usual route, giving the caravan master instructions to deliver the

Rabbi James to Nazareth and pick him up again on the return trip.

James craned his neck and looked behind as the city faded into the distance, its towers now blocked by hills and rocks, now revealed again, until finally they were gone from view. How completely the city of the Lord had burrowed into his heart. Though he'd been raised in Nazareth, Jerusalem was his home, and had been for so long. Each time he departed it, his thoughts echoed with the words of the psalm: *If I forget you Jerusalem, let my right hand wither.*

In the circumstances, that thought was, perhaps, a bit too mawkish, and James shook it off. This was only a trip to the family compound. He'd made the journey before, sometimes urgently, as upon Zacharias' death. His father and Mary had been surprised then to hear that John was to be raised in the Essene community, though Zacharias' logic in making such an arrangement seemed sound to them.

Other trips had been occasions of greater joy. They provided opportunities to meet new nephews and nieces, to marvel at the flourishing and expansion of the olive grove, to see how the household was enlarged when Judas' oldest son married and a new house was added beyond the compound's walls, and many other happy changes. For all of his years away, James' sense of closeness to his family had not diminished, nor his pride in their accomplishments.

There had been occasions, too, when relatives took the reverse journey, visiting him in Jerusalem. His father and Mary were on hand when he received ordination, known by the Hebrew term, *semikhah*, from the hands of Hillel. And of course, there were the Passover feasts when James' family members were welcomed as guests, first by his landlord, and later by James himself after he became master of the Synagogue at the Crossed Streets.

James smiled at the memory of one such Passover, which years later would be recalled as a humorous family anecdote but had also provided an insight into the character of Mary's son, Jesus. The boy was twelve years old at the time, having come to the city with his parents for the feast. Joseph of Arimathea arranged for the family to return to Nazareth with a train of pack animals that included both donkeys and camels.

After the activities associated with the festive season had been completed, including going up to the temple to make a special offering,

James accompanied his relatives to the embarkation point. There was delay in getting the beasts loaded and uncertainty about when the caravan would leave. Some other people who were to walk along had sent word they would be late and asked that the train not go without them. James introduced his family to the master of that caravan, whom he knew from many deliveries and removals of metal ingots outside the stone hut. Since Jesus was curious about the camels, the master offered to take him in hand and show him how they were fed, harnessed and loaded.

The city was emptying rapidly of pilgrims when the latecomers finally showed up, so James made his farewells amid great confusion. In the tumult of braying animals being prodded into their places along the queue, the procession departed, with Joseph and Mary assuming Jesus was still in the company of the caravan master at the lead. It was not until hours later, when they arrived at a caravansary to spend the night, that they realized the boy had been left behind.

They wanted to return to Jerusalem immediately, but the master restrained them from going. The dangers of this route, well traveled as it was, were too great for an older man and a woman to venture alone, he insisted. He knew that a donkey train would be coming in the opposite direction in a day or two, and he urged them to wait until it arrived. Recognizing the wisdom in this advice, Joseph promised they would stay at the inn, so it was three days before they were back in the city.

Frantically and in a most ineffectual way, they searched places they had visited during Passover, finally arriving at the stone hut. Amara, the serving girl, informed them that Master James was not at home but could likely be found in the Royal Porch at the temple. They hurried to the temple mount, and as they came into the court, there was Jesus sitting on the stairway to the upper level, amid a coterie of gray-bearded men dressed in the distinctive garb that marked them as doctors of the Law. Joseph and Mary were nonplussed to watch how the boy held the attention of these elderly rabbis, taking their questions and offering comments that appeared to provoke intense thought and considerable wonder.

James, who was standing by, came up behind them. "He has been engaged in conversations like this for the past two days."

Joseph and Mary both turned with a start.

"Has he been with you?" his father asked.

James laughed. "Am I my brother's keeper?"

Worn by the anxiety of their search, Joseph was not amused at the quip. James' raised hand was calming and his smile reassuring.

"Jesus became distracted and separated from the group after the caravan master left him to prepare for departure," he explained. "The fascinations of the city, I suppose. They can arrest the mind of a small-town boy, as I well remember. At any rate, Jesus strolled about the streets, not thinking. When he realized that the train had gone without him, he went to the temple. That night, he found his way to my door. I knew you would be back, once you discovered he wasn't with the train."

Mary emitted something like a choked sob, the sound of a mother's relief. Joseph exhaled deeply and put his hand on James' arm.

"Thank you for being your brother's keeper," he said with a grateful smile.

Comforted though she was, Mary still had words of admonishment for her son, that he should have wandered off in such a thoughtless way. Jesus was truly sorry for having caused his parents worry, but his odd reply left an impression on James.

"Why did you bother to search?" the boy asked in all innocence. "Didn't you know that I would be in my Father's house?"

Even now, after all the years, as James sat on the back of his camel, tossed to and fro by the animal's rhythmic motion, he could still hear his brother's young voice pronouncing that inexplicable phrase. Had Jesus' assumption—so naively evident to him—been a sign of things that lay ahead, events that might now be coming to ripeness?

CHAPTER TWENTY-FOUR

"Am I my brother's keeper?"

(Genesis 4)

The camels in the caravan bearing James to Nazareth had not been desert-bred or trained for travel in dry country, so their ability to go long distances without water was limited. Since the caravan master had no stomach for haggling with Samaritans over watering privileges when passing through their territory, he pushed the animals to press on all the way to the River Kishon in the Jezreel Valley, stopping there for water and a night's rest.

When they reached the day's destination, James prayed the evening service alone, since there were no other passengers or walkers with this train and the animal handlers and caravan master were busy tending to the camels and setting up camp. Most weren't Jews anyway, but rather Arabs from Syria. When he finished, he ambled about the meadow that ran between the road and the river, his mind drifting back to days past.

This was the spot where he had camped with Lucillus, Nachum and Mary on their furtive journey to Ein Karem so many years before. He'd rested here on other trips as well. Indeed, this was a place to stir many memories. One especially came to him now. It involved the saddest of his journeys.

Lucillus and Nachum had hurried to Jerusalem with distressing news: Joseph was ill and had asked that James be brought to him. This was before James established the Synagogue at the Crossed Streets, while he was still serving Gamaliel as proctor of students. Also, it was during the tenure of Valerius Gratus, when a cluster of violent incidents showed that the Zealots were once again testing the prefect's mettle. Gamaliel had worried that the company of Lucillus and Nachum might not provide adequate protection, and so insisted on sending three students along. This would comprise what he saw as an unchallengeable group of six going, with four to make a safe journey back.

They hastened to Nazareth. Joseph was in a very weakened condition when they arrived at the compound, but fortunately, he was clear-headed and able to raise himself enough to receive his son's embrace. It was obvious to James that he had come just in time.

"Father," he said with a crack in his voice from shock at Joseph's appearance.

Joseph could see the concern in his eyes. "My son, do not be sad that the Holy One is calling me to Him. My work is done. I have lived my life according to the Law of Moses. I leave my family in as good a shape as I could. I am content."

Mary and Jesus were there in the upper room, the chamber James and his father had shared years before. They knelt by the side of Joseph's sleeping mat. Other members of the family were present as well. Sons, daughters, wives, husbands, grandchildren had organized themselves so that several loved ones would always be in attendance during the last days of the family patriarch and the rest could be called when it became apparent the end was at hand.

Mary lightly stroked Joseph's brow with a damp cloth. James noticed droplets of water glistening in his father's thinned and now-completely silver hair. He couldn't tell if they were sweat or water from the cloth. Jesus sat with his eyes closed and a hand on the shoulder of this father who had taken him as his own son, raised him, cherished him under circumstances that would have confounded a man of weaker faith and a less loving heart.

At that moment it occurred to James that he had no idea how much knowledge Jesus possessed about his origins. The boy had been small when James left for Jerusalem, and in the years since, there was no mention of how much had been shared with him about Mary's belief that she'd borne the *Son of the Living God*. James had certainly never discussed it with Jesus on any occasion when they'd been together. He wouldn't have wanted to blunder into a subject Jesus' parents might not already have broached.

James, as all in the household, recognized that Jesus' birth and the incidents surrounding it were extraordinary, and he was amply aware of his brother's noteworthy gifts. But despite carrying the family secret, and also despite his relationship with Zacharias and the ongoing watch he kept over the boy, John, James had never been able to fully embrace the idea that Jesus could be the Messiah. And immersion in the sacred books did nothing to crack his reserve.

Perhaps it was just emotion that impeded his acceptance, a wall he could not surmount. Would the King of the Universe really touch James' own family in such a way? Was it possible for an ordinary child from an undistinguished place like Nazareth to accomplish the marvelous deeds by which Jewish tradition maintained the Anointed One would be recognized? Of course, it all came down to Jesus himself—someone whom James had to admit wasn't really ordinary.

But what did his brother know? If Jesus did have a special nature, was he aware of it?

These thoughts brought James to a realization of how completely removed he was from his family at this point in his life, despite the feelings of warmth and closeness. Jerusalem had been his world while the sun had risen and set day after day, year after year on the compound here in the little hill town. His brothers and sisters were aging. His nieces and nephews were growing up—some were grown. His dear father had become an old man and now lay before him about to die. James had been so far away. A sense of emptiness overcame him, and he felt that he was close to tears.

Joseph seemed to sense the turmoil in his son. He turned to Mary.

"My wife," he said, "would you please take everyone from the room for a few minutes? I would speak with James alone."

"Of course, my husband." With small gestures of gentle authority, she ushered everyone out.

When they were alone, Joseph said, "My son, you are distressed, and you must not be. You *cannot* be. We have come to the time when I must call you to a great service. I need you, James. I need you to do what no one else can."

"What is that, Father?"

"I hand the care of your brother over to you."

Taken aback, James said, "But Father, Josis is the eldest."

"Yes, of course. Josis has control of all the family's assets. He will provide for Jesus' material needs. But that is not what I mean."

James was confused.

"You, my son, are a promising scholar whose renown reaches even to Galilee. The Rabbi Ezra, my old and dear friend, tells me of the respect you are gaining in learned circles."

"I am merely proctor to the students of Gamaliel."

"But you will be more. Of this Ezra is certain, and so am I. Equally certain am I that all your learning, all the influence you will acquire— everything—it is for a purpose the Holy One has ordained. That purpose centers on your brother."

This near to his end, Joseph did not exhibit the extreme faintness of energy or the struggle to speak which James had observed when Zacharias was dying. Still, it was apparent that Joseph was taxed by his efforts. James could see now that the droplets on his father's brow were beads of sweat.

"You must carry on for me," Joseph continued.

"In what way, Father? What can I give Jesus that compares with the things he's gotten from you? You saved him from Herod. You raised and sheltered him. You taught him."

"And now *you* will help him to prepare for his mission and carry it out. That is the point of all your knowledge, of your involvements and connections, of the prominence you are gaining. I am sure of it. You must help him, and— And...my son...you must *protect* your brother."

"Protect?"

"You know the suffering that has always been the fate of prophets," Joseph said. "I cannot say where Jesus' path may lead. But someone sent to do the Lord's work faces terrible risks. Even the risk of death. I hate to think of such an end for him, especially while his mother lives."

Still Joseph was concerned for the well-being of Mary. Still he honored the promise made to Joachim so long before.

But now James had to know his father's true conviction about Jesus. No uncertainty, no ambiguity could remain on the question that had hung over the family these many years.

"Are you absolutely sure," he asked, slowly and in a tone of the utmost solemnity, "that Jesus is the *Son of God?*"

Joseph looked into James' eyes with a depth of penetration that left no misunderstanding. "I...*know*...that he is. I have been told it by the Holy One Himself. There is not the least doubt."

He reached up to take James' hands between his own.

"I remember the night we spoke, James," he said, "that horrible night after the Sepphoris crucifixions. I recall the uncertainty you expressed when I proposed that Mary's son might have been sent to deliver our people from Roman oppression. Do you remember that?"

"Yes."

"I could not answer your question then about whether Jesus was Messiah. But I can now. He is, James. He is. And I can tell you that I believe he will do more than defeat Rome, though what that all may be has not been revealed to me."

His grip on James' fingers was surprisingly strong for someone in a depleted state. James could *feel* his father's conviction in the press of those rough, leathered palms, a carpenter's hands.

"I fear, however," Joseph continued, "that your brother may pay a high price to fulfill his mission. You must do what you can to protect him from that—or at least to stave it off as long as possible. The will of the Holy One must be accomplished, no matter what, James. I have played my part to assist in that, and now you must, also."

"What is there for me to do, Father?"

"That I cannot tell you, my son. I don't know."

He released his grip on James' hands.

"You must wait for the Lord's promptings. Perhaps He will speak to you in the clear voice I have heard. Perhaps you will be led only by signs and circumstance. But you must respond when need arises." Once more the penetrating gaze. "You *must*, my son. You *must*."

James sat back on his heels and took a long, slow, thoughtful breath. What did he really have to give his brother? How could he help? What dangers was he capable of staving off, if dangers did come? He couldn't begin to know. But it was his father who asked this of him, his beloved father. "I will," said James. "I will do whatever I can, Father. I promise you."

Then he bent over and kissed on the cheek this man who had been the most important influence in his life. Joseph reached up, and they embraced again. When they separated, Joseph pointed toward the door.

"The others now," he said. "Get Mary."

"Yes, Father."

It was as if death had been held at bay expressly for the sake of this final sharing between father and son. During the next two days, Joseph's decline accelerated rapidly. The family kept watch, different individuals coming in to relieve the others. The stretch of time seemed ever more slow, ever more ponderous and draining.

Finally, late of a Sabbath morning, after a cloud of unconsciousness had laid upon him for several hours, Joseph, of blessed memory, Nazareth carpenter, builder, master of craftsmen and laborers, husband of Mary, son of Jacob, went to the Lord.

He was laid to rest beside his first wife, Escha, in a tomb hewn out of a rock face on the side of a hill beyond the olive grove, overlooking the compound. Everyone in town attended the ceremonies conducted by the Rabbi Ezra, who had to be assisted in walking because of his advanced years. The prayer for the dead was recited, and many tears were shed. Likewise, all called on the family during the days of receiving. Numerous messages of condolence came, many from Greek clients and acquaintances in Sepphoris.

Years later, the Rabbi James reflected on these things in a meadow near the River Kishon. The next morning, the caravan departed for Nazareth.

*   *   *

Passing the synagogue, riding atop his camel, James recalled the day when, as a student in the school of the Rabbi Ezra, he spotted Mary being carried by. A smile came to his face as he mused on the image of her small form tossed up and down, side to side with the camel's lope. The smile broadened into a wide grin when his caravan reached the far end of town and the family compound came into view. He called to the caravan master that they had arrived, and the master signaled the handlers to stop.

James found himself compassed about by wives, nephews, nieces—though fewer of the girls than on earlier visits, since there had been marriages. His brothers, Judas and Simon were not present. Presumably, they were with their flocks or attending to other family business. Mary and Josis greeted him warmly, and James read the passing of the years in their faces. Josis was now nearly as gray of hair and beard as their father, Joseph, had been at his end. Mary had acquired the look of a distinguished matron, though her face retained traces of its girlish beauty.

"James," Mary said, "how wonderful it is to see you. Your presence always brings joy to the household."

"Peace be upon you, Mary," he said. "You're looking well. Have you word of Jesus? When last I heard, he was in the east."

A motherly smile seemed to hold great import. James took note of it and flashed her a quizzical look. Her response was to aim a glance over his shoulder. James turned to see where it was directed. Jesus stood behind him.

"Peace be with you, brother," Jesus said.

"Jesus," said James in surprise. "I did not expect you to be here."

James found himself looking into a face he hadn't seen for nearly five years, a face that had changed. It reflected its age of just thirty—long and, in its way, elegant, with features that were more comely and distinctive than those of anyone else in the family. He had the impression that Jesus was starting to resemble his grandfather, Joachim, or what he could remember of the great landholder. Jesus had definitely gained a distinguished appearance, his closely cropped beard and flowing hair now showing the merest scattered beginnings of gray, and his dark eyes warm and engaging.

"Joseph of Arimathea told me you were reported to be in Arabia or even farther east," said James. "Word is you have covered much distance and have come to know many foreign climes moving along the trading networks."

"To which you gained me admittance, Brother," said Jesus, "and for that I thank you. Yes, my adventures have been many."

Their exchange was interrupted by the wife of Judas' eldest son. She lifted up her little boy so that *Uncle James, the family rabbi,* could see how much the four-year-old had grown since James' last visit.

"The family rabbi is impressed," James said, laughing. He touched the boy's arm, squeezing gently with thumb and forefinger to assess the muscle. "What a fine strapping lad indeed. I can see that Uncle Josis will soon be able to retire his ox cart when delivering those finely carved beams to the building sites. This young Samson will carry them."

The little boy squealed with delight, both at James' attention and at the tickling sensation produced on his arm.

When all welcomes had been extended and plans improvised for a family feast in James' honor, the household returned to its affairs. James, Josis, Mary and Jesus retired to the portico.

"So, Brother, where have you traveled with Joseph's caravans?" James asked.

"Many places," said Jesus. "I was first into Cappadocia, then up along the Euxine Sea to the Kingdom of Armenia, and then all the way east into Persia along the spice route and into the mountain land of the Afghans."

"When Jesus told me of his journeys, I was astounded," said Josis with a wide-eyed look of amazement. "Well beyond the frontiers of the empire."

Jesus laughed. "Yes, there was no sign of the Roman eagle in those far passes. Even Alexander never penetrated to the places I walked."

"When you came to me five years ago," said James, "I was— Well, Brother, I admit I was very reluctant to ask Joseph of Arimathea to accept you for such treks into unknown regions."

"Not unknown to those who travel there," said Jesus. "And it was at my own request, after all. I told you I desired travel, and asked your brotherly aid." He turned to Josis. "Not that I hadn't enjoyed working at your side. You taught me much, Josis, as Father had before. I value the skills I gained from both of you."

"Oh, I understood your wish to know the larger world," said Josis. "You were meant for much more than a Nazareth carpenter's shop or even the building sites at Sepphoris."

"Well, *I was afraid*," said James. "I worried what dangers you might encounter along foreign roads, and I dare say your mother did as well."

"That is true," Mary said.

"Well, here I am, safe and sound," said Jesus, beaming.

"For which I give thanks to the King of the Universe," Mary added. Jesus embraced his mother.

"How long have you been back in Nazareth?" James asked.

"Only two days."

"Then this feast the wives are planning honors both of us."

Josis laughed. "Hardly," he said. "We have been feasting since he arrived."

They all joined him in laughter, then James came to the purpose of his visit.

"I have news of your cousin, John," he said. "Pinchas, his teacher, writes me that John has separated himself from the community at Jericho and taken up some sort of preaching mission in the wilderness by the Jordan."

"Yes," Jesus said, "I know."

"You know?"

"I have seen him. In fact, I spent several days with him and took his baptism."

James was surprised at this unexpected turn. "But...how..."

"The letters of referral I carried from Joseph of Arimathea got me passage along the incense route for my return trip," Jesus explained. "From the Sea of Persia, I followed the Arabian coast, sometimes on land, sometimes by boat. At Aila on the gulf, I joined a pack train for Jericho. Word of John's preaching was everywhere in the region of the Salt Sea. I found him at Bethany Beyond the Jordan."

"Then...why did you not come to Jerusalem afterward?" James asked. "It is fairly close by. You could have stayed with me to rest before heading on to Galilee by the Samaria road. Joseph would have arranged further transport."

Jesus turned his head and gazed off across the court. "Yes... Well, I could have. But after I left John, I spent some time...in the desert. I had...an encounter."

"Encounter?"

"Let us call it a time for answering questions," Jesus said, turning his glance back to James. "But there were some men I met. Fisherman, down from Galilee. They were among those following John. They insisted I come to their home. The one—Andrew by name—thought it especially important that I meet his brother, Simon. So after my desert sojourn, I followed the river directly north."

"If you needed a time of reflection," James said, "I would have been happy to put you up in my house."

"Ah yes, the Synagogue at the Crossed Streets," Jesus said. "What a wonderful place that is. I recall the Passover feasts when we all used to lodge there."

It seemed to James that Jesus didn't wish to address this time he'd spent in the desert *answering questions*. With whom did he have this *encounter*?

"In any event, these friends, and some others, have come with me," Jesus said. "They're walking about the town and the countryside now. They wished to see the region where I was raised. But they will be back later, and you will meet them."

All of this information had put James off his purpose. And once more, it raised the question of what Jesus understood about himself. With some hesitation, he ventured onto that topic.

"Did you..." he asked cautiously, "Did you have any discussions with John about...well, about what he sees as this mission of his? Since receiving Pinchas' note, I have wondered what the object of his preaching might be—and this cleansing ritual he is conducting."

Jesus' eyes were closed, and he didn't seem quite prepared to offer a response to this inquiry. But James felt it important to probe further.

"Indeed," he said, "I've wondered if it might have something to do with...you."

After a moment, Jesus looked at his brother. "Yes, James," he said quietly, "it has to do with me. Over the years, I have come to an awareness of...things. Things I've never discussed with you. There were indications, you see...little signs that showed in how I was treated by the family...how I was kept apart from others. And, of course..." He glanced at Mary. "...from time to time, Mother and I have spoken, to some extent—"

Mary's face broke into an enigmatic smile.

"—and Father, too...a bit...before he left us. But I have never gone deeply into...well, what can one call it—my origin? my destiny?—not with anyone."

So he did know.

"The one specific thing which Mother and Father told me," Jesus continued, "was that they felt my cousin, John, might one day help me to discern my future path. Isn't that right, Mother?"

"Yes, it is."

"So when I came upon the great excitement he was creating in the Jordan Valley—and there is *considerable* excitement, I can tell you—it seemed that the time had come to seek him out."

Still proceeding cautiously, James asked, "What do you intend to do now?"

Jesus smiled, then said jovially, "Why, go to a wedding, of course."

"A wedding?" James was confused again. He looked at Mary, who directed him with her eyes to Josis.

Josis cleared his throat. "The younger sister of my daughter's husband is to be married," he said. "In Cana. The family is invited."

"It is in three days, James," Mary said. "You'll come?"

"The procession will go to the groom's home in Capernaum," Josis added. "So we'll be going there as well. But much of the celebration will be held in Cana, because the bride's father is very infirm and cannot travel."

Knowing that the caravan would return for him in little more that a week, James agreed to go to Cana, but not to Capernaum. Then he directed his attention back to Jesus.

"Well now, a wedding is one thing, Brother, but have you plans beyond that?"

The expression on Jesus' face was quite inscrutable. Not a smile. Not a frown. Not anything indicative. "All in good time, James," he said. "I am thinking. And I am praying." Then, with a twinkle: "Especially the latter."

The mention of prayer brought an end to Jesus' participation in this exchange. "It is good to see you, Brother," he said, rising from his seat. "We will speak again. I look forward to it."

And with that, he walked across the court toward the front gate. The small grandnephew James had joked with earlier was playing near Josis' shop. Jesus stopped for a moment, bent down to speak with the boy, and tousled his hair. Then he straightened up and went out of the compound.

James looked after. "He has changed, my brother. Somehow he seems less open than he was. He holds something back."

"Yes, James, he has changed," said Mary, an ambiguous note in her voice from her own uncertainty about what she perceived as different in her son.

"No man is unguarded in the way he was as a boy," Josis said. "At least he *shouldn't* be, not if he is wise."

"That's true," James said. "Still...I wonder if I was right in agreeing to ask Joseph of Arimathea to arrange passage for him on the caravans."

"It isn't the travel that has changed him," Mary said. "No doubt he was touched by his experiences in foreign lands, but there is more at work than that." She patted James lightly on the arm. "You know it to be true."

"Perhaps...as he said...the time has come," James said.

"I think so," Mary replied, nodding.

James turned to Josis. "What of these fishermen he mentioned?"

"Pleasant fellows," Josis said. "What a carpenter might call *a bit rough to the plane*. But that's fishermen, isn't it?" He grinned, amused at his own thought. "I have always found that men who make their living on the water have a very positive outlook. Maybe it's because their fortunes are so uncertain. They never know if their nets will be full. Then too, they frequently face danger, and it can come at any time. Seamen are a jolly bunch, usually. I have found it so whenever I've spoken with the sailors who bring us our lumber from Lebanon. Jesus' friends are much of the same stripe."

"They keep to themselves, though," Mary said. "There are seven who came with him, and since they have arrived, they've camped in the olive grove. Jesus sleeps with them out there."

It struck James as odd that, after so many years away, Jesus wouldn't spend his nights in his mother's house. A questioning look prompted Mary to explain further.

"They pray together," she said, "sometimes late into the night. And it appears that he instructs or advises them."

This James took without surprise. Somehow it seemed expected, though he didn't quite know why.

"They all come into the compound for meals," Mary continued, "so I suppose you'll meet them tonight at our feast."

"Yes," James said. "I shall be most interested to meet these jolly fishermen."

*   *   *

The feasting was ample, and if another abundant communal meal with extra mouths to fill placed a burden on the wives and daughters, they didn't show it. The entire household was gathered in the court, along with Jesus and his companions. The atmosphere was festive, everyone seated on stools, benches, or cross-legged on the ground, with animated chatter, children running about, and food steadily disappearing from trestle tables set up in the portico.

Jesus introduced his friends to James, and they did reflect Josis' description, a bit rough in manner and appearance, but amiable with a refreshing air of optimism about them. One member of the group, in particular, James found interesting: Simon son of Jonah, the brother whom Jesus said he'd been urged to meet. Simon was older than the others. James judged him to be in his forties, where his fellows—Andrew, Thomas, Philip, Nathaniel, James and John—looked Jesus' age or younger.

Simon was a big, powerful man with a ruddy face weathered by sea and sun. His hands were made hide-like from long years at the oars and the net lines. Perhaps because of his age, Simon received a certain deference from the other six friends. It appeared that he'd assumed the role of intermediary between them and Jesus. He made it a point to stay at Jesus' side. And several times during the dinner, James observed one of the others whisper something to Simon, which he would pass on to Jesus, then relay the answer back.

Mary's observation that Jesus prayed with these fellows and instructed or advised them didn't fully describe his position in the group. James understood his brother had been going about with them for some months, and he could see that a certain pattern or order had developed among them. Clearly, they all looked to his brother as a sort of leader.

What of Simon? It seemed his function was somewhat like that of James when he was proctor to Gamaliel's students. What were the thoughts of this more mature man? What did the fellow see in Jesus that made him willing to subordinate himself to someone so obviously his junior? An opportunity to explore that question presented itself later in the evening, when James came upon the big fisherman standing alone, bent over one of the tables in search of whatever food might be left.

"I see you are a man of good appetite," said James.

Simon straightened himself and laughed heartily. "Yes, Rabbi," he said in a broad, jovial manner. "I admit to it. Eating well is a habit I have passed onto my children, much to the overwork of my poor wife."

"Where is your home, Simon?" James asked, seeking to stir conversation.

"On the shore of Gennesaret, between Capernaum and Bethsaida, though nearer Capernaum. I am originally from Bethsaida. My brother and I fish the lake. We are part of a team that works the north end."

"Ah, the Sea of Galilee."

Simon laughed again. "That name overstates things," he said. "Not much of a sea. Just a big lake. But it's plentiful."

"Our Roman friends seem to have adopted it as their own sea," James said, "since Antipas built his new city of Tiberius."

"Yes, the Sea of Tiberius, they call it," said Simon. "As if they didn't have seas enough in the Mediterranean, the Aegean, and all the other parts of that great basin. Their *Roman lake.*"

James chuckled amiably. Presumptuousness in attempting to impose their own labels on everything was a Roman trait most Jews were likely to speak of mockingly.

"Who keeps after those fish, with you and the others here?" he asked.

"My sons. And there are more who make up the team, in particular, Zebedee, the father of James and John. He was *my* father's partner in the trade and helped to teach me the ways of marine life. Winter is coming, and they are pursuing the last big catch of the season. Warm times of year are much more hospitable to working on the water. I hope to find a large batch smoking when we return home. But those of us here...we have established a kind of fellowship in pursuit of a different kind of fish."

This was the opening James had been waiting for.

"Yes...I am interested in this *fellowship*," he said. "I observe that my brother holds a special place in it."

"He...does indeed..." said Simon, now eyeing James warily, not sure of the attitude behind that remark. "Jesus is a man of wisdom."

James sensed guardedness. Wishing to disarm it, he said in as sincere a way as he could, "The family has long been aware that my brother possesses special qualities. I am not surprised that others would be drawn to him."

Simon accepted that as an honest statement of familial understanding, if one that was somewhat incomplete.

"I trust you are aware, Rabbi, of what Jesus' kinsman, John, son of the great priest, Zacharias, has been prophesying along the Jordan?"

"I am aware that John is preaching."

"He is. And his message is very pointed. He is calling people to repentance."

"A praiseworthy endeavor."

"Yes, but with a specific goal: to prepare for the coming of the *Lord's anointed.*"

Simon observed in James the quiver of a reaction. He went on. "My brother, Andrew, and his friend, Thomas, both of whom you have met, heard about John and went down to take his baptism. They became interested in his message, and attached themselves to his company of followers for several weeks in hope that they might glimpse this *deliverer* of whom John speaks. They were on hand when a deputation from the priests' council quizzed John as to whether he himself might be the one whose coming he was heralding. John made it plain he was not."

James listened impassively. Simon's account of John and his doings accorded generally with the information contained in the letter from Pinchas.

"Andrew reported to me that, sometime later, Jesus came to the spot where John was conducting his cleansing ceremony. When he appeared, John recognized his kinsman, even though the two cousins had not been face-to-face since they were infants. But most astounding is how John referred to Jesus. My brother said that John called him the *Lamb of God.*"

James' reaction to this was clearly visible to the fisherman.

"I realize that is a shocking term," Simon said. "Andrew told me that everyone who heard it was *very* shocked."

"What did John mean by this description?" James asked.

"I don't know," said Simon, "at least not with complete certainty. But my brother came to me in a state of high excitement."

It was late, and the wives were starting to collect food bowls from the trestle tables and clean up the court. Simon and James moved away to a quieter, more secluded area.

"I am a practical man, Rabbi," said Simon. "Not always wise, I grant you, but inclined to want clear proof, and stubborn until convinced." A crooked smile broke on his ruddy face again. "Your brother calls me his *rock*—which I'm not sure is a compliment, and I suspect refers to the hardness of my head."

Another chuckle from James.

"But when I met Jesus, I understood what prompted John's outburst. There is something about him that impresses. It has to do with the direct and confident way he speaks the truth. And how he looks at you—I can't explain it—like he peers into your heart and knows your thoughts. I felt myself ashamed to be in his presence, an unworthy sinner."

Now the only reaction Simon observed in James was a thoughtful silence.

"You are his brother," said Simon. "You have known him since childhood, and so you may not see him as I do. That is understandable. I would probably see more in *my* brother if I wasn't related to him."

This melted James' serious countenance. The fisherman had a wit.

"I have observed Jesus and listened to his teaching for many weeks now," added Simon, "and his effect on me has not lessened."

"And now you have left your home and business to go with him?" James asked.

"Believe me, Rabbi," said Simon, "it was not an easy decision. As I explained, this is a critical time of year. But I knew I had to do it. And I can tell you there will be more who follow Jesus. I think there will be interesting things to see for those who take up with him."

James felt a strong desire to ask Simon if he believed that John had been right and Jesus was the Messiah. He liked this big fisherman, sensing in him a forthrightness that, in its way, was rather inspiring. If Jesus had chosen him as his right hand, he had chosen well. But James held back. Perhaps it was too early in Simon's association with Jesus to ask him to take a firm stand on such a momentous question.

"Simon," said James, "my brother has been abroad for five years. And the man who has returned...to be honest...I do not know."

A wise nod was Simon's response.

"Also...I am unclear about this mission he has set himself upon, and have no idea of where it might lead." James felt awkward in asking for the aid of a man he had only just met. But he saw it as necessary, and he sensed that Simon could be trusted. "If Jesus should ever come into any...difficulty... Well, please let me know if problems appear. I am not without influence in certain circles, and in my small way, I might be of help."

"I have heard of *James the Just*, Rabbi," said Simon, looking at him now with all appearance of the jolly fisherman set aside. "And I respect your concern. If help should ever be needed..."

"Thank you, Simon," James said. "May the Holy One protect you and your companions."

"And your brother, Rabbi."

CHAPTER TWENTY-FIVE

There was a wedding in Cana in Galilee, and the mother of Jesus was there.
Jesus and his disciples were also invited.

(John 2)

The family's wedding gift was a specially made litter on which the bride would be borne to the groom's home in Capernaum. Josis had constructed it, suspending the seat between two long, stout poles by which eight men could carry the girl, though she was so petite, half as many bearers would have sufficed. He padded the bottom and back, covering them with shearling from a sheep which his brother, Judas, had culled from the flock. After being borne to its destination, the poles could then be removed and the seat used as a chair.

Since he'd arranged for the litter to be delivered two days before the wedding, the bridesmaids had adorned its poles with plaits of late-season flowers and tufts of wheat heads. These were expressions of the traditional hope that the marriage would be fruitful. The maids looked forward to that moment when the bride would be lifted high and carried off in joy to her new life, their decorative handiwork displayed to all present.

The affair was well attended. Relatives of both the bride and the groom were on hand, along with a good representation of neighbors from the village of Cana and its surrounding district. Everybody was crowded into the court of the bride's family home, received by her father, who was set up on a stack of cushions, the withered legs with which he suffered in chronic pain wrapped in a blanket. His portly wife stood at his side, welcoming one and all, as proud mother of the bride, occasionally directing solicitous questions at her invalid husband, inquiring about his comfort and needs.

It was a scene very much like one James had witnessed four years before when he'd attended the wedding of Josis' youngest daughter, Beche, who was on hand now to welcome her relatives from Nazareth. She kissed Josis and Salome, and embraced all the other members of the family group, greeting James with special enthusiasm.

"Uncle James," Beche said with undisguised joy, "I haven't seen you in so long."

"Peace be upon you, Beche," he said, and pointed to her prominent belly. "I see you are exceedingly well. Number two is it?"

"Yes, Uncle, and hoping for your blessing when my little one arrives."

"My blessings you always have."

She presented the relatives to her mother- and father-in-law, who expressed their delight at having the family of Josis in their home once again. In introducing Jesus, who had come with his seven friends, Beche noted that this uncle had been abroad at the time of her wedding and so had not been present with the family then. Her in-laws welcomed him and his companions.

Beche's most portentous introduction, delivered in a voice of the utmost pride and solemnity, was for James. "Of course, you remember my uncle, the Rabbi James, from Jerusalem."

"Of course," her father-in-law said. "Welcome, Rabbi, welcome."

"Peace be upon you and all your house," James said, "on this special day for your family."

"Made all the more special by the honor of your presence." There was no doubt that this suffering man felt honored indeed. "Such a thrill, such a blessing."

He raised himself up as straight as he was able, then spread his arms widely, gesturing to the guests nearby. "My friends, my friends," he called. "Look who has deigned to attend my daughter's wedding. This is the famous rabbi of Jerusalem known to all as *James the Just*."

The crowd was duly impressed to be in attendance at the same function as such a well known figure. But the old fellow was just getting started.

"This is the man who declined a seat on the Great Sanhedrin," he said, clapping his hands and smiling in delight. "He is the scourge of the priestly class, the man to whom all turn for real insight and sage advice—even the priests themselves when they wish to learn true religion."

The gibe evoked laughter throughout the court.

"And he is uncle to *my* daughter-in-law." His relish of this connection could not be missed.

Accustomed to expressions of high regard, this exuberant display nonetheless made James feel as if he might blush. He glanced at Josis, whose face bore a lump in one cheek where the tongue was pressed betraying brotherly amusement.

"My son, my son," the father called to Beche's husband, "introduce the great rabbi to all of our friends."

Seeing James' embarrassment, the young man approached him hesitantly.

"Uncle?" he said quietly.

James' hooded eyes and a slight bob of the head noted his assent to be led about, and he went off with his niece's husband. All took the opportunity to bask in his celebrity as they made the acquaintance of the famous scribe.

In the manner of Jewish weddings, the celebration went on for many hours. There was music and dancing, the men frolicking in their circle on one side of the court, the women on the other. There were games of skill to occupy the younger boys, including bean-filled bags thrown into baskets, rope rings tossed onto spikes sticking in the ground, and other such amusing challenges.

Given the restrictions on the bride's father, it had been arranged that most of the festivities would be held in Cana, so the old man could be present. The groom arrived with his retinue of companions in mid afternoon to claim his bride. But instead of carrying her off to his home in Capernaum at the head of a procession of revelers, he exchanged vows with his bride under the wedding canopy here, then the couple remained to take part in the Cana celebration. They would leave later. Naturally, there was abundant feasting, with copious volumes of wine consumed.

The bride's father insisted that the great rabbi from Jerusalem be seated in a place of honor at his table alongside the parents of the groom who had come with their son's party. They too were excited at the prospect of such exalted company. James acceded graciously to the host's wish and seated himself, from time to time glancing mournfully at his family set off on the periphery.

Josis, Judas and Simon found his predicament comical, as James could tell from their faces. But Jesus' expression was not so readily decipherable. It seemed to mix sympathy for James' discomfort at being made the focus of awkward attention with satisfaction for his brother's eminence, which was acknowledged by all present.

The day passed into evening with no abating of the celebration. At one point, Mary became aware that there was a fuss among the servants tending refreshments. She observed the steward consult the bride's father, whose countenance changed to one of worry at the man's words. When the steward returned, there was heated conversation, which Mary, now standing close by, overheard. The wine reserve was low—about to run out, in fact—and the servants were deep in conjecture about where more wine might be obtained.

"We could ask a neighbor," said one servant. "Nearly all the town is present, and surely—"

"Impossible," the steward said curtly. "The master would be shamed." Then, in frustration, he asked, "How was the need so underestimated?"

No one had an answer. The steward looked around the court.

"Well," he said, "I suppose there are more guests than expected." He glanced in the direction of Josis' family. "Look at the size of this herd from Nazareth alone," he added, shaking his head. Just then he noticed Mary. "Madame, I—"

She cut him off, gently but with firmness. "Do not be distressed," Mary said. "Your hospitality has been gracious and more than ample."

The steward flushed with mortification, but Mary ignored him. She closed her eyes as if deep in thought, standing silently in this attitude for some seconds. Then she said, "My son may be of help," and went over to where Jesus was seated with his friends.

"Jesus," she called.

He rose and went to her. "Mother?"

"They have no wine left."

Jesus looked over at the servants standing by a row of large, stone vessels from which water had been drawn for the guests in their prayers of hand washing. Then he looked back at her. Mother's and son's eyes met, and he perceived her intention. He turned and trained his glance on James, seated at the head table with the parents of the bride and groom. He watched his brother for a moment, pondering the importance of James' presence to these people. Mary could see he was torn in his heart, filled as he was with consideration for his brother's position.

"Woman," he said lovingly, still watching James. "What has this concern to do with me?"

She set her eyes on him—the wordless look of a mother.

Another quick glance at James, then at Mary. "*My* hour has not yet come," he said.

Still she gave him the look. After a moment, she touched his arm and led him, gently and without resistance, to the steward. The man saw her approach and diverted his eyes.

Mary smiled kindly, gesturing to Jesus at her side. "Do what he tells you," she said.

The steward now looked at Jesus in puzzlement, then at Mary, then back at Jesus again, then back at Mary. This woman spoke with an assertiveness unusual for a female outside the confines of her own home—not stridently, but in a way that demanded response. Obviously, the son followed her lead. Perhaps he was aware of some nearby and unknown source of wine.

"Fill those vessels with water," Jesus told him.

This was an odd instruction. Did he think they needed to be rinsed out? The washing prayers were over. Still, if his intention was to provide wine to fill them—and the way this crowd was drinking, that wouldn't be a bad idea—the steward was willing to scrub each container himself. Whatever it might take to save the master's honor. Then too, he had already offended the fellow's mother. He gave an order for the servants to bring water, which they poured into the vessels.

Jesus extended his hands over them, and raised his eyes to the sky. He stood in this posture without speaking for a time, the passing of each second increasing the steward's anxiety. Finally, Jesus turned his attention back to the steward. "Draw some out," he said.

The steward was now totally perplexed. But having committed to his course, there was nothing to be lost in indulging him further. When he saw the contents of the ladle, the man's eyes bulged wide.

"Wine? Where has this—?"

He sniffed at the ladle, then poured its contents into a cup and tasted it. It *was* wine. And excellent wine at that. He went to the other vessels and looked inside. Each was filled to the brim, the bouquet of the drink rising and scenting the air.

"Give it to the head of the servers to be distributed," said Jesus.

Then he turned away and started back to where the Nazareth group was seated. The back of his head was only partly visible above his shoulders as he walked. It struck the steward that this fellow seemed sad to have done such an amazing thing. But how *had* he done it?

The steward looked down into his cup again, and hurried off to arrange for the serving. Mary was still there, a conflicted expression on her face. She saw Jesus plodding slowly away, and then she watched as the steward pulled his chief server aside. Gesticulating in an animated way, he explained what had happened to the water, and gave him the cup of wine to taste. The bridegroom, who was nearby, joined in their exchange, and Mary could see disbelief on his face as he heard the tale, which was already being spread throughout the court by the other servants.

When she turned back in her son's direction, she saw that Jesus and his friends were leaving the party. Josis caught her searching glance, and he raised his shoulders and palms to show he didn't understand why they were going.

James became aware that a buzz had developed among the crowd, though he didn't know its source or reason. He spotted Jesus and his friends walking toward the gate, and observed a troubled exchange of signals between Josis and Mary. Excusing himself from the table, he went over to where his family was grouped, seeing that Josis had gone to catch Jesus, and meeting Mary on the way.

"What is the matter?" he asked her.

"Oh James, I may have done a wrong thing," she said. "I may have pushed my son to begin something he was not ready to set in motion. I thought it was an opportunity given him by the Holy One, but now I'm not sure."

"What happened?"

She started to answer his question, but was interrupted by Beche.

"Mother Mary," she said, "everyone is talking about the wine and someone in the family. Do you know what it's all about?" Then she asked, presciently, "Does it involve Uncle Jesus?"

Mary did not want to attempt an explanation of something that was beyond explaining, something she surely didn't understand herself. She was spared the effort by Josis' return.

"Jesus and his friends are going to Capernaum," he said. "I asked him what had upset him, and he—he asked me to tell his mother that she was right and that she shouldn't worry."

Josis turned to James, and with a shrug said, "And he also asked me to convey his *apology* to you, Brother." Josis shook his head in bewilderment, then, looking back at Mary: "If we wish to see him after the wedding festivities are concluded in Capernaum, we can find him at Simon's house outside the town. He says that anyone in the area can direct us there."

Mary acknowledged Josis' message with an inarticulate sound, then turned to Beche. "Your Uncle Jesus did something which I really don't understand and cannot explain. But I can tell you that whatever the steward said he saw is true. Speak with him."

The abruptness of this reply was inconsistent with Mary's usually gentle, indulgent manner, and it left Beche unsatisfied. But she could see that whatever it was that happened had shaken her grandfather's widow, so she withdrew and went to find the steward.

A waving of her hands together drew Josis and James close to Mary, and she spoke to them as one who bore important news. "Jesus prayed over those stone water vessels, and—" She swallowed nervously before speaking the words, not so much because they were unbelievable, but because of what Jesus' act suggested. "And the water in them became... wine. This is the beginning of his mission," she said. "I am sure of it."

Josis and James looked into each other's faces, neither of which evinced anything that could be considered doubt. The family had lived with indications of Jesus' extraordinary powers from the time when he'd healed the broken leg of Noah, son of Simon and Zipporah. There had been other such acts performed innocently when he was a child. As he grew older, he became increasingly aware that his gifts were extraordinary, and he guarded them with care.

There was no way of knowing if he'd had occasion to exhibit these abilities while away on his journeys, nor if he'd revealed anything to the group of friends—followers, clearly—that had gathered around him. But his action with the wine was a very public display. Mary had realized this when she prompted him to do it, but she'd nonetheless felt something compelling her to urge Jesus along. His words to Josis confirmed that her instinct had been correct.

"We must be prepared for whatever happens, now," Mary went on. "This is the first sign which has been seen outside the family, and word of it will spread." She directed her attention at James, particularly. "The time has come for you to be especially attentive to your father's plea, James. Jesus may require your help."

A burst of air escaped James' nostrils as he made a small, quick, ironic laugh. "So I *am* my brother's keeper, aren't I," he said.

* * *

After the wedding party had left for Capernaum, most of his family among them, James returned to Nazareth. He walked in the company of several nieces and nephews who hadn't gone on to the groom's home, as well as another Nazareth family also related, by some clanship connection, to the bridal household. Such was the web of family ties across all of Galilee that it was unusual to meet somebody with whom one didn't have at least an indirect link.

His walking companions were much caught up in the excitement of the wine incident, and they pressed James for the secret of how Jesus had done such a remarkable thing. Was he a magician? Had he acquired the skills of an illusionist in the exotic lands he'd so recently visited? James insisted he had no explanation and was as baffled as anyone—which, of course, was only partly true.

The next day brought a rare time of ease for a rabbi normally much burdened by other people's woes and entreaties. It was a chance to walk in the olive grove, play with the children, and talk to those members of the household who had grown up during his years in Jerusalem, as well as some who had joined the family by marriage. This James considered a blessing, since there had been so few opportunities to interact with his nieces and nephews as adults.

Two young men, Judas' and Simon's youngest sons, he found especially amusing. Both now being of marriageable age, they regaled their uncle with humorous tales of how they found themselves objects of great interest among the matchmakers in the region. They were hounded with endless offers on behalf of respectable girls seeking husbands, each more beautiful and a far better cook than the one before.

Late in the morning, James called in for a visit with the Rabbi Ezra. It was a joy to sit with his old teacher again, though the stay was limited by those severe physical impediments with which the rabbi now had to live. They spoke mostly of James' work with the school of Gamaliel and the Synagogue at the Crossed Streets. The prominence and accomplishments of his former student were enormously gratifying to Ezra.

"I knew you would be a great man," he said. "The King of the Universe has truly touched you, my boy. You have been called for his ineffable purpose."

"If that is so," said James, "then He first touched *you*, because you surely have helped to prepare me. And for all you have done I will be forever grateful."

They embraced, and there was a tear in the old man's eye. Then they shared reminiscences about James' days in the class, about other boys he had known, and about the countless private conversations in which Ezra had led James to seek deeper meaning in so many passages from the holy books. Finally, James touched on a subject he had never raised with his teacher.

"Rabbi, how did you find my brother, Jesus, when you taught him?"

Ezra reflected on the question for a moment. "Hmm, yes," he said at last, "your brother. I have expected that, someday, you would ask me about him. I must admit to being extremely skeptical when your father, of blessed memory, revealed the story of Jesus' origins. My first thought was that, in his devotion to honoring the pledge made to Joachim, he had fixed on this wild account to protect a foolish girl who had fallen under the sway of some seducer. I've been a rabbi long enough to know there are many young women who carry a secret when they stand under the wedding canopy. Wise is the guest who does not inspect the bride too carefully."

James smiled at a truth to which his own experiences in Jerusalem could attest.

"But I knew Joseph to be a man of integrity, and the more I thought about it, the less it seemed possible that he would weave such a tale. So I decided to accept his words and to assess the boy for myself."

Ezra was starting to become fatigued. "I can only tell you," he said with a yawn, "that what I saw lent credence to Joseph's story. Jesus was extraordinary. His quickness in learning to read was impressive, but that was the least of his gifts. What struck me was his grasp of moral truths in the scriptures we studied. Very early I was hard-pressed to challenge him. I have never known a child so able to see beyond surface facts and penetrate to the heart of their meaning."

The rabbi's eyes were growing heavy, and James became concerned that their talk was exhausting him. Still, Ezra pressed on.

"But I should also tell you, James," he said, "that even today, rumors persist in Nazareth about Jesus and his mother. Joseph took pains to seclude the boy, which was wise, under the circumstances. But it left many questions unanswered, and people's imaginations have filled the gaps in some highly original ways. One of the most persistent theories is that Mary was raped while she was living in Jerusalem. Fanciful as the idea may be, it is said that Jesus is the son of a Roman soldier."

James' brow knit incredulously.

"As for me," Ezra said, "I am convinced that, somehow, the Lord's will is in your brother's coming to us, though what his mission might be I cannot say. If I am right, then your father's depiction of his birth is as believable to me as any." He reached out to touch James' hand. "But then, I am convinced that *you* have a mission as well. And the advantage you enjoy is that there is no similar cloud over your beginnings."

This was indeed an advantage James had over his brother. No one would ever challenge his legitimacy, and that was something for which to be thankful. But once more, the old family question poked at his mind, and he decided this was his opportunity, perhaps his only opportunity, to get Ezra's view. "Do you think that my brother, Jesus, is... Messiah?"

The rabbi's smile was astute. Wasn't this the logical question to arise within the context of their discussion? "Your father thought so," he said. "I cannot speak with his certainty. But I am disposed to think it possible. Maybe even probable."

Ezra had pushed on long enough, James decided. After sharing abbreviated mid-day prayers, he left the aged scholar to his rest. He paused for a parting glimpse of this man who had been such a formative influence in his life. Ezra, reclining on a divan, raised a hand in farewell, and James had the distinct impression that this was the last time he would ever see him.

*   *   *

When he returned to the compound, James was delighted to find Lucillus in Josis' shop.

"Now there is an old and familiar face," he said.

"James!"

"Peace be upon you, Lucillus."

They embraced.

"I was told you were here," Lucillus said. "I am so sorry I was not able to greet you when you arrived from Jerusalem. I was in Caesarea receiving a shipment of lumber from Lebanon."

"Still keeping the family business running," said James.

"I do my best," Lucillus answered with an overly humble smile.

They spent some minutes catching up on developments in each other's lives as well as on the progress of the carpentry shop and construction trade. Lucillus related how the business had experienced ups and downs in the years since Joseph's death, but that, overall, things were going well.

Then James said, with some hesitancy, "Have you spoken with anyone in the compound about the wedding we attended yesterday in Cana?"

"No."

James related the incident of the wine.

"You saw this yourself?" Lucillus asked.

"I did not witness the act, but I surely observed an abundance of wine and a great deal of excitement over its provision. The water vessels had been filled with just that, *water*. And Mary insists Jesus changed it to wine with a prayer."

Lucillus ran fingers through his by now well-thinned hair. "Well, I would not doubt the word of your father's widow. Mary is a most trustworthy woman. And it's true that we've seen other inexplicable things from her son over the years." He tossed a hand in an unconcerned way. "This seems like just the thing to set tongues wagging, especially in gossip-loving Nazareth. But it was inevitable that Jesus would one day reveal himself as someone out of the ordinary."

The hand gesture transformed itself into a pointed finger, which he directed at James. "I know the pledge you made to your father," Lucillus said. "And I fully expect you will be diligent in trying to protect your brother. But you must not be anxious about this. We have all assumed that Jesus had a destiny. Hasn't that been your family's most closely guarded secret?"

"But if this marks the start of his mission—"

"Then you will not be alone in watching over him," Lucillus insisted firmly. "The Holy One will be with you—and with Jesus. Whatever happens will be to the Lord's purpose." It was Lucillus' worldly Greek wisdom on display again, tinged with the faith of a God-fearer.

"You are right," James said, yielding to this sound reasoning. "Once more my old tutor gives me good guidance."

James' body lost some tension as he seated himself on the plank Josis was carving. "By the way, you will be interested to know that I recently met the new prefect of Judea, Pontius Pilate, and that I charmed him with my Greek. Naturally, I gave all the credit for my fluency to you."

"Ah, my most demanding student," Lucillus teased with a kindly chuckle. Then he asked, "What is your impression of this...Pilate?"

"I can't say I have one that's very clear," said James. "No doubt his intention was to win me with his genial nature. How much of that was a diplomatic pose I don't know. Our conversation touched on nothing political. He did ask if he might call upon me for counsel, should he need it. But that too could just have been a show. Or he might be hoping to establish a relationship that allows him to use my position as cover for some Roman mischief. Time will tell."

Lucillus was alert to the slight but discernible edge in James' remark. "Roman mischief?"

James understood why Lucillus had focused on that phrase.

"I have spent my adult life ministering to people ruled by an empire," James said. "The functionaries who represent that empire have varied in talent, wisdom and temperament. Some have been fools, others monsters. And I am fair-minded enough to recognize that some have been quite good, as imperial functionaries are measured. But all have come with a mandate from Caesar, and in the end, the objective of each has been to please his master. When Caesar's whims have required it, some mischief or other has been perpetrated on the people. I expect no different from the current prefect."

"I hear an echo of the Sepphoris road," Lucillus observed.

James' laugh was sardonic. "As may be, Lucillus," he said. "I attempt to serve my people and do the Lord's work as best I can. If Pilate asks my advice, I will give it. But my hopes for having any real influence are limited."

CHAPTER TWENTY-SIX

Be strong and courageous, being careful to act in accordance
with all the law that my servant Moses commanded you.

(Joshua 1)

A t the meadow along the River Kishon once more, the caravan broke out of its queue, the handlers leading their camels to the river's edge for watering before starting on the rise up into Samaritan country and thence to Jerusalem. A little way farther along the river another train had begun reforming for the road, but was stopped by what appeared to be a squad of legionaries.

"Can you see what's happening to them?" James called up to the caravan master from the ground.

The master was still in his saddle, neck craned, with one hand shielding his eyes against the glare of the morning sun. "It looks like some kind of inspection. Maybe trouble has broken out. I recall being stopped once when there was a search for Zealots. Dagger-men had murdered some tax farmer in Jerusalem. All caravans were checked. It happened years ago."

"I remember the incident," said James.

"They have finished," said the master. "Now, no doubt, *we* will have a pleasant visit with the friendly Romans."

Mounted soldiers approached, and the principales in charge drew his horse up next to the master's camel.

"Where are you bound?" he asked curtly.

"Jerusalem."

"From where do you come?"

"Caesarea Philippi," the master said, "by way of Nazareth."

This elicited great interest from the officer. "Nazareth?" he said. "We seek the Rabbi James of Jerusalem. We are informed that he has been visiting relatives in Nazareth."

"So he has," James said, stepping forward. "I am the one you seek. These men are taking me back to Jerusalem."

The principales hopped off his horse, stood at attention, and offered a sharp fist-to-chest salute, which took James by surprise. It was rare for a Jew of less than royal or priestly status to receive such a sign of respect.

"Rabbi," the man said, "My Lord, Pontius Pilate, instructs that you be brought to Caesarea Maritima immediately. He seeks your aid in a pressing matter."

"What sort of matter?"

"Some religious dispute. I'm afraid I don't understand it. Jews are complaining about defilement. My lord, Pilate, will have to explain the situation to you."

The caravan master called for James' camel to be brought up from the river, but the principales objected.

"We have a horse for the Rabbi. "It will be faster."

"I have never ridden a horse," James said, appearing somewhat uneasy at the prospect.

The principales looked at the camel, then at James. "Very well," he said. "Ride the camel."

The caravan master instructed one of the handlers to have the dromedary kneel so that James could climb aboard. When the animal was on its feet again, James pulled it up next to the master. As the principales remounted his horse, James thanked the master for his assistance, passing him a handful of coins to disburse among his crew.

"For you and your men," he said. "Please tell Joseph of Arimathea where I am. I will return the camel to the feeding ground at Jerusalem."

"Yes, Rabbi."

James departed with the legionaries. They rode at a modest canter, the soldiers holding back their mounts to accommodate James on his camel. During one of several breaks, the principales offered him some dried food, which he refused gently with an expression of thanks. The soldier didn't understand why he wouldn't eat. But then, Jews were such a perplexing people.

After some hours on the road, they reached Caesarea in the early evening. Along their way through the city, there were Jews and pairs of Jews, which became groups of Jews, which became crowds of Jews, growing more dense the nearer they got to the prefect's palace. Some recognized the Rabbi James, and word of his presence began to spread. That the famous scholar should be riding among legionaries was a source of confusion. Some feared he might be under arrest, and a murmur developed.

The main gate of the palace was guarded heavily, soldiers in full battle dress. James dismounted and was approached by a centurion.

"The prefect awaits you eagerly, Rabbi," the man said.

"What is happening here?" James asked. "Why are all these people jammed into the streets and squares? There are hundreds."

"Thousands, Rabbi. It is a protest."

James scanned the crowd. "A strangely quiet one," he said, looking about at various faces. "Most of these people are just sitting on the ground. What are they protesting?"

"*That* the prefect will explain, sir. Please follow me."

James was led into the compound, whose size and opulence were impressive, if not quite comparable to the prefecture in Jerusalem. But then, this palace was another accomplishment of Herod, whose passion for elaborate buildings had known no bounds.

They arrived at a deep portico whose Greek-style columns were set in two rows two stories in height. Wooden frames were installed between several of them, draped with heavy fabrics, forming a rough enclosure into which James was ushered. The interior was warmed by a fire burning in a large brazier, a bench on either side. Technically, James was still outdoors, though sheltered from the chill that overtook a seaside town on an evening this time of year.

"Please wait, Rabbi," the centurion said. He left James and went into the building, guards posted on either side of the door snapping to attention as he passed.

James stood next to the brazier, extending his hands over the burning coals, feeling the heat. A minute later, one of the drapes was pulled back and Pilate entered the enclosure.

"Rabbi," he said, and with a small gesture, dismissed the centurion and the guards, leaving him alone with James. "Thank you for coming." His face looked grim. "I trust the time spent at your family home was gratifying."

"Peace be upon you, Prefect," James said. "And yes, my visit was quite nice. I am, however, rather perplexed at this side trip—and curious as to how you knew where I was."

"Naturally you would be, Rabbi," Pilate said. "We inquired at your synagogue and at the Royal Porch. As you can see, there has been an incident in your absence."

"So I gather," said James. "What is the subject of this protest?"

"Something which I am quite unable to comprehend," Pilate said. "The garrison in the Antonia Fortress was recently relieved, quite soon after you departed from the city, as it happens. The standard of our new detachment bears a likeness of the Augustus. For reasons I cannot fathom, this is a cause of great offense to the people of Jerusalem. Now, I am well aware of the famous incident of the eagle standard during Herod's last days. But as I understand it, the problem at that time involved bringing a foreign symbol into the temple precincts. This is nothing of the sort."

"You know about our prohibition of graven images?" James asked.

"Of course," Pilate said. "But doesn't that refer to the worship of idols? This is merely a regimental emblem which is only displayed within the garrison or when the troops are in transit."

"How did the protest get started?" asked James.

Pilate glanced down at the ground for a second. "Well, here I have to admit that my men were not tactful," he said. "The emblem was posted on one of the fortress towers overlooking the temple grounds. But you must appreciate that the right to carry Caesar's image is an honor which the unit has received for conspicuous valor. The men are proud of it."

"Prefect," said James, "as I'm sure you understand, the fact that the Antonia Fortress is immediately adjacent to the temple is an irritant of long standing. This proximity, in itself, is a vivid symbol of Rome's control over Jewish religious life. You keep the high priest's vestments in that fortress. We can obtain them only during our holy days."

"Yes, yes. I concede that displaying the standard in the way it was done showed a touch of arrogance. It was a mistake, and those responsible have been disciplined. More to the point, we've taken the standard down. But even that isn't enough to satisfy your people. The crowd demands that Caesar's image be removed from the city, and this I cannot do. Not only would it insult the Augustus—and let me assure you, *that* will not happen—it would make me appear to be denigrating my own troops. Mutinies occur over such things, Rabbi."

"What has been done so far in protest?" James asked.

Pilate's muscular frame exhibited a slight shiver of frustration as he prepared to recount the events of recent days. "It all began with a lot of shouting when someone in the temple court or on one of the balconies spotted the image," he said. "That brought people streaming into the temple—and as word spread out to the countryside, streaming into the city as well. In a very short time we had angry crowds surging through the streets of Jerusalem. Many of the shop keepers were afraid they might be looted, so they closed their businesses. That has caused shortages of basic commodities, furthering inflaming the situation.

"It all happened so quickly," he continued. "I received word here by express courier, and sent reinforcements. But that was only two hundred additional men—all I could call in at the time. The most we've been able to do is try to keep as much order as we can."

"But how did all these people come to be here in Caesarea?" James asked. "I recognize some of them from Jerusalem."

Pilate gestured for James to be seated on one of the benches near the fire, then took the other for himself.

"When shouting outside the fortress brought them no result, some instigators began calling for a march on my capital. So they organized themselves and came here."

"Well," said James, "At least I saw no evidence of rioting when I arrived. Everything is quite calm."

"That is the oddest part of the affair," Pilate said. "There has been no violence at all. After the initial anger and a good deal of marching about, they just settled down to camp in the streets. The city's business has ground to a halt. The only people benefiting from this are the hucksters selling provisions. I sent my soldiers to clear the main thoroughfares. I even threatened bloodshed if people didn't return peacefully to their homes. But..."

Pilate's hesitation hung in the air for a moment like smoke from the brazier. "Rabbi, I know you Jews are a dedicated lot. Some would call you fanatical. But I was stunned by what I saw out there in the streets.

Hundreds of men fell to their knees, bent forward, uncovered their necks from beneath their robes, and dared us to kill them. I withdrew my men with a very weak threat to return if they did not rethink their stubbornness."

James pursed his lips at Pilate's account, his expression betraying, not surprise, but confirmation. "Well, Prefect," he said, "so you have discovered the Jewish soul. This is the very quality that made the Maccabees willing to sacrifice themselves in rebellion against the Seleucids. It is the spirit of dedication and resolve that has always sustained us."

"How am I to govern such a people?" Pilate asked almost in despair. "Caesar didn't send me here to kill half the population of Judea. But I cannot tolerate such a challenge—not to the Augustus, not to my troops, and not to my authority."

Pilate was confronted by a genuine dilemma, and James could see it would have to be resolved quickly. He pondered the question for a few minutes, then said, "My close associate, Joseph of Arimathea, faces a vexing and continual problem."

"What? Joseph of Arimathea? He is a member of the Sanhedrin, is he not? I believe I have met him. What are you talking about, Rabbi?"

"You may not be aware, Prefect, that Joseph is perhaps the largest operator of caravans in Palestine, and the problem he faces is robbers. It is especially acute along the roads of Idumea. His trains are regularly harassed by Idumean raiders."

Pilate couldn't see where Joseph's story was leading, but he sensed the rabbi had a point to make, so he bore with his rambling tale.

"Are there large garrisons to the south of Jerusalem?" James asked.

"Not really," said Pilate, "not this side of Sinai. Mainly small outposts and toll stations."

"This new cohort currently ensconced in the Antonia Fortress—from where did it come?"

"Joppa, and before that, Crete."

"I assume it has experience fighting in wilderness areas."

"No doubt, at some point in its history. It was formed in Gaul, but that was many years ago."

"Still... The southern caravan routes pass through many parts that are wild. It is in such places that Idumean raiders strike and then run away to hide."

Pilate grasped James' direction now. "And the troops in Jerusalem are uniquely equipped to hunt them down?"

"These men constitute the largest unit currently located so close to the problem area," said James, "is that not true? With their experience, if some emergency situation should arise along the southern routes..."

The prefect's face was a picture of skepticism. "You're suggesting an excuse to withdraw the detachment from Jerusalem," he said. "What Jew is going to believe this, Rabbi?"

"None," James said. "But it hardly matters. Men who are *willing* to die are not necessarily *eager* to do so. When your troops march out of the city to hunt the raiders—bearing their image of Caesar proudly—you may find many people expressing gratitude for a tragedy averted."

"They will think me weak."

"Then you can demonstrate otherwise at some future time. I pray the Holy One wills that you never have to. But meanwhile, the cohort with its objectionable emblem will have left Jerusalem for a perfectly good reason, not because you yielded to the demands of the crowd." He added, with a wry smile, "Perhaps this was your intention all along?"

Pilate mused on James' idea, and it struck him as barely plausible. Then he couldn't help laughing. Plausible or not, it was realistically the only option at hand. The prefect considered how this artifice might best be approached.

"It would never do," he said broadly, "for one of our foremost merchants—and a Sanhredrin member, at that—to have his trade ruined by these Idumean bandits. And after all, this criminality affects the well-being of the whole southern region. I would most certainly entertain a request by Joseph of Arimathea for assistance."

"I will speak with him right away," said James.

Pilate and James caught each other's glance, both trying to hold back their smiles and maintain a sense of official decorum. The prefect started to reach out and grip James' forearm in the comradely Roman manner, but then he wasn't sure if the rabbi would consider himself defiled by the touch of a foreigner. So he bowed slightly and said, "You have my gratitude, Rabbi. I will not forget this."

*   *   *

Subduing the Idumean raiders was given out as the reason for rotating the Antonia Fortress garrison, though as Pilate had predicted, the story was far from convincing. Some accepted it on the assumption that the presence of the Rabbi James had helped to bring such a resolution about, and this served to limit overt gloating at an apparent victory over the Roman oppressors. The protesters left Caesarea peacefully, the predominant feeling among them being one of relief that a crisis had passed. Days later, there were very few jeers and catcalls from onlookers when the cohort marched out of Jerusalem under its standard with the hated image of Caesar.

Joseph of Arimathea was amused to have played a part in prompting an aggressive military action, even though his written request for help didn't reach Pilate until nearly a week after the troops had departed. His amusement was heightened by the fact that this action wasn't really all that necessary. The Arab archers Joseph normally hired to accompany his southern-route caravans had been doing an adequate job of keeping bandits away. But he certainly had no objection to Roman suppression of this recurrent threat. Cleaning out those Idumean vipers' nests was long overdue. And besides, Joseph speculated that whatever gratitude might accrue to him for his part in solving Pilate's dilemma could prove useful.

The person who benefited most from the foolish and unnecessary incident of the standard, at least in terms of the prefect's admiration, was James. Pilate saw in this Greek-speaking rabbi an ally, or at the very least, a wise advisor on the incomprehensible ways of this very peculiar people.

James was a Jew who knew he was a Jew. He was no Hellenized sycophant like the companionable Jews of Caesarea. But he had the invaluable gift of tact. While his speech and manner established an unmistakable boundary, they did not irritate. Unlike with so many of these self-righteous Jerusalem Jews, you didn't get the feeling from him that your unclean pagan presence was barely tolerable.

Pilate wanted to know more about the rabbi of the Synagogue at the Crossed Streets, and he inquired of his staff whom they might know that would be able to ferret out whatever information existed. The consensus among his officers was that the person for such a task was the centurion, Cassius Longinus, commandant of the Antonia Fortress, so

Pilate had him sent for and brought to Caesarea.

Longinus snapped to attention before the prefect and saluted. Pilate bade him be at ease.

"You have extended service in Jerusalem, Centurion," Pilate said, "though I am told that your situation is somewhat irregular."

"Yes sir. After I received this injury—" He indicated his left eye, which bore a very visible wound and discoloration. "I was offered release with a cripple's pension. But I liked soldiering, and I liked Jerusalem. So I asked for a post in station. I was assigned to the permanent staff of the Antonia Fortress. Over the years, I've done just about every job there, and my legion experience made me able to work well with all the different cohorts rotating through. Your predecessor, Valerius Gratus, honored me with promotion. Of course, my rank is purely functional, with no social status."

"Of course." Pilate looked closely at the centurion's eye. "Are you able to see with that?"

"Not...clearly, sir," said Longinus warily. "But it has never proven a barrier to fulfilling my duties."

"No, no, of course not," said Pilate. "It is of no concern. And the reports I have of you are excellent."

Longinus relaxed somewhat, but he was confused as to why he had been summoned before the prefect.

"I understand," said Pilate, "you are married to a Jew woman."

The wariness returned. "Yes...sir?"

"How are you treated by the Jews?"

"I have a small house in the foreign quarter. My wife lives there—as do I when I'm not on duty. Things are less...Jewish...than in other parts of Jerusalem."

"Does your wife attend any of the synagogues?"

"Well...as much as any woman in Judea would, sir. Females here have fewer religious duties than we are accustomed to. There is no Jewish equivalent of Vestal Virgins or cultic priestesses. And even as regards the temple, that's mostly men's concern. A woman's primary obligations are in the home. For instance, they perform a prayer ritual involving candles on the Sabbath."

"Does your wife perform this ritual?"

Now Longinus was on his guard. "She...does...sir."

"Do you participate in it?"

Was Pilate accusing him of neglecting his sacrificial obligations to the imperial cult?

"Well, Prefect...this is merely a small devotional practice. It begins the traditional family feast which Jews hold every week. I assure you that I am scrupulous about all the religious duties of the legion. The post has always met its—"

"Centurion," Pilate said, seeing that the man was becoming fearful, "I am not interested in your spiritual predilections. As long as sacrifice is made on the Augustus' birthday, you have done your duty. I wish to know how you get along with the Jews."

A wave of relief swept over Longinus. "Oh."

"Does your position as post commandant create any resentments? From what I can see, Jews hate the Antonia Fortress."

"Ah...yes, sir. They do. But, as I say...the neighborhood in which I live is not typical. Even the synagogue with which my wife and I are— That is..."

"Yes, Centurion, go on."

"Well, sir, the congregation is mainly what are called, *God-fearers.* Those are people who follow Jewish laws and practices, at least most laws and practices. The men are not circumcised, you see, so they are not actually Jews. I must admit I have taken an interest in Jewish ways—as do many in the legions, I would point out."

He searched Pilate's face for a reaction, and was reassured by the lack of any expression suggesting disapproval.

"Then too," Longinus continued, "during my time in command, I've taken steps to ease ill feelings against the garrison. From time to time, I have ordered transport to be provided for grains and other foodstuffs collected by the synagogue of Rabbi Gamaliel for distribution to needy families. We haul these goods in from farms in the surrounding—"

"Did you say, *the synagogue of Gamaliel?*" Pilate asked.

"Yes, sir. They have a very well-organized—"

"Do you know the Rabbi James?"

"I know *of* him, sir, but I've never really made his acquaintance."

Pilate picked up a stylus lying on the table before him next to a wax writing tablet. He tapped it several times against the tablet's wooden frame. "Centurion," he said, "I am interested in the Rabbi James. He seems like someone who could be extremely helpful in our governance of this troublesome country. I wish you to call upon your Jew contacts to learn all you can about him. Family background, friends, business involvements—anything there is to know."

"Yes, Prefect."

"And be discreet, Centurion. Do not draw undue attention to the prefecture's interest in this man. Given the suspiciousness of these people and how quickly passions become inflamed here, his position would be compromised if he were perceived as a favorite of Rome."

"Yes, Prefect."

*   *   *

James' first day back in the stone hut passed quickly, absorbed as he was in writing. He was pleased to be at work again, responding to inquiries in the correspondence that had accumulated on his table. Soon enough he would be counseling men seeking insight in the quiet of the Synagogue at the Crossed Streets, and advising Joseph on issues before the Sanhedrin. The uproar over the image of Caesar had brought a measure of perspective to his concerns about Jesus. James would leave his brother in the hands of the Holy One—for now, anyway.

He was surprised when Amara brought his evening meal on a tray, not realizing how the day had slipped by. The African woman had remained with the house when Joseph moved out to the villa in Ein Kerem. Now, long married and with five children, she and her husband, a convert Jew from Ethiopia named Ephron, saw to all the needs of the establishment. She prepared the food, cleaned the rooms, and took care of James' laundry, while Ephron maintained the structures and tended to the grounds. Ephron had made many improvements. Along the stretch of yard that had once been stacked with metal ingots there now ran a long arbor woven with grape vines, the yield of which was increasing steadily every year.

Watching Amara through the window of the hut as she made her way back up the path to the main house prompted reflection. James' mind ran with thoughts, about the passage of time, similar to those that had struck him upon observing all the changes in the family compound at Nazareth. Where was the lithe and dusky young girl he had first met when he came here to lodge as a student? But then, where was that student? Both were the same, yet both were so different.

One constant remained in James' life. Not a day passed that he didn't think of Avigail. He prayed for her well-being, that the marriage made for her had proven to be good, that her husband treated her well, that she had been blessed with children, that she was healthy and contented. He held no bitterness toward her father. How could a student without means of his own and living far from his family and their resources have even thought of asking for the hand of such a girl? Still, the memory of their days together in the garden at the villa was a source of regret. After all these years, the ache had never completely gone away.

James returned to his correspondence after eating. The letters ran a familiar gamut of religious questions, queries about the Law as applied to an endless variety of circumstances, conflicts between friends and relatives, private dilemmas, and the occasional request for intercession on behalf of some bright son, grandson or nephew seeking a referral to the school of Gamaliel. He worked until well after sunset when the oil in his lamp had run low and sleep tugged heavily at his eyelids. Then he washed, said his nightly prayers, and turned in to bed.

The next morning found James on his way to the Royal Porch. Since leaving his position as Gamaliel's proctor to establish the Synagogue at the Crossed Streets, he and his colleague had maintained an arrangement whereby James would drop into the class from time to time. Gamaliel had inherited the outlook of his grandfather, Hillel, of blessed memory, and did not insist on making himself the exclusive center of his disciples' lives or their only point of scholarly reference—unlike so many other temple sages. He enjoyed it when James would come to participate in the discussions, offering another learned point of view.

Entering the temple, James was assaulted as usual by the ceaseless uproar in the Court of the Gentiles. The Sanhedrin's decision, years before, to allow bankers to operate a currency exchange in the temple had led to all the excesses which Zacharias and Joseph had feared. Once the money changers were established, vendors of doves began lobbying to offer their birds on temple grounds for the convenience of those traveling long distances to make sacrifice. Approval of this request opened the doors to purveyors of grains, herbs and wines, as well as to lamb sellers, and eventually even to brokers of bulls. They were all able to make the case that availability of their wares was conducive to faithful sacrifice and met a genuine need of the people. The percentage of income which these vendors were willing to pass on to the temple treasury made their inclusion inevitable.

And so it was that the Court of the Gentiles resounded with a cacophony of bleating and squawking, not to mention the cries of competing sellers eager to attract customers and the ever-present haggling over price and condition of the creatures on sale. All too common was the indignant complaint, generally made at full voice, that a particular dove had a broken wing or a particular lamb some hidden mark, making the animal insufficiently unblemished to pass inspection by the priests.

On top of all that, there was regular conflict between the vendors and the temple guards. Vendors were assigned spaces under the colonnades lining the east and west walls of the court, their rents predicated on how many spaces were contracted for. But the animal pens tended to grow outward from the colonnades toward the center of the court. Whenever they intruded too deeply into the common area, temple guards would insist that the added fencing be removed, causing great umbrage among the vendors who contended that the rules were too strictly enforced—arguments about which added to the ongoing din.

The scholars on the upper level of the Royal Porch did their best to ignore the noise—and for that matter, the pervasive smells associated with all those animals. When James arrived on this day, he found the Rabbi Gamaliel holding forth as best he could on the topic of a father's obligations to his son. By the Law, these included such necessities as providing food and shelter, having him circumcised, redeeming him if he is kidnapped, and arranging a marriage. Gamaliel focused particularly on the importance of a father teaching his son a trade. To stimulate discussion, he offered a favorite aphorism: *He who has a trade is like a vineyard that is fenced.*

Several of the students related how their fathers had taught them various skills. One, a young man named Saul, expressed pride in having learned the craft of making tents, canopies and pavilions as a small boy growing up in Tarsus of Cilicia.

James, adding his perspective to the topic, noted that he was unable to claim he had been sufficiently prepared for a trade, since his father had determined right from the start that James would be a scholar. He related to the class that, while his father had shown him the rudiments of woodworking, the primary occupation of James' childhood had been his studies with the rabbi in his hometown. It was not until later, during a period when his father was out of the country, that James really learned carpentry skills, and then from his eldest brother.

This candor brought forth a number of comments from the students. One argued that James' father *had* prepared him for a trade—that of the scribe—since he'd provided the means for education. To this James responded that it was fortunate he'd had the aptitude to vindicate his father's expectations, which drew scattered laughter.

In answer to James' quip, another student pointed out that no man can ever be sure that his son will master the craft he teaches him. But the young fellow from Tarsus found this defense of James' father to be weak.

"Forgive me, Rabbi," Saul said, "but I cannot help thinking that, in this respect, your father failed you."

There was a collective gasp from the other students who were shocked that such an impertinence would be directed at the famous rabbi. One young man seated next to Saul started to dispute him with some anger, but James held up a hand to forestall any argument.

"I am interested in knowing how you come to this view, Saul," he said placidly.

"The Law is clear on the responsibilities of a father," said Saul with youthful certainty and a cutting tone of voice. "Isn't it said that a man who does not teach his son a trade teaches him to be a thief? Becoming a rabbi is a noble ambition. I have journeyed all the way from Cilicia to pursue it myself. But this learning is a long and arduous path, and there is no guarantee that anyone will complete it. If I were to fall short of my dreams, I would yet have the skills my father gave me. But if you had proven to be less of a scholar, what would *you* have?"

All the other students shrank back upon themselves in embarrassment at Saul's assertiveness. But James remained unflappable.

"Your point is valid and well argued," he said with a smile, much to the relief of the class.

After the session, James asked his colleague about this confident young man from Cilicia.

"Ah, Saul of Tarsus," Gamaliel said, shaking his head. "If ever there was someone fired with righteousness and certitude, it is this tentmaker's son. Already in the time he has been here, I've had several urges to strangle him. But he has a brilliant mind—though one never in doubt, I hasten to say—and he presents his opinions in undeniably compelling ways. He is talented, and he will make a great rabbi...if he lives."

James laughed at Gamaliel's frustration. "He seems a bit older than the others."

"Yes, he spent some years in his family's business," said Gamaliel. "But for all that experience, he lacks a grasp of people and their feelings. He is able to make fine and subtle points in his arguments, but he is not subtle in relationships. The other students find him impatient and rather pompous.

"And there is an interesting irony," Gamaliel continued. "Saul fancies himself a great champion of the people. He calls himself a *Jew's Jew*, if you can swallow that. But at the same time, he makes quite a piece of the fact that his family holds citizenship in the empire."

"Is that so?"

"And it's due to no particular distinction on their part. Pompey made Tarsus the capital of Cilicia and granted Roman citizenship to the whole populace."

Again James laughed. "Well, it will be interesting to see where the young tentmaker ultimately pitches his tent."

* * *

Pilate had come to Jerusalem where he remained for several weeks, assembling a new force, cobbled together from units dispersed around the region, to replace the troops sent after the Idumean raiders. It would garrison Jerusalem until an entire new cohort could be transferred. On the morning he was to return to Caesarea, he received a note from Longinus informing him that data had been obtained about the *person of interest*. Pilate delayed his departure.

When Longinus arrived at the prefecture, Pilate dismissed his attendants so that the discussion of James could be held in private. "What have you found out about our friend, Centurion?"

"Some interesting facts, Prefect. The Rabbi James was born and raised in the town of Nazareth of Galilee. His father was Joseph son of Jacob, though there is disagreement among my sources about the precise designation of the grandfather. Some call him Heli, which may be another family name. In any event, the rabbi's mother seems to have been one, Escha. The couple had six children, four boys and two girls. James is the youngest of the lot.

"It is not a family of huge wealth," Longinus continued, "but they are far from poor. Their primary business is carpentry and construction, and the enterprise is now managed by the rabbi's eldest brother, Josis. They also have pastoral interests, with landholding to accommodate a considerable flock of sheep, and they grow olives and process the oil for sale."

"It sounds like a family of substance," Pilate said.

"Indeed," said Longinus, "and for a reason besides business. The father, Joseph, was a descendent of David, the great Jew king."

"Royal lineage?"

"Yes, Prefect. And there is more."

"Go on."

"The rabbi's mother seems to have died when he was small, and his father remained a widower for many years. But then he took a much younger wife, the daughter of one, Joachim, who was a man of wealth with numerous farmlands and tenancies. The wife of this Joachim was sister to the wife of a highly regarded temple priest—Zacharias by name."

"I have heard of this Zacharias," Pilate said.

"The young wife, whose name is Mary, had a son. This half-brother of the Rabbi James is called Jesus. It appears he was brought up in seclusion, and as an adult he has taken to traveling with caravans, so I could not learn much about him. I do know that he was taught by the local rabbi in Nazareth as a child, as was James."

"That no doubt reflects the family's means."

"And there is some indication that he learned the woodworker's craft. I assume he participated in the family business, at least for a time."

A fleeting scowl indicated Pilate's lack of interest in this Jesus. "The brother is of no consequence. What else do you know about James?"

"He came to Jerusalem around the age of fifteen or sixteen, and studied in the school of Hillel." Longinus took pains to draw Pilate's attention to the significance of that fact. "This is important, Prefect. In the days of Herod and Archelaus, Hillel was regarded as the main authority on the Jewish Law. His school exists to this day, under the direction of his grandson, the Rabbi Gamaliel."

"I have met the Rabbi Gamaliel."

"James became Gamaliel's assistant for several years. It was during this time that he gained his reputation as a religious authority in his own right and people started calling him *James the Just*. He has declined nomination to the Sanhedrin, though Gamaliel sits on the council and James is also close to another member, Joseph of Arimathea."

Pilate chuckled quietly at the name of Joseph, who had provided the request by which the offensive image of Caesar was removed from the Antonia Fortress. Then he turned away from the commandant, placed his hands on the sill of a window, and gazed out thoughtfully. "So the Rabbi James is a man of exceptional knowledge and erudition."

"He would have to be," said Longinus. "His reputation is widespread. Many people regard him highly and seek his guidance."

This was the first time that Longinus had ever seen his Jewish connections as benefiting him in his role as a Roman officer. He found he was enjoying this assignment of teaching Pilate about James and the world of Jewish religious scholarship—of demonstrating a certain expertise to his superior.

"Jews value learning above all things, Prefect," he said. "No Jew would ever follow some untutored country bumpkin, or even listen to him seriously. Only someone who spoke with knowledge and authority could gain people's trust."

Pilate turned back in his direction. "Yes, the Rabbi James certainly has knowledge. With his Davidic lineage—and being related to a temple family—I wonder if he might not be the perfect candidate for high priest. Gratus made four changes in that office during his term. If the need should arise again..."

"I...wouldn't think so, sir," Longinus interjected cautiously. "The Jews are very particular about blood. That the Rabbi James is descended from David is clear enough. But the priestly tie is only indirect, through his father's marriage to this niece of Zacharias. In actuality, the half-brother, Jesus, would have a more authentic claim to priesthood."

Pilate crossed his arms and leaned back against the sill. "Well, if not high priest, then perhaps something else useful. We shall see, Centurion. We shall see."

Then Longinus gave a small inward laugh.

"Centurion?"

"It is an odd coincidence, sir, that I should be poking about for information from this little town of Nazareth." he said. "I was in Nazareth once. In fact, it is there that I received my injury." He indicated his eye.

Pilate's interest in this piece of personal trivia was scant at best. "That will be all, Centurion."

CHAPTER TWENTY-SEVEN

A great prophet has appeared among us.

(Luke 7)

*J*ames was standing at the foot of a large cross. His father, his brothers and Lucillus were with him, though they were turned away and speaking among themselves. Are you going to Sepphoris? asked a young man, his naked body nailed to the wooden beams. No, James answered, I'm on my way to Jerusalem to become a rabbi. *Looking down at him, the young man said,* You have to go through Sepphoris. You always have to go through Sepphoris. Sepphoris is where you will find the peace of Rome. *And then the young man began to beat loudly upon the beams, and James wondered how he could do that while he was nailed. Then James realized that the sound was not that of wood, but of wood on metal.*

It was coming from outside the stone hut. James sat up and tried to shake the sleep out of his eyes. He tossed his blankets aside, then stood and wrapped himself in a cloak, draping it over his head to cover his uncut hair. Going out, he saw Ephron coming down the walk toward the gate where someone was beating on the iron bars with a walking staff.

"I seek the Rabbi James," the caller said.

"You cannot barge in on the rabbi in the middle of the night," said Ephron angrily. "Go away. Come back in the morning."

"I will speak to the fellow, Ephron," said James. "Who are you? What do you wish of me?"

"I am Tobias. I come from Jericho bearing words of the Elder Pinchas."

"It is alright, Ephron," said James, opening the gate. "I'll take care of the man."

James led Tobias to the stone hut as Ephron turned and walked back up the path muttering to himself at having been rousted out of his bed.

"Peace be with you, friend," said James, pointing toward the divan. "Rest from your journey."

Tobias sat, took several breaths to calm himself after a hurried and taxing journey. "Rabbi," he said finally, "Your kinsman, John, has been arrested." He reached inside his cloak, drew out a sheet of papyrus which was partially cracked from being hastily folded, and handed it to James. "This will explain."

James took the letter and then reached to open the shutter of his window. He sat on his chair at the table, reading by a shaft of moonlight.

Pinchas reported that John had taken his baptism ministry farther up the Jordan where he had begun to inject into his preaching harsh criticisms of Herod Antipas, the tetrarch. True to the pattern of his family, Antipas had seduced Herodias, his niece and the wife of his brother, Philip, and taken her away from her husband. This was reminiscent of the outrage Archelaus had caused through his dalliance with Glaphyra. It created a scandal, and it raised the possibility of war with the Nabateans, since Antipas had abandoned his first wife, the daughter of Aretas, the Nabatean king.

By now, this was old news in Jerusalem. James had heard the story months before, and couldn't understand why John would have fixed on the issue. Why attack Antipas so stridently now? The baptist's ministry had focused on general repentance, not on the rapaciousness and misdeeds of a half-Jew petty monarch whom most people dismissed as hopelessly decadent. Then too, why would Antipas care what was said about him by some itinerant Essene preacher?

Pinchas' answer to that last question crystallized all of James' anxieties about problems Jesus might face. John's following had grown so large it seemed to foreshadow a popular uprising, perhaps in support of the Nabateans. Or at least it raised the specter of such a prospect.

The letter noted that John had been seized by Antipas' troops and taken to the tetrarch's new capital, Tiberius, where he was being held in prison. It closed with a query as to whether there was anything James could do on John's behalf.

Anything indeed. If this was to be the first test of James' ability to intercede effectively in such a situation, it left him stroking his beard. Had he been overconfident in assuming he could help in case Jesus got into trouble? He felt reasonably confident he could bring some influence to bear if an incident should occur in Judea—but beyond? While the famous Rabbi James came from Galilee, the center of his reputation was Jerusalem. The Lord's city might be the heart of Jewish religious life, but it was outside of Antipas' territories and peripheral to the tetrarch's interests. Antipas only came to Jerusalem for the holy days, and not consistently on all of those.

James put the letter down and thought for a moment, then turned to Tobias. "Please inform Pinchas that I will speak with members of the Great Sanhedrin," he said. "The council is the ultimate authority on matters of Jewish Law—at least it's supposed to be. It isn't always able to extend its authority over long distances, but the men whom I will ask to appeal on John's behalf are all leading figures. Antipas will know their names, and perhaps he will pay heed to them. Also, I will send messages to certain rabbis. Some former students in the school of Gamaliel are now established in the region near Tiberius. They may know people close to the tetrarch who can exert some influence."

"I will convey your words to Pinchas," Tobias said.

"Good," said James rising to his feet. "We will all pray for John's safety and swift deliverance from this difficulty. Meanwhile, you must refresh yourself."

James led Tobias to the main house, where he found him some food, and set him up for the night in one of the sleeping rooms. Next morning, after Tobias departed for Jericho, James dispatched the student, Asher, his messenger, to Ein Kerem to track down Joseph of Arimathea. Joseph was not at the villa but in Jerusalem at his storehouse where a caravan was being loaded. The young man found him there, then returned with Joseph's word that he would come in the afternoon.

Joseph arrived later than anticipated, and so stayed for the evening meal. During the day, two men had come to the Synagogue at the Crossed Streets from Bethphage to spend time in reflection. While James' normal practice was to share meals with his retreatants, tonight he had food brought to a separate room so that he could dine with Joseph in private. When they had finished the prayers and begun eating, James conveyed the news about John.

Years on the Sanhedrin had honed Joseph's political instincts to a fine edge, and he urged caution. "I think that too great a show of support for your kinsman may increase the danger to him," Joseph said, "especially when that support is coming primarily from Jerusalem. Antipas knows the disdain with which he is viewed in temple circles. He may suspect John of being the agent of a larger conspiracy against him."

"But the priests themselves are suspicious of John," said James. "They have sent deputations to investigate and discredit him."

"Even if Antipas is aware of that," Joseph said, "he may think it a ruse to make John appear independent. Remember, John is the son of a priest, and his years among the Essenes don't change that. We must look at it from Antipas' point of view, James. Why would John set himself apart from the temple? This is a question that might come readily to the tetrarch's mind. You and I remember Zacharias' disgust with corruption in the priesthood and how he sought to keep his son out of the temple's reach, but Antipas doesn't."

James could not dispute Joseph's reasoning. It was known that Antipas had inherited the suspicious nature of his father, Herod. This assessment of the danger to John had to be accepted.

"What do you recommend?" James asked.

"What we need first is information," said Joseph. "I think your idea of enlisting some local rabbi is good. Perhaps one of Gamaliel's former students could obtain a clearer picture of how threatened Antipas feels and thus the actual degree of jeopardy in which John finds himself. I suggest contacting someone who is in a position to inquire—someone you feel confident would proceed carefully."

Joseph arranged for the carrying of a letter to one of James' former classmates, the Rabbi Caleb, in Ammathus, the well known town of the hot springs, located close to Tiberius, as well as Caleb's reply which came a week later. The message James received seemed an accurate sounding on John's situation. He was being held near Antipas' palace. And though in chains, John was not languishing. The placement of his cell was such that his voice could be heard in the street through a barred window shaft. John was making the most of his location by shouting reproofs of Antipas at the top of his powerful lungs.

Surprisingly, Caleb reported that the tetrarch had not moved John to a more isolated cell or ordered him to be beaten or tortured for his impertinent outbursts. John was even permitted visits by his disciples. And strangest of all, word was around that Antipas had actually called on him personally, apparently drawn by curiosity about this odd Essene *prophet*.

Which, by now, was what John was being called.

"It appears your kinsman is in no immediate danger," Joseph said, upon reading this account. "His celebrity is spreading across the region. People regard him as a prophet, rather than a rebel, which may afford an extra measure of safety, at least for awhile. Perhaps the best approach is to do nothing. Herod might conclude that he has a harmless madman in his prison and eventually let him go." Joseph chuckled. "Or maybe the tetrarch will become one of John's followers."

"Pardon my doubts about *that*," said James.

A passage appended to the end of the letter James found disturbing. Caleb noted that the Galilean countryside was abuzz with stories about another so-called prophet who had appeared on the scene, one Jesus of Nazareth. Could this Jesus be the younger brother of whom James had spoken years before? "If so," Caleb wrote, "you should be aware that not all of these tales are good. One tells of a controversy that erupted in the Nazareth synagogue after Jesus rose to read from Scripture. I have no details, but it appears Jesus made some outrageous claim that infuriated people who had been his neighbors. If I learn more about this incident, I will try and get word to you."

*　　*　　*

On his visits to Jerusalem, Pilate had taken note of a problem with the local water supply. The population had been growing considerably, both inside the city walls and in neighborhoods springing up beyond— an area which was coming to be called the New Town. Shortages of water were occurring, especially in the blisteringly hot summers, and year-round there was fierce competition at the public fountains. The squabbling among women filling their water jars was most unseemly.

A more plentiful and reliable supply of water would clearly benefit all in the city. It could hardly be seen as serving Roman self-interest. Rather, it would be a meaningful, and greatly evident, contribution to life in the Jews' cherished capital.

A survey of the district identified springs on high ground south of Jerusalem, and a determination was made that this water could be delivered by an aqueduct. The slope from source to city was adequate to maintain strong flow in the watercourse. And the building work required was well within the capabilities of local craftsmen under the direction of Roman engineers expert in aqueduct construction.

There was only one problem: money.

Valerius Gratus hadn't left much in the reserves for provincial improvements, and Pilate already had one construction project underway, the Tiberieum, a new public plaza in Caesarea, planned to honor the Augustus. Expense projections for an aqueduct sufficient to serve Jerusalem indicated that such a venture would cost far more than he had on hand.

What to do? Imposing an additional tax would certainly not gain the appreciation of the people. More likely, it would trigger a revolt. Even after so many years, memories of Archelaus' hated surtax were still bitter. And there was no possibility of diverting any of the revenues due to Rome. Pilate had a firm quota to meet.

There was one possible source of money. An open secret had it that the temple treasury contained more—*much* more—than needed to meet the costs of yearly operations and maintenance. This was a cause of great resentment among a public that considered the temple tax an onerous burden, one from which there was never any relief, no matter how much the priests' coffers were stuffed with wealth. People might actually see a new aqueduct as a worthwhile investment of the coins wrung from them by their religious leaders. But was such a use permissible under the arcane provisions of Jewish Law?

Pilate needed an answer to that question before he could pursue the idea. And he would have to obtain it from someone who was not only knowledgeable in the Law, but who would keep this query in strictest confidence. One name came immediately to mind: the Rabbi James.

Now deeper into winter, the seasonal chill and occasional rains made the court of Pilate's Jerusalem palace unsuitable for receiving guests. Pilate ordered an elaborate pergola erected, with a top of canvas and sides of animal skins, and warmed by an oversize brazier at its center, filled with burning coals, vented through a port in the fabric roof. He hoped that the rabbi would consider this structure sufficiently *out of doors* to be an acceptable meeting place.

The prefect was waiting within the enclosure when James arrived. He dismissed his assistants, and greeted his guest. When they were seated on benches opposite each other, Pilate thanked James for his advice in the awkward business of Caesar's image.

"My men are meeting with some success in removing these robbers from the southern routes," he said. "Joseph of Arimathea and the other caravan operators should see a marked improvement. And I'm pleased to note a broad public satisfaction that the irritating icon has been removed—with no offense, either to my troops or to the Augustus. All in all, Rabbi, the wisdom of your suggestion has been demonstrated thoroughly. For that I am grateful."

"It was a small contribution to the improvement of conditions under which my people live."

"Well put, Rabbi, well put," said Pilate. "It is precisely with that objective in mind that I wished to speak with you today." He rose and reached for a sheet of parchment lying rolled on a folding table. Spreading it open, he asked James to look. "If you would, Rabbi?"

James came and observed a map charting the landscape and topography between Jerusalem and the hills near Bethlehem.

"As I am sure you know, Rabbi," Pilate said, "the main source of water for Jerusalem has been the Gihon Spring that feeds the reservoir located by the Water Gate—what do they call it?—the Pool of Siloam. But that spring runs inconsistently. It is supplemented by rainfall collected in numerous cisterns around the city, and the yields of those are unpredictable, often negligible. I am told that, other than winter drizzles, there are only two periods of good, solid downpour every year."

"Yes," James said, "adequate water is a constant concern."

Pilate tapped a pointed finger on the map. "This plan traces the route for an aqueduct which I propose to build. If the assessment of my engineers is correct—and I have every reason to assume it is—such a conduit would provide an abundance of water in a steady flow year-round. So much water, in fact, that it would not only meet normal demand, but provide an emergency supply to the storage chambers under the temple mount. I'm talking about a capacity sufficient to sustain the city in the unlikely event of a siege or a drought so severe as to dry up the springs which are its source."

"That *would* be an improvement," James said. "When will you begin this project?"

"Yes, well..." Pilate hesitated. "That is an...unanswered question."

Without taking his eyes from the map, James said, "Money."

"Exactly."

"I would not advise imposing an additional tax," James said, "even a temporary one."

"Oh, I am well aware of the furor that would raise," Pilate said. "But, actually...there is another resource which might be tapped. Since an improvement to the water system would be of indisputable benefit to the city of Jerusalem, which of course is the spiritual home of the Jewish people, it seems to me reasonable that at least part of the effort be funded by the temple treasury. I am given to believe that there is ample revenue held in reserve there, but I'm not familiar with the provisions of your Law that govern such matters. So my question to you, Rabbi, is: Can these funds be put to such a beneficent purpose?"

James returned to the bench and seated himself. Pilate mirrored his movement, and the two men sat facing each other in silence while the rabbi considered this question.

Finally James said, "You are referring, Prefect, to what in Hebrew is termed the *corban*—that is, money offered to the temple in sacrifice. Essentially, these funds are considered gifts to the King of the Universe." He paused and thought further, then: "Yes. It is permissible, under the Law, to apply treasury reserves in excess of the temple's needs to purposes that serve the public good. This is because the Lord cares for the well-being of his people. Your project might meet that criteria."

Pilate found this encouraging.

"I think, however," James continued, "it would not be possible for the temple authorities, if they agreed to your proposal—and this is something which would have to be put before the Sanhedrin—I think they would not be able to transfer the money to the prefecture. Corban funds are sacred. It would be a profanation to place them into non-Jewish hands. So payments would likely have to be made by the high priest directly to those contracting for the various elements of the project."

"I don't see any problem with that," said Pilate, "as long as controls are in place to ensure that proper fees are paid for honest work." It occurred to him that he might have said something which could be considered insulting to the temple leadership. "Not that I suggest the possibility of any corruption," he added hastily.

James smiled wryly. "Heaven forbid the thought," he said.

Pilate perceived the sardonic edge to that remark, and smiled in return. "Well...one must account for things accurately." The prefect cleared his throat, then went on. "About the Sanhedrin," he said, "is it...strictly speaking...*necessary* to put this plan before that body? After the uproar over the standard and the protest in Caesarea, I have come to appreciate Jewish sensitivities—"

James smiled again.

"—and it seems likely that using temple funds could stir some negative feelings, despite the public benefit. Your people can be quite volatile, Rabbi, as I recently found. Anything that has a religious aspect causes no end of distrust and anger, especially when the temple is involved."

"I can't deny it, Prefect," said James. "But that argues for candor. I am not a member of the Sanhedrin, but my advice is to lay your plan before the council and confront any opposition that may emerge there. Better this than to face the wrath of the people, should they think you are trying to steal the Lord's corban."

Pilate thanked James profusely, expressing his respect for the rabbi's knowledge, wisdom and *discretion*, placing particular emphasis on that last word. He took his leave of James with an expectation that they would have the opportunity to speak again soon, in hope of deepening Pilate's understanding of Jewish Law and life.

James' confirmation that temple money could be applied to the aqueduct project was what the prefect had wanted, the call for candor less so. It seemed to Pilate that making a public appeal to the Sanhedrin was the quickest route to controversy. No. This was something best pursued in the back chambers of national leadership. The person he needed to speak with now was the High Priest Caiaphas.

* * *

James had not expected to hear from the Rabbi Caleb so soon. But on an afternoon only a few weeks after their correspondence about John's arrest, a man appeared at the gate. He was a regular attendee at Caleb's synagogue in Tiberius, he explained. Coming to Jerusalem on business, he had agreed to carry a letter. He would be returning in four days time, and was happy to stop by again for a reply. James thanked him, and the man departed on his business.

According to the letter, John's situation had not changed. He was still in Antipas' prison, still decrying the tetrarch's immorality in a booming voice audible in the street. However, Caleb did have some further information about Jesus of Nazareth, whom he now knew from other sources was indeed James' brother.

What had happened in the Nazareth synagogue was still somewhat unclear. From what Caleb had been able to learn, Jesus tried to make it seem that the Scripture passage he'd gotten up to read—words of the prophet, Isaiah—somehow referred to the preaching mission he was undertaking. This his listeners found presumptuous, to say the least, and they expressed themselves emphatically to that effect. Since then, Jesus was roaming about Galilee with a band of followers, holding meetings to which people were invited to come and hear him speak.

"Your brother must be a gifted orator," Caleb wrote. "He attracts crowds. Word is spreading, and the gatherings get larger as he goes. Also, I have heard tales, which I do not credit, about inexplicable occurrences ascribed to him. Supposedly, he is responsible for some surprising cures of people with chronic illnesses and bodily incapacities and such. But these rumors probably just reflect the novelty he enjoys right now. It has been my experience that whenever people happen upon an arresting personality, they are given to over-estimating the man's qualities. If Jesus and his group come to this area, which I'm told they do sometimes, I will try to attend one of his meetings and let you know what I observe. Meanwhile, I will continue to watch John's situation."

James sat back in his seat, hands falling into his lap, still holding the letter. Caleb might not credit these tales, but *he* did. Inexplicable cures were not at all surprising. James might have expected to hear of such things, after the incident at the wedding. Evidently, Jesus now felt free to reveal his special abilities, no doubt in the service of his preaching. Didn't it make sense? Rumors about such dazzling deeds would spread quickly, draw many people, and add substance to whatever message he was seeking to deliver. James was certain that his brother's mission was now fully in motion.

He set the letter aside, found a small leaf of parchment, and wrote a brief note to be carried back to Caleb. It thanked his friend for the facts provided, and expressed eagerness for any other information which might be obtained about either John or Jesus.

CHAPTER TWENTY-EIGHT

Blessed be the Lord, my rock,
who trains my hands for war, my fingers for battle.

(Psalm 144)

Shortly before sunrise on a morning toward the end of winter, the last unit of the Caesarea night watch was completing its patrol before going off duty. In a narrow lane beside the temple dedicated to the late emperor, Octavian, known as Caesar Augustus, a large, rickety-looking cart hitched to two ancient donkeys sat blocking the way. Inspection revealed that one of its wheels was turned outward and barely stood upright, the axle having cracked in a most unnatural way.

With the day's business soon to begin in the imperial city, the guards were intent on clearing the street of the injured vehicle. They were all the more eager because of the acrid smell given off by its cargo of straw heaped high and apparently soaked in bitumen or the oil extracted from it for use in lamps or something equally pungent. A distinct sulfurous odor was also detectable.

To no avail, they looked about for the driver, who had probably gone in search of help. The cart was immovable in its current condition. If the guardsmen tried leading the donkeys to the side of the lane, the wheel would collapse and the straw would tip, creating a stinking mess all over the ground.

The officer in charge instructed one of his men to seek assistance inside the legion barracks located on the opposite side of the whitewashed brick wall lining the street across from the temple. This was the billet for a cohort assigned permanently to the garrison of the prefect's administrative headquarters—Pilate's personal guard. The man hurried around to the entrance on the other side.

A few minutes later, a group of half-awake soldiers emerged from the barracks, came around the wall, and stood trying to focus bleary eyes on the cart. As they became more fully conscious, they reacted to the assault on their nostrils. Then some others came, carrying a long pole with which they intended to support the cart in an attempt to move it. At that moment, an arrow, flaming at its head, arced along the length of the street and embedded itself in the pile of straw.

For a brief instant, it looked as if the flame had been extinguished. A night-watch guard, spotting the end of the feathered shaft, reached to pull it out, as other soldiers scanned the lane, trying to see where the missile had come from. Then, as quickly, a ball of fire, accompanied by a deafening roar, engulfed the cart and all near it. Six men and both of the donkeys died instantly. At least ten other soldiers were turned into screaming human torches, flaming goo sticking to their bodies, consuming them as they ran.

The wall was scorched, and some of the bricks along its top actually dislodged by the sudden heat of the fire ball. The roof of the barracks built against it was ablaze. On the opposite side of the street, tongues of fire had thrust into the temple between its columns. Much of the colonnade and parts of the vast inner chamber were blackened.

The noise could be heard throughout the city. Pilate lurched from his bed and ran out onto a balcony to see flames leaping high into the morning sky. His wife, Procula, hurried from her bed chamber.

"What is happening?" she asked, half numb, half frantic.

"I don't know. Fire near the temple." He turned and called inside, "Guard!"

After the blaze had been contained and then put out, examination of what remained of the cart revealed that the axle had been cut. Questioning of the survivors brought accounts of the flaming arrow. The soldiers also described the noxious smell, which suggested some combustible substance, perhaps the pitch used for sealing the seams of ships or the black liquid obtained from pools found in certain parts of Arabia. Sulfur may have been included to make the mixture even more volatile.

This information was reported to Pilate, to whom it was already clear that the fire was intentional. Undoubtedly, it was an attack on his capital troops. Probably, it was intended as an insult to the temple of

Augustus. Definitely, it was a challenge to him. Could it be that the Jews of Caesarea weren't all as companionable as he had assumed?

Pilate ordered the immediate closing of the city gates, an embargo on ships leaving the harbor, and a thorough investigation, to include questioning of all Jews who worked for, or had regular dealings with, the prefecture. They were the ones most likely to be familiar with the routine of the garrison and the schedule of the security units. Such Jews were to be dealt with politely, but the danger of withholding any information should be made clear to them.

At the same time, there was to be a general canvassing of the city in search of anyone who might have observed the movement of the cart or who could possess knowledge about someone acquiring materials for igniting a large fire. Both citizens and Jews were to be questioned, and no particular restrictions were placed on the treatment of non-citizens lacking government connections.

As his officers were hurrying out to implement the prefect's orders, a centurion entered Pilate's receiving room, came crisply to attention, and pounded his chest in salute. "My Lord, Pilate," the man said, "this document was nailed to the post in one of the squares where official announcements are displayed."

He handed a leaf of parchment to the prefect. Pilate read the words written in large, bold, Greek characters. It was a message impossible to misunderstand: "The dagger is unsheathed."

Further investigation uncovered a rumor to the effect that Zealot groups had agreed to cooperate more closely under a new combined leadership. It was said that one man had emerged as the principal figure in this centralized command, though whom that might be was unknown. Pilate's interrogators pressed hard in search of details about the structure of this new controlling body and the identity of the man at its center. But nothing beyond the broad assertions of the rumor came from these inquiries, even those conducted with the aid of physical force.

Pilate suspected that both this story about a mysterious leader and the ominous parchment found nailed to the post had been put out to create an impression that the fire was the first act of a revitalized Zealot movement. Undeniably, someone had succeeded in performing a deadly and dramatic feat right in the heart of the most secure and

Romanized city in Judea. It had been a bold stroke, to say the least. But was it really a harbinger of some great revolt, or just a one-time— perhaps extremely lucky—trick?

While Pilate would take all necessary steps to counter any Zealot threat, he refused to be deterred from pursuing his own aims. It was one thing to crush a rebellion, quite another to quash the *spirit* of resistance. To do that, people's hearts must be changed. Perhaps the Zealots had given him a gift. Perhaps this was a chance to correct any misunderstanding about the prudence he had shown in removing Caesar's image from the Antonia Fortress and not shedding Jewish blood. He would respond firmly to any Zealot provocations, even as he brought water to the people of Jerusalem. That combination of strength and benevolence was the hallmark of the empire. It was what characterized the Peace of Rome.

*   *   *

News of the fire reached Jerusalem even before the gates of Caesarea were reopened. It was as if whoever planned the act had also arranged a means of quickly spreading word about it. James' reaction upon hearing of the incident was worry. He recalled how the prefect had feared being thought weak. If Pilate was convinced that some people believed him irresolute, would he ever again stay his hand when faced with a challenge? Indeed, what would be the effect of this bitter experience on his entire attitude toward the Jews?

Pilate's willingness to seek advice from a rabbi had appeared to indicate interest in accommodating Jewish concerns. The aqueduct plan suggested a desire to demonstrate the empire's good wishes for the life of its subjects. Would all of that be swept aside by this affront to the dignity of Caesar's vicar? Would Pilate reject his own intentions as naive, and bring down Rome's iron fist?

One hint about his attitude was provided by a rumor, which Joseph of Arimathea heard in the Sanhedrin and shared with James. It was whispered that there had been a private agreement between Pilate and the High Priest Caiaphas to use funds from the temple treasury to help finance improvements to the water system of Jerusalem. This didn't surprise James. He had never really expected that the prefect would appeal to a Jewish council about the aqueduct. Seeking approval for a Roman initiative would likely seem far too deferential.

That Pilate had decided to continue on with the project might be an indication that he still had hope of eventually softening the people's feelings about the empire. If so, it was a good sign that the prefect would consider public sentiment important. But his willingness to risk controversy by circumventing the Sanhedrin and making a direct deal with Caiaphas was a strategy fraught with danger.

James wondered if Pilate even cared about possible negative reactions to using corban money. Perhaps in a certain corner of his heart, he would welcome a show of public anger as an opportunity to answer any questions raised by his hesitancy in Caesarea. And this time, it wasn't likely that silent resistance would work. If men knelt down and bared their necks, they might not get up again.

All of these thoughts James shared with Joseph, who in his practical, political way saw in them a different and nearer cause for concern.

"I hope that Pilate is not reconsidering his trust in you," Joseph said. "It is of no small value to the nation that the Roman prefect has taken you into his confidence. If he should now decide that the ruse you proposed for removing the offensive image caused him to lose the people's respect, neither the nation nor *James the Just* will be the better."

James put up his hands in resignation. "What can I do?" he asked. "I suggested what seemed the best course at the time. Pilate accepted it then. We will both have to live with the consequences."

Joseph screwed up his face. "*Live*...is the key word," he said.

*　*　*

Ever since his student days, James had continued to take part in the distribution of food to poor families. Sometimes he went out into the countryside to collect gifts of fruits, vegetables, grains and eggs from nearby farms. Sometimes he helped with deliveries around the city. He always made it a point to remind the students with whom he worked that being a Jew involved more than believing a certain set of religious precepts, more even than keeping the Law. A Jew's faith specifically demanded good deeds and a heartfelt concern for those around him. As the sages put it, one must act in a way that helps to *repair the world—*

expressed in the Hebrew phrase, *tikkun olam.*

The young men were thoroughly familiar with how the Rabbi James would explain this imperative. What good is it, he would say to them, if you see people with nothing to eat and nothing to wear, and you merely wish them well? One must do the work of providing for their needs, or else faith and good wishes have no meaning. Some who had heard him making this point on numerous occasions, could repeat his words by heart, even capturing his characteristic inflections. It was their running joke which James himself found amusing.

On this evening, he was in the storehouse attached to the synagogue established by Hillel and now under the leadership of Gamaliel. All around the room, students were hauling, selecting and combining food items, assembling them into parcels for the evening's distribution. James stood by a long table measuring out barley from a tub. Asher, the student who carried messages for him, held open the mouth of a sack as the rabbi doled the grain with a wooden scoop.

Two young men who had just arrived to participate in the evening's activity were waiting for their first load to be assembled. They sat on a cart they would pull to make the deliveries. James happened to overhear their conversation, which centered on some military engagement.

"From what I heard, the tetrarch's garrison was taken by surprise and completely overwhelmed," said the one.

"Who attacked?"

"Nabateans—from Petra."

"Raiders?"

"No. They were forces of King Aretas."

"But why would he do it? Surely, this will bring in the Romans."

"Because of his daughter. Antipas set her aside so he could marry Herodias. It was a betrayal of the peace between the two realms."

This exchange pricked James' interest. "Where did you hear this?" he interjected with a tone of urgency.

The student stood and faced him. "The market plaza, Rabbi. It is being told throughout the city."

"Do you know when this attack happened?"

The young man shrugged. "Some days ago, I assume. Weeks, even. I don't know how the story came to Jerusalem. Caravaners, maybe. It would take some days, at the least."

James nodded without saying anything further to the students about the matter. By then his thoughts were in Galilee, wrapped in anxiety about the safety of John. The caution urged by Joseph of Arimathea had been well advised at the time. Intervention from Jerusalem might indeed have placed John in greater jeopardy. But if events had taken a turn such as the young man described, John's situation could hardly be more perilous. Now was the time to act.

He turned to Asher. "Have you seen the Rabbi Gamaliel?" he asked.

"The master was in the hall of the synagogue earlier."

"Get some others to pack the barley," James said. "I need you to go to Ein Kerem,"

"Yes, Rabbi."

By the time Asher returned to the city with Joseph's promise to meet in the morning, James and Gamaliel had contacted three other rabbis who headed houses of study, along with several Sanhedrin members. On the strength of James' family connection and his insistence that he was confident his kinsman—son of the great priest, Zacharias, of blessed memory—was not involved in any sort of conspiracy with Aretas, they agreed to sign a letter to the tetrarch begging clemency.

James and Gamaliel spent most of the night crafting their message in the most tactful of language. They tried to strike a balance between the authority of those scholars and counselors making the appeal and appropriate deference to Antipas, whom they addressed as *the revered leader of our fellow Jews in another wing within the House of Israel.* This was laying it on thick, but everyone knew of the tetrarch's inflated self-regard. Antipas was a son of Herod.

Next morning, Joseph lent his approval to their draft, suggesting only a slight change in a line referring to the jurisdiction of the Sanhedrin. A finished version was rendered and signatures of all the petitioners obtained, including those of three additional council members whose names Joseph thought might enhance the list.

It was decided that James should deliver the appeal to Antipas— mainly because of the personal tie, though not entirely. Political as ever, Joseph pointed out that the effort could not be presented as an official act of the Sanhedrin, even if a number of council members were participating in their private capacities. Of course, if the tetrarch should leap to other conclusions, then so be it. But the fact that James was not a Sanhedrin member, only a relative of John, would answer any questions that might arise in Jerusalem after the fact.

Gamaliel selected six of his students to accompany James to Tiberius, among them Asher, who being from the area, could secure lodging for the party. They were gathering in the court of the Synagogue at the Crossed Streets, making ready to leave in the early afternoon when a man called at the gate. James recognized him as the fellow who had carried the last message from the Rabbi Caleb in Ammathus, and a cold chill of apprehension swept over him. The man held out a small parchment roll. James took it, asked the fellow to wait, and went into the stone hut to read the message alone.

Caleb reported that there had been an attack on one of Antipas' frontier posts by forces of King Aretas. This accorded with what the student in the storehouse had heard. The action had apparently been of limited intent, probably only a show of the King's anger over the rejection of his daughter, and amounted to little more than a skirmish. But the Nabatean general succeeded in doing so much damage so swiftly that Antipas feared a massive invasion might be imminent.

In recent weeks, Caleb wrote, followers of John had taken to gathering in the street outside the prison to call for the release of their teacher. After the attack by Aretas' troops, Antipas was more afraid than ever that John and his people were in league with the Nabateans. Even though he considered John a prophet and continued to be interested in his preaching, he ordered him taken to the fortress at Macherus, a more remote location in the south of Peraea near the Salt Sea.

Then Caleb related a story which seemed to him very odd, but that was nonetheless in circulation throughout the region. Herodias had held a dinner in celebration of her husband's birthday, to which the chief officials of the court and several high-ranking officers were invited.

"I have heard that there was much raucous behavior," Caleb wrote, "in the manner of Rome, where Herodias lived for a number of years. One can only imagine the goings-on. I'm told that some of those in attendance found it quite offensive, even men in the tetrarch's inner circle. The evening reached its high point—or low, depending on one's perspective—when Herodias' daughter, Salome, performed a dance for the guests. This exhibition was, it appears, a bit on the lewd side, much to the delight of her stepfather. If the report of Antipas' reaction is correct, it would be consistent with certain tales about his leering fascination with the girl. But that is a matter for another discussion.

"What you will undoubtedly find troubling," Caleb continued, "is the account of a peculiar thing that happened next. I have been told that Antipas made some grandiose offering to Salome in thanks for her performance. She could choose any reward that appealed to her. It is said that what she chose was the head of your kinsman.

"Now, please restrain your anxiety, my friend, because I cannot confirm any of this. And such a thing would certainly be bizarre, even for the House of Herod. I am also unable to ascertain where this dinner took place. The royal family has not been seen in the capital for some time, so it might have happened in Macherus, where John was taken. The fortress is garrisoned by one of the largest contingents of Antipas' troops. It would be a logical place for him to go, if he anticipates fending off more attacks from Aretas. And from there, he could take refuge in Jerusalem, should his defenses fail.

"Unclear as all of this may be," Caleb concluded, "I would advise that, if you intend to intercede for John, you should not hesitate to do so now. Macherus is probably where you should make your appeal."

Sitting with his elbows on the table, James put his head in his hands, examining the situation and how best to proceed. Should he have acted earlier, despite Joseph's caution? If he hurried to Macherus now, would he find it already too late to save John? After a moment in which he was torn by guilt and indecision, James stood and hurried outside to the messenger from Ammathus.

"Please tell the Rabbi Caleb that I am going to Macherus," he said.

"Yes, Rabbi."

"Take some food inside the house, and rest before departing. How did you come to Jerusalem?"

"I walked with a pack train, Rabbi. I will have to find one with which to return."

"No," said James, "that could delay your return for too long." He gestured to Asher. "Take two of the others and go with this man to Ammathus. Ask the Rabbi Caleb to find out anything else he can about John. If the tetrarch is not at Macherus, I will go to Tiberius. If I have to, I will go to the ends of the earth to save the son of Zacharias."

James departed with the three remaining students. Their route would run around the north of the Salt Sea on the road that passed near Qumran. Leaving Jerusalem, it occurred to James that a slight diversion farther north would bring them to Jericho and the Essene community. This was located near a ford that crossed the Jordan into Antipas' territory of Perea and not all that far from Macherus. It was possible that Pinchas might know more about John and about Antipas' military situation than Caleb did all the way up in Galilee. Having more recent information would be an advantage in making an appeal to the tetrarch.

*   *   *

The Essene compound was on the far side of Jericho, accessible by a path that wound upward and then down into a secluded hollow among rough hills and rocky projections overlooking the river. James and his party were stopped and challenged as they approached a gate barring the way into a cluster of houses and low buildings set around an open square. One appeared to be a synagogue. Beyond were garden terraces, though with little growth evident in the cool season. There was also an olive grove, which put James in mind of home. Identifying himself, James asked to see Pinchas, and was instructed to wait.

After a time, an old man came up to the gate, walking slowly with considerable effort and difficulty. James recognized Pinchas, noting how much he had changed in the years since James and Elizabeth placed a small, frightened boy into his care. Other than that fateful night, James' only contact with John's teacher had been through their ongoing correspondence.

"You are the Rabbi James," Pinchas said, noting the white robes and turban.

"I am, sir. Peace be upon you."

"It is good to see you again, my son—though...I fear I have bad news for you."

James' face hardened in anticipation of the pain he had half-expected to confront.

"Your kinsman, John, has been killed," said Pinchas. "His body was sent to us, and we have buried it at Sebaste near the tomb of his father."

James closed his eyes tightly, took a deep breath, and then said, "So it is true that Antipas had him executed?"

"Yes."

"This odd story about the birthday celebration and...the dance..."

"Ah, you have heard that."

James nodded slowly, sadly.

"I cannot say what happened at that wicked feast," Pinchas said, "but I must tell you that Antipas has very cruelly retained John's head."

James winced unconsciously.

"We asked to have it, so that we could bury it with his body. But our request has so far been denied. I have no idea what monstrous intentions the tetrarch has for such a grim artifact. Perhaps he plans on using it to intimidate John's followers."

"Pinchas," James said, "it cannot be true that John was involved in any sort of plot against Antipas...can it?"

"Of course not," said Pinchas. "Antipas is a fool as well as a reprobate. John may have been harsh in his criticisms, but he would never have raised his hand in violence against him. We of the Essene brotherhood await the final battle between the sons of light and the followers of darkness. Herod's little worm hardly meets our expectations of the Evil One."

Pinchas could see the crushing sadness in James' eyes.

"I failed," James said. "I should have acted to save John, but I was advised to wait, and wrongly I followed that advice."

"No, Rabbi," Pinchas objected. "You could never have kept the son of Zacharias from pursuing his mission. And it is unlikely that, once he was in Antipas' hands, you could have convinced the tetrarch that John was no threat to him. Condemning Antipas' marriage was, of itself, too great a challenge to the royal house. What the tetrarch had done was an affront to the Nabateans and proof to Rome that he is not fit to rule. I believe Antipas' folly will bring him down one day, perhaps quite soon. But John chose his own path and sealed his own fate."

James managed a partial smile in appreciation of Pinchas' attempt to reassure him.

"In any event," the old man continued, "Antipas aside, I believe that John completed his main task. He always felt he had been called by the

Holy One to announce the coming of the Lord's Anointed." Pinchas lowered his voice. "John confided to me that Messiah has come. I trust you know who he is."

James glanced about at the students, then back at the old Essene sage who noted his concern. At a nod from Pinchas, the gatekeeper admitted James, who then walked off a short distance with Pinchas, leaving the students outside the preserve.

Now James spoke in hushed tones also. "Yes, I know to whom John referred," he said. "There is a conviction among my family..."

"And within John's."

"And within John's. His father and mother were convinced."

"Rabbi, do you know of the declaration Zacharias made upon the birth of John?"

"I have heard it mentioned. Zacharias was a great man, and his words highly regarded. I suppose that particular utterance would have been of interest, coming as it did after the odd illness that robbed him of his voice for so many weeks."

"Elizabeth had the words taken down," said Pinchas, "and she once related them to me. *You, child, shall be called prophet of the most high, forerunner of the Lord, preparing his way...*"

"Yes," James said, "I believe Zacharias was citing the prophets, Malachi and Isaiah."

"Elizabeth also spoke of another memorable utterance," Pinchas said, "made by her kinswoman, Mary. She is the mother of your halfbrother, Jesus, is she not?"

"She is. And it happens that I was present on that occasion."

Pinchas eyed him searchingly. "So then, Rabbi," he said, fixing James with a penetrating gaze, "do you share your family's conviction?"

James was silent for a second, turning his own eyes to the side. "I... know that my brother possesses...extraordinary powers. But I am— I am not sure I can claim to be convinced he is the Messiah."

"Word of those powers has reached us here," said Pinchas, "through several channels. We have heard about masses of people flocking to hear him preach—more than ever followed John. And there are tales of mysterious cures. Even the appearance of wine where there was no wine before. Do you know of these things?"

"Some stories have come to my ears. They are not inconsistent with things we observed in his childhood and— I was on hand also when the wine appeared."

"And I should tell you..." Pinchas said.

James' eyes were on him once more.

"I should tell you that Elizabeth shared with me the striking details of your brother's birth."

Now a certain tension was evident in James' posture and facial expression. "Pinchas," he said nervously, "Zacharias knew that you would be prudent and discreet in protecting and nurturing his son. And I have depended on that in our correspondence over the years. So you can understand that I—"

"Of course, Rabbi." Pinchas nodded assuringly. "Circumspection is especially important now, after the death of John. Jesus' mission must be given its full opportunity to flower. In the meantime, we of the brotherhood will be patient and attend to our preparations."

"Preparations?" James asked.

Pinchas' face was in profile, but James could see the smile that cracked on his lips, one that was noticeably sly.

"Isn't it as I said, Rabbi, the sons of light against the followers of darkness? If Messiah has come, then the consolation of Israel is at hand and our expectations soon to be fulfilled. This is what we have waited for. If your brother is the one, he will free the Jewish nation as promised. But for that he will need...an army." Pinchas turned and once more looked full-face at James. *"Blessed be the Lord, my rock, who trains my hands for war, my fingers for battle."*

CHAPTER TWENTY-NINE

Set me as a seal upon your heart, a seal upon your arm,
for love is as strong as death.

(Song of Solomon 8)

nthusiasm generated by Pilate's announcement of the water project was high as men lined up for what were said to be the best-paying labor jobs available in the Jerusalem district since the days of Herod's vast building schemes. There would be ample food on family tables throughout the area. Likewise, the wives were filled with anticipation of the day when fighting for access to the fountains would be a thing of the past. Additional water outlets were to be installed around the city, even some outside the walls to serve the satellite neighborhoods.

People marked the progress toward life's improvement first in the construction of the supply ponds on the heights near Bethlehem, then in the earthworks for the arch foundations along the route of the aqueduct, and then in the steady rise of a tower near where the city wall was being pierced for entry of the watercourse into Jerusalem. This tower would contain sluices for diverting some of the water to supplement the Pool of Siloam when the Gihon Spring ran slow, as well as for increasing the water pressure in the city system through a steep drop, to carry the remaining flow across town and finally into the reservoirs beneath the Temple Mount.

Optimism was somewhat dampened when part of the tower collapsed, killing several workmen and bystanders, and injuring others quite severely. A murmur of suspicion was heard in certain circles that perhaps the whole water project, being essentially a Roman undertaking, might be cursed. There was counter-speculation that the workers could have been drunk or bore fault for the mishap in some other way.

This possibility too was laid at the feet of Rome by malevolent gossips. Had Pilate not troubled himself to hire qualified men? Did he merely assume that there were plenty more Jews to replace any lives sacrificed to the pagan effort?

An investigation conducted by the prefecture discovered that the accident had been caused by defects in some of the stones, making for cracks that eventually gave way under the weight of the over-structure. The contractor who had provided the defective material disappeared amid speculation that the imperial galleys now had another oarsman.

Confidence soon returned as construction proceeded, though James remained anxious about public reaction when the truth of how the work was being funded came out. And surely, it was inevitable that information about corban money being used would eventually be known.

He had other concerns to dominate his thoughts, however, on issues closer to his heart. Pinchas' remark about how the Messiah would need an army had continued to ring in his ears over the months since the trip to Jericho. If Essenes were preparing for war on the assumption that James' brother was the long-awaited Deliverer, what plans were being laid by others aware of Jesus and the movement he was building?

And clearly, this was a movement. Word of the throngs coming to hear Jesus preach was now the street chatter of Jerusalem. Three of Gamaliel's students had gone up to Galilee in order to attend one of the meetings. Upon their return, they told of a remarkable incident in which some 5,000, gathered in an isolated area, had stayed so long listening to Jesus that they lost track of time and found themselves hungry. In some miraculous fashion, Jesus and his men had fed the crowd with only a few loaves and some fish.

Such stories were coming thick and fast these days, and they caused James great anxiety. They also reached the ears of Pilate. While this intriguing prophet was confining his circuit to Antipas' territories and other points outside of Judea—at least that's how it appeared for the present—Pilate by now knew the religious enthusiasm of the Jews all too well. It was only a matter of time before the movement, and perhaps its leader himself, would come into Pilate's jurisdiction, possibly to stay. And given Jewish attraction to moralistic rabble rousers, what was now merely interest could easily become fervor.

Fervor was something that demanded watchfulness.

What Pilate found most curious was that this prophet was the very same Jesus identified by the centurion, Cassius Longinus, during his research into the background of the Rabbi James. Such an interesting family this was turning out to be—blood from the House of David, priestly tie, business linkages throughout Galilee, and of course, James' own prominence in Jerusalem. And one more thing: the Essene wild man, John, executed by Antipas—he too was a relative, and it was said his followers were still going about promoting his cause.

Jesus was a man of connections and an attractive figure—definitely no *untutored country bumpkin*, as Longinus had put it. This was someone who could potentially be a problem. Perhaps a talk with the Rabbi James was in order to ascertain the goal of his brother's preaching and crowd-gathering—and, not least, to determine if James was playing a part in the movement.

Pilate had put effort into cultivating this reasonable, Greek-speaking Jew. James was helpful in defusing conflict over Caesar's image, the subsequent fire in Caesarea notwithstanding. And he had provided useful information about the temple and the corban. Pilate hoped for even more from their relationship, but he needed assurance that there were no dubious ambitions lurking beneath the equable surface appearance.

On the occasion of his next visit to Jerusalem, Pilate sent a request that the rabbi join him in observing the progress of the water project. And so it was that James found himself in the company of Pilate on a tour of the supply ponds and the first sections of the aqueduct. The two men stood on a rock jutting from the slope of the Bethlehem heights facing Jerusalem in the distance. From this vantage, the sequence of piers leading down the hillside seemed like a line of stone markers by which someone arriving here for the first time might find the city. Each pier was taller than the one before it, reflecting the fall of the land. Work on the near, shorter members had reached the point where the piers were beginning to flare outward into the shape of the arches that would carry the watercourse at a gentle grade sufficient to maintain flow.

Pilate was pointing forward, sighting the line with his hand. "As you can see, Rabbi, after the sixth pier, the structure will proceed in two levels. The bottom row of arches, capped by a horizontal beam, supports the upper layer. This provides stability by distributing weight more evenly. There is a limit to how high you can build the piers safely—a lesson we have learned at great cost. Some of our more imaginative designers have created elegantly graceful arches soaring up to the sky, only to watch them crumble very inelegantly from the disturbance of an earth tremor or even a strong wind."

"You have refined these techniques greatly," James said.

"They are what permit us to build cities in regions not naturally hospitable to the habitation of men." The note of pride in Pilate's voice spoke for itself. "Perhaps more than any other structure, the aqueduct marks our civilization. You will find them from Britain to the easternmost desert wastes, and always they show the distinctive Roman hand."

James had made no mention of how this impressive enterprise was being financed, and he did not plan to do so. Pilate had chosen to disregard his counsel. Any protest which might erupt when the temple treasury was finally revealed as a contributor would be Pilate's problem. Which raised a question in James' mind about why he had been invited on this tour. Having pursued a course James had advised against, why would Pilate focus their entire time together on the construction? It didn't take long for James to realize that this jaunt was merely an excuse for a very different conversation.

"I find it interesting your family is so much discussed these days, Rabbi," said Pilate as they strolled back up to the pond site near the summit of what local folk referred to as the *Spring Hill*.

"My family?" James responded, curiosity vying with a wave of apprehension.

"Yes," Pilate said in as offhand a manner as he was able to feign. "Isn't the Galilee preacher, Jesus, your brother? He is causing quite a stir, I'm told."

So *this* was the motive that underlay Pilate's cordial invitation—not the aqueduct at all. The prefect wanted to talk about Jesus.

"He is," James said, "and he's becoming quite well known."

"And such a wide following," said Pilate, "people from all walks of life in Galilee and Perea, the Decapolis territories, too, I understand. What is it about your brother that draws crowds?"

"His message is inspiring. He calls people to righteousness, to live more fully in faith."

"Well, that seems a traditional Jewish appeal," said Pilate. "Many of your great seers have spoken of the insufficiency of sacrifice, compared to purity of heart."

"You have been studying again, Prefect."

"I try to know the people I govern." This Pilate said with a certain glint in his eye, like a schoolboy out to impress his teacher with how well he had mastered a lesson. "But really, Rabbi, there has to be more than a message. Your brother must possess great charm."

"Jesus is a warm person, and extremely bright and insightful. He always was. I recall how deeply he affected a group of temple sages when he was about twelve years old. He expounded on the Law with surprising wisdom, for a lad."

Pilate found the notion of a precocious child interesting but beside the point. "Your doctors of the Law might get excited at such a show, Rabbi, but most people are not moved by intellect. It is *personality* that attracts crowds. Jesus must be quite dazzling in his public utterances."

"Perhaps so."

"Have you not witnessed his preaching?"

"No. As you say, Jesus has conducted his ministry outside of Judea. My work keeps me mostly in Jerusalem. So my awareness of his activities depends on the reports of others."

It struck Pilate as odd, if not unbelievable, that a man of James' prominence in Jewish religious life would be so detached from a spiritual movement gaining such wide attention—one led by his own brother. But he had not known James to prevaricate. Indeed, this rabbi always seemed the very soul of an honest man.

"You should understand," James went on, "that my brother and I were never deeply involved in each other's lives. Primarily this was due to the considerable gap in our ages and my leaving our hometown of Nazareth to study in Jerusalem. I knew him when he was a little boy. We have been together on various family occasions over the years. And I arranged for him to travel with the caravans of my colleague, Joseph. But other than that, we have lived very much apart."

This was a plausible explanation.

"I see," said Pilate. "And what about your cousin, John?"

It was plain that Pilate was on a well considered hunt for information. He had obviously prepared for this talk.

"Jesus' cousin, actually," James said. "Jesus and I are half-brothers, and it is his mother, Mary, who has the family tie."

"Of course, of course. But did John take part in your brother's mission? I understand he preached with great intensity."

How forthright could James permit himself to be with Caesar's vicar? After a moment's thought, he decided it was best to conceal as little as possible. Only the essentials.

"I believe that John considered himself to be something of a herald. But I can't say whether he and Jesus ever consulted on the matter or specifically devised that role for John. And John was an Essene, so it's natural that his calls for repentance would have been very impassioned. That reflects the fierceness of Essene devotion to the Law."

"They do see themselves as set apart, don't they?"

"Very much so, Prefect."

"Is Jesus an Essene?"

Here James hesitated. "I don't...think so," he said. "My family has always held the views of the Pharisee party. However, it's possible Jesus has been influenced by Essene thinking. I, myself, have great admiration for the piety of the brotherhood. I try to emulate them in my own way. Perhaps Jesus does, as well. But once again, I must admit that I don't know his heart."

Pilate smiled amiably, even as he kept on probing. "Your brother speaks a lot about the poor," he said.

"As any good Jew might. Kindness toward the unfortunate is a key point of Jewish morality, the giving of alms a religious obligation."

The prefect's laugh brought a curious look from James.

"Rabbi, it has been my experience that your people consider anyone who isn't Roman to be *the poor*. It's more often a political distinction than one of wealth. I think even your high priest considers himself *poor*, and clings to that identity with pride. In fact, I must say I've never seen a country with so many rich *poor* people."

James couldn't help but smile. "Well, we Jews tend to use the word *poor* to indicate our utter dependence on the Holy One," he said. "Still... there is truth in your observation, Prefect."

Pilate smiled once more in response, but then his expression turned serious, and he spoke with candor. "What I wish to know, Rabbi, is whether this ministry of your brother's has a rebellious aspect. I'm told he refers to himself as...*Son of Man*. That strikes me as the sort of colorful—not to say grandiose—moniker with which Zealot leaders like to flatter themselves. I don't find such titles comforting."

James drew in a breath. Here was the point to which he had long known the growing interest in his brother's mission would come. Surely, Jesus was bound to fall under the watchful eye of the Roman authorities, even without setting foot in Judea. James wondered if Pilate had agents in attendance at Jesus' meetings, taking down his teachings and carrying them back to Caesarea.

"I do not think my brother is political," James said. "Yes, his words imply a call for justice. But I've assumed he is speaking from a moral point of view about what is a moral imperative. Are we not expected to deal with each other justly? It is the will of the Holy One, blessed be He—a will that finds expression in the teachings of your own philosophers. As to the title, *Son of Man*, that phrase is of common usage. It appears in several of the psalms, as well as the Book of Job. The Prophet Ezekiel also uses it. Perhaps Jesus merely wishes to emphasize his bond with other men—that all Jews are brothers. I'll admit my knowledge about his preaching is limited, but I believe I can assure you that Jesus is no Zealot."

Pilate looked off in the direction of Jerusalem, not answering for a time. Then he said, "Even if he isn't, there are those who might find some means of exploiting his celebrity for other than *moral* purposes."

He set his gaze directly on James. "I suggest, Rabbi, that you find an opportunity to counsel your brother. Make him understand that Rome has no objection to repentance and righteousness. Indeed, I would hope that all people might live up to their better natures. However, it is a fact that movements—no matter how well-intentioned—can go astray. Or they can be misdirected by people who intrude upon them with other motives."

Then Pilate swept a hand about to indicate the construction so much in evidence before them. "We Romans are known for our aqueducts, Rabbi, but the empire is also remarkable for its extensive system of roads. It is another of our contributions to civilization. And it has given rise to a saying that is widely repeated and very apt. *A road can be paved with the finest of stones, but it may still lead to Hades.*"

*   *   *

James knew that Pilate's suggestion was as good as an order. He would have to find Jesus, get a fuller picture of what his brother really was preaching, and warn him to temper his messages with prudence. And he would have to do it soon. There must be no hesitation, as had been the case in the failed effort to protect John.

Maybe Jesus really was Messiah. Wasn't that one interpretation of the phrase, *Son of Man,* as it appeared in the book of Daniel? *I beheld a vision in the night, like a Son of Man coming with the clouds of heaven.* James recognized the implications of his brother's words, though of course, it would hardly have been wise to point out this understanding to Pilate. As Pinchas had said, Jesus' mission must be given its full opportunity to flower.

But where to find Jesus? If he had really caused an uproar in Nazareth as violent as reported, it was unlikely he'd base his ministry there. The meeting Gamaliel's students attended had been held near Capernaum, which as James knew, was the region on the shore of Gennesaret where Simon lived. Perhaps that was the place to start.

Over the course of two days, James organized his affairs to allow for an extended absence from Jerusalem, traveling to wherever Jesus and his band might be found. That could be anywhere in Galilee, Perea, Syria, the Decapolis territories—who knew? Their presence had been reported in all of these regions. It was even said they made occasional forays into Judea.

Gamaliel assigned the three young men who had located Jesus in Capernaum to accompany James as escorts, in the hope that past success might contribute to success in the present. Eager for a second chance to hear the Rabbi James' brother speak, they refrained from mentioning that their prior accomplishment had been largely due to good luck. The student Asher also joined in for the value of his local contacts. Joseph of Arimathea provided camel-back transport, and the group departed.

The caravan to which they were attached followed a route east of the River Jordan, making stops at the Decapolis cities of Pella and Gadara. The students, none of whom had ever ridden a camel before, found it awkward and a little scary, so a handler was assigned to instruct the young men. After the first day, they felt more confident controlling their animals.

At Gadara, the caravan headed northeast to Abila. James and his companions split off on their own at Hippos on the eastern shore of Gennesaret. Before leaving town, they heard an odd tale. Apparently, Jesus had visited the area and, while there, exorcised a corps of demons from a man who had been possessed for many years and roamed the countryside creating terror in the region. As it was told, Jesus banished the demons into a herd of swine, which abounded in that pagan country, sending the poor beasts in a mad rush headlong into the lake.

Feelings about this incident were quite torn. Astonishment at seeing the old troublemaker released from his long possession was mixed with fear that there might be more demons about, as well as some anger over the loss of valuable pigs. Jesus and his band had been asked to leave the region in terms that were not pleasant. Suspicion among some of the gentiles was that this Jew wonder-worker had taken the opportunity to destroy a herd of animals he considered unclean and repulsive. James did not identify himself as the wonder-worker's brother.

Reaching Bethsaida, the travelers encountered numerous people who were not only aware of Jesus, but who had heard him preach, some multiple times. Local comments revealed much excitement about the progress of Jesus' ministry. And the familiarity and affection with which he was spoken of made it clear that this area—the north shore of Gennesaret—was the center of his activities. Here he was referred to commonly as *the rabbi*, a discovery James found unexpectedly disturbing.

"Rabbi?" he muttered in a bewildered tone to no one in particular. "Whose disciple was he? Who gave him certification?" The questions were laced with the slightest annoyance.

A number of area residents were related to some of Jesus' men. Knowing that Simon lived between Capernaum and Bethsaida, James asked for directions to his home. They located the place, one of a cluster of modest houses set about a slight rise overlooking the lakeshore. All around, large nets suspended between posts to dry in the sun marked this settlement as a community of fishermen.

They were received at the gate by Simon's wife. She expressed her delight at meeting the famous rabbi from Jerusalem, whom to James' surprise, she termed *the brother of the Lord*. Her husband and the others were not here, she told him. Rather, she believed they were in the north, probably at Caesarea-Philippi.

James and his companions were ushered in and feted with a more-than-ample meal plus an invitation to spend the night before continuing their journey. The meal was accepted gratefully, but James insisted that they'd best be heading on afterward, since a long trek still lay ahead. They departed with many thanks, and followed the Jordan north, making good progress until the sun was low in the sky. That night they camped along the river, below Lake Huleh where the camels could be watered and grasses abounded.

*   *   *

Caesarea-Philippi was set on the famous heights that marked the western end of what had once been called the Land of Bashan, near the mountain called Hermon. The road into the city bustled with market traffic as James and his companions approached the main gate. James instructed three of the students to remain outside grazing and guarding the camels. The other, Asher, he took with him into the city to inquire if anyone knew of Jesus and his whereabouts. When they were through the gate, Asher suggested that they seek out the local synagogues, since they had heard that Jesus was known to preach in such settings when he visited new regions.

Typical of cities built by the Herods, the appearance of Caesarea-Philippi owed much to the influence of Greco-Roman architectural design. Colonnaded buildings and broad plazas were very much in evidence, especially so since this was the capital of Philip's tetrarchy, as reflected in the city's name. Being here reminded James of his trips to Sepphoris as a boy in those days before the great tragedy that now seemed so long ago.

From questioning a guardsman of the city watch, they learned of a synagogue nearby that was especially welcoming to visitors, being a place where the Jewish tradesmen and farmers, in town to ply their wares, would gather to pray. The guardsman cautioned them that, this time in the afternoon, the place was likely to be unattended, except for some wives who gathered in the court for their own prayers and gossip.

He ventured that it was mostly gossip, since these women were known for unseemly boldness, self-will, and pestering other people. Why their husbands, or the synagogue leaders, tolerated such indecorous behavior was beyond him.

James thanked the guardsman, and set out to follow his directions to this welcoming synagogue. He remarked to Asher that gossipy women might be just who would be aware of a wandering preacher attracting crowds in the region.

"If they are truly so bold, Master," said the student, "maybe they have gone out to hear Jesus themselves."

"Maybe so."

The synagogue court was as the guardsman had said. Some half-dozen women were present. At the entry of the two men, they drew together, the younger women tugging at their veils demurely, partially concealing their faces. One young mother, who was holding a baby in her arms, rose from the bench on which she had been seated. Another pulled the small child beside her up against the folds of her robe. These women in no way seemed especially bold to James, but rather were behaving in the way of any proper Jewish female at the approach of unknown men. Then one of them, an older and somewhat stout woman, stepped up to the visitors.

"Peace be upon you, sirs. Is there some way we can assist you?"

James offered a slight bow of greeting. "I am the Rabbi James, master of the Synagogue at the Crossed Streets in Jerusalem. This young man is my assistant, Asher son of Elihu. We are searching for a preacher who leads a band of disciples and may be visiting this city. Have you heard of the man, Jesus of Nazareth?"

At the mention of that name, the women's demeanor changed noticeably. They seemed to stand straighter, with raised confidence, those who had covered their faces letting their veils fall aside.

"We know of him quite well," the stout women said. "All of us have heard him speak, and we consider ourselves students of his teaching."

James and Asher exchanged glances.

"*You*...are students?" James asked. "Women?"

"Oh yes, sir. The Lord has as wide a following among women as among men. There are even some women who go about with his company, serving him and aiding in his ministry. It happens wherever he travels. Several of us here have done it during the weeks he's been in this region. Women are especially helpful when the elderly and infirm seek the Lord's curative powers. We lead and support them as they come forth to receive his healing touch."

"Your husbands permit this?" James asked incredulously.

"Our husbands are his followers also. Actually, it was my own and two others who went down to Capernaum to ask if Jesus might come here. A group of us had heard the Lord speak in Galilee, and we were pleased to bring the good news of his mission back here. Of course, many other people heard of Jesus as well. His fame has been spreading in these parts for awhile, and now Jesus himself has come to us."

This was unimaginable to James. His brother surrounding himself with women? And this attitude of veneration that seemed to have built up—*The Lord? The Lord?* That was how Simon's wife had referred to Jesus. Was it common parlance among his followers?

"Where can I find Jesus?" he asked.

The stout woman thought for a time. "I do not know, sir. He and his band keep in motion. It seems they intend to cover much of the country hereabouts, though they have not yet entered the city itself. I cannot say where they might be at the moment. But...wait."

She turned to the other women. "Kiva, take the good rabbi and his man to your mistress. She will surely know how to find the Lord."

A tall, slim girl stepped out from among the group, came forward, and curtsied. James thanked the stout woman for the information provided. Then he and Asher followed the girl, Kiva, out of the synagogue court and through the streets of the city. As they went, she explained that she was servant to the widow of a wealthy man who had been named Zimran, a holder of vast estates and plantings. He had died just two years before, following a difficult illness. His widow had assumed the management of his properties, but she was grooming her eldest son, a young man of twenty, to take over the business.

"My mistress is a great lady," said Kiva, "intelligent and widely read. She is an admirer of Jesus, and is helping to build up his ministry in Caesarea-Philippi."

It occurred to James that Kiva herself, servant though she was, seemed quite intelligent, and as self-possessed as the stout woman in the synagogue court had been. Perhaps this was what the guardsman had described as boldness. Did all females who came into contact with Jesus acquire such confidence?

The imposing home to which Kiva led them attested to the late Zimran's wealth. While set tightly among other large buildings, both private homes and commercial structures, the house towered in three full stories above a luxuriant walled garden, rising to a high tiled roof that shined a bright red-ochre in the late-afternoon sun.

Many Jews spoke with disdain about Caesarea-Philippi because of certain pagan associations. Its most celebrated landmark was a temple dedicated to Caesar Augustus, and coins minted for the city by Philip bore the late emperor's likeness, a practice considered idolatrous. But this opulent home was a clear indication to James of how some Jews were able to accommodate themselves to a thoroughly Hellenized environment, doing quite well in the process. Ambivalent as he might feel about that reality, James was mindful of the success his own family enjoyed building the lavish Greek homes of Sepphoris.

Kiva took them into a large entry hall, bidding them to wait while she sought her mistress. James stood patiently, gazing around the impressive room with mild interest. But Asher was feeling quite dazed by the sumptuousness of the furnishings, the stunning floral-patterned mosaic covering the floor, and the richly colored tapestries that faced each other from opposite walls.

After a time, the girl returned with a woman whose bearing marked her as a person of substance, someone long accustomed to the company of authoritative, respected men, and totally at ease in their presence. She was a handsome woman of about James' age, with deep blue eyes and a braid of black hair, flecked with strands of gray, encircling her head, visible beneath a veil of silk. He recognized her immediately. It was Avigail.

The slightest catch in her voice cracked the veneer of cool sophistication, though only for an instant, as vision confirmed that this was indeed the Rabbi James of Jerusalem. "Peace...be upon you, James," she said, recovering herself.

"Avigail." His utterance of her name was almost breathless.

Asher was puzzled.

"It has been a very long time," she said.

"A very long time."

"You are well?"

"Quite well." He paused. "My condolences at the loss...of your husband, of blessed memory. It is two years now?"

"Thank you. Yes, two years. And *your* family...in Nazareth?"

"Continuing to grow. Children, grandchildren—more than I can count these days."

She smiled. But the situation was awkward. Both stood stiffly. Then she gestured toward Asher.

"Your companion?"

James was stirred from his self-consciousness. "Oh...yes. My assistant, Asher son of Elihu."

Asher bowed his head, feeling a certain self-consciousness of his own in the presence of this strong and striking woman. "Madam."

Avigail smiled once more. "Asher son of Elihu," she said, "you look hungry." She turned to the girl. "Kiva, this young man would benefit from the hospitality of our house. Provide him a meal. I would speak with the Rabbi James."

Asher took a step, paused, then started again, departing with the girl in some confusion. He had never been dismissed in such a peremptory way by a woman he did not know, and yet it seemed right that this woman's orders be obeyed.

When they were alone, Avigail extended her hand in the direction of an adjoining room, the far end of which was open to the gardens at the side of the house. The interior itself was filled with numerous plants, tall and low, growing in urns. There were couches along the side walls and two Roman-style chairs set in the center of the space. This was obviously where guests were received.

"Do be at ease, James."

They each took one of the chairs, facing each other.

"It is difficult to be at ease," he found himself saying.

Avigail nodded. "Yes. It is."

Her mature loveliness—the figure stately now, rather than the wispy girlishness he remembered, and the delicate features of her face composed confidently after a life of high position—it all made for a female presence that struck James with great force. It was how she had affected him years before, only more so, and it unsettled him.

"You seek Jesus," she said

"Yes. He is my brother."

"I know."

His eyebrows raised slightly.

"You spoke of your brother years ago—the child of your father's second wife."

"Of course."

"And... And I have been aware of the Rabbi James. Of the renown you have achieved among the temple sages and the leadership of Jerusalem." She hadn't intended to reveal her continuing interest in the progress made by that studious young man who claimed her heart so many years before. But she couldn't help herself. "The good counsel of *James the Just* is known here in the north."

An unintentional, slightly quivering smile was James' reaction to this. "I strive to give good counsel. But perhaps my...*renown*...is a bit overstated."

She turned the subject back to his search. "Jesus and his companions arrived several weeks ago, and have set a circuit which they are following throughout this region. There is a house on one of my properties. I have given them the use of it. They return there each night after the Lord has completed his preaching."

That term again: *the Lord.*

"Are you a follower of my brother? It seems he is well known hereabouts."

"Yes, I am. I became aware of his ministry some months after my husband's death. Word had spread about this interesting young rabbi who was causing such excitement in Galilee. It was said that he had wondrous powers and spoke uplifting truths that changed people's lives. At that...particular time...my life was in need of...uplifting. So I went down to Galilee with several friends. Esther, the woman who sent you here with Kiva, was one of them. Her husband accompanied us, grudgingly I must say, though his attitude changed when he heard Jesus' words. We were *all* changed."

It was becoming clearer and clearer that his brother was having an impact. The anxiety James felt increased with each new revelation of Jesus' fame.

"What do..." James searched for the right words. "How are Jesus and his mission viewed by those in authority here?"

"I think that there is...a measure of concern."

"Concern?"

"Frankly, yes. His arrival and the interest it caused were at first dismissed as Jewish *enthusiasm*—something to be watched, but no immediate cause for worry. The gentile character of this region must be apparent to you. Jews are not the dominant part of the population within the city itself, though are somewhat more present in the surrounding countryside. But Caesarea-Philippi is the capital of the tetrarchy, and the Jews who do live here have done well." She raised a hand to indicate their surroundings.

"It is a magnificent home," James said.

"Thank you. It more reflects my late husband than it does me. He was a man who valued the tokens of accomplishment. My tastes are simpler." A smile came to her lips. "Although I will confess, one does get used to such surroundings."

He returned her smile. "Your father was a man of means," he said. "Surely your childhood home in Rabbah must have been—"

She laughed slightly, self-deprecatingly. "Not like this."

James found it gratifying that a life of wealth had not robbed her of the inner core of sincerity he had once found so appealing.

Avigail continued. "But something unexpected has happened. Greeks have begun to take an interest in Jesus and his message."

"Many?"

"Enough to attract attention. My eldest son, Rouvin, represents our business, and he comes into contact with the Greek merchants and some government officials as well. He tells me there is consternation over how many non-Jews are attracted to the Jewish preacher from Galilee. It seems to them like something different from gentiles taking an interest in Judaism and becoming God-fearers. That is a more familiar situation which they find annoying but not alarming."

"*Are* they alarmed?"

"Not yet. But they are aware."

"What of the tetrarch, Philip?"

"I don't know his feelings, but I assume he has been informed about the Lord and is keeping a watchful eye. When I go to Jesus' meetings, I always notice some very attentive men in the crowd who whisper constantly among themselves."

James wondered if some of those men weren't agents of Pilate.

"Of course, Greeks are not the only ones wary of Jesus. The crowds always include some Jews who like to test the Lord and try to maneuver him into saying something foolish. They fancy themselves scholars, and perhaps they are. Some speak from the Pharisee view, and some are clearly Sadducees. Often they are quite hostile."

"How does he deal with this harassment?"

"With humor, usually. Jesus is a man of boundless wit, though sometimes he counters their probes with remarks that are very compelling. And even his humorous comments make you think." Then she looked at James questioningly. "But...surely you are familiar with his preaching. I've assumed you support his ministry."

James placed his elbows on the arms of the chair and brought his hands together, one over the other. "I...have not been involved," he said. "In truth, I've yet to hear my brother preach."

"Really?" Avigail found this astonishing. "Is there any sort of quarrel between you?"

"Not at all," James said. "It's just that we have lived so separately. And Jesus started his preaching after he returned from a long journey. I didn't know he was back, and I was completely unaware that he had undertaken such a mission until some time after it began."

"Well then," said Avigail, "you must experience one of his meetings, and see for yourself what others have discovered."

"Is he a rousing speaker?" asked James.

Avigail shook her head. "Not in the sense of being loud or dramatic, no. He speaks in a very even voice—calming, really. Yet all can hear him, even those far away. And his manner is irresistible. He forces you to examine yourself, penetrates your heart. It's remarkable really."

James wished to pose what seemed to him a delicate question. He hesitated for a second, then asked, "What about...the healings?"

"Oh yes," Avigail said. "I've witnessed them. People come to Jesus with various illnesses. Some are blind. Others lame. I know some of the ones who've been cured. Whatever you may have heard, it *is* true."

A long moment of silence followed, during which James considered Avigail's observations, while she just sat watching him. Then a word began to form on her lips, a thought which demanded to be expressed.

"I have always been sorry at how we parted," she said, "without even getting word to you."

James looked into her beautiful, womanly face and held up a hand. "There was much danger," he said. "Samuel was right to take you and your mother away quickly. I myself was caught inside of Jerusalem when they closed the city."

"But I was never able to explain what my father had—"

"There was nothing to explain. He did what was best for you in arranging your marriage—which a father has every right to do. It was for the best."

As had Avigail before, James indicated their surroundings with a gesture. "Look how it turned out," he said. "I was in no position..." He left his sentence unfinished.

Their eyes locked. Across the space between them. Across the time that had separated them. After all these years, it amazed Avigail to discover that she could still feel the horrible throbbing ache that had overwhelmed her, paralyzed her, when Samuel announced the marriage contract. She reached out a hand to James. He did the same, and the tips of their fingers met. Never before had he touched her, not even when they were young. It would have been far too presumptuous, too intimate a thing to be proper. It wasn't proper now.

The moment passed. She withdrew her hand. Again they sat without speaking.

Then: "Let me...show you my gardens." She said the words with difficulty, her face turned away as she attempted to wipe a tear. "I am very proud of my collection of flowers. The seeds come from as far away as Egypt and Macedonia."

She led him out the open end of the room. James looked across a court bedecked with blooms and foliage of all colors. He spotted a small boy seated under a canopy beside a young man in Greek dress.

"My younger son, Jesse," said Avigail, aware that James had noticed, "with his tutor."

James was transfixed by the scene. It was like watching himself years before with Lucillus, discussing the myths of Olympus.

"I have five children," she went on, "the two boys and three girls. My eldest daughter is married. Jesse is seven years old and very quick in learning. He takes in Greek and Latin so easily, and of course he studies with our rabbi. I think he will be a scholar."

"Of course he will," said James, "if he has his mother's mind."

She smiled, both at the compliment and in maternal pride.

"Keep me apprised of his progress," James said. "Write to me—the Synagogue at the Crossed Streets. I am associated with the school of Gamaliel. When it is time, we will see if the boy might be placed."

Avigail again felt tears welling in her eyes. Without looking at James, she said, "Thank you. That is very kind."

CHAPTER THIRTY

*Seeing the multitudes, he went up onto the mountain. When he had sat,
his disciples came to him, and he opened his mouth and taught them.*

(Matthew 5)

The house where Jesus and his men were staying was located too far across the range of hills to reach before dark. James decided it would be best if he and his companions spent the night in a caravansary just outside Caesarea-Philippi. He arranged for food and lodging, plus livery for the camels. The five-man party ate, prayed the evening service with another contingent of travelers, and turned in.

But James had difficulty falling asleep, his peacefulness torn asunder by thoughts of Avigail. All of the musings on what might have been, which he'd believed were set aside years before, returned now. When he finally did drift, he slept fitfully, waking several times through the night.

Next morning, they were off along the route Avigail had described, until they reached the place they sought. It was a low stone house containing three rooms, built beside a barn—a spare but comfortable habitation—set in a wide valley among vineyards and fruit orchards that clung to the surrounding hillsides. Jesus and his band were gone. The estate manager, who by now was accustomed to people coming in search of the Galilean rabbi, explained that Jesus had left for another of the meetings he was holding in the area. The man provided directions to the site where the gathering was to take place. Once more, James and his companions were on the road.

It was mid-afternoon when they started coming upon groups of people that appeared to be converging on a common destination. Most were on foot. A few rode donkeys. And some, with obvious physical impairments, were being carried or assisted in walking. James called out to several people, asking where they were headed. The reply, invariably, was that they were going to hear the famous preacher, Jesus. This news stirred eagerness among the three students who had gone up to Galilee to hear him before.

Catching their enthusiasm, Asher said to James, "It looks like we have finally found your brother, Master. Our efforts are rewarded."

"So it appears," James said.

The groups became clusters, which soon gathered into a crowd that streamed its way up through a canyon opening out at the top into a broad hollow. The encircling slopes, while irregular in contour, created a natural amphitheater. James slowed his camel, signaling his companions to do likewise. He wished to remain behind the crowd in hope of not being spotted by Jesus or his men. They dismounted and tethered their beasts in a grove of low trees that filled a side glen. Just slightly above they found a vantage between some cleft rocks, from which to view the scene.

Jesus was standing atop a small mound on the far side of the hollow, his eyes closed, lost within himself—perhaps praying? James noticed Simon and several other figures he recognized from his trip to Nazareth on the occasion of the wedding. The hills all around were covered with people, few open spots still visible, a clatter of voices resounding across the hollow.

After a time, when the last arrivals had found places to sit or stand, Jesus stirred from his absorption. He looked about at the many faces, then lowered himself onto a stone which had apparently been carried to the top of the mound for use as a seat. The crowd took this as a signal that the meeting was to begin, and silence fell.

A broad smile lit up Jesus' face as he sat, to which the onlookers reacted with delight, a thrill sweeping through the crowd. The energy present across this basin was palpable to James, and he realized that his brother possessed an attractive power that was far more than just the curiosity piqued by newness. There were men, women, even some babes in arms and children of assorted ages. Judging by clothing and other adornments, these people represented a wide sampling of the local populace drawn from various levels of wealth and social standing. Some were ragged and not particularly clean. Others were arrayed elegantly.

Most were Jews. That was obvious, marked as they were by their striped robes, tassels and headgear. But spotted throughout the assemblage were men and women in Greek dress, and no small number of them. James understood now why Avigail had said there was concern about the breadth of Jesus' appeal. He could imagine that the Jewish leadership in the region might be just as perplexed over this enthusiasm as the leading gentiles. Here were Jews and Greeks sitting together with surprising ease. James had never seen anything like it before.

A long moment of silence followed, then Jesus began to speak. He offered no words of welcome or introduction, but launched into a series of pronouncements, describing different behaviors or conditions of conscience and the moral results appropriate to each.

"Blessed are the poor in spirit," he began, "for the Kingdom of Heaven is theirs."

The crowd reacted with an instant surge of excitement. It was as if Jesus had begun to sing a well known and much-beloved song. Clearly, some of these people—perhaps most—had heard him speak before and knew his message, which likely was consistent wherever he preached.

This opening statement brought Pilate's remark about *the poor* to James' mind. The Prefect was right that many Jews used the word *poor* to indicate themselves, as apart from the gentiles. Was that the meaning Jesus' listeners had grasped—at least the Jews in the crowd? Were they reacting positively to being told *they* were blessed because they were *Jews?* Probably not. Jesus had said *poor in spirit,* which was a different thing entirely from what Pilate had spoken of.

Of course, it was easy to see how someone who didn't understand the expression might be misled. To a Jew, it spoke of one's longing for the King of the Universe, feeling the *poverty* of despair at being far from the Holy One. To a Roman, however, *poor in spirit,* especially when attached to the word *kingdom* could easily sound political. But then, did Jesus always say *poor in spirit* when he preached? Did he ever just say *poor?* This James didn't know.

Reaction to Jesus' second statement, "Blessed are the sorrowful, for they shall be consoled," was less elated, the onlookers now being drawn into the consoling quality of his presentation.

"Blessed are the meek," Jesus said next, "for they shall inherit the earth."

This was certainly a consoling thought—or it could be taken as such. But it raised another question in James mind. Was *the meek* a variation on *the poor*? And if so, was Jesus still talking about the *poor in spirit*? To whom was Jesus referring, merely people who have kind hearts and gentle natures? Or was there another connotation to *meek*? And what was suggested by the idea of *inheriting the earth*? Might some in the crowd sense a more pointed meaning? James wondered if Pilate or another authority could have agents at this gathering. There was no way to tell. They would be dressed to blend in.

"Blessed are those who hunger and thirst to see right prevail. They shall be satisfied."

Again James felt the gnaw of a question. What did Jesus mean by hungering and thirsting for *right*? Was this a call for righteousness— for each individual to *do* right? Or was it a demand for the redress of wrongs—for justice? And if justice, what kind? Political justice? James realized that these sayings of his brother bore a variety of interpretations, and he was beginning to feel a tiny knot deep within the pit of his stomach.

"Blessed are those who are merciful, for mercy will be given them."

This was straightforward enough. Nothing political there. Any rabbi or temple sage could say the same thing. James took a thoughtful breath. Perhaps he was reading too much into these simple statements, letting himself become preoccupied with Roman mistrustfulness. It was because of Pilate that he had embarked on this search for Jesus. Now Pilate seemed to be hovering over his shoulder like some suspicious ghost. James knew he had to be at ease, let himself hear Jesus' voice, take in the message as a whole, then make a more detached judgment.

Examining his brother's words from a scholarly point of view, James recognized a construct known as *beatitude*, which appeared frequently in the wisdom sayings and was a recurring motif in many of the psalms. Often it involved a rhythmic give-and-take between virtue and reward, sin and retribution. Sometimes beatitudes employed poetic imagery, as in the famous psalm: *Happy is the man who will not follow the counsel of the wicked... He shall be like a tree planted by rivers of water...* The words James was hearing Jesus use now were more direct—less poetic than a psalm—but there was a definite echo in terms of style.

"Blessed are those whose hearts are pure, for they shall see God."

Nothing political there, either. But *God?* Such a forthright public use of that term struck James as taking a bit of a liberty. It wasn't the Holy Name, of course—which could never be spoken—but it gave James some slight discomfort, nonetheless.

"Blessed are the peacemakers, for they will be called God's sons."

Again the word, *God*—used in an even more intimate context. James scanned the crowd. Some people appeared to have been similarly surprised at the usage. Others were unmoved—probably the ones who had heard Jesus preach before.

"Blessed are those who are persecuted in the cause of right. Theirs is the Kingdom of Heaven."

The *Kingdom of Heaven* again—this time, as a reward for enduring *persecution*. Not just *hungering* for righteousness, but *suffering* for it.

"Blessed are *you*, when you suffer insults, persecution and all sorts of falsehoods—for *my* sake."

His sake?

"Rejoice! Be glad! For you will be rewarded abundantly in Heaven. The prophets were persecuted in the same way before you."

James understood his brother was launching a movement. And it was now unmistakable that he was organizing it around himself. But what kind of movement would it be? Pilate was worried enough about its possible rebellious aspect to have called James in. Perhaps his words, offered in a friendly, if cautionary, way might actually be a more specific warning. And not without reason. James knew that the Essenes were thinking of armed conflict. Did Pilate know?

The knot was growing larger, but James was determined to retain his sense of balance and proportion. He had to be what he was: a scholar, a doctor of the Law, someone who could see into the heart of words and grasp their true meaning.

Again he cautioned himself about jumping to conclusions. Granted, the question of whether Jesus was Messiah had hung over his family since Mary had conceived and given birth under such extraordinary circumstances. And yes, the traditional expectation among Jews was that, when Messiah came, he would lead a revolt to free the land from foreign invaders, restore the kingdom, cleanse it of pagan influence, bring a golden age.

But was that the only understanding possible? Mightn't the Holy

One send his anointed with a more spiritual purpose? The words of the prophet, Isaiah—his description of the Lord's *servant*—came to mind. Isaiah wrote that the *servant* would be filled with the Lord's spirit to teach all nations the way of the Covenant. It was true that some interpreted the figure of the *servant* as the whole people of Israel, but others read the passage as referring specifically to the Messiah. Either way, this *servant* was presented as the gentlest of creatures who would not shout to make his voice heard or break even a bruised reed.

Jesus was gentle. James had observed for himself that Avigail's description of his brother's voice and presentation was accurate. Even without speaking loudly or dramatically, Jesus made himself heard by all. If he was indeed the Lord's anointed, surely he could follow a path that didn't depend on violence, that didn't risk the nation's destruction or a recurrence of the Sepphoris road. Maybe, by the grace of God, he possessed some means of *persuading* the Romans to leave. It seemed unlikely, of course, but if he really had the King of the Universe at his back, anything might be possible.

Hadn't the Lord used a reluctant and inarticulate Moses to lead the Children of Israel out of Pharaoh's Egypt? Hadn't He brought another pagan empire to conquer Babylon, making possible the exiles' return and the temple's restoration? Those acts had been extremely unlikely. Yet if such unlikely things had been done in ages past, was it really such a leap to believe that Messiah might be given some unexpected means to fulfill the purposes of the Holy One?

James realized that he was letting his mind drift into distracting conjecture. He tried to shake off his speculations and focus on his brother's sermon.

Jesus next made two statements employing straight metaphors. He told those present that they were *the salt of the earth* and *the light of the world*. James might have dismissed such rhetoric as attempts to flatter the audience, except that Jesus quickly turned these compliments into challenges. He admonished his listeners not only to persevere in their virtues, but to demonstrate them openly.

"If salt becomes tasteless," he said, "is there anything with which to season it? It is worthless, and may as well be tossed on the ground and walked on."

In the reference to light James heard a distinct echo of Isaiah, who wrote that the *servant* would be *a light to the nations*. Jesus explained how those who are called to light the world were supposed to conduct themselves: They should be like a city on a hill, shining for all to see.

"No one lights a lamp and then puts it under a basket," he said. "Rather, they put it on the lamp stand to illumine the whole house."

The level of excitement in the hollow rose once more as the assembly responded with strong approval of this image. James was beginning to grasp the nature of his brother's appeal. Jesus called people to be better than they assumed they were. Or perhaps he was simply providing them with the assurance that it was *possible* to be better. Either way, he was able to touch the secret, innermost part of each soul that longs for *good*, for *right*, for *sanctity*.

One didn't have to be Jewish to feel such a longing. Pilate had said he hoped people might live up to their better natures. Looking out across the crowd, James could see that the Greeks present were as moved by Jesus' exhortations as the Jews were. Indeed, how many men who sought James' own counsel in the Synagogue at the Crossed Streets, or spent their days in reflection there, were seeking ways to transcend the weaknesses, failings and burdens that held them back from becoming their best selves? It was an ideal common to all.

Then, unexpectedly, Jesus' tone shifted, and he spoke with a seriousness that showed he wished no misunderstanding. "Do not think," he said, "that I have come to abolish the Law and the prophets. I did not come to abolish, but to fulfill."

James' ears pricked up at this.

Not a letter of the Law should be changed until the end of time, Jesus insisted. Anyone who set aside even the smallest of the Law's demands, and led others into doing as much, was to be regarded as lowest, while those who kept all the Commandments would be greatest.

This was reassuring. Evidently, Jesus intended to keep his ministry within the traditional bounds of Judaism. There would be no novel doctrines proposed, as had been the case with some false teachers and would-be Messiahs who appeared from time to time. Avigail had said that scholars often came to challenge various points of Jesus' preaching. Well, no matter how his message might be criticized, Jesus was a Jew, and a dedicated one. Anybody listening to these words would have to acknowledge that. The Rabbi Ezra had taught him well.

But then Jesus said something that struck an odd chord. "I tell you this, unless you can show that your fidelity exceeds that of the Pharisees or the doctors of the law, you will not enter the Kingdom of Heaven."

The student, Asher, found himself caught up short and turned to James, perplexed. "Master," he whispered, indignation in his voice, "you are a doctor of the Law, and we aspire to be so—the other students and myself. Has your brother no regard for scholarship?"

James shook his head. "I don't think that's what Jesus means," he said. "I think he's just saying that one must strive mightily to uphold the Law in all its aspects."

Asher considered James' reasoning and was placated, though still a bit baffled.

Meanwhile, James experienced his own reaction to the mention of the *Pharisees* as a group whose virtue Jesus' followers should surpass. It seemed to him that the comparative point would have been made more clearly if Jesus had said the *Essenes*. After all, the brotherhood was known primarily for its adherence to even the minutest of legal strictures. Pharisaism, on the other hand, was one of the major divisions of Jewish religious thought, its roots going all the way back to the days of the Maccabaen revolt.

James would have been the first to admit that, among the Pharisees, there was an ample number of hypocrites and the weak-willed. But also there were people of firm adherence and unquestioned piety—a great many of them. And of course, most of the rabbis were Pharisees. Hillel had been a Pharisee. Gamaliel was a Pharisee. James, himself, was a Pharisee.

Jesus went on to illustrate the rigor he expected of his followers. He cited the Law's prohibition of murder, but then observed that even harboring angry thoughts could subject one to divine judgment. In addition, he urged the settlement of legal disputes by mutual agreement, rather than exploitation of the law courts or the stubborn insistence on having one's rights.

He touched on the delicate subject of adultery, and his teaching on that matter caused more than a few embarrassed faces. It was not just the *act*, he insisted, but the *intention*—what he called *committing adultery in the heart*—that was wrong. James had to chuckle at the wilder flights of rhetoric Jesus used to make his point. Such as: *If your eye is the cause of your sin, pluck it out and throw it away!* Or: *If your right hand is your undoing, cut it off!* It was amusing to imagine how much secret lust might be revealed by having a bunch of one-eyed, mutilated sinners wandering about.

As if Jesus' standards on adultery weren't stringent enough, he next declared that the widely accepted practice of a man giving his wife a bill of divorce was immoral. Many listeners were stunned when he insisted that a legal marriage, unencumbered by irregularities such as incest or unchastity, could not be broken. Jesus drew a clear line, stating that any man who divorces his wife makes her an adulteress, and someone who marries a divorced woman commits adultery himself. James found his brother's position especially interesting, in that it evoked the old controversy between Shammai and his own master, Hillel, who had maintained that divorce could be permitted as long as provision was made for the protection and support of the wife. Jesus' stand was like that of Shammai.

A certain amount of grumbling in the crowd suggested to James that enthusiasm for Jesus' message was no longer uniformly high. The pronouncements on adultery and divorce had caused some divisions among his listeners. Here and there, a few even got up and started making their way out of the hollow. Jesus seemed not to notice, or perhaps he chose to ignore the defections, but he continued in his teaching.

He spoke out against swearing elaborate oaths, insisting that saying what one meant and standing by one's word were the true marks of an honest man. "Let your *yes* mean *yes*, and your *no* mean *no*," he said. The crowd's approval of this position was much broader than for his rules on adultery and divorce.

Laughter was heard when Jesus chided people who display their piety or their worthy deeds in ostentatious ways. "There is no need for a flourish of trumpets over your acts of charity," he said, smiling wryly. "When you give alms, do not let your left hand know what your right hand is doing."

Similarly, he criticized showy and extended public prayers. "Don't babble on like pagans who think that the more words they say, the more their appeals will be heard." This brought an amused response from the Greeks present, to whom Jesus' description of pagan prayer had the ring of familiarity.

When the laughter subsided, he recited a prayer to be used in daily devotions. It began by appealing to *Our Father in Heaven*—which James recognized as a form of supplication used by some of the rabbis. Jesus' prayer then offered praise to the Holy Name, as well as a call for the coming of the Kingdom—perhaps a reference to the Messiah?—and a plea that the Lord's will might prevail on earth as readily as above.

Three further pleadings followed. The first was a simple request for sustenance in the form of *our daily bread*. The second begged forgiveness for wrongs done. To this Jesus added a proviso: *as we forgive those who have wronged us*. He explained that forgiveness should be expected only when we are willing to forgive others, even those who have done us grave harm.

The third pleading—to be delivered from *evil* and protected from the test of *temptation*—struck James as extremely subtle. The prophets had written about a time of trial to come. Was this the test of which Jesus was speaking? Was it a reference to the final judgment? Was it another possible hint about the coming of Messiah? All these options were worth pondering.

The afternoon wore on as Jesus continued his discourse. Some in the assembly, especially some of the older folk, appeared to tire and took their leave. Several of the children grew fussy, prompting their parents to remove them. But most people stayed to hear him cover a formidable array of challenging and thought-provoking points. These included: the need to concentrate on higher values rather than material possessions; not passing harsh judgments on others; keeping sacred things sacred and having confidence in the providence of the Holy One; discerning the difference between authentic teaching and attractive but false ideas; and much more.

James marveled at his brother's ability to maintain the crowd's interest. He was also impressed at Jesus' adeptness at using familiar sayings to reinforce his points. A smile of recognition came to James' lips when he heard the line, *Treat others as you would have others treat you.* This was a variation on Hillel's famous dictum: *Never do to others what you would not want done to yourself.*

Finally, late in the day, Jesus concluded the presentation by exhorting his listeners to go forth and apply his teachings—to make them the firm foundation of their lives—*like a man who builds his house upon a rock.*

So many ideas had Jesus covered that James felt tired from trying to absorb them all. But there was no denying his brother was a powerful preacher. James could see inspiration in the eyes of the people making their way out of the hollow. He could see it in the eyes of his student companions, especially the three who had heard his brother speak in Galilee.

How did Jesus do it? His speaking style was so reserved. There were a few rhetorical flourishes, yes, a bit of humor now and again, some exaggerations for emphasis' sake. But no loud outbursts, no dramatic poses or wild gesturing. He just...spoke.

And how had he developed this air of authority that so enveloped him? He'd had no rabbinical training. Where did he obtain all of his knowledge? Surely not just from the Rabbi Ezra. During his travels, perhaps? Had he visited the great libraries, like that in Alexandria?

"Rabbi?"

James was so immersed in his thoughts that the greeting didn't register on him.

"Rabbi?"

When he became aware, he turned at the sound of the voice, recognizing the fisherman.

"Simon."

"I saw the white robe and turban among these rocks, and thought it might be you. It is good to see you again, Rabbi."

"And you, Simon. Peace be upon you."

The big fellow was grinning with eager expectation. "Well, what did you think of your brother's preaching?" he asked genially.

James nodded. "He is an effective speaker, and there is much wisdom in his words."

"High praise from a learned man like you."

"My brother appears to be quite learned himself—more so than I realized."

"I'm sure he will be pleased that he was able to surprise you."

"Was what I heard here today the message he delivers in all of his meetings?"

"Basically," said Simon. "He uses different sayings and parables to illustrate his points, depending on the group he is addressing and the particular truths he wishes to emphasize at the moment."

"His views were very warmly received," said James, "except for the points about adultery and divorce."

Simon laughed. "Ah yes, adultery and divorce. We always lose a few from our gatherings when he mentions those."

"Most remained to the end, though," said James. "It was remarkable that so many would persevere in that way. Jesus' ideas are very challenging. A lot to think about."

"People love him, Rabbi." Simon stretched out an arm toward the hollow. "Look."

James peered through the rocks in the direction Simon indicated. He could see that Jesus was surrounded by groups of avid followers, including some of the physically impaired James had noted on the way to the meeting.

"What is he doing?" James asked.

"Healing," said Simon. "The sick, the crippled, the blind—there's always a flock of them. He never turns any away."

James watched in silence as people approached Jesus on crutches, were led by companions, or carried on litters. Jesus would touch them or stretch out a hand over them, or merely look at them. Sometimes he seemed to be praying, sometimes he spoke not a word. But after each encounter, the person who had sought his aid would light up in a spasm of joy, proclaiming himself cured. Crutches, canes or other aids were flung away. Sometimes a formerly crippled person would jump or dance. Always, a thrill spread among the witnesses, with exclamations of amazement and many thanks to the Holy One.

After watching for a long time, James turned back to Simon. I have heard about this healing," he said. "It happens all the time?"

"They come in such numbers that the master finds himself worn out from the onslaught. He has to seek quiet places, often in the wilderness, for prayer and respite."

"Simon," James said, "have you decided whether you believe my brother is the Messiah?"

Simon mused on the question for a moment, then looked at James. "Jesus has revealed much about himself to those of us in his company. And there is the evidence of what I have seen for myself." He paused, measuring how much he should share. Then he said, "Yes, Rabbi, I believe that Jesus is the *Anointed of God.*"

James reflected on these words. Simon was a man whose instincts were to be trusted. "Has he encountered any...difficulties?"

"Difficulties?"

"I understand there have been challenges to his teaching."

"Oh, that," said Simon. "Men claiming to be scholars have called him out on several points. They enjoy setting puzzles, tempting him to say something that makes it appear his teaching is in conflict with the Law. But that is to be expected when a man receives great acclaim and gains a large following."

Simon chuckled at a recollection. "Once we came upon a woman accused of adultery. Some neighbors demanded she be stoned, and the local rabbis supported them. Jesus intervened. He saved the woman, and taught a very sound lesson in the process."

"How so?" James asked.

"He posed a clever proposition. He suggested that the first stone should be thrown by a man who was without sin in his own life. That brought all the clamor to an end quickly."

James laughed. "Clever, indeed," he said. "But tell me, Simon... The people who challenge him—are they always different, or has there ever been someone who shows up again and again?"

A knowing smile from Simon now. "Yes, Rabbi, there are some we've seen more than once, and in different places. I have speculated about an organized effort—perhaps merely to learn about Jesus—"

"Perhaps to discredit him?"

"That's possible. But it is suggestive, I think, that the challenges rarely occur in front of large crowds. These men seem wary of appearing antagonistic in front of Jesus' followers."

"What is your plan now, Simon? Will you return to the house provided you by the Mistress Avigail?"

"Oh, you have met the widow of Zimran?"

"Yes," James said tersely.

"She has been highly supportive of our mission," said Simon. "A very generous lady. We will return there this evening. That is, when Jesus has finished with these sufferers. It may take some time."

"Then my companions and I will go there and await your arrival. Perhaps we might stay the night with your company? I am eager to speak with my brother."

"Jesus will be delighted, I'm sure. I will inform him."

"Thank you." In parting, James mentioned the hospitality he and the students had received from Simon's wife.

"Oh, yes, yes," the fisherman said. "That sounds like my dearest. Feeding visitors is the joy of her life."

James took his leave with Asher and the others.

*   *   *

The students were pleased to learn that they would spend the night with Jesus and his men. All along the road back, they kept up a steady chatter about Jesus' presentation. The three who had heard him before compared the similarities and differences between today's talk and the one they attended in Galilee.

Only Asher expressed a reservation, still wondering if Jesus' call for personal holiness didn't somehow imply a devaluation of learning. The other three saw no such suggestion. They insisted that Jesus was asking people to embrace the Law for themselves, to bring the principles of Judaism into their hearts, rather than just following rules or the decisions and dictates of religious authorities.

"But where does that leave *us*?" Asher asked. "Aren't we preparing to be religious authorities? I admire the high moral standard Jesus is setting, but is every man to be his own doctor of the Law? Is there no longer any need for the scholarly and the wise?"

James kept an ear attuned to this exchange, but didn't contribute to it. Rather, he rode his camel in silence, the animal keeping its rolling, rhythmic pace. James' own reflection on Jesus' call to holiness took a slightly different path from that of the young men.

Someone able to embrace the Law as fully as Jesus was demanding, he thought, would surely be an upright person, conducting himself honorably with those around him. But Jesus' emphasis was clearly on the individual heart. The Law, on the other hand, was part of a Covenant made between the King of the Universe and a community, the whole people of Israel. Each individual Jew was a party to it, and its moral precepts were instructions about how they were to live together within that community.

Jesus had said nothing about Israel as a people. And of course, a considerable number of those present weren't Jews. James observed it for himself, and Avigail had said it was a consistent pattern. So, would the fulfillment of Jesus' vision mean that Israel was to be Isaiah's *light to the nations*? Or would it mean that Israel *didn't matter*, that Jesus' appeal was not just to Jews, but to *all* people? If the latter were the case, what would it mean that Jesus was Messiah? Perhaps he wouldn't even *bother* to free the Jews—gratifying to Pilate, maybe, but of what value to the Jews?

These were questions for which James could see no answers. Maybe even Jesus couldn't answer them, at least not at this point in his mission. And anyway, they were beside the point of James' mission. His concern was how his brother's intentions were being perceived—by the Romans, who sensed a threat, and by others, who might view the groundswell Jesus was creating as an opportunity for a violent uprising. James' objective was to warn his brother to be prudent, and then to assure Pilate that there was nothing in Jesus' activities to worry about.

When they arrived back at the stone farmhouse, James informed the estate manager that Jesus and his party would follow along later, then asked that arrangements be made to feed the camels. Fodder was provided. The manager's wife, accustomed to Jesus' comings and goings, had already begun cutting vegetables and building her fire in preparation for the evening meal.

It was nearly two hours before the company returned. Immediately upon spotting James, Jesus went to his brother and embraced him.

"Peace be upon you, Brother," he said. "Please forgive my tardiness. There were so many in need of attending."

"So I saw, Brother," James said, "and may the Lord's peace be with you. Your discourse was most engaging. I am glad to finally hear you preach. Your fame spreads everywhere."

Jesus laughed at that. "Ha—my fame."

"You are much admired."

"Everywhere but in Nazareth."

"Well, it all makes for much to talk about," James said. "I would beg some of your time. Perhaps later?"

"My time is yours, Brother."

Introductions were made all around, James meeting some members of Jesus' inner circle who hadn't been present on the occasion of the wedding. He found it interesting to learn that these twelve men were being referred to as *apostles*. The name was apt since, as James learned, Jesus had taken to sending them out in pairs to represent him and spread his message beyond the meetings at which he himself preached. Further, it had apparently become common among people aware of Jesus to refer to that message—the core of his teaching—as the *good news*, an expression which Esther, the woman at the synagogue, had used.

Prayers, eating and other end-of-day activities were completed. James' students found it especially exhilarating to be able to pray the evening service with Jesus and his group. James, too, felt a special brotherly warmth. Here he was, side-by-side with Jesus, both wearing their phylacteries. It was an experience they had shared too rarely through the years.

Later, James and Jesus went off to a quiet spot out past the barn and the stock pen, which now contained the camels. The beasts had settled, and a soft wind in the fruit trees and the rippling of a nearby stream were the only sounds to break the night's stillness. A smooth rock protruding from a hillside provided a place to sit.

"Do you see the family?" James asked.

"Occasionally," Jesus said. "I pass through Nazareth on some of my journeys. When I do, I confine myself to the compound."

"I have heard a story about some disagreement in the synagogue."

"Oh yes, there was a definite disagreement." Jesus' face wore a vague smile at the recollection. "I announced the start of my ministry. It wasn't received well."

"There is an old saying," said James, "about how a prophet is never honored in his native place."

"Yes, I quoted it at the time."

"Has this...disagreement...caused any problems for the family?"

"Fortunately, no," Jesus said. "They have long been accepted as part of the town—as *you* were, Brother. Only *I* was set apart. I was a mystery to the people of Nazareth."

James nodded. "That is true, Jesus. Father made the decision to shield you. It must have caused you pain."

"Well," Jesus said with a passing shrug, "I was never lonely. There were always plenty of children in the compound."

"I imagine that being isolated in such a way was why you were so eager to travel and see the world."

Jesus said nothing, but gazed absently in the direction of the stream. James was mildly disquieted at the lack of a response.

Finally Jesus turned back to him. "But I am glad you came, Brother," he said. "You and I have lived so much apart. That has always been a misfortune."

"Yes, Jesus, I have wished to know you better."

"So, then... What did you think of my talk? Would it impress the sages of the temple?"

"I can remember when you once impressed the sages of the temple."

"And *I* remember Father and Mother being very perturbed about that."

This occasioned the sharing of a laugh. When it had passed, James decided now was the time to address the purpose of his visit.

"Brother," he said, "there is a particular reason I have come here."

"I assumed so," Jesus said. "You are a man with many demands upon him. For you to leave Jerusalem, there must be a need."

"Yes...well... I have had several conversations with Pontius Pilate, the prefect of Judea."

"You move in exalted circles."

"Hmmph... That's as may be, Brother. For some reason, Pilate has taken it upon himself to seek my counsel, though he does not always follow my advice." James shifted uncomfortably on the rock. "In any event, he has heard about you and your preaching ministry—about the wide following you have acquired—and it fills him with anxiety."

"Anxiety? Why should the prefect of Judea be anxious about me?"

"It is not you...exactly," James said. "Pilate fears large movements that attract crowds and stir up the people—anything that might unsettle the...*peace of Rome*. He wonders if your mission either represents or might give encouragement to Zealot resistance. I suspect that your acclaim disturbs the peaceful sleep of his household."

Laughter from Jesus again. "Far be it from me to disturb the sleep of Pilate."

"The point is, Jesus, I would like to be able to tell the prefect that your mission offers him no cause for alarm."

"Do you think me a Zealot, Brother?"

James put a hand on Jesus' arm. "No, I do not. At least, there's nothing I heard today that would unsettle the...*peace of Rome.*"

"That is twice you have spoken the phrase, *peace of Rome*," Jesus said, "and both times with acid in your voice."

James drew his hand away. He paused before giving a response. "Yes... Acid is the word, isn't it. I once witnessed the peace of Rome, and found that it left a very acidic taste—like drinking vinegar."

"Tell me, Brother..."

"It— It was when you were small. After the uprising in Sepphoris. The legions put down that rebellion with such ferocity. Then hundreds were crucified—"

"The Sepphoris road," Jesus said. "Father once told me about the Sepphoris road. And you were young yourself. It was a horrible thing for a boy to see."

Now it was James who said nothing.

"Do you recall, James—in my talk this afternoon—when I spoke about the need to forgive those who have harmed us?"

"Yes, Brother, and I'm bound to say it was one point I didn't fully comprehend. Would you ask me to forgive the Romans? Can I forget the Sepphoris road?"

"But James, you *must* forgive. Or else you will never be *able* to forget. The Sepphoris road will haunt you always."

Jesus put his hand on James' arm as James had touched him before. "Brother," he said, "you no doubt noticed that some people left the meeting today when I brought up certain awkward points. That happens a lot. There are things people don't wish to hear, and they will go to great lengths to avoid them. But I can tell you that no one ever leaves when I speak of forgiveness. They all realize that what I ask is difficult. But they also know I'm right, and they all wish they could do it." He made an open-handed gesture. "A few succeed."

Still James said nothing. Jesus let his advice sit for James to consider.

"But you can tell Pilate that I have no plans for rebellion, and I do not encourage others to pursue it. Would people's lives be improved if the Zealots were to succeed in driving out Rome? It would take more than the restoration of our own kingdom to bring genuine improvement. We have had our own kingdom in times past, and how many of our kings have led us down the path of idolatry, dissipation, and defeat in war."

"Surely you care for the future of the Jewish people."

"I do," Jesus said. "You may be sure I do. The Jewish people are my people. I was born a Jew. I live my life as a Jew. And I will die a Jew. You saw today how I make a point of defending the Law in my preaching. I stand up for the Covenant. But besides the Covenant by which we live as a people, there is a Covenant for each person individually. And I want every man and woman to understand that they must honor *this* Covenant as well. That is the essence of my message. If Pilate loses sleep over it, there is nothing to be done."

"Yet, you *are* building a movement."

"I prefer to call it my *assembly*."

James was somewhat puzzled. "Assembly? I attended your assembly today."

"That was just a gathering," Jesus said. "I'm speaking of the *whole* assembly, the assembly of my faithful ones, the people who have absorbed the *good news* and will take it to the world."

"It will be good-enough news to Pilate that this assembly is no threat to Caesar."

A smile from Jesus. "Well now, Brother, I did not say that. Caesar may one day find himself *in* my assembly."

The pitch of James' head indicated his skepticism. "I have a hard time imagining such a thing. Still...to the point, Brother—*take care*. Your words are inspiring. I can attest to it. But guard that what you say may not be turned against you or taken to justify actions you would not approve."

Jesus shrugged again. "Who can account for what others do?" he said. "But I am in the Father's hands."

"Well," James said, "there is no better guard than he. But if I can be of help..."

"Your brother's keeper?" Jesus said, still smiling.

James laughed at that, in a subdued and slightly discomfited way. "Just know that you can call upon me."

"I will, James. I will."

CHAPTER THIRTY-ONE

The good man conducts his affairs with honor.
The just man never wavers.

(Psalm 112)

The day after his return to Jerusalem, James went to the temple to make a sin offering for his indiscretion in touching Avigail's hand. It hadn't been a terrible offense, but it nagged at his conscience. He prayed that she be enfolded in the forgiveness sought by this sacrifice, and that her life be filled with blessings. The latter plea was an echo of a prayer he'd made for years after she'd departed to marry.

It was clear that blessings had come to her and time had treated her well. She was still beautiful and intelligent, and now a distinguished and wealthy widow with a fine family and a magnificent home. Her earthly welfare would soon be in the hands of her eldest son. Would her spiritual welfare be in the hands of Jesus? She was obviously devoted to his cause.

Most perplexing to James, though: Dare he even think of her again, to consider the possibility of salvaging some portion of the life they might have shared? So much time had gone by. Each was very different from the young person of years past. And as well known and admired as he'd become, James still was not a man of wealth. He lived a frugal life, a scholar's life. What had he to offer a woman in Avigail's position?

All this was the stuff of pondering and prayer. For now, following the weeks given over to searching for his brother, there was much to catch up on. The first item of business was a letter to Pilate, and he set his hand to it straight away.

He had attended one of Jesus' meetings, James wrote, without making his presence known. Therefore, he was convinced that the words he'd heard were his brother's authentic teaching. Nothing in them suggested sympathy for the Zealots. And in conversation later, Jesus declared emphatically that he did not advocate violent resistance to the empire.

"I realize, Prefect, that you will weigh my views in light of the fact that Jesus and I are related. Nevertheless, it is my belief that when he speaks of the coming of the Kingdom or of people striving to be part of the Kingdom, Jesus is referring to a commitment of the heart, a kind of spiritual perfection. You could also use the terms *vindication* or *salvation*, concepts that appear frequently in our sacred writings. From a Greek philosophical point of view, you might liken it to a serene acceptance of fate or giving assent to the will of a higher power, though the parallel may not be exact.

"While Jesus places greater emphasis on personal conviction than other rabbis might, he insists on adherence to *Torah*, the Law of Moses. In each of the behaviors and conditions which he says will be blessed by the Holy One—such as being *poor in spirit*—I see implications of what in Hebrew are termed *mitzvot*, obligations of charity or observance. This is entirely consistent with traditional Jewish piety, since we believe that faith is incomplete when it does not find some tangible expression.

"An important theme in his message is justice. I assume he applies this both to dealings between individuals and to the treatment of persons by the realm. But justice is, itself, intrinsic to the Law. Jesus asks us to treat each other fairly, which of course would contribute to the building up of a more humane community. But I certainly did not hear my brother call for changes in the structure of temporal society or to any of the class relations within it.

"I was impressed with the warm affection felt for him by those drawn to his preaching. But his appeal is moral, and does not conduce to the sort of mindless fervor one might expect to see in a rebellious movement. This is reflected in the behavior of his followers, which is entirely peaceable. There is no indication at all that people are moved to disobedience of civil or religious authorities.

"I have therefore concluded that neither Jesus' teaching nor his popular attractiveness represents a threat to the peace of Rome. This is my impression as a doctor of the Law, and I believe it to be accurate."

James choked at using the phrase *peace of Rome*. But he knew it would resonate with Pilate, so he accepted the irony. In conclusion, he noted that he had urged his brother to be prudent in his public remarks, so that his message might not be misinterpreted. Then he offered a formulary wish for the prefect's good health, and assured Pilate that he could continue to call upon him for any assistance that might advance the good of the Jewish people.

The parchment on which this missive was written made for a scroll of modest size, which James tied with a piece of linen ribbon and sealed with wax. Having kept Asher away from Gamaliel's class for so long, James had released the young man from any messenger duties for the next few days. So James himself carried the scroll to the prefecture to have it presented to Pilate. An officer informed him that Lord Pilate was in Caesarea. The message would be conveyed to him there by the next courier.

* * *

With a fair degree of confidence that there was nothing in Jesus' preaching and healing ministry likely to raise immediate problems—and hoping his report would relieve Pilate's worries as well—James immersed himself once more in his normal activities. He resumed his counseling in the Synagogue at the Crossed Streets. He answered the usual inquiries about life concerns or points of the Law. And he made a special effort to assist with Gamaliel's classes. The one commitment he was not able to fulfill right now was helping with distribution of food to the poor. He felt bad about this, but he needed his evenings, the mound of correspondence to which he'd returned still looming high on his table.

There was no response from Pilate to his letter, which James took as a sign of the prefect's satisfaction. If Roman agents were continuing to monitor Jesus—and if their reports were honest and accurate—they would confirm James' observations. He was most likely to be called in again if Pilate was receiving contradictory information, and after several weeks, James assumed this was not the case.

Avigail remained in his thoughts. But as time passed, her image became less vivid to him, and the idea of a renewed relationship less of an actual possibility. Even if he went to Josis and asked for his share of the family assets—which it was his right to do—he found it difficult to imagine how he could adapt his life and daily routine to the presence of a wife. And not doing so wouldn't be fair to her.

Yes, he would continue to think about marriage. There was no way he could push thoughts of Avigail completely from his mind. But being realistic, marrying wasn't a practical possibility. Not right now, anyway. For that matter, he couldn't be certain that Avigail would consent to it. Her life, her family, all her connections were in the north. Jerusalem was another world.

As months passed, the prospects for that world were brightening. The aqueduct progressed to where the first flow of water into the city from the Bethlehem heights was imminent and anticipated with great eagerness. If people were not quite ready to credit Rome with actual sympathy for Jewish welfare, they were at least willing to grant that this civic improvement was being brought about by Roman initiative and engineering prowess.

These expressions of public contentment made their way to the ears of Pilate, who found them gratifying. Perhaps all that bile over the unpleasant episode of Caesar's image was finally in the past. Was it too much to expect that some nugget of Jewish approval might make its way back to Rome? If so, good words would be timely. A troubling bit of news had come to Pilate, and it was cause for worry.

Aelius Sejanus, prefect of the Praetorian Guard and second only to Tiberius himself in the imperial administration, had been implicated in a conspiracy to overthrow the emperor. Though Pilate was far from Rome and couldn't possibly have participated in the plot, it had been Sejanus who raised him from army ranks and put his name forward for the post in Judea. Pilate and Sejanus were known to have had a long relationship, the elder man seeing potential in Pilate and cultivating it assiduously. After the failed move against the Augustus, anyone connected to the now-executed Sejanus might be subject to harsh scrutiny. Success in Judea would go a long way toward blunting any ill wishes Tiberius might harbor against Pilate.

It was on another of his inspection trips that the prefect's hopes came to a crashing halt. Disturbances had broken out around the city. There were crowds in the streets, shouting and carrying on in that peculiarly impassioned Jewish way, and disrupting work on the various elements of the water system. Pilate was at the prefecture when news of this unrest came to him. He sent officers to determine the reason for the uproar, and issued an order that the garrison in the Antonia Fortress be prepared for deployment.

The report on the cause of this commotion was like a blow to Pilate's midsection. Word about *corban* money being used to fund the aqueduct had gotten out. How had this happened? Pilate and the High Priest Caiaphas had agreed to keep knowledge of the details of their pact limited to only those few officials directly involved. The prefect had even transferred Roman funds to the temple treasury so that all dispersals to Jewish contractors would be made by priests.

True, there had been early rumors in the Sanhedrin about *corban* money being used. But in the absence of proof, they had faded quickly without causing any significant problems. Pilate's initial concerns were set aside as the aqueduct rose and the general enthusiasm grew. So why had this become an issue now? The only possible answer was that someone inside the temple was trying to sabotage the project, undermine Pilate's position, compromise Caiaphas, or all three. There were Zealot hands in this, Pilate was convinced.

James became aware of the clamor on his way to the Royal Porch, where he was to participate in one of Gamaliel's classes. A crowd of angry men had gathered in the Court of the Gentiles. Their shouts of *Defilement!* rang across the temple mount.

He encountered two rabbis of his acquaintance who provided quick explanations of what everyone was so excited about. This left James shaking his head at the inevitability of the situation. He'd advised the prefect to be open in seeking temple funds, to face any objections right at the start, to make his case that use of the money was legitimate under the Jews' own Law. But his words had been to no avail.

Now this.

It was probable that he would be consulted again, so he hurried back to the Synagogue at the Crossed Streets. By the time he arrived, the shouting was everywhere and gangs of angry men, and even some women, were forming throughout the city. No message came for James from Pilate, but by midday, the presence of Roman troops was evident. The garrison had left the fortress, various units moving into the

Tyropoeon Valley and other parts of the city to take up defensive positions from which they could quell violent outbreaks. Three such units marched right past James' front gate.

The shouting continued, and there were scuffles between some protesting groups and guards of the watch. Pilate had ordered his own men to refrain from drawing blood unless absolutely necessary, and none of the incidents that occurred during the afternoon were serious enough for the legionaries to take action.

That changed after sunset. With garrison units having been dispersed around the city and even into some neighborhoods outside the walls, there was surprisingly little security at two key points along the aqueduct route: where the watercourse entered the sluice to the cisterns under the temple mount, and the supply ponds in the Bethlehem heights. These lapses were exploited with devastating effect.

A band of men, armed, masked and dressed in black, approached the temple mount water-entry point under cover of darkness. Only a partial squad of legionaries guarded the position. The soldiers were brought down quickly by a hail of arrows loosed from the shadows. Then the attackers climbed a wooden framework yet to be removed from under the last archway of the aqueduct. They coated the beams with a liberal dose of pitch, and set them ablaze. So intense was the heat that the arch collapsed, taking much of the last pier with it.

Unexpectedly, the unit from which the dead legionaries had come was closer at hand than the attackers realized, and the sight of flames brought quick retaliation. With no clear avenue of escape, the men dressed in black decided to make a stand inside the temple. They were pursued by the Roman troops all the way into the inner court where they were overwhelmed and hacked to pieces, some of their blood spattering the altar of sacrifice.

Meanwhile, a second group, armed with both swords and pickaxes, attacked the completely unguarded well site above Bethlehem, doing extensive damage to the supply ponds and watercourse. A stream of water cascading down the hillside alerted some legionaries nearby, but the attackers escaped into the darkness before the soldiers could make it up the heights.

Other incidents occurred around the city overnight. A company of soldiers guarding the water tower by the Pool of Siloam was attacked by archers, but the legionaries' swift response in combining their shields into a protective covering demonstrated Roman military discipline. With only one man injured, the soldiers let the archers spend their arrows, then swiftly broke from their formation and slaughtered most of the attackers.

A barrage of flaming arrows shot into the grounds of the prefecture was similarly ineffective, mostly landing in the main court. There was no significant damage to anything but some garden beds and the pergola in which Pilate received the Rabbi James. Attackers were more successful in separate ambushes of guards at two of the city gates.

All of this convinced Pilate that word about the *corban* had been spread with the intention of fomenting civil unrest, which was then used as cover for attacks on the aqueduct. There was no question that he'd been right about the Zealots.

Couriers dispatched to other posts in Judea brought additional troops to the city within days. But they were largely unnecessary. Pilate ordered a swift and brutal response from the Antonia garrison. The streets of Jerusalem ran red as armed combatants, unarmed protesters, and even some unfortunate bystanders fell to Roman swords and javelins. Pilate was determined not to be seen as timid, after having spared the protesters in Caesarea.

James was heartsick over the slaughter, and wished the prefect had called upon him before unleashing his troops. Could he have done anything to help avoid disaster? There was no way of knowing, but he would have wanted to try.

The tragedy took on an added measure of sorrow for him when he heard a rumor about the Zealot band that had been killed in the temple. It was said they were Galileans. Was there the slightest chance that any were from Nazareth? Could James have known some of them?

There was no doubt these men had attacked the legionaries, but people were incensed that Roman troops pursued them into the holy place. A bitter saying was already in currency, that *Pilate had mixed the blood of these Galileans with the blood of the sacrifices*. This James dismissed as a typical reaction of the gut, the kind of thing that gets repeated in anger, obscures the truth, and creates a legend. Galileans or not, these men were murderers, assassins. To flirt with the idea that they were martyrs did nothing to redress the deaths of the innocent.

James found small solace in the fact that, bloody as the Romans' response to the attacks had been, it wasn't the Sepphoris road. There were no mass executions. Jerusalem hadn't been put to the torch. The spiritual center of the nation's life was intact. This incident was painful, but things could have been much worse.

Pilate was less comforted. He took it as a personal insult that the aqueduct—the very project with which he had hoped to demonstrate Roman goodwill and his own concern for the Jewish people—was the Zealots' main target. He also was unnerved by the extensive planning that was evident. Obviously, the fire arrows shot into the prefecture and the assaults at the city gates had been designed to distract the attention of his troops. Like the fire outside the temple of Augustus in Caesarea, this highly coordinated action was accomplished with intent and precision.

Pilate's judgment was confirmed by information extracted under torture from a wounded combatant. The man's words—the last he would utter before having his neck broken—gave substance to the rumor of a central command over the Zealot groups. They also put a name on the alleged commander—an odd name, one which the prefect intended to discuss with the Rabbi James. The leader was known as *Jesus bar Abbas*, Jesus the Son of the Father.

* * *

The only parts of the pergola still standing in the fire-scarred court of the prefecture were the upright posts. Pilate intended no disrespect to the rabbi, but things being as they were, concerns about Jewish ritual purity couldn't be a priority just now. Much to his discomfort, James—having been summoned from his home—was ushered directly up the wide stairway into the praetorium and along a corridor into Pilate's audience hall.

Once Herod's throne room, the large and ornate chamber opened at one end onto a deep balcony overlooking a plaza outside the royal compound. This terrace was where the prefect sat when Caesar's vicar was called upon to pronounce Roman justice in Jerusalem.

James waited, accompanied by his officer escort. After a few tense minutes, he heard footsteps on the marble floor. Pilate entered, gestured for the officer to leave, and walked over to James. James noted that Pilate's face was set in an expression he could only describe as grave.

"Thank you for coming, Rabbi."

"Peace be upon you, Prefect."

"I am not feeling peaceful," Pilate said.

James nodded. "No, I imagine not."

Pilate led James to a pair of bulky marble seats off to the side of the room. The two men sat at a right angle to each other.

"Forgive the need to meet inside," Pilate said. "As I'm sure you saw, our outdoor facilities are somewhat compromised, and I am much pressed by events."

James appreciated Pilate's recognition of his religious disadvantage. "I understand," he said.

"And...not to forget—" said Pilate, "my thanks also for the note about your brother. I am glad you were able to offer him a word of caution. What you describe, and what I have heard from other sources, suggest he is a man of wisdom. I should like to meet him someday."

James nodded once more.

"Which brings me to a question, Rabbi..."

"Yes?"

"We have learned—and it should come as no surprise—that the protest of recent days was instigated by the Zealots."

"I assumed as much. They seem to have taken full advantage of the public disturbances."

"We have also obtained knowledge confirming earlier indications that at least some of the Zealot groups have merged into a consolidated organization under a single command."

"That is very troubling," James said.

"It is indeed." Pilate leaned forward, his weight on one elbow resting on the arm of the marble seat. "Rabbi, have you ever heard the name, *Jesus bar Abbas?*"

"*Bar Abbas*—son of the father. No, Prefect, I have not."

"Is this a conventional Hebrew name?"

"Well... *Jesus* is quite common. My brother's name... But for someone to be denoted, *son of the father*, of course raises the question, *which father?* To whom does it refer, the Holy One? It sounds like an artificial construct, an assumed identity."

"My thoughts, as well," said Pilate.

"Is this a Zealot figure?" James asked.

"It appears to be *the* Zealot figure. We believe Jesus bar Abbas is the Zealot commander."

James mulled this over. It would be natural for a Zealot leader to emphasize his religiosity. The Zealots insisted that they acted in the name of the Jewish people—the people chosen by God—in trying to cleanse the land of pagan influences. So their movement was religiously inspired, at least partially.

"It occurs to me," Pilate said, "that this name has a certain similarity to the expression your brother uses to describe himself—*Son of Man?*"

"Prefect, you can't believe—"

"No, Rabbi, I don't think your brother is Jesus *bar Abbas*. But it is possible that this person could, in some sense, be trading on your brother's celebrity. I did warn you about unscrupulous people taking advantage of his movement."

"Yes," James said uneasily, "you did."

A moment passed as Pilate let James reflect on this complication in silence. Then he said, "On another matter, Rabbi—the issue of *corban*—what do you recommend at this point?"

James shook off his worry about Jesus. "I can only repeat my earlier advice," he said. "Go before the Sanhedrin. The high priest can explain the legality of using temple funds for civic improvements. There will be an open discussion. This far along in the project, I can't see the council doing anything other than agreeing the work should be completed. That will be proclaimed to the people, who despite all the clamor and protest, have been looking forward to the water. I think this is the only thing you can do to ease the situation."

"What I should have done in the beginning," Pilate said quietly.

James did not respond. He realized he was receiving what was, in essence, Pilate's apology for not heeding his advice.

"We will retain additional troops in and around the city to provide extra security for the aqueduct," Pilate continued. "I don't know how long they will be needed."

"Can you estimate how much time repairs will take?" James asked.

Pilate leaned back in his seat. "Construction was very nearly complete before the attacks," he said. "My engineers think we should be able to restore the damaged elements and bring the entire project to its conclusion in a month or so."

"I suspect," James said, "that once water begins to flow, people will accustom themselves quickly to the new abundance. Any lingering reservations about use of the *corban* will be conveniently overlooked."

The prefect's cheerless visage melted somewhat, and he gave a quiet laugh. "You are, no doubt, right."

"What will not be as easily forgotten is the blood that was spilled." James knew he was treading on sensitive ground now, but he felt that something needed to be said. "You must understand, Prefect, that even though most people might not take up arms against the empire, Zealots do command a certain respect. There is wide admiration for their willingness to sacrifice themselves in the cause of freedom. They are seen as patriots."

"Patriots who prompt the deaths of their own countrymen," replied Pilate sharply, "who even shed Jewish blood with their own hands."

"A point well taken," James said. "But bitterness over this incident is real. And it will last."

Pilate was stirring in his seat. James held out a hand of calm.

"I know that stoking resentment is one of the Zealots' goals," he said. "And this puts you in an impossible position. You receive blame when you are unable to protect Jewish lives, and you receive blame when your own people take them. Your quandary is clear to me, Prefect."

That James understood his situation seemed to drain some of Pilate's umbrage.

"What are you trying to say, Rabbi?"

"Your current need is to secure the aqueduct until it is in operation and people come to depend on it. The Zealots won't attack it again after that. They would face the public's anger for its loss. In the meantime, you must strike a delicate balance. Legion presence must be obvious enough to dissuade anyone from making mischief. But your security measures should not be seen as so heavy-handed as to worsen the already hard feelings. You must be prudent in displaying your strength, and your men must be extremely restrained in applying it. Time and discipline are your allies, Prefect, belligerence your enemy."

Pilate took a deep breath. He could hear wisdom in James' words, though he did not like being lectured by a Jew about military direction, a subject that went to the very heart of his authority. After an awkward moment, his manner softened again, and he yielded to the truth.

"Thank you, Rabbi," he said sincerely. "I will take your valuable observations to heart."

James was satisfied that he had been able to make his argument for restraint, by which he hoped to avoid further shedding of Jewish blood. Upon leaving the prefecture, he went directly to the synagogue of Gamaliel, where he sought out the ritual bath. It was not currently in use, so he underwent the *mikvah* ritual, cleansing himself after being inside Pilate's hall. He recited the prayers by rote, even as he found his mind drifting to the name, *Jesus bar Abbas*.

Was Pilate right that this Zealot leader had so styled himself in hopes of exploiting the popularity of James' brother? If it was a veiled reference to Jesus of Nazareth, the *Son of Man*, than surely this *bar Abbas* was placing himself in a higher position—as *Son of the Father*. When considered from that point of view, the strange moniker made sense, and its implication was obvious. Attractive as the Galilean preacher and his message might be, the way of Zealotry was superior. For any true and committed Jew, *bar Abbas* was the logical one to follow.

* * *

Pilate issued orders that his troops were to be vigilant in protecting the aqueduct as well as the crews and materials needed for the repairs and finish work. But he insisted that extreme care must be taken that soldiers not behave in ways seen as provocative or insulting toward the people of Jerusalem. He stressed to his commanders that they would be held personally accountable for any incidents prompted by hostility or misbehavior on the part of their subordinates.

It was especially important that men who hadn't served in the city before, of which there were many in the companies brought in during the emergency, learn to suppress their anger at apparent Jewish contempt. They were likely to encounter it. Jerusalemites considered themselves above their fellow Jews in other parts of the country; they did little to mask their attitude toward Romans, whom they regarded as ignorant pagan brutes.

Legionaries must conduct themselves with dignity and politeness. They should smile whenever possible. And if they received complaints about the aqueduct, they should note that this project was a cooperative effort between the prefecture and the temple.

The High Priest Caiaphas called a special session of the Great Sanhedrin, which was convened in the Court of the Gentiles, since Pontius Pilate, *Praefectus Iudaea*, would be in attendance. All the moneychangers and sacrifice vendors were informed that their booths would have to be closed for the day and animals removed from the court, which caused much grumbling against Pilate.

James watched the proceedings from the upper level of the Royal Porch. Caiaphas first addressed the council, explaining the legality of applying any treasury funds in excess of the amount needed for maintenance of the temple and performance of its normal functions to projects of civic improvement or charitable intent. Surveying the assembly below, James wondered how many members of the august body might be inspired by that information to consider *corban* money available to fund good works in which they had special interest. His long-ago Greek studies with Lucillus came to mind. Caiaphas, he thought, might very well be opening *Pandora's Box*.

Pilate then rose to make his appeal. James noted that he wore the toga edged in purple, denoting him as vicar of the Augustus. It had been specified that neither he nor any officers accompanying him should wear military insignia or any badges that bore imperial heraldry within the temple.

The prefect declared that the aqueduct was a prime example of Caesar's concern for the well-being of his Jewish subjects, and noted the monetary commitment the provincial administration had made to the project. Taking a small leaf of parchment from one of his engineers standing behind him, he briefly described some of the technical aspects of the construction as well as the volume of water the aqueduct would provide on a continuous basis when complete.

He expressed his certainty that the honored representatives of the Jewish nation could recognize the many benefits of the water-system enhancement to their people and to the life of Jerusalem—which was, of course, the spiritual home of Judaism, a religion that held a position of the utmost regard and tenderness in Caesar's heart.

Finally, this legate of the greatest empire the world had ever seen, with great self-possession, humbled himself to thank the council members for their kind attention, their understanding, and the gift of their valuable time. It was the closest he came to an apology for not bringing his plan to the Sanhedrin in the first place. No one expected anything more.

There followed a debate about the aqueduct and whether it met the criteria required for temple funding. This was conducted by several doctors of the Law, among them Gamaliel, and involved a number of abstruse arguments on both sides of the question. After about two hours, a vote was called. As James had predicted, the Sanhedrin gave its approval to allocating *corban* money for completion of the project.

Repairs and additional construction were accomplished in just over a month after the special Sanhedrin session. Water began flowing, much to the delight of the populace. Security measures were eased through the succeeding weeks, and the extra troops were removed to their posts around the country. There was lingering annoyance among some of the legionaries about having had to smile at Jews.

CHAPTER THIRTY-TWO

*"If anyone would come after me, let him deny himself
and take up his cross and follow me."*

(Matthew 16)

Pilate's hope of gaining credit for the improvement of Jerusalem city life did not come to fruition. Everyone recognized that the aqueduct had been initiated by the Romans. But in most people's minds, *corban* funds paid for it, which was to say that their own gifts to the temple paid for it. The critical contribution of the provincial administration, in terms of both money and engineering prowess, was virtually ignored. In fact, it didn't take long before people ceased to think about the project very much at all. They quickly became accustomed to the enhanced availability of water. It was like the aqueduct had always existed. Pilate was left wondering if the whole effort had been worth the trouble.

As always, there were other things to occupy the public's mind. One of them was Jesus. Over the next few months, news of him spread everywhere. His sayings, repeated by those who had attended his meetings, were discussed in synagogues, in marketplaces, and over countless tables. Much was said about the modest way in which he and his companions lived, wandering the country, dependent on the hospitality of others for food and shelter. Their willingness to sacrifice even the simplest comforts in order to spread a message of love, righteousness and forgiveness prompted wide admiration.

People who had somehow found out that Jesus of Nazareth was related to *James the Just* inquired as to when the rabbi would prevail upon his brother to bring his ministry to Jerusalem. Visitors from other territories where Jesus' fame had spread assumed he was based in the Lord's city, and were surprised to find that he wasn't holding forth in the temple precincts.

But amid all this interest, there were occasional questions about whether what Jesus taught was fully in accord with the sacred writings, and if not, to what degree he might have deviated. Increasingly, reservations were also heard about his healing of the sick. No one disputed that these actions were impressive. In cases of people suffering severely for long years, or bearing deformities or incapacities from birth, his cures could only be described as miraculous.

It was *the way* he did it.

General agreement among the rabbis held that to heal the sick was a form of work, regardless of the intentions of the healer or the benefits to the recipient. As such, it was subject to Sabbath restrictions. Jesus performed his healings on all days of the week, including on the Sabbath. Most people were willing to excuse his flouting of the rules for the sake of someone being freed from a heartbreaking malady or a burdensome physical impairment. But the issue was serious to the learned men.

James encountered this concern among the students. Speaking to the class as it met in Gamaliel's synagogue one day, he was queried about why his brother was so lax in honoring the sacredness of the Sabbath. This prompted a discussion about the appropriateness of the healings. But one student also related a tale he had heard about Jesus' men picking grain on the Sabbath.

"I know nothing of this grain incident," James replied, "but as to healing—under the Law, it is always the case that urgent need overrides Sabbath restrictions. You wouldn't wait to aid an injured person who requires immediate attention, even if helping him means you must travel farther than a Sabbath journey. The Holy One has given us His Law to protect us, not to cause us harm."

"But Jesus doesn't just heal those whose illnesses are critical," another student argued. "Most of his cures seem to involve long-term conditions that could wait for Sabbath to pass."

The point was valid, but James felt the young man was failing to grasp a larger truth.

"As I understand my brother's teaching," he said, "Jesus places the highest value on *love*—call it *charity*, if you will. He insists that love for our fellows demands that we act for their good. The Law, or anything else, for that matter, should not become an obstacle to our doing this."

"There is something that bothers me more than disregard for the Sabbath." A familiar and annoying voice cut across the group. It was the voice of Saul, the tentmaker's son from Tarsus.

James spotted him standing in the rear.

"Forgive me, Rabbi," Saul said, walking forward, "but I find it greatly troubling that your brother chooses to associate himself with the most disreputable of characters—notorious sinners, even women of ill repute. It is known that he is a favorite of tax farmers. He has at least one of them among his followers. Not to mention that another of his men is said to have consorted with Zealots—though I must say I have more respect for Zealots than for tax collectors."

James, of course, had heard about his brother's dubious associations. *Simon the Zealot* was brought up frequently by people wondering how Jesus chose his apostles. Often enough, James had struggled to explain Jesus' choices. He even knew—which apparently, Saul did not—that there were rumors suggesting that a second of his brother's companions had Zealot sympathies.

That was one, Judas Iscariot, whom Jesus had assigned the job of managing the company's travel purse. The meaning of *Iscariot* was obscured by a play on words that gave rise to two very different assumptions about Judas' roots. One was that it referred to his home place, the Judean town of Kerioth. But that name was often rendered in a Romanized form that was very close to the Latin word, *sicarius*, meaning *dagger-man*, which raised all manner of questions.

"No disrespect, Rabbi—" Saul went on.

No disrespect, indeed. James tried not to roll his eyes.

"—but I believe that your brother weakens his own position by surrounding himself with such individuals."

"Does he?" James asked. "Is there nothing to be learned from the fact that people who might otherwise be lost to sin have had their lives transformed by my brother's words and good example?" Perhaps it was largely a reaction to all the questions and comments going around about Jesus, not all of them kind, but James felt himself losing patience with this young prig from Cilicia. "It seems to me not a bad thing when a man is turned from violence or from a life devoted to wringing money out of his own countrymen."

Saul was undaunted. "Oh, of course I am pleased that Jesus has such a salutary influence," he countered, "but reputation persists. It would be a shame if upright Jews are dissuaded from hearing your brother's message just because they don't wish to mix with those close to him."

"Ah, Saul, you are indeed a *Jew's Jew.*"

Laughter rippled across the class as the rabbi turned Saul's favorite self-characterization back upon him.

"But I think my brother has had little difficulty in getting upright Jews—and all other types of Jews, for that matter—to hear his message. Even his disreputable companions seem quite able to convey it."

James held to the practice of giving students wide latitude in their comments, in the same way as Gamaliel and like Hillel before. But there were times when he permitted himself the pleasant fantasy of hitting the tentmaker's son over the head with a tent pole.

The student, Asher, rose to speak, still bothered by something he had witnessed at Jesus' meeting months before. "Master," he said, "I have heard from many sources that your brother continues to be highly critical of Pharisees—which, in fact, you and I observed for ourselves. I am as unable to understand it now as I was then. He is not a Sadducee or an Essene. Why does he do this?"

James' hands opened wide to indicate his own perplexity at the question. "I can only assume he wishes to point out the harmful effects of hypocrisy," he said. "Perhaps he feels on firmer ground criticizing the shortcomings of his own people. If so, there may be charity in it."

Saul too had heard of Jesus' harangues about Pharisaical hypocrites, and he saw no charity in them whatsoever. There was so much that seemed questionable about this sage of Galilee. But then, as the old saying put it, could anything good come out of Nazareth?

The discussion continued, James leading the group into a deeper consideration of the meaning and rewards of Sabbath rest. Many of the students offered stories of family experiences related to Sabbath and the challenges of keeping it, especially the difficulties their mothers faced preparing food in advance to keep their families fed while avoiding work on the rest day. One young man admitted, awkwardly, that his mother sometimes paid a gentile woman to cook on Sabbath—what in Hebrew was called hiring a *Shabbos goy.* While this practice was permitted in strictly limited circumstances, it tended to subvert the importance of Sabbath, and so was held by the rabbis to be less than honorable.

It was after the lesson was ended, when he had finished praying the evening service with the students and all the others departed, that James' attention was drawn to a faint sound. The synagogue was dark and quiet. He stood silently, trying to discern the character of this noise, which was very much like that of someone gagging or retching.

He followed it down a short passage off the synagogue hall to an alcove that was shielded from view on three sides. There, deep in the shadows, he could just make out the form of someone lying on the floor. The body was twitching, arms flailing about. It was Saul. James knelt down and gripped him by the shoulders, holding his torso firmly against the paving blocks.

"Saul... Saul... Saul..." he repeated calmly. "Be at peace, son. Be at peace. The Holy One is with you."

After some minutes, the twitching body calmed. Saul lay still for awhile, James having released his shoulders. Finally, the young man looked up and realized who was there.

"Rabbi..." he said. "I— I am sorry."

He tried to rise, but James' hand against his chest restrained him.

"Lie still, Saul. Rest. Recover yourself."

Saul looked up into James' eyes. He quickly turned his head away and attempted to cover his face with a hand, but James could see the look of shame. The young man began to weep.

After a time, James asked, "How long have these fits been coming upon you?"

Saul's voice cracked with emotion, but he was able to say, "It has been a thorn in my flesh...since I was a child."

He paused, then brought himself to a sitting posture and peered through the dark into James' eyes. "My father was reluctant to let me come to Jerusalem because of it. But I was determined to be a rabbi, and particularly to study in the school of the great Gamaliel. I begged him over and over. Finally he relented."

"Is Master Gamaliel aware?"

"No." Saul stared down into the folds of his robe, gathered across the contour of his crossed legs, the look of shame in his eyes again. A long silence, then: "I think I have a demon, Rabbi."

James considered this. "It is possible," he said. "There is a story going about that tells of how my brother drove a demon from someone who was given to fits such as yours. But I think these falling episodes can be caused by other things as well. They are more common than many realize. Greeks call it the *holy disease*."

Which brought a slight smile to Saul's face. "Holy?" he asked. "Is there holiness in me?"

James smiled in return. "Perhaps. Somewhere."

They shared the humor of the moment. Then worry came into Saul's eyes.

"What should I do, Rabbi?"

"Confide in Master Gamaliel," James said. "He is a wise man, and a kind one. He will understand."

Saul stared off into the darkness. This would be a difficult thing to do. The Rabbi James was undoubtedly right about Master Gamaliel. But it would still be difficult.

James and Saul left the synagogue and descended the stairs beside the bridge that crossed over the Tyropoeon Valley to the temple mount. They walked together for a time through the lower city. Few words passed between them on their way, James letting Saul ponder how he would tell the Rabbi Gamaliel about his fits. They parted at a small square in which one of the new water fountains had been installed, Saul heading off to his lodgings and James to the Synagogue at the Crossed Streets.

Entering the front gate, James passed the stone hut and went to the main house to inquire of Amara about the evening meal. He was met with a surprise when he entered the front room.

"Brothers!" he exclaimed.

It was Josis and Simon, along with Simon's son, Noah.

"How wonderful it is to see all of you." James embraced each in turn. "Why have you come to Jerusalem?"

Josis answered. "For happy reasons and for sad reasons," he said, his face set in an expression that showed his ambivalence.

"What has happened?"

"Lucillus has died," said Josis.

James absorbed this blow. His eyes closed as he let himself down on a nearby couch. "My old tutor and friend. May he rest in the arms of the Holy One."

"He was returning from Sepphoris, from inspecting the building sites. His heart..."

James smiled in wistful remembrance. "He was still visiting the sites."

"I urged him to let others do it. But Lucillus insisted I was mistaken in thinking him old. He told me, *I have crossed the empire from Carthage to Palestine. I can surely make it between Nazareth and Sepphoris.*"

"Such a thing sounds like Lucillus," James said.

"We buried him near Father's tomb," said Simon.

"That is good." And James' memory was overflowing with past exchanges in Greek and Latin, with tales of the gods on Olympus, the heroes of Troy and Marathon. It had all helped to make a studious boy's childhood, and it was all precious to him.

After some minutes drifting in recollection, he turned back to his brothers. "And now, what is a *good* reason for your being here?"

"The olive business," Josis said. "You knew that Simon and Judas acquired a second grove."

"Yes."

Simon spoke with excitement. "Our yield of oil exceeds what we can sell in the vicinity of Nazareth. We are seeking new markets."

"Sepphoris?"

A slight shake of Simon's head. "The Greek merchants have their own suppliers. Lucillus had suggested that we look to Jerusalem. He thought we could get better prices here."

"Lucillus had a good head for business," said James in admiration of his old mentor. "I can speak to Joseph of Arimathea about transport."

"We had hoped for that," said Josis.

"But there is even better news," said Simon. "Noah will be a father."

"Now that *is* good news." James rose and embraced his nephew once again. "Your wife blossoms and is well?"

"Yes, Uncle."

"Praise to the King of the Universe." He turned to look at Josis. "The rest of the family?"

"All enjoy good health," Josis said. "Our household prospers."

"Excellent. And Mary?"

The flicker of a moment before Josis answered. "Mary is...fine. But she is part of the reason we have come."

James sat again, and bade the others to do likewise. As they found seats, Amara entered and announced that dinner would be within the hour. When she left, James indicated that his brother should proceed with the tale.

"A very odd incident occurred some time ago," said Josis. "We had heard that Jesus was preaching fairly close by. Mary asked if Simon, Judas and I would take her to him so that we might visit. We thought it a fine idea, and located Jesus speaking in a synagogue. I asked some people there to say that his mother and brothers were outside. They did. But his reaction was not at all like him."

James cocked his head in interest as Josis' story unfolded.

"He seemed to care not at all that we were there. In fact, he very much dismissed us as unimportant to him, claiming instead that those who choose to follow him and heed his message are his *real* family. Mary tried to make light of it. She insisted he wanted people to understand how important it was that they take his teaching to heart. But we could see that she had been surprised, as were we all. We mentioned nothing later when we finally met with him. It turned out to be a pleasant visit. But somehow...he wasn't the same as he had been in the past. His manner was subdued, as if great weight pressed upon him."

"Do you think Mary was correct in how she took the meaning of his remark in the synagogue?"

"Probably," Josis said. "He was pleased to see us—especially so to see his mother. But since then, we have become aware of a change in his preaching."

"What sort of change?"

Josis looked over at Noah.

"I recently attended one of his outdoor meetings, Uncle," Noah said. "Jesus made many of the points I have heard him make before. But there was...an emphasis...that was different. He appeared anxious that his listeners understood something about following his way."

"Understood what?"

Noah thought for a moment, then: "That it would be...*difficult.* He used many parables and sayings that spoke of counting the cost of some great enterprise—a king preparing for battle and assessing his forces, a man planning to build and being certain he is able to carry out his plan."

James gave a shrug. "Sensible advice."

"Yes, but aimed at a very specific point," Noah said. "It was the cost of following *him* that he was talking about, of being part of his movement. And the implication was that this cost would be high."

Simon interjected. "Other people have reported these sayings too. We have heard similar things from different sources. And— And there is more." He nodded for Noah to continue.

"Jesus spoke of how he would cause conflict," Noah said, "even in families. He saw fathers and sons falling out, daughters opposing their mothers and their mothers-in-law, all because of him. He even went so far as to say his intention was not to bring peace, but...a *sword*."

"A metaphor, surely," said James.

"I took it as such," said Noah, "but the whole tone of his sermon was peculiar. Not that the talk wasn't uplifting in parts. Jesus spoke of kindling a fire and fanning the world into high fervor. Those parts were quite rousing. But I think—" He paused, then completed his thought hesitantly, "I think...he frightened some people, Uncle. Quite a few walked out of the meeting."

James was absorbed in Noah's account. He sat with one hand to his face, rubbing the tips of his fingers back and forth across his lips.

Noah took a long breath before going on. "Jesus used an expression which I have never heard before, and which I found unnerving—even though it didn't really make very much sense. He called upon all of his listeners to...*take up their crosses* and follow him. I believe he meant for the cross to represent some kind of sacrificial burden, but to me it could only mean...hideous death. I suspected a lot of the other people who heard him say this were equally confused."

To James it brought back a picture of the Sepphoris road. Did Jesus anticipate such a gruesome end? Why should he? Crucifixion was the Romans' ultimate punishment, the one they reserved for seditionists and rebels. There was nothing in what Jesus was saying or doing to put him in danger of that.

James weighed Noah's words against his own impressions of Jesus. "Well..." he said reflectively, "I was struck by the change in our brother when I saw him on the occasion of the wedding. But he had been away for all those years prior, and a man grows, matures over such a period.

Then, when I myself attended one of his sessions months ago, I was most taken by his power as an orator. This surprised me, because I never knew he possessed such ability. But he had been preaching for a long time at that point. Certainly, he would have become accustomed to speaking before large crowds and refined his presentation.

"Then too," he went on, slowly, purposefully, "a man to whom people turn for guidance or example, and on whom they lavish praise and respect..." A pointed finger for emphasis. "I've seen the awe in which our brother is held by so many—Jews and gentiles alike. Fame has its consequences. In my own small way, I have been the object of people's interest and admiration. It can be gratifying, but at the same time, there is a cost to be counted in that. If you wish to speak of sacrificial burdens, I can tell you that other people's expectations weigh heavily. It changes a man."

"That may be, Brother," said Josis. "You are the one to know. We live simple lives, and we take you at your word. But we fear there is more happening to Jesus than what you describe."

"What do you mean?"

Again it was Noah. "Things he says about himself now. He seems to believe that he—in his own person—is essential to people's very lives. So much so that he has taken to telling his followers they must somehow *consume* him."

"Consume his words," James said, "absorb his teaching."

"Yes...that... But something more as well—that they must feast on him, flesh and blood."

"Oh, you know how Jesus uses vivid images."

"Yes, I do," Noah said. "But this was different. This was a whole new mystical aspect of his message which I had never heard before. I found it disturbing, and so did many others. A lot of people simply got up and walked away. It was too hard a teaching for them to accept."

James could understand that. If Noah's account was accurate, it suggested that Jesus had begun to push at the bounds of Jewish thinking. It was true that Judaism had known its share of mystics and seers. But this idea of consuming flesh and blood sounded like something one would find in the various mystery cults that flourished throughout the empire.

Now it was Josis who spoke. "Jesus has conducted his ministry for over two years now. And in that time, it has never been clear to us what the object of this preaching is or how it reflects the destiny which the family has always speculated about."

"Do you think he is moving toward some revelation?" asked James.

Another moment of uneasy silence—then from Noah: "Jesus was my playmate, Uncle. I have known his character since we were both little children. I was the one who would climb to the highest roof in the compound on a whim. He was the one who examined and contemplated and then knew exactly the right thing to do or the right word to say for any situation in which he found himself. Some hand directed him that did not direct me. If his thoughts and manner have now taken these unexpected turns, I can only conclude that there is meaning in the change."

* * *

James took Josis, Simon and Noah to see Joseph of Arimathea, who was quite interested in the abundance of olive oil produced by James' family. Joseph told them he could arrange for the oil to be sold in Jerusalem and, if their output was great enough, other towns in Judea as well. With a slight alteration in the route taken by one of the pack trains that passed through Galilee, shipments could be picked up in Nazareth. Joseph would handle the sales and payments for a percentage of the receipts. Simon agreed to Joseph's terms, speaking for both himself and his brother, Judas, his partner in the olive business. Josis, as eldest and family head, approved.

James' guests remained in Jerusalem for three days, scouring the marketplaces for items not readily available in Galilee, making sacrifice in the temple to give thanks for the family's good fortunes, and resting over Sabbath. All enjoyed the evenings of conversation in the Synagogue at the Crossed Streets. The brothers shared reminiscences about their father, Joseph. Josis and Simon spoke of their mother, Escha, bringing to James' mind the stories his father had told of her. And of course, everyone had much to say about the family retainer, Lucillus.

James considered this interlude a rare blessing. He noticed how his brothers were aging, especially Josis. It made him wonder how many more opportunities he might get to be with them. The warmth of their time together and the laughter over days past caused him to renew his acquaintance with an old ache for the home he'd left so long before, a life steadily fading into the mists of memory.

*   *   *

In the weeks after the departure of his brothers and nephew, news and conjecture about Jesus increased greatly. There were reports of meetings being held now in various parts of Judea, and excited talk from some who said they had attended them or knew others who did. Eventually, a rumor circulated to the effect that the Galilean prophet and his company were coming to Jerusalem, though no one seemed to know when this might happen or what was the rumor's source. Gamaliel reported that Jesus was discussed in the Sanhedrin, with some members expressing discomfort at the size of his following.

"Your brother's popularity is worrisome to many of our leaders," he remarked to James.

"Why? Jesus preaches nothing different from what the rabbis teach. He upholds the Law."

"With compromises."

"With love," James said adamantly. "He maintains that *the Sabbath was made for man, and not man for the Sabbath.* Which sounds to me very much like something your grandfather would have said. Hillel was always willing to interpret the Law broadly when it was necessary for human needs to be met."

"And for that, criticism of the Rabbi Hillel was not unknown," said Gamaliel. "But James, you must consider, my grandfather did not hurl reckless charges at the scribes and temple priests. I don't dispute for a moment that hypocrisy reigns among our eminent men. But I can understand how hypocrites might not enjoy being referred to as *whitewashed tombs* and other of Jesus' picturesque images."

James waved away Gamaliel's observation. "Jesus has said nothing worse about the temple circle than the Essenes say all the time."

"The Essenes do not command a mass movement. Their numbers are small, and their communities isolated. They have set themselves apart from the main run of Jewish life. Jesus, on the other hand, has thrust himself right into the center of it."

James paused questioningly. "Do you really think my brother's influence is that great?" he asked his colleague.

"It's *huge*," said Gamaliel, "and it grows bigger all the time. Many... *many*...people—throughout Judea, Galilee, the Decapolis, and beyond—are pinning their hopes on Jesus to change their lives. His movement collects Jews, gentiles, even Samaritans. It is a *phenomenon*, as the Greeks would say. You know all too well how it's drawn the attention of the Roman authorities."

James' head fell forward, and he was silent. Then he raised his eyes to Gamaliel. "Yes. That I do know. And I thank you for your good counsel. But...dear friend...you have never told me of *your* feelings. Do you share the worries of others in the Sanhedrin?"

Gamaliel shifted in place. "No, James," he said. "I do not fear your brother. Indeed, I can see that Jesus and his preaching help many people to be better Jews, and this is all to the good. I admit I do not feel in need of his message to make *me* a better Jew. And that is not pride on my part, merely confidence in my own faith. Moses and the Commandments and the prophets are sufficient for me. As to the impact Jesus may have over the longer term...I suspend my judgment, for now. In the final measure, it is a question of authority. If his movement reflects the will of the Holy One, it will succeed to great effect. If not..."

"Yes. You are right. Your answer is an honest one. I respect it."

Then Gamaliel looked at James with knit brows, an expression of deep searching. "And what of you? What do *you* think?"

James' hands came together, his palms flat against each other in front of his face. He looked very torn. "I confess to being a man of two minds," he said after a breath. "I have lived with the mystery of Jesus for most of my life. I remember the unusual circumstances of his birth. I know the inexplicable things he has done. I have heard the arguments for his special destiny put forth by my father and by his mother, Mary. I have witnessed the power of his presence over great crowds of people, felt the strange charge of his words. I have defended his teaching and his behavior, and tried to deflect some of the criticism he receives."

His palms separated, and his eyes closed tightly. Gamaliel thought he saw the glistening of a tear seeping out from under one of James' eyelids.

"Yet, even now...*even now*," said James, "I do not know who my brother is."

CHAPTER THIRTY-THREE

A voice came out of the cloud, saying,
"This is my beloved Son. Hear him."

(Mark 9)

That Pilate had been able to complete the aqueduct in the face of such bold provocation apparently gained him favor with the emperor. His report on the affair brought congratulations from Tiberius for a swift response to the attacks and single-mindedness in following through on the project. Pilate had succeeded in demonstrating Caesar's goodwill, despite this Zealot wickedness. The actual extent of that success Pilate knew was debatable. But of most immediate importance, nothing in his ongoing correspondence with Rome suggested that Tiberius held any ill feeling toward him over that other wickedness, the attempted coup by Pilate's mentor, Sejanus.

To the contrary, Tiberius was so pleased with the aqueduct that he instructed Pilate to make some expression of Caesar's blessing on the capital city of the Jews. The prefect should demonstrate in a public and permanent way Tiberius' regard for the Jewish people and the critical role played by Jerusalem in the commerce and security of the eastern empire. Pilate was delighted to set his mind to the task. He would devise something tasteful, appropriate and respectful of Jewish sensitivities. But not just now. There was other business to attend to.

A series of quick Zealot strikes around the country showed that the new unified command intended to keep pressure on Caesar's vicar. None of these actions was as spectacular as the attack on the aqueduct or the fire in Caesarea. There were assaults on toll stations, the waylaying and murder of a military courier, and the assassination of a tax collector in Samaria. That was of particular interest, since it suggested to Pilate that the Zealots were seeking to strengthen their operational ties across religious boundaries. It was unlikely that old animosities could be overcome enough to enlist large numbers of Samaritans in what was essentially a Jewish cause. But the attempt indicated a change in Zealot thinking.

Occasionally, over the years of imperial occupation, the Romans would obtain random bits of information about insurrectionist groups, which sometimes helped in foiling plots. But mostly the legions depended on their highly refined defensive tactics, followed by harsh reprisals intended to dissuade people from giving aid to the resistance. The reprisals succeeded largely in fanning people's resentment against Rome.

Pilate realized that the Zealots' more sophisticated organizational scheme required better information. He was not facing a marauding army whose path could be traced by scouts and lookouts. While there were a few small Zealot bands that kept on the move among the hills and desert wastes, Pilate reasoned that most groups were likely made up of men living ordinary lives by day and indulging their rebellious proclivities in secret. Essentially, the movement was based in the towns and villages, and Pilate had the means for penetrating there.

The network of tax collectors had long provided the empire's most extensive contacts with its subject peoples, far more than the vassal monarchies on which it usually depended for regional administration. The tax farmers were always able to buy local stooges willing to sniff out who had the money. If revenue could be collected, so could facts, rumor and gossip, some of which might be useful.

Agents of the prefect spent weeks making discreet contacts with tax collectors, who were motivated to help since they knew themselves to be Zealot targets. Before long, intelligence began trickling in. Most of it was worthless, but some showed promise. No visible changes in unit deployment were made as a result of these findings. Pilate did not want to do anything that might draw attention to his sources. If there were fresh attacks, his troops could deal with them. Everything would remain as it was until he had enough information to pursue his primary objective, the killing or capture of the Zealot leader, Jesus bar Abbas.

*   *   *

It was in the fall when James received clear confirmation that his brother had entered Judea and was conducting his ministry within Pilate's domain. He soon realized that Gamaliel had been right about the extent of Jesus' influence. People flocked to attend his brother's meetings, even from the Jerusalem district. They would return home fired with enthusiasm, urging friends and relatives to go hear this young rabbi they had begun calling the *Nazarene*.

Jesus' party followed an erratic route through Judea and Samaria, heading west toward the Plain of Sharon, then back to the east, even crossing the Jordan into Antipas' territory, then back into Judea again. The nearer they got to the Lord's city, the larger the crowds and the more heightened the anticipation.

To his surprise, James found that Jesus' cousin—now commonly referred to as *John the Baptist*—was remembered and admired widely. Where most people once dismissed him as an oddity, the current assumption was that the son of Zacharias had not only been a prophet in his own right, but Jesus' forerunner.

Many of those who had been John's disciples continued to proclaim his virtues and his message of repentance. Interestingly, not all allied themselves with Jesus' movement. Some joined in criticizing its apparent laxity toward the Sabbath, which they saw as contradicting the strict Essene discipline by which John had lived. This put them in something of a dilemma, since they knew John had subordinated his own mission to that of his kinsman. And there was a definite irony in their agreeing with the religious leadership so despised by the Essenes.

But the greater public faced no such conflict. A growing consensus held that Jesus was bringing a refreshing new vitality to Jewish life. James heard this frequently from men who came to the Synagogue at the Crossed Streets and also in much of his correspondence.

Jesus' personal gifts were widely remarked upon. People said he radiated sanctity. You had only to approach him to feel the aura of holiness, though the sensation was experienced in different ways by different individuals. Some reported being exhilarated in his presence, others felt joy, as of long-held hopes finally realized, still others a deep and abiding calm.

Most compelling, Jesus didn't just heal the sick, it was held that he actually raised the dead. Two instances were cited, the son of a widow from Nain, and the daughter of a Galilean synagogue elder. James didn't know if the stories were true or just adornments to the many legends rapidly growing up around his brother. Regardless, no one who saw Jesus or heard him speak remained untouched.

However, James did come across those who complained that, uplifting as Jesus' preaching was, and while his healing powers were a marvel, his moral demands seemed far too challenging, even harsh. And to some, the things he suggested about difficulties his followers might face had an ominous sound. Of course, there were also people who simply stayed away, dismissing all the excitement, all the stories, all of Jesus' fame and wonder as an illusion conjured up through a kind of religious trickery. They would never allow themselves to be drawn into false frenzy.

There was one aspect of Jesus' healing practices that some Jews found even more offensive than his daring to cure on the Sabbath. That was how, when he cleansed a sufferer of disease or corrected physical abnormalities, he would sometimes also pronounce sins forgiven. The very idea rang blasphemous. It raised suspicions of heresy. James heard about this forgiving of sins, and it made him uncomfortable.

Serious reservations about Jesus were to be found most readily among those in positions of leadership, especially in the temple circle. These were the nation's highest religious authorities, the men charged with enforcing adherence to the Law of Moses and protecting the purity of Jewish belief. But they were also affected by some hard, practical concerns that had a more immediate impact than issues of doctrine.

And so it was that Joseph of Arimathea came to James early on the day before the Festival of the Dedication of the Temple was to begin, to deliver a message he had been given by representatives of the priests' council. After their usual greetings and James' instructions to Amara to prepare a place for his guest at the morning meal, the two men stood outside the door of the stone hut. James wished to enjoy the sunshine of the pleasant winter morning for a time. They prayed together in the open air, which was crisp but yet warm enough to be inviting.

When they had finished and were putting away their phylacteries, Joseph said, "You know that I have heard your brother speak."

"Have you?"

"He held one of his meetings near my hometown. The crowd was large. I had no idea he attracted so many."

"What was your impression?"

Joseph stroked his beard, and his head took to bobbing slightly as he searched for words with which to describe a feeling that was in the process of becoming a conviction. "He interests me, James. Your brother is a man with something to say. Great love envelopes him, and he is uniquely able to impart it to others. I am beginning to understand the strange story you confided to me so long ago about Jesus' birth, and also to appreciate what our friend, Zacharias, saw."

"I'm sure my brother would be pleased at a respected member of the Sanhedrin speaking so generously on his behalf," James said.

"Speaking with *you*," Joseph said in a lowered voice, his manner suddenly subdued. "I'm not sure I would express myself openly to my colleagues in the Sanhedrin or the temple—some of them, anyway."

"What do you mean?"

"My visit here has a purpose, James."

"And what is that?"

A beat of hesitation, then: "The priests find Jesus vexing."

James laughed. "That does not surprise me," he said. "Our leaders are always vexed by the fear that Jews might encounter holiness and joy outside the smoke of the altar fires. The priests have never fully accepted the fact that men gather to pray in synagogues."

"There is more truth in what you say than even you may realize," said Joseph warily.

"What troubles you, my friend?"

The task Joseph had been given was distasteful to him, but he found the resolve to carry on, for James' sake.

"The aqueduct project very much depleted the temple's reserves," he said, "especially since there were extra costs involved in repairing the Zealot damage. This has drawn attention to the fact that sacrifices have decreased significantly, which means that money offerings are below expectations. It has been happening for some time, but the shortage is especially apparent since Jesus brought his preaching ministry to Judea. The priests suspect Jesus' followers of believing that their faith in him and in his teaching somehow relieves them of the need to make sacrifice."

James was a blank. "That is absurd," he said after collecting himself for a moment.

"They cite Jesus' claims to forgive sins," Joseph said.

"But..." James searched his memory. "I know of nothing Jesus has said that would discourage people from making sacrifice. I'm sure he regards the temple as sacred. Besides, I don't really know what he means by this forgiving of sins. Forgiveness is a central point of his ministry, so perhaps he intends the expression merely as some sort of blessing."

"To forgive sin is to claim power which only the King of the Universe possesses," Joseph said. "I will admit to you—and to *you* alone— that I have felt the exercise of this power by your brother. I don't quite know what to think of it, myself, but I do know it is real. However, our priests would only believe it if they allowed Jesus to lay his hands on them, and I do not see that happening any time soon."

"What would they have Jesus do?"

"At the least, he could urge his followers to increase their sacrifices and sacrificial gifts. That would likely meet many of the objections. But—" He hesitated again. "Some would be satisfied only if he were to recant these claims of forgiveness. I know this, James, because I've been asked to have you instruct your brother to do just that."

James reacted visibly. "*Instruct* my brother? I can hardly *instruct* my brother."

"You counseled Jesus about Pilate's concerns."

"I advised him to be prudent. What the priests ask is a bit more than that."

Joseph was becoming agitated. He shifted nervously on his feet. "I understand how difficult a position this puts you in, James. But, please believe me, the distrust of Jesus in the temple—of his movement, of his influence among the people—is very great, very great indeed. It was one thing for him to be wandering around Galilee, preaching and drawing crowds. It's another to have him approaching Jerusalem. The priests came to me because they know that you and I have been friends for so many years. If you are unable to...well, to *caution* Jesus...I fear steps will be taken that may affect him severely."

"What do you think they might do?"

"Caiaphas could bar him from the temple," said Joseph, "possibly have him removed from Judea. Jesus is a subject of Antipas, who would benefit greatly from some priestly gratitude. If Jesus were deported back to Galilee, he might end up in the tetrarch's custody like John. And you know what came of that. I don't think Caiaphas would want to involve the Romans. At least, that wouldn't be his first choice. He has borne enough abuse over giving *corban* funds for the aqueduct. But a number of options are open to him, and in the worst case, he could charge your brother with blasphemy."

"That would be highly unwise," James said. "Jesus is so popular at this moment, arresting him might cause a riot. It could be like Herod and the eagle standard."

"Moments pass," Joseph said, "moments pass. Caiaphas will wait for the right opportunity. If Jesus should do something that challenges the authorities, that provides an excuse to move against him..." He reached out and laid an imploring hand on James' arm. "Counsel him again, James. I know you can't tell your brother what to do, but you can advise him to proceed carefully—and maybe to offer a word to the crowds about the importance of sacrifice and supporting the priests."

"But people already pay the temple tax, while the priests get fat on the food offerings."

"That is not good enough," Joseph said. "The low level of the treasury reserve only increases the priests' worry. Religious life is changing, James. The Essenes are small in number, but their disdain for the temple is widely shared. More and more people turn to the synagogues for prayer and encouragement in their faith. Now Jesus appears with his message of love and brotherhood, raises questions about the need for strict adherence to established rules and customs, and gains a tremendous following along the way. This is a fearful thing to the priests. And to many of the rabbis, as well, I must say. Your brother has not been circumspect in his remarks about the doctors of the Law."

A quick snort was James' acknowledgement of this last point.

"Men who feel threatened can be dangerous, James," Joseph said.

James rubbed the palm of one hand across his forehead. "Yes, my friend. Yes, yes, I know."

"Speak to him. Please."

"I will speak to him," James said with a sigh. "I will try to make him see he must be careful, if he wishes his movement to last."

"If he wishes *himself* to last," said Joseph.

"Yes," James said, "that too."

In his heart, James suspected that his brother's pronouncements about the forgiveness of sins were more than blessings, more than words of encouragement, more than figures of speech. He even suspected that they had been foreshadowed in Zacharias' proclamation at the birth of John, that curious utterance which Elizabeth had taken down. The great priest said that his son, who came to them so late in life, would be called the *prophet of the Most High* and that he would bring people *knowledge of salvation by the forgiveness of their sins.*

This could have been a prediction of the calls to repentance that undergirded John's baptism ministry. But then, John never claimed that he, himself, had the power to forgive sins. More prophetically, Zacharias' words could be read as referring to Jesus, who didn't hesitate to make that claim. And now, Joseph of Arimathea testified to having experienced Jesus' forgiving power directly.

If the suspicions of the priests were correct, if some people did assume that receiving forgiveness from Jesus made sacrifice unnecessary, then he represented a significant threat to the religious leadership, to the temple, to traditions that had long marked, measured and directed the life of the Jews. Caiaphas wouldn't tolerate that. He couldn't.

James had Ephron make some inquiries as to whether anyone might know Jesus' present whereabouts. Several people thought the Nazarene was near Jerusalem, but no one Ephron spoke with was sure exactly where.

Early the next day, James went to the temple to meet Gamaliel and the students on the upper level of the Royal Porch. They would participate in ceremonies celebrating the miracle of the light. Afterward, he intended to ask around himself about Jesus.

The Court of the Gentiles was beginning to fill for the event. James paused at the top of the stairs and looked out over the gathering. Some men, obviously walking together, were making their way through the larger crowd. In its center was a figure recognizable even though his face was partially obscured by a prayer shawl. It was Jesus. James hurried down the stairs and out into the court.

"Brother," he called.

Jesus turned at the voice. They met, and James went to embrace him. Surprisingly, Jesus pulled back, instead taking James' hands and enclosing them between his own.

"Peace be with you, Brother," Jesus said quietly.

This greeting was disarming—uncharacteristically muted. "And... with you...Brother," James said. Josis' story of how Jesus had been cool to his mother and brothers came to mind.

Greetings were exchanged with Jesus' companions.

"Peace be upon you all. It is good to see you."

While each nodded or offered a pleasant word, the manner of the whole company seemed oddly restrained. Even Simon, who when James was taking his leave of the group at Avigail's estate, had given him a boisterous farewell clap on the shoulders, now put out his hand with an almost hushed, "Peace, Rabbi."

James looked questioningly into the big fisherman's eyes for a second, then turned back to Jesus. "Are you in Jerusalem to preach?"

Jesus raised a finger to his lips, and with his other hand, drew the prayer shawl farther forward around his face. "Not just yet," he said. "We are here for the celebration."

"I too," said James, "with Gamaliel and the students. But Brother... we must speak. Important considerations have presented themselves. Perhaps you and the others might come home with me later?"

"We will speak, James," Jesus said tersely, and then turned away.

The reunion had been brief and its ending abrupt. James found himself left standing amid the throng, which was, by now, packing the Court of the Gentiles. But confused as he was, his intention was to meet the class, so he headed back to the stairway. Climbing the steps against the flow of traffic was difficult, rabbis and disciples now on their way down for the ceremonies. Gamaliel and some of his students appeared at the top. When James spotted them, he worked his way over toward the rail, with the begging of many pardons, to await their descent. Just then, his attention was diverted to a clamor of raised voices cutting through the din of the crowd below. Others on the stairway heard it as well.

"What is this fuss?" Gamaliel said when he reached James at about the midpoint of the flight.

James was looking off in the direction of the outcry. "I cannot tell." He saw some men gesticulating angrily with raised arms, and then realized they were addressing Jesus. "Those men are hollering at my brother," he said.

"Your brother?" Gamaliel asked. "Jesus is in the temple?"

"He came for the festival. I just spoke with him."

James turned and started hurriedly down the stairs. He struggled to cross the court, picking his way through all the people as best he could. But so thick was the crowd, that it took several minutes to accomplish his purpose. When he reached the altercation, he could see that some of the men accosting his brother were holding rocks in their hands as if they intended to stone Jesus.

"Stop this!" he called. "Stop it immediately!" He waved to some sentries standing their posts in the colonnade of the Royal Porch. "Guard! Guard!"

Heads turned at James' cry. One of the assailants heard it and recognized him.

"It is the Rabbi James," he said.

James glanced about for Jesus, whom he now saw pushing through the crowd in the direction of the gate with his companions. When he looked back, the men with the rocks were off in the opposite direction.

Two temple guards appeared. "What is the problem, Rabbi?" one asked.

"There was an altercation," James said, still trying to spot those who had threatened Jesus. But they had melted into the flood of people. James expelled some breath in a burst. "No matter. It is over. All the parties have fled."

"People are worked up for the festival, Rabbi," the guard said.

"Yes, of course." James gestured in acknowledgment. "My thanks for the prompt response."

Bowing slightly, the guards departed to their duty.

Gamaliel was standing behind James. "I think Jesus and his men have left the temple. I saw a small band heading for the gate."

The press of bodies pouring into the court blocked any view through the opening.

"Please take the students in," James said. "I must find my brother."

Again he pushed against the crowd. When he eventually made it outside, after some labored minutes, he stood on tiptoes and craned his neck trying to spot Jesus and his group. Finally, he saw Simon standing out apart from the flow of traffic. James went to him.

"Simon, what happened in there? Where is my brother?"

The fisherman took his arm and drew James to a side walkway that led down from the temple entrance to a lower terrace away from the main flow of bodies. He deposited his large frame on a parapet, gesturing for James to join him. It was comparatively quiet here, and they could talk.

"Jesus told me to remain and wait for you," he said. "He and the others have left the temple mount. I will catch up with them later."

"What was that dispute about?" James asked. "It looked like those men were going to attack Jesus."

"Those ruffians have been following us around for some time," said Simon. "They claim to be scholars, but I think them just thugs. They taunt the Lord, trying to make him speak against the temple or say that he is the Messiah."

"Did they intend to stone him—right there in the court?"

"Threats. Nothing more. We've been threatened on other occasions. When people are hostile, Jesus either talks them into perplexity or else eludes them as he did just then with your help."

"Well," James said, "I must speak with my brother. Where can I find him?"

"Jesus decided that—after this little uproar—it would be best to get out of Jerusalem. We have been staying at the home of his friend, Lazarus, in Bethany. Lazarus and his two sisters have provided us a base while Jesus preaches in the regions east and south of the city."

"Bethany?" said James. "That is little more than a Sabbath journey. I had no idea you were so close. Why has Jesus not contacted me?"

This walkway too was starting to fill with people and noise.

"Come, Rabbi," said Simon, rising from the parapet. "Let us find a more peaceful spot."

They made their way down into the Tyropoeon Valley, heading toward the Synagogue at the Crossed Streets. People were bound for the temple from all directions, but down here, the flow was more spread out as they came either alone or in small groups. The noise was much less.

"Rabbi," said Simon, "I saw how you reacted to the way Jesus greeted you in the Court of the Gentiles. Also, I realize you would have expected him to alert you to his presence in the region. Understand, please, that your brother does not seek to avoid you. Not at all. Your place in his heart is secure, as are those of all his family members. But some things have happened in the past months. He is different from when you last saw him, and we are all affected by it."

"Different in what way? I know his fame has increased, but—"

"It is not fame," said Simon. "The Lord is unmoved by celebrity, or even controversy."

"He seems to have generated much of *that*."

Simon answered with a grunt. Then he repeated, "Some things have happened."

"What things?"

The big fisherman's stride broke slightly, but he kept walking, though more slowly than before. "There was a— how can I put it—a vision? An appearance? Two of our fellows and myself went up with Jesus into the heights near Caesarea-Philippi—Zebedee's sons, James and John. It was when we were still staying at the house provided us by the widow of Zimran, after your visit. We followed Jesus to the top of a high bluff and sat. It was late in the day. We were quite tired, and I think we drifted off while Jesus prayed. Then, out of nowhere, two men appeared. This woke us, you may be sure. It was quite startling. We took the men for—"

Simon halted in mid-pace, James with him.

"Rabbi...the men were...Moses...and the prophet, Elijah."

James showed no reaction, so Simon continued his account.

"It was as if they had come to do homage to Jesus," he said. "And rightly they should, for a heavy cloud then accumulated over the place, and...there was...a voice. All three of us heard it, Rabbi. The others would attest."

"What was this voice?" James asked.

"It was the voice of God, Rabbi."

Still no visible reaction from James.

"The Holy One called Jesus...*my beloved son*."

Mary's words echoed in James' mind: *Son of the living God*.

"Throughout this whole time, Jesus had taken on a strange and very remarkable appearance."

James' eyes narrowed in curiosity, but still he said nothing.

"He...*glowed*...Rabbi. A sort of *light* came from him. It was like nothing we have ever seen—and I can tell you, we have seen wondrous things since we've been following Jesus."

A moment's silence, then James asked—not in a dismissive way, but merely questioning—"You did say you were asleep?"

"We considered that. Yes, we considered it. The three of us have discussed it many times. We were all awake when these things occurred. We know that to be true, and we agree on what we saw there."

After reflecting, James said, "The prophet Malachi has written that Elijah must come before the great day of judgment."

"Indeed," said Simon. "That is why we reserve him a place at the Passover table. But Jesus told us the prophet has already come. And after what I saw on that hilltop, I don't doubt it."

He paused, scratched the side of his head, and then said, "By the way, Rabbi, the Lord didn't really want us to speak of this incident. But I felt you should know. And anyway, no one ever keeps quiet when he tells them to. The whole country rings with words Jesus insisted should remain secret. He often laughs about it."

They resumed walking, and James said, "Why didn't he want me to know he's in the area?"

"Maybe to protect you, Rabbi."

"Protect me?" This was a turnabout. James had been charged by his father with protecting Jesus.

"The vision on that mount is only one of a number of things that indicate these changes which have taken place," said Simon. "For some time now, Jesus has spoken to us about what would befall him in Jerusalem. This will no doubt disturb you, Rabbi—it certainly has disturbed all of us—but the Lord expects to die here."

James felt a shiver of unease.

"He has either told us this directly or hinted at it several times. We are all worried—although I must say the whole thing is very unclear. He says he will die, but at the same time, he suggests that he will be alive. We can't tell if this is another of his confusing parables, but he speaks with the utmost conviction. We always complain when he makes reference to this, but he will hear no argument on the matter. I once objected fiercely, and he scolded me as he had never done before. He actually called me *Satan*."

"That was rather severe."

"Very. But he is intent on our taking his words seriously. And he insists he has to be here."

"Why does he expect to die in Jerusalem?" James asked.

"I cannot say, Rabbi. He has been confronted many times by hostile types—much as you witnessed in the temple. And I know there is grumbling about some aspects of his teaching."

"And about the things you do on the Sabbath?"

"Ah...you know of all that," Simon said. "Yes, the Sabbath has been a point of contention. But to my mind, nothing the Lord either says or does would put his life in peril. Still, he insists it will happen, and I think he doesn't want his fate to bring harm upon anyone in his family. At least that is what I presume he's thinking in staying away from you."

Simon touched James' arm, bringing a worried glance in response.

"You may not know this, Rabbi, but we have been in Jerusalem on other occasions. Jesus has visited the temple without revealing his presence widely. He has even done some limited teaching—before very small and carefully chosen groups put together by several of his followers here. Each time I asked if he intended to call upon you, or if he would like me to fetch you to him. Each time he said no. I think he respects the sensitivity of your position among the rabbis."

This explained a few secondhand accounts of people meeting Jesus when James questioned whether it was likely they had left the city. Concern for the family might also be the reason behind that awkward reception in the synagogue of which Josis had spoken.

Simon was eager to be on his way. Jesus wanted to revisit the spot across the Jordan where he received the baptism of John. It was a long walk. Simon and James lingered for a moment.

"Simon, please tell my brother that I appreciate his concern for me."

"I will, Rabbi."

"I suspect he is over-worried. But for the time being, I will not press myself upon him. In that case, however...I would ask you to convey a piece of information to him."

"Of course."

"There is reason to believe that the priests council is eager to accuse Jesus of trying to turn his followers away from the temple." James gave the fisherman a quick summary of what Joseph of Arimathea had said about the treasury deficit and the decline in sacrificial giving, then: "If there is any way for him to make plain in his preaching that he does not disparage sacrifice— He *doesn't*, does he?"

"Of course not," said Simon. "Jesus cherishes the temple. Whenever we come, we recite the psalm—*My zeal for your house consumes me.*"

"Then perhaps he might do something that makes his reverence for the temple more explicit. Something that would pacify the priests."

"I will speak with him about it, Rabbi."

"Please, Simon...make him understand that this is important. I know he has encountered challenges and resistance in Galilee and other parts. But in Jerusalem the criticism will be much more intense. He must appreciate that there is more at stake here."

"Yes, Rabbi. I will tell him."

And with that, they parted to warm farewells.

CHAPTER THIRTY-FOUR

My enemies whisper together against me;
they imagine the worst for me.

(Psalm 41)

W inter passed without any notable disruption of normal life in Jerusalem. There was occasional news of blood spilled around the country by Zealots—much of it Jewish blood—and of legion responses to the offensive acts. Interest in Jesus remained high. People wondered when he would finally hold one of his meetings within the city walls, a step which his supporters felt would have great symbolic significance for the future of the movement. Instead, he persisted in going from small town to small town.

He preached primarily in Peraea, east of the Jordan, though it was said he had also gone into Idumea and even all the way west to Philistia. This fueled speculation about when he intended to make his entry into Jerusalem. Occasionally he was sighted on the Mount of Olives, a triple-peaked ridge overlooking the city, covered with tombs, gardens, olive groves, and a few elegant villas. But the nearest he ever came to stay was Bethany, and he maintained a very discreet presence when he was there.

During this time, Pilate occupied himself with the general run of administrative tasks involved in governing, but two projects made particular claims upon his interest. One was the design of a series of ornamental shields, each of which bore a message from Tiberius noting some feature of the province upon which the Augustus pronounced his blessing. Pilate and his wife had composed these legends in response to the emperor's instructions about demonstrating his high regard for the Jews. They had obtained approval of the wording from Rome.

The shields were being fabricated at the arsenal in Caesarea, with expertly hammered gold surfaces and Tiberius' sentiments rendered in Greek, Latin and Hebrew. Naturally, each included a small annotation that these tokens had been dedicated during the tenure of Pontius Pilate. The unveiling would take place before a carefully selected group of Jewish leaders at a special ceremony held on the grounds of the prefecture in Jerusalem. While the shields were intended to signify Roman goodwill, Pilate saw too many risks in an open event before a crowd of volatile Jews. The invited guests—prominent men of authority and respect—would be relied upon to make the people aware of Caesar's magnanimous gesture.

The other activity that engaged the prefect's mind was stalking the Zealot commander, Jesus bar Abbas. Information from the tax farmers and their minions was beginning to reveal certain patterns. A number of houses around Judea had been identified as possible hiding places for bar Abbas. It seemed he kept on the move. Individuals suspected of providing aid to the Zealots—possibly, to bar Abbas himself—had also been identified. Pilate and his officers were laying plans to spring their trap, though conditions were not quite ripe. Soon, however, very soon.

For James, the winter months were a time of reflection on the ceaseless chatter about his brother. Everything Jesus was doing, which provided the substance of that talk, affirmed a persistent feeling that the mission was headed toward some kind of climax. If so, the questions that had hung over the family for so many years might soon be resolved—for better or for worse.

And thus things proceeded into the warmer season, when farmers were making their plans to sow once more and everyone set their minds to the upcoming Passover. One afternoon, some days before the festival was to begin, James received a young boy who bore a message from Joseph of Arimathea. There was urgent news of Jesus—so urgent that James must come to the storehouse at the caravan station as soon as convenient. *Our leaders are taking steps,* Joseph wrote cryptically.

James hurried out, following the boy, who retraced the route he had just come. They arrived at the storehouse, outside the city walls, where Joseph was conferring with the master of a pack train being readied. He spotted James and held up a pointed finger as a signal to wait. When he finished giving his instructions, he came to James and led him through a tangle of camels and stacked bundles to a grove beyond the paddock where the beasts were harnessed and loaded.

"It seems a strategy has been decided upon to meet the threat of your brother," Joseph said in an agitated manner that showed he was worried.

"What is being done?"

"I chanced upon one of the Levites who had asked me to speak with you all those weeks ago. He inquired as to whether you talked to your brother as requested, because it didn't seem that Jesus had added anything to his preaching about the temple—at least nothing that sounded like a plea for more giving. Apparently, revenues are still down, and the priests are very disappointed. I told him that you and I discussed Jesus, and you agreed that you would advise him. I said no more than *advise*. You are committed to nothing."

James nodded.

"The Levite started to laugh, which certainly piqued my curiosity. When I inquired as to what was so funny, he told me—and in a very snide way—that there may be less to worry about with this *Nazarene fraud* than they thought. That is the expression he used, *Nazarene fraud*. He is a smug little *mamzer*, that one.

"So I asked what he meant, and he said a story was circulating that Jesus had several women in his retinue, and one in particular was a known harlot. The women had apparently come all the way from Galilee, which could only suggest one thing about this *so-called prophet*. I asked him who was spreading the stories. He laughed again. That was all he did—just laugh. So I knew."

Joseph's face took on a deep scowl. "It is obvious that this is how they intend to discredit your brother," he said.

"The tongue is like a fire," said James. "It can set a heap of wood ablaze, and soon the flames are beyond control. These slanderers had best be careful, or else it may burn them." He turned away, shaking his head slowly. "But...I should have expected that such an idea would suggest itself."

"What do you mean?"

James' eyes were staring off in the direction of the camels. "My brother has helped many people of dubious backgrounds to leave their sins behind, which is something I think is often misunderstood. One of Gamaliel's students commented to me on the *disreputable* types who attach themselves to Jesus."

"Your brother inspires people to seek virtue," Joseph said. "A good thing."

"But it doesn't necessarily *look* like a good thing," said James, facing Joseph again. "It wouldn't be hard to impugn Jesus for the failings of those around him or to misrepresent his most innocent associations."

"James, you must warn him. It is despicable that they would be hatching so vicious a plot. I tell you, they are afraid of Jesus."

"I will go to Bethany."

"Bethany?"

"Jesus is staying there."

"Oh, yes...I had heard that. Well, if any women *are* among his group, tell him he must send them away. There should be no hint of scandal."

James agreed, and departing said he would let Joseph know how Jesus responds to his cautionary words.

It had been arranged that a man was coming to seek counsel later that day in the Synagogue at the Crossed Streets, so James returned home. Also, Asher was due to pick up correspondence in need of delivery. It would be a simple matter to send him to Bethany to find out whether Jesus was there or off on another preaching trip.

When Asher did arrive, he came with important news of his own. "Rabbi," he said, "have you heard what Jesus did in Bethany?"

"Bethany? I was about to send you to Bethany. What happened?"

"A man died—a friend of your brother, so I'm told. Jesus was sent for while away on his travels. When he returned, he actually restored the man to life, called him from his grave. Can you imagine, Rabbi? This actually happened right in Bethany. Word is through the temple, and several people have told me of it directly. I'm convinced it's true."

"Do you know the dead man's name, by any chance?"

"I think it is...*Lazarus*."

"That is the fellow who has opened his home to Jesus' group. When did this happen?"

"Within the last day or so. But I should tell you, Rabbi, Master Gamaliel said the incident has disturbed some of the priests. I don't know why. I think it's exciting. People are praising the King of the Universe for such a miracle."

"Yes, well... It does not surprise me that the priests aren't giving praise for this miracle," said James.

He gathered up some letters for Asher to deliver, and instructed him to find the home of Lazarus and confirm that Jesus was still there. If he was, Asher was to get word to Jesus that the Rabbi James would come to speak with him.

"Tell my brother he must not leave town until we have spoken."

"Yes, Rabbi."

When James' counseling session was finished, he went to the synagogue of Gamaliel to sound out his colleague on the priests' reaction. There he prayed the evening service with Gamaliel and the students. After prayers, the two rabbis were alone. They sat in one of the gaps between posts that lined the edge of a mezzanine surrounding the meeting area, raised about a knee height above the main floor.

"It is good you came," Gamaliel said. "You need to know that your brother was discussed in the Sanhedrin today. The incident in Bethany. Are you aware of it?"

"I have heard about the incident, yes."

"Caiaphas himself was present in the council, and he spoke against Jesus by name. As I understand it, whatever your brother did in Bethany was met with great enthusiasm, but it also frightened some who witnessed it. Giving the high priest his due, he was responding to complaints about witchcraft brought to him by several people who had been on the scene and came to Jerusalem to express their fears."

"Do you think those fears were genuine?" James asked. "Or could these so-called *witnesses* be agents of the priests?"

"Who can say? But several of the priest-members on the council called for Jesus' arrest, or at the very least, his interrogation. There were even wild charges that this raising of the dead might cause the Romans to take some action."

"Complete nonsense," James said. "Pilate cares nothing about Jewish religious disputes, though he has expressed worry about large popular movements. As for witchcraft, the Romans love their auguries and magicians."

"I agree," said Gamaliel. "It's plain the real fear is that Jesus' act will be taken as so powerful a sign as to make him more attractive than ever. A council member even said as much. Caiaphas responded to that with a conjecture about one man dying in order to avert disaster for the whole nation. The remark was actually rather ambivalent. In a way, he seemed to be dismissing the concerns about Jesus. But at the same time, I got the impression he was taken with the idea of making a sacrifice of your brother."

"But why such a furor over this?" James asked. "Stories about Jesus raising the dead have been around for some time."

"Yes," Gamaliel said. "But true or not, those other incidents didn't happen in the Jerusalem district. Bethany is on the very doorstep of the Lord's city. I can understand why Caiaphas and the others would find this alarming."

James leaned back on his hands where he sat on the edge of the mezzanine. "So can I," he said, pondering the implications of such an act. Then, quickly, nervously, he rose to his feet and began pacing about. "Earlier today, Joseph informed me of a plan among the priests to spread salacious rumors about Jesus, in hopes of discrediting him. What you tell me now far exceeds that in its threat to my brother."

"I'm afraid so," said Gamaliel. "After this, they may not need salacious rumors."

He rose from the mezzanine and went over to where his friend was pacing. "You know, James," he said, "there is something in all of this which you should consider."

James stopped and looked at his fellow rabbi.

"I do think," Gamaliel said, "that the reaction of Caiaphas and the others to these wondrous things Jesus does may be more extreme than is warranted. But the questions they ask about your brother are not without merit."

"Surely you don't defend—"

"I do not defend their preoccupation with his movement's effect on the temple treasury," Gamaliel said firmly. "And I surely cannot justify the petty viciousness of spreading rumors. One would think such a base tactic beneath our exalted leaders. But there is an essential concern here, and it is valid."

Gamaliel observed a tightening of James' expression. He knew that his friend's first instinct would be to defend a brother, so he took care to frame his thoughts precisely.

"The temple is the center of Jewish life," he said. "And yet, there have been times when we had no temple. There was no temple in Babylon where so many of our forebears were carried off. Even today, while the temple stands in Jerusalem, tens of thousands of Jews living in the Dispersion will never see it. And—who is to say—it could again be that the temple is taken from us, or we from the temple—may the Holy One protect us from such a time."

"What is your point?"

"Patience, my friend," said Gamaliel. "We are rabbis, and it requires effort to unfold all the many layers of our reasoning."

A fleeting smile from James at this truth he knew well.

"Whether or not we have had the temple," Gamaliel went on, "we have been Jews. We have survived. Specifically, we have survived *as a people*. We survived in Babylon. We survived the depredations of the Greeks and the Romans. We even survived Herod. *How* did we survive? By *being* Jews. By doing the things Jews do—keeping the Law, praying the services, honoring the Sabbath. Now your brother comes to us, inserting himself into the center of our Jewish life."

"Jesus defends the Law," James said. "He exhorts us to live righteously and to serve the Lord, as all the prophets have done."

"Yes, but he does it in a way that is very different from the prophets. He calls us to...*himself*. The whole focus of his ministry, as I have observed it, is himself. *His* words. *His* example. *His* promises. *His* very being."

James thought about Noah's account of Jesus insisting others must consume him, body and blood. But he said, "People respond to the message."

"Oh, no doubt people respond. People respond everywhere he goes, and with elation. What he says has strong appeal. He speaks to people's hearts. He stirs many deep human longings, for love, for brotherhood, for decency, for forgiveness. He touches all of this, and he does it powerfully. But a question remains: By what authority does he do it? By what authority? You and I have discussed the matter before. And behind all the priestly fuss and bluster, it is this same question Caiaphas and the others are raising."

"And let us go one step further, James," Gamaliel said. "If we choose to follow the path Jesus lays out for us...if we fasten ourselves onto him...if living as Jews becomes less important to us than living by *his* words and *his* example and *his* promises...are we still Jews?"

James' hands were open in front of his body as if he was about to make an urgent, heartfelt argument. Then they dropped to his sides, and he stood limply in the center of the meeting floor. He had no answer for this colleague, this mentor, this man of wisdom who had done so much to help shape his thinking and set the direction of his life.

Gamaliel reached out and laid a hand on his shoulder. "James," he said quietly, earnestly, soberly, "I have heard many calls among the people for Jesus to bring his ministry to the city. I think it would be better if he absented himself from the region for a while. Might you suggest to him that he return to Galilee?"

"Yes," James said, "I intend to do just that."

"And quickly, James. Quickly."

*   *   *

Back in the stone hut, later that evening, James was unable to concentrate on his correspondence, and equally unable to rest. He stepped out into the court and tried praying, but found his anxiety intruding on this as well. He settled on just gazing up into the heavens trying to grasp some sense of the Holy One's presence and comfort.

His reverie was interrupted by the sound of the front gate opening. It was Asher back from his deliveries and his trip to Bethany.

"Rabbi," the young man said, "I have come from Jesus."

"He was at the house of Lazarus, then?"

"Yes, though I had to wait for him to return from preaching. He said he will speak with you tomorrow."

James nodded. "I will go to him."

*   *   *

The next morning's early rising was facilitated by the unease with which James passed the night. His sleep had been fitful and erratic, and the morning found him praying with his head fogged and his phylacteries applied sloppily. Breaking his fast helped him achieve some measure of alertness, however, and he set out for Bethany, leaving the city through the Water Gate by the Pool of Siloam.

A typical array of invalids and sufferers had begun to accumulate, seeking the healing effects attributed to the water when stirred up. It occurred to James how many people there were who could benefit from his brother's healing touch. Little wonder Jesus was the focus of high hopes.

Tomorrow was Sabbath, so the road was busy with market traffic, both vendors and buyers, headed for the city. Business would be more brisk than usual with Passover only a week away. James wondered if anyone from the family might appear at his door for the festival. His relatives knew they could always count on comfort and hospitality in his house, but whether anyone availed themselves of it depended on the demands of business back in Nazareth.

The spring morning was warm by the time James reached Bethany—unseasonably so. He followed the directions Asher had provided to the house of Lazarus, a single-story, mud-brick residence set in a yard ringed by garden beds and a low wall. Several women sat under a shade roof extending out from the house, busy at meal grinding, wool carding and other domestic tasks.

Recognizing one of them immediately, James broke into a hearty laugh, and called out across the wall, "Mary!"

She looked up and spotted him— "James!" —then set her task aside and came to him.

"So you are one of the suspicious women who follow Jesus. *His mother.*"

"What?" She was perplexed by the remark.

"I will explain, Mary. I will explain. Peace be upon you."

"And you, James. Come in." She pulled open the gate for him.

Touching the scroll of the commandment set in a post, he entered and followed her to the sheltered porch where four other women sat. There, Mary introduced the Rabbi James to Mary and Martha, sisters of Lazarus, another Mary, from Magdala, near Tiberius on the shore of Gennesaret, who had come down with her to Bethany, and an old woman, also named Mary, whom James dimly recognized.

"Do you know me, child?" the old woman asked.

James stared at her, trying to connect a face with a vague memory.

"I am your aunt," she said, chuckling cheerfully, "wife of your father's brother, Cleophas. I haven't seen you since you were a boy. And now, a famous rabbi."

"Aunt Mary—of course. I thought you were in Alexandria."

"I returned to our home city of Bethlehem when your uncle died. I wished to end my days in our promised land."

"Your aunt heard that Jesus was staying here," Mary explained, "She came to see him."

"My aching bones needed a healing touch," said Aunt Mary. "I was getting around pretty well, for my age. But since he laid his hands on me, I do even better. A wonder, your brother."

Mary leaned down and embraced the old woman where she sat combing a bunch of wool. "Aunt Mary is staying with us for Passover. We have shared delightful reminiscences of our days together in Egypt."

"Such a sweet child Jesus was," Aunt Mary said. "And today—a prophet of God." She held up her hands, wiggling all ten fingers vigorously. "He has loosened these old joints. Thirty years younger I feel. A wonder. So...we have a rabbi and a prophet. Such a family!"

James laughed. "Where *is* our prophet?"

"Jesus and the others have gone up to the Mount of Olives to pray," Mary said. "There is a garden there, surrounded by thick groves. It provides some blessed seclusion. He is constantly besieged by people seeking healing or words of guidance. Now and then he must draw away, to find a few minutes' respite. But he knows you were to come today, and he will be back."

A number of people milling about in the street, eying the house attested to this onslaught with which his brother had to bear.

"But James," she said, "what did you mean by *suspicious women?*"

James laughed again. "There are those who have an interest in dissuading people from flocking around Jesus," he said.

"I am well aware of *that*," said Mary, "too well aware."

"It seems that some of them feel no compunction about spreading stories that cast Jesus' morals into question. They are claiming he associates with fallen women—one, in particular, whom it is said has an extremely blighted character."

The sound of a throat being cleared. "That would be me, Rabbi," said the woman from Magdala.

Mary turned to her and admonished her sharply. "Don't say that. You were ill-used, and we all know it." Then she faced James again. "Mary of Magdala is a woman who was wronged in many ways and has been the subject of cruel gossip. Jesus helped her to free herself from a hard and bitter life."

"Your son *saved* my life."

James inclined his head toward the woman in what was almost a bow. "I am pleased to hear about another of Jesus' good works. But I fear the gossip continues."

"Well, I am Jesus' mother," said Mary. "This woman is my friend, and she has been a true servant of my son's ministry. Let those with wicked tongues make of that what they will."

"Ah, Mary," James said, "still as good-hearted and loyal as ever." He addressed the others. "This is the slip of a girl who won the respect of a household full of very stubborn and resistant women. *Nazareth* women, the toughest there are."

"Bah!" Mary said, waving a dismissive hand.

"But tell me, Mary," he said, "why are you here? Have you come for Passover?"

"Jesus asked me to, and arranged for my conveyance. He contacted Mary—"

Aunt Mary interrupted. "There are too many Marys under this roof," she said. "How can the rabbi keep us all straight? It is very confusing."

Everyone laughed.

"Well, the son of Mary from Nazareth...*me*...contacted Mary from Magdala...*her*...who arranged with some of the other disciples there to accompany...*me*. They were planning to celebrate Passover in Jerusalem anyway. So they came to Nazareth to deliver Jesus' invitation, and now here we are, staying with Martha and...*Mary*...in Bethany."

"And after all that," Aunt Mary said, "another Mary shows up—*me*."

More laughter, with James shaking his head in amusement.

"What of my brothers and nephews?" he asked. "Did anyone else from the family come along? And how is everyone in the household, anyway?"

"All are well," she said. "Noah is a father now."

"Ah, the baby has arrived."

"A fine boy."

"Praise to the Holy One."

"But..." Mary took James and turned him away from the others. She spoke more seriously. "Jesus made it clear that, of all his relatives, he wished only me to come. Only his mother."

"Again he distances himself from the family."

"More than ever."

"Josis advised me of this."

"I know."

A noise beyond the wall drew their attention. People in the street—by now a small crowd—were stirred to interest at the arrival of a group of men. It was Jesus and his companions.

James could hear many crying out in supplication, "Lord, Lord, Lord..." As a tide of bodies engulfed his brother, Jesus pronounced a blessing over the crowd, assuring the people that he would attend to their needs individually. But then he begged their indulgence. It was necessary for him to speak with someone here. He would return to them in a few minutes. The crowd accepted his promise, parting to let him pass. He came through the gate into the yard, leaving his apostles to gather the people and lead them in prayer.

"Peace be upon you, James," said Jesus.

"Peace to you, Brother."

James refrained from trying to embrace him, in mind of the temple court and the reserve he had encountered at their meeting there. Jesus greeted his mother and the other women, then extended a hand to James as an invitation to join him inside the house. James followed.

The room was cool, illuminated only by a bank of three small windows in the wall opposite the direction of the morning sun. The contrast was such that James' eyes took a few seconds to adjust. Jesus seated himself on a bench that ran the length of a long table in the center of the floor. James could see that he was praying, so he stood and waited. Finally Jesus glanced up at his brother. He gestured to the bench, and James sat beside him.

"You have the look of one who worries, Brother," Jesus said. "Are your worries about me?"

"Yes, Jesus, they are." James shifted, drawing one leg up on the bench to face his brother more directly. He had resolved during his walk to Bethany that he would waste no time easing into difficult topics. Jesus needed to know the situation as it existed, and he needed to hear these facts unvarnished. "I am informed that the Sanhedrin has discussed the...incident...here."

"Ah, yes," Jesus said. "Lazarus, my dear friend, and our host. He was a follower of John, and he became one of our earliest supporters. Lazarus has gone away for the present. There has been some talk that his life is in danger."

"In danger? Why?"

"Because I raised him. He is living proof of the power of God's love. His sisters were concerned for him, so he has gone. For awhile."

"Was he really dead?"

"Four days, by the time I arrived."

James took a deep breath. Such a simple confirmation of such an incredible event. But this was Jesus, his brother, the center of so much that remained inexplicable in the family's history.

"His sisters may have reason to worry," James said. "What you did here has caused much consternation in Jerusalem."

Jesus nodded.

"I believe *you* are in danger as well, Brother."

Another nod.

"The priests see your ministry as a threat," James said. "These miraculous acts of yours—they suspect the motives behind them. I imagine that the possibility of outright deception has crossed their minds, too. Either way, they feel you are diverting people from true worship. Some even fear your movement will prompt intervention by the Romans."

Jesus smiled. "I recall that, when we spoke near Caesarea-Philippi, you warned me about Pilate."

"Their concern about the Romans is unfounded," said James. "Pilate is satisfied that you are not organizing any resistance to the empire. But the danger you face from our own leaders is real. What are your plans, Brother? Do you intend to bring your ministry into the city?"

A pause, and then: "That has been my intention."

"I recommend against it," said James. "In fact, I urge you to leave

these parts. And the sooner the better. Go across the Jordan into Peraea. Or return to Galilee. You have already been denounced in the
Sanhedrin. If you try to set up in Jerusalem—or even if you remain
here in Bethany—I expect you will be arrested."

"Do I trouble them so, Brother?"

"They see in your teaching and your approach to the Sabbath a
specter of dangerous novelty. And the size of your following terrifies
them. They worry that you are leading people away from the temple,
and that this will cause loss of the temple's support."

"James, you know the temple is my Father's house."

An image came to James' mind of that precocious twelve-year-old
expounding before the doctors of the Law—and of two parents, perplexed and exasperated after searching for him.

"Yes, Jesus, I do know that," he said. "I know that you have never
spoken against the temple, and that you never would. But even so, you
show people a way of living—a way of believing—that is different from
what the priests offer them. The priests offer sacrifice, and they dread
the thought that Jews might cease laying their souls before the King of
the Universe in the form of burnt offerings on an altar. It didn't begin
with you, Brother. Religion is changing. Jewish life is changing. The
influence of the Greeks has been working on us for some time, and
that's only one source of change. But your followers see in you a clear
and definite alternative—*so* clear and definite that it poses a challenge.
That challenge is the source of danger to you."

Yet another nod from Jesus.

"Go back to Galilee, Brother," James said. "Build your movement,
spread your influence. I believe you have much to teach the Jewish nation, much to offer the people you and I both love. Take your time and
become strong. Lay so broad a base of support that no one will be able
to stop you."

James leaned forward, his eyes drilling into his brother's, his hands
gripping the edges of the bench. "You do not have such strength now,
Jesus. If you move into Jerusalem now, they will crush you. All you have
worked for will be swept away."

There was no response at all from Jesus. His gaze dissolved into a
blank stare over James' shoulder in the general direction of the three
small windows.

"Please, Brother," James implored him, "listen to me."

Jesus' eyes gently closed. He was praying again, immersed in a communion of which James could not be part. Seconds passed, James bearing the increasing weight of his brother's extended silence. He could hear his own breath. He could feel his own pulse. Then a sensation of chill fluttered across his shoulders, and his body shivered inside his robes. And somewhere in the depth of his being, he came to know the black agony of realizing that his words would not be heeded—and of comprehending what that meant. A crisis lay before them, and Jesus would do nothing to avoid it.

"Simon told me you expect to die in Jerusalem."

Jesus stirred, and his attention returned to his brother. He still said nothing, but his eyes were open now, moist with sorrow. James looked into those sad eyes and nodded his head slowly. He rose and started for the door, then paused when Jesus spoke to him at last.

"It is ordained, Brother. The Son of Man must die and be raised again. It is my Father's will."

Without turning around, James said, "Is it your mother's will?"

*   *   *

James regretted the remark almost immediately. It had been pointless and petty, even childish, a sting to one sibling from another. If Jesus was convinced he was doing the will of the Holy One, the wishes of his mother would not dissuade him, no matter how much he loved her.

For three years he had conducted his ministry, leaving home and family to wander from town to town, living very much in a manner set out in tales James had heard about the holy beggars in the east, those ragged men of the forests who carried their rice bowls and prayed to a thousand gods. Surely to take up such a life of faith demonstrated single-mindedness.

James did *not* regret giving Mary a compassionate and highly visible embrace, even if it shocked the other women and all the people standing in the street beyond the low wall. He understood now why Jesus had wanted her with him at this time, and he ached for what she might have to endure if the priests moved against her son, as seemed inevitable.

But mostly, James was heartsick at the thought that he was failing in the promise he had made to his father, Joseph. He was failing at being his brother's keeper. Jesus would do what he felt called to do, regardless of any entreaties. Did James have power to shield him from the consequences, or to minimize their impact? He doubted it.

What he did have was a library, in the Synagogue at the Crossed Streets. It was extensive, consisting of the collection that had come to Joseph of Arimathea with the purchase of Zacharias' villa in Ein Karem. Joseph had given the papyri, scrolls and manuscripts to James so that scholarly use would be made of them. James added to his holdings over the years, and made these materials available to Gamaliel and the students.

Sabbath was spent in an examination of writings from the Prophet Isaiah, particularly the dissertation on the Lord's *servant*. Study of the holy books was permitted on Sabbath—indeed, encouraged—but James realized that reading the prophets for a purpose other than pure knowledge or spiritual insight came very close to work, stretching the rule. So be it. This was a matter of urgent necessity, and human need overrode the Sabbath.

James concentrated on Isaiah's depiction of how the servant would suffer. There seemed a rough parallel here. Perhaps Jesus saw himself in this role. If so, James hoped there might be something in the book to demonstrate that it would be wrong to intentionally seek such a fate. But after poring over the text and shaving its finest points in his most rabbinical way, he had to admit he'd found nothing that might sway his brother. If Jesus was bent on self-sacrifice, Isaiah's portrait of the suffering servant would probably encourage him.

So James was left with the thought that, if it came to Jesus being brought before the Sanhedrin, he could at least ask to speak in his brother's defense. And though James wasn't, himself, a member, there were several distinguished counselors he could count on to do likewise, among them Joseph and Gamaliel. Then too, there might actually be *many* willing to defend Jesus. The *Nazarene* was enormously popular. Some rabbis, even some priests and Levites, might see a benefit in standing up for him—those who weren't strongly indebted to the temple leadership.

Which prompted an ironic thought. Might it be possible to find support among the Sadducee faction? Surely they took pleasure in Jesus' harsh criticisms of the Pharisees. And since they concentrated so intensely on fulfilling the ritual demands of the here and now, rejecting even the idea of an afterlife, they would care little for speculations about what he meant by the *coming of the Kingdom*.

It was an unlikely prospect, however, and James' musings on it didn't last long. The fact was, Sadducees constituted a majority in the priesthood. They were the ones most affected by any threat which Jesus' movement posed to the temple and its solvency. There would be little incentive to even give him a fair hearing, much less spring to his defense.

The one factor in this situation which James saw as an advantage was Pilate. If the priests so feared Jesus that they would charge him with blasphemy—a capital crime—they would have to take him before the prefect. Rome reserved for itself the power to execute. Even the highest authority in a province under direct imperial administration had to make its case for death to Caesar's vicar.

Now, it was true that extra-judicial killings did sometimes take place. Most common were the more-or-less-spontaneous stonings that occurred in the countryside and the villages for such offenses as adultery or blasphemy. The Romans tried to suppress the practice, which had it roots deep in Jewish tradition. But whether or not those who carried them out would be prosecuted depended on highly variable legion resources.

In the cities, where Roman police power was concentrated, it was a different matter. If Jesus was tried, found guilty, and sentenced to death in Jerusalem, he would ultimately stand before the prefect. And there, the relationship between James and Pilate might possibly make a difference. This in mind, James was pleased that he would soon have another opportunity to be in the prefect's company. He had been invited to the unveiling of a collection of imperial tokens dedicated to the Jewish nation. The event was scheduled for the very next day.

CHAPTER THIRTY-FIVE

The multitude said, "This is the prophet,
Jesus, from Nazareth of Galilee."

(Matthew 21)

Pilate was beaming. James wondered if the six objects set up on stands along one wall of the prefecture court and covered with linen sheets could be the cause of such overt good cheer. He watched this broad, powerfully built man, who represented Caesar in Judea, pick his way glowingly among the guests.

Aided by an officer who was fluent in Aramaic, the prefect made pleasant chatter with priests, Levites and scribes, most of them members of the Sanhedrin. These were the leading men of a nation that, at this moment, seemed to James very small, almost inconsequential, compared with the mightiest empire the world had ever known.

Only Caiaphas, among the temple elite, had sent regrets at not being able to attend. The high priest needed to seclude himself in preparation for the observance of Passover, he wrote in response to the invitation. It was a most transparent bit of nonsense. The truth was that feelings in some quarters were still sensitive over Caiaphas' secret dealings with Pilate on the aqueduct and he judged it wise to keep his distance. The prefect understood.

Pilate finally came to James, a look of genuine pleasure in his face. "Rabbi," he said. "I am delighted you could join us. Thank you for taking time from your many important tasks."

"Peace be upon you, Prefect," said James. "I am pleased to hear small snatches of Aramaic from you as you welcome your guests."

"Languages have never been my strength," Pilate said. "Certainly, I am no scholar like you. But the tongue of your people is so colorful, and this day is so special, I have done my best to master a few simple phrases. I'm glad my humble efforts please you."

James had to smile. Pilate was working so hard at being gracious. "What makes the day special, Prefect?"

"*That* you will know in a little while," he said with a twinkle.

There were several more dignitaries to be greeted. Then the prefect stepped onto a raised platform to address the group as a whole, his words translated by the officer. After a few formulary welcoming remarks, offered on behalf of Caesar as well as himself, followed by good wishes for the upcoming holy time of Passover, he took a dramatic pause.

Pilate surveyed his audience with a look that blended gravity and satisfaction. "Honored leaders of the nation," he said. "Eager as I am to present the tokens which our beloved Augustus has commissioned to express his respect for the Jewish people, there is important news bearing on the welfare of your community."

He had the attention of all. One could never be sure how Rome interpreted Jewish welfare.

"It is my honor to announce that Caesar's legions have captured the bandit, bar Abbas, chief of the Zealot renegade forces, on whose hands is much blood, both Roman and Jewish."

Suspended breathing. Not a sound from the crowd.

"We also have in our possession two of his henchmen and a large cache of weaponry stolen from various military supply depots. A number of other bandits and several individuals known to be providing aid to the rebel gang were killed."

None of his listeners was quite sure how to respond. The Zealots brought great disturbance to Jewish life, and the blood of many Jews had indeed been paid to their cause, willingly or otherwise. At the same time, these rebels did enjoy a certain recognition as patriots. No Jew here in the prefecture court could be sure how the man standing next to him really felt about Zealotry, or as it was often called, the *Fourth Philosophy* of Judaism (the other three being Pharisaism, Sadduceeism and Essenism).

Pilate's relish was not going to be dampened by the open mouths and empty eyes before him. He pressed on with details of the operation, which took place near Herod's old summer palace at Masada. The careful gathering of suggestive facts, combined with dogged tracking of Zealot movements, had identified a hidden lair used by bar Abbas in the hills overlooking the Salt Sea. Three crack auxiliary units had converged stealthily, assaulting the hideaway in the middle of the night. Bar Abbas and the other two captured rebels had been brought to Jerusalem, and were now being held in the Antonia Fortress.

The awkward silence that followed Pilate's announcement finally gave way to a few reserved congratulations. Muted as the reaction was, Pilate knew there would be some present who were deeply—if privately—relieved to hear that these infamous murderers were in Roman hands. He did not expect such sentiments to be expressed openly, and he moved on to the actual subject of the day's event.

"But now, my distinguished guests, we have come together for a more refined and exalted purpose. On the direct instruction of Tiberius Augustus, I have had rendered a series of beautifully gilded memorial shields, each of which expresses Caesar's pride in a particular feature of your ancient and noble land."

James laughed inwardly at how thickly Pilate was laying on the flattery. He must have received strong pressure from Rome to make this elaborate show. Or else, maybe ingratiating himself with the Jews was key to some secret plan for advancement. A better post beckoning?

"The Jewish people occupy a place of special warmth and fondness in Caesar's heart. He considers your nation, with its rich heritage reaching back beyond the days of Solomon and David, a vital link in the great chain of empire."

At a signal from Pilate, a line of six guards saluted. Each man then stepped smartly to one of the stands, grasping its linen covering. A second signal, and the sheets were pulled away. The burnished gold facings of the shields glistened with such brilliance in the morning sun that the onlookers had to cover their eyes. Several distinct gasps were heard. All of which was exactly the effect Pilate had hoped for.

"Each shield has been designed in a heraldic shape signifying one of the legions that has served in Palestine," Pilate explained. "As you can see, each bears a message from Caesar. They will be mounted along the wall of the prefecture facing the public plaza—a permanent reminder of Caesar's respect and admiration. Feel free to examine them at your leisure."

Everyone was duly impressed, and also—after the announcement about bar Abbas—pleased to have something for which they could applaud heartily. Loud, extended clapping broke out. The prefect smiled and glanced up at a balconied window on the top level of Herod's old residence. He was clearly enjoying himself. James followed the line of his gaze upward. A woman stood in the window, watching the proceedings with a broad smile of her own.

Since Procula had coauthored the inscriptions, she insisted on accompanying her husband to Jerusalem for the unveiling. It was her expectation that she would mingle with the guests, basking in the excitement of the event, and enjoying some adulation as the prefect's wife. Her husband explained to her sadly that, in a truly civilized country, that would be an entirely natural thing to do. But this being Jerusalem, and Jews being Jews, she would have to content herself with observing from above. She was not pleased with that situation, but she nonetheless enjoyed the reaction of the crowd.

Pilate stepped down from the platform as the guests swarmed to view the shields up close. He came to James.

"There, Rabbi," he said, "I told you it was a special day."

"So you did, Prefect—a day of triumph for you, on several counts."

James was pleased that Pilate sought him out as someone to whom he could speak with ease. That might prove important, should his brother be brought before the bar of Roman justice.

As they chatted, James' attention was drawn to a growing murmur among those inspecting the shields. There was much agitated pointing at the messages from Caesar and shocked expressions on flushed faces. The readers were unmistakably upset. Then the crowd moved away from the row of stands and regrouped in a corner of the court. Pilate noticed this marked change. He and James exchanged glances, neither able to fathom what was going on.

Gamaliel, who had also been invited to the unveiling, came out from among the Jewish guests now conferring quite animatedly among themselves. He approached Pilate uneasily, having been deputized for the task by the others because of his proficiency in Greek.

"Prefect... Rabbi..."

James knew Pilate was acquainted with Gamaliel and had already welcomed him to the event, so introductions weren't necessary. "What is wrong, Master Gamaliel?" he asked.

"Begging the Prefect's pardon," said Gamaliel deferentially. "There is some concern about Caesar's messages."

"Caesar's messages?" said Pilate, taken aback. "What is wrong with Caesar's messages?" He looked at the shields, then at Gamaliel. "They compliment your people profusely. One of them recognizes the essential role played by Judea as a center of trade and commerce."

The prefect was, perhaps, a bit too defensive. But pride of authorship inclined him to justify the effort he and his wife had put into crafting the inscriptions. "Another message notes the piety of the Jewish people. These words were framed with the utmost care and sincerity. They express the emperor's most heartfelt wishes. I don't see how they could cause any concern."

Gamaliel glanced at James, then over his shoulder at the huddled group. Finally he attempted to make the nuances of Jewish conviction understandable to a man born into a profoundly different culture.

"You see...Prefect," he said reluctantly, "each message begins with the phrase...*The Divine Tiberius.*"

James flinched.

Pilate was confused. "That is the customary title. It's how everyone in the empire refers to Caesar."

"Not quite everyone, Prefect," said Gamaliel.

What Jewish eccentricity was this that objected to such common parlance? A title was merely form, its use a simple courtesy. Pilate felt complete dismay, then anger, then a pressure building within himself he was unable to contain. Unmindful of Gamaliel's ritual purity, he grabbed his arm, dragged him to one of the stands, and pointed to the shield it bore. James hurried after.

"There," the prefect said in disbelief, "read that: *The Divine Tiberius expresses his love for the great beauty and variety of the Judean landscape, its broad vistas, its pleasant climate, its verdancy and abundance.* What could possibly be wrong with that?"

"Yes, the sentiments are lovely," Gamaliel said, "and very much appreciated, you may be sure, Prefect. But referring to Caesar as *The Divine Tiberius* ascribes to him the status and virtues of the Holy One."

Pilate felt himself totally at sea. "No one asks you to worship Caesar," he said, stunned. "Jewish reservations on that point are too well known."

"Nevertheless, Prefect," Gamaliel said, "to display such an appellation publicly would be unacceptable to Jews."

Pilate's eyes widened, and a heavy moment descended. A redness came into his face, beginning at the throat and rising to the top of his head.

"*Jews?*" he fumed. "Unacceptable to *Jews?* What other indignities must I bear for Jews? I took great pains to avoid a repeat of the controversy over Caesar's image. There are no images at all on these shields, only words—and beautiful words at that. I built you an aqueduct to make life better in your sacred city, and all I've gotten for my troubles are violence and resentment. No wonder your own Scripture calls you *a stiff-necked people.*"

James tried to inject a note of calm and clarity. "Prefect, perhaps I can explain—"

"Thank you, Rabbi," Pilate cut him off sharply. "You have been my honest advisor, and I am grateful for that. But right now I will hear no more explanations about the sensitivities of Jews." He turned and stormed off toward the stairway leading up into the praetorium, calling to the guards, "Cover the shields."

James and Gamaliel were left standing alone, looking dumbly at each other. Pilate's wife gazed down from the window, perplexed. The guards replaced the linen sheets.

* * *

James walked with Gamaliel back to his synagogue where the students were conducting their own discussion in the absence of their teacher.

"Do you think you can calm Pilate's anger?" Gamaliel asked his colleague as they approached the front door. "He does seem to value your insights."

"I've been fortunate to have his ear," James said with a shrug.

"Let us hope that continues."

"I *do* hope," James said. "But whether it does— Well, we shall see."

They parted, Gamaliel heading to the ritual bath to restore his purity, and James descending the steps beside the bridge leading over to the temple mount. He came down into the Tyropoeon Valley. As he made his way home, he became aware of excited talk among people he passed, and then of increasing numbers heading toward the south end of the city. By the time he reached his front gate, threads of walkers were becoming a crowd.

A thought occurred that perhaps word of the golden shields had already spread and people were gathering to protest. But nobody was heading in the direction of the prefecture, which would have been the locus of such a demonstration. He stopped a man striding earnestly toward the south and asked him where everyone was going.

"Haven't you heard?" the man said. "It is the prophet, Jesus of Nazareth. He is approaching the city with a vast throng—advancing on the Water Gate. I think finally he is bringing his ministry here."

"Jesus?"

"Yes. Word came this morning. Everyone is rushing to meet him. What a wonderful day!"

*　　*　　*

The captain of the Water Gate civil guard detachment was alarmed to see such a mass of travelers coming on the road from Bethphage and Bethany. A cloud of dust billowed up from hundreds of scuffing feet, dense enough to obscure the base of the Mount of Olives. Children frolicked about, adding their laughter and squeals of delight to the growing ruckus.

More guardsmen had already been sent for, and the captain was now consulting with an officer from the Roman watch. Should they install the eye of the needle and try to slow entry into the city? The officer advised against it. This crowd appeared peaceful—happy, in fact. Why provoke joyous pilgrims? Mood could shift so quickly in Jerusalem, gaiety turning to anger at the flick of an eyebrow.

The officer had seen long service in Palestine and much Jewish peculiarity. But what strange doings were these? The crowd was paying homage to a very ordinary-looking fellow riding on a donkey colt that seemed barely able to carry his weight. Young boys were casting down cloaks and palm fronds in his path, then collecting them and running to spread them in front again as the march progressed. Meanwhile, people from inside the city were streaming out to join the crowd or finding vantage points inside the gate from which to watch the procession pass through. This was treatment due some distinguished royal personage, not a rather unimposing Jew. Who was this fellow, and why had his arrival stirred such eager interest?

James came on the scene just after Jesus entered the city. He climbed on the stoop of a house built where the street sloped upward, and so was able to see over the crowd as his brother passed before the Pool of Siloam and then under the first arch of the aqueduct after the water tower.

The neighborhood echoed with the Hebrew expression, *Hosanna*—save us. "Save us, Son of David!" people shouted, "Save us!"

By long popular usage, the phrase had come to be understood as an acclamation for a leader or hero. But taken literally, it could raise the question, *Save us from what—Rome?* Pilate would not be comforted by such a call, James thought. Would this revive the prefect's worries about Jesus trying to incite some kind of revolt?

More shouts: "Blessed is he who comes in the Lord's name!" and again, "Save us, Son of David!" over and over.

Just then, James saw that Jesus had spotted him standing on the high point. Their glances locked for a second, Jesus' face set in an expression that was quite inscrutable, half a smile, half a distant weariness. The procession moved on through the lower city.

Arrival of more civil guardsmen added to the confusion, until finally—through a variety of animated hand gestures—the captain succeeded in arranging his men along the sides of the crowd to accompany it on its way. Such a demonstration could provide opportunities for filching attractive items from the fronts of market stalls along the route or slicing scrips from the belts of distracted walkers. The presence of the guards was intended to suppress such impulses, though that became increasingly difficult as the march went on and more people joined.

There were plenty to do so, the city experiencing its annual influx of visitors for Passover. By the time Jesus and his mass of followers neared the center of Jerusalem, a mob had accumulated. Much of normal city business had ground to a halt.

Pilate was with Procula, engaged in venting his frustration over the gold shields, when the officer who had been at the Water Gate came to apprise him of this new situation.

"What has caused the disturbance?"

"It appears to be a celebration of the Jew prophet from Galilee," the officer said, "that Jesus of Nazareth whose name is everywhere. He's making a triumphal entry into the city."

"Is he, indeed?"

"I have heard of this prophet," Procula interjected. "Many people champion his cause, even in Caesarea—and not only Jews, Husband. His teachings have aroused much interest, and I'm told he is credited with miraculous healings."

"Yes," Pilate replied, "we have followed his activities closely." He addressed the officer. "Alert Longinus at the Antonia Fortress. Have him ready the garrison, but don't bring them out of the compound. I want no legion presence unless the civil guard is unable to maintain order."

"Yes, Prefect." The officer saluted, turned, and departed quickly.

*   *   *

It became apparent to James that Jesus was headed for the temple mount. And while Passover always brought masses of people into the sacred grounds, the sight of an independent preacher at the head of such a huge procession would not please the priests. To the contrary, it would be a sign of his influence among the Jewish faithful. If Jesus could lead the masses into the temple, he could lead them away.

James turned into a side street and sprinted along an alternate route, trying to get ahead of the crowd. What he would do when his brother arrived at the temple he didn't know, but he was determined to be on hand. By the time he made his way up the stairs to the Royal Porch, he was panting heavily. He found that word was already around that the Nazarene was on his way. This added to James' worry, though he wasn't sure why. No one would try to stop his brother from praying in the holy place, whatever the priests might think about it.

The student, Saul of Tarsus, was just outside the court and noticed James.

"Rabbi," he called. "Are you alright? Your face is flushed, and your robes are all soaked with sweat."

James waved a hand. "Yes, yes. I am fine. I was running—to be here when my brother comes." He paused, glancing down at himself. "I suppose I don't look very dignified at the moment. You have heard that Jesus is marching through Jerusalem?"

"Everyone has," said Saul.

"Have you seen any of the priests? What do they think of this?"

"I don't know," said Saul, "but the vendors and money changers are most excited. With such a hoard on the way, they expect business to be even more brisk than usual at Passover."

"Hmmph—they would."

A dull roar could be heard, thousands of voices in a collective murmur growing in intensity. James and Saul went across the terrace where a sizable group had assembled. Looking down from the parapet, James saw Jesus dismount his colt. The throng of followers was gathered around him, flooding the plaza at the base of the temple mount and up the street for blocks behind. He could pick out the faces of Simon and several of the others from Jesus' inner circle.

An occasional spear could be seen along the edges of this human sea, suggesting the impossible task faced by the guardsmen charged with containing all these people. The noise of the crowd had disrupted classes in session, and all along the upper level of the Royal Porch students and rabbis were taking in the strange vista.

Jesus ascended the stairs, followed by his apostles and then, at a respectful distance, by the first ranks of the crowd. When he reached the top and came to the temple gate, he saw James and smiled.

"Brother," he said.

"Welcome back to Jerusalem, Brother," James responded guardedly.

Onlookers standing about found themselves absorbed in this scene of the famous Rabbi James greeting his even more famous kinsman, the Galilean prophet, Jesus of Nazareth.

Mindful of Saul's presence, James turned to indicate his companion. "Let me introduce one of our students," he said to Jesus politely. "This is Saul, of the tribe of Benjamin, a promising scholar who comes to us from Tarsus in Celicia."

Jesus peered into the young man's eyes. "Peace be upon you, Saul of Tarsus."

Saul nodded his acknowledgement, but his inner response to this greeting was a vague unease. He did not feel the warmth or the sense of serenity reported by many others upon meeting the Nazarene, though there was nothing in Jesus' visage or the way he uttered Saul's name that should have denied him that experience.

James took note of Saul's queer expression and placed a hand on the young man's back, by which he intended to ease the anxiety now clearly evident. A thought occurred unexpectedly, James not knowing why, or from where, it had come. He leaned in close to Saul's ear.

"Perhaps you might like to share with my brother the great burden you carry," James whispered. "He may be able to help."

Startled, Saul glanced quickly at James, then at Jesus, and then back at James again. His eyes were filled with distress. Like everyone, Saul knew of the unusual powers ascribed to the Nazarene. But if he were to ask Jesus to be healed of his strange affliction, would the falling disease appear, right in public, here at the very gate of the temple? And what if it was no disease, but a demon, as Saul had always feared? Would Jesus call the evil spirit out of him in the plain sight of all present? The idea was too dreadful, too humiliating to contemplate.

Saul looked at Jesus once more, and he was suddenly overcome by a withering, unbearable, lifelong shame. Jesus returned his anxious glance with a gentle, inviting smile lighting his face and seeming to say, *Trust me.* For some seconds, his eyes rested upon the student, so gripped by fear and the horror of disgrace. Jesus waited. James watched.

Saul didn't speak, but rather backed away awkwardly. At last he said, "No...thank you, Rabbi."

Jesus nodded his head in the young man's direction, then looked back at James. "I must go," he said.

James reached out and took his brother by the hand, holding it with a marked firmness. "Go with...*care*," he said.

Again, Jesus smiled. He extracted his fingers from James' grip and moved on toward the Royal Porch. James exchanged a quick glance with Simon as the apostles proceeded after.

Squads of temple guards had, by now, positioned themselves at each of the gates, in response to the mass of people seeking to follow the Nazarene inside. It had been judged that the crowd was greater than could be accommodated within the Court of the Gentiles, which already held a considerable number of people. And since entry into other parts of the temple was restricted, effort was made to direct the flow to a single gate for admittance.

A plan was hastily improvised whereby people coming in might be kept moving along a narrow walkway across the court and out the far side. In this manner, those eager to see the prophet would have their chance without interfering with the day's sacrifices or impeding the cash exchanges and sacrificial purchases. Two lines of guards were being arranged to form a corridor into which visitors were directed. Those wandering beyond the designated path—and there were many who did so, trying to get close to Jesus—were blocked and herded back between the cordons.

Jesus was aware of this activity and mused over the futile effort to restrain these spontaneous outbursts of faith and enthusiasm. But his attention was primarily directed elsewhere. He wandered about the court observing the transactions taking place in the vendor stalls and at the tables of the money changers. Simon took note of a rising disgust in his master's face. He recalled how Jesus had expressed unhappiness with this trade on earlier temple visits.

At the stall of a dealer in lambs, Jesus bent down to retrieve some discarded lengths of rope with which animals had been tethered. Walking toward the center of the court, he unknotted and straightened the cords, arranged them in his hand, and began to braid them. Simon watched this action, which seemed so casual and pointless. But he had come to know that everything the master did had a purpose, and he was curious about what Jesus intended.

Despite the animals and the mass of people, the Court of the Gentiles had taken on an eerie quiet and was now the center of interest throughout the entire temple complex. People even left the high altar to observe the behavior of this famous visitor from Galilee with his impressive cadre of followers. Caiaphas had sent a delegation of priests to keep watch on these doings as well. They entered the court by the raised walkway that capped the colonnade running along the east wall, and descended the stairway at the far end of the Royal Porch to confer with the captain of the guard. As further seconds passed in silence, they too caught sight of the prophet's odd behavior, and wondered at the point of this inexplicable foolery with the cords.

Then Jesus took the rope braid in his two hands and, unexpectedly, jerked the ends quickly outward, creating a loud crack which, like the sound of lightening, echoed across the court. The onlookers felt a jolt of surprise, and before they realized what he was doing, Jesus raced over to one of the money-changer booths, swung the rope braid over his head like a whip, and brought it crashing down on the tabletop. The banker standing behind the table leapt back, gasping in fright as he sought to avoid being hit. Stacks of coins bounced and scattered at the impact.

Jesus next ran to a second money-changer booth and kicked over the table completely. The two bankers manning that stand scrambled about the ground on hands and knees, gathering up coins and spewing curses while Jesus hurried on to the stall where he had obtained the ropes. He pulled a bolt from the gate of a small pen, cracking his whip over the heads of the lambs inside so that the frightened animals ran out into the court, bleating loudly as they went.

All who watched were stunned.

The captain of the guard turned to the highest ranking of the priests who had come from Caiaphas. "What should I do, Master?" he asked.

The priest saw that more of Jesus' followers were pouring in through every opening, pushing the guards aside, breaking apart the cordons. These wild actions of Jesus were getting the people's blood up. Everyone was eager to see what the prophet was doing, and egging him on.

Jesus continued going from stand to stand, tearing open the pens, freeing doves from their cages, overturning more tables. The people cheered at each wild act, while some of the vendors and money changers fled from the court screaming, "Mad man! Mad man!"

In reply, Jesus hollered back, "Scripture says, *My house shall be a house of prayer*, but you have made it a den of thieves."

The court erupted into complete pandemonium, the crowd roaring its approval. How many of those present had felt gouged purchasing sacrificial animals at exorbitant prices in this tightly controlled market, or paying the money changers' outrageous fees for currency exchanges?

This frenzy caused the ranking priest to grab the guard captain by his arm. "Restore order," he shouted, "restore order now."

"I'll bring that criminal down," the captain said, throwing off the priest's grip and reaching for his sword.

"No!" cried the priest desperately. *"Don't touch the Nazarene.* We'll have a riot, and we must not spill blood in the temple."

James, who had come into the court with Saul and climbed the stairs to the upper level of the Royal Porch, was standing with the students and rabbis, watching the tumult from above.

"Father in heaven," James moaned in a near-stupor of disbelief, not realizing that he was voicing his thoughts aloud, "stop my brother. Please stop him. What is he doing? Turn him from this madness. He's attacking the temple. Caiaphas will have him killed."

Down on the floor of the court, Simon stood watching Jesus' actions, and he was filled with a similar fear. The words of the psalm came to his mind, but this time with a new and sinister meaning: *Zeal for my Father's house will consume me.*

Was this the start of the final sequence Jesus had predicted, when he would be given over into the hands of those who would take his life? The Lord had said he would die in Jerusalem.

The student, Saul, standing at James' side, was numb with rage at the spectacle below. *This* was the man Rabbi James had suggested he ask to heal his sickness? *This* was someone before whom he should humble himself and risk personal disgrace? This mocker? This vandal? He turned away from the appalling scene and made his way down the stairs to a small room off the court where he knew cleaning implements were stored. Inside, he lay down on the floor and prepared for the shaking he could feel coming on.

By now, the guards had lost control. The court was jammed with bodies. Animals ran about in panic. Waves of frightened birds flew overhead, their droppings making a sprinkle on the crowd. The walls rang with shouting, braying, bleating, squawking—every manner of uproar.

Simon went to Jesus. "Lord," he said, "let us take the opportunity of this confusion to go."

Jesus looked at his assistant, heaved a deep sigh, and let the rope braid fall from his hand. He nodded his ascent and slipped out of the court with the rest of the apostles. A handful of people followed after, begging to be healed.

From the upper level, James could see his brother depart. Then he slumped forward, arms on the parapet, head in his hands.

CHAPTER THIRTY-SIX

*"Render to Caesar the things that are Caesar's,
and to God the things that are God's."*

(Mark 12)

hy did Jesus do it? James was at a loss to understand his brother's motives. Up to this point, the ministry, as James followed it, had been generally positive in tone, focused on moral uplift and spiritual renewal primarily through charity, service to the sick, and forgiveness. It was true that many people thought Jesus presumptuous in assuming he could flout the rules of Judaism, and were quite put off by that. But if the family's expectation was correct, if Jesus was indeed the Lord's Anointed, then mightn't it be within his purview to call for reforms, both of the faith itself and of how people practiced it?

This was a question worthy of debate by the rabbis, though it was looking unlikely to James that such a debate would ever take place, at least in reference to his brother. Jesus had attacked the temple, and he would be lucky to escape with his life after such an affront.

Thinking back on the strained conversation they'd had at the house of Lazarus in Bethany, James suspected that Jesus' act in the Court of the Gentiles was anything but spontaneous. He'd sensed then that Jesus planned some kind of statement. But why this? What point could he possibly wish to make?

Was Jesus chastising the vendors and money changers for exploiting the people through inflated prices and fees? Charge them with greed as one might, the merchants and bankers did perform an important function in the temple. They facilitated sacrifice. James had been among those who opposed their installation on temple grounds at the time the proposal was put forth. But even he had to admit these services were merely measures of convenience. People were perfectly free to bring their own sacrificial animals, as well as to obtain ritually suitable coinage elsewhere before coming to the temple.

On the other hand, did Jesus see something profane in the temple treasury receiving a percentage of the profits? Mercenary as the arrangement might appear, that income did help to keep the temple tax from being even more onerous than it already was.

Then too, could Jesus be calling, in an ironic way, for a kind of balance and moderation? Was he saying the commercial activity was legitimate, but had gotten out of hand, debasing the sacred atmosphere of the temple? If so, his violent rampage rather undercut the point. What he, himself, had done was neither balanced nor moderate. And it certainly wasn't sacred.

The only explanation that seemed to make sense was the one James most feared to contemplate, that Jesus was demanding a change in essential Jewish religious understanding. Why should he attack the animal vendors, unless he objected to animal sacrifice? Why drive out the money changers, unless he saw giving *corban* as pointless?

Was he saying there was some way other than sacrifice to atone for sin or invoke the blessing of the Holy One? That was a deeply disturbing possibility. Because if this was what Jesus meant, then he was going well beyond anything which the prophets, who criticized insincere or unworthy sacrifice, had ever said. He was not only attacking the temple, he was setting a new direction for Judaism—one that probably didn't include the hereditary priesthood, since it was the priests who conducted the sacrifices.

To make such a change would be to cast out onto wholly uncharted seas. And this was a prospect at which James and every other faithful Jew must tremble. Because it might very well mean that laws and rituals and traditions that had helped to sustain the Jewish people through war and exile and conquest would be nullified. Under such altered circumstances, would Judaism still be Judaism?

Gamaliel had seen these implications in Jesus' teaching. Now this wild act in the temple made them tangible to James, and he pursued them a step further. He asked himself whether those who chose to follow Jesus—the mass of believers he called his *assembly*—might really be the heralds of a whole new religion. If so, what was such a faith to be like? Without the temple, would it be based entirely on synagogues? Following the lead of Jesus himself, would it place strong emphasis on preaching? What role would it play in Jewish family life and the community of Jews? Would there still be a community of Jews?

James had assured Pilate that his brother was making no plans to rise up against Rome, and he still believed that. But in a way, Jesus' behavior posed questions even more vexing and dangerous. James simply had no idea what was in his brother's mind, and he wondered if even Jesus did. With the best of intentions, Jesus might seek to lead the Jewish nation toward a bright and glorious future, all the while actually bringing it to a dark abyss.

*   *   *

The next morning, James sent Asher to Bethany to find out if Jesus was there, and if so, to deliver an urgent reprise of James' earlier advice: *Leave Judea as quickly as possible.* Asher returned some time later, still bearing the small leaf of parchment on which James had scratched out this message, and bringing a piece of troubling news. Jesus was not in Bethany. He was back in Jerusalem.

"His mother told me that Jesus and his men rose early to pray in the garden he frequents," Asher reported. "From there, Jesus intended to return to the temple."

The temple? Did Jesus *wish* to be killed? Was he taunting the priests, daring them to arrest him, seeking some kind of martyrdom?

James and Asher hurried to the temple mount—Asher to his class, and James to find his brother and implore him to flee. Jesus was easily located, sitting on the lower level of the Royal Porch, teaching. He was attended by the twelve along with a substantial group of other people, both men and women, who filled half the length of the colonnade and spilled out into the terrace in front of it.

A squad of temple guards stood by observing at a distance, showing no apparent intention to do anything about this impromptu gathering. James assumed they had been instructed not to threaten Jesus in front of his followers. Yesterday had revealed the unwillingness of the temple authorities to risk provoking a riot by molesting the Nazarene. Jesus was probably safe while he was in public. But for how long?

Moving to a visible position in the Royal Porch, James stood listening to his brother speak. Jesus would notice him there. Jesus always seemed to know when James was around. But it was Simon who sought him out.

"Peace be with you, Rabbi," the big fisherman said in a low voice.

James nodded in reply. Simon cleared his throat and tilted his head to one side as a request for James to follow him. They walked out toward the far edge of the terrace.

"I'm sure I know why you have come," said Simon.

"My brother must flee," said James. "After what he has done, his life is in peril. You and the others must convince him to leave Judea. Go into pagan territory. The priests will have him killed if he remains here. It is only a matter of time."

"Yes, Rabbi, I understand. But he will not go. He has made his will plain on the matter. He intends to stay in Jerusalem."

"Is he determined to die, Simon?"

Simon's broad chest seemed to collapse inward, and his voice caught. "Ye— Yes, Rabbi," he said weakly, "I believe he is. He is convinced that this is his destiny, and he has accepted it. He *insists* on it, truth be told. There is nothing any of us can say to persuade him otherwise."

"Then what has been the point of this ministry? Of all his preaching and healing and traveling about? What does it accomplish?"

"I don't know, Rabbi, I don't know. I have asked myself the same question, and I have no answer. The wondrous things we have seen... I cannot tell you all the marvelous hopes he has aroused in us, and in so many others as well." Simon shook his head sadly. "I am not able to understand why it has to end like this—or how it *could* end like this, if this mission has been the will of the Holy One."

James turned away and put a hand to his forehead, massaging his temples in an attempt to think, to comprehend. Then he looked at the fisherman again.

"If my brother will do nothing to save himself, perhaps there is yet something I can do," he said. "I don't promise anything, Simon. I *cannot* promise. But when they move against him—and they surely will— get word to me."

"Yes, Rabbi."

"I will...*try*...Simon. I will try. That is all I can say."

"I know you will, Rabbi."

Simon returned to Jesus' group, and James went inside, heading for the stairs and up to where Gamaliel was teaching. On the way, he discovered several of Gamaliel's students. Apparently, they had absented themselves from the class and were instead listening to Jesus. The young men shrank self-consciously when James passed by, not knowing if the rabbi would be pleased to find them interested in his brother's talk or annoyed to see that they had deserted their master's class.

At the far end of the upper colonnade, James found Gamaliel and gestured that he needed Asher again. His colleague nodded in assent.

As usual, James' instinct was to speak with Joseph of Arimathea, and he dispatched Asher to arrange a meeting for that afternoon. Then he positioned himself beside a column to await the end of the class session. Gamaliel perceived that James wished to speak with him, brought the discussion to an early close, and dismissed the students who were present, among them Saul.

"I am sorry to be such a distraction," James said, "and to claim so much of Asher's time."

"Fortunately," Gamaliel replied, "he is a young man well able to divide his attention. And as for my class—you probably observe that it is somewhat under-attended. Jesus provokes great interest among my disciples. These days, their attention too is divided."

"It is of that I wish to speak with you."

"No doubt. Your brother's boldness has placed him in danger."

"If he is brought before the Sanhedrin, he will need support."

"I will speak with some of the rabbis who are members."

"Thank you, my friend."

"But James..." Gamaliel approached the point gingerly. "There is a good deal of suspicion to overcome, even among those who would be most intent on seeing that no injustice is done to Jesus. Your brother has spared little criticism for the doctors of the Law."

James said nothing.

"In particular, those of the Pharisee party."

A long, frustrated breath from James, then: "I know."

"And..." said Gamaliel, "after that absurd demonstration of yesterday..."

"Do what you can, my friend. That is all I ask."

*   *   *

At the appointed hour, Joseph of Arimathea came to the Synagogue at the Crossed Streets, bringing with him Nicodemus, a friend and fellow council member with whom James was also acquainted. Nicodemus was a jolly and quite rotund fellow known for a curious mind and an ongoing interest in new ideas. Joseph had often told him he should have been a rabbi, from which proposition Nicodemus would always demur.

"Oh no," he would say. "My thoughts are too unoriginal. No student would find them interesting. I just reflect on what others propose and support those ideas that strike me as constructive."

His humility endeared him to many on the Sanhedrin—his open-mindedness less so.

"You know, I met your brother some time ago," Nicodemus said to James. "We had a long and most fascinating conversation about how one may achieve a vivid awareness of the Holy One—or rather, a relationship with Him. Jesus called it being *born again*. It is an intriguing doctrine. We discussed many other points as well. I am quite convinced he brings something worthwhile to Judaism."

"Do you consider yourself one of his followers?" James asked.

Nicodemus paused for a moment, scratched his glisteningly bald head, then said, "Yes, I suppose I do. In my position I would be loath to make any sort of public declaration about that, especially just now. But I feel a distinct affinity for Jesus and his message."

"In present circumstances," Joseph said, "it would be wise for you to keep any interest in him to yourself."

"By all means," James added. "My brother will need credible men to speak for him—those who can plausibly be seen as untainted by personal loyalty."

"I understand," said Nicodemus. "Oh yes, I surely do understand."

At James' request, Joseph and Nicodemus made a list of those council members they felt could be counted on to resist any pressure to bring a quick conviction in the Sanhedrin.

"These are good men," Nicodemus said, "men of principle. They might be offended at Jesus' action in the Court of the Gentiles, but they will give him a fair hearing. I am certain of that. If he makes a good case for the reform he is demanding, they will listen and judge him fairly."

A second list was compiled—of those members who would be inclined to vote against Jesus.

Joseph tapped his finger on that list. "Not all of these fellows are lackeys of the priests," he said. "But they will not be receptive to any criticism of the temple. *Some* might be turned around...perhaps...but it will take a more compelling argument."

"Jesus is a most persuasive speaker," Nicodemus said.

"True..." said Joseph, his voice fading with something less than full confidence.

James stepped in. "That is, *if* he will speak in a straight-forward way. Jesus presents his points indirectly, and he has refined the technique to where it is very effective in his preaching. But there are some who consider his parables and metaphors not so much illuminating as evasive. I don't know if this approach would find ready acceptance in the Sanhedrin."

"Surely he would be direct in presenting his argument there," said Joseph. "His life would depend on it."

"Yes...well...how much Jesus cares about his life is an unanswered question just now," said James, prompting Nicodemus and Joseph to look at each other uneasily. James went on, "At any rate, it is vital to make contact with all those whom you say will consider my brother's case fairly—and to do it right away. We cannot afford to wait, as we did with Jesus' cousin, John. And I must depend on *you* to reach these men, as well as on Gamaliel, in the case of the rabbis. I am Jesus' kinsman. An appeal on my part would be put down to family tie. Also, I'm too much the outsider to temple circles. Besides, I think my influence would be best spent elsewhere."

"On Pilate?" Joseph asked.

"Just so. A charge brought against Jesus would likely be one of *blasphemy*. That is a capital offense, and a death-penalty conviction would have to be taken to the prefect for confirmation and execution. This is Jerusalem. No one is going to drag my brother outside to stone him here. That would risk the ire of the people and an angry Roman response. The priests don't want either. They'll judge that everything must be done in compliance with the law. Then too, the more they can spread responsibility for Jesus' death over the Roman occupiers, the better."

"I think your assessment is correct," said Joseph. "All procedures will be followed strictly."

"Indeed, indeed," said Nicodemus. "They know the Jewish people have no desire to harm Jesus. Not all agree with his teachings, to be sure, but he is widely admired as a man of faith and commitment, not to mention his ability to banish infirmity. And after doing what he did in the temple court, certainly no one doubts his courage."

"You concentrate on Pilate, James," Joseph said. "We will make the most of our contacts on the council. You can depend on us."

*   *   *

Calling at the prefecture, James was informed by the officer of the watch that Lord Pilate was engaged in preparations for a dinner that evening, at which he would host the Tetrarch of Galilee. Antipas was in Jerusalem for Passover with his wife, Herodias, and they were to receive an official greeting. The next day the prefect would be similarly occupied, as he planned to conduct the tetrarch on a tour of the Jerusalem district. He particularly wished for Antipas to see the aqueduct and the other improvements to the city's water system. Consequently, Lord Pilate—much to his regret—would not be able to receive the Rabbi James until the day after.

James mused that these hours in the company of Antipas might not be the most pleasant for Pilate. It was said that there was a rivalry between the prefect and the tetrarch who clung to the dream of reunifying his father's kingdom. Rumor had it that Antipas' agents in the court of Caesar were quick to play up any problems besetting Pilate. Apparently, they had made a great fuss over the protest against Caesar's image on the regimental standard. James figured they would do as much with the recent objections to the gold shields.

That unfortunate incident had put strain enough on Pilate's mood. Now there would be no counting on his attitude after having to keep up a show of good fellowship with Antipas. At the very least, Pilate would be tired of guarding his words and forcing himself to smile. This did not bode well for James' hopes.

Uncertain of what else to do at the moment, James decided to go back to the temple to see if conditions there had changed since morning. He would have to give Gamaliel, Joseph and Nicodemus time to conduct their various consultations with Sanhedrin members. And he had virtually ignored his work in the Synagogue at the Crossed Streets since the question of Jesus' safety in Jerusalem had taken over all his thoughts. Correspondence sat unanswered, and he hadn't made himself available to anyone coming for counsel in days. This he felt quite bad about, but worry over his brother dominated every waking hour, even creeping into his dreams.

Jesus and the twelve were gone when James arrived at the Royal Porch, though some of the people who had gathered to hear him teach still lingered, discussing the prophet's words. From them James learned that his brother and the apostles would be spending the night in rest and prayer on the Mount of Olives and then returning in the morning for another teaching session.

James grasped the significance of this plan. It was obvious that Jesus didn't want to go back to Bethany, where his mother and the other women might be placed in danger should the house of Lazarus be raided in the night. If these followers knew he was on the Mount of Olives, the temple authorities would know it too, which was probably his brother's intention.

*   *   *

The next day brought a note from Joseph that he and Nicodemus had spoken to several council members—with mixed results. Some promised their support right away, and others to remain open-minded if Jesus should be charged. But it looked as if the wild antics in the Court of the Gentiles would prove an even greater obstacle to gaining sympathy than anticipated. Some members who found Jesus' message appealing were having second thoughts about his judgment. Several questioned his sanity, and at least one gave voice to the possibility that maybe he really was toying with heresy. All of which brought a familiar knot to James' stomach. He could only hope that Gamaliel would report better results.

Putting the note aside, James headed out to the temple once more, catching sight of Pilate and Antipas along the way. They were on their tour, accompanied by a retinue of soldiers that included both prefecture staff and the tetrarch's personal company of guards. James thought he might have caught Pilate's eye, though he'd made no effort to do so. He would never attempt to intrude into such a highly official entourage. Still, he couldn't help entertaining the idea that Pilate's glance showed his longing to be in the company of anyone other than Antipas.

James arrived to find Jesus' followers already gathered in the Royal Porch and his brother leading them in the morning service. He took a position just inside and joined the prayers, then settled himself to listen to Jesus' words of the day.

Whatever lesson was planned, Jesus' attention was quickly diverted by a series of questions from several rabbis whom James knew were extremely protective of their status as doctors of the Law. They had even criticized James for setting up the Synagogue at the Crossed Streets, which despite its affiliation with the school of Gamaliel, they considered a rogue operation.

The rabbis challenged Jesus about the authority by which he, as an uncertified layman, presumed to teach. Jesus' response seemed to James not precisely on the point, but shrewd nonetheless. He asked them if they thought the baptism offered by John had been from God or devised by men.

James could fairly well read their minds as they deliberated on how to answer. If they said it reflected the will of the Holy One, the next logical question would be why they hadn't accepted it and believed John to be commissioned by God. If, in contrast, they said John's baptism was of human origin, they risked angering the people who considered John a prophet.

The weak answer that came was that they couldn't be sure—to which Jesus replied that he then felt under no obligation to tell them the source of his own authority. There was laughter throughout the colonnade, including from James.

Then Jesus offered a parable about vine-growers who had leased a vineyard but refused to pay their rent, even going so far as to kill the owner's son when he came to collect. This the rabbis saw as directed at them, perhaps a veiled charge that they themselves were failing in their obligations to the one who had provided the bounty of their scholarly prerogatives. They knew they were being insulted but, aware of the crowd, their only response was an insipid, *God forbid.*

Jesus wasn't content to let them slip away to nurse their wounds. He quoted a line from the famous psalm: *The stone which the builders rejected has become the corner stone.* Just for emphasis, he insisted that anyone tripping over the stone would be injured and anyone on whom it fell crushed. It was clear enough who was the stone and who would be crushed. The rabbis found this suggestion quite impudent.

Amused as James was to watch his brother score such debilitating strikes on these pompous and self-inflated scribes, he realized this exchange would do nothing to help his case if Jesus did stand before the Sanhedrin. The hostility of his questioners was only increased by Jesus' triumph over them.

The rabbis conferred in a tight circle, arriving at a question that set their faces in the most sinister of grins. One of them stepped forward. "Master," he addressed Jesus with an edge of understated sarcasm in his voice, "is it, or is it not proper for us to pay taxes to Caesar?"

James could see in the fellow's eyes that he thought this had finally stumped the upstart, would-be prophet. Everyone paid the Roman tax, fearing the consequences of not doing so. But the question of whether, by the Law of Moses, it was truly moral to give Jewish substance to the pagan overlords remained unsettled. This was a sore point continually exploited by the Zealots. It had been the essential question behind the controversy over using *corban* to fund the aqueduct.

A wistful smile played on Jesus' face, which his questioner took as a sign of nervousness. If Jesus affirmed the legitimacy of the tax he could be called a traitor to his people. If he held that paying the tax was wrong, Pilate might be alerted that he was undermining the empire.

Jesus looked up. "Show me a silver piece," he said to the rabbi.

James held his breath as he watched the man take a coin from his scrip and hand it over. Jesus examined it, front and back.

"Whose image is this?" he asked.

"Caesar's, of course."

Tossing the coin back, Jesus said, "Then give to Caesar what is Caesar's, and to God what is God's."

The rabbi was rattled by Jesus' quip, so taken aback that he missed the silver piece and had to bend over to pick it up off the ground as peals of laughter swept the crowd. James looked at Jesus, who was now staring directly at him, the wistful smile still on his lips. James too smiled and nodded in his brother's direction.

Jesus was quick, no doubt about that. He could use humor to devastating effect, and his words weren't just funny, they were wise. James hoped they wouldn't fail him when the critical moment came.

Though people had gathered to hear Jesus teach, they weren't disappointed that the discussion had taken a combative turn. In fact, they found the battle fascinating. The rabbis persisted in trying to maneuver Jesus into saying something that might discredit him before the crowd. But he put on a dazzling display of verbal parry and thrust, deflecting each effort and revealing the facile nature of his opponents' arguments.

The debate continued throughout the morning—and it surely was a debate—covering a number of topics and drawing an increasing crowd of onlookers. At one point, discussion turned to the temple itself, prompting Jesus to make a disturbing prediction. The time would come, he said, when everything standing here would be thrown down, not a stone remaining upon another.

This narrative had a predictably chilling effect on Jesus' audience. James reflected that it seemed to be a pattern in his brother's speaking that, after raising his listeners' spirits, he would introduce a subject that dampened their mood, even driving some away. Looking around, James saw a few people leaving now. He recalled the talk given near Caesarea-Philippi when Jesus had introduced the difficult topics of adultery and divorce.

James was satisfied that Jesus could hold up quite well under the incessant attempts to cast him in a bad light. And though he didn't want anyone to assume he was reacting negatively to his brother's remarks, he decided he'd had enough of this contest. There was nothing more to be done in preparing a defense until he could speak with Pilate. In the meantime, he really had to catch up on his correspondence. So when the discussion had moved on to another topic and the crowd was absorbed in Jesus' words, James took his leave. He was descending the stairs to the base of the temple mount when he heard:

"Rabbi."

He turned and saw that once more it was Simon.

"A moment, if you would, Rabbi."

"Yes, of course, Simon."

They found a private spot behind a wall at the bottom of the stairs.

"Something is afoot," said the fisherman. "I think the priests are preparing to move against the Lord."

"Why do you say that, Simon?"

"Last night we were followed, and then we were watched in the garden where we spent the night on the Mount of Olives. I recognized one of the temple guard officers who has been observing the Lord's teaching sessions in the Porch."

This confirmed James' assumption about why they hadn't returned to Bethany.

"Also," said Simon," one of our circle—Judas, the one who is called Iscariot—he has been spending time away from our group lately."

"What significance do you see in that?"

Simon hesitated for a second, then said, "For awhile now, I have suspected he has become—well...perhaps a bit disillusioned with our ministry. Judas has connections with the Zealots, Rabbi. I don't know if he was ever deeply involved in their activities, and it looked like he had put all of that behind him. But I think he still hopes the Lord will take more direct action—that he will be...*bolder*...in calling people to a new life."

"He expected that Jesus would call them to a political movement?"

"He has misunderstood the mission."

"Do you think he is conspiring with the temple authorities?"

Simon shrugged. "I can't make an accusation," he said, "but neither would I be surprised."

"A spy."

"It is possible."

James considered this. "Well...the Zealot movement probably is not in the best of shape right now," he said. "I have no idea how they're organized, but the fact that Pilate has bar Abbas in custody must cause difficulties. If my brother were executed—and of course, it would be for the Romans to execute him—the anger of his followers might be exploited to stoke a rebellion."

Simon nodded. It was more than a nod, actually, his entire upper body swayed forward and back as if he were shuckling in prayer. "Yes,

Rabbi," he said, "some might have that thought."

"Where will you go this evening?" James asked. "If this garden is known to the priests, then perhaps you would be better spending the night somewhere else."

"Jesus will not hide," said Simon.

"No." James shook his head. "My brother is making himself as visible as can be. Where will you spend Passover? I don't suppose he would go back to the house of Lazarus. You are welcome to take the unleavened bread with me in the Synagogue at the Crossed Streets."

Simon raised a hand in objection. "I don't think the Lord would want that. He stays away from Bethany to protect his mother, and I'm sure he would stay away from your home for a similar reason. There are disciples in the city with whom arrangements can be made."

"I'm sure there are many who would be honored to host your group," James said. "But if circumstance should change—"

"Of course, Rabbi," said Simon. "I will keep you informed."

CHAPTER THIRTY-SEVEN

To do justice and judgment is
more acceptable to the Lord than sacrifice.

(Proverbs 21)

Amara had been in a flurry of activity since before sunrise, cleaning the interior of the main house in anticipation of Passover. She'd set her husband, Ephron, to policing the grounds and burnishing the copper band around the archway at the front gate. James knew the onslaught would soon reach his doorstep and he would be ejected from the stone hut. He hurried to complete a letter he was writing in answer to one of the many requests for his advice, which had been left sitting for the past several days.

The approach of the feast gave a measure of urgency to the question before him. His inquirer had asked if a particular circumstance justified exemption from the fast required of all first-born sons. Abstaining from food was an expression of gratitude to the Holy One for sparing the first-borns in Egypt. It applied during the day before the ritual *Seder*, the Feast of Unleavened Bread.

The inquiry was typical for this season. Receiving such questions had become a kind of Passover custom for James. This one was a bit difficult to answer, since some of the specifics had been stated unclearly. The best James could do was to explain the principles involved and to provide a few general guidelines and analogies by which he hoped the inquirer would be able to make his own judgment in the matter.

Another seasonal custom—one James had established at the first Passover after he'd opened the Synagogue at the Crossed Streets— was to invite some orphaned children to share in the feast. His work with Gamaliel's students in the food distributions put him in contact with many needy individuals, so it was always a simple matter to identify prospective young guests. Even those *Seders* at which relatives from Nazareth were present always included a few stray urchins. And often it was the youngest among these who got to ask the traditional four questions by which the purpose and elements of Passover were explained to children.

Other than the three ragged little guests scheduled for this year, the only people sharing James' *Seder* table would be Amara, Ephron and their two sons and three daughters. No one was expected from Nazareth. And according to Simon, Jesus was making other arrangements for himself and his men.

Of course, there was Mary—in fact, there was a gaggle of Marys—in Bethany. If Jesus was trying to keep his mother at a safe distance, it was unlikely he would have her with him at the feast. If so, what plans did she have? She could, James assumed, spend Passover at the house of Lazarus. But might she rather be with a relative during these days in which she must surely be feeling considerable apprehension about her son?

It occurred to James that there might be a particularly good reason for extending an invitation to Mary: getting her away from Bethany, getting her out of sight altogether, in fact. He didn't know if anybody in the temple was aware of Jesus' mother being so close by. But if this was known, it might strike someone that her presence could provide a means by which to exert some sort of pressure on Jesus.

Such a situation wasn't at all unthinkable, and James saw that it must be avoided. He should arrange for Mary to be brought to Jerusalem in an inconspicuous manner. As much of an outsider as he was to the temple circle, his personal stature would provide her a measure of protection. No one would make an official attempt to remove her from the Synagogue at the Crossed Streets. And he could have some of Gamaliel's students stay on the grounds to guard against any unofficial mischief.

Asher was due to pick up the morning's messages for delivery. There were five small parchment rolls sealed with wax on James' table when he arrived. James handed them to the student, instructing him to make Bethany a stop on his route and to speak with Mary about staying in Jerusalem for Passover. She was welcome to come by herself, or to bring along Aunt Mary and the Mary from Magdala, if she liked. There was plenty of room in the main house to accommodate them all for a few days.

After Asher departed, James went to break his fast, finding nothing set out with which to relieve his morning hunger and Amara deep into her cleaning regimen. Embarrassed at having neglected his needs, Amara called to one of her daughters to prepare something quickly for the master.

"Forgive me, Rabbi," she said. "My girls and I are caught up in preparations. You must be starving."

"There is no problem, Amara, I assure you." James tried to calm her. "A bit of fruit and some bread will do."

Amara ran off, returning a few minutes later with a tray bearing a bowl of oat porridge along with bread and a plate of grapes. These she set before James. Her daughter brought a basin of water and a towel.

James recited the prayer for washing as he cleaned and dried his hands, then the blessing of bread, and began to eat.

"Oh—Amara," he said, catching her as she was about to return to her work, "there may be more at the feast tomorrow. I will know later today how many."

"Yes, Master," she said, turning to go. Then she stopped and faced him again. "Please don't forget, Rabbi—you have been so busy lately— please remember that, as master of the house, you must perform the search for leaven after sunset tonight. Ephron is setting up a place for the fire out in the court, so we can burn the *hametz* in the morning."

The pre-Passover ritual was a special pleasure to James. Amara's children would place pieces of bread containing yeast around the house for the master to discover as he walked through the darkened rooms carrying a candle and a large wooden spoon. Ephron would instruct the children where to put the bread so that James would be sure to find it—fulfilling the requirement to cleanse the premises of all *hametz*, to be burned the next day. The ritual searching was highly formularized, Amara having already done the actual work of ridding the house of leaven.

This had all been so very exciting to the children when they were small. They would squeal with delight at each discovery and feel proud of the critical part they played in preparing for Passover. Even now it was still fun.

Which brought another idea to James' mind. "Amara," he asked, have you disposed of your stock of yeast?"

"I put it out behind the house. Ephron will destroy it."

"Is there a lot?"

"A full jar." Amara was perplexed.

"I'll take it with me," James said. "I have a call to make today, and it might prove useful."

Amara looked at her daughter, shrugged, and said, "Yes, Master."

*   *   *

The officer who admitted him to the prefecture court thought it very odd that the Rabbi James should have this homely domestic object with him. It was the sort of plain, covered jar used for flour, beans or some other bulk food item. If he hadn't known this was the famous Jewish scholar held in such high regard by Lord Pilate, he would have been suspicious about whether the jar concealed a weapon.

A new set of awnings shaded the section of the court where James and Pilate usually met. At the officer's request, James seated himself, placing the jar on a low table at the side, to await the prefect's arrival. His gaze drifted about as he recalled the unfortunate developments that had attended the unveiling of the gold shields just days before. James hoped Pilate's anger over the rejection of the emperor's gift had cooled. Much might depend on the attitude of Caesar's vicar. After a few minutes, Pilate came down the stairs and strode over to James, who rose to his feet.

"Good morning, Rabbi," Pilate said.

"Peace be upon you, Prefect."

They both sat.

"I am sorry to be unavailable the last two days," Pilate said. "I've been hosting the Tetrarch Herod Antipas."

"Of course, Prefect—an important function of state protocol."

Pilate grunted quietly, which James took as expression of his feelings, either about state protocol or about Antipas.

"How may I help you today?" Pilate asked in a businesslike voice.

"Well, first...I was concerned that you might have questions about— That is, Prefect...about the reaction to the shields. I am quite anxious for you to understand that what happened did not reflect any lack of gratitude. My colleagues realized that the gift was intended as a show of Caesar's good will. And I know that *your* heart was in the effort. It is not easy for someone—for a non-Jew—to grasp the depth of feeling in our devotion to the Law."

Pilate pursed his lips. The incident had obviously left a bruise.

"If sometimes we Jews appear to be overly guarded—"

"I understand, Rabbi," Pilate interrupted. "Please inform the priests and learned men that the shields have been taken to Caesarea. They will be displayed in the Tiberium, our great public square." He looked directly at James now, as if underscoring his words. "And they *will* be displayed, Rabbi. Not in Jerusalem, as I had originally intended—but they will be displayed."

James said nothing.

Pilate turned his eyes away and spoke less emphatically, almost thoughtfully. "Perhaps that is a more appropriate location anyway. So many travelers coming to Palestine enter through the port of Caesarea. Maybe the messages on the shields are best directed at them."

James let the point sit.

Having had his say, the prefect now seemed relieved of his annoyance. He looked at James again with a much milder expression. "Is there anything else I can do for you, Rabbi?"

"Actually, there is, Prefect." James had devised an artifice by which to encourage Pilate toward better feelings about Jewish religious sensitivities and, hopefully, to reinforce their good relationship. He couldn't be sure it would work, but circumstances justified the risk.

"I have come with a business proposition," James said and pointed at the jar sitting on the low table next to him. "This vessel contains yeast. I wish to offer it for sale to you."

Pilate eyed the jar with a raised brow. "You want to sell me yeast?"

"Yes."

James' crooked smile intrigued Pilate. "I didn't know you dealt in such commodities, Rabbi," he said.

"I don't," said James, "not normally. But this jar of yeast reflects another aspect of Jewish Law—one which you might find interesting. As I am sure you know, preparations for our Feast of Unleavened Bread include clearing our homes of all substances that can cause rising or fermentation, as well as any mixed or prepared foods that contain such ingredients. These items, which are called in Hebrew, *hametz*, must be collected and destroyed. But, Jews are not a wasteful people. If we have a store of such materials—which of course would have value—then the Law permits us to sell it...to a non-Jew."

"And you want to sell it to me."

"Exactly. Perhaps your wife can use it for baking."

A hearty outburst of laughter showed that Pilate found this idea most amusing. "My wife is the daughter of a senator, Rabbi," he said. "She is a hostess of admirable grace and tact, but cooking is not among her many gifts. I can tell you quite frankly that, if we had no servants, I would starve."

James chuckled in response. The thought came to him that he really knew very little about this Roman knight. He didn't even know if Pilate had children. He must pose the question on some appropriate occasion. But that was for another time.

"I should point out to you, however," he said, "that the Law also allows for buying the leavening back after Passover."

"Ah," said Pilate, "so the sale is just symbolic."

James shook his head. "No, no. Not at all. It must be a genuine business transaction that actually removes the material from my possession. You are perfectly free to refuse my offer to repurchase it, or you can sell it back to me at a higher price and make a profit—whichever you wish to do at the time."

Pilate laughed again. "You Jews are certainly great keepers of your Law," he said. "But you are equally adept at figuring out how to have your own way."

It was a point which had to be granted. But also, it provided an opportunity for a rabbi to explain something about how Jews understood the Holy One.

"The King of the Universe gives us the Law so that we may live in ways that are ordered to His will," James said. "But He knows that human needs must be met. Thus, He shows Himself to be both the God of justice and the God of kindness."

Pilate reflected upon this—another example of that unfailing Jewish spiritual logic. "Alright, Rabbi," he said, taking a gold coin from his scrip and placing it on the table beside the jar. "I shall purchase your yeast."

James eyed the coin. "A most generous payment."

"A very special yeast," said Pilate. "And I do not intend to sell it back to you."

"In that case, " said James, nodding, "your gold piece will purchase much food for distribution to the poor of the city." He picked up the coin and placed it into his own scrip.

Now Pilate chuckled over this unanticipated business transaction. Procula would be amused. He would have to tease her about baking him a loaf of bread. Then he said, "So, Rabbi, shall we get to the real point of your visit today?"

This brought a start to James, followed by a quick clearing of the throat.

"You are concerned about your brother," said Pilate. "He caused quite an uproar, both with his grand entry into the city and with his protest against the merchants in the temple. The priests are not happy, and you are worried that he will be arrested."

James took a long, slow breath. "To be honest, Prefect, I am somewhat surprised he hasn't been already."

"Of course you realize they fear him," Pilate said. "That much is obvious. He commands great respect among the people, and your authorities are apprehensive about moving against him. This pleases me, I must say. I do not desire having to put down a riot."

"But how long will they stay their hand?" James asked.

"You could make a better estimate of that than I could," said Pilate. "These are your leaders, and the temple is their jurisdiction. I suppose it all comes down to how far your brother will go in provoking them."

A sigh from James. "I wish I knew."

"Let me tell you this, Rabbi. An inquiry has already been made about what the provincial administration is prepared to do if the situation should become too threatening. The question was raised casually, of course. I suspect that, after the business of the shields, your priests are feeling a bit wary of *me* too."

James was rubbing his fingers unconsciously, uneasily.

"Well, let them be so," Pilate continued. "Rome acts when Rome sees the right. I will do my duty when my duty is clear. And at this point, all I see is a rather foolish and headstrong young man with some sort of vague, Jewish religious complaint. As long as he presents no threat to the peace of Rome, he is not my problem."

The peace of Rome.

"I appreciate that, Prefect," said James. "And please know that I would not presume to comment on your duty. But if it happens that my brother should be brought before you—"

"Then he would receive a fair hearing under the just principles of Roman law."

"Yes, Prefect. I know he would." James hesitated, then: "I cannot say what prompted Jesus to make the display he did. But he is not a criminal. Whatever may be said about him—and you might be told any number of wild tales—my brother is a man of deep conviction and great love. I have known him from when he was a small child, and I can attest to that. If I have any credibility in your eyes—"

"Credibility?" Pilate said, smiling, surprised that James should be uncertain of his standing in the prefect's eyes. "Let me assure you, Rabbi...*James the Just* has great credibility."

The two men exchanged a glance, and each nodded to the other— Pilate in respect, James in thanks.

But the conversation was finished. It had come too close to the heart of Pilate's official responsibilities. James understood that, no matter what personal regard he might enjoy, the man who spoke for Caesar could accept only so much advice from someone who was his provincial subject. And James' kinship with Jesus was an added complication in the circumstances Pilate might soon be facing.

The prefect came to his feet. James mirrored the movement. Then Pilate bent over and picked up the jar of yeast from the low table. With another smile and a slight laugh, but no further word, he turned and took his leave. James watched him ascend the stairway.

*   *   *

Asher led Jesus' mother and the other two Marys, along with two bulky young men drawn from Gamaliel's class, by a circuitous route through the warren of streets in the lower city. James hadn't told him to take any particular measures to avoid being followed. If anyone wished to find out where Mary was, they had only to ask at the house of Lazarus. But Asher decided for himself on extra precautions.

Anxiety was written upon Mary's face when she arrived in late afternoon. At their greeting, James took her aside and related the substance of his talk that day with Pilate.

"He knows his duty, and he will do it," James said. "We must have no illusions about that. But his concern is merely to keep the peace. Right now, he doesn't see any basis for invoking Roman justice—which means he would question any charge of a capital crime. The priests would have to fabricate some elaborate charade in order to ask Pilate to take Jesus' life."

"Oh James, would they try such a thing?"

"They *are* afraid of his influence," James said. "His popularity raises the specter—in their minds, at least—of his creating some kind of broad religious movement that diminishes the importance of the temple. Maybe even some alternative form of Judaism. At least that's how I assess their thinking. If I'm correct, they'll call him a heretic, no doubt, but I don't see how they can kill him. Only the prefect could authorize it, and Pilate has no interest in religious disputes."

Mary looked less than convinced. "But you *do* think the temple authorities will arrest him."

"Unless he demonstrates that he intends no further harm..." said James, "that his rampage in the Court of the Gentiles was a one-time occurrence...maybe even that he regrets the rashness of his act and really does respect the leadership. If he were willing to make a statement like that?"

"He wouldn't." Mary shook her head. "There is no chance of it. My son has taken his stand. He will not back down. And at this point, even if he refrains from any further criticism of the priests and scribes— even if he says not another word—his presence in the temple is, itself, a reproach to the leaders."

A nod, a partial shrug, loose movement of his hands—James was at a loss to disagree. "I fear you are right, Mary."

Ephron prepared a room for the three women guests. And he set sleeping mats outside in the court for Asher and the other two young men who, in this time of the Rabbi James' special need, had volunteered to sacrifice celebrating Passover with their master, Gamaliel. The unplanned presence of these added visitors put a special burden on Amara and her daughters. James felt bad about that.

Perhaps because he, himself, was an outsider when he'd first come to this place as a student to board, he was never quite able to think of Amara and her family as his servants. He and the African woman had both reached maturity within these walls. After being master of the house for so many years, James considered Amara, Ephron and their children, if not quite kin, then dear family retainers.

Amara could read the rabbi's slightly guilty expression, and hastened to assure him that she and the girls were up to the extra cooking and related preparations.

"I have no doubt of it," he told her, gratefully.

"Just one thing, Master..." she said.

"Yes?"

"It is your aunt, Rabbi... That is—my daughters and I do have things quite well in hand. I realize she only wishes to be helpful..."

A sideward glance revealed the wife of Cleophas inspecting the *Seder* plates, bowls, cups and other implements.

"I understand," he said. And then, striving for the utmost in tact, he appealed, "Please try to be patient, Amara. Perhaps you could assign Aunt Mary some task that would...well, that might make best use of the skills and knowledge a woman of her years must surely possess—while not interfering with your own excellent work, of course." James could see that Amara was skeptical. "It is the festival season, after all. And as you say, she does wish to be helpful."

"Yes, Master," Amara said with a spirit of willingness and an echo of resignation.

After some thought, she settled on asking Aunt Mary to make a careful scan of the house against the possibility that some minute speck of *hametz* might have been overlooked. Amara was certain the cleaning had been thorough, but a mature woman with an eye drawn to examining household things might find such a duty gratifying.

The instinct proved correct. Amara's confidence in her cleaning was rewarded when Aunt Mary later confirmed that all was indeed as it should be. The younger woman thanked the older for her rigorous scrutiny. Aunt Mary was pleased to have her decades of experience recognized.

She was also somewhat moved by the ritual search of the house carried out that night by James. Witnessing everyone's enjoyment brought a wave of nostalgia for the old days in Alexandria when her own sons and daughter had been small and so completely caught up in the thrill of participation. Tears came, along with a comforting embrace from Mary.

The evening closed on a graceful note, though sleep did not come easily to everyone. Mary lay awake in the darkened bed chamber, its blackness pierced only by a shaft of silvery moonlight falling upon her lower section from the single window. Her mind was crammed with the worries that had been multiplying ever since Jesus sent for her to be brought from Nazareth.

What was in store for her son, the strangely inspired child given by the Holy One, the curious, mystical youth who had sought remote and exotic places, the resolute young man consecrated to a mission of preaching and healing and transforming lives? Would he at last reveal himself as the Lord's Anointed, join all the Jewish people to his own personal destiny, and shine the light of the Covenant more brightly than ever upon the nations? Or would his journey come to a sudden end in an orgy of blood, anguish and pointlessness? And if such failure was to be his true fate, would he have brought it on himself? Such were a mother's thoughts. Mary pondered them in all their shades and variations against the soft murmur of sleep emanating from Aunt Mary and Mary of Magdala, reposing near her in the dark.

Lying in the stone hut, James was similarly unsettled. Sleep eluded him also as he weighed the uncertainties. One thought offered some small comfort: If the temple authorities had done nothing to Jesus yet, then his safety was assured through at least the following week. The next day's sunset would bring the start of Passover. Practically, it would be impossible to convene the Sanhedrin with a legal quorum of 71 members during the festival. There was still time to find some way to defend his brother. Or maybe common sense would yet prevail and Jesus could be persuaded to leave the country.

*   *   *

Morning brought a rush of activity in advance of that night's Feast of Unleavened Bread. Ephron was squatting beside a fire pit in the court burning the *hametz*. Amara's daughters were putting the house in final order, under the watchful eye of Aunt Mary. Jesus' mother and the

Mary from Magdala were helping. The sons were dispatched to collect a lamb raised for the Rabbi James' *Seder* table by a farmer outside the city. And Amara herself had scurried off to the market square for fresh greens and other last-minute items.

James was trying to place himself in the proper frame of mind for his day's major responsibility: presentation of the paschal offering in the temple. Later, he would meet Amara's sons on the mount, take the lamb for entry into the sacred enclave, and deliver it up to be slaughtered. That duty wasn't just a practical function, it was an act of worship for which spiritual preparation was as important as the house-cleaning and removal of leaven.

He had risen early to immerse himself in the ritual bath as a precaution after the talk with Pilate yesterday. There was nothing about the meeting that should have defiled him. But since only the circumcised and ritually pure were permitted to take part in the paschal sacrifice, and the rabbis continued to debate what degree of contact with non-Jews compromised one's ritual standing, an extra step seemed justified. Now, having prayed the morning service with the three students, he was leading the young men in a brief study of some scriptural passages relevant to Passover and discussing their significance.

Asher was having difficulty concentrating on the topic, since he was a first-born and faced a day of fasting before that night's meal. It was his yearly confrontation with the reality that nothing so focuses one's thoughts on eating as having to abstain from it.

In the late morning, James received a note from Gamaliel. The approach of the feast was making it difficult for him to contact fellow rabbis, he reported, and so he had set the effort aside for the time being. However, he had been able to speak with several on the Sanhedrin who promised to resist any attempt to force an action against Jesus. Not that they were supporters of the Nazarene—to a man, they objected strongly to Jesus' criticisms. But some saw his challenge to the temple leaders as compatible with their own desire to reduce priestly dominance of the council. That bit of pragmatism struck James as interesting. He mused on how his brother seemed to touch so many differing and deeply held ambitions, one way or the other.

James met Amara's sons at the temple and took the lamb—male, one year old, unblemished—to queue up for entry. The worshippers were admitted in groups of thirty to the inner court. As the gates were opened and they passed through, all shared a common reaction. To approach the high altar with the great sanctum looming up behind, its immense pillars and shining white marble facade, the golden spikes of its crenellated ridge gleaming, always brought a catch to one's breath.

At Passover the experience was especially dramatic. You were met with a wild cacophony of prayers, animal bleating, trumpet blasts, and the singing of psalms by a choir of Levites. The effect, at once celestial and ear-splitting, jolted you from the world of earthly concerns.

The lambs were taken and slaughtered in the ritual way, a single, quick stroke of a blade honed to the keenest edge. The blood was caught in golden cups, rounded on the bottom so they could not be set down and the liquid congeal. These vessels were then passed from hand to hand along a line of priests. The entire corps of temple clergy took part in the meritorious act of conveying the blood to the altar for sprinkling.

The carcasses were hung on hooks. The entrails were removed, cleansed of excrement, and salted in preparation for burning. The air was thick with smoke from the holocaust, rising in a column visible for miles, its pungent stench detectable throughout the city. Eyes stung whenever a shift in the wind disrupted its ascent and concentrated it within the court.

This frenzied scene, the most tumultuous in a yearly calendar abounding in fervid ceremonial made James ponder a question that regularly intruded on his thinking: *How was it that animal sacrifice found favor in the eyes of the Holy One?*

Scripture insisted that it did, and laid out in minute detail the instructions for its correct conduct. Rabbis explored the appropriate disposition of mind required for the act to be truly efficacious. But even if those offering their lambs did so with the utmost purity, devotion and love of their fellows, as the prophets had insisted made sacrifice pleasing to God, how did the deaths of animals move the Lord's heart?

The fact was that, despite his careful attention to all the sacred tasks of Jewish life, James had profound doubts about the blood ritual. And he knew from his counseling in the Synagogue at the Crossed Streets, as well as from many written inquiries, that others questioned it too.

CHAPTER THIRTY-EIGHT

You shall eat it in haste:
it is the Lord's Passover.

(Exodus 12)

The youngest of the three orphaned children at the table, a pale and spindly lad named Gefen, had the honor of asking the four questions. In answer, the Rabbi James explained what made this night different from all others, noting why only unleavened bread was consumed, why bitter herbs were eaten in place of ordinary vegetables, why the herbs were dipped—not just once, but twice—and why the feast was conducted with everyone in a reclining posture.

The *Seder* was an actual meal centered around the lamb sacrificed in the temple. But it was also a religious service, the elements of which unfolded according to an order inspired by Scripture and formularized through long and hallowed tradition. These included prayers and blessings, hand washing, the sharing of four goblets of wine, retelling the Exodus story, and eating the ritual foods, including the bitter herbs and the unleavened bread from which the festival got its identity. Even the method for cooking the lamb—roasting, usually on a spit over pomegranate wood—was prescribed.

But while ritual was paramount, the feast was intended to be a joyous family celebration. It had been so in the past for James, but this year, the atmosphere was unmistakably subdued. At several moments during the meal, James and Mary caught each other's glance, each recognizing the preoccupation they shared.

Where was Jesus partaking of the feast? Was he reclining at table in the manner of free men? That was the significance of this posture prescribed for eating the meal, since the Holy One had made His people free. If Jesus was eating the bitter herbs that commemorated the bitter lot of the Jews in their slavery, would he soon taste the bitterness of captivity—or worse? Would his mother shed salty tears for her son as the salt water in which the greens were dipped recalled the tears shed in Egypt? So hastily prepared was the first Passover meal that the leavening in the bread had no time to rise. This was because the Jews were waiting in eager anticipation of escaping their bondage. But James knew that Jesus planned no escape.

Mulling such parallels troubled James' mind. But perhaps the most disturbing *Seder* image of all was that of the lamb. Did Jesus intend to make a kind of sacrificial offering of himself? If this was what his brother had in mind, the word *blasphemy* might be more apt than the Rabbi James cared to consider.

These thoughts James tried to set aside so that he might enjoy the feast—this memorial of liberty, this hallmark of Jewishness. And for the most part, he was able to share in the felicity of the meal which ran long into the night.

After a time, though, everyone's enthusiasm was bound to wane. The children were finding it difficult to stay awake, and even the adults were contemplating sweet repose, when a pounding was heard at the front gate. Ephron went to inquire, returning with a young man James and Mary recognized immediately. It was John son of Zebedee, one of Jesus' apostles. He was out of breath and his face reddened. Beads of sweat glistened in his hair and what were the beginnings of a sparse beard. James stood and looked at Mary who rose from her place and came forward. Collecting himself, John bowed before James.

"Rabbi," he said in a shallow, breathy voice, "my master has been arrested."

A gasp from Mary. The room went silent. All were attentive.

"We were in the garden on the mount," he said, "the place called Gethsemane. We went there after our *Seder*. Temple officials, their attendants, and a unit of guards accosted the Lord there. Simon tried to put up a defense. He had a sword and went to fend them off. One man was injured. Jesus ordered that no one resist. Simon and the rest of us withdrew."

Mary gripped James by the arm, her mouth open, eyes wide with alarm.

"When did this happen?" James asked.

"Just now," said John, "within the hour. Simon sent me to alert you."

"They would move against Jesus during the festival?" Mary said, aghast.

James thought for a moment, then in an abrupt motion, cut the air in front of his chest with a fist. "Of course they would," he said. "There would be no possibility of attracting a crowd on the night of *Seder*. I should have foreseen this."

"But it is unthinkable," Mary insisted.

"*That* is the point," James said, rebuking himself. "It is unthinkable, and so I didn't think of it. No one thought of it—but the priests."

"Someone else thought of it, Rabbi," John said. "One of our company, Judas."

"Iscariot?"

John nodded. "It was he who led them to our place of seclusion."

"How can that be?" Asher blurted out from across the room, shocked. "One of Jesus' own men would betray him?"

Now it was James who nodded. "Simon told me of his suspicions about this Judas."

"For some time Judas has been acting in a strangely detached way," said John. "And at our feast tonight, the Lord seemed to confront him. They had a very odd exchange, and then Judas departed, even before the supper was finished."

"Where is my brother now?" James asked.

"I don't know, Rabbi," said John. "The guards first took him to Annas, the former high priest. He questioned the Lord for a time."

"Annas?" Mary said. "Annas is father-in-law to Caiaphas and no longer holds office."

James stroked his face thoughtfully. "Annas has a villa on the Mount of Olives," he said.

"Yes, it is located very close to the garden," said John. "Perhaps that is where they gathered before they came for the Lord."

"Perhaps," James said. Then, addressing Mary: "I think the involvement of Annas suggests this was a thoroughly organized plot. His son-in-law may be high priest now, but Annas wields much power out of sight. Pilate's predecessor, Valerius Gratis, removed Annas from office, but he didn't remove the office from the family. That is why Caiaphas holds it to this day—such is the influence of Annas." He turned back to John. "Jesus is no longer at the villa?"

"No, Rabbi. We followed the guards as they took him away, though at some distance. They brought him to the city, and we were delayed at the gate, holding back until they passed through and moved on before we dared enter. Simon continued to follow. I came here."

"Were they headed toward the amphitheater?" James asked.

"Possibly," said John. "Yes, I think so."

"They're taking him to Caiaphas," said James. "Why were you not all arrested?"

John hesitated. "I am not sure, Rabbi," he said. Perhaps the guards were distracted by what happened after Simon's action."

"Distracted?"

"The man Simon wounded—his ear was damaged. There was blood all over him. But Jesus healed him, right on the spot. I think after seeing that, everyone forgot about the rest of us. They just seized the Lord and departed quickly. He went without objecting."

"Asher," James barked decisively.

"Yes, Rabbi?"

"Go to Master Gamaliel, and have him meet me at the high priest's residence. Your two companions will stay here to guard Jesus' mother. If anyone wanted to use her as a means of threatening her son, now would be the time."

"Threatening him?" Mary said. "To do what?"

"Recanting, giving up his ministry, confessing to some absurd crime—who knows?" James said. "We must consider all possibilities. If necessary, we will get you out of Jerusalem."

Mary planted her feet firmly on the floor, glaring at James. "I stay with my child," she said.

There was no point—and no time—to argue with a woman whose firmness of will James knew so well. He turned to Ephron. "Joseph of Arimathea is at his city residence for the festival. Go tell him what happened. Bring him to the house of Caiaphas as quickly as you can."

"Yes, Master."

Asher and Ephron departed to carry out James' directives.

"What are *you* going to do, James?" Mary asked.

"Whatever has been set in motion tonight," he said, "I must do what

I can to stop it—or at least to slow it down. I knew our spiritual leaders intended to attack Jesus, but I thought they would stay within the Law. Now I see how foolish was that assumption."

He took John by the arm and pulled him toward the door. "To the high priest," he said. Then pausing, he looked at Mary. "I promised my father that I would keep my brother safe. Pray for me, Mary, that I can fulfill that pledge."

James hurried outside and along the path, pausing only to grab a cloak from the stone hut. He went out through the front gate, John following closely behind. They made their way across the city amid a large number of people in the streets. As was usual during the festival, officers of the night watch were on patrol but curfew had been suspended to allow those who were guests at the tables of others or who participated in joint feasts to return home. Despite the lateness of the hour, a genial atmosphere prevailed as people exchanged greetings of *Chag Sameach*—Joyous Festival—sometimes with an exuberance that suggested consumption of far more wine than was ritually demanded. The cheerfulness was lost on James and John, whose sole focus was the danger facing Jesus.

John pointed out a particular two-story house they passed on their way. It sat at the far end of a lane running from a small plaza in which one of the new water fountains had been installed. "Down there is the place where we held our *Seder* tonight," John said. "In the upper room of that far house."

James peered down the lane. "There?" he asked. "Among the Essenes?"

This was a part of town known as the Essene Quarter, still called such even though only a small number of the brothers continued to reside here. Most had removed themselves to the compounds in Jericho or Qumran to await the final battle. Which brought to mind Pinchas' remark about an army. If Jesus were to be killed, would the Essenes take it as a sign of the end? Would the Essenes rise?

"Jesus sent Simon and myself to arrange for a room where we could celebrate the feast," John explained. "All he told us was that we would meet a man carrying a water jar and that fellow would take us to the place. Sure enough, when we entered the city, the man made himself known to us. We followed him to that fountain, where he filled his jar, and then to the house."

In what ironic circumstances James seemed to find his brother. The location of their *Seder* was quite close to the home of Caiaphas. Of course, it had long been considered humorous that the priestly abode should be situated in a neighborhood identified with the Essenes, so well known for their estrangement from the temple.

The high priest's residence was a handsome Greek-style structure that was impressive but didn't quite merit the name *palace* given it by some. In many ways, it reminded James of the fine houses his family built in Sepphoris. It faced one of the main thoroughfares in this part of town, a broad and elegant street that ran from the north end of Jerusalem to the principal market of the Upper City. A number of important buildings dotted its route, including Antipas' Jerusalem villa and several wealthy and prominent synagogues.

Here too, the festive spirit was evident. Knots of people loitered about, engaged in jovial chatter around fires hastily built for warmth against the night chill. One such cluster stood outside the high priest's residence in a wide front court that was separated from the street only by a low wall with an open gate. Gathered around a large brazier were several temple guards along with the house servants who had been ejected from the inside while a proceeding was underway.

And one other as well—John spotted Simon lurking nervously by a window, apparently trying to catch what he could of words being spoken within.

"There is Simon," John said, pointing.

James scanned up and down the street, then across into the court, then up and down again. "Let us stay here." He watched the big fisherman's furtive listening for several seconds. "Simon may hear more if we draw no attention to him, and that could be helpful. We must wait for Joseph and Gamaliel. I would not be welcome in there, so we can do nothing until they arrive."

Gamaliel and Asher came first, approaching in another direction from which James and John had come. The four men found a secluded spot in which to speak.

"Whatever kind of tribunal Caiaphas is conducting, it cannot be lawful," said Gamaliel.

"I fear the high priest is not paying close attention to legalities," James said. "He wants to remove my brother with as much dispatch as possible. Please, friend, you sit on the Sanhedrin. Go in and do what you can."

Gamaliel nodded agreement. "Asher said you've sent for Joseph."

"Yes. I assume he is on his way now."

"Hurry him in too as soon as he comes. I will need every voice that can speak."

"Are there others we might recruit?" asked James.

"This late on the night of the feast? I doubt it."

Gamaliel hurried across the street and up some steps to a portico where a guard came forward to challenge him at the front door. James and the others couldn't hear the exchange, but from Gamaliel's emphatic gestures they discerned that the rabbi was insisting on his rights as a council member. After a moment, the guard stepped aside and admitted him.

It was growing colder now, and many of the loiterers had begun fading into the night. One of the fires was abandoned, so James, John and Asher claimed it for themselves. They hunched over the few remaining embers that smoldered lowly but still radiated some heat. James noted that Simon must also be cold. He had left off from his skulking about and found a place at the brazier among the servants. A young woman spoke to him, and he drew back, waving a hand.

Footsteps announced that Joseph of Arimathea had arrived.

"I sent Ephron home and came as quickly as I could," Joseph said. "What is happening?"

James provided a brief explanation. Without further word, Joseph turned away and crossed the street, looking quite determined. He too was challenged at the door, and a repeat of Gamaliel's confrontation scene played out. James could hear Joseph shout, "I am a court officer." Once more the guard relented and stepped aside. The presence of Gamaliel and Joseph gave James a small spark of hope that a miscarriage of justice might yet be averted.

Meanwhile, Simon was approached by a second woman. James saw that he looked agitated. He shook his head and gestured again, an expression of what seemed like fear now on his face.

Time passed and the embers burned out as James waited with Asher and John. They found the remains of another abandoned fire some lengths up the street and enjoyed what warmth was still available. Each pulled his cloak tightly around himself against the chill, now sharp. They would have felt the cold even more severely, if not for their shared worry about Jesus.

"Rabbi," asked John, "the high priest *will* allow Rabbi Gamaliel and Master Joseph to speak on your brother's behalf, won't he?"

"They are both senior members of the Sanhedrin," James said. "They cannot be denied their right to be heard. And they both enjoy the advantage of never having championed Jesus' cause in public, which gives them a measure of credibility."

"The Rabbi Gamaliel is not a follower of Jesus at all," Asher said. "That is known."

"Yes, and I'm glad it is," said James. "It allows him to argue for proper application of the Law without being accused of favoring my brother. As for Joseph...well, he *does* believe in Jesus' teaching, but he has kept his sentiments to himself."

The sky was beginning to show the first glow of morning light when the sound of a voice drew James' attention across the street.

"No!" Simon shouted at another bystander. "I tell you, I do not know the man."

Just at that moment, the door of the high priest's residence opened and Jesus was led out and down the steps by a squad of guards. His hands were bound, and he looked tired, his face blank. The crowing of a rooster could be heard faintly in the distance.

James noticed that as he walked toward the open gate, Jesus turned his head in Simon's direction. The big fisherman was fixed by his master's glance and froze in place. A trembling overcame him as Jesus passed by, and his face broke into a look of deep shame. He actually began to weep. As Jesus was led away, prodded along by the guards, Simon ran out through the gate and fled in the opposite direction.

Gamaliel and Joseph came hurrying across the street, their faces seared in anger.

"What happened?" James asked anxiously.

"A travesty happened," said Gamaliel. "The Law was totally abused. I feel like I have been insulted as a Jew."

"False witness," Joseph sputtered. "False witness—in brazen defiance of the commandment. A disgrace! They painted Jesus as a Zealot, as if all his preaching was aimed at promoting insurrection. They even brought in liars to trump up nonsense."

"The fools couldn't even get themselves to agree with each other's stories," said Gamaliel.

"Did my brother defend himself?"

"Hardly," Gamaliel replied. "Caiaphas focused on something Jesus said in the Porch about destruction of the temple. I was told about his remark at the time. Apparently, he was speaking prophetically of evil days to come. Everyone who heard him there understood what he meant."

"Yes, I know. I was in the Porch when he said it."

"Caiaphas made it seem as if your brother was threatening to tear the place down himself."

"How did Jesus answer such an absurd charge?"

Gamaliel gave a shudder of exasperation. "Your...*brother*..." He paused to shake off the emotion. "Jesus walked right into Caiaphas' trap, James. He said he would raise *this temple* again in three days. It was another provocation. He was talking about himself—*this* temple—the temple of his own body. He was daring Caiaphas to kill him."

Joseph jumped in to expand on the account. "And then the high priest asked Jesus directly, *Are you the Son of God?*"

James' stomach tightened immediately. Here was the question to which his family believed they knew the answer—but the one they had always dreaded would someday be asked.

"What...did my brother say...to that?"

"At first he seemed to equivocate," said Joseph. "He replied that those were *Caiaphas'* words. But I sensed that he wasn't finished. I held my breath, hoping that his explanation would somehow deflect the question, the way I'd seen him do before with some witty riposte. Instead, he went on about how the *Son of Man* would be seen at the right hand of God and coming from heaven on a cloud. You've heard how he calls himself *Son of Man.*"

"And that was enough for the high priest," Gamaliel added. "He knew he had him at that point. Caiaphas tore his robe and shouted *Blasphemy!* Joseph and I protested the whole business. We said the hearing was illegal—held at night during the feast, held outside of the official chamber, held without a quorum—"

"How many members were present?" James asked.

"Thirty, at the most," said Joseph.

"And most of those were priests," Gamaliel said. "The scribes and lay elders I could count on one hand—all close allies of Caiaphas, anyway. That so-called *court* was selected carefully."

"Then there could have been no actual verdict," said James. "It didn't meet the requirements of a legitimate session."

"We raised that very objection," Joseph said, "several times."

"Not that it did any good," said Gamaliel. "The court rendered a finding, and the high priest declared it valid."

James was stunned. "That is outrageous. Caiaphas dares to ignore the Law and yet calls my brother a blasphemer? This cannot stand. It *will* not stand. The Sanhedrin won't allow its authority to be usurped in such a way. You two must demand a special session of the full body."

"There is no time," Gamaliel said. "Caiaphas ordered that your brother be taken to Pilate. He's asking...for Jesus' death, James."

The moment. The confirmation of all James' fears. He felt his head beginning to spin, but he forced the sensation away. He needed his mind to be absolutely clear.

The high priest could not call for an audience with the prefect right now. Short of a civic emergency or special need of state, Pilate kept strictly to his routine of personal preparation, daily briefings, and administrative tasks. James was never able to see him until at least mid-morning. Caiaphas would be aware of this schedule.

Unless—unless an arrangement had already been made. Did Pilate know about the false court? Was he waiting to receive the prisoner and render a confirming judgment of his own?

No. James was sure that the prefect would not intentionally collude in this malfeasance. Even if he felt some obligation for Caiaphas' help with the aqueduct funding, Pilate regarded the concept of Roman justice too highly. Which meant that Jesus would have to be held someplace for awhile.

"It's too early for Caiaphas to bring my brother to Pilate. If Jesus is to be presented before the provincial bar, where would he be lodged until a hearing is convened?"

"In provincial custody," Gamaliel said.

"What facility?"

Gamaliel shrugged. "Well...if Pilate were at his government seat in Caesarea, Jesus would be transported there. But since the prefect is currently in residence in Jerusalem...the cells in the Antonia Fortress?"

"That is what I think as well," James said. "I must go there and speak to Jesus. He has to realize that Pilate is his only hope."

"Do you trust the ethics of our Roman overlord?" Joseph asked.

"I have nothing else to trust, and neither does Jesus. I must convince my brother to speak forthrightly in his own defense."

"He hasn't taken your advice on that so far," said Gamaliel.

"I know..." James said with a note of irresolution. "But what else can I tell him? His life is at stake."

Gamaliel and Joseph nodded resignedly.

James looked up at the sky, which was getting light but not all that much. The sun had not yet peeked above the eastern hills. He asked if Gamaliel and Joseph thought it might be possible to recruit some of their fellow council members to come later in the morning and join in an appeal to the prefect. They could register an objection to the illegal proceeding on behalf of the Sanhedrin. At the very least, that would alert Pilate to the duplicity of Annas and Caiaphas. Whoever might be gotten—even if only a handful—it would be a help.

The pair departed, promising to make a supreme effort.

James instructed Asher and John to return to the Synagogue at the Crossed Streets, inform Mary of what was happening, and remain with her, providing what support and comfort they could. Then he headed off to the Antonia Fortress.

He did not hurry, and he did not attempt to follow the squad of guards transferring Jesus. He knew it would be impossible to get near his brother on the street. Instead, he turned east of the amphitheater and walked along the ridge above the Tyropoeon Valley to Gamaliel's synagogue and then across the bridge to the temple mount.

He kept up a steady but modest pace, restraining his nervous inclination to hurry, and tried to think of anything he might say that could somehow break through his brother's stubbornness. Traversing the western face of the temple, he reached the fortress gate. By now, Jesus should have arrived and the guards have had time to turn him over to the Roman garrison. Presumably, he would be in a cell.

The figure in white robes and turban was an unexpected sight to the principales in charge of the sentries at the gate. Who was this distinguished-looking Jew, and what was his mission at so early an hour?

Except for the local provisioners, Jews avoided the Antonia Fortress with its taint of pagan uncleanness.

"I am the Rabbi James, master of the Synagogue at the Crossed Streets and a doctor of the Law. You have received a prisoner named Jesus?"

"Yes," said the officer.

"I wish to speak with him."

"For what purpose?"

"For religious counsel." Which James hoped was sufficiently vague while sounding sufficiently plausible. Even a non-Jew might reason that someone charged with blasphemy would surely be in need of religious counsel. Then too, the principales might assume that James was Jesus' spokesman before the court, which would be equally satisfactory.

Having never before received a request about religious counsel for a prisoner, the principales told James to wait and then went inside the arched gateway. James observed him give a sharp salute to a higher-ranking officer who happened to be in the forecourt. Presently, the two came out through the gate.

"This is the man, Centurion," said the captain.

"I am Cassius Longinus, commandant of the Antonia Fortress."

James' attention was drawn momentarily to an odd disfigurement of the man's left eye. "Peace be upon you, Centurion. I am the Rabbi James."

A glint of recognition in the Roman. "Yes... You are the Jewish advisor to Lord Pilate."

James hesitated on hearing himself described so, but only briefly. "That is correct," he said.

The centurion turned to his subordinate. "Admit him and take him to the prisoner." Then to James: "The Jerusalem garrison welcomes you, Rabbi. We are honored by the presence of so respected a guest."

"Thank you."

James was taken to a stairway that led down to a guard post below ground. The principales turned him over to a jailer, gave a word of instruction, and a heavy, iron-framed, plank door was opened. James entered a dark corridor lined on either side with similar doors, each of which bore a small hinged port, unbolted and open. The air in this narrow and gloomy passage carried a mixture of stale odors, among which he identified human waste, mold, and the smoke from a torch held in a wall bracket, providing the only light.

The jailer led him the entire length of the corridor to a door at the far end. He selected a key from among those on a heavy ring and opened the door to a wide space divided into three cage-like chambers by thick metal bars. Dim but natural light from open shafts above the far wall revealed the dark figures of three men, each lying in his own cell on a heap of dank, musty straw.

"The center one," said the jailer, then pointed behind himself. "The door will be left open." He went back into the corridor and returned to the guard station.

James blinked, trying to make his eyes adjust to the shadowy space. All three men were still, and the sound of snoring could be heard. It didn't seem possible that his brother could have settled himself to sleep so readily in this eerie, unnerving place, even though he had looked tired coming out of the high priest's residence.

"Jesus?" James whispered, to no response. "Jesus?"

The man in the middle cell stirred and brought himself up on an elbow, his face in shadow from the light shaft behind. "Well, well..." he said. "Peace be upon you, James son of Joseph."

The voice was not that of James' brother, but it was familiar.

"Do you not remember your old classmate in the school of Hillel?"

James knelt down at the bars and struggled to make out the obscured face. At last his vision became clear and he was able to connect the features into an image he recognized.

"Jedediah..."

"Ah, you do remember." He sat, hunched but upright, legs crossed. "How is it that the famous Rabbi James comes to visit me?"

"What are you doing here?"

"Enjoying the hospitality of our Roman friends. I fancy I am their most honored guest. Surely, you must have heard about my arrival."

James paused. Thought. Knew. "You are...*bar Abbas*."

Jedediah smiled. "Some know me by that name."

"So," said James, "you found a way to take that...*action*...we once spoke of."

"And did you find your way to improve the life of the people?"

"A small way," said James. "I answer questions. I offer advice. I interpret the Law. I serve as best I can."

"Then we both serve—each in his own manner."

A moment of quiet, an awkward space in time. The two other prisoners continued their snoring in the background.

"Do you still think about the Sepphoris road, James?"

James said nothing.

"Does the *peace of Rome* still grate on you?"

"I...*remember*," said James. "I try *not* to hate."

There were innumerable questions James might have asked his old classmate after all these years. He had often thought about the prickly and secretive young man who forsook the path of learning for the course of violence and blood—and who had offered James the opportunity to do likewise. At the same time, James realized that, actually, he had nothing at all to say. His own course had been so different. It had not taken him down the Sepphoris road, which now seemed to be Jedediah's destination.

But curiosity prompted him on one point. "Why did you adopt the name, *Jesus bar Abbas?*"

Jedediah laughed. "Is it family pride inquiring?"

"Family—?"

"Your brother, of course." Jedediah spoke in a grandiloquent way that was clearly meant as mockery. "If he could become so famous as the *Son of Man*—an identity earned through no accomplishments at all, other than much talk and the raising of pointless hopes—then surely I, who have brought such tangible progress to the cause of the Jewish nation, deserved a more exalted identity. I am...the *Son of the Father*. Appropriate, isn't it?"

James expelled a small burst of air through his nose. He looked about, feeling the oppressiveness of this grim enclosure in which the Zealot leader, *bar Abbas*, was to spend his last days. He considered Jedediah's fate. "Then, may the Father be with you," he said.

"Did you come to offer me a blessing, James?"

"I came to find my brother."

"Your brother?"

"He has been arrested."

Jedediah sat up straighter, his interest piqued. "Arrested? So, your family has been touched by the *peace of Rome* once again."

"It is not Rome that arrested him. It is our own leaders. They are calling him a blasphemer. Has anybody been brought into this place during the past hour or so?"

"Well, James...elegant as these quarters may be, my view is somewhat restricted. I do not think, however, that there is anyone here but my companions and myself."

James got to his feet. "Then I must go."

"So soon?" There was now actual bile in Jedediah's voice.

"I have to find my brother," said James. "I have to defend him."

"Your brother's keeper, eh?"

"I will pray for you, Jedediah."

"I will pray for your brother. He may yet prove useful to the cause of the Jewish nation."

The man in the right cell stirred. "Who is here?" he asked in a groan.

"Go back to sleep, Dismis," Jedediah said. "It is just an old friend."

James paused at the doorway. "Peace be upon you, Jedediah."

"That is not...likely...Rabbi."

James walked the length of the corridor to the guard station. The principales was still waiting there.

"Jesus bar Abbas is not the man I came to see," James said. "Where is Jesus of Nazareth?"

"The Jew prophet?"

James nodded.

"I don't know."

"Is he not a prisoner within the fortress?"

"No. Those three are the only prisoners we hold right now."

James thanked him, climbed the stairway up into the forecourt, and went out through the front gate.

CHAPTER THIRTY-NINE

The crowd shouted, crying,
"Crucify him, crucify him!"

(Luke 23)

J esus could be glimpsed being led up the stairway into the praetorium when James arrived at the prefecture gate. He was still
bound, flanked on either side by legionaries.

"I must speak with Lord Pilate," James demanded of the guards.

The officer at the entry post held his hands open outwardly,
apologetically. "I'm sorry, Rabbi. The prefect will be interviewing that
prisoner who was brought here this morning on orders from your Sanhedrin. Some of the chief priests and rabbis are in the court."

James recognized several faces—members of Caiaphas' inner circle—along with the squad of temple guards that had brought Jesus
from the high priest's residence.

"I know about this prisoner," he said. "Why was he not turned over
to the garrison at the fortress? Isn't it usual to place a prisoner into provincial custody when requesting a trial before the prefect?"

"You are correct, Rabbi," the officer said. "It was quite *unusual*
for them to present him here. But I understand this is something of a
special case. The man is a very renowned figure, Jesus, the Nazarene
prophet. Given his popularity among the Jews, I think the authorities
were eager to avoid parading him around in the streets. We informed
them that Lord Pilate would be occupied for some time, but they insisted on waiting here in the court."

James was beginning to despair of his ability to anticipate the high
priest's moves at all. He knew that Caiaphas wished Jesus eliminated,
but he had assumed it would be done according to either the Law of
Moses or the law of Rome. Now he saw that his expectations were

being thwarted at every turn. Such duplicity was worthy of Herod or Archelaus, not the steward of God's holy temple. Little wonder the family of Annas had retained the high priesthood in spite of changing political fortunes. These were people without scruples of any kind.

A crowd was forming in the plaza outside the prefecture. Word of Jesus' arrest must have begun to circulate. James took in the scene, his glance settling on various figures. This assemblage did not seem like the typical array of curiosity seekers one would expect to see gather in response to an unusual occurrence. It was nothing like the throng that had cheered Jesus on his entry into the city. The people he saw before him were not representative of the wide variety of classes, trades and ethnic types normally observed in the streets of Jerusalem. James got the feeling they were hard characters, lowlifes, even derelicts. They evinced no real interest, but seemed rather to be waiting, chatting idly or not speaking at all.

Then, in contrast, Joseph of Arimathea appeared with two other men whom James recognized as lay elders of the Sanhedrin. They strode purposefully across the plaza, Joseph spotting James at the gate. Greetings were exchanged, and James thanked the counselors for coming. He explained the high priest's circumvention of the standard process and that Jesus was currently being interrogated by Pilate.

"After what Gamaliel and I witnessed in Caiaphas' house," Joseph said, "it is no surprise that rules are being bent here as well." He went up to the officer at the gate. "We are members of the Sanhedrin with an interest in this matter," he said in a voice that was almost ceremonial.

The officer looked at James, who nodded authoritatively. Joseph and the two others were admitted. James strode in at their side. If Caiaphas wasn't impeded by technicalities, neither would he be.

Their arrival was noted by the priests and scribes, who were gathered under the new awnings where James had met with Pilate, as if they were all too delicate for the morning light. The temple guards, not so privileged, stood in the sun. Joseph observed that every one of the priests and scribes present had earlier taken part in the travesty at the high priest's residence.

"Keep an eye on those *mamzers*," he whispered to James. "They are here to demand your brother's head, and they won't go quietly if Pilate doesn't give it to them."

James conversed for several minutes with Joseph and the two others. They speculated about how Pilate would conduct his part in this farce, and agreed that, somehow, the prefect had to be made aware that the proceeding in Caiaphas' house violated the Law.

The crowd outside the prefecture had grown to where it could be heard over the walls. James went back to the gate and looked out. There was somewhat more variety now. A few women were present, though most had the same bedraggled look as the men. James began to suspect that these people weren't casual onlookers at all. Had they been recruited to support the priests in demanding Jesus' death?

A stir drew his attention back inside. Two legionaries were descending the wide stairway to take up a position on either side of the bottom step, their javelins and shields ported in guard bearing. All assumed Pilate would follow, but several minutes passed with no one else appearing. James stood, waiting, thinking. He wondered what instructions the priests and scribes had from Caiaphas, and considered what he might say to counter their falsehoods.

Glancing toward the upper level of the praetorium, James noticed Pilate's wife standing in the window from which she had watched the unveiling of the golden shields. The woman looked uneasy. James wondered what the elegant wife of a Roman knight, the daughter of a senator, might be thinking about the religious disputes of a land that must seem very strange to her.

"Rabbi James..."

Someone had come up behind him. It was Gamaliel accompanied by a short man, round of body and face with wisps of hair as starkly white as his beard.

"Rabbi Zephan has graciously come to assist in the defense of your brother," Gamaliel said.

"The best which Rabbi Gamaliel, could find at short notice, I'm afraid," said Zephan with the jollity for which he was known. "But I'll make my feelings clear and stand for no skirting of justice."

James offered as full a smile as his anxious state permitted. "I could ask for no one better," he said. "Peace be upon you, Rabbi. My thanks for your help. I know my brother would offer his thanks too."

"Your brother has done nothing to keep himself from this end," Zephan said, wagging a finger in a scolding manner, even as his face retained its grin. "He would have greater support from among the rabbinate, more voices to speak for him, if he wasn't so unrelenting in his complaints. We are not all a bunch of *whited sepulchers.*" The point was sharp, but not bitter.

A shrug and a shake of the head from James. "Too true, Rabbi."

"I brought several students as well," Gamaliel said, "for moral support, if nothing else. That mob outside is just a bunch of vagrants and good-for-nothings dragged off the streets. I saw one of Caiaphas' pages handing out coins so they'll make the right noises at the right time. My lads may be able to provide some counterweight. They can be loud when they want to be."

A pair of doors opened at ground level, and a column of soldiers marched out into the court. Then a hush fell as Pilate appeared at the top of the stairs. The priests and scribes rushed from under the awnings and clustered at the base of the steps, engulfing the two guards. Jesus could be seen behind the prefect, flanked by two legionaries. Several officers were also present.

"Men of the Sanhedrin," Pilate called, "you have charged the prisoner, Jesus of Nazareth, with blasphemy as well as with inciting the people to disorder and insurrection. I accept your religious judgment as to the question of blasphemy, a matter on which I cannot comment. It is for you to say who may have affronted your god. That is no business of Caesar. As for the charge of incitement—"

Here Pilate paused ever so slightly. James thought he detected a tiny bit of discomfort in the prefect, and he felt his own tension increase.

"It is true that, in recent days, certain actions of the accused have unsettled the public peace. However, I see no evidence of any intent to precipitate a revolt. On the basis of what has been presented to me at this point, the punishment of death is not warranted."

James wished to feel hopeful at that statement. But the reaction of the priests and scribes did nothing to ease the knot he'd carried in his stomach for the past few hours.

One of Caiaphas' key suffragans extended his arm and pointed to Jesus severely. "This man has misled the people and caused uproar throughout all of Galilee and Judea, from his native place of Nazareth, right into the heart of the Lord's city. He is a *menace.*"

"Galilee, you say?" The hint of a smile played on Pilate's lips. "Ah yes, he is a Galilean, isn't he." The prefect turned to look at Jesus, as if an idea had just sprung freshly into his head. "Jesus of Nazareth—yes, of course. He is a subject of the Tetrarch Herod Antipas. And as it happens, His Excellency is in residence here in Jerusalem for the duration of your holy festival."

The prefect gestured to one of his officers.

"The prisoner will be taken to the Tetrarch for an assessment of his guilt. The ruler of Galilee should judge one of his own."

To the open mouths of the delegation, Jesus was led slowly down the stairs by the officer to whom Pilate had directed his signal. The guards at the bottom, holding their shields out in front of themselves, pushed everyone back away from the stairs. When Jesus reached the bottom, the column of soldiers standing by instantly split and moved to surround him, and the group proceeded as a body toward the gate. James tried to catch his brother's eye, but Jesus kept his head bowed in a posture of humble submission.

The priests and scribes were engaged in a furious huddle discussing this turn of events. A similar conference had coalesced among Joseph, the two fellow lay elders, and the Rabbis Gamaliel and Zephan. For his part, James trained his gaze up the stairs at Pilate, whose eyes, he saw, were fixed on him. The prefect turned to another of his officers and said something, then left. The officer descended the stairs and came to James.

"Lord Pilate wishes to meet with you, Rabbi," he said.

The suffragan priest who had spoken out against Jesus called to the commander of the temple guards. He gave him some instructions, and the commander conveyed them to one of his subordinates. That guard and another instantly started for the gate. The priests and scribes retired to the awnings to continue their consultation.

James waved to Gamaliel, jerking his head in the direction of the stairway. Gamaliel, whose first reaction was concern for James' ritual purity, took a half step in his direction, but caught himself and nodded in return. Of course James would accept any spiritual taint which entering a pagan building might bring—Passover or not. His brother's life was at stake.

James followed the officer up the steps, along the corridor, and then into the audience hall. Pilate was there.

"Do not worry about Antipas, Rabbi," the prefect said. "He will dither for a few minutes, probably beg your brother to perform some wondrous feat, and then send him back here. The tetrarch is not going to seal the conviction of a man who is beloved of so many people in Galilee and Perea. Not after what was done to John the Baptist. He will want the blood of Jesus to be on *my* hands, and if Jerusalem is torn apart by rioters, report it all gleefully to Rome."

"Then why did you send my brother to him?" James asked.

"I needed a little time."

"For what?"

"I intend to offer the people a choice."

"Choice?"

"You have a custom of releasing prisoners as part of a festival celebration, do you not?"

"Yes, at the jubilee year."

"Can it apply to other occasions?"

"It can," said James. "But it doesn't happen very often—and hasn't for quite some time."

"Well, perhaps we shall revive that custom for Passover," Pilate said. "I cannot just turn your brother loose. He is charged with a crime—several crimes, in fact. But I *can* listen to the voice of the people."

"Prefect, you must realize that Caiaphas is not finished making his case against Jesus."

"I know that," Pilate said. "And I must tell you, Rabbi, if the case he makes is damning, I will have to do my duty. Caesar would hear about it if I failed in the proper exercise of Roman justice. He would hear from Antipas, from Caiaphas, from Annas, and from many others as well. So I make you no promises."

James understood.

"But at least," said Pilate, "you brother has a chance."

"Will you allow me to speak in his defense?"

"Of course, Rabbi, justice would demand it."

James stood quietly, head sunken, looking at the marble floor. He was very close to feeling overwhelmed by the situation—the unimaginable danger his brother faced, the tragedy that was so possible, so near and vivid. To himself, or to no one in particular, he muttered, "I cannot believe it has come to this. I do not understand how it has happened."

Hearing the remark, Pilate said, "It has come to this because your brother is a man of vision and courage—though I must say, of very *little* prudence—and also because your family is so respected in Galilee."

James looked up. "My family—?"

"Your father was a man of accomplishment, held in high regard. Joseph the Nazareth Builder—correct? He was respected well beyond the circle of Jews in your town. He was respected even by those you would call the *Greeks*. He prospered. He acquired the means—and the intention—to make *you* a man of learning. Your brother benefited from these factors as well, I'm sure. Moreover, he benefited from the situation of his mother, a temple virgin, and from her kinship ties. His grandfather was a man of wealth. His uncle was a temple priest. His cousin *should* have been one. And of course, there is the lineage of David."

Had Pilate looked so deeply into the family background? Why?

"These are the kinds of connections that draw the interest of others, Rabbi. People do not follow an ignorant nobody. They *will* follow a man of pedigree. That's something Jews and Romans have in common, let me assure you. It is the way of the world. If your brother had come from humble origins, from obscurity, he could never have acquired such fame or enjoyed the devotion of so many as to threaten the religious leadership of your country. I doubt he would be facing *me* at this moment. And even if somehow he did succeed in making trouble, he would have been disposed of quickly and easily." Pilate's head was cocked at a slight angle now. "This situation is no mystery, Rabbi. Not really."

"But...what if my brother is doing...the will of the Holy One?" James asked gingerly.

"Then your god placed him in a family that could give him a good start," said Pilate.

The prefect had other business to attend to. He invited James to make himself comfortable, and headed out of the audience hall. Of course, under present conditions, the rabbi was unlikely to be very comfortable, no matter where he might seat himself.

As Pilate had predicted, the squad transporting Jesus returned him to the prefecture within little more than an hour. The officer in charge reported that there had been a delegation from the temple at the tetrarch's Jerusalem villa when Jesus was brought in. Pilate found it amusing that sly old Caiaphas may have anticipated his maneuver. The priests there made accusations against the prisoner to Antipas, but the tetrarch brushed them aside, intent on probing into Jesus and his ministry. He was particularly interested in the healings, the raising of the dead, and other reported marvels.

"The Nazarene would not pander to idle curiosity," said the officer. "I had to admire him. He remained silent, which annoyed Herod Antipas greatly. So much so that he abetted some of his officers in mocking Jesus by giving one of his elegant royal cloaks in which to dress the prisoner. He insisted Jesus be shown off wearing it when we marched back to the prefecture."

Pilate screwed up his face in a disgusted way. "It is good that Antipas' trollop of a stepdaughter isn't in Jerusalem just now. One lewd dance, and you would have had to wrap the Nazarene's head in that cloak."

"I must also tell you," said the officer, "that the tetrarch sends his warmest regards to Lord Pilate. He thanks you for your hospitality over these days and for the tour of the water system. He also said that he is grateful for your providing him an opportunity to meet the famous prophet, though I fear he was being slightly sarcastic. He insists that you and he will be dearest friends from this day forward."

"I'm sure we will," Pilate said dryly, "at least until the next chance to stab me in the back."

The prefect gave instructions for all the visitors in the court to be escorted out into the plaza below the terrace that extended from the end of the audience hall to the top of the prefecture's outer wall. The Sanhedrin delegation was removed first, followed by Gamaliel, Joseph and the others. When they were all outside, Joseph spotted Nicodemus picking his way across the plaza.

"I have only just heard of this proceeding," Nicodemus said. "Jesus is to stand before Pilate? How did this happen?"

Joseph and Gamaliel gave Nicodemus a quick summary of the situation, from the sham trial at the home of the high priest, to Jesus' being taken to Antipas and brought back again.

"We had hoped to speak in Jesus' defense," said Joseph. "But so far, we have not accomplished very much of anything. And out here, it doesn't look as though we will get a chance to speak at all."

"Where is James?" Nicodemus asked.

"He is inside with the prefect," Gamaliel said. "It seems that any defense of his brother is in his hands alone."

Servants prepared the terrace for a trial. Pilate's throne was carried out through one of the two tall, arched doorways that opened onto the terrace. It was placed on a raised platform in the center to serve as the *Seat of Justice*, from which the prefect would render his verdict. Pilate's personal standard was set up on one side, the eagle of Rome on the other.

Soldiers of various ranks and functional designations came and went, each performing some relevant task. Two cornicenes, the unit buglers, carried their instruments. One officer bore the fasces, a ceremonial ax wrapped in a bundle of white birch rods, which was the insignia of a Roman magistrate. Another carried a small lap desk with parchment sheets, styli and a pot of ink. He went out onto the terrace and sat on a stool off to the side, ready to take down an official record of the proceedings.

This bustle of activity continued for some time, until finally, Pilate came back into the audience hall with several of his subordinates. He was now clothed in full military regalia, including a gilded breastplate bearing a representation of eagle's wings, and a scarlet cloak that draped from his shoulders.

James rose from a low bench that spanned the width of a shadowed alcove on one side of the cavernous hall. He had sat there, ignoring the preparatory activities going on in front of him, trying to pray, trying to hope. The prefect did not glance in his direction, but rather bore himself in a manner that made it plain he was now acting in his most official capacity. This was the vicar of Caesar, the ultimate repository of law and judgment in Judea. Whatever personal affinity Pontius Pilate had for the Rabbi James, it could not bear on the decision to be made.

At a sign from the officer supervising the arrangements, the two cornicenes stepped through the arched doorways, and came to attention out on the terrace, one at either end. In perfect unison, the men raised their horns to their lips and sounded a musical flourish signaling the start of the trial. A ripple of excitement passed through the crowd, stirring even the most ragged and uninterested of the onlookers and bringing the plaza to a hush.

Two columns of officers, six in each, marched out onto the terrace and positioned themselves to the right and left of the throne. These were followed by the fasces bearer, who took his place at the forward edge of the terrace on what would be Pilate's right. Lastly, the prefect himself came out, stepped up onto the raised platform, and assumed his position on the Seat of Justice.

He had just sat and was about to call the session to order when there was a disturbance in the crowd. The line of soldiers posted along the prefecture wall beneath the terrace strained to see what was happening as a gap opened among the onlookers. A phalanx of temple guards approached, muscling bodies out of the way. In the center of the squad walked the high priest.

Pilate felt a surge of pique at this ostentatious entry, undoubtedly timed to assert Sanhedrin prerogatives. He had not expected Caiaphas himself to attend, since there was an ample delegation representing the leadership. Such a grand arrival held a message, and it wasn't hard to decipher its meaning. These Jew priests must have considered the Nazarene prophet an even greater threat to the temple than Pilate had realized. They wanted him dead, and Caiaphas was telling the prefect they would not have it any other way.

Standing just inside the hall by the arched door on the right, James reached the same conclusion. He thought of Pilate's remark about Caesar hearing from Antipas, Caiaphas, Annas, and others. And he feared it would be very hard for the prefect to resist this pressure.

Pilate rose from his seat and swept a hand broadly out toward Caiaphas. The distinguished visitor would have to be acknowledged.

"The prefecture is honored by the presence of Lord Caiaphas, High Priest of the temple and Pontifex of the Jewish religion," Pilate said. "My Lord Caiaphas, for what purpose do you present yourself before the Seat of Justice?"

Caiaphas was not a tall man, nor in any way physically imposing. But he had perfected the manner and comportment of authority. All his movements, down to the most subtle hand gesture, evinced meaning and purpose. He also benefited from a voice, which, while not deep, carried well. So that whenever he appeared in public he was able to convey the impression of a man who spoke with God.

He straightened himself to his maximum height and called back to the prefect, "I appeal for the execution of a blasphemer and traitor."

"Then we invite you to take part in this proceeding," Pilate replied imperiously.

Caiaphas and his retinue were directed in through the gate. The high priest ascended the narrow stairway running up along the wall from the prefecture court directly to the terrace, his cadre of temple guards remaining below.

"We welcome you, Lord Caiaphas," Pilate said, resuming his seat, "and we express our deepest gratitude for your assistance in the true and proper application of Roman justice."

Both the statement and the fact that it had been delivered while sitting down were pointed. The high priest was left to stand before the Seat of Justice and the eagle of Rome.

"I charge the man, Jesus of Nazareth," said Caiaphas.

Pilate nodded at the high priest, then turned and, over his shoulder, called, "Bring out the prisoner."

The order was passed along inside. James watched as his brother was led into the audience hall from the corridor and across to the arched door on the left. Jesus wore the purple robe given by Antipas, his hands were tied, and he kept his eyes turned down. A mix of sounds rose from the crowd when he emerged onto the terrace. Some onlookers chuckled at the sight of the robe.

"What is the man's offense?" Pilate asked.

"He is a heretic," said Caiaphas, "and has blasphemed against the Holy One of Israel by claiming to himself the status of a god."

"These are offenses according to your Jewish laws. They are not crimes against the empire. Why bring him before Caesar's magistrate when you could judge him for yourselves?"

"If he were not a criminal, Prefect, we wouldn't have brought him to you. But we lack the right to execute, and the man, Jesus, has not only blasphemed, he has committed treason against Rome. He calls himself a *king*."

Pilate looked at Jesus. He had already received the high priest's bill of particulars from the Sanhedrin delegation, and had questioned the prisoner in private. But for the sake of the record, the prefect asked, "Are you the king of the Jews?"

There was a long silence, during which James observed that his brother neither spoke nor lifted his eyes from the floor. The prefect was patient for some seconds. He wanted this matter settled cleanly, and he suspected that Jesus was reluctant to answer the question out here on the terrace where Caiaphas would then make some exaggerated show of horror before the crowd. If that was indeed what the Nazarene was thinking, Pilate too had no taste for dramatics from the high priest. He rose from his seat once again.

"We will continue the testimony inside."

He stepped off the platform and walked back into the praetorium. Complaints and moans of disappointment could be heard from the crowd. Jesus was led in after, and the high priest followed. The soldier who was taking down the proceedings hurried in with his lap desk and situated himself to continue writing. James approached quietly from across the room.

The prefect repeated his query. "Are you the king of the Jews?"

Another pause, then Jesus said, "Do you ask this for yourself, or have others said it of me?"

"I am not a Jew," Pilate said. "The chief priests of your own nation have brought you before me. What have you done to cause this?"

"My kingdom is not of this world," Jesus said. "If it were, I would have servants to fight on my behalf. They would not see me handed over to...*the Jews*."

James couldn't believe his brother would make a joke. But Jesus' sense of humor hadn't failed him, even as he was facing such peril. Referring to Caiaphas and the other priests as *the Jews* was to invoke the common sarcasm by which people derided religious leaders who presented themselves as *more Jewish than the Jews* while they really were grasping hypocrites living well on the people's wealth.

"Then you *are* a king," said Pilate, appreciating the sarcasm and trying to suppress a smile.

"*You* say I am," Jesus replied. For the first time, he looked up and eyed Pilate directly. "I was born and came into the world to bear witness to the truth. Those who abide in the truth listen to me."

Pilate fixed on Jesus' eyes, then glanced at Caiaphas and shook his head slowly, as if reflecting on the observations of a lifetime. "What *is* truth?" he said with a shrug, not really expecting an answer.

After a moment of thought, Pilate walked back outside and addressed the crowd. "I do not find guilt in this man," he called, "not by the standards of Roman justice. But since he has offended against your religious statutes, I will have him scourged."

Some of those down in the plaza started applauding and assumed it was time to leave. But the priests and scribes of the delegation that had brought Jesus to Pilate began a chant: *Crucify him! Crucify him! Crucify him!* The others, who had been paid for their attendance, realized they weren't supposed to be satisfied with a mere scourging and joined in the demand.

Pilate ordered Jesus taken out to a small court in a back part of the prefecture where punishments were administered. James grimaced at the thought of the ordeal his brother would undergo. It was well known that the Roman manner of scourging was no mere application of the lash. Jagged metal knobs at the ends of leather thongs ripped wide ribbons of flesh from the victim. The effect was not only severe pain, but loss of so much blood as to cause devastating shock to the entire body. Not all who experienced it recovered.

Again James tried to catch his brother's eye in hopes of conveying some sign of compassion or support. And again Jesus kept his face turned downward. He was led out of the hall.

Caiaphas was now standing behind Pilate on the terrace. "This is not sufficient, Prefect," the high priest said as the chanting continued.

Pilate turned, glared at him, and went back inside the hall.

"The Sanhedrin has submitted a long list of charges," Caiaphas said, following him in. "There are matters that touch on concerns of civic order, and they have not been addressed. The Sanhedrin has found this Nazarene guilty of—"

"The Sanhedrin has done nothing at all," said James, thrusting himself into the matter for the first time. "The so-called court bringing this bill was not legal."

"That man should not be here," Caiaphas retorted, pointing a finger at James. "He is the criminal's brother. His views on this are tainted, and he is not a member of the Sanhedrin."

"But I am a doctor of the Law," James said firmly. "I was certified so by the great Hillel. And I attest that your meeting was not a legitimate session of the Sanhedrin. It was held in the middle of the night. There was nothing close to a quorum of seventy-one members, as required by the Law. And it was conducted in your home, not in the temple. No verdict arrived at can remotely be considered legal."

"Is that so, Lord Caiaphas?" Pilate asked.

The high priest stood stiffly erect. "There are precedents for extraordinary scheduling, as the rabbi well knows. The Sanhedrin has met in emergency session before, and its authority rests with the high priest. Where the high priest sits the council sits."

"But the council did *not* sit," James countered, "only a carefully selected group of priests."

"Were your colleagues, Gamaliel and Joseph, not present? I seem to recall them being in attendance, as were several other rabbis and lay members. And regarding the issue of quorum, urgent necessity overrode formality, just as urgent necessity overrides the restrictions of the Sabbath—a point which your brother makes with some frequency, I'm told. Has he not said that *the Sabbath was made for man, and not man for the Sabbath?*"

It was appalling enough to James that a sham court proceeding—totally without legal validity—had been used to trump up false charges against his brother. That Jesus' own words should be quoted in support of such a farce made Caiaphas' effrontery all the more enraging. But before James could say any of this, Pilate intervened.

"There is nothing to be gained in debating the fine points of your arcane statutes," he said, annoyance in his voice now. "I am the one who makes the ultimate judgment as to whether crimes have been committed." He gestured toward Caiaphas and said, "Explain these accusations against the rabbi's brother."

"Certainly, Prefect," said Caiaphas. "We find Jesus of Nazareth guilty of perpetrating numerous civic disruptions. The pattern has been recurring and consistent. The large public gatherings for which he is well known have been occasions of raucous behavior and—"

"That is a complete falsehood," objected James. "I attended one of his meetings, and the people present were orderly and attentive."

"Only one meeting?" Caiaphas shot back. "That hardly seems like adequate exposure to a series of wild goings-on spanning nearly three years."

The high priest glanced at Pilate, whose face clearly showed that this allegation hadn't rung true. The descriptions of Jesus' meetings provided by the prefect's own agents did not suggest a pattern of raucous public behavior.

"Regardless of their atmosphere," Caiaphas said, adjusting his argument, "they have drawn substantial numbers of people away from their pursuits, causing significant disruptions in normal commercial activity. When thousands of farmers, craftsmen and merchants go plodding about the countryside seeking...*wisdom*—" He pronounced the word snidely. "—from some self-anointed prophet, they aren't generating the revenue from which Caesar's taxes must be paid."

Caiaphas found Pilate's reaction to that point more encouraging. He followed up with another example of commercial disruption.

"Also," he said, "as is well known, the fishing companies on the Sea of Tiberius have agreements about permissible sizes of catch. These are critical to maintaining plentiful stocks of the various species on which the fishing families depend for their livelihoods and the populace for its sustenance. We received complaints that Jesus instigated over-fishing in a portion of the lake, inciting one crew to take enormous catches. This abrogates a long-held compact and encourages an irresponsible competition as the other crews attempt to even the catch. The entire lake could be depleted, devastating the local economy."

"You go some distance to find a complaint against my brother," said James with a flat smile.

"Are the fishermen of Gennesaret not Jews?" Caiaphas retorted. "Is Galilee not an imperial protectorate? But our concern isn't only with the conduct of business. We know of at least two instances when the man's inflammatory preaching nearly caused a riot—even in his own native place, where he was virtually thrown out of the town. What does that say about his ability to inflame passions? He rouses people's anger because his teachings and his actions contradict all that promotes order and serenity in life."

"They do no such thing," James insisted sharply. "My brother preaches love and charity, repentance, virtue."

"*Virtue?*" the high priest said, his voice rising in mockery. "Virtue? Let me tell you how he promotes virtue. In one town where he spoke, your brother intruded into the effort of a local committee admonishing a woman whose notorious behavior and immoral life were a public scandal. He defended this harlot and absolved her of her sins—as if he had any power to do so."

"I have heard of that episode," James said. "And I find rather interesting this term you use to describe what the...*committee*...was doing. *Admonish*, you said, *admonish*. Yes, they were going to *admonish* her in a very direct way. They were going to *stone* her. And my brother *stopped* that illegal act."

The high priest's smile was so derisive as to be almost a sneer. "Yes, Rabbi," he said. "And what *I* find interesting is that the woman at the center of this shameful incident became one of your brother's disciples, following him and his band around from place to place, no doubt serving their every need."

"What sort of insinuation—"

"There are even some very credible stories about a shameful public display in which a woman caressed your brother's feet with her hair—though I cannot be entirely sure it was the same woman. But same or different, it was a disgrace."

James felt a burst of breath escape him. He hardly knew how to answer such an outrageous accusation.

"And, in fact, *you* are now harboring the person I mention in *your* home."

James' face darkened to an angry crimson. So, temple agents *had* been observing Mary and the other women. Asher may have been right in trying to throw them off the trail, though apparently not successful in doing so.

"Well, if you know that," he said, "then you must know that the woman became a close friend of Jesus' mother—who, I'm sure you *also* know, is at my house as well. Can you possibly believe that his mother endorses the sinfulness you imply?"

Caiaphas turned away, his lips still curled, sneer-like. "There are questions enough about Jesus' mother," he said, "and about the family that would shelter her. People in Nazareth recall a very queer and secretive wedding, followed by a long disappearance."

James was now filled with rage. Was this an attack on his beloved father? His fists clenched, and he took a step toward Caiaphas. Fortunately, a quick-witted officer stepped in front of him.

"*Stop this!*" barked Pilate in a commanding voice. "You are leaders of your people. Conduct yourselves accordingly." He focused on Caiaphas. "Lord High Priest," he said, "I appreciate that the prisoner has caused some distress. But you ask for a condemnation to death, and yet I do not see a crime that warrants such a finding. In fact, I'm not sure I see a crime at all."

"The man is a thief," Caiaphas yelled. "He and his companions stole grain from a field in harvest and consumed it brazenly."

The prefect glanced at James, who was trying to calm himself after Caiaphas' outlandish accusations. James looked at Pilate and spread his hands, unable to offer any explanation for his brother's action.

Pilate turned back to Caiaphas. "A punishable offense, if it can be proven. In fact, we will consider it punished by the scourging he is receiving right now. But it is not worthy of death."

"Then how about this," said Caiaphas, the sneer having settled into a smirk, "*sedition.*"

"Sedition?" asked Pilate. "What has he done that is seditious?"

"He has attempted to undermine the tax-collection system by inducing publicans to abandon their duties. We have evidence of at least two tax farmers who left the practice to become disciples of Jesus—one in his inner circle of so-called apostles. We suspect there are more."

"That is nonsense," said James. "Why would my brother even consider such a thing?"

The high priest glared at him. "Because he has Zealot ties." Then, turning back to the prefect: "They include two of these apostles, one of whom, Judas son of Simon, called Iscariot, led us to Jesus so we could arrest him."

"If my brother is a Zealot, why would his comrade betray him?" James asked dismissively.

"A disagreement over method and expectation," Caiaphas said. "This Judas believed his master would take more decisive action, while Jesus apparently chose a more gradual approach."

"And where is this Judas?" Pilate asked.

"He is under our surveillance," Caiaphas said. "We can produce him any time."

"Prefect, this is an absurdity," said James, "a total concoction."

Caiaphas wheeled on him. "Is it, Rabbi? Then what is the significance of your brother calling himself a *king*, if he does not propose to lead a nation?"

"Jesus has explained that," James said. "His kingdom is *not of this world.* He said it plainly. It is a spiritual mission."

The high priest addressed Pilate. "Prefect, I am sure you know of the Jewish tradition that insists a *Deliverer* will come."

"Of course," Pilate said, "the one called *Messiah.*"

"Are you fully aware of the implications of his coming?"

"I know that Jews pray for the restoration of Solomon's kingdom and for this...*anointed one*...to bring it about. If you will excuse my saying so, Lord Caiaphas, it is a vain hope. The accomplishment of such a dream would require resources which your people do not possess. Any revolt against Caesar and his legions would have to be carried out on a scale which I doubt you are capable of mounting."

"Perhaps..." Caiaphas said, "perhaps. But it may interest you to know that there are certain groups around the country accumulating weapons and actively training to use them. Are you familiar with the Essene brotherhood and its doctrine of the final battle between the Sons of Light and the Sons of Darkness?"

Pilate's certitude appeared to waver slightly. "We...receive occasional bits of information about the Essenes."

"Are you aware," Caiaphas pressed on, "that Jesus of Nazareth has followers among the Essene brothers?"

"It appears he has followers across the entire—"

"But you do realize, Prefect, that his cousin, the so-called Baptist— John—son of the priest, Zacharias, of blessed memory, was an Essene? Don't you find these personal connections strangely coincidental? A blood tie to the brotherhood? Zealots among his close companions?"

"Lord Pilate," said James, "Caiaphas is spinning a web of innuendo. My brother has nothing to do—"

"It may also interest you to know," the high priest pressed on, "that at the trial earlier this morning, Jesus confessed to being Messiah, and laid claim to a seat beside the power of heaven."

"That is a metaphor," said James.

Caiaphas pointed a finger. "Yes, Rabbi, it is a metaphor. It's a metaphor that suggests invoking God's own force. And all Jews understand how Messiah is to use that force."

Then to Pilate: "This Jesus—this peaceful prophet—has laid out his program for all to see, if only they will look. When I say that he is a blasphemer, I am not making some esoteric religious point. The Jewish nation endures because we cling to a strict and clear understanding of how the Holy One has structured our beliefs and our practices and the life of our nation. A man who presents himself as Messiah—a man who makes the claims Jesus makes and who raises the hopes he raises—such a man upsets everything. Such a man makes people long for things that cannot be and covet things they do not have. Such a man stirs their hearts to grand visions of overturning the settled order. Such a man has the ability to drown the nation in blood."

James could see that Pilate's face had lost a bit of the resolve he'd earlier shown about Jesus' innocence.

"Prefect," James said, an air of desperation creeping into his voice, "Caiaphas points to possibilities, conjecture, what someone with my brother's popularity *might* do. He cannot prove that Jesus intends to pursue such a course or that his ministry has any involvement in rebellious plots and preparations. My brother has spoken throughout the land for three years. Thousands of people have witnessed him do so. And in all that time, no one has ever heard him call for insurrection or seen the least sign that he has any interest in such things. It simply isn't true."

Pilate had withdrawn into his own thoughts. "Yes...Rabbi..." he said vaguely.

He drifted aimlessly about the room for several minutes, lost in contemplation. Even if Caiaphas' charges were a bit overblown—and they certainly did seem to be—was it possible that this odd movement of Jewish religious enthusiasm held the prospect of real danger? Pilate's first instinct, when he'd originally heard about the prophet from Galilee, was to be on his guard. That was why he'd sent men to infiltrate Jesus' meetings. It was true that they reported no seditious content in his preaching. But then, perhaps content wasn't really the issue. Perhaps Pilate's inclination to question the huge numbers of people flocking around the Nazarene had been more to the point. Perhaps the reassuring reports, from his own agents and then from the Rabbi James, had blinded him to a genuine threat.

The Rabbi James. The Greek-speaking scholar. The civilized Jew. Pilate liked the Rabbi James, enjoyed being in his company, respected his opinions, and valued his insights into how Jews thought. James had been right about reaction to the aqueduct. There was no reason to believe the rabbi had misled him about Jesus or his ministry. But James was the man's brother. It was natural to expect he would see the best in his kinsman and not wish to dwell on the possibility of harm flowing from the excitement that followed his brother everywhere.

Yes. The Rabbi James was intelligent. He was sincere. But maybe in certain ways he was naive. Caiaphas, on the other hand, was deeply cynical and corrupt at the core. But it was just possible that, in this case, he might be right. And there was not the slightest doubt that the high priest would move heaven and earth to bring down Caesar's wrath if Pilate made the wrong decision about this Nazarene.

The officer who had taken Jesus away entered from the corridor and stepped quickly over to Pilate, who by now had wandered to the far end of the hall. "The prisoner has been disciplined."

Pilate shook himself out of his reverie and nodded. "Bring him in." "Yes, My Lord."

The prefect touched his officer's shoulder to stop him. "And the other?"

"He is at the ready."

"Good."

Pilate strode resolutely across the room to the arched door and out onto the terrace, resuming his seat. The crowd stirred at his return.

Jesus entered the hall from the corridor. James emitted a sudden, loud groan to see his brother's condition. Jesus looked dazed and disoriented. He took short, jerky, irregular steps, barely able to keep himself erect, and had to be prodded in the right direction by the shields and spear butts of his guards. He still wore the royal cloak of Antipas, but the purple fabric was soaked through with splotches of blood, especially across the back, which was almost entirely discolored. Droplets of blood left a trail on the marble floor as he lurched his way along.

His face and hair were drenched with blood as well, running in rivulets from around his scalp and brow. This flow was caused by what, to James, was the most horrifying sight of all, a wreath of prickly vines, the needle-sharp thorns digging into the skin of Jesus' head. It was some warped parody of a crown or perhaps the victory laurel awarded to the winner of a Greek athletic match.

Pilate, too, was taken aback on seeing Jesus' condition. The men administering this discipline had gone too far, and the prefect would have to deal with that later. For now, the prisoner was as the prisoner was. To Pilate's disgust, some in the crowd found delight in this hideous display, squawking and cackling like the ugly carrion birds they resembled.

James saw that Caiaphas was keeping his face blank, determined not to show any reaction. But as the high priest stepped out onto the terrace, his minions took up their chant once more: *Crucify him! Crucify him! Crucify him!*

The prefect looked at Jesus, who was unsteady and in obvious excruciating pain but surprisingly composed, eyes still turned down.

"Where...are you...from?" Pilate heard himself ask in a dazed, wondering manner that seemed almost beyond his control.

Only silence.

"You still refuse to speak? Don't you realize that I have the power to release you or to crucify you?"

Without raising his eyes, Jesus said, "You would have no power at all, if it had not been given to you from above." The strength of his voice was a contrast to his ruined condition. Then his eyelids rose, he took Pilate's glance, and spoke as if sharing a confidence. "The one who delivered me to you has the greater sin."

Pilate's own eyes shifted to the high priest, then back to Jesus.

At that moment, an officer appeared beside the Seat of Justice. "Forgive me, Lord Pilate," the man said. "There is a message—from the Mistress Procula."

Startled by this intrusion, Pilate said, disconnectedly, "My wife?"

"She was insistent that you read it, My Lord—*very* insistent."

Pilate took the small leaf of parchment and scanned it rapidly. It concerned a dream about the Nazarene prophet from which Procula had awoken in much distress. With the surprise early arrival of the delegation from the Sanhedrin, Pilate had not spoken with his wife that morning. She was convinced of Jesus' innocence, and she urged her husband to have nothing further to do with this matter. He held the message for a moment, uncertain of what to think about it. Finally, he shook his head in dismissal, handing the parchment back to the officer who withdrew.

The prefect straightened himself in his seat and called, once more in his commanding voice, "Bring out the other prisoner."

The idea of listening to *the voice of the people*, of letting the crowd have a say in Jesus' fate, was even more appealing now than it had been before. It would help to defuse criticism of the final verdict, giving Caiaphas and any other of Pilate's antagonists less to complain about in Rome. And it could give the Nazarene a chance to escape death if he truly was innocent—or truly popular with the people.

At the sound of new activity in the hall, James turned from his position at the arched doorway. Soldiers were bringing in another man, this one with his wrists clamped in a set of manacles held at waist level by a chain looped around his back. It was Jedediah.

James immediately grasped what the prefect intended. The crowd was to choose between a prophet and an insurrectionist. It was a last chance to save Jesus' life. But it did not reassure. James recalled a saying of his brother, cited widely in one form or another, about those who build tombs for the prophets whom their fathers killed. It was one of the accusations Jesus had hurled at the Pharisees. Might it now come back upon him?

Jedediah spotted the old classmate who had visited his cell. The look they exchanged was awkward for James. Here was the man who might represent his brother's survival, but whom he had no desire to see die, regardless of how much blood was on the hands of *Jesus bar Abbas*. As he passed out onto the terrace, Jedediah gave him a smile that was at once sad and ironic, the abrasive mockery he had shown earlier now vanished.

An unknown, chained figure appearing on the terrace created confusion among the crowd. Pilate rose from his seat and extended both hands toward his audience.

"People of Jerusalem," he said, "you see before you two men accused of crimes." He pointed to Jesus. "Here is Jesus of Nazareth, called by some a prophet, but charged by your high priest with blasphemy and sedition." He pointed to Jedediah. "And here is the notorious brigand, Jesus bar Abbas—"

A massed in-taking of breath could be heard across the plaza as everyone realized this was the captured Zealot leader.

"—accused of insurrection, theft and murder, including attacks on Roman legionaries as well as on citizens of your own nation. According to the ancient custom, I will release one of these two criminals to mark the occasion of Passover."

Caiaphas stepped boldly and quickly up onto the platform and stood right next to the Seat of Justice, his mouth close to Pilate's ear. "This will not do, Prefect."

Pilate turned and faced him, eye to eye. "Lord Caiaphas," he said, "would you forbid Jews from judging Jews?"

The high priest backed away, and Pilate turned to address the crowd again.

"It is for you—people of Jerusalem, people of your own race and religion—to decide which of these two men shall go free and which shall go to the cross."

Immediately, the priests and scribes of the Sanhedrin delegation started up a new chant: *Give us bar Abbas—release bar Abbas! Give us bar Abbas—release bar Abbas! Give us bar Abbas—release bar Abbas!* They signaled wildly for the hired voices to join in, and soon the chant was being repeated across the plaza.

The mass of onlookers had increased throughout the morning as more people heard about the trial and came into the plaza out of curiosity. Gamaliel, Joseph and their companions recognized the urgent need to counter Caiaphas' minions. They started an opposing chant: *Release the Nazarene! Release the Nazarene! Release the Nazarene!* Gamaliel's students pushed through the crowd desperately entreating others to take it up. James could see their frantic efforts.

The competition in shouting grew to a tumultuous clamor, but it was becoming clear that the advantage lay with the faction supporting bar Abbas. Those onlookers to whom James' colleagues appealed had neither sufficient numbers nor clarity of purpose. Pilate waited, giving time for Jesus' support to gain strength. Out of the corner of his eye, he glanced at Caiaphas, whose satisfied grin was becoming more apparent and more obnoxious.

"The people are speaking, Prefect," said the high priest. "You have your duty to them, and you have your duty to the empire. If you let the Nazarene go, you are no friend of Caesar."

At that moment Pilate would very much have liked to free both bar Abbas and the Rabbi James' brother in favor of executing Caiaphas. But this choice was not available to him. He glared angrily at the high priest and, at the end of his patience, asked bitterly, "Would you have me kill the *king of the Jews?*"

Caiaphas answered coldly, "*We*...have no king but...*Caesar.*"

There was no point in letting the uproar persist any longer. Pilate surveyed the crowd below with a look of disgust. He turned to his adjutant and instructed him to have a basin of water brought out along with a towel. The officer, unsure of what the prefect intended to do, sent for the specified items, which were delivered to the terrace by a servant boy a minute or two later.

Pilate raised his arms for silence and, when the noise had abated, called out, "People of Jerusalem, you shall have your choice."

A cheer rose, which Pilate cut short with his next remark. "*Your* choice—one with which *you* will live. I hope you consider this justice, because I wash my hands of the whole affair." With that, he splashed in the water, then held one dripping hand out in front of himself and pointed the other at Jesus. "I am innocent of this man's blood. The responsibility is yours."

To another cheer, less enthusiastic this time, the servant put down the basin and dried the prefect's hands and arms with the towel. Pilate glared at Caiaphas, who smiled serenely. Then the prefect lowered himself onto his chair, all energy seeming to have gone out of him. He rested the weight of his upper body on an elbow.

"Have the Nazarene taken to the Antonia," he said to his adjutant. "Longinus will prepare for a crucifixion. Alert the garrison, in case of any disturbances."

The air and the hope had gone out of James, and he collapsed back against the archway. He looked at his brother, whose eyes were still turned down, the lines of blood now dry on his face and hair. Then James' own eyes moved to Jedediah, on whom it was beginning to dawn that he would not die this day.

"There are two other condemned prisoners being held, Lord Pilate," the adjutant said. "Shall we execute them at the same time?"

Pilate waved the question away. "Why not," he said, turning to the soldier who was taking down the proceedings. "Let the record show that the man, Jesus son of Joseph, from Nazareth of Galilee, has been convicted."

He rose, stepped off the platform, and went inside the praetorium, taking care not to look in the direction of the Rabbi James.

CHAPTER FORTY

Out of the depths I cry to you, O Lord. Hear my voice.
Let your ears be attentive to my supplications.

(Psalm 130)

Everything now existed somewhere just beyond the limit of James' awareness. Without thinking, or even knowing, he descended the stairs from the terrace down to the prefecture court and wandered out through the gate. Gamaliel, Joseph and the others spotted him shuffling slowly, head down, across the plaza, oblivious to the crowd now breaking up, deaf to the cries of some who were still calling out their objections to the verdict.

Joseph approached him first, his heart aching for this dear friend he had known and loved since taking him into his home as a youth. Artless in the face of James' palpable shock, all he could think to say was, "They led Jesus out a side gate to avoid the crowd."

The Rabbi Zephan spoke next, his round face devoid of its customary smile. "We never had a chance to make a defense for your brother, Rabbi," he said. "We never had a chance."

Nicodemus, the other two council members, and several students offered words of sympathy or comfort, along with expressions of outrage at what had transpired. Only Gamaliel was silent, observing that none of these attempts at commiseration were registering on James. The classic words of condolence came to his mind: *May the Holy One comfort you together with all the other mourners of Zion.* But it was not yet time to offer such a sentiment. That would come when Jesus was dead.

James made his way toward the Tyropoeon Valley, taking an erratic, meandering course back to the Synagogue at the Crossed Streets. Joseph started to follow, but Gamaliel held his arm and signaled to the others that they should leave the Rabbi James alone.

"There is nothing we can do for him," he said to Joseph. "At the moment, James is lost in confusion. But soon he will be in his grief and need our help."

"Yes," Joseph said. "You are right. For one thing, an arrangement must be made for the disposition of his brother. I have had a tomb prepared. It was to be for my own rest and that of my dear Chava, but..." With his thumb he indicated the prefecture behind him. "I could ask for permission to take the body. That would relieve James of at least one concern."

The only thought at all clear in James' mind right now was the horrible question of how to tell Mary that he had failed so completely. Her beloved son—his brother—was condemned to die in the most agonizing and shameful way imaginable, and James was unable to believe that the blame for it lay on anyone but James himself.

His walk home took much longer than it normally would, though in his disorientation, James had no idea how much time had actually elapsed. Upon arriving, his mind somewhat clearer now, he knew that the only way to tell Mary what happened was to speak directly. He gathered up his courage and was about to go through the gate when he remembered to touch the scroll of the commandment in its niche. Feeling the small roll of parchment under his fingertips somehow confirmed his purpose and gave strength. He walked up the path to the door of the main house and went inside.

Amara was there, her eyes wet with tears. "Master James," she said. "We have heard what happened. Word of your brother is all through the city."

"Where is Mary?" James asked anxiously.

"She and your aunt and Mary of Magdala have gone to Skull Hill."

"The execution place?"

"She insisted she must see her son at the end. She *insisted*. The young man, John, is with them. Asher went in search of you, to tell you where they are. Oh, Master James..."

James turned and ran out of the house, down the walk, through the gate. He made his way along the streets of the lower city to the temple mount, sometimes running, sometimes slowing in order to recover his breath.

People had massed outside the Antonia Fortress, as always happened whenever word spread that someone was to be executed. How many of these had been among the throng hailing Jesus when he entered the city just days before? Which of them were admirers, which detractors?

From across the crowd, the slow tattoo of a drum indicated that the march of the condemned had already begun. James climbed up onto a wall surrounding the court of a corner house. From this vantage he spotted his brother's head, which still wore the thorned crown.

Jesus, in simple garb now, the purple cloak gone, walked between two lines of soldiers, their javelins carried horizontally to serve as barricades against the mob. His back was bowed under the weight of a thick wood beam that was to serve as his gibbet. He lurched along for several paces, sometimes blocked from James' sight by the crush of onlookers, each straining to gawk over or between the surrounding heads. Two other prisoners trod slowly along bearing similar loads. James assumed these were the men he had seen asleep in their cells that morning.

At one point Jesus stumbled. A reaction went up among the crowd, and James stretched to see, balancing on the wall. He watched as two soldiers lifted the heavy timber and a third pulled Jesus to his feet. Jesus took the beam once more and attempted to move forward, but his steps were slow and shaky, almost staggering. James saw him stop and peer into the face of a woman standing at the side. Was it Mary? James couldn't tell. The distance was too great and his view obstructed. Then the soldiers dragged a husky fellow from the crowd and forced him to help Jesus with his burden. The procession went on, around a curve and into a narrow street, out of James' sight.

Large crowds always raised special concern about order, prompting added security measures. With such a jam of people and extra guards on duty at the city gate nearest the execution site, more than a half hour elapsed before James was able to reach the gate and make it outside the walls. It had become unusually dark, and he heard some people talking about the sun being blotted out. But a rain had begun, which was not unusual for spring, and in any event, weather was hardly a concern on this most horrible of days. He ignored any talk of the sun.

As he approached the foot of Skull Hill, he could see his brother suspended above the ground. He froze in place at the sight, feeling as if his guts had been wrenched out. Jesus was stripped of his clothes. He hung there entirely naked except for the circle of thorns around his head.

His arms were nailed to the beam, which was being hoisted to the top of a thick, roughly hewn wooden pole sticking up out of the earth. It was one of several standing in a line under a framework equipped with ropes and pulleys to lift the condemned.

The top of the pole was cut into a square peg shape that projected up from the end. This, James knew from his carpentry experience, was called a tenon. The beam was raised above the pole, and positioned over the tenon, guided by soldiers climbing on the framework. James hadn't noticed, when Jesus was carrying the beam, that a square hole, or mortise, was cut into one face to receive the tenon and allow the timber to balance securely.

Jesus grimaced and struggled for breath when the beam was dropped into place, the vertical and horizontal pieces now creating a form resembling the Greek letter, Tau. The two other prisoners were being raised up similarly to hang on either side of Jesus. A soldier perched on the framework tacked a crudely painted sign above Jesus' head. From where James stood, the lettering was too small for him to read. At the same time, soldiers on the ground held Jesus' feet, one over the other, at about the height of a man's waist, and drove a long, sharp spike through them. James saw his brother writhe and scream at the pain.

James made his way slowly up the hill. He could hear shouts of mockery and derision from some of the onlookers. Perhaps these hecklers were more of Caiaphas' minions. He watched his brother exchanging words with the other condemned men, clearly straining to do so, and then speaking to some people standing near the foot of his cross. But James was still too far away to make out what Jesus said or who the people were.

The crowd had thinned somewhat by the time James neared the crest of the hill. Many of those who earlier had been attracted by the death walk were falling away, uneasy now at the sight of human figures hung up to die. Curiosity had been displaced by realization, pity, even compassion, and stragglers were heading back toward the city gate in varying states of upset.

Others, however, pressed closer to get a better view. Crucifixion could hold a perverse and grisly appeal. The bloodied, discolored, ruined form, the screams and ceaseless writhing of the victim—these were so horrifying that frequently witnesses found themselves overcome by illness. Soldiers charged with carrying out the grim task preferred to do the job drunk.

Yet the completeness with which this ancient method of terror shredded all dignity, reducing a man or woman to a worthless *thing* nailed on a post as a public spectacle, could be ghoulishly fascinating. No matter how many times one turned away in revulsion, the urge to look again was often irresistible.

Of course, there was also the simple allure of nakedness, a sight rarely glimpsed outside the darkest, most private confines. But for the truly depraved, of which there were always a few on hand, crucifixion offered the pleasure of watching someone suffer—of witnessing the effect of excruciating pain, humiliating torment. To those with a certain set of mind, that opportunity was beguiling.

James' own response to the frightful display before him was an odd detachment. Here was the nightmare from his youth all over again, though now with his own brother at the center of the ghastly drama. And after all the worry of past days, after the outrage of the trial, the heartbreak of the verdict, he found he couldn't quite accept that this was actually happening. He walked on without clear intention, pulled up the slope in slow and heavy steps like those conjured in dreams, finally arriving at the foot of Jesus' cross.

He looked up at his brother's face. It mirrored the unreal quality of this whole situation, seeming hardly to be Jesus' face at all. Rather, it was twisted, contorted by the agony of pierced flesh and displaced bone bearing the dead weight of a body not yet dead, strangling the breath, roiling the brain with a screaming mad craving for relief and no relief possible.

Which pain to endure next? Which next—the wrenching of forearm bones with each upward pull trying to relieve the lightening-bolt shooting through splayed feet with each downward push trying to assist the collapsing lungs in a desperate gasp for air—which next? How long to endure each pain until it can be traded for another? A circular struggle with no end but death.

All of this was written on Jesus' face, which looked as if it had been crafted into a mask meant to symbolize torment in one of the tragedies Greeks liked to watch in their vast amphitheaters. The eyes were open, staring. The skin was drained of color but overlaid by streaks of dried blood, sweat, grime. An image flashed into James' mind—the young man dying on the Sepphoris road—that picture carved so deeply into his memory.

Unmoving, James stood, barely able to breathe himself, gazing up into the agonized visage for minutes he could never have thought to count. Then he fell to his knees and, with a cracking voice, cried out in despair, words competing for space in his throat with the choking wave of a sob, "Forgive me, Brother. I failed you."

Jesus stirred. His head bent slowly forward, eyes downward, and the two men beheld one another, Jesus above, James below. Was it a play of the light on this angle of Jesus' face, the random twitching of muscles in his lips, an effect of his unimaginable misery? Did James perceive the merest shade of a smile?

Someone touched him from behind. Turning, he saw it was Mary. Her eyes were red and swollen, her face stained with tears. But the grip of her hands on his shoulders was surprisingly firm and controlled.

"Come, James," she said.

He got to his feet. The other two Marys and the disciple, John, were there, a few steps away, along with several other women who were followers of Jesus and had come to support his mother. James went with Mary to the group. No one spoke, but they looked upon him with sad, sympathetic eyes, red like Mary's from crying. He sensed the bond between them and was grateful for their presence.

Turning back in the direction of his brother, he looked up, his attention drawn to the sign nailed at the top of the cross. "Jesus of Nazareth, King of the Jews," it read in three roughly scrawled lines—one in Aramaic, one Greek, one Latin.

On the far side of the cross, a group of soldiers, manifestly under the sway of too much wine, were engaged in a vulgar Roman gambling game which James had seen played years before on the streets of Sepphoris. He noticed that the prize over which they were contending was a heap of clothes, among which he recognized the robe Jesus had worn when he was carrying the beam. It was an old, worn-out legion cloak. James felt a flush of indignation and an impulse to claim it for the family. But then he almost laughed at himself over the absurdity of such an idea. In the face of his brother's ordeal, could this sad, threadbare artifact even matter?

The centurion in charge of the execution detail, Cassius Longinus, approached with another soldier who carried a bucket and a long staff. Longinus picked something out of the pail, which James could see was a wet sponge. The centurion took the staff from the other soldier, stuck the sponge on its end, and held it up to the side of Jesus' face.

"Drink," Longinus called up. "It will help."

James wondered at this act—a small token of kindness on the part of a Roman officer? Jesus put his tongue to the sponge and then jerked his face away, wincing at the sharp pains in his arms and feet caused by the sudden movement.

"Alright," said Longinus, taking down the sponge.

There was a cup of wine near the gambling soldiers, an earthen goblet with a thick base.

"Hey, you sots," Longinus called. "bring me that drink."

A soldier got unsteadily to his feet and took up the vessel.

"You need it...Centurion?" he said, his speech slurred. "Have a good swill."

"Go back to your foolishness," Longinus replied, taking the cup and sniffing at it. "Sour," he said. "Not that it matters for what you need to get through this day."

Then he squeezed out the sponge with one hand, its contents dripping onto the ground. James caught the distinctive smell of myrrh and realized that the centurion had offered Jesus something to reduce his pain. But now Longinus poured the sour wine onto the sponge, put it back on the staff, and lifted it up to Jesus again. Jesus tested the sponge with his tongue, and then sucked some of the wine.

At that, he lifted his eyes toward the sky, paused, and spoke in a voice James could only just hear, "Father, into your hands, I commend my spirit." His eyes began to lose focus, and his head started to sway on his shoulders. Barely able to hold it erect, he said, "It is finished."

At the sight of Jesus' head collapsing onto his chest, Mary let out a sound—the doleful blending of a scream, a moan, a shriek—a mother's wretched wail of despair at the loss of her only child. James' eyes now brimmed with tears as he took her in his arms. He thought back to the other-worldly sounds that had come down to him from her upstairs room on that strange night at the beginning of her motherhood. What an other-worldly sound now emanated from the pierced heart she was left with at the end.

The rain became heavier. After some time had passed, Longinus observed that all three of the condemned appeared to be dead. He sent a runner to inform Lord Pilate, and then rousted the soldiers from the stupor into which they had drifted after their game. When they were on their feet—somewhat unsteadily—he instructed them to break the legs of the two Zealots. This would make the bodies collapse entirely, squeezing the last of the air from their lungs to ensure that they were completely gone.

"Sabbath is coming," he said. "The Jews will demand that these corpses be down."

"You should know, Centurion," one of the inebriated soldiers mumbled. "You're practically a Jew yourself."

With his men in their current condition—the better to do their revolting work—Longinus was inclined to tolerate what, under other circumstances, he would consider disrespect. "Just hurry along," he said, picking up a javelin. He walked to Jesus' cross, and thrust it into the side of his chest. Some blood seeped out when he withdrew the weapon, along with what looked like water.

This dripping became a flow, and one of the drunk soldiers spotted it. In his giddy state, he grabbed up the vessel that had contained the sour wine and caught some of the blood and watery fluid. Laughing, he offered it as a novel drink to his besotted fellows. They declined, employing some unpleasant Roman oaths, and he set the cup down near the heap of Jesus' clothes.

What remained of the crowd broke up, and people started down the hill, some shaken by what they had witnessed, others discreditably amused. The rain was heavy now, with occasional crashes of thunder. Longinus herded the men along to the work of dismantling the crosses and removing the bodies. Soldiers scrambled awkwardly up on the framework to refasten the pulley lines to the beams. One knocked the sign down from Jesus' cross.

All that had happened and the emotion it stirred were too much for James. He felt drained, his thoughts unclear. Then, with the bustle of activity among the soldiers and Mary attended to by the women, his mind fixed on an opportunity. He knew it made no sense, but he was drawn by some raw, indefinable need over to where the gambling game had been held. There he bent down and took both the robe and the cup filled with Jesus' life fluids. Foolish as he knew his action was, he would not see these things in the hands of those who had killed his brother.

The deed went unnoticed by the solders, who were struggling to accomplish their tasks with fogged heads, clinging dizzily to the framework in the rain. James returned, walking slowly with an expression that was almost a daze, rain dripping down his face and beard, robes and turban soaked. The disciple, John, saw what he had done and offered to take the items.

"The rabbi should not concern himself with these," he said kindly.

"My brother..." James said. "They are from my brother..."

"I understand, Rabbi." John took the robe and cup, concealing them under his own cloak.

"His mother—" James said next, "we must bring her back to my— back to the Synagogue at the Crossed Streets." Thoughts raced, focusing only with great effort. "She can stay as long as she likes."

John hesitated, then said, almost apologetically, "Jesus placed her into my care. I don't know why, Rabbi. I would have thought he'd want her back in Nazareth with the family."

This information contained meaning to James, helping him regain his presence of mind. "Of course," he said. "Jesus tried to protect her when she was in Bethany. Perhaps my brother thought there may yet be some danger to her. And it could be so. Caiaphas' men were watching my home. Do you have a place to take Mary?"

"The house where we held our Seder," said John. "I believe the others are there."

"Then go," James said. "Contact me if you need anything."

"Yes, Rabbi."

The sound of a painful cry made James turn back in the direction of the crosses. He saw Longinus stooped over, holding a hand to his left eye.

The soldier who had carried the bucket and sponge asked, "What is the matter, Centurion?"

"Oh—" said Longinus. A pause, and then: "Sharp pain. But...it has passed." He straightened up and looked around. Shook his head. Looked once more. "Peculiar. Very peculiar. My eye... I see clearly through it—I... I haven't seen clearly through that eye in years. Not since I was wounded in that town in Galilee." He looked up at the figure of Jesus. "*His* town," he said thoughtfully, raising a pointed finger toward the body.

The soldier peered closely at Longinus' eye. "Centurion," he said, "your scar is gone."

The other soldiers had removed the spike from Jesus' feet, and were straining to lift the cross beam off its place on the vertical pole. They brought it down, laid the body out on the wet ground, took the circle of thorns off his head, and started to pry out the spikes that pinned his arms to the beam.

Longinus studied Jesus' face carefully. Thinking. Thinking. "This was...a righteous man," he said, nodding his head slowly. "Without doubt."

James and John observed this exchange. They now glanced at each other, saying nothing. James gestured toward the women.

"Take them," he said. "I must see to my brother."

"Yes, Rabbi."

John suggested to the women that they should go. It required extra prompting to convince Jesus' mother.

"The rabbi will take care of him," John said to her.

Finally she agreed, and they all started down the hill. After several steps, Mary stopped, asked the others to wait, and went back to James. Facing him, her distress now under better control, and intent on relating something important, she said, "He forgave them, James."

"Mary?"

"Before you arrived, Jesus begged forgiveness of the Holy One for those who were taking his life. Right from the cross. He said they were merely ignorant of what they were doing, and he forgave them."

This was beyond James' understanding. He could find no words by which to take the measure of such a thing. Jesus *forgave* his tormenters, his executioners? All James could think to say was, "I hope he forgave me."

Mary took his hands in her own and held them for some seconds, eyes closed, seemingly in prayer. Then she turned and went to the others. The group departed.

James stood watching the soldiers as they hauled off the three cross beams, packed up their tools, ropes and tackles, and placed the bodies on litters to carry them down the hill. There was a cart, drawn by two oxen, on which the corpses were loaded. James followed along as the cart rumbled toward the city gate.

With the thick clouds and steady rain, it was impossible to tell what time of day it might be. Was the start of Sabbath close? James found it difficult to care. Some familiar faces were emerging from the gate as the execution detail approached. It was Gamaliel and Joseph, followed by Mary of Magdala and one of the other women who had been with Jesus' mother. Joseph spotted James and hurried to him.

"I spoke with the prefect," Joseph said. "He gave me an order to have your brother taken to my tomb." Joseph showed a parchment sheet bearing Pilate's seal.

"Your tomb? But that is for—"

Joseph put up a hand, palm forward. "It is for your brother," he said.

James closed his eyes. "Thank you, my friend."

Carrying a folded linen cloth he had brought to use as a pall, Joseph went to consult with the Centurion. He handed over Pilate's order and pointed the direction to the tomb, which was back along the outside of the city wall beyond Skull Hill. Longinus was not pleased at having to turn the cart around and go in the direction they'd already come. But he was still marveling at the unexpected clearing of his vision and couldn't help wondering if—somehow—Jesus was responsible for it. He gave the order, and the return trip was begun, Joseph leading the way.

Gamaliel approached with the women as the lumbering beasts were driven in a wide circle.

"Mary's friends stayed behind to see where Jesus was to be placed," he said.

"Of course."

They walked along, following the cart, saying nothing, each lost in private thoughts. The party advanced beyond Skull Hill and came to the gravesite, a row of vaults cut into the rock face of a low ridge. Joseph's tomb was open. A heavy stone that was carved round to permit its being rolled across the entrance stood to one side. This was a simple resting place for a man of Joseph's stature. But James knew his old landlord as someone with simple tastes. No showy monument on the Mount of Olives for him. Joseph of Arimathea wouldn't jostle for prominence with the other leading men in death, as he never sought to aggrandize himself in life.

Just then, Nicodemus appeared, winded and carrying a small ceramic vessel. He went to James and removed its stopper. James caught the scent of myrrh.

"For your brother's preparation," he said. "It's not much, but...for now."

James nodded his thanks and then turned to look inside the shadowed chamber. Without expecting it, but without surprise that it should occur, he felt a disturbance, a tremor in the pit of his guts. It spread rapidly throughout his entire body until even his hands and feet shook. A moan rose from some core of sorrow deep within, transforming itself into a long, disconsolate, fearsome yowl not unlike that of a wild animal or the sound he had earlier heard from Mary. Gamaliel put his arms around James' shoulders and held him as his friend sobbed and the Sabbath came upon Jerusalem.

CHAPTER FORTY-ONE

"Greater love has no man than this,
that he lay down his life for his friends."

(John 15)

N ext morning, the city was abuzz with rumors of strange and inexplicable occurrences many believed were connected with Jesus' death. Some reported having felt a quaking of the earth. Others told of people long dead sighted walking about the city—though most often, the accounts were actually of hearing such things from others who had heard them from others still. Tales circulated about damage to the temple, one telling how the veil inside the Holy of Holies had been mysteriously torn.

Some of these stories reached James' ears through Amara, who immersed herself in the morning gossip coming back from synagogue. After the events of yesterday, James was in no mood for fancies.

"Nonsense," he said curtly and a bit more gruffly than he'd intended. "Many people were devoted to my brother. His life was known for remarkable incidents, so it would be expected that people assume remarkable things about his death."

"Well, there is one thing which may interest you, Master James," Amara said. "You know that Judas, the one who betrayed your brother to the priests?"

"Yes?"

"He has taken his own life."

"Taken—"

"It is said that the priests paid him to do what he did to Jesus. But he was filled with remorse for it, and he hanged himself."

A suicide was more plausible than tales of dead people roaming the streets of Jerusalem. It wasn't hard to imagine a man who had followed Jesus for three years being plagued by guilt over his own treachery. In any event, this story would be confirmed or disproved in time. Meanwhile, James did wonder at the quality of that surveillance Caiaphas had said they were keeping on Judas. Then again, could the High Priest have had a hand in this death? It was a loathsome idea, but not unthinkable after what James had seen happen to his brother.

And he *had* seen it, every heart-rending moment of it. After a long night of scant sleep—and what little he'd gotten fitful at that—James was beyond disbelief. Jesus was dead. James had helped Joseph, Gamaliel and, interestingly, the centurion, Longinus, carry the body into Joseph's tomb. He had placed his brother on a stone slab cut from one wall. He had straightened the long, linen cloth laid under Jesus and then drawn over his head and along the length of his torso and legs. He had done all of these things, and he knew, as well and as painfully as he could ever know it, that his brother was gone.

He also knew that the family was unaware of what had happened. Everyone would have to be informed, and this sad duty was his to carry out. He would go to Nazareth, and he must exert himself mightily to arrive before rumors made their way to the compound—which they surely would. Jesus was too famous for James to believe that word of his death wouldn't spread. Any caravan passing through the Jezreel Valley could put off some traveler who had knowledge of the execution. Any legion squad transiting to Sepphoris could bring the shocking news. James must get ahead of that. Joseph could arrange his transport to Nazareth, but there would be no departure today. Today was Sabbath, and travel impossible.

Pilate also planned to depart. He had originally intended to remain in Jerusalem until the completion of Passover as a show of respect for the festival. But the unpleasantness of the trial made him decide to put the holy city of the Jews behind him as soon as possible. He longed for the refreshing sea breezes and comforting Greek atmosphere of Caesarea. Insulted by the rejection of the shields, disgusted by Caiaphas' duplicity, impatient with the schemes and inanity of Antipas, and eager to avoid a guilty confrontation with the Rabbi James, he had ordered that his cortege be ready to leave in the early afternoon.

Procula was relieved at this change in their schedule. She had been most annoyed at the restrictions imposed on her by Jewish propriety.

No women at public functions, indeed—what civilized people would hold to such a convention? Now, after her unsettling dream about the Nazarene prophet and the verdict issued by her husband—which in her view, though she would never tell him, was most unwise—she was eager to be on her way.

The prefect was in conference with his staff officers when he was handed a message. Another Sanhedrin delegation had arrived in the court. They were requesting that a guard be put on the Nazarene's tomb.

"A guard? Why does a corpse need to be guarded?"

"They are most adamant, Lord Pilate," said the officer bearing the message.

Pilate was at the end of his patience with adamant Jews. He suspended the conference and went down to the court.

"What is the meaning of this request?" he asked the senior priest in the group, the same one who had led yesterday's delegation bringing the Nazarene and the complaints against him.

"My Lord Prefect," the priest said nervously with no doubt about Pilate's exasperation, "the imposter, Jesus, made bold prophecies about rising from the dead after three days, and—"

Pilate gave a loud and disdainful snort. "A man who is able to do that will hardly be kept in his grave by guards."

The priest waved his hands excitedly. "No, no, Prefect," he said. "Certainly we do not believe this conceit. The man was a trickster. But it might come into his followers' heads to sneak off with the body and then claim that he had fulfilled his promise through some miraculous power. And that imposture would be worse than the first. We must protect against any such plotting and deflate this heretical enthusiasm so many of our people have fallen into. The man is dead, and we want no heroic legends growing up around his memory."

The prefect had to admit this made sense. Jesus may have met his untimely end as the result of an injustice—one in which Pilate, himself, had played a part—but it wouldn't do to encourage the spread of wild stories about him which could be exploited for dubious purposes.

He turned to one of his officers. "Go to the Antonia," he said. "Have Longinus post a detail to secure the Nazarene's tomb. Send word to me in Caesarea if anyone tries to tamper with it."

"Yes, Prefect."

Pilate dismissed the delegation abruptly—almost rudely so—went back inside the praetorium, and resumed the meeting with his officers. When that session was finished, he gave further instructions about the departure for Caesarea, then sifted through some documents, choosing several to be batched up and taken with him. At midday a servant brought in the light meal, which the prefect normally took while working. The tray set before him contained some broth, fruit, cheese and a small loaf of hard-crusted bread, along with a cup of wine.

The bread riveted Pilate's attention unexpectedly, prompting a slight catch in his breath. "Yeast," he said to himself.

* * *

James arranged with Joseph to be on a caravan scheduled to depart Jerusalem the next day.

"Its route can be diverted somewhat to get you nearer to Nazareth," his friend said. "How many will be going?"

James turned the question over in his mind. "I must speak with Mary to see if she is able to travel. If so, perhaps one or two of Jesus' men will accompany us—the young fellow, John, in particular. My brother apparently gave him the task of caring for her."

"Let me know," said Joseph. "I will have mounts for all."

James made his way across the city to the Essene quarter, headed for the house John had pointed out as the place where Jesus and his company held their *Seder*. Catching bits and snatches of conversation along the way, he became aware that his brother's death was the day's main topic in the streets. He also noted that views on the occurrence were quite divergent. Some people bemoaned the tragic end of a righteous man, while others expressed relief that a movement which might have become a source of division was quashed early on. A conversation in one of the fountain plazas captured the split perfectly, and James stopped to listen.

"Jews must stick together," a short man holding his phylacteries was saying. "With the Romans pressing on us and so many of our own who go over to Greek ways, we don't need anybody teaching different doctrines."

A hunched old fellow sitting on a bench threw up his hands. "Bah!" he said. "Put two Jews in a room and already you have three opinions. What does it matter the doctrines this Nazarene taught? He had a good heart. It was just Caiaphas and his gang who objected."

"A crime," said a wrinkled crone who appeared to be the old man's wife. "It was a crime what they did, turning the poor young rabbi over to suffer under Pontius Pilate. No Jew should have to endure such treatment. And setting that Zealot, bar Abbas, free—another crime. If anybody can bring Rome down on us, it's him and his blood-thirsty bandits."

"Well, maybe the Zealots will finally do something someday," the first man said, "and drive the legions out."

"They'll do something," the crone said. "They'll get us all hung on crosses. That Jesus is the one who should have gone free."

James mused that his brother seemed to be as controversial in death as he had been in life. He wondered how long Jesus' memory would continue to inspire disagreement.

The lane to which John had drawn James' attention was deserted this morning. It was short and closed at its end by the court wall of the house where Jesus' *Seder* had been held. Only one other house opened onto it, the rest of its length being lined along both sides by the rear walls of courts opening onto other streets. His brother had likely chosen this location because of that privacy.

A knock on the wooden gate brought no response, though James could hear a scurrying of feet on the other side. He knocked again, and a voice—almost a whisper—finally came. "Who is there?"

"It is James, the brother of Jesus," he replied.

"Rabbi?"

"Yes."

The gate opened, and James recognized one of Jesus' men, who peeked out into the lane, checking to see if anyone else was nearby. "Come," he said furtively.

James entered, and the gate closed quickly behind him. He was directed along a stone path through a narrow yard that contained several small fruit trees, then off to one side where a stairway led to a room on the upper level. Mary was there with Simon, John and some of the others.

"Welcome, Rabbi," said Simon. "Please forgive our caution. We have worried about repercussions from yesterday. Caiaphas' thugs—like those he put into the crowd to call for Jesus' death—they may be around, searching for more victims."

"I understand," said James. "I witnessed their doings firsthand. But nothing is happening in the streets—not that I saw on my way."

He knelt down on the floor where Mary was seated. Her eyes were dry of tears, but she looked drained.

"Have you slept, Mary?" he asked.

"Not very much, James," she said. "Aunt Mary came back with us and sat up beside me through the night. I am grateful to her, but—"

"Yes," James said. He patted her hands. "Of course. I go to Nazareth in the morning to inform the family. Joseph of Arimathea is providing transport. If you wish to come—"

She shook her head. "Not now, James. Not yet. I cannot face the questions—the telling and retelling—it is too soon." Tears came.

"As you wish, Mary. I will see to it." He turned to Simon. "How long can you remain in this house?" he asked.

"As long as we need to, Rabbi," he said. "When it seems safe, we will probably go back to Galilee. Without the Lord, we don't know— Well, we must take time and pray and decide what we should do."

James nodded, then turned back to Mary. "If you wish to stay in Jerusalem, you are always welcome in my home."

"Thank you, James."

There was some further talk, though very subdued, as suited the mood of the day. James asked Mary if she had a message for the family. She wished only that he convey her love and her concern for them all.

"Tell them they must be strong," she said, "as their brother was."

James embraced her and stood to take his leave.

Then Mary said, "I know you tried to save him, James. You tried your best. I am sure of it."

James felt a constriction in his throat.

"Your father would be proud of you."

James could say nothing.

"And do not worry about me, James. The Almighty has done great things for me. I am the mother of his son. I am blessed among women."

Now there were tears in James' eyes.

"I will pray for you, James...as I always pray for you."

Unable to look back at her, James went out of the room and down the stairway. Simon followed. At the bottom, James stopped and tried to speak with the man who had been Jesus' chief apostle, but tightness in his throat impeded him. He paused, turned toward the wall of the court, took a few slow breaths. Recovering himself, he faced the big fisherman again.

"You were with my brother for three years, Simon," he said. "Please tell me, what was he really trying to accomplish?"

Simon glanced away, his eyes falling on one of the fruit trees. He examined a cluster of buds at the end of a branch. "I heard the Lord speak of many things," he said. "I saw him work many wonders and move many hearts."

"Did he *change* hearts?" James asked. "Were people made better by his teaching?"

"Oh yes, Rabbi. No question. Well...not everyone who came into contact with him was changed for the good, I must admit. Some listened and then walked away. But that was because not everyone can grasp what lies at the heart of his message."

"What is that, Simon?"

"Love," he said. "Jesus taught that we are our best and truest selves when we act in love—not simple emotion, mind you, but sincere intent. When we can do this we are best as people. We are best as Jews. Love is the greatest sacrifice, Rabbi."

"*Sacrifices offered in righteousness*," James said, quoting the psalm.

"And offered from the heart," said Simon, "with the purest of motives, wishing to do best for our fellow men, and seeing the right and sensible way to do it. That is what Jesus taught that the King of the Universe desires of us. We Jews have always known this. In a sense, Jesus said nothing new. But it was the saying of it, in itself, that made the difference—and the living of it."

"Do you still believe my brother was the Messiah?"

Simon brought his hands together in front of his chest, his head tilted forward and turned slightly. "Just now...it would be...difficult to claim that," he said. "But, I am willing to wait before I decide otherwise. Jesus promised he would not be defeated by death. Perhaps it is for us, those who followed him, to see that his teaching survives and his example is not lost."

"You are a man of great loyalty, Simon."

The fisherman's expression changed. Something came into his eyes. Was it shame?

"Me?" he asked in a tone of surprise, almost shock. His eyes darted about self-consciously. Then he spoke in a near-whisper. "You are known for good counsel, Rabbi, and I have need of it now. Something happened which I have not shared with the others."

"Yes?"

Where to begin? Simon was struggling. "Jesus told us what the priests would do to him, but I protested stupidly. In my boldness and vanity I declared that I would defend him to the end, lay down my life. I was a fool, and the Lord knew it. *You will deny me,* he said—as he put it, *three times, before the cock crows.* And he was right. I followed when they took him to Caiaphas' house, and I waited outside, trying to hear what was going on in that parody of a trial."

"I saw you there," James said.

"You did?"

"I was across the street waiting for Joseph and Gamaliel to come."

"Ah! Then you witnessed my folly for yourself."

"I saw you looking upset."

"The servants pegged me for a Galilean from the way I speak, and they asked if I was one of Jesus' men. Three times I denied even knowing him—the third just as a rooster called the morning light. It was exactly as the Lord had said." He shot James a shame-filled glance. "I behaved cowardly, Rabbi. I am not worthy to call myself Jesus' friend."

A sigh from James. "I failed in my duty to protect him," he said. "Am I worthy to call myself his brother? Mary says my father would be proud of the effort I made, but I do not think it. I let my father down. So we both have something for which to reproach ourselves."

They stood without speaking for a time, sharing their remorse. Then James said, "But Mary told me something else. She said that Jesus forgave his executioners."

"Yes, I know. It is astounding."

"Then, maybe he forgave us too, Simon. And if that is the case, all we can do is trust in him and carry out the tasks we have been given—

do what we feel is owed."

"That isn't doing very much, Rabbi. It doesn't seem nearly enough."

"No, it doesn't. But if we have his forgiveness, what more is there to ask?"

*   *   *

The conversation with Simon repeated itself in James' mind several times during that day and evening. He wondered if the advice he had given him was correct. Should he rather have told Simon to go to the temple and make a guilt offering for failing Jesus? Should James go and make one himself?

It would have been traditional. More than that, it would have accorded with the Law. But somehow James didn't feel it was needed. And this realization brought him up sharply. Whose forgiveness did James consider more important? That of his brother, or that of the Holy One? If Jesus was truly Messiah, perhaps the first implied the second.

But Jesus died on a cross. He decidedly had not accomplished what Jews always expected Messiah would accomplish.

And yet, to have Jesus' forgiveness felt to James like enough.

Perhaps the priests were right. If Jesus could inspire such deviation from the normal Jewish understanding of how to expiate guilt, if one could feel forgiven without an offering in the fire of the altar, maybe the temple really was threatened. If even James, a doctor of the Law who did not consider himself his brother's follower, could harbor such thoughts, maybe Jesus really would have taken Judaism in a new direction.

Throughout the remainder of his Sabbath, James pondered these implications. They were in his mind until sleep finally carried his mind away and he slumbered in surprising peace.

He awoke recalling no dreams or disturbances in the night. When he had eaten and prayed the morning service, he rolled some clean linen, a spare tunic, and his phylacteries into a sack, took leave of the household, and went to meet Joseph where the caravan was loading. Ephron was left with instructions to tell anyone coming to the Synagogue at the

Crossed Streets that the Rabbi James would be unavailable for some weeks. Correspondence was to be accepted and left to accumulate in the stone hut. It would be dealt with upon James' return.

The train was packed and ready to depart by mid-morning. Once more, James felt the familiar rolling sway of a camel as the great beasts queued up, took to the road, and fell into their steady, rhythmic gait.

Travel was never easy, whether walking or riding. But it provided such a complete change from the normal routine that it did bring a certain refreshment of mind. Not too many hours passed before James noticed his mood had lightened. He was able to observe the passing sights with a modicum of pleasure, even though he knew a difficult task awaited him at the compound in Nazareth. Informing the family would be painful, but that pain lay yet ahead. As the sage had written, there was *a time for silence and a time for speaking.* This was a time for silence, and after everything that had happened, silence was much appreciated.

A caravansary came into view as the sun was getting low. James was given a private room at the request of the caravan master whose instructions from Joseph were to secure the best accommodations for the rabbi. Having shed his cloak and tunic, James was washing himself with water from a large pottery bowl when a knock sounded. He dressed again and opened the door, expecting the tray of food ordered for him.

Instead, there stood a man wearing a turban in the Persian style, his face concealed by a cloth draping from its crown. The visitor let the covering fall away, taking James by surprise.

"Hello, Rabbi."

"Jedediah. What are you doing here?"

"I came to speak with you, and have taken some risk in doing so."

James cocked his head outside the door and looked around, checking to see if anyone in the caravansary's common room was watching. "You'd best come in."

His visitor entered, James closing and securing the door behind him.

"I am surprised to see you outside of Jerusalem," James said. "I couldn't believe Pilate would really let you go."

"He didn't," Jedediah said, "not entirely. I was followed after the trial, but I evaded those on my tail. There are people willing to assist me in Jerusalem, more than you might imagine. They got me out of the city—in a very undignified way, I should note. The method involved crates and bales. But, one travels as one can. Still, I can't move about with complete openness."

"What do you want, Jedediah?"

"Ah, the rabbi comes right to the point. That is good. I really mustn't linger." Jedediah smiled in the cynical manner he'd shown when he and James talked in the prison. "I wish once again to raise a subject we discussed years ago. You were not disposed to consider it in those days. But perhaps your attitude has changed after what happened to your brother—that latest testament to the *peace of Rome.*"

Jedediah waited for a reaction. The only one observable was a slight narrowing of James' eyes, which was enough to encourage him.

"Your brother has suffered a wretched death, brutal and unjust."

"A death that saved your life."

"True," Jedediah said. "But if Pilate had not backed himself into a corner and let the people choose me over Jesus to live, you may be sure I would have accompanied your brother to that hill of skulls. It could still happen, if I were captured again." He tugged thoughtfully at the cloth running down from his head covering. "Actually, I am quite amazed the prefect didn't learn from the experience of Herod Antipas in that matter of the Baptist. Pilate made exactly the same sort of re-grettable bargain—regrettable to him, of course, not me. But let that be a lesson to you, James. Never promise what you don't wish to deliver should things go against you."

James had no taste for levity about his brother's death, and he was impatient with this visit. "The point, Jedediah?"

"Of course. Forgive me, Rabbi. I have indeed come with a purpose, and I'm sure it isn't hard for you to fathom what it is. Jesus was beloved among the people. There is great anger at what happened, and rightly so. His death was one more act of oppression on the part of Rome, and as such, it provides an opportunity."

"Pilate didn't arrest Jesus," said James.

"Caiaphas didn't send him to the cross," Jedediah countered. "But somehow, working together in this convenient relationship by which our freedoms are crushed and our wealth stolen, the temple and the empire managed to see your brother dead. It *happened,* James, and you know *how* it happened. Such wrongs always happen when the interests of our leaders correspond with the interests of our oppressors. And these things will continue to happen until we Jews free ourselves from the monstrous evils besetting us."

"I am not a Zealot, Jedediah."

"No. You are *James the Just*, wise advisor to all who seek wisdom— even Pilate."

This brought a start. James' surprise was readable on his face.

"Come now, classmate, you think your relationship with our Roman overlord isn't known? Jews serve in the prefecture, and some are greatly sympathetic to our cause. Your comings and goings are noted. Incidentally, you have been under special observation since I evaded my pursuers. That is how I was able to follow you today."

James was on his guard now. Had he been marked as a collaborator by the Zealots?

"Yes, Jedediah, I have offered my advice to Pilate. And I believe that whatever respect my counsel has gained in his eyes works to the betterment of our people's condition."

Jedediah noticed a stool and seated himself, which gave James a measure of ease, even if a short measure. It didn't appear that Jedediah intended to spring upon him.

"The tragic death of your brother is an opportune moment," Jedediah continued. "Jesus was building a considerable movement. His teaching was widely admired, and his following grew daily. He called people to holiness, to sincere fidelity to the Law. He may have been a little loose with some of its particulars, but it was true Judaism, nonetheless. And true Judaism cannot accept the endless suppression of liberty and ceaseless assaults on the Jewish heart by Roman injustice, Greek superstition, and a priestly class that has sold its spiritual patrimony for a cut of Caesar's gold. I assure you, many people who admired your brother understand that this situation cannot go on forever. And if Jesus had lived, he would eventually have had to address that reality."

"If so," James said, "he would have addressed it in peacefulness and charity, as he addressed all things."

"Hmmm... One wonders, James, one wonders. I am told there were times when Jesus advised his followers to arm themselves. Didn't he say that he had come to *bring a sword*, to *sow fire upon the earth*?"

"My brother spoke in metaphors, and they were often quite vivid. But he was not a violent person, as anyone who ever heard his preaching can attest."

"Ah yes, all that loving of one's enemies and turning of the other cheek—some of his most quoted sayings." The cynical smile again. "Most quoted and least lived."

"If your hope is to take over my brother's movement," said James, "I think you will be disappointed. Right now I'm not sure that even his teaching will survive, much less any movement. The men of his inner circle are frightened for their lives and may not be able to keep together. Without them, there can hardly *be* a movement. Who would the people follow?"

"They would follow...*you*."

James was nonplussed. "Follow me?" he said. "Why should they follow me? I wasn't one of Jesus' disciples. I had nothing whatever to do with the ministry, and in fact, I was quite worried that his activities would bring him to harm."

"You were proven right in that," said Jedediah.

This remark James waved away. "Then how can you think of me as Jesus' successor? If the movement is to go on, it must be led by Simon and the others."

Jedediah rose from the stool. "Who would follow a bunch of bedraggled fishermen?" he said. "Jesus was the attractive figure, and you are the obvious heir. You are his brother. You are the renowned rabbi. You are *James the Just*. If Simon and the others have any sense, *they* will recognize that. It's a wonder they aren't already begging you to take up the mantle of leadership. You are a natural asset."

James found himself laughing at the very idea. "Jedediah," he said, smiling and putting a hand to his forehead, "assuming this movement has any validity aside from Jesus' own personal attraction—and it possibly might—I would be the very last person they should choose to lead it. The key to my brother's appeal was the authority with which he taught. It was rather bold of him to claim such authority, but people recognized it in his words and manner, and they followed him because of it. To put that authority into the hands of his kinsman would be to turn the movement into a sort of *family religion*. It would become either like the household deities of the eastern cults, or like the temple priesthood with all of its inherited prerogatives and corruption. If my brother was anything, he was a reformer, and what you propose is not the path of reform. Far better to build an organization—what he called an *assembly*—that is not run by Jesus' relatives and can stand on its own."

Jedediah folded his arms and leaned casually against one wall of the room, looking James up and down. "Perhaps *James the Just* is as humble as people insist," he said. "Or maybe his vision is merely too limited."

"I cannot be Jesus' successor," James said. "And in any case, I suspect your interest is not in religious reform."

"Do not be too sure," Jedediah said, pushing himself off from the wall. "James, James, James... Caiaphas and Pilate killed your brother. This is the moment to strike at the entire rotten structure that allowed it to happen—a structure that has crushed the souls of the Jewish people for generations. Jesus has created a powerful weapon with which to strike down that structure, and the fact that it is religious in nature gives it its power. The religion of the Jews and the fate of the Jewish nation are inextricably bound together. Righteousness is as much a political concept as a moral one. *James the Just* can speak for righteousness, for that purity of religion which your brother preached. You can speak for true Judaism, James. And you can show people that Judaism can only *be* true when it is free."

"I will not ask Jesus' followers to become an army."

"James, how many crucifixions must you witness? How many times must you walk the Sepphoris road before you admit your hatred of Rome? You can't watch the oppression suffered by your people and not burn with anger, not cry out for justice. You are a Jew, and you have a Jewish heart."

James found the stool Jedediah had been sitting on before. He placed himself on it, put his elbows on his knees, and held his face in his hands.

"There is much truth in your argument, Jedediah," he said in a low voice becoming slightly ragged from frustration. "Many times I have wondered if I am doing anything worthwhile for our people. I know full well that my efforts at ingratiating myself with Pilate have yielded very limited results. But what is the alternative? The power of the empire is too great to be broken by armed resistance—at least by the Jews. We are too divided, too separated into factions. We haven't been united as a people since the days of the Maccabees."

He took his hands away from his face and fixed his eyes on this insurrectionist and murderer, this man of action, this *bar Abbas* whom, on one level, James recognized as a patriot.

"Haven't you proven that yourself?" James asked. "What have all your plots and attacks and assassinations accomplished, other than futile loss of life? I cannot see that what you wish me to do would possibly lead to anything but more of the same. My brother's call to turn the other cheek might be too much to ask of someone who sees injustice all around. Perhaps it's an impossibility in any circumstance. But *your* path— Your path Jesus would never take. And I cannot lead his followers there."

"Futile or not, James, I would lay down my life for the cause of Jewish freedom."

"I know you would, Jedediah. I pray you do not have to."

"Is there anything for which you would lay down yours, Rabbi?"

James paused, reflecting. "In all honesty, I cannot say. Perhaps...*love*. That is what Jesus' man, Simon, told me was at the heart of my brother's preaching. And he was right, my brother's message was about love. So perhaps I would be willing to die for love—including love for our people. But I would have to know that it *was* love in which I was acting. And I don't see love in what you propose."

Jedediah took a few undirected steps around the room, a sigh of resignation escaping him at one point. "I want you to know, James," he said, "that I do not think you a coward or a traitor. But I do think you foolish. Your brother has died for no purpose. His teaching has come to nothing and will be forgotten. You are letting that happen when it could have been otherwise." He shook his head. "Such a waste."

There was a window, narrow and somewhat high off the floor but sufficient to meet the need of the moment. "If I might have that stool?" Jedediah said.

James stood. Jedediah took the stool and carried it to the window.

"I think I will depart by a different route," he said. "I have learned not to retrace my steps. A bit over-cautious, perhaps, but advisable for one in my situation."

Using the stool to reach the window, Jedediah worked his legs through and perched awkwardly on the sill, gathering his robes and stuffing them around himself in the restricted opening. "Goodbye once more, James son of Joseph," he said. "Perhaps we will meet again. Only the Holy One knows. Meanwhile, you have chosen your brother's path. I hope, classmate, that it takes you to where you can find true freedom."

"And I hope you find peace, Jedediah. That is freedom in itself."

Jedediah smiled, this time without the taint of cynicism, and recited the final blessing of Passover, "*Next year in Jerusalem rebuilt.*"

He slipped out the window and dropped to the ground. After a few seconds, James heard the sound of horses being mounted and then trotting away into the darkness of the night.

CHAPTER FORTY-TWO

A friend loves at all times,
and a brother is born for adversity.

(Proverbs 17)

The next day James' caravan traversed the highlands of Samaria. James thought about his reply to Jedediah's question of last night. For what would he be willing to lay down his life? *Would* he die for love, as he had suggested? It was a grand assertion predicated on quite a lot of love and no small amount of courage as well.

But then, for what had *Jesus* died? Was he acting in love, or out of some fatalistic conviction that the cross was his unavoidable destiny? He had told his men that death awaited him in Jerusalem. Yet he could have turned away from that horrible end at many points along his path. He didn't have to keep on with his challenges to the priests and the scribes and the Pharisees. He didn't have to make his violent exhibition in the temple court. He didn't have to remain silent when he was given the chance to speak in his own defense.

But he did do those things. And what was the point? What had he been trying to prove?

The caravan descended from the hills and made its way along the valley floor heading northwest. This was the alteration of its route arranged by Joseph of Arimathea. It would bring James to a point from which he could reach Nazareth with only a day's walk. And since the Jezreel Valley, so familiar to him, was well settled and its central road so heavily traveled, he felt confident making the trek alone.

A new growing season had started in this great fertile basin of Galilee watered by the River Kishon and the many streams and rivulets running down from the mountain ranges hemming it on both sides.

This was the renewal of a timeless process by which life itself was renewed, evident in the tillage of the fields and the buds bursting forth on the trees of so many orchards. Again James recalled the words of the sage, who observed that there was *a time for sowing and a time to harvest what has been planted.*

The sage had also noted that there was *a time for weeping and a time for laughing.* James was about to bring the family its time for weeping. It would be awhile before they reached a laughing time once again.

Late in the afternoon, the column drew up at that meadow by the riverside where James had camped on so many other trips. As shadows drew long, the animals were watered and fed, and fires built for preparation of the evening meal. Mats and blankets were spread for the night's rest, the caravan master ordering a shelter of animal skins erected for the Rabbi James, another of the small perquisites ordered by Joseph.

When James had eaten and prayed the evening service, he walked down to the riverbank, beyond a grove of low trees, for a few minutes of quiet contemplation before turning in. The sky was clear and star-filled, the moon large, bright and unseemly close. It was reminiscent of another night, many years before, when he had stood in the portico of his father's house looking up into the endless depth.

Stillness. Only the occasional bleat or rumbling groan of a camel, a few insect noises, faint lapping of water. The crispness of the air, the shining moon disk overhead—what the creation story termed the *lesser light,* though it didn't seem lesser as it obliterated the darkness of this evening. It was a moon for which caravaners pray to illumine the night. James allowed himself to be washed in its radiance, to feel as if it was lifting him, transporting him, bearing him away. He basked in the feeling for a time, for no time, for forever. He could not measure the minutes that transpired, but only waited, waited. Waited in the silence. Waited in the light. Waited in the time.

"Peace be with you, Brother."

The voice was familiar, the sound as clear as if heard through the night air enveloping him. But surely, he was hearing it in his mind.

"Peace be with you, Brother," the voice repeated. Jesus' voice. A memory. An echo. A waking dream.

"Peace be with you, Brother."

James turned slowly. A form came into view, shining in moon glow.

The sudden inrush of his own breath made James swoon. His legs grew wobbly, and steadiness of balance eluded him. He listed sharply to one side, then tried to catch himself, ending up on his knees in the grass of the meadow before the figure of his brother.

"Jesus..." James heard himself say, as if the name had been spoken by someone else.

The figure reached out, hands open and apart, an invitation to stand. James rose without thought or conscious effort, staring into Jesus' face, his eyes wide, brows raised, mouth open as he did so.

He struggled to find words amid a jumble of dazed and scattered thoughts. "This cannot be. How... I saw... You were..."

Jesus smiled. A brother's smile. A lifetime of a smile, comfortable as a childhood recollection. But not real. This couldn't be real.

"What *are* you?" James demanded. "What is this I see?"

"You see your brother," Jesus said.

"No," said James. "I saw him die. He died on a cross."

"That is true. You saw what you saw. But I have been raised."

"Raised?"

"If you had stayed in Jerusalem, the others would have told you."

"The others? They've...seen...?"

"Yes. They have seen. They sent word to you, but you were gone. You had your duty to perform—as you have always done your duty. And so I've come."

James tried to marshal all his intellect, all his knowledge, all his common sense. But this was beyond sense. Jesus was dead. James had witnessed his awful end. And yet here he was. Here. Now. Words failed. Knowledge and intellect failed.

"You—" James began after a breathless pause, set on a new line of supposition, the only one plausible to his addled mind. "You have performed many wondrous deeds. Is this another? A deed even more wondrous, by which somehow you escaped death? It must be that you were never dead. Surely, it was all an illusion. A trick. Yes, of course, a trick. But...*how?*"

"You are ever the scholar, James. And as such, you grasp at some formulation by which to explain what you do not understand." A small burst of laughter from Jesus, brief and amused. "Be assured, you are not the only one who will find it difficult to accept, or who will think my death just an appearance. But what I tell you is true, Brother. I was dead, truly dead. And I am dead no longer."

Like a wall through which one cannot pass, the experience of watching his brother die would not let James accept the living being on which his eyes now fixed. Jesus couldn't be alive. Jesus couldn't be standing before him on this riverbank. Yet, in spite of what James knew to be impossible, he reached out his hands, placing them on his brother's shoulders. Jesus let him feel the solidity of his presence, then took a step back as James absorbed what could not be but was.

Suddenly James began to feel a shaking within, reminiscent of the tremors by which he had been gripped at Jesus' tomb, but now of a surprisingly pleasant nature. He began to laugh, to giggle as a child would, awash in floods of joy and relief ever more intense until they overwhelmed him and he sat on the ground, forcing himself to be still.

"You are *alive*, brother," he said when he had regained a degree of composure. "You are *here*. Simon told me of how you promised to overcome death. I gave it hardly a thought—and, to be truthful, I think that when I last saw him, he no longer hoped. But...you have done it. You have done it."

James toiled to bring himself back to his feet, but he was still not entirely recovered, so he remained seated on the ground. His head turned slowly from side to side as he tried to force himself to clarity, the childlike giggling upon him again. "This is—what...astounding? The word is insufficient, Brother. This is...a marvel...a *miracle*."

That last term forced his mind to focus on the implications of his brother's living presence. A miracle. A miracle. Who could make such a miracle happen? And for what purpose? His laughter ceased, and he brought himself to a stiff posture, staring up into Jesus' face.

"If you were truly dead, Brother, then please, answer me this: What the family has always suspected—is it true? Are you...Messiah?"

The lids of Jesus' eyes closed for a second, then opened again, and his smile was now wistfully detached. "Some will say I am. Some will say I am not. Those who deny will insist that I failed to do what was expected of God's anointed. Others will say I did more but did it differently than how anyone had anticipated."

He brought a hand to his face and fingered his beard. The other, open-palmed, he held forward, James catching a glimpse of a wound in the wrist.

"But what is *your* view, Brother? I know that you have pondered the question since I came into the family. It has been a challenge to you in every circumstance, pursuing you each day of your life."

James passed another moment in silence, a smile on his own lips mirroring that of his brother. "I know the circumstances of your birth, Jesus," he said. "I know the gifts you showed as a child. I know the conviction shared by my father and your mother. I watched you die, and now I see you standing here alive."

"Then you have the advantage over many others who must make their choices in the absence of such tangible signs. Yet, with all you have seen, Brother, the answer still eludes you."

"Yes," James said. "It is true. I have...withheld my judgment for all these years. But as you say, I am a scholar. I share the conceit of the learned. I want proof."

Jesus swept his forward hand downward across the front of himself, his fingers wide. "Will this not suffice?"

James started to speak, but found himself devoid of the air needed to do so, a wave of emotion interrupting his breath. It was something like fear, though he didn't really feel afraid. Perhaps it was shame, though over what he wasn't quite certain. In a flash of time without time, he experienced an insight unlike any he had ever known in his scholarly life. He mused on it, measured it, weighed it, evaluated it, and finally, he accepted it.

"I thought I had to protect you, Jesus. I thought I was supposed to be your keeper. But I didn't see what was before me all along. I saw only as a man sees...as a scholar sees...as a brother sees. If I had been able to see as God sees, I would have run to you for *your* protection."

He brought himself to his knees. "You are more than Messiah," he said slowly, soberly, yet in a way that filled him with an unexpected and unfathomable joy. "You are the Son of the Living God. You are the Holy One of Israel. You are the King of the Universe."

The moonlight on Jesus now seemed to have become more intense. Or *was* it moonlight? James recalled how Simon had described a glow emanating from Jesus during that strange apparition on the hilltop. He felt another wave of emotion, and thought he might break down into sobbing. But he did not. It occurred to him that he should beg

Jesus' forgiveness for misunderstanding what had been obvious. But, strangely, to make such an appeal seemed unnecessary. What remorse could he demonstrate that Jesus did not already know he bore?

Still, for some inexplicable reason, he felt that it was appropriate to ask. "Please forgive me, Brother," he said. "I did not recognize you. I couldn't believe that you were the Lord."

"And yet," said Jesus, "not believing, you stood by me. You did your duty as a brother. You tried to keep faith with the promise you made to your father. And all of this you did in love."

"Very deficient love," said James. "Very weak faith. I failed. I did not fulfill my promise. I was unable to keep you from harm."

Jesus laughed again, a deep, warm, hearty laugh. "Oh, Brother, Brother," he said, "your duty was never to keep me from harm."

"But, my father..."

"Joseph didn't realize that the cross was waiting for me from the first. It was to be my confirming sign—like the healings I performed. Whenever I cured someone's illness, I did them good, yes, but the point of the sign was never physical well-being. It was to validate the authority by which I spoke the truth. I had to die and rise again, James. It was necessary so that all could discover, as you have, that...*I Am.*"

The Name. The Holy Name. The unutterable Name.

Jesus let it hang in the space between them so that his brother could absorb it. Then he reached and took James by the hand, bringing him to his feet, and said, "Your duty was not to protect me. It was to learn... to become wise...to serve others...to give of yourself...*to be a good Jew.* And these things you have done, Brother. That is why people call you *James the Just.*"

At this, tears finally broke through, and James' face became streaked with them. A sensation of love and forgiveness washed over him, a feeling of contentment that exceeded anything he'd ever known. He might have compared it, inadequately, to his memories of skipping about the court as a small child, exploring the sheep meadow and the olive grove on a warm, sunny Galilee day, playing with his nephews and nieces. Perhaps it felt something like knowing, when he was a youngster, that he was welcome and wanted at each table in the family compound, or like the joy he felt discussing the holy books for hours on end with the Rabbi Ezra, or listening to the wonderful Greek tales of Lucillus.

Or maybe it was like sitting tucked under his father's arm, warmed by Joseph's stories about the mother he knew only in his heart. It was vaguely like all of these cherished memories. But it was more. Much more. So very much more.

He basked in the experience, crying unashamedly, a broad smile on his face, until Jesus said, "Now, Brother, I have a new task to set before you."

It took a moment for James to shake himself out of his ecstasy.

"Yes, Jesus?" he asked finally, blearily.

Jesus waited for James' attention to become focused, and then said, "I've told my followers that I came first for the lost sheep of the House of Israel, though not only. My message of love and repentance and forgiveness of sins—what I have called my *good news*—is meant for the salvation of the whole world. My apostles and those they appoint will carry this teaching to the nations. That is how the Law of Moses and the words of the prophets and the psalms will be fulfilled. But this salvation is from the Jews, Brother, and so Jerusalem is the starting point. As the work is undertaken, Simon and the others will need a base in the holy city, a congregation to support and encourage them. Someone must establish it and lead it. For this task I want you."

"Me, Brother?" James said, taken aback. "But I know little of your teaching. I've not been a follower. I only heard you preach that time near Caesarea-Philippi and those few days in the temple. Many of your sayings are reported to me, of course. One hears of them all over. But really, my knowledge is so very shallow. I am ill-equipped to speak in your name."

"Simon will instruct you," Jesus said, confidence in his eyes as he regarded his brother's confusion. "He has been with me from the start. Understanding has sometimes been a struggle for Simon, but he is coming to realize the full meaning and import of my words, as I always knew he would. That is why I call him my rock. He will teach with my authority, and you can depend on him.

"However," Jesus went on, "in Jerusalem I need a true Jerusalem man—someone trained in the manner which Jews recognize as the way of the learned. You were a student of the Rabbi Hillel, whose wisdom and insight I hold in highest regard, a great sage whose words will be remembered and repeated down through the ages. You carry his certification as you will carry my consecration, and these will be *your* authority. I know you will find a way to perform this duty, Brother, as you have always found your way."

James didn't know how to even begin thinking about such a duty. He was now to play a part in Jesus' mission? Everything that was happening to him was so unexpected, so startling. But it was his brother's desire, so he could not decline.

"Yes," he said. "I will consult Simon, and I will do my best." Then he laughed to think of his own deficiencies and misunderstandings. "I am yours, Brother," he said. "But please, give your blessing to a poor fool in his stumbling efforts."

Jesus smiled warmly and shared the moment of levity, but then his expression turned serious.

"James," he said, his brows furrowing, "you must know that what I have laid upon you is really an impossible task—one at which you can succeed for only a time. As a Jew, I understand full well the forces that have always tended to divide our people, and I must tell you that they will continue to be felt.

"In a sense, my teaching about love will make the divisions even deeper. Some people will resist it, maintaining that love consists solely in keeping the Law, while others will conclude from my words that the Law is kept by love alone. Both of these views are in error. They result from incomplete vision, lack of perspective. I have tried to demonstrate true righteousness, where proper observance and proper intention are in balance. How I taught my apostles to conduct themselves was meant to provide a model for others to follow, though to be sure, my men are not perfect. Even now, there are rivalries between them. But they are trying.

"You will find that not all in Jerusalem grasp the teaching. Some people simply cannot understand. Others refuse to. And even some who assume they do will be led into false and destructive interpretations. Be prepared for great confusion and controversy, which will spawn abusive criticism and harsh reaction on all sides.

"You must struggle against these forces, James. You must do your best to push back the day when divisions become so deep as to appear no longer reconcilable. Keep my people together, Brother. This is the mandate I give you. Keep my people together for as long as you are able. As long as it takes for my assembly to be established on a firm footing. And know that, when the break does come, I will not blame you. What will be will be—even though to think of those who follow my way becoming separated from their fellow Jews is painful to me. It is like another crucifixion."

James perceived the sacredness of Jesus' heart on this matter, a mercy for the people of God that was truly divine. He understood the need for unity, and shared his brother's hope.

"I will try, Jesus," he swore. "I will labor for this as hard and long as I can. I promise you."

He closed his eyes and attempted to absorb the full magnitude of this task his brother had assigned him. There would be much to learn and much work to do. There would be recruiting and organizing, seeking out those who felt called to Jesus' message and those in search of answers the *good news* might provide. It occurred to him that, at least, he had a facility to serve as a meeting place for this Jerusalem congregation, the Synagogue at the Crossed Streets, well located and already known.

A clever thought came to mind. Perhaps the Synagogue at the Crossed Streets would become the *Synagogue of the Cross*. He opened his eyes, intending to propose this idea, thinking his brother might find it useful, or at least amusing. Jesus was gone.

*   *   *

The shelter restricted James' view of the stars. He would rather his bedroll have been set out under the sky. But since the caravan master had provided the enclosure on orders from Joseph of Arimathea, James accepted it as a token of hospitality and reclined on his mat inside of it. In any case, this was a night on which he had things far more wondrous than stars to contemplate.

The family's suppositions, a source of so much anxiety over the years, were finally validated. Indeed, they had been unimaginably exceeded. It was the presence of the Holy One himself the family had sheltered, the earthly incarnation of God.

Which, of course, raised another question, one of imponderable immensity: If the Holy One had become a man—by Mary's definition, the *Son of the Living God*—had he somehow stepped down from his position as creator, ruler, father of all? This could not be. God had to remain as King of the Universe, his spirit at work in all of reality, or else reality would cease to exist.

Wasn't that the truth implicit in the Holy Name? On Sinai Moses had asked how he should refer to the Lord when addressing the people, and God had told him: *I Am Who Am.*

Indeed, God was reality itself.

This was a conundrum of exactly the sort James' rabbinical colleagues could parse in infinite ways. It would, no doubt, be fascinating to see the theories and formulations put forth to explain it, once Jesus' resurrection became widely known. But all of that was beside James' concern of the moment. His immediate objective was to inform the family of this wondrous thing that had happened. And for all of James' knowledge and scholarly training, he felt quite incapable of answering even the most basic questions his announcement would prompt.

Could he say with certainty that, having returned from the dead, Jesus remained an actual human being? James was convinced that a living person stood before him. His brother seemed real enough in terms of appearance, which James had seen, sound of voice, which James had heard, and solidity of body, which James had touched. Of course, knowing what he now knew, could James be sure that Jesus was ever actually human?

More grist for the rabbis to speculate upon. It was becoming all too clear that to speak about Jesus raised all kinds of imponderable questions.

Tomorrow. Or the next day. He would face this problem in the future. Perhaps his remaining hours on the road would best be spent praying for the ability to explain in simple terms what had happened. If he was to participate in Jesus' saving work, which was his brother's intention for him, the gift of simplicity and directness might be the most useful asset he could possess.

*   *   *

James arose at the sound of the camel drivers rousting their beasts. For a moment he questioned whether the experience of last evening had been real. It now seemed almost like a dream. But no. He shook off both his sleepiness and the sense of unreality lingering from the night. What had happened had happened. Of this he was sure.

After breaking his fast with a light meal of fruit and flat bread and praying the morning service, he was ready to set out on the last portion of his journey. He would be in Nazareth by nightfall. And if all went well, he would be back in Jerusalem in a month, since Joseph of Arimathea was arranging for another caravan to divert through the hill country of Galilee and pick him up at the family compound. He thanked the master for all his help and kind consideration, gave him a handful of coins to distribute among his men, and started off on foot along the Jezreel Valley while the train headed in the opposite direction.

In the early evening, after hours of steady walking, broken only by occasional stops for rest, nibbling on some hard cheese and dried figs, or attending to natural functions, James came to the spot where the Nazareth road veered off the main highway up into the hills. This was home territory now, and being close to his destination brought a surge of renewed energy to offset the weariness he could feel creeping upon him after the day's exertion.

He progressed up the rise, passing the grove where he, Lucillus, Nachum and Mary had slept on that long-ago night of the hurried and secret departure from Nazareth. She had been carrying a child inside her, mysteriously conceived and a cause of much consternation to his father. That journey was only the first of many travels that would bring James to this strange end. He could not have known then how his life would be shaped by his brother, or have ever imagined the inexplicable way in which their destinies would converge. But then, there was so much he could not have imagined—not in the wildest fancies of a scholarly boy who dreamed of being a rabbi.

His brother was the *Son of the Living God*. And who would ever think of that?

Nazareth was in twilight as he reached the edge of town. He passed the potter's kiln, walked along the market street by the house that had belonged to Joachim, paused for the slightest moment outside the synagogue once of the Rabbi Ezra, went across the square with the well at its center, and beyond to the far side of town.

The family compound was in sight. He came to the front gate and touched the scroll of the commandment.

EPILOGUE

The caravan from Tyre which Joseph of Arimathea had assigned to pick James up was delayed, and didn't arrive at the family compound for nearly six weeks. During that time, stories began to make their way into Nazareth to the effect that the son of Joseph the Carpenter, of blessed memory—Jesus, that so-called Nazarene prophet whom Pilate had executed—was mysteriously alive. Most people who heard the stories dismissed them as foolish rumors, the product of wishful thinking on the part of Jesus' followers.

At James' advice, his family members kept their own council when neighbors inquired as to whether they had heard any of these fantastic tales attached to their kinsman. It wasn't easy for the family to be so discreet, because James' account of the wondrous conversation he'd shared with his resurrected brother had occasioned great excitement and joy—once he'd convinced everyone that it was true.

When his transport finally arrived, James departed with many expressions of hope, and a few more words of caution. If he was to pursue his mission of establishing a Jerusalem base for Jesus' movement, as his brother wished, James knew he would have to proceed carefully. Also, who could say what ill feelings his activities might stir, and whether they might bring harm to the family.

James found himself retracing the route back to Jerusalem. On the second night, his train was stopped at the caravansary on the Samaria road, where it was again arranged for him to occupy the private chamber in which he'd spoken with Jedediah on the way to Nazareth.

Picking his path jaggedly through the crowded common area to the small room, James encountered someone with whom Joseph of Arimathea had dealings. The man was a trader in the delicate polished and pleated linen cloth woven in Egypt, as well as in the red Egyptian clayware for which James' father had once made crates, and other goods from the African coastal region. Some years earlier, this fellow had consulted James for rabbinical guidance on a point of family concern.

"Rabbi," the man said, "peace be with you."

James returned the greeting.

"How do I find you here on the Samaria road, Rabbi?"

"Returning from Galilee," said James. "A visit with my family."

"May the blessings of the Holy One be upon them all."

"And upon your family, my friend."

"How long have you been away, Rabbi?"

"A few weeks."

"Then you have not heard of the strange doings in Jerusalem?"

"Strange doings?" This James offered in a neutral way, sensing the need to be circumspect.

"The prophet Jesus, the one Pilate crucified."

James pricked up his ears at the mention of his brother, though he tried not to show too much interest. "What of Jesus?"

"It is said all over the district that the man still lives."

Struggling to hold his face in a blank, noncommittal set, James asked, "Lives?"

"That is the word. It's been told me by many people. Some who claim to have seen him—or know of someone who has."

"You have not seen him?"

"No, Rabbi."

"But...people are convinced of this?"

"Many are, yes. And his men—of this Jesus I mean, the ones who had followed him about the countryside when he was preaching—they are out in the streets and squares everyday telling all who will listen that Jesus has returned from the dead. Can you imagine? Even in the temple. They made a most amazing display of themselves just a couple of days ago, preaching and proclaiming in a variety of languages."

A fragment of memory caught in the man's mind. His head leaned to one side as he asked thoughtfully, "Rabbi...don't you have some family tie——?"

James ignored the question. "So not everyone accepts this idea that Jesus lives."

"Well...no. Some say it's a hoax. The priests and Levites in particular. And some of the rabbis as well. They are quite fierce in their denials." He laughed in a deep and hearty way. "Actually, I think they regret the whole business—the trial and crucifixion, I mean—for all the attention it brought to Jesus and his words. They would rather Jesus had never come to Jerusalem, I'm sure."

"And what of Pilate?" James asked. "Has the prefect seen Jesus?"

"Pilate has not been in Jerusalem since the whole unfortunate affair, or so I'm told."

James' brow knit as he looked at the man directly. "And what do you think, my friend?" he asked. "Do you believe that Jesus is alive?"

The merchant shook his head, which set a fringe of graying brown locks swinging slightly from under his cap. "I don't know what to believe, Rabbi," he said with a shrug. "But it does seem that something unusual happened."

James looked away, casting his gaze across the other travelers in the large, congested space. There were wayfarers of all types here—men, women, rich, poor, gentile, Jew, slave, free—the broad, motley representation of the empire, of the whole world, which one customarily encountered on the road to Jerusalem.

"Yes," James said. "Something unusual happened. Something very unusual."

AUTHOR'S NOTE

This book is a work of speculative fiction, based on incidents in the New Testament, re-imagined and elaborated on extensively. I have not attempted to create a "fifth gospel." Rather, I've tried to fill in some of the gaps between facts given in Scripture with inventive suppositions about *how things might have been*.

The Holy Bible is the most durable and influential book in the history of the world (a compendium of books, really). Yet anyone who reads it objectively must admit that the portrait it offers of life in Christ's time is often painted in broad strokes with little historical perspective or everyday detail.

Many of the situations presented in my story are suggested by the non-canonical writings of the early Christian period. These are the "gospels" and "testaments" that didn't make it into the Bible. Yet they reflect beliefs and traditions maintained by communities of people who identified themselves as followers of Christ.

Some of these traditions have resonance in Church practice to this day. For instance, a feast still found on the liturgical calendar, *The Presentation of the Blessed Virgin Mary in the Temple* (celebrated by both Catholics and Orthodox on November 21), is assumed by some scholars to reflect a tradition that Mary was raised in the temple at Jerusalem. Likewise, a view held primarily among Eastern Christians is that Joseph was considerably older than Mary, a widower with children, when they married. That idea is not disputed by Catholic dogma, and even some Protestants find that it sheds light on many questions about the relationship between Mary and Joseph (and about what Catholics and Orthodox maintain on the subject) that otherwise go unanswered by Scripture.

In addition to the non-canonical works, I drew on many other print and online sources, most of which cite two authors whose accounts figure prominently in virtually all histories of the period: the Jewish general-turned-historian, Flavius Josephus (c. 37-100 C.E.), and Eusebius, Bishop of Caesarea (c. 260-339 C.E.), who compiled an account of the Church's first three centuries.

Pulling all of these various informational threads together and weaving them into a story presented some challenges which I was able to confront only by taking a good deal of creative license. But I have hewn to one central commitment, that *I would not contradict the Bible.* Extract from it selectively? Yes. Adapt and embroider? Most elaborately. And, to be sure, do a bit of hedging now and then to bridge the variations between different Gospel accounts. But not contradict.

For instance, I have described the principal circumstances of Jesus' birth largely as traditionally told (except for the date of Christmas), despite the fact that scholars have long struggled with a conflict between that event and the time of the great census which the Bible tells us found Joseph and Mary in Bethlehem. The discrepancy between the Gospel accounts and other documentary evidence of the period is as much as ten years. I also had to address variations with which the four evangelist/authors of the Gospels list events in Jesus' ministry. I mainly followed the order given in the Book of Luke while including some episodes mentioned by the other Gospel writers.

In order to move my plot along, making the things happen which I wanted to have happen at times that seemed to make the most sense, I have taken a loose approach to *sequence* and *duration.* Biblical incidents are referenced with some arbitrariness on my part. And while the major non-Scriptural historical events cited in my story are real, I have reconfigured them freely and either compressed, extended or shifted the time in which it is believed they occurred. Naturally, most of the narrative details are imagined, since two thousand years later, there's no way of knowing exactly how events unfolded.

But then, this is a novel, not a historical treatise or catechetical tract.

No doubt there are many points in the book which can be debated, and I've likely gotten some details wrong. But my goal has been to tell a plausible story about human beings confronting an extraordinary situation—indeed the most extraordinary situation imaginable: *God present in human form*. I wanted to explore how different individuals (both historical figures and made-up characters) might have behaved, presenting motives and feelings that would ring true to readers today.

Because, despite the passage of twenty centuries and the differences in cultural context, human nature is consistent. The people of Jesus' era really were very much like us. In particular, I felt it was important to paint a detailed picture of the political currents in First-Century Palestine, especially as they affected reactions to Jesus and his movement.

It's easy to get a shallow, Sunday-school impression that the Jews of Christ's time were a bunch of thin-skinned spoilsports, very confused about what was really important. Why would anybody want to kill someone who went around preaching love and offering a lot of uplifting homilies? And healing the sick to boot! Well, there were reasons why Jesus was seen as a threat, and I have attempted to suggest some of them.

It has been my experience that people often need *a way* to think about religious ideas and questions of faith. While the Bible speaks with profundity on all the great themes of human existence and has an indisputable track record for changing lives, it very often raises as many questions as it answers. That's why well-organized, scholarly Scripture study, conducted within an informed historical context, is a critical component of effective religious education.

In my story I have tried to offer a way to think about the great events that befell the Holy Family, most particularly James, whom the Bible names as head of the Church in Jerusalem and calls *the brother of the Lord*. I would not begin to claim that all my suppositions are correct. But I do claim a certain kind of inspiration in coming up with them—surely not of the caliber experienced by the Gospel writers, but sufficient to keep me going whenever the well of creativity seemed to have run dry. I offer a sincere prayer of thanks for that, gratefully acknowledging His help and guidance.

Bill Kassel

www.billkassel.com